LEGACY OF THE LOST

A Donna DeShayne Adventure

BELLA FAYRE

Published and Distributed by:
UCAN Publishing, LLC
P.O. Box 51616
Myrtle Beach, S.C. 29579
www.ucanpublishing.com

Interior Layout and Cover Design:
TWA Solutions
www.twasolutions.com

Proofreading:
Star Editing
stareditors@gmail.com

ISBN: 978-0-9909310-7-2
Library of Congress Control Number: 2019915804

First Print: November 2019

For inquiries, contact the publisher.

For Mary and Joe.

"Death is not the greatest loss in life.
The greatest loss is
what dies inside us while we live."

Norman Cousins

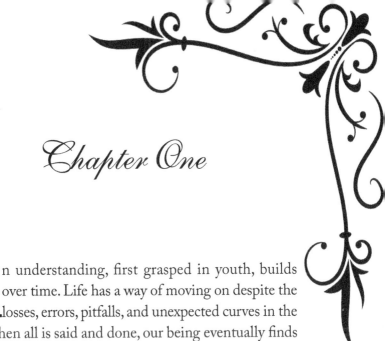

Chapter One

An understanding, first grasped in youth, builds over time. Life has a way of moving on despite the losses, errors, pitfalls, and unexpected curves in the road. When all is said and done, our being eventually finds its stride, homeostasis, and balance, despite an unsettling, even brutal arrival result. The receiver must process input to reach a conclusion to be learned from and lived with. Not all are lucky in this endeavor. For some receivers, the outcome is unforeseen and unwelcomed.

In the present case, the follow-up was welcomed. Circumstances were purposely contrived that, while a bit unnerving at first would, in the end, afford a place to hide. It wouldn't be forever. For now there would be no questions regarding the past, no inquiries related to previous actions. Welcomed silence on multiple fronts culminated in supreme satisfaction. Finally! Finally, the wrong had been righted!

Years before it was apparent the indifference had to be addressed. The flagrant withholding of years of support on multiple fronts had to be discovered, questioned, confirmed, and dealt with in no uncertain terms. Those who allowed their greed to draw them into the mix would be dealt with directly. Outside, intruding interests had to be eliminated. It was the only way. The greedy would understand the consequence of their actions! There were results to one's decisions. How hard it would be for some to find the lessons of outcome. So be it!

For a quiet and unobtrusive observer of dysfunction, the years of cataloged neglect and disregard would bring a personal conclusion that some were not worthy of mercy or forgiveness. The lack of conscience, the denial of responsibility would only do harm, in some cases for generations. The spiritually informed could take one of two paths. Either sit back as a passive observer, watching the dysfunction take hold in another generation or create a path toward decisive action in protest. The latter was the clear choice.

By the grace of divine providence, a controlled environment would allow withdrawal and final assessment in the short term; a blessing, when all was considered. One had to understand and accept the trade-offs to be able to surmount the unforeseen travails of life.

There was little to complain about in the aftermath. No one would suspect. For a time. There was still work to do and as before, there would be assistance. For now there was a peace, a serenity, and sense of accomplishment. Finally.

Blame was not to be placed on the fourth wife. The woman, after all, was not at all worldly or informed, though she possessed a cunning to those who could recognize it. The problem was, no one was looking. This woman was used as a tool to further the agenda of a highly passive-aggressive mate who had just enough standing to affect the future of generations, disregarding the past intentions. The timing for this wife was fortuitous. She would realize an unexpected windfall upon the death of her second husband. How could she know the real history after five short years of marriage, especially from a husband so good at manipulating the unsuspecting?

Young by comparison, days were now spent observing others dealing with their own struggles. Anonymity was found in hiding among an unsuspecting population. A sly smile appeared most days. Those around her had no idea she had the ability to create and orchestrate such brutality. How could they? Most were unpretentious and vulnerable. They had no idea a murderer struggled to speak to them, feigning interest in their struggles. They had no clue why the smile appeared or the distant look of satisfaction in the eyes. They had no idea a personal insult had been dealt with in no uncertain terms. They had no inkling an affront had been adjusted. They had no hint of the legacy of the lost.

Chapter Two

Coastal South Carolina -Spring- Current Time

Donna was luxuriating in her time at home. She had received no urgent calls from law enforcement agencies for nearly two weeks. Heavenly! She was determined to tackle projects that she had long ignored because of sojourns away from home. It was spring cleaning at its finest for a woman who was accustomed to organization.

She started with the bedrooms, continued through the living room and kitchen, and finally worked her way to Ken's office. Her partner and lover for nearly twenty years, Ken was a detective with the county police department. She often referred to him as her 'everything man.' They were a match made in heaven. Most important to Donna, he made no demands on her. Similarly, she made no demands on him. Each understood the spiritual side of the other and acted accordingly. It was what positioned their relationship for success early on.

As a forensic psychiatrist, Donna's expertise in criminal behavior had propelled her to nationwide recognition. She had not strived for notoriety; it just happened. In recent years, she was the go-to-gal for law enforcement agencies across the nation that were grappling with stubborn scenarios. She loved her work, but it often took an emotional and physical toll. For a start, there were the long periods of time away from home. Ken was understanding during these times, but she would long for his embrace while away. It could be weeks before they reunited in an explosion of long-overdue need, emotional, physical, mental, and sexual.

Today, after a night of unbridled passion, she was energized for cleaning. Ken's office was next on her agenda. This was tricky because of the confidential material he sometimes had on his desk, so she first asked Ken for his approval. "It's fine with me, but don't move my stuff, if you can help it. I have some sensitive issues I'm working on," he responded as he kissed her seductively before leaving for the morning.

The kiss sealed it! Donna was project-oriented. Give her a task, and she would find her stride. She attacked Ken's home office with a fervor. First on the list were the windows. They hadn't had attention in months. After restoring them to clean and glistening, she next took on the blinds, baseboard, and cabinets, and even dusted the walls. Draperies were vacuumed: Flooring cleaned.

When she neared Ken's desk to dust, she noticed a binder titled "Case 20617." Normally, she and Ken never discussed their cases. They were both highly respectful of the other's domain and rarely crossed the lines. On a few exceptional occasions, the conversation was along the lines of outflow of thoughts leading to possible conclusions. Each understood the intent and guarded the sacred ground of discretion.

Donna continued dusting, but found herself drawn back to the case binder minutes later. Her insatiable curiosity was piqued. She put down her cleaning tools before taking a seat at Ken's desk. Her hand hesitated, but she eventually opened the file. In it she found material related to a haunting criminal escapade. She was eager to talk with Ken.

Returning to her project, she continued for a time until she was satisfied Ken's office had received a proper spring cleaning. Late in the afternoon, she headed for the kitchen to stir the beef stew she had prepared in the crock pot that morning. The aroma was inviting. She was in the middle of making a salad when she heard the garage door open. Ken was home earlier than usual.

She greeted him at the door between the kitchen and the garage. "You're early. What's the occasion?" she asked kissing him warmly before taking a lick of her crock pot stirring spoon to assess the flavor.

"You! It's not often you have such a long stretch at home, and quite frankly, I'm loving every minute of it. My, what smells so good?"

"Stew," Donna answered with a slight bow. "Carole and Gavin are coming over early to have dinner with us before our card game tonight. They're bringing dessert."

"Perfect! Let me take a quick shower and then I'll help you set the table," he threw over his shoulder as he headed for the bedroom.

"It will be a warm evening. Maybe we can eat on the porch," she suggested.

Ken gave a thumbs-up signal as he headed quickly for the shower in the master bedroom.

Donna's best friend was Carole Tandermann. Though there was nearly a twelve-year-age difference between the two women, they had clicked from Donna's early childhood.

Carole was the one who encouraged Donna to seek an education in psychiatry and later asked her to join her own psychiatric practice in South Carolina. That was where Donna's career as a forensic psychiatrist took flight.

Carole's husband, Gavin, was a former FBI agent and fifteen years older than Carole. The couple had been devoted to each other for nearly thirty years. Having no children of their own, years earlier they had informally 'adopted' Lacy Sue, her husband Saul Larson, and their then newborn, Mary. Prior to that, the little family did not have a connection to grandparents. It was a rescue orchestrated by the gods. Lacy Sue and Saul eventually added a set of twins they named Carole and Gavin, in honor of their defacto grandparents, an indication of the gratitude and honor Lacy Sue and Saul felt for the Tandermanns.

Just the year before, Gavin, thanks to Donna's dogged endeavors, connected with blood relatives he never knew existed, and he was reveling in a new sense of belonging and heritage. The experience instilled in Gavin a keen interest in genealogy. Since then, he had become quite proficient in the research process.

After her retirement from psychiatry, Carole founded a successful business venture in Beans coffee cafés along the Grand Strand, the name given to a 60 mile stretch of coastal South Carolina. Carole, witty, fun, and endearing, never met a stranger, nor did any new coffee blend escape her notice.

Carole and Gavin arrived on time, bringing dessert. After dinner, Carole, with her usual wild and witty abandon, shared an encounter at the market earlier that day. "So…I'm paying for my groceries when the woman before me returned to the register complaining she had been charged incorrectly. She was quite loud and rude. I had noticed that as she was walking away with her cart, she dropped her receipt and quickly picked it up from the floor. There happened to be another receipt nearby and this is the one she picked up. Lo and behold! I would have thought her rant would evaporate when I fetched the other receipt, which was still on the floor, and asked her whether it was hers. After examining that receipt, she slunk away in utter embarrassment, never even apologizing to the poor cashier for her tirade.

"The story doesn't end there! On my way out to the car, I saw this woman again. This time while she is unloading her groceries, one of her bags spills out onto the parking lot... oranges, grapefruit, lemons, and apples, mind you! She is really irritated now, so irritated she is cursing as she gathers her fruit. When a vehicle exiting the parking lot unavoidably runs over one of her oranges, the woman responds by throwing a lemon at the vehicle! Wow! Beam me up, Scotty! I stayed in my car until she completely cleared the parking lot. That woman certainly needs lessons in anger management."

"Welcome to my world," Ken quietly replied as he set up the table for their card game.

The others were temporarily silenced by Ken's comment. A county detective for over twenty-five years, he had pursued the bad guys, given relief or condolence on multiple levels to victims when possible, all while facing significant challenges in his pursuit of the truth.

"I sometimes forget, Ken, you are more than educated in the mindless ways of humanity," Carole said. "Forgive me for my insensitivity."

"No forgiveness necessary," Ken said as he busied himself dealing the initial hand. "It is what it is, Carole. The misplaced soul is everywhere. It remains our job to recognize it in the context of accepted societal standards. Once someone breaks the standards, we are compelled to act."

Ken rarely spoke of his work, and even now he was couching his words. Gavin was the first to respond. "I can't imagine what you have witnessed."

Ken looked up from dealing. "Enough to last a lifetime, I can assure you."

"What keeps you going?" Carole asked, her voice more subdued than usual.

"A paycheck, for one!" was Ken's witty retort. The others laughed.

"Really, though," Carole prodded.

Having dealt their hands, Ken sat back contemplating his answer. "The long and the short of why I do what I do is that I love people. Kind, caring, and innocent people. They are everywhere. They give when they can, they carry their burdens and they often act to protect one another. The kind and caring heart is in every neighborhood and on every street corner, but, unfortunately, they often go unrecognized.

"The bad guy occupies the headlines, uses up endless tax dollars in the court system, remains a burden on society and, sadly, often wins because of unprincipled attorneys padding their bank accounts with amoral billable hours. These are the real enemies. The guys who look the other way to achieve a measure of wealth on the backs of the innocent. It's a disgusting web of deceit. It is only when the little guy says, 'I've had enough,' that society engages."

"Here, here!" Gavin added. "That's when you come in."

"You had your share of experiences when you were with the FBI, Gavin. I'm sure there is no shortage of stories you could tell."

"Speaking of shortage," Donna interjected toward a more pleasant subject. "We're playing for pennies tonight. I hope I have enough. I raided our penny jar."

"I brought ours as well. Can't have enough pennies!" Carole added jovially.

"Oh....so we've graduated from M-&-M candies to pennies?" Ken queried.

The girls looked at each other and giggled. "Too many calories!" Carole explained. "Besides, you guys keep eating from the winnings!"

"I vote for M-&-M's for the next game. Even when you lose the occasion is sweet," Gavin countered.

The card game ended with Carole winning the pot. "It's a dirty job, but someone has to do it," she said while drawing the mound of pennies toward her.

"Spare us from looking so smug," Donna humorously returned.

Donna and Ken walked Carole and Gavin to the end of their driveway. The Tandermanns lived across the road.

"Hey, I almost forgot," Carole said as they approached the road. "The Landscape Yard is open for business and offering a spring sale. Gavin and I plan to visit in the morning. Care to join us?"

Donna looked at Ken. He nodded in agreement. "We're planning on our usual spring and summer plantings. Yes... We will join you," Ken replied.

"How about meeting us at 9:00 o'clock for breakfast? The Landscape Yard is just a block over."

"Perfect! The weather tomorrow afternoon will be ideal for planting," Donna said.

Having selected their plantings after breakfast with Carole and Gavin, Donna and Ken spent the next afternoon gardening. Ken was usually in charge of the vegetable garden, while Donna oversaw planting annuals in the usual beds, though in recent years she leaned more toward perennials with annuals planted in between.

"I can't remember the last time we worked together in the yard," Ken yelled over from the vegetable garden to Donna, who was on the side of the house within earshot.

"I love getting in the dirt. There's something so balancing about it," Donna mused aloud.

"Especially if Mother Nature cooperates with her magical rains," Ken returned.

They both went back to their tasks, each lost in thought. Donna finally broached the subject that had been bothering her since the day before.

"I have a confession to make," she said, approaching Ken as he knelt over a tray of tomato plants.

"Will I have to arrest you?" he threw over his shoulder, still focused on his project.

"That would be an adventure," Donna mischievously returned.

Ken turned to look at her and smiled. "I'm already thinking of the possibilities."

Donna shook her head.

"So, what's this confession all about?"

"Yesterday, I discovered the case file on your desk and spent a good hour or more reading it."

He smiled broadly. "You can't help yourself, can you?" he returned good-naturedly.

"It's a curse I'll have to live with until the day I die."

"I have a confession to make as well. I purposely left it on the desk knowing you wouldn't be able to keep your hands off of it."

"You didn't!"

"I did. I set you up!"

"Why couldn't you just ask me to review it?"

"I didn't want to intrude on your time at home with a case. I've been struggling with it, and I figured if I left the binder on the desk, your insatiable curiosity would get the better of you. I want you to be the one to decide whether you want to take a closer look or not. I would understand if you declined."

Donna nodded her head in understanding. "The thing is," Donna began hesitantly, "the whole affair is already in my head, but I have questions. Lots of questions."

Chapter Three

GOTTLIEB AND TRUDY

Stuttgart, Germany – Late Spring-1911

Trudy was suspiciously eyeing her second daughter but instinctively she already knew. They had thirteen mouths to feed, another just add to their burden. Kathe was not like her other children, nine sons and another older daughter. This one was restless, adventurous, and provocatively daring. This one was a handful. The young woman intuitively knew she possessed beauty, often flaunting her mature and buxom body to any male heart she met. She had a teasing nature, void of complete honesty with those in her still-young life. Yes, this child was different. Her parents would come to rue the day she was born.

The family lived on a hillside in a mountainous region of Germany outside of Stuttgart. Their acreage was considerable, but the constant upkeep for their livelihood had always been arduous. Sons were a necessary component to till and care for the land. Their nine sons were an investment in the family's survival. The two daughters were an offset to help their mother in the support of the men. This was simply how it was. Sons were recognized. Daughters remained an undervalued support system.

It came to a head when Gottlieb asked the whereabouts of their second daughter, Kathe.

"Kathe has gone up the hill again, I suspect," Trudy replied wearily.

Gottlieb questioningly looked at his overworked wife. She had once been a thing of beauty. Still somewhat young, she was now worn and haggard, a far cry from her youthful days. Her face and body bore the signs of one with too many chores and no respite in sight. He was not much better. Bestowed in his youth with an outstandingly handsome physique and features, he was the presumed catch of every female in the region. How beautiful a man he was in and out of their bed in the early days. The ensuing years had not been kind to either one of them. They aged under the weight of their responsibilities and workload. Supporting the thirteen of them drew on their strength and fortitude.

She added further unwelcomed news. "There have been no bloody rags for several months."

The look of bewilderment on her husband's face was obvious. "What are you saying?"

The woman sighed deeply, the weight of her responsibilities obvious in her downtrodden demeanor. "I suspect she is with child."

Her husband froze with disbelief. "How is this possible?"

Trudy wearily lifted her head from her butter-churning task to look at her husband. Oh, how the years had changed their union. He was once everything to her, courting her handsomely and promising her the world. The world, as it turned out, was nothing but hard work. It wasn't completely his fault. She wanted another world, different from her mother's, but alas, she would eventually see she was much the same as her mother, overworked, with little relief in sight. It was the life of a farmer's wife, with children, many children, bred to work the land.

Her tone held a measure of discordance. "Do you forget how it was with us? How we stole away to be together? Do you really think it is somehow different with our children? Does it not dawn on you that when you have daughters, you face such challenges, especially in this god-forsaken land?"

The expression on Gottlieb's face was as if he had been slapped. He looked at his wife for a time, the understanding crushing his heart. He stepped forward, embracing her for the first time in many months.

"I have failed you. I am so sorry. You deserve a better life," he somberly said while holding her. "I wanted so many things for you, but it has all become a burden. Don't you think I see it?" he asked with more than a hint of angst.

It had been a long time since he held her in such a manner. So busy were the both of them with work and accompanying responsibilities they had forgotten what had brought them together in the first place. She had once luxuriated in his embrace, smelling his manly scent while enjoying his masculine hold in their lovemaking, but over time it had become rushed and abrupt, and then not at all. For her, the desire was gone; the consequence of overwork and exhaustion.

Yet she remained prudent and realistic. Someone had to be. "I fear we have come to the point of mere survival," was all she said as she disengaged from his embrace. She was, by far, the more astute of the two. She could see the horizon and their future. They were not getting any younger, and the long periods of loneliness had taken their toll, setting up a hard and fast resolution in her psyche. The man she had fallen madly in love with in her youth, the man with whom she had bred so many children, no longer had a hold on her. She was spent, both in love and in energy.

He stepped back, pained by her words, but he understood. He had for some time, yet hearing it from her mouth added to his discomfort. With each year since their union, she gave birth to a child. They were cautioned that a twelfth pregnancy would be life-threatening to the mother and possibly the child. She had almost died with the birth of their youngest daughter, Kathe. The doctor cautioned it was too many children too close together. In many respects, she was relieved by the warning. Their method of birth control was clearly not working. The doctor's directive was clear, giving little option. From that point on, she emotionally and physically withdrew from her husband. She had little choice. He had done the same. There were now too many who needed care. If something happened to her…she dared not to think about the eventual consequences.

Gottlieb gathered himself after a time to question his wife regarding their youngest daughter. It was almost a welcome distraction. "Who would be the father?"

Trudy looked at him long and hard. *How easily the male gender missed the nuances of life, even the obvious ones,* she thought. After giving her reply some thought, she finally answered, "I suspect it is the Jewish boy over the hill. Kathe has befriended his sister. They all go to school together. We can only know for sure by asking."

"When do you expect a birth?" he questioned, clearly agitated about having one more mouth to feed and protect. The responsibility was clearly on him and his wife. The import of this news filled him with misgiving and elation…misgiving for the added responsibility and elation for the impending first grandchild.

"Early winter would be my guess."

He inwardly groaned.

The winters were hard on the family for a number of reasons. First and foremost were the long periods of isolation and confinement. The winter storms and accompanying snowfalls could be fierce, further isolating them on their hillside dwelling. Their home was small for the number of inhabitants. An additional member would worsen their overcrowding. During the height of the winter, there was little to entertain them. Neighbors were far away and the harsh weather made travel nearly impossible. Trudy spent winter hours mending their clothes, or making new ones for the upcoming year. She saw to their meals, which served as a distraction from the boredom. Educating her daughters on wifely chores took additional time. She taught her daughters well.

Gottlieb though, along with his sons, grasped for reasons to be present. The animals had to be fed and the eggs from the chickens gathered, but other than that, the male members were house-bound. On the rare occasions when the weather broke, some would hunt, though the pickings were often slim.

During these isolated times, Trudy, though still somewhat young and overworked, would question society's acceptance of the everyday standard: The female gave birth to offspring, and yet everything belonged to the male. There was rarely a path toward a birthright for the female. Trudy, her mind always questioning, pondered the inequity in the equation. How was she, a female, less than a male in birthright? Who determined this departure and designation? A female? A male? A council of both in the far distant past? In these lonely and desolate hours of winter, she questioned and hoped that a future generation would find an answer to her questions. Her innate intelligence had already nudged her toward casting aside much of present-day thinking about the holy writing's position that the woman was to follow the lead of her husband.

Highly observant, and given to suspicion, she surmised that holy writings, written by a man, would trend with the political leanings of the day, even if it meant changing original writings to favor political notion. How ingenious, she often thought…using the faith of the populace to advance a political track! Yet, there was no one to whom she could speak of such thoughts and leanings. Even her husband would reject her position as contrary thinking toward the church. So, she held her own truth. Hers was a lonely world.

The early winter saw the birth of their first grandchild; a grandson. He was named Burkhardt. The initial elation of a healthy birth was tainted by the fact the boy was not only conceived illegitimately, but had Jewish blood as well. The Jewish grandfather decided the child should be recognized as a Swiss citizen. As they were just an hour from the Swiss border, it was arranged for the birth to take place in Lucerne, Switzerland, fully arranged and paid for by the Jewish family. The designation was lost on the German family, but not for long.

Shortly after the birth, Kathe and the child returned to Germany to the already crowded home on a hillside near

Stuttgart. Then to the grandparents' complete surprise, four weeks after the birth of their grandson there was a hard knock on their door early one afternoon. The day before had produced a rather abundant snowfall that would normally stop all movement for a time. Most would not have ventured out in these conditions. That was not the case this day.

Gottlieb opened the door with caution. His sons were behind him ready to act in defense if it was necessary, for rarely did anyone come to their door in such conditions unless it was threatening.

To their surprise, the man standing in the doorway was elegantly dressed in heavy woolen wear, appropriate for the weather. There was another man standing behind the first, dressed just as elegantly. Their bearing was regal. Gottlieb looked beyond the men to the majestic coach and horses that had brought them.

"I represent Burkhardt's father and grandfather. May we come in?" the first man asked. "You will find the reason for our visit interesting."

Gottlieb, unaccustomed to such formal requests, replied, "We have little to offer, but we have hot tea and warmth. We would be happy to share what we have." He stepped aside to let the unexpected visitors enter their humble dwelling.

Hurrying to heat water for tea, Trudy presented their guests with simple biscuits made that morning, complete with butter and honey. The men were grateful for the repast and the display of hospitality.

The sudden presence of guests elated the family. They had been isolated on the hillside, with their neighbors tied to their homes by the winter weather. Until now, they had little to distract them.

After small talk, a bite or two of the biscuits, and a sip of hot tea, the men stated the reason for their visit. The first one introduced himself as the estate manager of the affairs of the child's Jewish grandfather, and the other as an attorney representing the Jewish family.

"What we are about to propose is for your ear's only," the attorney began, eyeing the family gathered about.

Gottlieb understood and immediately waved the family to the other end of the small house.

Lowering their voices, the estate manager cleared his throat before speaking. "The child's grandfather would like to make a gesture toward Burkhardt's future. He is proposing a generous transfer of money to you for the care of the child. In return, you may make no claims regarding paternity, nor shall the terms of this agreement be revealed beyond family members. The transfer of sums will be realized in three parts, as follows. One third will be transferred immediately, one third will be paid upon the child reaching the age of eight years old, and one third will be paid upon the child reaching the age of sixteen. Upon the final payment at age sixteen, and with the assurance this matter has not been compromised by the revealing of the terms, the matter shall be considered closed. We have papers you should review before deciding," the representative said, nodding to the attorney who respectfully took his cue, politely sliding the paperwork toward Gottlieb.

The manager and attorney sat back. They had already calculated the outcome. It would be accepted by the peasant family without question. In reality, it was more money than Gottlieb and Trudy could ever imagine; a windfall for people like themselves with struggling means. Yet, the representatives of the child's wealthy Jewish grandfather allowed the scene to play out to the satisfaction of the German grandfather. They allowed the questions, an expected rebuttal or two, and even displayed a deep concern for the German family's situation. It was, in the end, all about the signature on the agreement. Gottlieb made a bold attempt at being astute in such matters, but the other side knew differently. They had researched his history and means. Without question, the offering was a godsend for ones of such little means.

The papers were signed. The representatives took their leave after civil and honorable overtures. Their job was done, their mission accomplished. The legal ministrations on behalf of their employer were now a matter of record, never to be challenged or revealed.

Having closed the door behind the visitors, Gottlieb stood back against the door and reviewed in his mind the entire encounter. His response was one of pure elation. He sighed in satisfaction. Finally! Finally, they had enough money to make a difference in their lives. No more would their future depend on the weather, or the price of grain, or the price per pound of cattle. No more would they beg for the continuance of their overdue account at the general store. In fact, he would go in, when the weather allowed travel, to pay his entire account in full! How grand the experience would be; how he would relish the look on the proprietor's face when he did so! He laughed to himself, and then out loud. The family gathered around, questioning his good humor.

No longer would Trudy be overburdened with work. They could hire someone to take on many of her current responsibilities. Maybe, just maybe, if she were not so exhausted, she would come back to his bed. Oh, how he had missed her!

The first thing he was determined to do when the weather thawed was to add an extension to their dwelling. They desperately needed more space. He sat down the next morning and drew an outline of their expansion.

Trudy looked over his shoulder as she served breakfast to him. "What is this?" she asked.

He smiled up at her. Even in her care-worn, exhausted state, she was still beautiful to him.

"Our future," was all he said.

"We have the means for this now?" she asked, still puzzled by his buoyant mood since the departure of the visitors the day before.

"Yes, and much more, if we are careful," he returned, inwardly seeking her approval.

"I suspect it is because of the child," she probed with caution.

"Yes, an unexpected blessing in many ways," was all he said.

Two years later:

On a gloriously sunny morning, in stark contrast to the demeanor of Gottlieb and his children, the family gathered with friends and neighbors to bury their beloved Trudy. She was one of the early victims in a great pandemic that overtook many corners of the world and became known as the Spanish flu. Months later, Gottlieb would also bury his son, Franz who, while serving in the German army, was also felled by Spanish flu. The malicious disease eventually extinguished, by some accounts, twenty to fifty million people in an eighteen-month period. Troop movement from a military base in Kansas to Europe and other locations amplified its speed of infection as troops fought the Great War.

Gottlieb lingered over his wife's grave long after the others had left, still trying to come to grips with the stark reality of her death. It had been good between them the last two years. Indeed, adding more space to their home coupled with outside assistance relieved Trudy of much of the burden of running a household. He had noted a transformation in her almost overnight. She smiled more, was more engaged in conversation with him as well as the rest of the family, and took the time to be more attentive in her dress and grooming. He had even purchased bolts of fabric so she could make new dresses for herself.

They had developed a routine of spending time outside after sunset, listening to the sounds of nature around them while holding each other's hand. It was on one of these occasions Gottlieb inquired of her if she was agreeable to coming back to his bed.

"I have missed you beside me," he admitted. "It's not enough for me to admire you from a distance. Surely, you must feel the same."

Trudy looked at her husband for a time before responding. A decidedly lessened work-load had allowed her body to rest and her spirit to be renewed. A physical desire for her husband had been intensifying. "The longing I have for you grows with each day. Yes, I feel the same, Gottlieb. I fear, however, the problem remains. I cannot bear another child for fear of death. You must understand this. I am just as pained as you are by our separation."

Gottlieb's heart melted. It was all he needed to hear. "What if we had the means to prevent another birth?"

"What are you saying? The method we have used in counting the days when I am not fertile has proven to be a dismal failure. We cannot take a chance on such an unreliable method."

"Perhaps another method then?" he asked softly.

"What method? I am not educated in these matters, I fear."

"A German company sells these," he replied, reaching into his breast pocket to transfer to her palm a small packet. "I understand they sell them all throughout Europe, Australia, New Zealand, and Canada. It is placed over my member to constrain the fluid."

She looked aghast, all the while eyeing the packet. Finally looking at her husband, she responded. "How have you come to know of this?"

He wasn't going to share that, since they had come into a measure of money, he was learning the ways of the more affluent members of society. The poor, he learned, were far less informed in such affairs.

"It doesn't matter. What matters is that you and I are together again, with you in my bed. Won't you please consider it, Trudy?"

She thought long and hard before speaking. Finally, with an almost husky voice, she said, "Gottlieb, I wish to come back to our bed. Please take me there."

He remembered, as night began to fall while still sitting by her grave, how delirious that night had been for both of them. Deprived of pleasure for so long, both gave way to lustful and, heretofore, abandoned need. They had revived, through the darkness of the night, what they thought had been lost, awakening in each other the dormant longing and soulful response so present in their younger days. How glorious to be together again! Now, free from the fear of pregnancy, they could fully luxuriate in each other's love, encasing each other in a cocoon of trusting devotion.

Sitting there, remembering, he felt a hand placed gently on his shoulder. It was the hand of his son, Max. "Father, it is time for you to come home. It is late. You haven't eaten, and the air is becoming chilled."

"She doesn't want to be alone in the dark," was the sad reply.

Max was taken aback, unprepared for a response of this type from his stalwart father, a man he had known to be commandingly in control. Recognizing the reply as unbridled grief, he offered an unorthodox solution. "Perhaps Mother would be comforted by the light of a lantern through the night, Father."

Gottlieb, not looking up, simply nodded. "Yes. Yes, then she would not be afraid."

At once, Max placed his lantern on the grave of his mother, illuminating her headstone. Helping his father to his feet, he guided him toward home in the dark; he repeated the gesture of placing the lantern for some time thereafter.

Germany – 1915
Germany had been at war for nearly a year. In the end, World War I would take the lives of nearly ten million combatants and the political map of the world would reflect the demise of four empires. Triggered by the assassination of Archduke Franz Ferdinand, heir to the throne of the Austro-Hungarian Empire, by a Bosnian-Serb in June 1914, it took only a matter of weeks for Austria-Hungry to attack Serbia.

As if overnight, major powers formed alliances, creating two opposing factions. One was the Allies, comprising

France, Britain, Russia, and later Italy. The other was the Central Powers of the German Empire, the Austro-Hungarian Empire, the Ottoman Empire, and the Kingdom of Bulgaria. The conflict spread across the globe.

Amid this worldwide turbulence, Gottlieb and his family did what they could to support Germany's war effort. He invested with pride in German war bonds. During this time, however, he suffered the loss of two of his sons, Klavin through a hideous death on the battlefield, and Yuri from the Spanish flu. By the grace of God, the rest of his children survived, leaving him now with seven sons, two daughters, and a grandson.

When America entered the war in April 1917, declaring war on Germany, the tide turned against the German war effort. Nearly eighteen months later, Germany agreed to a halt in confrontation, effectively ending the war.

Germany's economic plight was becoming increasingly clear, especially upon the announcement by Gottlieb's son, Max, that the general store had refused the family further credit. "I was stunned. We have never been denied credit, Father. How are we going to do the plantings this year?"

Gottlieb put his head down in a gesture of shame. Finally looking up, he decided to be honest with his children. "I deeply regret that I've done something very foolish. I invested the bulk of our monies in German war bonds. I was so sure Germany would be victorious. We would have been if it weren't for the Americans entering the war."

His children looked at him questioningly. "Are we going to be all right, Father?" his older daughter, Sigrid, asked with more than a hint of trepidation.

"I honestly don't know. Germany is now under the thumb of the Versailles Treaty and the German mark is in free-fall.

Prices for goods are already starting to rise. Rumor is we will soon be facing prices for goods beyond our current means. We will need to be very careful to conserve what we can. There is a meeting of the farmers tomorrow. All of us are facing the same plight. Some fear a revolution."

"Father, I can go to the city. The government is embarking on transportation projects and building power plants. I can send money back to the family," Hans projected.

Gottlieb nodded. "If need be, Hans. We shall see."

In time, and with no other choice, three of Gottlieb's sons, Max, Franz, and Peter, left the farm for jobs in the city, leaving the other three, Joseph, Heinrich, and Friedrich to work the farm. This arrangement was short-lived as the German economy could no longer sustain the social programs with little revenue coming into its treasury. Hyperinflation indeed took hold with a vengeance. The buying power of the German mark disintegrated. By the end of 1923, a hundred thousand marks would not even buy a loaf of bread. Six years later, adding insult to injury, the Great Depression of the United States engulfed the world's economies. Those countries, including the United States, who had loaned money to Germany after the war, were now asking for accelerated payments in an effort to bolster their own economies. Germany was approaching near collapse.

Gottlieb's newly married older daughter, Sigrid, announced that she and her husband, Greuton, would be moving to America. Gottlieb was dismayed by the decision. His daughter urged him and her brothers and younger sister to join her in the immigration effort, but all refused, at least for a time. The house he had enlarged was now much too big. Things were changing so quickly. He grew increasingly lonely for Trudy, often going to her grave to speak with her about the disconcerting events facing the family. He was worried. In addition to the economic woes of the country, there was a new threat on the horizon.

A new political party had evolved from Germany's working class, a class of people who lacked hope, the most dangerous kind. The German Workers' Party promoted outrage for the terms of the Versailles Treaty and its harsh treatment of Germany. Furthering anti-Semitism in favor of German pride, the new party loudly spoke of the injustices of the Weimar government toward the middle class, a group that had not benefited from new government policies or wage increases. The German Workers' Party blamed their plight on the ruling class, communists, trade unions, capitalism, and wealthy Jewish business owners. The fierce promotion of a "Greater Germany" was taking hold in the psyche of the working class.

Gottlieb grew fearful for his grandson. Through the years, the child's teasing uncle would often mock him about his Jewish bloodline. Burkhardt learned to laugh it off. It was the only thing he could do. He knew he was different. Not German. Not Jewish. Even on the playground he was often faced with his dual identity. His grandfather protected him as best he could against those who advanced the fanatical idea of a pure German heritage, but he feared it could severely affect his grandson in time if he didn't act.

Chapter Four

Present Day – South Carolina

The evening after they completed the plantings and gardening, Donna and Ken sat on their porch while they took a closer look at Ken's case binder.

Donna, ever dogged, was the first to speak about its content. "There's a police report of the crime scene, but no photos, no forensic evidence, no suspects," she asserted with an air of impatience. Turning to Ken, she asked quietly, "Why?"

He knowingly nodded and then reached behind him to produce another binder. "The photos are graphic; the forensics are disturbing," he offered as he passed the folder in Donna's direction.

Donna hesitatingly reached out for it and then stopped. "So you're saying…'Go slow?'" she asked.

Ken shook his head in protest. He felt torn. As a detective, he wanted to solve a crime, but another part of him was reluctant to involve his significant other in the process, especially using her time off!

"Donna, you need to enjoy your vacation," he finally said, in surrender.

She eyed her lover of twenty years. "No way, babe! I'm already hooked. You need to give-up-the-goods on this one." Her tone sounded unyielding.

Ken sighed in resignation. He knew his woman. After all, he had purposely put all of this in play, knowing Donna would take the bait. He felt a guilty twist in the pit of his stomach. Before he could protest further, she inquired of him, "I assume there are persons of interest?"

Ken looked at her directly. "Not a one."

She was unnerved by his response. "There is no such thing as the perfect crime, Ken. Surely something has been overlooked."

"If that is so, you are my only hope. I have examined the evidence from every angle. I have spent hours and hours examining the crime scene and forensic reports. I have asked every local expert I can think of, and every person even remotely involved with the victims, and still I come up with nothing."

Donna's heart went out to Ken, knowing how proud he was of his investigative skills. He was clearly unglued by this case. She went to him, kneeling before him while cupping his face in the palms of her hands. Leaning her forehead against his, she simply said, "You have given hope to those needing hope, solace to those lifted by a kind word, and guidance to the many who have temporarily lost their way. Don't ever forget you're good at catching the bad guys. This is just a bend in the road. It will be solved. I sense it at my very core."

Ken appreciatively smiled at Donna. "I take it you're in?"

She smiled back and kissed him before saying, "I'm in!"

Donna took the next several days to peruse, with keen intent, the contents of the two binders. The first offered a detailed overview of discovery. It included, word-for-word, the 911 call from the crime scene. Clearly, an overwrought person had inadvertently discovered the deathly scene. Donna, later in the day, provided Ken with her condensed version.

"If I have my facts straight, a couple in their mid-fifties were murdered in their home on a Tuesday evening, and were discovered by a member of their Bible study group just moments before the group was to meet. I reviewed the 911 call. The guy placing the call was clearly unhinged. The report indicates he was taken to the hospital hours later, as a result of a panic attack.

"The crime scene photos are of interest. The victims, Simon and Wanda Lundy, were seated in chairs with tape over their mouths and their arms tied behind their backs with duct tape just below the elbows. Their wrists were deeply slashed. Not just one wrist, but both wrists for each victim. The murderer, however, had a thing for clean. It was arranged for the blood spill from the couple to drip into a bucket placed just behind each of their chairs. A controlled blood flow... how interesting! What do we know about the couple?" Donna asked, not looking up from the photos.

It was already in the report, but Ken felt it an advantage if he reviewed it again verbally. "The victims were a white couple, married nearly twenty-seven years. They had two grown daughters and four grandchildren. They also owned Lundy Vintage Automotive, well-known for restoring vintage automobiles. Both were faithful church members, for years hosting a weekly Bible study. The husband was very active in the church. There was no criminal record for either one. No traffic violations. No unpaid taxes. They were, by all accounts, the ideal neighbors and friends."

"Yet they were methodically killed and left to be found by their Bible study group hours later."

"What are you suggesting?" Ken asked.

"I sense the timing of the killings is telling. I also sense that containing the blood spill is significant. The killer is most likely a neat-freak and obsessively orderly. On another note, I sense there had to be more than one person doing this killing. There was no evidence of a break in, so it had to be someone the couple let into their home. Since nothing was stolen, this had to be personal."

Donna took a deep breath before continuing. "The fact their home was violated with a murder just hours before a meeting of a church group translates, at least to me, as an intentional message."

"The message would be?" Ken encouraged without finishing the sentence.

"That God cannot always save you," Donna answered somberly.

❦

Ken could see Donna was deeply engaged into his case when he entered her home office several days later and found the photos from the murder scene mounted on her timeline board on the wall above her desk. She was busy studying the official police report.

"There was a chair placed in front of the victims," she commented, noting Ken's entrance. "What do you make of that?"

"Currently it's surmised the murderer sat in front of them to watch them die," he answered.

"I agree, but I also feel the couple received an accounting of their sins while they were dying. The scene is too planned, too controlled for anything to be left to chance. The person responsible for this needed the victims to understand why this was happening to them."

"I agree."

"Another thing," she continued, "the forensic report includes fibers of hair from the victims and others. Have the others been identified?"

"Yes. You probably haven't gotten that far, but the list is in the back of the binder. All have been cleared, by the way," Ken added.

Donna immediately turned the pages to the back of the binder, looked at the list, and then looked up at Ken. A puzzled expression crossed her face. "Really? All of these people on the list, family included, and not one suspicious character?"

"Not a one. All are as pure as the white wind-driven snow. You can see why this case rattles my cage."

"I completely understand," Donna sighed.

"The thing is, the family wants the property to be released so they can put it up for sale. They've been breathing down my neck. I'm reluctant to release it because it's a crime scene but I may have to before too long."

Donna looked up. "Would you take me there?"

Ken was startled. "You want to go to the home where the murder happened? Why?"

Donna replied with a question. "Do you want this case solved or not? I'll invest the time, but I need to get a feel for where it happened. I need to absorb the family who lived there. This is how it works for me, Ken. You know this."

He was embarrassed. She was right. He had drawn her into this and now was questioning her method. He could have kicked himself. "Yes. You're right, of course. Forgive me for being so insensitive. How about tomorrow morning? Once your questions have been addressed, I'll call the family and release the property by the end of the week. I don't think I can hold it much longer anyhow."

The next morning, they decided to take separate cars. Donna remembered she had an appointment to have her nails done in the early afternoon, and she thought it would be easier if she had her own vehicle, since she would be on that end of town. Dressed in jeans, a favorite lacey top, and work shoes, she followed Ken in his car to the home of Simon and Wanda Lundy.

They drove up to a lovely, nicely placed and landscaped home in a well-established neighborhood just outside the town limits. The home sat back from the road with a somewhat long, double-wide graveled driveway. Donna could picture the driveway filled with vehicles on Bible study night, nicely accommodating the visitors without their having to park on the grass. The grounds had large, mature trees accenting the inviting look of the property. The only thing that looked out of place was the glaring yellow police tape surrounding the house and grounds.

When she exited her vehicle at the curb, Ken was waiting for her to join him as she walked up the driveway to the walkway leading to the front door. He smiled wickedly.

"Do I dare ask why you are smiling?" she questioned.

"It's you in those jeans. You wear them well," he replied, winking at her.

"Keep your mind on your work, Detective," she returned with a hint of humor.

"Oh, yeah. My work," Ken responded teasingly. Donna laughed. He then turned to lead them up the front steps where he produced a key from the temporary lock system placed on the doorknob. Before entering the house, they put on shoe booties and rubber gloves to protect the crime scene from contamination.

Upon entering Donna was immediately drawn to the open living room. Still present were the two side-by-side folding metal chairs where the victims had sat tied and gagged as they were dying. She remembered them from her review of the crime scene photos. The chairs were about two feet apart. Directly in front of the two chairs, but placed at least five feet away, was the lone folding metal chair the murderer sat in while watching the intended targets die slowly. Donna examined the scene for some time, picturing the anguish of the victims as they bled-out.

She looked around the living room. It was tastefully arranged with couches and arm chairs along with a display case of family photos. Again, she imagined the group of Bible students gathered in this setting.

Moving on to the rest of the house, she entered a well-appointed kitchen, moved on to an inviting sunroom toward the back of the house, before finishing a quick review of the three bedrooms, one of which was used as a study. Nothing stood out as unusual. She then went back to the study. Ken followed, studying her face.

Donna scanned the study. "No computer?" she inquired.

"A laptop. It's clean. No incriminating evidence. We'll be returning it to the family once we release the property."

Donna noted a wooden file cabinet and opened it, only to find it empty. She looked at Ken questioningly.

He understood. "All of the files from both the home and their place of business have been copied, photographed, catalogued, and boxed. They will be returned with the release of the property. So far, we're not impressed by the contents. Nothing indicates they had anything to hide or had any enemies."

"Yet, they were murdered in their own home. Nothing was stolen, no damage done to the property, no threatening letters or other means of communication, no clue left behind. They definitely had an enemy. Friends don't murder friends."

"You can see why we're baffled and feel like we've hit a brick wall," Ken commented.

"This is a tough one, I agree." Donna left the study and wandered about the house noting the placement of things and the decorative settings. Everything appeared normal. A normal family having a normal day. Almost.

She then wandered into the sunroom. On the one end stood a large flat-screen TV surrounded by two reclining chairs and a loveseat. Donna could imagine the couple watching a movie at the end of the day with their feet up. The other end of the room was filled with numerous house plants. Some were dangerously close to dying from lack of water. Donna went to the kitchen to retrieve a container of water, making her way back to the sunroom to water the plants. Ken was shaking his head with a smile on his face.

"It's my green thumb," she stated, noting his expression. "It aches when I don't water dying plants," she said wryly. "I assume the small shed in the back has been accounted for," Donna said looking out the window beyond the plants toward the backyard.

"Just the usual riding lawn mower and garden tools, et cetera. Nothing unusual there."

Donna, thoughtful, stood for a moment and then re-entered the living room taking one more look around, especially at the photos of the family so proudly displayed.

"What do you think?" Ken asked, breaking her self-induced spell.

She turned to him slightly, her eyes still scanning the photos. "A lovely family, a beautiful home, a successful business by all accounts, loyal church-goers, and respectable community members. The perfect life. Too perfect. On the surface."

Chapter Five

BURKHARDT

Stuttgart, Germany - 1936

Gottlieb made a decision regarding Burkhardt. Agonizing as it was, he felt he had no choice given the circumstances of his grandson's birth. Kathe, his mother, was away again with another boyfriend.

Gottlieb had written to his daughter Sigrid, and her husband Greuton, now settled in America. They agreed to his request. Within four weeks, Burkhardt was accompanied to the docks of Hamburg, Germany, by his uncle Frederic, who would oversee his nephew's boarding of the *SS Albert Ballin*, an ocean liner of the Hamburg-America line that had completed its maiden voyage just eight years previously.

His grandfather wanted Burkhardt to understand he was not sending him away because of anything he had done wrong.

"I don't understand, Grandfather. If I've done nothing wrong, then why am I being sent away?"

Gottlieb grappled with his explanation, eventually deciding to be reply honestly.

"You are being sent away, my son, for your protection. You have Jewish blood from your father's side. Jews are increasingly unwelcomed in Germany and I'm afraid it will get much worse. Your aunt and uncle are willing to look after you in America and keep you safe."

"Will I be allowed to come back?" Burkhardt asked.

"Yes, my child. When things in Germany are whole again you can make your own decision to return. In the meantime, your safety is my main concern. Please do this, Burkhardt, so as not to cause me to worry."

Reluctantly, Burkhardt agreed, not really understanding the political climate unfolding that could imperil his future. He said a tearful goodbye to his grandfather. His mother, Kathe, sent a note conveying her disappointment at not being able to bid a proper farewell, and promising to visit him in America. It would be years before she did so.

Finally, arriving at the docks in Hamburg, he looked up at the imposing 602-foot-long cruise ship, the SS *Albert Ballin*, accommodating 1,650 passengers that would be his home for his four-week journey to America, eventually arriving in the New York harbor. For all of his youth, he had been sheltered in a quiet hamlet outside of Stuttgart. Now, at sixteen he was facing a journey for which he was not prepared. He grew more anxious by the moment as he boarded the large vessel with a single cloth satchel of his belongings after saying goodbye to his uncle. He promised to write but, never did.

Despite his apprehension, the ship represented a departure from his previous rural experience and proved both exciting and revealing. His accommodations were in steerage, a designation reserved for those with lesser means. In fact, he would find in this assigned level hundreds of passengers placed together in a single large hold with long rows of shared bunks with straw mattresses and no bedding. Little privacy was afforded, and little effort was made to segregate the males from the females. There were no windows on these decks, just air vents at strategic locations. The air was often hot and stifled with wretched smells accumulated over time. Minimal presence by staff afforded a simple sweeping of the rows between beds and the transfer of fresh linen once a week. The showers and toilets were divided, designated for male and female. Children roamed everywhere seeking a place to play. Only when their parents brought them to higher deck levels could they experience the sun and spray of the ocean. Those levels were guarded and confined to steerage passengers only.

Meals for those in steerage were miserable, presented in huge kettles and ladled out into dinner pails with passengers pushing forward in a disorderly fashion to garner their meals. The exception to this was the first and last night, when the ship ordered a more presentable fare, possibly to secure a final memory in the minds of steerage passengers who might make a recommendation to future passengers. Burkhardt was never clear on the intent, he just noted the difference. Otherwise, he and others in steerage were limited to porridge and soups with stale bread. Rarely did fruits and vegetables appear, and when they did, they were quickly gobbled up. Milk was at a premium. It had to be demanded by parents with children, but it was eventually supplied. Drinking water was grudgingly given as well.

Steerage passengers were never encouraged to go to the upper decks, but Burkhardt found a way, discovering corridors reserved only for the staff. On the upper decks, another level of comfort he couldn't have imagined was revealed to him, and he took advantage of it whenever he could. The upper levels fit a station in life held by those who could pay the price of the fare. The second level was more humane, with four to a cabin and a dining room with more choices offered.

The first level was unlike anything Burkhardt had ever seen. Those on this level had their own cabins, not having to share with anyone else unless it was prearranged. The dining rooms were well-appointed with waiters and busboys busying themselves filling the requests of the guests seated at lace-covered tables with colorful cloth napkins folded as flowers and placed as centerpieces. Each place setting was adorned in the finest china and silverware. Crystal glassware was presented for each beverage offering. Almost any dish could be ordered to the complete satisfaction of the first-class passenger. The presentations were a sight to behold. It was Burkhardt's first exposure to evidence of class, for those who could afford and for those who could not. He clearly understood why he was in steerage.

Protected by his grandfather in a hamlet near Stuttgart, these lessons were never taught, for there was no need for such information. In his mind, in his sheltered corner of the world, his family congealed in their endeavors to just be, never comparing or over-reaching in their expectations. It was a balanced existence, though fraught with the never-ending need to survive. He wouldn't truly appreciate all of this until years later. What he immediately understood upon his perusal of the upper decks was that wealth and means could advance your station, affect your future, and provide a recipe for comfort and well-being.

Burkhardt watched and observed and as he did so a thought occurred to him. It just might work. He had nothing to lose. One afternoon, he entered the secret corridors he had discovered and found his way to the lodging area for the onboard help: waiters, bartenders, cleaning and laundry personnel, et cetera. Even here, there was a strict code of station. Those with more oversight held accommodations befitting their station. They were separated from the general help and had their own dining room. It was somewhat better than what he was experiencing in steerage, but not by much.

Every day, fresh laundry would be delivered to the rooms of the waiters, busboys, and other staff personnel. Uniforms provided by the ship's laundry department had to be crisp and clean at all times as part of the experience for the upper-tier guests.

On one occasion, Burkhardt eyed a freshly delivered uniform in his size and walked off with it. Finding a closet, he quickly donned the uniform and combed his hair neatly. He even had the presence of mind to scrub and trim his nails, understanding his hands would be observed. Looking down at his feet, he knew his shoes would give him away. He found a pair of shoes to his liking on the floor of one of the sleeping rooms and simply replaced what he was wearing.

With more confidence now, he headed to the upper-tier dining room and stood by the other waiters, waiting for direction. In his secret perusals, he noted waiters were often given a gratuity for service well-rendered, especially if a drink or two was delivered to the table of an especially boisterous guest, one who was already well on the way to drunkenness. Invariably, the inebriated guest would be assisted to his cabin and the waiter would be handed a monetary reward. At times it was even necessary to put the guest to bed, thus having access to their wallet. Lifting a bill or two, not so much as to be obvious, and replacing the wallet would ensure an extra night's return for those who dared.

Burkhardt spent the first several evenings learning the ropes of the dining room. No one on the staff suspected he was a guest from steerage. He would change dining rooms often to avoid recognition. Finding a place to hide a dinner pail, he would often dump the remains of a meal or two into it to eat at a later time. He was amazed at what people would leave on their plates.

Avoiding conversation, he simply nodded his head when given direction, but his work was always flawless and of high caliber. The tips began to come his way. A drink here. A cocktail there. Special attention to gravies and sauces per the request of the guests. Always something personal and memorable. Before long, his stash of money increased. Coming aboard ship with little money, he understood through rumors and conversations with others in steerage, that money could make the difference when they finally reached America.

Befriending several other young men his age, Burkhardt learned to play poker shortly after boarding the ship. There were many such games in steerage…a way to pass the time, but also a way to lose what little money one had. For Burkhardt, the game proved an advantage. Through these games, he was often able to add to his growing bank of funds. Understanding the need to protect his money, he would determine to play at different times with various groups so as not to draw attention to his success. Theft was a usual occurrence for those not protecting their belongings. Upon discovering a loose floorboard near the steering compartment of the ship one day, he retrieved from the kitchen garbage bins a glass jar with a lid. In this jar he stored his funds under the loose floorboard until the day he disembarked. One couldn't be too careful.

Burkhardt observed, watched, and learned. His still young and innocent mind was beginning to understand the art of survival. Too many, he noted, remained victims of their circumstances. In watching, he learned one can transcend a situation by simply being aware of when to pivot toward a more self-satisfying outcome. The pivot, many times, was just a tilt of awareness or a subtle action…nothing earth-shattering, but still helpful in the big picture. So be it.

Before long the SS *Albert Ballin* neared Liberty Island in New York Harbor, New York City. What a grand sight to behold the copper statue, the Statue of Liberty, a gift from France to the United States. The figure of the robed woman who held a lighted torch raised above her head with her right hand while her left hand carried the date of America's Declaration of Independence, July 4, 1776, welcomed the ship's passengers as she had for many before them. There was not a one in the steerage department who was not able to recite the inscription by Emma Lazarus on the statute:

"Give me your tired, your poor,
Your huddled masses, yearning to be free.
The wretched refuse of your teeming shore.
Send these, the homeless, tempest-tossed to me.
I lift my lamp beside the golden door."

A chill reverberated through Burkhardt as many in steerage stood on the rails of the ship as it neared America. As the ship was in full view of the Statue of Liberty the passengers on all three passenger levels of the ship recited loudly the quote, many weeping with hands placed over hearts, the hope and dreams their new home represented evident in their display of reverence as the ship sailed into the New York harbor.

It was time for all passengers to disembark. As was customary, the first-tier passengers exited the ship first, but everyone boarded a transport ferry to Ellis Island. Most, if not all, were not seeking citizenship in the United States, but were already citizens, returning from business or vacations overseas. The process, however, would take most of the day.

On day two, the second-tier passengers disembarked. Though of lesser means than the first tier, this group faced little in the way of challenge to their entry as long as they had an American sponsor of some station vouching for their welfare. First-and-second tier passengers were considered by the government less likely be a burden to the public in their new country.

Day three began the processing for those in steerage. This could last several days, as immigration officials eyed this level of passenger with far more scrutiny. The disembarkation process for this group was in alphabetical order, after cordoning off country of origin. The mood among steerage passengers could only be described as tense. This tier, the lower-class passengers, were transported to Ellis Island on over-crowded barges or ferries. They would often have to wait for hours on the barges to enter Ellis Island. No food, water, toilets, or protection was afforded during this process.

Burkhardt waited for his name to be called, spending the first two days playing poker with those also waiting. In fact, he was not called until the third day. Given the tense political leanings of Germany, those Germans seeking a home in America were given careful scrutiny. Burkhardt descended from the ship with others of his nation for the beleaguered walk toward the Registry Room, where doctors examined each entrant for physical and mental issues. A white chalk on the immigrant's clothing by the doctor was an indication of possible health issues. An "H" represented a possible heart issue. An "LCD" indicated contagious disease. The rapid-fire physical health inspections were suspect at best. The least suspicion of the overall health of anyone from steerage resulted in a chalk mark on the lapel of that one's coat. The coded chalk marks indicated the designation: B=back, C=conjunctivitis, Ct=trachoma, E=eyes, F=face, Ft=feet. G=goiter, H=heart, K=hernia, L=lameness, X=mental retardation, and a circled K=insanity.

Burkhardt passed his physical with a sigh of relief, but noticed those who did not. A family he had befriended on the ship had not passed the exam. Burkhardt watched from a distance as they made their way through the line of doctors. The parents were examined first and then the older of the two girls in a type of assembly line of medical examinations. The doctor overseeing the eye exam looked at the parents after probing their older daughter's eyes a second time. He marked the child's clothing with a white chalk mark. The dreaded eye exam in which the doctor flipped up the eyelid with either his fingers or a hairpin often revealed the common and contagious eye disease known as trachoma, prevalent in southeastern Europe. The daughter had the disease.

The mother let out a muffled cry when she realized their efforts to enter America were thwarted with this discovery. The father put his hands on his wife's shoulder to quiet her so as not to draw attention.

Burkhardt swiftly came up behind the doctor and slipped a wad of money into the man's hand, pointing discreetly to the young girl in front of the doctor who had just been marked, and then walked away just as quickly. The doctor simply nodded an understanding and removed the white chalk mark from the child's clothing with a damp cloth, deftly moving on to her younger sister next in line.

The parents looked at each other in disbelief and then at Burkhardt, who was already in line at the next station of entry, his back to them. Gathering his family, who had now passed the physical exams, the father stood behind Burkhardt in line. Burkhardt felt a hand on his shoulder but refused to turn around to be engaged by the man. He simply looked forward in an attempt to discourage any conversation.

Now, divided into groups per the ships manifest, the passengers waited to answer a list of questions related to their entry into America. In these inquiry rooms, several questions had to do with how much money they had, and whether they were being met and/or supported by a relative. Documentation in such matters was handed to the inspectors. The long journey had left many of the immigrants exhausted and anxious. The inspection process and language barrier added to the mix of confusion for the detainees. Misunderstandings were common when giving answers despite the presence of interpreters and interviews often ended in rejection.

Burkhardt moved forward with the rest, but his paperwork did not reveal his true financial situation because of the additional money he had managed to garner while on board the ship. Eventually, after what seemed like hours of answering many questions, Burkhardt was handed an Inspection Card, indicating approval to enter. He would be one of more than 63 thousand entering America through the Port of New York in 1936 alone, a total in excess of 97 thousand nationwide.

Passing through the process area, Burkhardt scanned beyond to see if he could get a glimpse of his Aunt Sigrid and Uncle Greuton. It was necessary for the inspectors to confirm the right of claim his aunt and uncle made on his behalf in efforts of entry into the country. He was overwhelmed with relief when he noted them waving at him. They were accompanied by their friend Henry, who had sponsored their immigration to America nearly two years previously. Hearing his name called, he stepped forward. Aunt Sigrid and Uncle Greuton came forward as well, confirming their sponsorship of their nephew. Finally approved for entry, Burkhardt was handed his immigration papers. He hugged his family, noting Aunt Sigrid was very pregnant.

"When?" he managed to ask, regarding the birth.

"It shouldn't be much longer," Uncle Greuton proudly responded.

"You are well?" he inquired of his aunt.

She blushed before responding. "I tire easily, but then I rest. Now, let's go home and celebrate your arrival."

Burkhardt nodded his approval, but dropped his satchel suddenly to the ground, turned and kissed 'The Kissing Post', a column famous for being kissed by joyous immigrants entering America. His aunt and uncle smiled in amusement. Just as Burkhardt was about to take hold of his satchel to join his family, the father of the family whose daughter had initially been rejected because of her eye disease approached him. Burkhardt looked beyond and noted the man's family was busy in their joyous union with their sponsor as well.

The man held out his hand to Burkhardt. "I cannot repay you," he said sadly, shaking his hand.

"There is no need. I wish you well," was Burkhardt's reply, returning the handshake.

The man became teary. "I will always remember the young boy who saved our family, and I will pray for that young man every night." With that the man turned to rejoin his joyous group.

Burkhardt smiled and allowed himself to be led by his family and Henry to Henry's automobile, a vehicle that had seen better days. He was in America, and in transit to his new home in a place called Newark, New Jersey. He turned to get another glimpse of the stately Statue of Liberty standing majestically in the New York Harbor as they wound their way out of the parking area. He saluted the stately figure as well as the ship, the SS *Albert Ballin*. He would never know the ship was taken by the Nazi government in their master plan to invade Poland, and sunk less than two years later.

With each turn of the vehicle down New York City streets, Burkhardt felt more impressed by the place. His hillside home near Stuttgart could not have prepared him for the hustle and bustle of a city pregnant with activity. He craned his neck for a better look at Ellis Island as the vehicle wove its way through Manhattan.

Since the inception of Ellis Island operations, New York City had been transformed into a metropolis. Always a hub for entertainment and business, an energy had taken hold in recent years, based on new sources of building material, such as steel and also abundant labor. Both empowered the city toward an abundant growth evidenced by towering buildings, eventually known as skyscrapers. The New York skyscrapers were a marvel for a new and enthusiastic age.

Burkhardt looked out the car window and marveled at the miracle before him in the sky above. The New York skyscrapers had grown to be the tallest in the world. It was an optimistic age at the start. From the New York World Building of 1890 at 309 feet, through the Woolworth Building of 1913 at 792 feet, to the art-deco Chrysler Building at 1,046 feet in 1930, to the famous Empire State Building at 1,250 architectural feet the following year. Burkhardt was witnessing the endorsement of new inventions and processes that would make all of this possible.

The elevator and the transformational process of converting pig iron into strong and low-cost steel made all of what he was eyeing a reality. The introduction of plate glass and electric lighting provided the substance to underscore the New York skyline in its final reality, a masterpiece of engineering. The people of the city would look up and marvel. The immigrants approaching the port of New York would look beyond the Statue of Liberty to a city distinguished by the skyscrapers and become speechless in the wonder of it all, their hearts surging with hope.

It seemed no time before Henry pulled to a curb and announced, "Here we are."

Burkhardt noted a congested street in a busy town. "Where are we?" It seemed their destination was less than an hour's drive from the port.

Uncle Greuton turned around in his seat in the front row to face his nephew. "We live in Newark, New Jersey. We have a small flat on the second floor and have established a butcher shop in the space below," his uncle explained, pointing to simple signage that said 'Meats and Poultry.'

The four made their way up a dark staircase to a door on the second floor. Aunt Sigrid unlocked the door and announced, "Make yourselves comfortable while I see to lunch. It won't take long."

Burkhardt looked around the apartment. It was small, but comfortable. A baby added to the mix would present a challenge for space, no doubt.

"Uncle, is your business doing well?" he asked.

"It is beginning to get some footing. There is a large German population, so we have that going for us. We take orders and deliver to the beer gardens and the German restaurants. Your Aunt Sigrid prepares the salads early in the morning before opening for the day. We are not rich, by any means, but we have enough."

"Is there work for someone like me in this city?" Burkhardt hesitantly asked.

Henry engaged himself in the conversation. "Your aunt and uncle struggled mightily, Burkhardt. The shop has a small following now, which is good. The economy is not so good, however."

"This is true," Uncle Greuton conveyed. "Our coming to America was ill-timed in many respects, I'm afraid. The stock market crash two years ago, just after our arrival, cast America into a major economic depression. Thousands are out of work and without means. Not only here, but worldwide. Our business is fragile, as are all businesses, but we are surviving."

Henry leaned forward to offer his own observations. "To top it off, last year, in the Mid-west, there was something called a Black Blizzard, a massive dark dust storm that took up the topsoil and swept thousands of tons of dirt across the whole region. It has happened several times since with devastating results to the farmers. Almost 35 million acres of cultivated land have been lost. There is no longer any topsoil in which to grow crops."

"What does all of this mean?" Burkhardt asked in alarm, silently thinking that he might have been better off if he'd stayed in Germany.

His uncle provided an assessment. "It has added to the number affected by the stock market crash. It is estimated that 3 million farmers are unemployed because of this Dust Bowl."

"So, there is no work?" Burkhardt concluded questioningly.

It was Henry who spoke up. "The three of us have a plan. I own a small luncheonette. I need a dishwasher. The one I have currently is unreliable. You can stay in the back room and earn your keep by washing dishes and making sure the place is clean. Breakfast and lunch will be included. I won't be able to pay you much."

"You may have your dinners with us," Aunt Sigrid added as she entered the room with a tray of sandwiches and fruit. Setting down the tray, she explained further. "As you can see, our home is small, and now with a child coming, there is little room," she stammered.

Burkhardt nonetheless was pleased by the offer. "This is all very generous of you. You will not be disappointed."

"Then you can start tomorrow," Henry concluded.

Chapter Six

ANNA

Newark, New Jersey – 1938

Anna was the only daughter of five children born to Irish immigrants who settled in America just twelve years before Burkhardt's arrival. Her father, a mason, traveled to New York from their home in Newark, New Jersey each day to construction sites where work could be had. Her mother served as a maid for a well-known hotel in the city. Anna and her four brothers, Connor, Sean, Jack, and Liam, the youngest, were recognized in their Irish neighborhood for their flaming red hair and rambunctious manners. They were a handful for their hard-working parents. Now seventeen years old, Anna earned money by waitressing at Henry's luncheonette.

Loud, open, and forever chewing gum, Anna greeted every customer with a hearty "Hello!" The regulars loved her. She always gave them a little something extra without charge, and they left a bigger tip, as a reward. She was quick...very quick. Quick to take what didn't belong to her, like tips from the other waitresses or food to take home. Henry observed her in acts that she thought she'd cleverly concealed, but he remained quiet. Anna brought in the customers, and Henry needed all the customers he could muster in this abysmal economy. He understood that Anna's bohemian ways served as a refreshing distraction from the weariness and despair of those seeking work when none was available. Therefore, he tolerated the intolerable and ignored her wily ways. After all, Anna brought in the business.

Those times when she sang an Irish ballad during lunch at full throttle or when she danced a jig with a drunk were fun to Anna. To her, the world was a joy ride. To the customers, however, down-trodden by the journey of life, the song and the dance made a positive difference in their otherwise dreary existence.

So, they came to the luncheonette for a glimpse of the golden girl with the flaming red hair who could make them feel alive again, forget their troubles, and laugh once more. Anna's joy was infectious in a society that had lost so much on so many levels, and for those who would never recover their dignity after nearly nine years in the Great Depression. For such customers, the luncheonette became their glimmer of hope...their passage to what was and might still be their reason to continue.

It wasn't long before Burkhardt became mesmerized by the young waitress. Immediately upon being introduced by Henry, Anna commented on his name. "Burkhardt. German, right? Too formal! From now on we will call you Burk."

Each day, between washing dishes, or sweeping and mopping floors, and cleaning toilets or windows, Burk watched Anna entertain the customers with her quick wit and teasing manner. On more than several occasions, her four brothers came into the luncheonette at the height of the lunch hour, and before you knew it, the five siblings were singing a buoyant Irish ballad with a rousing harmony of voices heard beyond the luncheonette and onto the sidewalk and street. Within minutes faces were planted against the glass, peering into the café to get a glimpse of the singers, while the diners enjoyed their hearty meals and unexpected entertainment.

Over time, as Burk observed by helping Henry in the kitchen, discovered he had a knack for producing excellent combinations. At first he prepared the vegetables for stews and soups. Then he moved on to gravies and sauces. In no time, using his experience as a waiter aboard the ship, he was presenting appealing, hearty dishes. Henry was relieved to have the kitchen backup. Having to be at the luncheonette each day was beginning to take its toll. Perhaps soon he could use Burk to take over some of the responsibility of meal and menu planning.

After a short time, Henry and Burk decided to divide the responsibility of the kitchen, with Burk planning most of the meals and menu, while Henry prepared the pastries and desserts. Burk had an idea to increase business, and he shared it with Henry one day after an especially busy lunch hour.

"The place is closed at 3:00 p.m. each day. It's a shame we can't open for dinner."

"That would take more work and more help. I don't think we can swing it," Henry returned.

"Let's give it a try. How about on Wednesday nights we announce Irish Night with an offer of Irish stews or corned beef and puddings for dessert? Maybe Anna's brothers can sing their Irish songs for a small fee and tips. On Friday nights we can sponsor German Fest with sauerbraten, red cabbage, spaetzle, and apple strudel, or German bratwurst with all the fixings," Burt put forth excitedly.

Henry was beginning to warm up to the idea. "I know a couple of fellas who just might be interested in playing some German music."

"On Saturday, we can advertise Italian fare with family-style servings of pasta and meatballs and all the makings of an authentic Italian dinner," Burk added. "Three nights a week from 5:30 to 9:00. That should be manageable. They'll come from all over."

Henry was silent for a time, mulling over Burk's suggestion. "I like the idea, but let's start out slowly with Irish Night on Wednesdays for now and gauge the response. We'll need time to prepare and advertise. We can begin in two weeks."

In no time, news of Irish Night spread quickly. To cut down on the need for extra help, Burk and Henry decided to serve cafeteria style, with people paying for their meal at the end of the line. Uncle Greuton and Aunt Sigrid took turns on these evenings, receiving the monies, and clearing or cleaning tables when necessary. The extra money helped, now that their baby was born, a beautiful little girl they named Rose. Anna and her brothers would sing Irish ballads in return for tips and a decent dinner. It was a shining success.

Before long, German Fest was added on Friday nights, followed by Italian Night on Saturdays. Henry's luncheonette was becoming much too small. Word had gotten around of the good dinners and entertainment to be had at a reasonable price. Before long, Burk suggested they see about obtaining the small empty shop space beside the luncheonette to enlarge the premises. It was a daring move in an economy still rocked by the Great Depression, but business had sufficiently justified the added expense.

On nights off, Burk would often join Anna's brothers to play poker or attend outings to the Irish pubs. The Irish pubs were a gathering of hard-drinking young men. Anna kept up with her brothers' spirited partying, often becoming quite drunk herself by the end of the evening. Burk was usually the only one in the group sober enough to guide Anna back home. Anna always thanked Burk the next day for looking after her. The couple developed a liking for each other and began dating, though for Burk, a fascination with the redhead with the spirited temperament had happened long before.

One evening, Burk spent the night at home in the one room he was still allowed at the back of the luncheonette. It was a rare occurrence since he always sought time away from the luncheonette when he was off work, for a change of scenery. Anna had told him she would be attending a Catholic mass but would stop by later in the evening to say goodnight.

A light tap on his door indicated her arrival. He opened the door to find Anna taking a quick nip from a flask. "I thought you were going to mass," he said, observing her putting the flask in her dress pocket.

"I did already," she said stepping in but not before amorously kissing Burk as she sashayed her way toward the bed to sit at its edge. She reeked of alcohol, he noted, but was alluring, all the same. Retrieving the flask from her pocket, she took another swallow. "I thought we could party a bit. I already confessed my sins, so I need another reason to go to church to confess next week," she commented with slurred words.

"You need to go easy on that stuff," Burk commented.

"Nice and easy," she replied with a giggle, taking another swallow before handing him the flask to join her.

She was especially sexy and demanding this night. Burk had no sexual experience, but he didn't need it. Anna took charge, guiding him to an explosive first experience meant for the gods.

"That was nice," she said afterward. She then reached toward the floor for her dress, retrieving a pack of cigarettes from a hidden pocket, then lighting one while she lay beside him.

"I didn't know you smoked," was all Burk could say, still recovering from his trip around the world.

"There's a lot you don't know about me, honey," she returned huskily and mounted him once again.

❦

It was common knowledge Burk and Anna were dating, the two often joining her brothers for a Sunday afternoon at Coney Island. Separated from the main part of Brooklyn by a three-mile creek, Coney Island was a popular beach resort and amusement center, with a two-mile boardwalk, famous for its wooden roller coaster and hot dogs.

This Sunday, the men rode the roller coaster without Anna, who declined complaining of a sick stomach. Then, while Anna was in the restroom, her brothers surrounded Burk, cornering him in an out-of-the way alcove near the coaster.

"You gonna marry her, right?" the older brother, Sean, asked.

Burk was surprised by the question. "Someday," he replied weakly, clearly perplexed.

At that point, the youngest brother, Liam, stepped forward, getting directly into Burk's face with a menacing glare. "Not someday. This week, before our parents find out."

"This week? Are you mad? We haven't even talked about marriage. We're just having a good time," Burk replied confused by the posturing of Anna's brothers.

"Too good a time, if you ask me," Sean replied. "You'd better make this right or else," came the threatening tone.

The puzzled expression on Burk's face led one of the brothers toward a possible conclusion. "Maybe he doesn't know," Liam suggested.

"Know what?" Burk asked, clearly perplexed.

The brothers looked at each other before responding. "Well, I'll be. You don't know, do you?"

Burk looked at the four brothers and then looked beyond them at Anna in the distance coming toward them. "What should I know?"

Jack, the next older brother replied. "You should know that our sister is pregnant and she tells us you're the father!"

Burk felt faint, his face draining of all color. "What? This is the first I've heard. How could you know before me?"

"She's been getting sick a lot lately. She finally told us last night," Connor, the third brother, confessed.

When Anna drew up to the group, she knew her secret was out by the look of disbelief on Burk's face.

"You didn't!" she said loudly with her hands on her hips in a defiant stance toward her brothers.

"Someone had to," Liam defensively retorted. "We did it for your own good. Do you know what will happen if our parents find out? You two need to get married right away. This week! We can claim the baby came a bit early. No one has to know but the six of us."

"It will take time to plan a wedding," Burk stammered, still reeling from the news of his impending fatherhood while trying to buy time for his freedom.

"No time for a wedding. Go down to the courthouse and get married there and then claim you eloped," Sean said, thinking it through hastily. "Our parents will be upset, but at least you'll live to tell of it."

Things were going much too fast for Burk. Afraid of Anna's brothers and father, he reluctantly agreed to being marshalled toward matrimony to prevent Anna and the family from being marred by scandal. The next week, on a Thursday afternoon, the four Irish brothers met Burk and Anna at the courthouse to witness the marriage of their only sister to the German immigrant. Burk was clueless about how to care for a baby. For that matter, so was Anna.

After the ceremony, all had a quick dinner and then Burk, Anna, and her brothers apprehensively presented themselves at the home of their parents, where the young couple announced their marriage. Anna's mother cried. Her father's face turned a crimson red, his anger and disappointment obvious in balled fists. Anna's parents had hoped for an honorable wedding of their daughter to an Irishman of some stature, not a fast turn-around to a German-Jewish immigrant of limited means who spoke broken English. How could this have happened?

Anna's mother quickly surmised her daughter was pregnant, but kept this assumption to herself so as not to enrage her husband further. She was the pragmatic one. What is done, is done, she concluded. There was no reversing the inevitable. No one would witness, though, the disappointed tears she shed on her pillow for many a night. Thankfully, her daughter and sons were taking special care so as not to reveal the bride's true plight. Perhaps, just perhaps, they would keep their reputation as a family in-tack. Yet, Anna's mother worried. She had noted her daughter's drinking and partying were becoming more frequent. The neighbors noticed as well, one even commenting on Anna's seductively playful manner. While beautiful, and vivacious, with her long, flowing red hair, Anna was much too young to be a mother. She had not gained the maturity required to take on the responsibility of motherhood.

"Where are you to live?" Anna's father asked brusquely three days later while Burk and Anna visited for the family's Sunday dinner. "Two people can't live forever in the back room of that luncheonette."

Burk drew back, clearly afraid of his father-in-law, but glad he could provide an answer. "We have secured a one-bedroom flat in Montclair," Burk shared. "We moved in yesterday."

"Where in Montclair?" Anna's mother probed.

"Claremont Avenue," Anna returned before taking a bite of the Irish stew.

The parents looked at each other before responding. "That's the nigger part of town," Anna's father responded with growing agitation. "You want our grandchild born there?"

Anna stepped in before the conversation turned heated. "Actually, Father, it is on the edge of the Negro section of Montclair; besides, we can afford the rent."

Burk was not understanding his father-in-law's ire, not having been exposed to racial or ethnic conflict. The world scene was changing decidedly, however. Even in Burkhardt's small hamlet near Stuttgart, Germany, all would come to know of ethnic cleansing. He had no idea of the animosity between the Negro and the Irish in this new country of his, though both groups were vilified by their fellow countrymen.

Anna's four brothers helped defuse the situation by discussing the 1938 World Series. The family were ardent New York Yankees fans. The Yankees' opponent in this year's standing, the Chicago Cubs, lost to a Yankee sweep in four games. The distraction served its purpose. Anna's father was somewhat mollified and retreated to his room for the rest of the evening.

Despite her pregnancy, Anna went about her business as usual. Though working each day, she continued to party and drink. Burk wondered what this activity was doing to the baby.

"Maybe you should let up on the drinking," he said one morning after she came home drunk the night before."

"No respectable Irishman gives up the drink," she sarcastically shot back.

He knew it was pointless to argue. Anna had a stubborn streak and Burk was no match for her caustic rebuttals.

Seven months later:

Early in 1940, Anna gave birth to a robust male child she and Burk named John. He was absolutely beautiful and had a sweet nature, already seeming wise, as though he was an old soul who had returned to the earth-plain many times. Quiet and compliant, this child would immediately win Burk's heart. He was mesmerized as he held his newborn son in his arms, walking him around the hospital room shortly after Anna gave birth.

"Are you going to hold him all day with that goofy smile on your face?" she railed from her bed when the boy was just hours old.

"I just might," he returned without looking at the mother of his child. "He's a handsome one, he is."

It didn't seem motherhood had any effect on Anna. She appeared to lack any maternal instinct. It wasn't long before she began complaining of how much time baby John took up. Finding a neighbor, friend, or family member to care for the baby for a few hours, Anna would steal off to spend time at a nearby pub, at times not returning home at all. Burk, with increasing frequency, would take the child with him to work, where he stayed until Anna's arrival. Placing the baby in the back room, Burk was forced to stop work periodically to check on the infant.

"We can't have this, Burkhardt," Henry was forced to declare one day. "The child should be home with his mother. It's too disruptive for you to bring him here."

Burk nodded while preparing the menu for the day in feigned acknowledgement. "If only I knew where the mother was," he replied under his breath.

Eventually Anna would appear for her waitress shift at the luncheonette, often looking a bit hung-over. Her drinking was getting worse, but she managed to pull herself together enough to ingratiate herself to the customers and earn bigger tips. She laughed and joked as if she were the sun. She hugged and teased, and in so doing, she lured those torn from their moorings by an unforgiving economy; those who had lost everything and were now living on the streets. For many, Anna was the sunshine in their day, and she luxuriated in their recognition.

Burk watched his wife, who entertained the sullen customers who sat each day on the stools in the luncheonette, but who appeared to be unmoved by the crying baby in the back room. He was often angry and undone by her calculated antics for attention, and then ended up completely forgiving her as she made passionate love to him in the night. She indeed had a hold on him. She wasn't an easy woman to tame. It was what made her so alluring.

Two years later, Anna produced another boy; this one they named Gus. Burk took one look at his second son and knew it wasn't his. The whole family questioned the paternity, knowing Anna's wandering spirit could not be contained.

Aunt Sigrid did what she could to support Burkhardt, but she herself was overwhelmed by a second child of her own. Their meat market was beginning to prosper and their participation in Henry's highly successful themed dinner nights commanded much of their time. Presently, Henry was operating six nights a week, adding a Scandinavian menu on one night and an Americana menu of fried chicken and ribs with all the fixings on another night. There was no way they could rescue Burk each time he asked for help. To Aunt Sigrid and Uncle Greuton, Burke's difficulty indicated that Anna was more interested in partying than in caring for her two young children. It wasn't their place to assume full time responsibility for the children.

The situation was clearly deteriorating when Anna, less than a year later, announced she was pregnant once again. It was doubtful Burk was the father. The occasion proved more alarming because of two occurrences within months of each other. The first was Anna's arrest for disorderly conduct while in a drunken state, and the second was of her mother's unexpected death by heart attack. After the arrest, Anna took to the bottle with even more frequency. Her drinking was out of control. She was clearly addicted. Henry had no choice but to dismiss her from employment. She had become more of a liability than an asset.

Burk was almost relieved by her dismissal. Not having her at work each day created a buffer and prevented the frequent embarrassing scenes she caused. He assumed, incorrectly, that her dismissal would allow her to spend more time with the children during the day. The little girl, Lorraine, now nearly a year old, was not a happy baby. Burk wondered if it was related to Anna's drinking while pregnant. In any event, the child was difficult to pacify, crying often and sleeping fitfully, giving rise to excuses Anna made up to disappear during the day. Burk would often come home to find the children in the care of a teenage neighbor who had no idea where their mother had gone. Often the children were hungry and dirty. To make matters worse, rumors of Anna being seen with other men had increased.

"Your brother, Liam, tells me you were at the bar last night with the guy down the street," Burk ventured one morning. "I thought you were meeting your girlfriends."

Anna turned to him with a snarl. "Liam needs to mind his own damned business," she shot back.

Burk looked at her for a time before venturing further, knowing he was going to be bombarded by a sarcastic, demeaning reply. "You're a mother, Anna. We have three children who need care. They need three meals a day and baths at night. The neighbors have been stopping me in the hallway concerned about their crying. They are threatening to call the police."

She turned to Burk with balled fists. "So, let them call. In fact, if they are so concerned, let them come and raise them!"

Burk was shocked. "You can't mean that!"

Anna said nothing in reply. She simply grabbed her handbag and left, never looking back.

Chapter Seven

Present Day – South Carolina

Donna had spent several days evaluating the statements of each person who came for Bible study the day of the murder. After she reviewed the background checks done on every member of the group, she placed photos of them on the wall. Ken was right; they were clean as a whistle.

She painstakingly reviewed the personnel files of the Lundys' automotive supply and restoration shop employees, finding that the files lacked sufficient detail. That evening she mentioned to Ken the absence of elements in the company's employee files.

"You know how it is, Donna. Most small businesses are fairly lax in their upkeep of files and records."

"I understand, but we might be missing something important. I saw you interviewed the employees. Does that include past employees?" she inquired.

Ken marveled at how thorough she was. "Yes, just one past employee, but was cleared."

"I'd like to speak with the employees, both past and present. Do you think it will be a problem?"

"Suit yourself, but since the owners are gone, they've closed the place to new business. You'll have to visit them at their homes. If I remember, a list of their addresses is in one of the binders."

"I saw the list. I'll call one or two of them tonight to see how their day is looking tomorrow and then proceed from there."

After dinner, Donna called the employee she determined from the records had been employed by Lundy Vintage Automotive the longest. Sam Carpetta answered on the third ring. After explaining who she was and what she was hoping to accomplish, Donna asked Mr. Carpetta whether she could meet with him in the morning.

He seemed hesitant. "I already told the police everything I know. I don't know what more there is to say. Do the police know you're snooping around?"

Donna took on a more authoritative stance before answering. "I am engaged in this matter at their request, Mr. Carpetta. If you feel you need an introduction from Detective Daniels before meeting with me, I can certainly have him call you this evening to verify my engagement as a consultant."

There was a pause on the other end. "No, that won't be necessary. It's just I don't see what you can accomplish that the police haven't been able to do, that's all."

Donna was beginning to dislike the guy, but forced herself to respond respectfully. "Sometimes, Mr. Carpetta, a different approach and perspective can yield positive results."

"Maybe," he half-heartedly replied. "Tomorrow morning is not good. I have work to do. How about late afternoon about 3:30? I'll try to be available."

Having agreed to the time and then ending the conversation with Sam Carpetta, Donna then telephoned Eden Parish, listed in the employee records of Lundy Vintage Automotive as a paint specialist. Mr. Parish was far more engaging and helpful than Sam Carpetta had been. Again, Donna explained to Parish who she was and the purpose of her call.

"I'd be happy to help in any way I can," Eden Parish responded. "The Lundys were wonderful people. They gave me a job when I needed it most and I've tried to return their kindness by doing some of my best work. I still can't get over what happened. It's never going to be the same without them."

Donna ended the conversation by setting a time for their meeting, after verifying Eden Parish's address.

Late the next morning, Donna pulled into Eden Parish's driveway. He was waiting for her on the front porch, seated in a rocking chair with an iced tea in his hand. As she came up the steps, Parish stood to greet her by shaking her hand. He was rather young, in his mid-forties, tall, and somewhat angular. Though not especially good-looking, nonetheless, he possessed a captivating smile and sincere manner.

"How about joining me for an iced tea, Dr. DeShayne?"

Donna eyed a pitcher, and extra glass on a side table. "I'd love to," she agreed.

Seated and comfortable, Donna took a sip of her tea before beginning her interview.

"I was remembering our conversation yesterday, Mr. Parish. You seemed to have had high regard for Simon and Wanda Lundy."

Eden Parish appeared to almost shrivel within himself before responding emotionally in a near trembling voice.

"They were the closest thing to family I had ever known. I'm an only child. My parents died when I was young, so I really had no family to speak of, just a grouchy old aunt I had little to do with. She's gone now, thank goodness. I ended up doing drugs and such, just getting into trouble with no real future... or plans for that matter...but I found I had a love for cars and paint restoration.

"The Lundy's encouraged me to go to body-shop school. They even paid for half the tuition. It was the first time in my life someone was looking after me. They took me to church and it was there I was introduced to a whole different way of seeing the world. I got off drugs and made a lot of good friends in the process."

"That's quite a success story," Donna acknowledged. "It's not often someone pays for another's schooling."

"Oh, it wasn't a handout, rightly. They promised to hire me after I received my certification, and we arranged I'd pay them back a little every pay period. I feel a little guilty...I still owe them for half the loan amount and now they're gone."

"What are you going to do for work now?" Donna asked tentatively.

Eden Parish straightened a bit more in his chair, eager to share. "I'm finishing up on some orders we took before the Lundy's were...before their deaths. I've been talking with the Lundy children. I'd like to buy the business and pay them monthly. We just need to agree on an amount. They're working with their accountant."

"I'll bet you're relieved," Donna replied, interested.

Eden twisted in his chair to get a better measure of Donna. Finding no hint of ill intent, he continued. "You see, I just bought this home two years ago. Imagine me, an orphaned former drug addict being able to buy my own home. A dream come true. I come home every day and give thanks for my blessings, and I owe it all to the Lord and the Lundys. Their deaths threw me for a loop, for sure. Then I began to see the opportunity to own my own business. Who would have thought?"

Donna nodded a bit before continuing. "Would you know, Mr. Parish, whether anyone held a grudge toward Simon or Wanda? They seemed to be highly upstanding people from what I've been able to establish so far."

"Now that's the thing. They *were* upstanding people. They would do anything for anyone. They spent a great deal of time drawing folks into the church. That's how I ended up addicted to God instead of drugs," Parish replied rather proudly. "I can't imagine anyone disliking, much less murdering them."

"I see," Donna returned slowly. "What was the Lundys relationship with Sam Carpetta?"

Eden Parish seemed uncomfortable with the question, fidgeting in his chair before pouring himself another iced tea. Donna thought the additional drink may be his way of buying time to decide on his answer. After taking a long, deep swallow from his glass, he finally addressed Donna's question.

"Sam's a great auto body restoration guy, but he could be difficult."

"In what way?" Donna probed.

Parish cocked his head before responding. "He's moody. One minute he's as soft as a new kitten, the other minute he is growling like a bear about something. Unpredictable is how Simon described Sam one day. It got to the point Simon was forced to keep Sam away from the customers. Sam took issue with the decision. It ended in a heated scene with Sam storming out of the garage. I didn't expect him to come back to work, but lo and behold, he shows up the next day as if nothing happened."

"Do you get along with Mr. Carpetta, Mr. Parish?" Donna asked in an attempt to get a handle on the dynamics of the employees and owners of Lundy Vintage Automotive.

"Pretty much. I just stay out of his way," came the reply. "It's easier that way. Besides, Sam goes to the same church. I don't want to bring any conflict into the church."

Donna thought for a moment before continuing. "If you succeed in securing the Lundy's business assets, will you retain Sam Carpetta?"

Parish looked at Donna questioningly. "I haven't given it any thought, really. I'll cross that bridge when I get to it."

Donna thought Eden Parish already knew the answer, but decided to end her questioning, thanking Eden Parish for his time and the iced tea. She walked back to her vehicle, sitting in it for a time before backing out of the driveway. He was a nice enough guy, she concluded. It was an interesting fact the Lundy's had financed his education, with him paying them back. It was even more interesting Eden Parish had purchased a new home in the last couple of years. Apparently being an automotive restorer paid very well.

That evening, Donna related to Ken her meeting with Eden Parish. They were having a glass of wine on the porch on what was proving to be a lovely evening.

"So, is he a good guy?" Ken asked quietly.

Donna thought about the question before answering. "He *appears* to be a good guy. I really don't know what he is. He has been squired through school, church, and employment by the Lundy's. So my judgment is on the back burner for now. Oh, by the way, Sam Carpetta was not at his home this afternoon per our agreed upon time."

Upon Donna's pronouncement, Ken immediately retrieved his cell phone and dialed a number. Donna listened, intrigued by his posturing.

"Mr. Carpetta, this is Detective Ken Daniels with Horry County Law Enforcement. If you remember, sir, we met previously. It's my understanding you failed to appear for an interview with Dr. DeShayne this afternoon. I am hopeful your reason for not appearing is due to an unavoidable occurrence. In any event, Mr. Carpetta, we will expect you at the County Law Enforcement Center in the morning, ten o'clock sharp. I trust I have your complete agreement as to time and place," Ken postured authoritatively.

"You people have nothing better to do than harass law-abiding citizens, I see," Sam Carpetta sarcastically replied. "Some of us, Detective, work for a living and don't sit behind a desk scratching their ass, pretending authority. You can bet I'll be there in the morning, but you'd better have a good reason for dragging me in. I can pretty much guarantee you're not going to pay me for my lost hours at work, are you? You must be desperate to conjure up this poor excuse for not solving a crime! Shame on you, Detective!"

"Nonetheless, Mr. Carpetta, you *will* appear, I trust." Ken then ended the call.

Ken was taken aback by the venomous response of Sam Carpetta. He thoughtfully stood for a moment before turning to Donna. "Whew! Was he ever angry! I don't remember him being so volatile in our previous encounter. I would have remembered, for sure," Ken mused. "What has changed, I wonder?"

"Perhaps it's because he's out of work. With the demise of Simon and Wanda, Lundy Vintage Automotive has been closed, at least temporarily, though Eden Parish tells me he is negotiating with the Lundy children in the hopes of securing ownership," Donna recounted.

"Is that so?" Ken returned.

He looked at Donna intently knowing she was bothered by something. "You have an issue with his buying the business?"

Donna turned to Ken with a smile, always counting on him to bring home the obvious. "It's a wonder to me how a former drug-addict-orphan finds his way to such a state of accomplishment. I'm not saying it's not possible, but the odds of one climbing their way to the top are few and far between."

"You are suggesting that purchasing the assets of Lundy Vintage Automotive is climbing one's way to the top?" Ken asks with a hint of sarcasm.

Donna gathered herself before responding. "Here's how I see it. The Lundy daughters are recovering from the deaths of their parents. There are lingering interests that need to be attended. The business for one, and the Lundy home for another. If I were them, I'd welcome any overture to take matters off my hands. The business for sure. How fortuitous that Eden Parish comes forward to rescue them from the business side of things."

Ken ponders Donna response. "The guy is trying to solidify his future," Ken counters.

"I might do the same thing if I were in his shoes."

"Maybe," Donna quietly replied.

The next morning, Ken and Donna waited for Sam Carpetta to arrive at the Law Enforcement Center. He did so right on time, but his attitude was less than inviting. Escorted into a nearby conference room, Carpetta glared at the couple after sitting down. "You've got twenty minutes and then I'm out of here! Some of us work for a living," he harshly declared.

"Mr. Carpetta, I believe you are out of work with the death of the Lundys unless you have found employment in the interim. May I remind you that if you had kept your appointment yesterday with Dr. DeShayne, this inconvenience for both of us wouldn't have been necessary," Ken countered evenly.

"So what is it you want from me this time? I told you everything I know," Carpetta spat back.

Donna leaned forward to address the scowling personality across the table. "Two people were viciously murdered in their home, two people you worked for. In your mind, doesn't this occurrence demand a little more cooperation from you in the hopes it brings the guilty party of this revolting crime to justice? After all, two people you knew well, even going to the same church, were maliciously assaulted and killed. Does this not anger you?" Donna asked with a measured air of angst.

Carpetta sat back, somewhat shamed by Donna's question. "How do you know we went to the same church?" he asked in a much more subdued tone.

Donna looked at the man who now appeared contrite. "Eden Parish mentioned it in passing," was all Donna said.

Carpetta looked down at his lap in a gesture of surrender. Donna sought to further reclaim the man's interest. "Eden Parish also mentioned you were a top-notch restorer of older vehicles. He seemed quite impressed by your capabilities."

"He said that?" Carpetta questioned, clearly taken aback.

"You seem surprised by his endorsement," Donna furthered.

Carpetta was slow to respond. "It's just that we've had a rivalry of sorts between us. I guess you can call it professional pride. It's not really personal, though. The guy is difficult to dislike, if you know what I mean."

Donna and Ken smiled.

The icy manner was melting. He continued, "The thing is, I've been out of work for nearly three weeks. It's been hard to find employment in my field. I'm under a lot of pressure. I'm not usually so hard to get along with."

Donna remembered Parish's comment on Carpetta's mood swings, but chose not to go there. "I know you've been asked this before, but would you know if anyone had it in for the Lundys in the form of a grudge or a hostile dispute?"

Sam sat back, more engaged now in assisting in the investigation. "I've worked for them for nearly eight years, and in all that time, I've not witnessed one sour note of discontent from anyone dealing with them. They were very well-respected. People came from all over the country to have their collector cars restored. Their passing has left a hole in the industry, I can tell you that much."

Ken proposed a question of his own. "Did you ever notice anything off between Simon or Wanda, or the family as a whole?"

"Never. Wanda oversaw the front end shop for parts while Simon oversaw the restoration end of the business in the back. The one daughter, Joanna Carnes, came in a couple of mornings each week to do the bookkeeping and payroll."

"Do you know both daughters?" Donna inquired.

"I met the other daughter briefly a while back. She and her husband are very involved with the church. They travel, visiting related churches in the district. They rarely get home to visit."

"Is there anything else you can tell us about the Lundy's?" Ken asked. "There's nothing too small."

"Nothing negative, really. I can be hard to get along with. It's my diabetes, but Simon always found a way around my moods. He had a thing for people, especially the elderly. They just liked him and his wife. Simon and Wanda would have folks come to the shop after work for private Bible study. They would use the kitchen in the back."

"Have you met the people who came for Bible study at the shop?" Ken queried.

"I know one who became a member of the church. His name is Nathan Bennett. He's a single guy who lives alone. He's a welder by trade, but raises dogs on the side; Huskies, I think. He would bring his dog, Camelot, to the shop when he met with Simon for private Bible study."

Donna and Ken were busy taking notes. This information was new to them. "Any others?" Donna asked, not looking up.

"There's a middle-aged couple who would come for private Bible study on a different day than Bennett. They've even been to church with the Lundy's from time to time. I noticed they were at the funeral. I don't know much about them, but they seemed to be pleasant enough. I only met them the one time."

"Do you know their names?"

Carpetta thought for a bit, and then shook his head. "No. I'm not good with names."

Two Days Later:

"Ms. Carnes, this is Detective Ken Daniels from the County Law Enforcement Division. I'm calling to inform you that your parents' properties, both their home and business, have been released as crime scenes. You are free to handle your parents' affairs in any way you see fit."

"Thank goodness," Joanna returned. "I appreciate your phone call."

"By the way," Ken continued, "we're seeking the name of the couple who had private Bible studies with your parents at their shop. Would you know their names?"

"Oh, that would be Blake and Laura Miles," Joanna returned.

Ken was taken aback. "Wasn't Mr. Miles the one who discovered the crime scene and called the police?

"Why, yes. I would have thought you knew."

"We were only told your dad had private Bible studies with a couple. We didn't know it was Blake Miles."

"Oh. I understand. So I'm free to sell the property and the business, then?"

"Since it has been surrendered as a crime scene, you are free to make any decision regarding the properties you deem necessary. If I can be of support in any way, please do not hesitate to contact me."

"I will," Joanna assured the detective. "I still have your business card."

❦

Within weeks Eden Parish had taken ownership of Lundy Vintage Automotive and decided to keep the name due to the company's nationwide reputation for outstanding work and service. Sam Carpetta agreed to stay on, not really having a choice, but all the same, relieved he was working again.

Joanna Carnes placed a "For Sale by Owner" sign in the front yard of her parents' property. She was hoping the sale would allow her to own a home of her own. Currently, she was renting.

Donna's dogged approach in the investigation continued. There was an answer. There had to be.

Chapter Eight

HILDEGARDE

Montclair, New Jersey–1944

While the country was still healing from the Great Depression, it was now under the second-term leadership of President Franklin D. Roosevelt. Though economic recovery in FDR's first term rapidly improved from 1933-1936, the country relapsed into a deep recession in 1937. It would stay that way until America's entry into another world war. Despite this national economic setback, the luncheonette held its own, even growing at a slow but acceptable pace.

Anna had been gone for weeks and, in the end, never did return to her husband and children.

Burkhardt feebly attempted to care for the young ones, but the task proved overwhelming. Following the many concerned complaints from neighbors to city officials, the children were eventually taken into protective care and, by court order, were placed in an orphanage. The judge ruled the parents unfit, unavailable, and unviable for the parenting of the three under-age children. Aunt Sigrid, Uncle Greuton, and Henry spoke before the court, but none could assure the court of stable care for the long term. Burkhardt noted that during this entire process Anna's family was conspicuously absent.

Burkhardt grieved the outcome, visiting his children often. They seemed to be prospering without him, benefiting from consistent eating, sleeping, and bathing routines, as well as supervised play with other children in the orphanage. All of it was more than they had experienced with their parents. No more would they cower in the corner while adults fought in angry and drunken rages. No longer would they be looked after by disinterested teenaged neighbors when their mother left for the day, resulting in hunger and filth. The orphanage, to these youngsters, served as a respite from their often frightening abandonment.

Most weeks the man who claimed to be their father visited them. How could they know, or even care whether he was really their father? So many men had been paraded before them in their lives. For now, they were enjoying the routine, food, and clean bedding. They actually feared that the man who visited might have the authority to take them away from this pleasant environment and return them to their former existence of neglect and want.

Burk continued to work for Henry. Business was good, but Henry had developed a health condition that caused him to miss work with increasing frequency. The burden of compensation for Henry's absences fell on Burk, but he managed, with the children in the orphanage, to cover all bases, gaining confidence as he went along. He hired two additional waitresses and a helper in the kitchen, and even expanded the pantry to allow for a much-needed prep station.

Henry came to work when he could, but eventually had come to a decision. One day, after an especially busy lunch hour, Henry approached Burk with an offer.

"Would you be interested in buying the business from me?" Henry inquired of Burk. "I think I need to spend my time regaining my health," he explained.

"I have no money to buy you out," Burk declared honestly, mindful of the overall expense of the operation.

"We can work something out. Perhaps a monthly payment arrangement?"

Burk considered the offer. "Perhaps," he replied. "Let's talk again. We may be able to will come up with a plan we can both live with."

Within weeks, Henry and Burk signed papers, transferring ownership of the luncheonette to Burk. While Burk proved to be an excellent cook, he was lacking in money management skills. It didn't help that he gambled money away at weekly poker games. He became adept at 'robbing Peter-to-pay Paul,' and he was often late with his monthly payment to Henry. If truth be told, Burk unconsciously liked to live on the edge of monetary collapse. It somehow fed his need for excitement. This became more obvious as time went on.

Luckily, his staff of waitresses and kitchen helper were dependable. One waitress in particular was often early for her shift or left late after seeing to the needs of the customers. Hildegarde was a thin woman of German descent. Her father had served in the German army as an officer in World War I. She told Burkhardt that her parents had established a steamship ticket agency in Elizabeth, New Jersey, after immigrating to America. Burk also discovered through conversation, that Hildegarde was the second youngest of twelve children, and the youngest of only three girls in the brood.

Quiet by nature, Hildegarde spoke little, and to him, seemed vulnerable for some reason. Always respectful, she was a hard worker and a keen observer. At one point, she came to Burk to let him know she had seen one of the waitresses stealing the tips off a table served by another waitress. They quietly conspired to watch for future happenings. Sure enough, it happened again. Burk dismissed the woman that very afternoon, after recovering the stolen tip money by threatening her with a criminal charge of theft.

Watching his disgraced employee leave the restaurant, Burk commented on his dilemma in Hildegarde's hearing. "This leaves us short-handed for tomorrow," he said.

There was a knowing quiet before Hildegarde responded. "I know someone who can step right in," was her nearly inaudible reply.

Sure enough, the next morning Hildegarde walked in with another woman in a waitress uniform, introducing the woman to Burk as her sister, Caroline. The two couldn't be more different. Caroline was taller and somewhat hefty, while Hildegarde was thin, almost boney. While Hildegarde was quiet and reserved, Caroline was outgoing and talkative. While Caroline looked as if her clothing was straining to contain her large frame, Hildegarde's uniforms, in contrast, were often too large and baggy, almost suggesting an effort to hide her body. Burk observed a hearty appetite in Caroline, but a rather small or non-existent one in Hildegarde.

Burk was focused these days on Hildegarde, partially because she seemed in need of protection, but of greater interest was Hildegarde's keen mind and ability to assess an environment, whether it be personal or business. He was not good at such things.

Burk was in the throes of sexual deprivation since Anna's exit, often finding willing women to address his need. In considering Hildegarde, though, he found he was not as attracted to her as he was to Anna. Anna reeked of sexuality and wild abandon. Hildegarde, however, was more restrained, appearing almost doubtful of her worth and in the end, not as physically attractive as Anna. Anna had a voluptuous presence in both body and spirit. Hildegarde's presence was far less so. She often hid and drew back, as though pained by her appearance. Despite these deficits, Hildegarde, to Burk, represented a possible replacement for the mother of his three children. He knew the court needed to be presented with stable parenting from two parents. She came from a good family who owned a prospering business and had no record of run-ins with the law. That was important.

Several months later, Burk asked Hildegarde to a movie. It would be their first date. *Gone with the Wind* had recently exploded across the big screen to enthusiastic audiences everywhere, presenting an epic historical romantic film set during the Civil War and reconstruction.

It had been a wise choice for Burk. Hildegarde was mesmerized by Olivia de Havilland's portrayal of Melanie, and Vivien Leigh's role as Scarlett O'Hara. Many other film goers idolized Clark Cable in his role as Rhett Butler or Leslie

Howard as he brilliantly portrayed Ashely Wilkes. *Gone with the Wind* was the talk of the town, earning acclaim far and wide for both the stars and film.

Walking home afterward, holding her hand, Burk noted Hildegarde was animated more than usual in her review of the movie. She clearly loved it! The following week, he gave her a copy of *Gone with the Wind*, Margaret Mitchell's only known book. You would have thought he had given her the keys to the kingdom. She hugged him fiercely in gratitude. It was enough for Burk. Hildegarde wasn't Anna, in any sense, but he felt from her a sense of trustworthiness and the presence of a quiet grace, new to him until now.

Several weeks later, after three dates and one walk along the shoreline and dinner after, Burk bit the bullet and engaged Hildegarde in a serious conversation. He had no idea what the outcome would be.

"I am visiting my children this weekend. Would you like to meet them?" Burk asked hesitantly.

She considered the question. "I didn't know you had children. Where are they?" she finally queried.

Burk bowed his head in shame, and recounted to Hildegarde the drama of Anna and the three children. Hildegarde was stunned.

"All three are in an orphanage?" she asked in disbelief. Her life experience had not included the reality that some children did not live in loving homes. Her naïveté would be her undoing for years to come.

"I visit them every week," Burk offered in an attempt to explain and seek forgiveness. Truthfully, he would sometimes miss visits for various reasons, mostly to gamble or to date women.

Three days later, Hildegarde accompanied Burk on his visit with his three small children…two sons, both under six years old, and a daughter, nearly two years old. This was a whole new world to her. She could not have imagined the overwhelming surprises ahead for her.

In the ensuing months, Hildegarde accompanied Burk every week in his visits to the children. The young ones were guarded at first, never smiling, but Hildegarde often brought presents and treats, and engaged them in games during their visit. Slowly, very slowly, their fear lessened, and they responded to her questions about their week's activities, health, and concerns. Burk was pleased. It appeared Hildegarde was becoming emotionally attached to his children.

The facility personnel noted the consistent visitation schedule day, time and length. They observed the gifts of clothing, shoes, and treats, as well. The woman accompanying the father, they observed, seem stable and genuinely caring toward the children.

In time, Burkhardt asked Hildegarde to marry him. To his surprise, she said agreed, but insisted he ask her father for her hand in marriage. Burk accompanied Hildegarde to the home of her father and mother. They lived in a neighboring community called Elizabeth. Turning off a paved street onto a graveled road, they proceeded a mile onward before coming to a rather large home enclosed in a somewhat forested area. Burk noted how private the setting was. Exiting the vehicle, however, the first thing he noticed was a flag pole on the grounds bearing an American flag, and then another flag right below it; a Nazi flag.

Burk froze in place. Hildegarde looked at him questioningly. "Are you all right?" she asked, clearly bewildered by his demeanor.

"I didn't expect to see the Nazi flag," he said. He then gathered himself. "Your parents *do* know I'm a German-Jew, right?"

"What difference does it make?" Hildegarde returned innocently. Clearly, she was indifferent to the political leanings of the time.

Beckoning him toward the house, Hildegarde took his hand and guided him toward the front porch. Burk was becoming increasingly uncomfortable. Was this a trap? He remembered she mentioned her father established a steamship ticket agency in Elizabeth shortly after arriving in America. Was the business a cover for sinister operations supporting the German Nazi party? All manner of thoughts were going through his head as Hildegarde opened the front door and yelled for her parents.

"Papa, Mama, I am home and have brought a friend," she bellowed toward the interior of the home while looking back at Burk who was now sweating.

"Are you all right? You don't look well," she inquired of her future husband.

"I'm fine," he managed to stammer before bringing himself under control.

Hildegarde's mother rushed toward her daughter, embracing her warmly. "Your father is on an overseas call, but will join us shortly. This must be your friend, Burkhardt," she said extending her hand to him in greeting.

"It is a pleasure to meet you, Mrs. Zimmer. Hildegarde speaks of you and your husband in the most glowing terms," Burk managed to say while shaking his future mother-in-law's hand.

Ushered toward the back of the house into a large kitchen, he was introduced to one of Hildegarde's nine brothers. The youngest of the family, Peter, was making himself a sandwich at a sideboard filled with meat, cheese, bread, fruits, and desserts.

"So sorry to have to eat and run," Peter said before sitting down to eat. "I have to be at work soon, and I'm running a bit late," he said, before taking a quick bite of his sandwich.

"Help yourself to something to eat, Burkhardt. We are quite casual on Saturdays. We all serve ourselves," Mrs. Zimmer invited.

Midway through lunch, Mr. Zimmer entered the kitchen. He was a tall, imposing man with an impressive handlebar mustache and commanding stance. His handshake was forceful, while he looked directly at Burk in a prolonged assessment before letting go.

"Please, finish your lunch," Hildegarde's father gestured to Burkhardt's half-eaten plate of food while he turned to the sideboard to fix a serving for himself. He noted that once again his daughter was not eating.

Settling himself at the table he looked at Hildegarde and Burkhardt, already surmising the reason for their visit. Hildegarde had never brought a boy home before, though she had been in other relationships. She seemed content these days to be with her girlfriends. Until now. He wondered whether this young man was aware of her illness. They had certainly struggled with it as a family in recent years, baffled by its hold on her. He could only hope that finding love would be her cure.

"You need to see the doctor about this. There's definitely something wrong with your stomach," Burk commented shortly after their marriage, having observed Hildegarde vomiting in the bathroom once again.

"It's nothing," she managed to say while rinsing her mouth.

He suspiciously eyed her. "How can you say such a thing? You obviously cannot hold down your food. That's not normal."

"It must be a bug of some sort. I'll see the doctor next week," she promised, not really intending to make an appointment.

Burk nodded and kissed his wife goodbye for the day before heading out the door for work. He wasn't one to make waves. Life was finally stable. Hildegarde was taking care of the children and keeping a clean home. That was the most he could hope for. She didn't cook, so he would bring home supper for her and the children from his luncheonette at the end of the day, and then go out again several nights a week to play poker with the guys.

Offhandedly, he mentioned Hildegarde's stomach problem to his Aunt Sigrid several days later. "Maybe she's pregnant, Burkhardt," Aunt Sigrid suggested.

Burk was taken aback. "Do you think?" he asked.

"Surely her visit to the doctor will reveal the source of her discomfort," Aunt Sigrid said reassuringly.

In time, Burkhardt inquired of Hildegarde what the doctor had said, assuming she had gone. Hildegarde came up with a response. "Oh, he thinks it's an ulcer and gave me some pills. I feel better already. I'll be going back next month for a recheck."

Satisfied that the problem had been addressed, and especially relieved she wasn't pregnant Burk allowed himself to become distracted in the weeks ahead. He never fully grasped that Hildegarde had an eating disorder, purging herself after eating in a desperate attempt to remain thin. Her parents had agonized over her disease, even sending her back to doctors in Germany for a cure. It would eventually kill her, leaving her body with nothing with which to fight her eventual cancer.

The possibility that Hildegarde deceived him never entered Burkhardt's mind. There was a new waitress at the luncheonette who reminded him of Anna. Like Anna, she was outgoing and seductive. Witty and wily, she would often make him laugh. He realized he missed Anna, especially in the bedroom. Hildegarde was dutiful enough, but just that... dutiful. She wasn't at all inclined toward sexual adventure, and her thin frame was not all that appealing. Burk liked his women full and curvaceous. He ventured off from time-to-time to engage in back room trysts with the new waitress, one of many such departures over the years.

Metuchen, New Jersey – January 1952

Hildegarde sat in a 1950 Henry J with the children, watching their home burn to the ground. She was grateful the two older boys from Burk's marriage to Anna were away from home that night, working at Burk's diner. It was a chilly night and she was very pregnant with another child. She kept the car running for warmth. The children were crying. She felt alone and helpless.

Panicked phone calls to her husband before leaving the burning house proved fruitless. She ushered the children to her car after calling the fire department, who appeared nearly thirty minutes later, the damage already proving extensive. The firemen did what they could, but the destruction was too great on the end of the house where it had started. The rest of the house was drenched in the spray of the fire hoses and a falling snow that had started earlier and didn't stop for nearly twelve hours.

Her only recourse was to call her mother-in-law, Kathe, who had immigrated to America four years previously with her third husband. The children were cold and scared, as was she, and the house was uninhabitable for the foreseeable future. As it turned out, her mother-in-law took in the three older children, while her sister, Caroline took in Hildegarde and the younger children. Burkhardt showed up hours later with no excuse for his absence.

The immediate cause of the fire was determined to be faulty wiring. The home, after all, was nearly sixty years old. They had moved there after losing their home in Montclair because of unpaid property taxes. Burkhardt claimed he had a friend who was willing to rent the home to him until he was in a position to purchase it.

Hildegarde went into labor in the wee hours of the morning, no doubt related to the stress of the house fire. She was delivering several weeks early. This baby, a girl, would be followed by another girl fourteen months later. This last one would be weaker and frail, but a survivor, nonetheless.

With no room for Burkhardt, he retreated to the back room of his luncheonette until the house was rebuilt, this time with two additional rooms. Hildegarde became distant with her husband, long suspicious that he had strayed into the beds of other women. He denied the claim, but he couldn't explain his often late arrivals home smelling of perfume. The unfaithfulness was just one of a long list of disappointments for Hildegarde.

"How long are you going to punish me for something I didn't do?" Burkhardt railed one night after unsuccessfully attempting a move into the bedroom of the now-renovated house.

"There are enough children already. Find your pleasure with your women," Hildegarde replied with an air of disgust.

"Maybe I'll just do that," Burkhardt declared heatedly. "In the meantime, I'll leave you to your cleaning frenzies. They seem to satisfy you more than I do!" he said before leaving the room, slamming the door behind him.

Indeed, Hildegarde was a compulsive cleaner, working feverishly through her days. Some would consider some of it necessary with so many children and an absentee husband. Her cleanliness, however, went far beyond the norm. Twice a year, she would attack the house in spring and fall cleaning rituals that lasted for days, often to her near exhaustion. In between these occasions, she cleaned daily with a driving compulsion.

Despite the emotional distance between the two, Burk brought dinner home each night from his luncheonette. He had taken to turning the three and one-half acres of property on which the house sat into a mini-farm as if he was replicating memories of his hillside home in Germany. Having finally purchased the home, he had a two-story chicken coop built and an attached cow barn. In another corner of the property, there was a pig-pen with a goat corral nearby. Dogs, cats, and geese roamed the property.

Burkhardt was staying home more, occupied by the care of the animals, while his wife cared for the children. There was an unspoken truce between them, though neither said much to the other.

One Saturday morning, there was a knock on the front door. Burk answered and was greeted by a middle-aged couple selling Bibles and Bible literature. Burk listened to their talk of God while they read scripture to him. This was all new to him. He wasn't inclined toward religion of any sort, but this couple affected him. Their warm and caring manner was genuine and infectious. Burk took the literature. The couple promised to come back, and indeed they did the following week. Each week, the couple took time with Burk, sharing with him the scriptures, citing passages of hope and deliverance.

Soon, both Hildegarde and Burk were attending the church the middle-aged couple attended. They became avid adherents to church teachings, fearless in their faith and raising the children in their new-found belief system.

For Burkhardt, it was the beginning of finally feeling as though he belonged, of being accepted without question. When their young son was hit by a car while crossing a busy street, the church rallied around the family, bringing meals and words of encouragement until the crisis passed. Burkhardt was never so moved or grateful for the child's survival and for the support of church members.

In time Burk and Hildegarde volunteered their home as a Bible study site for a small group from the church, one of several homes that served church members offered for this purpose. Every Tuesday evening, a group came to study and learn scripture. On Saturday mornings they used the home to host an introduction of door-to-door evangelizing, in which Burk and Hildegarde participated with relish.

"Brother Burk," one of the elders from the church addressed the new recruit. "We have noticed your dedication and zeal for the Lord. We'd like you to assist us in our activities to shepherd the flock. Would you consider taking on that responsibility?"

Burkhardt was stunned. They wanted to use him? A German-Jew with a decided accent and cumbersome ways? What could he possibly offer this group that had been so gracious to him and his family? "I would be honored," he finally stammered.

"Wonderful!" the elder replied, warmly embracing Burk. "As you know, we have a gathering each year at our convention and, we must feed the flock just as Jesus would. With your restaurant experience, we could use you in the kitchen to help with food preparation."

"How long would you need me?" Burk asked.

"Why, for the entire week," came the reply. "Three meals a day."

Burk agreed, having no idea the commitment he was making. Not only would it take him from his luncheonette, but from his animals as well. He needed to make preparations for his absence. The dishwasher at the eatery could probably come feed the animals each day, and he could probably prepare food in advance for the customers. Thankfully, he had a dependable short-order cook for the front end and a baker in the back kitchen.

It wasn't long before Burk was appointed an elder in the church, with responsibility for the welfare of those assigned to his home Bible study group. In some cases, he would be judging the sins of those under his charge, visiting those who were ill, and giving Bible lectures, not only in his church, but also in associated churches. He relished his involvement, as well as being a part of the circle of influence in the church.

There was nothing he wouldn't do to advance church teachings by evangelizing wherever and whenever he could.

Hildegarde cared for their eight children as well as she could, rarely seeing her husband except for dinner, and then he was gone for the evening, either to a meeting with other elders or visiting those under his charge. While she regularly attended church, she secretly seethed at being left to care for the children without consideration for her need to rest and have time to herself. To compensate for the lack of support, she began to drink, sneaking cases of beer into the house and hiding them under her bed. Fortunately, the older children looked after the younger ones.

"You're going to bed early again tonight?" Burk questioned her one evening.

"I got up early to read," was her made-up excuse. "I'm behind on my Bible reading."

"I've been asked to attend Elder School. It will be held in upstate New York," he shared off-handedly while adjusting his tie before heading out the door to attend a meeting of the elders.

She looked at her husband intently. "For how long?"

"Three weeks. All of the elders from this region have been invited."

"Do they really expect a man with eight children to leave his family for three weeks?" she countered indignantly.

"Hildegarde, you know very well that we must sacrifice ourselves to save lives before the end comes. It's the will of the Lord."

Hildegarde never replied. She simply went up to her bedroom and began to drink.

Spring – 1975

The funeral director gathered the family in a side room just before the memorial service for Hildegarde, who had died at home after an unexplained illness.

The director seemed agitated as he addressed Burkhardt. "Am I to understand that your wife died at home?"

Burkhardt, now sixty-four years old, nodded. The manager shook his head in disbelief, looking down at the papers in his hand. "Your wife was riddled with cancer, and yet I'm to understand she had no pain medication to lessen her suffering. Who was her doctor? Surely no competent physician would allow her condition to go unattended!"

Burkhardt simply shrugged his shoulders and stammered. "She was seen by several doctors, I think."

The man stared at Burkhardt with more than a hint of exasperation. "You think? Don't you know? She should have been in hospice care at the very least. In all my years of practice, I have never seen a more inadequate response to the needs of the dying. Shame on you!" The director walked out of the room, so disgusted that he never said another word to Hildegarde's husband.

Burkhardt looked contrite. The rest of the family stood in stunned silence, not knowing what to say or how to respond. They carried on with the memorial service, which was attended by many compassionate church members.

Inquiry months later by one of the children into the whereabouts of Hildegarde's ashes would yield a nonplussed response from Burkhardt. "Oh, I suppose the funeral home still has them."

Chapter Nine

Present Day – South Carolina

Donna was becoming discouraged. Her work assisting Ken in solving the Simon and Wanda Lundy murders was going nowhere. She and Ken had interviewed Nathan Bennett the day before. They learned he was out-of-town for the entire month in which the Lundy murders took place, visiting his sick father in Oregon. His father died during the early part of his visit; Bennett had stayed on a couple of more weeks to assist his mother.

"Ken, I can understand why you have become so discouraged with this case. It's a tough one. I don't think I'm being much help to you," Donna commented one morning over breakfast.

"If you can't solve it, then no one can. I may just have to accept that someone got away with murder," Ken replied, before taking a bite of his toast.

"I'm still working on it but unless a miracle happens, I may have to throw in the towel. I'll let you know."

Just as they were finishing breakfast, Donna's cell phone rang. The caller was Lacy Sue Larson, Carole and Gavin's adopted daughter.

"Hey, girl," Donna answered. "What a nice way to begin the day. Everything all right?"

"Everything is really good with us, but I thought you would like to know Herta Cohen was admitted yesterday after taking a fall. She has a cracked right femur. She asked me to call you to let you know."

"Oh, no! I hadn't heard. Will she be okay?" Donna asked.

"I think she'll be all right, but, given her age, these things have a way of taking a sudden turn, if you know what I mean."

"Yes, I do know what you mean. I'll be sure to visit her today. Thanks for letting me know."

Donna turned to Ken. "That was Lacy Sue. Mrs. Cohen is in the nursing home recovering from a cracked femur after a fall. I think I will visit her this afternoon."

Just then Donna's phone rang again. "Donna, this is Suzanne Siegel, Herta Cohen's daughter."

"Oh, yes, Suzanne. I just heard about your mother from the director of the nursing home, Mrs. Larson. I'm sure you're worried for her."

"I am concerned, but she's in good hands. I'm glad to know Mrs. Larson called you. Mom wanted you to know," Suzanne shared.

"I have plans to visit her this afternoon, unless you know of some reason why I should not."

"Please do. Mom will be delighted. She thinks the world of you and speaks of you often.

"I feel the same about her, Suzanne. Will you be there this afternoon as well?"

"I rarely leave her side. Yes, I'll be there."

Donna made her way to Lacy Sue's office upon entering the nursing home before visiting Mrs. Cohen. She hugged her grown god-child who was now managing the affairs of not only the nursing home, but also the assisted-living center associated with it. Donna was extremely proud of this woman who had transcended a traumatic experience to become a respected community professional.

"Mrs. Cohen will be thrilled to see you, Donna. I know I am," Lacy Sue commented as she hugged her mother's best friend.

"You look busy," Donna commented looking at Lacy Sue's desk filled with files.

"We've admitted several new patients, including Mrs. Cohen, to the nursing home and a few people have applied to move to the assisted-living facilities. I'm going over all the paperwork. My assistant is on vacation."

"Lucky you," Donna returned with a wink. Donna left Lacy Sue's office after securing Mrs. Cohen's room number.

Entering Mrs. Cohen's room, she found Suzanne seated by her mother's bed working on a crossword puzzle. Mrs. Cohen's eyes were closed.

"Is she sleeping?" Donna asked softly.

"No, I'm not sleeping. I'm just checking the back of my eyelids for cracks," the aged woman teased, though her voice was weak.

Donna and Suzanne laughed. "I can always count on you for humor, Herta," Donna said while making her way around the bed to hug her friend. "Are you comfortable?"

"I am. My daughter has seen to my every need. I feel I am such a burden. She has better things to do than watch over me."

"There is nothing more important than you, Mom," Suzanne countered. "Besides, Sally will be here by the end of the week to help."

Donna looked questioningly at Herta. "My younger daughter. Sally lives with her family in Utah, but is taking some time off while I recuperate. So what adventure are you working on these days, Doctor?"

Donna smiled at the older woman, who knew of her many sojourns away from home consulting with law enforcement agencies on their tough criminal situations. "I have had the luxury of being home for the last two weeks catching up with myself and household chores," Donna shared.

"Oh, I'm sure your Ken is delighted," Herta responded.

"Well, he's eating better, I can tell you that," Donna returned with a hint of humor.

Donna began relating her progress to date in her spring cleaning and gardening efforts as well as her latest reads. The three women talked until an orderly came into the room announcing it was time for Mrs. Cohen's physical therapy session. After the older woman was transferred to a wheelchair, Suzanne and Donna followed her and the orderly down the hall to the physical therapy room. Before Herta entered the room, Donna hugged her friend goodbye, assuring her she would visit again during the week. Donna noted there were two other patients in the physical therapy room working through their supervised routines.

Exiting into the hallway, Donna turned to Herta's daughter. "Listen, Suzanne, I had a thought. I could certainly come and sit with your mother most afternoons. Surely staying here all day is exhausting."

"Oh, Donna, I couldn't ask you to do that."

"You didn't ask; I offered. Let me come at least one or two afternoons this week, until your sister arrives. Surely, you have things you need to catch up on. It will give me a chance to spend more time with your mother."

The women agreed to a schedule for the week. Before leaving the center, Donna popped her head into Lacy Sue's office to inform her of her departure and the arrangement she had made with Suzanne to return later in the week.

"Oh, I forgot to tell you!" Lacy Sue commented. "Mary is buying a house."

"What? I didn't even know she was looking!"

"Neither did I, but she told us that when she compared a rental payment with a home loan payment, the loan payment was just as doable. The house is a fixer-upper, but she thinks she can handle it over time."

"Good for her. Wow! Our little girl has grown up."

"I'm very proud of her. I'll let you know when the closing is. The house is part of an estate settlement. An old lady lived there. Apparently it is quite dated and the old woman left many things behind, destined for the trash heap."

"Sounds like Mary has her work cut out for her, but she is more than capable."

Two days later, Donna returned to the nursing home to spend the afternoon with Herta. While Herta was having physical therapy, Donna briefly visited Lacy Sue in her office.

"Any word on Mary's closing?" Donna asked Lacy Sue from the doorway.

"It's scheduled for tomorrow afternoon. We're planning on a trash haul Saturday morning and cleaning on Sunday."

"Count me in for both days," Donna called, leaving before Lacy Sue could protest.

Returning to the physical therapy room, Donna waited on an upholstered bench in the hallway. After a short time, the door opened. Expecting to see Herta, Donna looked up and saw instead, a patient she had seen wheeled out the day before. Shortly after, Herta emerged.

"She did great," the physical therapist reported as Donna took charge of the wheelchair.

Donna suggested they enjoy the garden for a few minutes before returning to the room. Herta was more than agreeable to the change in scenery. It was a beautiful day, and the courtyard was adorned in flowering shrubs and plants native to South Carolina. Bird houses, statuary, and fountains completed the inviting picture. Other patients were enjoying the cool, refreshing breeze as well. After a time, Donna left Herta on the patio and headed for the refreshment room to get a drink and cookie for the both of them. On her way back to the square with their treats, she noticed a couple who appeared to be in engaged in intense discussion in a far corner of the hallway. It was a peculiar scene. She decided to take a shortcut back to Herta, thus bypassing the occupied couple.

Two Days Later –

Donna and Ken drove to Mary Larson's new home the first thing Saturday morning. Lacy Sue, her husband, Seth, and their twins…little Gavin and little Carole…were already there, along with grandparents Gavin and Carole. Two pickup trucks, Seth's and Gavin's, were backed into the driveway. Ken had driven his over as well, just in case.

"Are we ready to go to work?" Ken asked the group as he and Donna exited their vehicle.

"I'm anxious to look at the house first. Can we?" Donna asked.

"Sure," Mary answered. "Let's all go. Along the way I can tell you what needs to be removed."

It was obvious the house had been neglected and was in need of TLC, but Mary had wisely looked beyond its current condition to see its potential. A brick ranch-style house, it sat on a wooded lot with mature trees and, while the grounds also required attention, the setting was inviting.

After the tour, they spent the morning hauling out worn and outdated furniture, much of it to be taken to the dump. There were very few pieces worth keeping. The kitchen was very dated. They decided to empty the kitchen cabinets of dishes and glassware, which they boxed and set aside to be donated to a local charity. The girls concentrated on emptying the kitchen cabinets while the guys hauled out the furniture.

After a break for lunch, which Gavin had brought for the group, they resumed their work.

The guys started the afternoon tearing out the kitchen cabinets with the decision made to replace them with newer ones. The ladies hauled things from the closets and storage areas. By mid-afternoon they had emptied most of the house, even taking down the old, worn draperies and window blinds.

Seth and Gavin drove their pickup trucks, now full with discarded cabinets and furniture, to the dump, while Ken and the women moved into the garage. They set aside tools that were still useful, while relegating old paints and solvents to a corner for disposal at the county's recycling center. Pulling on a cord hanging from the garage ceiling, Donna brought down a set of stairs leading to a storage space. Climbing the stairs, she found several boxes.

"Hey, there are boxes up here. I'll need help getting them down."

Ken came to lend a hand, replacing Donna on the stairs and passing the boxes to her and Mary.

Donna opened the first box and realized they were accounting ledgers, bank statements, and old files. The second, third, and fourth box looked about the same. All were marked with the word "Estate" in bold, black letters, and each box was dated. Based on Donna's initial assessment, all four of them apparently contained estate records for a nearly twenty-year period.

Curious, Donna opened the fourth box, which contained the closing period of accounting and retrieved a bank statement. She was about to toss the paper back into the box, when she glanced at the bank statement again. The first line of the heading indicated it was the financial statement for an estate, but the second line of the heading is what caught Donna's attention. The second line read, "Simon Lundy, Personal Representative.

"Mary, didn't you say you bought this house from an estate?" Donna asked.

"Yes," Mary answered. "Why?"

Donna looked around the garage with a far-away look in her eyes. "What are the odds this house belonged to a trust in which Simon Lundy was named as executor!"

Ken looked stunned. "Our Simon Lundy?" he asked with an incredulous tone.

"I think so," Donna returned quietly, still thinking and scanning the contents.

"Then it means all of this paperwork needs to be examined," Ken said with a sweeping hand over the boxes. "We can't take anything for granted."

"I agree," Donna countered.

"Mary, may we have these records?" Ken asked the young woman, avoiding any mention the current investigation.

"I certainly don't want them. They mean nothing to me, Uncle Ken. Take them if you wish."

❦

By the end of the following week, Ken and Donna had sorted through the paperwork in the four boxes they found in Mary's upper attic.

"It seems each box was full of papers representing four separate estates for which Simon Lundy and his wife Wanda served as executors," Ken summarized. "Now, what are the odds someone would serve as personal representative to four estates unless they were an attorney, which Lundy was not?"

"Indeed," Donna concurred. "It's apparent the house Mary purchased was part of an estate and the old woman who lived there benefitted from a trust as part of that estate, but who are these others?" Donna asked, sweeping a hand over the other three boxes.

"That's what we're going to find out," Ken returned.

"We should ask Joanne Carnes. She just might know some of these people from her association with the church," Donna ventured.

"It's as good a place as any to start," Ken agreed.

Ken telephoned Joanne Carnes the following morning. "Mrs. Carnes, this is Detective Ken Daniels."

"Is something wrong, Detective? I wasn't expecting to hear from you. Are you calling to let me know you have arrested those responsible for my parents' murders?

"I'm afraid not. Believe me when I tell you we are working diligently on solving this case. Which is why I am calling. We have come across some papers that are in need of explanation."

"What kind of papers?" Carnes inquired with a note of hesitation.

"Accounting papers, mostly ledgers and bank statements. I know I'm asking a great deal of you, but is there any chance you can come by the Law Enforcement Center and see whether you can identify these files for us?"

"Are they accounting papers from my parent's business? Lundy Vintage Automotive? If you remember, I did most of the bookkeeping for my parents. To answer your question though, I can try to identify whatever you have. Would this afternoon be all right? I'll be in the area. It shouldn't take long, right?"

"This afternoon would work very well," Ken replied, pleased by her cooperation. "No, it shouldn't take long at all."

Joanna Carnes was a bit early for her appointment. "I finished up my business ahead of schedule," she said by way of explanation when she spotted Ken in the foyer.

"We appreciate your cooperation, Mrs. Carnes. It *is* Mrs. Carnes, correct?"

"Yes, but I'm divorced. Where are these papers you want me to look at?"

Ken took her into the conference room and introduced her to Donna. "We've asked Dr. DeShayne to assist us in our investigation."

Donna had the paperwork lined up on the far end of the conference room table in date order. There were four stacks of records corresponding to the four found boxes.

"What kind of doctor are you?" Joanna asked, eyeing Donna intently.

"I'm a forensic psychiatrist, Mrs. Carnes. I'm usually called in on difficult cases," Donna answered succinctly while making a sweeping motion toward the four piles of paper. "I took the liberty of arranging them in date order."

"Where did you find all of this?" she asked scanning the organized papers on the conference table."

"We found these records in boxes in the upper garage storage area of a deceased woman named in a current trust your father and mother were overseeing," Ken continued in explanation. "It appears they relate to estate matters, four of them, with your father serving as executor for each. Do you recognize the names on the binders, Mrs. Carnes?"

Joanna looked over the four sets of paperwork, taking her time with each one. She finally looked at Ken with a puzzled expression. "I only know of one, Detective. This one," she said pointing to the last stack. "I didn't know they had control over these others. I wonder why they didn't tell me."

Ken and Donna looked at each other. "Who is this person?" Ken inquired placing his hand on the one stack Carnes had recognized.

"Brother Burkhardt was a member of the church. An elderly gentlemen with a bit of money. My father and he were rather close. I knew my father had been asked to oversee the terms of this gentleman's will, but I didn't know about these others," Carnes said with a gesture toward the other three stacks.

"So, you don't know who these other people are?" Donna asked for clarity.

"Oh, I know who they are, all right. I just didn't know my father represented these other estates as well."

Donna cast a quick glance at Ken. "How do you know these others, Mrs. Carnes?"

"They were members of the church as well," she revealed.

Donna was quick to respond. "Your father must have been highly valued to have four people from the church entrust their last wishes to him."

Joanna smiled slightly. "He and Mom had a way with the elderly. They were always visiting them, having them over for dinner, doing little errands or chores for them, visiting them at the hospital or driving them to doctor's visits. They'd been doing that for years."

"I see," Donna replied. "Did these people not have families to see to their last wishes?"

"I know this last one had a large family," Joanna disclosed. She walked from one pile to the others, examining each name as she went. "I don't know about these others. Some of these folks have been gone for a while." She then looked hopefully at the detective. "Is this important? Will it help solve my parents' murders?"

"We are examining every bit of information that comes to us, Mrs. Carnes. We are not overlooking anything in the hopes it leads to the arrest of the person responsible for your parents' deaths," was all Ken replied.

Ken walked Joanna Carnes to the front entrance of the Law Enforcement Center, thanking her for her time. Returning to the conference room, he found Donna busy on her iPhone.

"Did you know?" she asked as he reentered the room, "that an executor of a will or estate in the state of South Carolina is entitled to be compensated each year until the estate is settled?"

"I would think so. It can be a lot of work," Ken returned. Donna didn't respond, but kept reading her phone search. "What are you thinking?" he finally asked.

"I'd like to go over these papers before I comment. I will say, however, that the murders of Simon and Wanda Lundy could be just the tip of the iceberg."

Donna carefully reviewed all of the papers retrieved from the storage space above the garage. Creating a large wall chart, she constructed a flow chart of dates and names, including the size of each estate under Lundy's care.

"Uh, oh!" Ken said, entering her office late one afternoon several days after their meeting with Joanna Carnes, "I know when I see something like this you're in your 'pit bull' state."

"Something like that," Donna muttered with a pen in her mouth while pinning a note to the chart. Straightening up and taking the pen out of her mouth, she turned to kiss Ken in greeting.

"Find anything, yet?"

"Nothing substantial. It seems the first three estates were small compared with the fourth. I've listed them by financial value as you can see. The first three took anywhere from two to five years to settle. The fourth was just being settled now. Mary's purchase of her home was the last physical-asset-related matter to conclude in this estate after nearly eighteen years of oversight by Lundy."

"Eighteen years? Why so long?"

"The trust provided for the wife to live in the home with all expenses paid by the trust until her death before the children could receive their inheritance."

"That's not so unusual. Most wives stay in the house, willing it to their children upon their death."

"Yes, but this wife wasn't their mother."

"Ouch!"

"Yes, ouch. For all nine of them. Waiting eighteen years for their inheritance is only half of it. The wife was number four!"

Chapter Ten

DOROTHY

New Jersey – 1976

Within thirteen months of Hildegarde's death, Burkhardt, now nearly sixty-six, married Dorothy, a woman he had known from the church who owned a home and had personal savings. Burkhardt himself was broke, living in a rented home and running a food truck and catering business from its basement after losing yet another home to unpaid state taxes several years before Hildegarde died. Dorothy wouldn't know of such matters until much later.

Dorothy had worked all of her life, having raised four children; two boys and two girls, now grown with children of their own. Her husband died ten years before, leaving her to oversee the care of her now aging mother and a mentally-challenged aunt that lived together.

Burkhardt moved into Dorothy's home after their marriage; a lovely bungalow-type dwelling with a fenced-in yard. She also assisted Burkhardt in his catering business often working long hours preparing food destined for occasions the following day. It was not unusual for the weekends to be especially busy with catering for a wedding reception or two along with other occasions of celebration. Holidays were especially demanding.

In time, the business moved out of the basement into a storefront location. Above the storefront was a two-bedroom unit where Dorothy placed her mother and aunt, overseeing their care through the day while she worked below.

Burkhardt was again comfortable and solvent. Still very active in the church, he was managing both his business and escalating church responsibility, not to mention increased monetary contributions toward the church's needs.

After fourteen years of marriage to Dorothy, Burkhardt made a decision. "I need to think about retirement in the next year or so. I'll be selling the business. We will need to relocate so that we don't outlive our money."

"Relocate where?" Dorothy asked, surprised by her husband's decision.

"South Carolina. It's cheaper to live there. Besides, my daughter Karen lives there with her family and raves about it."

"I'll need to bring my mother and aunt," Dorothy declared.

"Of course. We'll find a home suitable for all of us."

Within months, Burkhardt and Dorothy found a home they liked in South Carolina and paid cash for it upon the sale of Dorothy's home. Before the move, however, her mentally-challenged aunt died. That left just the three of them to relocate to their new home.

Six months after moving into South Carolina home, Dorothy's mother fell ill and was hospitalized.

"Where's Dorothy?" asked Karen, Burkhardt's daughter by Hildegarde, when she encountered him at church services that evening.

"Oh, her mother is sick and in the hospital," was the reply.

"What are you doing here, then?"

Burkhardt was taken aback by Karen's snappish tone. "I have responsibilities here."

"Your first responsibility is your family!" Karen turned away in disgust and headed to the hospital to support her step-mother.

Two days later, Dorothy's mother died. Dorothy began to realize that her distraction by the move and the care of her mother and aunt had prevented her from seeing Burkhardt's tendency to be self-absorbed and obsessive in his church activities. Since relocating and transferring his membership to a new church, he was more involved than ever. While Burkhardt was thriving, Dorothy was lonely.

Not long after her mother's death, Dorothy made an announcement. "I have a doctor's appointment this week. I have a lump on my breast," she said to no one in particular as Karen served dinner. It was one of their frequent meals with her father and step-mother.

"You're kidding!" Karen commented. "How long have you had it?"

"About a year, but it's getting larger. I think I need to have it checked."

"I would hope so. A year! What took you so long to say something?" Karen asked with a hint of alarm.

Dorothy didn't answer. Burkhardt kept eating as if nothing was amiss. Karen was viewing the scene in disbelief. She had great affection for her step-mother. Indeed, Dorothy had been kinder to her than her own mother. It seemed as if her father and step-mother were in deep denial of the potential consequences of the situation.

Medical testing revealed the shocking truth three weeks later. Dorothy was diagnosed with metastatic breast cancer. It was discovered in the lymph nodes and had already spread to the bone. Karen knew her step-mother had limited time and wondered whether the diagnosis would have been different had it been treated a year earlier.

Dorothy seemed resigned and Burkhardt simply stepped up his involvement in the church, often leaving his wife by herself. Karen would assist, often taking her step-mother to the doctor, and then the hospital when her bones began to shatter. There was little that could be done other than making her comfortable.

A member of the church had devised a system of supportive straps he used for his cancer-ridden wife to lessen the pressure and discomfort she felt from lying on the bed for long periods. He offered it for Dorothy's comfort after his wife's passing. Hydraulically operated, the straps could raise the patient higher from the bed for bathing, sheet changing, and general care. The patient was suspended an inch or so from the surface of the bed. That, along with periodic infusions of morphine, would allow Dorothy a bearable passing.

Karen was seething at Burkhardt's seeming indifference. He would leave his home for hours on far too many occasions to make house calls on sick people from the church while his own wife lay dying of cancer. Karen spoke to the hospice nurse of her resentment.

"Some people, if they can't manage the circumstances around them, project their energies to something they can control. This may be the case with your father," the nurse offered by way of explanation.

"He seems so removed, so uninvolved," Karen observed to the caretaker. "He leaves early in the morning and doesn't come back until mid-afternoon. It's almost criminal. I've had to arrange for church members to sit with her on those days I have other commitments."

"Try to see it from his view. He knows he's going to lose his wife. That can be hard. Some just go into denial as though nothing were happening."

Karen listened to the nurse's exercise in compassion, remaining silent, but underneath she was still fuming at her father's lack of concern.

Before long, Karen was forced to make the dreaded phone call to her step-sister. They had agreed that, when Karen felt Dorothy's time was near, her step-sister would take time off from work to help care for their mother in the final days. The girls took turns sitting with Dorothy through the days and nights, taking shifts so that each could sleep. Burkhardt rarely came into the bedroom where his wife lay, and when he did it was only to announce dinner was ready. The women took turns eating so Dorothy would never be left alone.

Dorothy died during a night of torrential downpours. The funeral was attended by a large number of family and church members. The family was saddened. Dorothy had been good to them. Karen and her step-sisters made sure to secure Dorothy's ashes, not allowing Burkhardt to have a say in their retrieval, and made sure she was placed in an honorable cremation garden in New Jersey near her former husband, mother, and aunt.

Less than three months later, Burkhardt made a phone call to Karen.

"I'm getting married," he announced unceremoniously.

Karen was shocked. "What do you mean you're getting married? Mom isn't even cold yet! Who is this one?"

"Mrs. Straighter," was all he said.

"Darla Straighter? You've got to be kidding me! You gave us Dorothy and now you want us to accept Darla Straighter? You need to wait awhile and think about this."

"How long do you want me to wait? I'm almost 88 years old. I don't have time to wait."

Six months later Karen received another phone call from her father. "I got married yesterday."

Chapter Eleven

Present Day – South Carolina

Donna approached every investigation as if it were a puzzle with many pieces. Over time, the puzzle would start to take shape, the images and placement becoming more cohesive and convincing. The acquisition of the four estate files, in Donna's mind, was very much a part of the puzzle. How they would eventually fit together was another matter.

Donna dedicated another wall in her office to the timeline of the four estates overseen by the Lundys along with a list of the subsequent payments from each estate made to them over the years for their oversight. The fourth estate, as with the other three, revealed the names of those who would eventually inherit.

"Learn anything?" Ken asked, perusing the newly placed information.

"A couple of interesting things. I had my forensic accountant go over the fourth estate. Nothing was amiss financially at first blush, but it did appear that Lundy disbursed funds to the children during the course of his oversight."

"Why is that interesting?"

"The children are what the trust refers to as second-tier beneficiaries. That means they only can inherit what's left of the estate once their step-mother dies."

"So?"

"So they shouldn't have received any monies before her death without court permission. The estate is an irrevocable trust. Its terms cannot be changed or altered without court consent. There were four distributions made to the children over a sixteen-year period. The first one was approved by the terms of the trust, the next two were done without court approval, but the fourth, apparently, had court approval. There are papers indicating the court's decision."

"So, Lundy broke the terms of the trust on at least two occasions."

"Yes. I wonder whether he got permission from the fourth wife to do so," Donna mused aloud. "Ken, I think we need to interview each of the beneficiaries starting with the one who lives locally, Karen Coppick," Donna suggested, pointing to the list of beneficiaries on her wall.

"I agree," Ken replied. "What about the couple who went to the Lundys for Bible instruction?"

"I have been calling them, but they have not returned my phone calls. I hope we have the right phone number."

"I'll send a unit over to see whether they still live at the address Joanna Carnes gave us. In the meantime, I'll get a hold of Karen Coppick."

Two days later, Ken and Donna pulled up to a lovely brick home in a well-established neighborhood less than two miles from the home Mary purchased from the trust.

"She lived close to her father," Donna commented.

Karen Coppick greeted the doctor and detective respectfully, offering them something to drink as they seated themselves in the garden room.

"You're investigating the Lundy murders," she began the conversation.

"We are, yes. How well did you know them?" Ken asked.

"I've known them for years," was all she said.

Donna saw they would have to prompt her for more information.

"How did you come to know them?" Donna asked.

"From the church."

"You belong to their church as well?" Ken inquired.

"Belonged. I no longer belong," came the terse response.

Donna and Ken glanced at each other. They waited for Karen Coppick to explain, but she didn't. Ken took another approach.

"How well did you get along with your father's last wife, Darla Straighter?" he finally asked.

Karen looked at the both of them. "What does *she* have to do with the Lundy murders? She's not involved, is she?"

Donna jumped in. "We're attempting to understand family dynamics. Surely your step-mother knew the Lundys from the church. Are we correct in our assumption?"

Karen gave a slight smile. "They were thick as thieves," she answered finally.

"What do you mean?" Ken prompted.

"Darla Straighter worked for Mr. Lundy for a time before she married my father. Simon would visit my father often before my step-mother, Dorothy, died."

"How did you feel about that?" Donna prompted, sensing there was more to this story than met the eye.

Karen shrugged. "Mr. Lundy was an operator. Even my step-mother knew it. She asked me to keep an eye on the situation after she was gone."

"What situation?" Ken questioned.

Karen looked down, as if attempting to find the words. "My father had come into some money. It was known that Lundy borrowed from him while married to my step-mother, but supposedly he paid it back."

"Do you know how much Lundy borrowed?" Ken probed.

"I don't know. I never asked."

"How did your father come into the money?" Donna asked. "Was it an inheritance of some type?"

Karen shook her head before responding. "It was a stroke of luck. He had a Certificate of Deposit with a local bank. The bank decided to go public and let its customers know. My father took the CD and bought shares of stock in the bank. The stock split every three months for the first several years, making my father a millionaire. The bank was eventually absorbed by a larger regional bank, and it no longer exists, but before then its stock paid off very well. He would tell me to invest, but I never did. My biggest mistake."

"Wow! That's quite an investment success story!" At this point Donna took another tack. "Were you close to your father, Karen?" Donna probed.

"I used to worship the ground he walked on," she replied in a sad voice.

"Used to…?" Donna prompted.

Karen looked up with a neutral expression, though her eyes were focused beyond. "It all changed when I left the church," she sighed. "My reality shifted. I took another look. I researched and studied and then made a decision more in tune with my new understanding. I finally made a decision that was, in the end, against the will of the family members who remained in the church."

Donna held her breath before speaking. "That couldn't have been easy."

Karen turned to Donna. Her expression was one of determination. "Nothing is easy when you're bucking a system that restrains free will and expression, but I had stepped over the line. I had a different insight and freed myself from the mind control and the entrapments that support a manufactured spiritual authority."

"Bravo!" Donna said while Ken listened intently.

Karen smiled weakly. "Thank you," she said.

"Was that why your father didn't choose you to be his Personal Representative?" Donna probed.

"Oh, I was, for the first will," came the chilling answer.

"First will?" Ken asked sitting up in rapt attention.

"There were three wills. Lundy finally gained the control he wanted with the third one."

"What happened to the other two?" Donna asked in disbelief.

"I left the church, so I was no longer trusted at that point. My brother Joshua, who was a stalwart church member, became the executor of the second will, but when he received a copy, he found it convoluted and unclear in its intent. It would have created countless problems after my father's passing. My brother and I sought to obtain addendums in the interest of clarification, even having people from the church witness my father's agreement to the changes. Then, after my father's death we discovered the third will, with Mr. Lundy named as executor."

Donna looked hard and long at Karen Coppick before speaking. "That must have been a slap in the face."

Karen's face twisted in remembrance. "I knew what Lundy was after. He was after the yearly executor's fee. In his twenty years of oversight, he realized nearly $250,000 for doing virtually nothing. The irony is that it is all perfectly legal."

Donna picked up the bitterness in Karen's voice. The woman went on. "What's more ironic is that my father was explicit in his verbal wish that he didn't want Darla's five grown children to have any part of the monies. Now here's the long and the short of it. Darla received a handsome sum every month from the trust with no responsibility for the upkeep or maintenance of the house or her medical expense. Those expenses would be the responsibility of the trust.

"In addition to the monthly trust allowance, she was also receiving pension payments from her deceased first husband, along with social security payments.

"It doesn't take a math genius to figure out her kids ended up a lot better than my siblings and myself, I can tell you that much. I'll bet my last dollar she laid aside enough funds from her 'earnings' to leave her children a handsome sum.

"The only thing left was the house, and it is in such a shambles, it had to be almost given away."

Ken and Donna eyed each other from across the room, not revealing that they were close to the person who purchased the house.

"How was your relationship with your father before he died, Karen?" Donna asked quietly.

Karen Coppick shook her head before answering. "It was non-existent toward the end. I figured out what he was really all about. All the pieces fell into place. My eyes were opened.

In our last conversation, I told him I wanted nothing to do with him. He used every woman he married, and then tried to use me. I reminded him his other wives had wishes for their children, wishes that would never be realized because of his lack of family loyalty."

Karen then looked imploringly at Ken and Donna. "To me, it's a spiritual process to support the physical bloodline and further whatever spiritual intent there may be. It was a law recorded in the writings of Moses and others who followed the dictates of early teachings. It is supported in this country when wills and estates include the term "*per stirpes*," which translates from the Latin as "my roots," and, indicates the children of the one who passes. My father was easily influenced, always wanting to look good in front of the church. To the church, his children looked ungrateful. They only know what they've been told by an old man who came into a bit of money and who waved it over his family in carrot-and-stick displays of self-importance. The church never knew there was not one, but three wills, of which the third would be the final legal document. "

Donna looked at Karen and understood. "You seem bitterly disappointed."

Karen returned Donna's gaze. "I'm disappointed, but I'm no longer bitter. It's been a spiritual lesson for me, Doctor. I can stand back from my bitterness and resentment and understand the behavior of those who don't grasp the spiritual dimension of life. My father practiced his religion but was not a spiritual man. He was deeds oriented. Underlying the deeds was his ego. He enjoyed the recognition he received as a leader in a church that many members experienced as more fear-based than love-based. Religion does not always encompass spirituality, although the two can blend beautifully."

Donna was impressed by Karen's perceptivity. "Do you attend a church now, Karen?"

"No. I avoid exclusivity," she replied. "Religion can be both good and evil. It can unite and it can divide. I appreciate the value of the sense of belonging and hope it offers to those who need it, however."

Ken edged forward in his seat to ask the ultimate question of this woman. "Mrs. Coppick, who do you think murdered the Simon and Wanda Lundy?"

Karen shook her head before answering. "I've asked myself that question a million times, Detective. I simply have no answer for you, but I'll say this. Whoever it was did our community an enormous favor."

Ken and Donna returned home. The conversation with Karen Coppick was very much on their minds, though they said very little to each other on the subject until much later. While they enjoyed a glass of wine, Donna prepared a chef salad for dinner topped with shredded ham, turkey, and hard-boiled eggs.

Ken was lingering at the counter when he finally asked the question. "What do you think of our visit today?"

Donna hesitated before she answered. "She clearly didn't like Simon and Wanda, but do I think she killed them? No, I don't think she did."

"She admitted to her bitterness and resentment," Ken noted.

"*Former* bitterness and resentment," Donna corrected. "Remember, there are eight other beneficiaries who may be bitter and resentful enough to commit murder, not to mention the fourth wife's children who may feel cheated out of recognition by the estate."

Ken nodded. "Finding those estate papers has presented a host of other possibilities that, until now, were not on the radar. I have a lot of interviews to arrange."

Just then Ken's phone rang. Donna took the prepared salads out to the sunroom table and refilled their wine glasses while listening to Ken's side of the conversation.

"Yes, Mr. Miles. We've been trying to reach you," Ken said to the man on the other end.

"I'm sorry, Detective. I've been away. My mother-in-law took a spill and we've been supporting her recovery. My wife, Laura, is still with her and won't be returning for some time. Is there something you need?"

"We're still investigating the Lundy deaths. We'd like to ask you some questions related to your finding the bodies. I'm sorry to have to do this, but it's important."

Blake Miles hesitated a bit before responding. "I'll help in any way I can, Detective. I don't know what more I can say on the subject though. Quite frankly, I'm trying to forget it. It was gruesome."

"I completely understand, Mr. Miles. I'm hoping I won't have to bother you again after this. May I come to your home, let's say, tomorrow afternoon?"

"I'm working late tomorrow afternoon and am just in the middle of a move to another home. Can we make it first thing tomorrow morning? I mean very early...about 7:00? I've got movers after that. They'll be here by 8:00."

Ken agreed to the time and acquired Blake Miles' current address before hanging up. He joined Donna in the sunroom.

"We've got an appointment with Blake Miles early tomorrow morning. I'll take you to breakfast afterward," he said with a smile.

"You'd better," Donna returned lightly.

The next morning, they presented themselves at Blake Miles' apartment with a knock on the door. He answered immediately. Blake Miles was a fully bearded man. Donna noted he wore his beard well-trimmed. It suited him. Ken introduced Donna.

"I have a full pot of coffee ready. Can I pour either one of you a cup?"

"I'd love one," Donna returned. "How thoughtful of you."

Blake busied himself in the kitchen before bringing out a tray with three cups of coffee, along with milk and sugar. "Sorry for the styrofoam cups. Our dishes are packed."

"Are you moving from the area?" Ken asked.

"No, we're moving to another property that's far more affordable. We've saved a long time for a home of our own and the time has finally come. Now, how can I help you?"

"All the best to you on your new home," Ken said, acknowledging the man's accomplishment. "We're aware, from our previous conversation, you were the first to discover the bodies. We recently learned you and your wife took private Bible instructions from Mr. and Mrs. Lundy at their place of work."

"We did, yes. For about eight months before their deaths."

"It's our understanding you also attended church with them on occasion. Were you planning to become part of the church?"

Blake smiled at the two before answering. "I must confess, Detective. We never intended to join the church."

"I don't understand," Ken admitted.

"Let me explain. My wife and I are avid students of religion. All religion. This group is interesting because of its vision of a doomsday survived by only a handful of people. We wanted to study its teachings and felt the only way to do that successfully was to present ourselves as eager students. It's not hard to penetrate the church. They are willing to speak to or teach anyone if it means saving a life."

"So you faked your interest?" Donna asked, surprised by the man's honesty.

"More or less," came the reply. "We wanted to get a real feel for how people of this church lived and interacted with each other."

"What is your conclusion?" Donna continued to probe, intrigued by the admission.

"There are some who genuinely believe the teachings of the church and others who are, what my wife and I call 'surface believers,' ones who use the church more for social interaction and job opportunities than as an avenue to demonstrate real faith."

"In which group were Mr. and Mrs. Lundy, if I might ask?" Ken inquired, his interest piqued.

"Now, they were slick. Very slick. They appeared to give heart, mind, and soul to the teachings of the church. Laura and I really thought they were sincere, at the outset."

"What changed all that?" Donna queried.

"I guess becoming too close to the couple. If you observe and listen, you can learn a lot."

Miles didn't appear to want to go any further in explanation, but simply concluded by saying, "Apparently, someone else listened and observed as well."

Ken sat back, watching the man before finally speaking. "Mr. Miles, are you saying that you're not surprised by the killings?"

"Oh! I'm not saying that at all! No one needs to die in such a hideous fashion. I'm just saying I'm probably not the only one who noticed a disconnection between what Simon and Wanda preached and how they lived, that's all."

"How so?" Ken probed.

Miles smiled slightly and simply shrugged. "They were greedy. Simon would often borrow money from those in the church, even though he didn't have to."

"Why would he do that?" Donna asked.

"To create a condition of trust. He always paid back the lender before the sum was due. The lender could then consider Simon someone they could trust and rely on."

"So you're suggesting that Simon Lundy purposely created an environment for future predatory use," Donna prompted.

"It's only my opinion," came the reply.

"I see," Ken replied. He went in a different direction. "It's been a while since we interviewed you right after you discovered the bodies. Sometimes we interview again to ascertain whether any other significant memory of events has surfaced. Have you thought of anything noteworthy that may have an effect on this case? Anything at all?"

"Like I told you on the phone, I can't say I have anything further to add other than what I've already said."

Donna had a question. "Mr. Miles, I haven't fully read the report you gave when you discovered the bodies. I plan to do that shortly. Was your wife with you as well, sir?"

"No, she was home with a migraine. I was going to attend Bible study by myself that evening. I came early to drop off a power saw I borrowed. When no one answered the door after a couple of tries at knocking, I walked in. That's when I discovered the bodies. I'm just glad my wife wasn't with me. She didn't need to see all of that."

"You've been in the Lundy home on other occasions not related to Bible study?" Ken probed.

"Simon and Wanda were always inviting groups over for dinner and picnics. They were quite the entertainers and very good at arranging group games. In some respects, I'm going to miss them. They took us in. I mean really took us in."

"What do you do for a living, Mr. Miles?" Donna probed.

"I'm a pharmacy technician."

"Does your wife work as well?" Ken asked.

"She has a little business cleaning homes."

Leaving Blake Miles with Ken's business card, Ken and Donna thanked the gentleman for his time, having noted from the window near where they sat the arrival of the moving company's truck.

On their way to breakfast, they discussed the interview.

"It appears Blake Miles wasn't impressed with his spiritual guides," Ken began.

"I found his position somewhat confusing. On one hand, he indicates the Lundys weren't what they appeared to be but, on the other hand, he comments he is going to miss them, that they were a lot of fun.

"What I find peculiar is the fact that Blake appears to be in his late forties or early fifties, and yet they are just now buying a home. There's no indication they have children so they don't have the expense of child-rearing."

"Your point?" Ken questioned after Donna hesitated.

She sighed. "Maybe I'm reading too much into it, but shouldn't they have been homeowners long before now?"

"Maybe they had a financial setback. The Great Recession did that to many."

"Maybe. Oh, by the way, Carole and Gavin are coming over tomorrow night to play cards. I hope that's all right."

"Sounds great! They're always a lot of fun. I just hope we go back to M-&-M's for the kitty."

Donna laughed.

❦

Donna spent the following day in a state of unrest. She tenaciously reviewed all the facts known thus far, perusing the timelines on her wall carefully; finding nothing. Something was gnawing at her sub-conscious, though. She hated such occurrences, when fragmented impressions tugged her awareness only to stay at the edges of her mind. These were the worst for an overly-focused woman so determined to reach a conclusion. There were too many unanswered questions, too many players in the game, too many avenues yet unexplored. This case beat all. She was afraid she was not up to the challenge; that was the greatest concern of all.

While putting together a vegetable platter and dip, along with a plate of cheese and crackers for the card game that night, she pondered her last conversation with Karen Coppick. She began to wonder whether Karen's father, Burkhardt, having four wives and a number of children, had left anyone out of the trust. That might cause someone to retaliate. Why, though, target the executor? She learned long ago the mind could create illogical reasoning. Was this an example of that?

On simple impulse, she called Karen Coppick. Their discussion was revealing. The conversation showed Karen to be a thoughtful soul, understanding the nuances of human interaction far more than anyone Donna yet had encountered in her consulting work. Burkhardt's daughter was both brutally honest and circumspect in her review. She gave Donna reason to apply other considerations to this case.

Just as she ended her call, the doorbell rang. Gavin and Carole were right on time. "Gavin made éclairs, my favorite!" Carole proudly pronounced as she placed the tray filled with not only éclairs, but cookies as well, on the sideboard.

"Uh oh! There goes my waistline," Donna declared with a twinkle in her voice, while hugging her friends in welcome.

"Mine, too," said Ken as he grabbed an oatmeal cookie. "Donna keeps telling me I'm looking more like the Pillsbury Dough Boy as I age. The problem is I'm surrounded by good food. How does one walk away from that?" he protested as he filled the bowls in the middle of the table with M-&-M chocolate-covered-peanuts for the card game wagers.

Donna, Carole, and Gavin took one look at the bowl of M-&-M's and howled in laughter. "What?" Ken asked, confused by the round of hilarity. No one dared point out the obvious.

"Oh, I almost forgot," Carole said reaching into her oversized bag. "Mary asked me to deliver these to you. They look like bank statements. They belonged to the old woman who lived in Mary's house. She found them in the very back of a top shelf in one of the closets." It was a considerable stack.

"Thanks…I think," Donna returned, accepting the bundle.

Carole caught the doubt in her friend's voice. "Not going so good, eh?"

Donna sighed while stealing a glance at Ken. "This is the puzzle of all puzzles. We're missing something. I'd hate to see this relegated to a cold case file. That would really have me bummed."

Ken put his arm around Donna. "My beloved is letting her perfectionism show."

The card game ended with Gavin winning the pot. Donna was more quiet than usual, but periodically threw in a playful dig when losing a hand. As they were clearing the table for coffee and éclairs, Donna posed a question.

"Gavin, how are you doing with your genealogy hobby?"

"I think I've gone back as far as I can go with my family, but every time I say that I end up finding another connection."

"Would you like another project?"

Ken and Carole looked at each other with questioning glances.

"What do you have in mind?" Gavin responded.

"I wish to research a family, going back to at least the 1900's."

"Does this have something to do with the case you and Ken are working on?" Carole asked.

"It does," Donna said. "Are you game? Do you have the time?" Donna asked Gavin hopefully.

Gavin nodded before responding. "I think it would be fun. Give me what you know." For the next thirty minutes Donna shared what little she knew of the family she wanted researched.

§

The following week was occupied with interviews, mostly by telephone, with the second-tier beneficiaries of the trust. All were polite and willing to answer questions. Most were restrained in their responses; a few were brutally honest. Donna took copious notes on the responses of each participant. In between her telephone interview, she kept her weekly appointment to sit with Herta Cohen at the nursing home, which was a welcomed distraction. Herta was progressing nicely, negotiating the halls with the help of a walker. It was always a pleasant experience being with this Holocaust survivor who transcended her experience with fortitude and humor.

Each week after Herta's physical therapy sessions, she and two other participants were wheeled out of the therapy room. Donna, as usual, waited in the hallway just outside the physical therapy room for her friend. As she turned her head toward the lobby Donna noticed a face she recognized coming down the hallway.

"Oh, Dr. DeShayne. It's good to see you," said Blake Miles walking toward her to shake her hand. "Are you here to visit someone?" he asked.

"My friend who is recovering from a fall," Donna replied, noting his lab coat. "Are you here on business?"

He smiled warmly. "I deliver prescriptions to this facility from the hospital pharmacy department."

"That's right," Donna returned. "Now I remember. You're a pharmacy technician. Is your mother-in-law feeling better?" Donna asked, recalling that his wife had been away caring for her mother, who was not well.

"She's much better. How kind of you to remember. Who is it you are visiting, if I might ask?"

"Herta Cohen, a friend of mine."

"Yes…the name sounds familiar. I would only recognize names for people who had prescriptions called into the hospital."

"Will your wife be home soon?"

"Very soon, I'm pleased to say," he said as he pushed his cart down the hallway. "Nice seeing you again," he threw over his shoulder.

Donna watched Blake Miles head down the hallway with his prescription cart. It appeared he was keeping pace with a resident in a wheelchair. She kept her eyes on him until they both rounded the corner and were out of sight. Just then, Herta was wheeled out of the physical therapy room.

"What's my treat for the day?" Herta asked in an almost child-like fashion. Donna had established a routine that, upon the successful execution of physical therapy, they would go for a treat and then play cards.

"Hmmm," Donna mused. "I'm thinking of a double chocolate brownie topped with vanilla ice cream!"

"Sold!" Herta agreed. "Take me to your Leader!" The two women laughed, caught up in the joy of their continuing friendship and mutual devotion. Donna wheeled the older woman to the day room where she had stored homemade brownies, complements of Gavin, and a pint of vanilla ice cream in the freezer. The women luxuriated in their indulgence.

"Tell Gavin," Herta managed to say while stabbing the last piece of brownie with her fork, "that he is a godsend." At that, she playfully plunked the brownie piece into her mouth, and purred while chewing.

Donna laughed. "Herta, you are a delight to watch. You're such a chocoholic!"

"It's my addiction," she giggled in satisfaction as she licked her fingers.

Donna was in her office the next day reviewing the bank statements Mary Larson had found in the closet in her new home. There were at least six years' worth. After the first year, she noted a pattern. When Ken came home from work, Donna initiated discussion of her findings while they sat on the back porch, eyeing the birds at the new bird feeder.

"What smells so good?" Ken asked as he sat down on a lounger after taking a shower.

"I put together a crab-stuffed flounder with a side of macaroni and cheese," she replied.

"You spoil me!" he returned.

"You're worth spoiling."

"What have you been up to today?"

"I reviewed the bank statements Mary found in her new home."

"That sounds awfully boring. Anything revealing, though?"

"I think there is, but I'm still working on it. There are the usual monthly expenses, but then there is an expense occurring monthly with no explanation. I'm zeroing in on this one."

"Who is it payable to?"

"Cash."

"Hmmm. That can be for anything."

Donna nodded knowingly. "I would have thought the same. There is, however, a companion withdrawal from the trust account for the same amount just days before the transfer into the personal account of the widow with no explanation."

Ken looked intrigued. "What are you thinking?"

"I don't know yet, but it's suspicious to say the least."

"In what way?"

"A separate draw from the trust to the widow above her usual monthly funds with no explanation? Then it is drawn out again from the widow's account in the form of "Cash" without explanation? Someone is either daring or simply stupid?"

"Stupid is more like it. Given the fact the trust is involved it sounds like a trail we need to follow," Ken said with concern.

"That's what I was thinking."

Chapter Twelve

A few days later, Gavin telephoned Donna about the initial findings of his genealogy search.

"I'd like to share with you where I am with this. Do you have some time today to get together?" Gavin asked.

"I have all the time you need."

"Let's meet over lunch at the Rivertown Bistro. Is it all right if I bring Carole?"

"Of course! We're overdue for a lunch. Would it be okay if I also invited Ken?"

"By all means!"

The four friends met at a popular local bistro for lunch and spent the first hour sharing recent events related to Mary Larson's progress on her new home, and the twins' extracurricular activities. By the time dessert was served, they were ready to get down to the reason for their get together.

"So," Donna began the conversation. "What have you discovered?"

"The usual family connections as you might guess. Knowing the husband had four wives, I decided to go backward instead of forward."

"And?"

Gavin cleared his throat and sat up straight. "Everything appears normal up to a point. Every marriage and death were substantiated, until, eventually, I hit a brick wall."

"What do you mean?" Donna asked.

"I mean, I got back as far as the first wife…Anna…"

"And?" Donna coaxed impatiently.

Gavin frowned. "I'm new at this tracking thing, but it's not really rocket science. I discovered the record of her marriage to Burkhardt. There are also records of the births of three children, but never a record of a divorce!"

Donna raised her eyebrows. "What does that mean?"

Gavin again cleared his throat, clearly uncomfortable. "She simply disappears. Pure and simple. There are no records of her after the marriage and the birth of the children."

"How can that be? Surely she must be dead by now. At the very least there should be a death certificate," Donna declared with more than a hint of disbelief.

Gavin did not answer for a time, but when he did it was unsettling. "It's possible she didn't want to be found. Remember, she left a husband and three children behind. Maybe she was ashamed of that. Or, she may have been hiding a secret. It was easy, back then, to get lost and never be discovered again. The records were scant, even now, anyone can go off the grid and simply disappear. It's done all the time."

Donna was dismayed. "Why would she do that? After all, she was a mother."

Gavin, a former FBI agent, knew the human psyche all too well. "Some women are mothers, Donna, but not motherly. The responsibility of caring for a child can be overwhelming for some women, and not a happy event to be celebrated."

Donna shook her head in disbelief. "So, she allowed her three children to be placed in an orphanage!"

Gavin caught Donna's judgmental tone. "Consider this. It may have been her attempt to give her children a better life, one she could not provide because of her inability to prioritize their needs and welfare. Not all biological mothers can nurture, Donna."

Donna took note of Gavin's non-judgmental position. "So you're saying she did the right thing allowing her children to live in an orphanage?"

Gavin hesitated before responding thoughtfully. "I'm saying we can't judge when someone is overcome by a fear so great it results in behavior that is not what is generally considered normal or expected. In the face of overwhelming pressure, there is no normal, there is simply reaction. Reaction is the mind's way of coping. In its wake they often experience regret, remorse, or shame."

It was a long time before Donna commented. She looked at Gavin long and hard. "I can understand why Carole adores you. You should have been a psychiatrist, Gavin. Your insights are remarkable. As a psychiatrist myself, I should have thought that through."

"Thank you. I've seen a lot of facets of human nature over the years."

"Haven't we all? So, where do we go from here?"

"Have you interviewed all of the children from the four marriages?" Carole asked. "I'd like to be a fly on the wall for those, I admit."

Ken smiled. "We've interviewed only those who are beneficiaries."

Carole grimaced. "Not all the children where beneficiaries?"

Donna noted Carole's surprise. "The five children of the fourth wife were left out."

"Wow! Talk about splitting hairs. In their shoes, I would be rather peeved in being omitted."

"I thought that as well. However, in reviewing the bank statements you handed me the other night, I realized the fourth wife was doing okay for herself. In addition to a healthy sum of money from the estate each month, she was also receiving a pension from her former husband, in addition to social security."

"Oh, how clever," Carole commented softly.

Donna looked at her friend. "What do you mean? What's so clever about being left out of an estate?"

Carole sat back playing with the wrapper of a straw left on the table before she spoke. "The five children will get their inheritance. It just won't be through the trust. If what you say is true, there was enough money coming in to the fourth wife to set a good sum aside for her children. They probably got a handsome sum when she died."

Carole had captured Ken and Donna's earlier conclusion, as well. It was as though, she too, had spoken to Karen Coppick. "As it turns out, the only thing left of the estate when the fourth wife died was a house in need of repair."

"Mary's new home," Gavin confirmed.

"Yes," Donna answered. Looking at Ken she said, "So the five children of the fourth wife would not necessarily harbor ill-will in the whole affair."

Ken nodded, but said nothing, still processing Carole's comment.

"I would love to know what size estate the old woman left, and who the executor was in that case," Carole said thoughtfully as she stabbed a French fry on her plate.

Donna looked at Ken. "Can we get that information?"

He nodded again. "I can have it by tomorrow."

"Getting back to my research results," Gavin said, "I have another piece of information that will add to your workload, I'm afraid."

Donna looked at Ken. They both shook their heads. This case was complex. What else could get in the way?

"Go on," Ken prompted, almost reluctantly.

Gavin sat back, reviewing his notes before continuing. "The long and the short of it is that this man Burkhardt's second wife, Hildegarde, was married two times before him."

"What!" Donna nearly yelled. The other patrons in the restaurant looked toward their table. Ken placed his hand over Donna's in both a signal of support and to remain calm.

The group went silent. Carole and Gavin were still trying to gage the possible consequence of this finding, while Ken and Donna were already imagining the possibilities.

"Are there any children born of these unions?" Donna asked shakily.

"Is that important?" Carole asked with concern for her friend.

Donna didn't answer. Instead, Gavin continued his summary with a softer voice, not wanting to upset Donna further. "Donna, if you remember," he gently ventured forth, "you provided Karen Coppick's phone number to me. I appreciate that you paved the way for permission to call her. She told me that after her mother's death she found a black satchel under her mother's bed that held papers. In the paperwork, she found two Mexican divorce certificates. I researched the names and dates she provided me from the divorce certificates for both marriages. Each marriage lasted less than a year."

"Wow! Both? What are the odds?" Carole pondered aloud while stealing a pickle from Gavin's plate.

"Why a Mexican divorce?" Donna probed, looking at both Ken and Gavin. "Are they legal?"

"Back then one could obtain a Mexican divorce by mail even if you were married in the United States to another U.S. citizen. There were companies advertising a legitimate "same-day" divorce. They made it easier, faster, and less expensive than a divorce in the U.S. but it had to be valid in Mexico for it to be valid in the United States," Ken answered.

"So they had to jump through Mexican hoops first? Do all states recognize them?" Donna prodded.

"Let me say this. One has to be very careful about a claim of divorce if it was obtained through Mexico. The laws have changed since then. If a Mexican domicile was not established then a Mexican divorce permit would not be granted. The U.S. court system will not recognize any divorce, Mexican or otherwise, unless the couple's place of residence is located within the jurisdiction of the court. Both parties have to be notified of the proceedings. One can no longer secure a Mexican divorce without notifying one's spouse, though such requirements may be state-specific."

"Could it be that one or both of Hildegarde's divorces were illegal?" Carole asked, wholly absorbed in the conversation.

"Anything's possible. Nothing about this case is obvious," Donna returned with a hint of dismay. "I think I need to have another conversation with Karen Coppick."

"Why? What's bothering you?" Ken questioned.

"Everything at this point. Nothing is coming together. We have interviewed nearly two dozen people and have not even the hint of a trail. Karen knows the whole family history, though, and I'll bet she has more to say if properly questioned."

"With me she only answered the questions I posed and went no further. Be prepared to ask follow-up questions," Gavin suggested while handing his typewritten report to her. Gavin was always going to sound like FBI, even years after retirement.

Donna turned to Ken. "I think I need to speak with Mrs. Coppick alone this time. It's a woman-to-woman thing, and she knows I'm a psychiatrist. She may feel safer and say more without a law enforcement officer sitting beside me. Do you mind?"

"If it moves this case forward, I'm all for it. I'm every bit as frustrated as you are."

🙟

The following day, Donna placed a call to Karen Coppick, daughter of Burkhardt and Hildegarde. "Mrs. Coppick, thank you for being so cooperative with Mr. Tandermann."

"I hope it was useful information," Karen returned.

"Much of it was and some of it raised other questions. I hate to inconvenience you further, but would it be possible for us to meet again? I am curious about several things in Mr. Tandermann's report."

"What kind of things?" she asked with a measure of hesitation.

"I have a copy for you of Mr. Tandermann's report. I have underlined some findings which I hope you can clarify. Would you mind?"

"I'm not a suspect, am I?" she asked with a trace of alarm.

"I can assure you, we are deeply appreciative of your cooperation. We have no current reason to suspect you of any wrongdoing. My purpose for the meeting is to further the investigation and to get an idea of family dynamics. That is all."

"Will it be just you?" she inquired. "The detective made me worry he was going to arrest me, from the way he was staring at me."

"Detective Daniels can be focused in a conversation, so I can see how you might feel intimidated. Only you and I will be meeting. Why don't we choose a neutral place, say Starbucks?" Donna knew she could never tell Carole she met Karen Coppick at a Starbucks instead of one of her Beans café. She would never hear the end of it, for sure.

Karen hesitated before she answered. "I suppose that will be all right. How about tomorrow morning? I'm busy the rest of the week."

Both arrived at the same time and walked into Starbucks together. The setting for a conversation was perfect. The café was fairly empty and Donna found a table in a somewhat secluded corner of the room. Donna insisted on paying for Karen's choices of coffee and pumpkin bread. She left the table to place the order, leaving Karen with her copy of Gavin's report. She glanced over at Karen while waiting for their order, and saw that she was absorbed in her reading.

Having secured a tray, Donna settled in at their table, sliding Karen's order toward her without disturbing her reading of Gavin's report. Finally, she looked up. "This is quite comprehensive. I'm impressed."

"I'm glad. Gavin knows his stuff," Donna replied in an attempt to keep the conversation light. "Is there anything that surprises you or that you would dispute?"

"Not really. It is about what I've already known, or suspected."

"I'm aware you already knew of your mother's previous marriages. I'm sure it was a surprise at the time."

Karen sighed. "Oh, it was a shock at the time. No one said a word all those years. When I confronted my father he simply said that my mother didn't want anyone to know. So nothing was said. Divorce at that time was rare and somewhat scandalous. They were Catholic at the time, and the church was against divorce."

"Do you know whether there were any children from the first two marriages?"

"I asked that at the time. My father was very dismissive of my inquiry, even a bit annoyed, so I never brought up the subject again."

"Why do you think both marriages ended so quickly?"

Karen shook her head. "I don't really know, but I suspect my grandfather ended them."

Donna raised an eyebrow. "Why would he do that?"

"I can only guess. My mother was a tragic figure. It took me years to understand that. When she was only days away from dying, my aunt came to the house for the day in a show of support and to give me a bit of a break. At one point we sat on the front porch and visited. She told me something very revealing."

"What was it?"

"She told me that when my mother was seventeen, her father shipped her back to Germany to be cared for by German doctors. My mother simply stopped eating. She spent months there, at first on feeding tubes, and then with supervised meals where someone monitored her eating. They fattened her up and sent her home, but never dealt with the emotional issues that remained, the underlying cause of her food addiction. She would purge every night after eating dinner, her only real meal of the day. She would wear clothing way too big for her as well. I now understand she felt body shame and attempted to hide herself in baggy, oversized clothing. It was just the way things were in the home where I grew up. The dark moods, the obsessive cleaning rituals, the eating disorder, not to mention the displays of anger when she lashed out at us children with whips secured from bushes outside the home which she used to attack us for the slightest departure from her rules. I now see it as a sickness and one big cry for help. I spent my entire youth avoiding her."

"Who cared for you?"

"Fortunately, I had an older sister. Four years older than me, but far beyond her years. I and my younger sister, Mary, were looked after by her. My older sister seemed to know my mother was unavailable."

"Then what?" Donna asked with keen interest.

"The whole family was pretty much involved in the church. I eventually married a believer as well and we ended up living on a ministerial farm in upstate New York for a time. Be mindful. We were hook, line, and sinker into the church."

"What effect did this have on you?" Donna prompted.

Karen looked at the psychiatrist intently before answering. "You have to understand that I was subject to the will of my husband and the church in this environment, but I also saw the flaws and the misdemeanors in behavior by the church, the extension of the ego in making decisions for a host of supporters. In time, as I questioned, I began to suspect it was a sham. That is when my belief system began to slowly erode. I said nothing to my husband at first, but simply observed the hubris and the process of the church. We eventually left the ministerial farm to go to the care of my father, who was left alone after the death of my mother, Hildegarde. It was a fruitless gesture. It was obvious my father had already picked a replacement in marriage. In a little more than a year, he had remarried…the third wife…Dorothy."

"Were you at ill-will over his decision?"

"At first I was, but then I came to know Dorothy. A good and capable woman, who in time came to understand she married a deceiving mate."

Donna cocked her head. "In what way?"

"My father had nothing before he married her. He lost my childhood home due to unpaid state taxes and lived in a rented home until my mother's death. After my mother died he moved again and operated his business out of the basement of a rental home. The next thing I know, he's seeing Dorothy and they marry!"

Donna looked at Karen with sympathetic eyes. "And…?"

"She had a home fully paid for and he was suddenly living in a lap of convenience. I didn't see it at the time, but I figured it out later on."

"So he married her for her money?"

"I wouldn't say that. She owned a simple home and he lost one. He was an elder in the church, and she believed in the leadership of the church. It was a recipe for misplaced expectation on her part."

"So your father was deceptive," Donna concluded out loud.

Karen hesitated before answering, coaching her reply. "I would say my father was more an opportunist. He saw the deficits and the advantages and weighed the balance to see if it would translate into an outcome in his favor. Not a foreign concept to those in the know. She, on the other hand, was banking on the righteousness of an elder from the church. I'm afraid she got taken. She understood that in the end."

"She had children," Donna forwarded.

"Four grown children...two sons and two daughters. The children knew their mother had surrendered her will to this man who owned nothing."

"Were they angry?"

"I don't think angry is the word. Disappointed is more appropriate. They were powerless to stop the inevitable."

Donna nodded in understanding. "So I'm guessing they did not embrace their new step-father."

Karen smiled. "They were polite enough, but only to preserve the relationship with their mother. I am almost certain of this."

"When your step-mother died, your father married again shortly thereafter."

"Less than a year," Karen added.

"How did you feel about that?"

Karen was slow to respond. "At this point I had left the church and so I was in a mindset of reality. I was able to take a long hard look at my family of origin; my father especially."

"And...?"

"I'm almost certain that, while my step-mother was dying, my father had already picked a replacement from the church."

Donna's head whipped up in surprise. She was slow to respond. "Why would you say such a thing?" she asked in an obvious display of surprise.

Karen took a moment, assuming a meditative pose. "There was always a replacement," was all she said at first.

"Go on," Donna prompted quietly, not wanting to break stride in a trust that had been obvious throughout their dialogue.

"If I review the past, I can see Dorothy was a replacement for my mother Hildegarde, and the fourth wife was a replacement for Dorothy. These women were picked months before the death of the wife before. I'm almost certain of this."

Donna took a deep breath. "*Whew!*" was all she said at first. "That would make your dad fairly calculating."

Karen looked up with a neutral expression. "It bears consideration," she shared, almost inaudibly.

Donna shifted in the conversation slightly to bring about a revelation. "Your dad was religious, though."

"Just so you know, I've considered this. I believe the church teachings were important to him in some respects, but the grounding the church provided was monumental for a man who was illegitimately conceived and fostered through his grandfather. The demarcation was immense given the time period when illegitimacy was frowned upon. I believe the occasion left a considerable mark on my father in his effort to be acknowledged and received. The church provided the avenue. It provided status and affirmation."

Donna sat back considering the reply. "After Dorothy, your father married Darla," was her quiet reply.

"Yes. This time, however, this wife was not a victim like the others, but the victor. She received the bulk of wealth the family should have rightly received. There were three other wives who had wishes for their children. My father ignored all three of them in his final bequeath."

"You are angry," Donna returned with a hint of certainty.

Karen hesitated with a thoughtful look before responding. "You've asked that question in a previous conversation and my answer is the same. I admit, I was at first. We all were. I've come to understand, though, not all have a spiritual leaning. Many just get through their days surviving and invoking whatever support they can get along the way. That was my father."

Donna sat back digesting the wisdom of this woman she had come to respect. Even so, she had to ask the following question. "Karen," she began with hesitancy, "can you say with any certainty that any one of the beneficiaries was capable of murder? Not all may be as benevolent as you."

Karen's head did a quick jerk of attention in a resolute response. "No! Not a one! All are upstanding and respectful. That's not to say we don't have our issues. Who doesn't? Murder, however, is not in our equation, I can assure you. You'll have to look elsewhere, Doctor!"

Chapter Thirteen

DARLA

South Carolina - 2006

On a bright autumn day, Darla buried her ninety-four-year-old second husband, Burkhardt. Though there was little support from Burkhardt's children, church members stepped forward with food and emotional support in the initial days of her loss.

Days after the funeral, Darla was visibly comforted as she sat listening to the executor of the estate read the terms of the trust. She breathed a sigh of relief. Although Burkhardt had hinted at his financial holdings, she was never privy to the details. Now she knew she wouldn't have to worry about money. Even the home and its maintenance would be seen to by the trust until her death, along with a healthy allowance for her each month. How grand!

Though there was a twenty-year difference in their ages, she had gotten along well enough with Burkhardt. While he was somewhat obsessive in his worship, he was, nevertheless, recognized in the church. That had to count for something. It had given her a long-sought-after status among the members of the church. Finally she was recognized.

Shortly after the reading of the trust, Darla was informed of Burkhardt's family's anger regarding its terms. When they were told they were reduced to second-tier beneficiaries and would have to wait for their inheritances until after Darla's death, they were not happy. The terms confirmed that the estate was designed to support Darla, and what was left over would go to those named as second tier heirs. It was a bitter blow to Burkhardt's children, but, Darla concluded at least verbally to her friends and family, Burkhardt knew what he was doing. Besides, she reasoned inwardly, there would be enough coming in to put aside a sizeable estate for all five of her own children. They, too, would receive an inheritance, though not mentioned in Burkhardt's will. The monthly allowance alone would see to this. *Thank you, Burkhardt!*

Seventeen years after Burkhardt's passing, Darla died. Alone. She was found late one afternoon in her bed, having passed during the night. No one attended her through the weekend, concluding, erroneously that she was well enough to be left alone. Her children and other church members were attending a weekend-long Bible seminar at the time. It was obvious she struggled in her final hours.

In due course, the estate was settled. After the sale of the home, the second-tier beneficiaries would realize a fraction of the original wealth of the estate. The funds were gone. The annual accounting they received reflected its slow demise leading up to Darla's death. Their only solace was in the realization they were finally free of the estate executor, Simon Lundy and his wife, Wanda. Some couldn't have been more pleased.

Chapter Fourteen

Present Day – South Carolina

Donna took a phone call in the middle of dinner with Ken, Gavin, and Carole at The Library, a sophisticated, yet casual, restaurant nestled in the heart of Myrtle Beach with a to-die-for offers on the dinner menu and superb service. They were celebrating Ken's fiftieth birthday.

When Donna returned to the table minutes later, Ken saw a puzzled expression on her face. "Is there a problem?" he asked.

"I've been called to Atlanta. Another investigation without a resolution," she said before settling herself at the table and spearing a delicious vegetable on her plate.

"When do you leave?" Carole asked.

"They want me there by Tuesday."

The group resumed their meal until Gavin spoke up. "What does this do to your investigation here?"

Donna smiled benignly before answering. "It's a distraction, for sure."

Ken came to his beloved's defense. "In all fairness, I've used Donna's free time to work on a mystery I haven't been able to solve. She's given it rigorous attention, I must say."

Placing her hand on Ken's, Donna said, "Just so you know, I'm hooked, both on you *and* on the case."

The day before she left for Atlanta, Donna visited Herta Cohen at the nursing home.

"They tell me I can go home by the end of the week," Herta announced with glee.

"Way to go, Lady Love!" Donna returned as she gave her friend a congratulatory hug. "I'm off to Atlanta for a few days, but I wanted to see you before I left."

"You are always the faithful one." Herta fell quiet. Donna sensed her friend wanted to tell her something and waited for it.

"I'm an old woman. I've lived my days, Donna. Days when I experienced the very worst of humanity and the very best of the human spirit. To end my days with your support and kindness has been a blessing, Dear Heart. I want you to know this."

Donna teared. How she loved this wonderful woman with a catastrophic history. Donna hugged her older friend. "I was blessed the day you entered my office, Herta. What a gem you are!"

The two women parted with a mixture of joy and sadness. Donna asked a question of her older friend before she left her room. Her reply was revealing, as well as a bit unsettling.

Donna departed for Atlanta the following day, opting to drive, rather than fly. In her experience, a long drive often cleared her mind. For the first hour or so, she reviewed the facts related to the Atlanta case. She then let her mind rest, enjoying the radio, listening and singing along to oldie tunes she knew and loved.

Arriving in Atlanta, she checked into her hotel, called Ken, and had a restful night. The next morning, she reported to the contact person for the case in question. She spent the entire day painstakingly reviewing the facts presented. Asking questions of the detectives, she soon found a flaw in their assumptions. By guiding the evidence to other possible outcomes, the group soon hit upon another possibility, this one a winner. By midmorning the next day they had their suspect!

With a positive outcome assured, Donna checked out of the hotel and made a call to Ken from the road. "I'm heading home this afternoon. I should be there by dinner time," she announced to her partner.

"Wow! Already? Your review must have been successful."

"It was. I just received a phone call saying that they already have their man!"

"Good for you!" Ken declared, clearly proud of Donna's accomplishment. "Be careful on the drive home. I need you in one piece."

"*I* need me in one piece," she replied jokingly.

The trip, for Donna, was cathartic in many respects. She mentally reviewed the Atlanta case, after which she again listened to oldies on the radio. After singing along for an hour or so, her mind returned to the Lundy case. As she mentally stepped through it from the beginning, she targeted the anomalies that stood out, becoming increasingly unsettled. It was beginning to make sense. Maybe. She needed to be careful not to get ahead of herself.

She made a call to Gavin and explained what she needed without revealing the reason for her request. Gavin, always attuned to nuances because of his FBI background, responded to Donna's request. "I hear what you're asking, Donna. You have a hunch on Ken's case, I assume."

Donna paused before responding. "Let's just say it's a long-shot and I'm grasping at straws," she finally replied.

Gavin knew otherwise. "That's not the Donna I know. The Donna I know does not make a request like this unless she's on the verge of a resolution."

Donna sighed. "I can only wish, Gavin. Make my day!"

Disconnecting, she reviewed her chains of thought once again as she drove down the interstate north toward home. Step by step, interview by interview, encounter by encounter, she carefully isolated the source of her angst behind her unsettled feelings. By the fourth hour of her drive, her senses were fully engaged. Careful not to let emotion override logic, she began to tease out the beginnings of a plausible theory. Maybe, just maybe, she was onto something.

Donna checked the time on the dashboard. It was still early enough. She telephoned Karen Coppick. Donna was looking for more clarity around the dynamics of Karen's family and asked questions she had not previously considered. Karen, as always, was forthright in her responses. It was revealing. For Donna, it may just be the catalyst in helping Ken solve his case.

Highly encouraged when she ended the call, she allowed herself to clear her mind by listening to the music again. Before long her phone rang. It was Gavin. Donna engaged Bluetooth so as not to take her hands off the wheel and become distracted.

"Hi...I didn't expect to hear from you so soon," Donna greeted him.

"Normally, I would have waited, but I've come across some interesting parallels. Care to hear them now or should I wait until the morning after you've had a good night's rest?"

"Now, Gavin. You know I don't have the patience to wait for anything, especially something having to do with this case. Tell me what you've discovered or there won't be a good night's rest."

For the next twenty minutes or so, Gavin revealed his findings in his usual methodical manner. Donna stopped him on occasion to clarify aspects of his summary and, when satisfied, prompted him to continue. In the end, the information aligned with the thought fragments already circulating in her mind.

After Gavin concluded his report, Donna was quiet. "Donna, are you there?" he finally asked.

The sound of Gavin's voice forced her to mentally surface. "I'm here, Gavin...just thinking. We have more pieces of the puzzle now, but not all. It's just a gut feeling, mind you, but what you have just provided certainly puts us on track."

They spoke for a few more minutes while Donna shared her reservations, doubts, and suspicions. Before ending the call, she asked one additional favor.

"I'm on it," he returned. "I think you have this in the bag."

"Not yet, Gavin. Ken will tell me whether I'm on the right track," she answered before ending the call.

If truth be told, she had no idea whether Ken would support her line of reasoning. It was a bit out of the box, even for her. She struggled with the various facets of her conclusions, and yet the back-story was compelling enough to fit recent history and a cause-and-effect scenario.

She placed a quick call to alert Ken of her impending arrival. As she pulled into the driveway, there he was, waiting for her. How she loved this man! He was always there, always present! She kissed him warmly.

"I ordered Chinese. Whenever you're ready," he told her as he embraced her.

"Perfect! I've missed you!"

"It's only been three days," he replied.

"Three days too long," Donna returned.

Ken knew her dining preference and had ordered her favorite; egg-drop soup followed by sweet and sour shrimp with brown rice. It was his favorite as well. They dinner after he presented his special gal with a glass of her favorite wine.

"You spoil me," she whispered before sipping from her glass.

"I plan on spoiling you all through the night," he replied seductively. Their twenty-year match was that of two ideally suited souls who had found each other after lifetimes of searching.

"So, how was Atlanta?" Ken asked as they began their dinners.

"Interesting," was Donna's understated response. She shared a bit about her visit and the case on which she was consulting. She waited for the end of dinner to unveil her newest assumptions and suppositions in the Lundy case, along with Gavin's findings and today's conversation with Karen Coppick. Ken listened without interruption, acknowledging the plausible points in Donna's open and, as always, thorough review. He couldn't argue her position. It was well-defined and defensible.

"Whew!" he eventually said. Ken was immersed in thought for a very long time. Donna knew better than to interrupt his musings, which usually ended up being highly productive.

Finally, he spoke. "You just might have something here, but there are a couple of minor flaws in your assessment. It's been my experience that minor flaws often translate into major foul-ups in solving a crime." Ken then shared two of his reservations.

He was right! Donna got up immediately from her chair and went to her office. Ken wasn't far behind. She grasped the binder with photos from the crime scene until she found what she was looking for. It was evidence of what simply wasn't there! She then pointed out the anomaly to Ken.

He smiled. She just might be onto something, but he would need a bit more convincing.

They surrendered themselves to a shared love through the night. Not an unusual experience given their mutual devotion, but this night was especially moving. Perhaps it was because of their short separation or simply an unleashing of desire. It wasn't the first time, and it wouldn't be the last. There really didn't have to be a reason. It was just the way it was between them.

Donna awoke the next morning to find Ken already gone from their bed. She looked at the clock. It was late! He hadn't woken her, allowing her to sleep. Shuffling to the kitchen, she found the Keurig primed for brew. Another of Ken's acts of thoughtfulness. She smiled and waited for the 'cue-to-brew', an expression her coffee-connoisseur friend, Carole, often used. While her cup was filling, she sighed with satisfaction after her night with her knight. She knew she was a lucky woman.

After showering and dressing for the day, she headed for her home office. There were details dancing in her head. A knock at the front door interrupted her train of thought. It was Gavin.

"Hey, Carole and I are on the way to Home Depot for a new grill, but I wanted to make sure you got this before we left," he said handing a folder to her.

"Am I going to like what's in it?" Donna asked looking down at the folder.

"I'm not sure, but it's interesting. How it fits into your case I can't begin to guess, but it came up in the genealogy review you asked for."

Donna opened the folder and began to read while heading back to her office, but suddenly stopped. She looked up, contemplating what she had just read and the related possibilities. *Yes, of course!* She smiled. It was all beginning to make sense.

Chapter Fifteen

Donna spent the better part of two days creating a summary of her suspicions and conclusions, much of which could be documented. Her office wall grew into a grand database of information. She knew Ken would require an in-depth accounting. He would ask questions, lots of questions. She knew he would, initially, perceive her conjecture as a reach. Her instincts, though, told her otherwise. There were still a couple of areas worthy of further investigation, but she felt she had a back-story and motive congealing.

Over dinner one evening, she surprised Ken with a request. "I'd like to come to your office tomorrow afternoon and present what I have so far. Do you have room in your schedule?"

He looked up, watching her face, and knew she had a game plan. "You would rather do it at my office than here?" he questioned.

She nodded. "Yes. I think your entire team needs to hear what I have uncovered and let me know if I'm barking up the wrong tree."

"They won't pull any punches, Donna. They'll give it to you straight."

"That's exactly what I'm hoping for."

The next morning, Donna went to the printers to copy several pages of her graph so each person attending her afternoon presentation would have a point of reference, allowing for questions and clarifications.

The hour finally arrived. Donna was nervous… an unusual state for her given the many times she had sat before law enforcement teams in the course of her career.

There were four at the table, including Ken and his right-hand man, Detective Caleb Blackwell. Caleb gave Donna a warm hug when she entered the room. He and his family had been friends of Ken's and Donna's for years and were often at their home for summer barbecues. The other team members were Detectives' Steven Pratcher and Leon Niles, whom Donna had met in the past and liked.

"Donna felt it advisable for us to review her findings on the Lundy case as a team. I'll let her take it from here," Ken said without fanfare.

For the next hour, Donna meticulously unfolded the details of the Lundy murders, details already known to the detectives. She then handed each a copy of her graph, which included anomalies and unanswered questions that, until now, prevented the case from being solved. At this juncture, Donna presented her suppositions and inferences, being careful not to appear inflexible in her position.

The group asked questions, to some of which Donna had to simply answer, "I don't know." For the most part, however, the questions drew an informed response, often highlighted with supportive data and facts.

When she finished, she simply sat down and waited for their feedback.

Blackwell was the first to respond. "I wouldn't have put this together, but it has some merit," was all he said at first. "If what you're suggesting is true, someone has been watching the watcher for years."

"Of all those who have been interviewed, who do you think our suspect is?" Leon Niles asked Donna directly.

Donna smiled, anticipating the question. "Someone we haven't interviewed."

The group looked at each other questioningly. "You mean we still don't have our suspect?" Ken asked, his voice conveying disbelief.

"Oh, I didn't say that. I just said the culprit was not on our interview list."

"So what are we waiting for?" Caleb asked.

"The right time," Donna replied evenly. She then laid out her notions and suppositions before finally suggesting a course of action.

After Donna's presentation, Ken assigned two of his detectives to continue pursuing details and leads. He and Donna went to the nursing home the following day, the day Herta Cohen was to be released to go home. Though Donna was thrilled to see Herta finally go home to the care of her daughter, she knew her own visits at the facility would continue for a short time. While Donna walked down the hall with a small bouquet toward Herta's room, Ken went to the office of Lacy Sue Larson, the administrator of the facility. Ken had held a telephone conference with Lacy Sue the day before, but wanted to address her concerns in person. Understanding her priority was the safety of the other residents, Ken assured her all precautions would be taken, taking special note to isolate the situation.

Also that morning, Detectives Blackwell and Niles, dressed as orderlies, integrated themselves into the nursing home staff, moving through the halls with linen carts or mopping floors while alert for anything out of the ordinary. Workers hired by the Department had previously installed video cameras in strategic locations to record questionable activity.

Donna walked into Herta's room and noted Herta was sitting in a wheelchair. "I wanted to see you off properly," Donna said to the aging woman, handing the small spray of flowers to her.

"Oh, Donna, how thoughtful!" Herta said, her voice choking. "It *does* feel good to be going home. Suzanne has gone for the car."

"I'll walk with you to the front door," Donna offered, when a nurse entered the room to assist with Herta's wheelchair.

Following Herta and the nurse through the hallways, Donna observed the two detectives in their role as laundry personnel. They met her eyes but made no acknowledgement as she walked by.

Once Herta was settled in the car, Donna gave both mother and daughter a warm embrace. "Now, remember, I'm available whenever you need backup."

"What would we do without you?" Suzanne replied appreciatively.

As the car drove away, Ken joined Donna on the sidewalk, having finished his conversation with Lacy Sue. "The plan is unfolding nicely. The more we dig, the more we find. Your suspicions are spot on, Donna." He then shared a couple of new discoveries.

"We need a plant, someone who appears to need nursing care, but can observe from the inside and feed us information. It won't raise suspicion when you are seen in the building again if you have someone else to visit."

Donna could think of only one person who could fit the bill. "Carole would be ideal."

"Normally I would agree with you, but I'm leaning more toward Gavin, given his FBI background."

Donna nodded. "Yes, I see your point. He would be the logical choice."

Donna and Ken went directly to Gavin and Carole's home, where they found them setting up their new grill on the back porch.

"What brings you two over this time of the day?" Gavin asked, looking up while setting the propane tank in its holder to connect the gas line to the grill. Carole stood nearby, ready to hand Gavin a wrench.

"Wow, that's a nice grill," Ken said admiringly.

"Got it on a huge sale," Carole returned proudly. "We'll be grilling the whole summer away."

Gavin sensed Ken and Donna had something important to share. He got up from his knees, with Carole's assistance, and took a seat at the patio table.

"How's the case coming?" he asked before either could say anything.

"That's really why we're here. We may have it solved," Ken returned, glancing at Donna.

"But…" Gavin knowingly encouraged.

Ken gave a condensed version of their findings, leaving out much of the detail. He then told Gavin they needed a decoy resident at the nursing home to complete their operation.

Gavin looked at Carole and then at Ken before responding. "I'm the logical choice given my FBI background. My age helps as well."

"What?" Carole boomed. "I don't get to be part of the fun? No fair!"

Ken smiled, and Donna laughed. "You have a point, Gavin. Normally, we don't use civilians in law enforcement situations, but your credentials make you the logical choice. You'll have to agree to sign off on liability."

"Understood," Gavin replied, his past FBI experience already engaged.

Carole looked alarmed. "What liability? Should I be concerned?"

Ken considered the limits of his authority before responding. "Using a civilian on rare occasions always comes with a risk, but I don't think Gavin will be in any real danger. We'll have undercover agents on the scene at all times. We will set Gavin up with a two-way transmitter for use in the unlikely event of a threatening situation."

"I'm familiar with them," Gavin commented.

Ken cleared his throat and looked at Donna before continuing. "I have received confirmation of a great many of your assertions. I want to get Gavin settled in tomorrow morning and have you visit him tomorrow afternoon, as the concerned neighbor. Carole, you can sit with your supposedly recovering husband through the day to make it look authentic, but understand, neither one of you should engage the party on any level. Your presence there is simply to allow Donna access to thc facility. Understood?"

"I am so ready!" Carole bellowed. "Will we see the arrest?"

"It's not likely. We'll be confining the apprehension to a sector of the facility that will be off limits for a time, but we will inform you of our intention before we take action. At that point, neither one of you is to leave Gavin's room until we say so."

"Gavin, we'll see to it you get physical therapy that day to make it look believable."

"Oh dear," Carole quipped. "*That* should be interesting!"

Donna and Ken smiled while Gavin grimaced. "You really are going to make me do physical therapy?"

"We are. Everything has to appear normal," Ken explained.

"This is going to be fun!" Carole giggled, enjoying her husband's discomfort.

Gavin was admitted to the nursing facility with Lacy Sue overseeing the admissions process. Carole played the role of the dutiful wife, asking appropriate questions of the staff and being present for her husband's admission and eventual room assignment. Lunch and dinner were served to the newly admitted patient. A nurse came into the room to announce Gavin's schedule for the next day, including physical therapy later in the afternoon. Everything looked normal on the surface. Few knew the real goings-on.

Carole eventually left for the night, but not before making a rather loud broadcast to her husband. "Now, here's your call button," she announced, handling the apparatus with care before laying it beside Gavin. "They will bring you a snack at about eight o'clock. If you need to go to the bathroom during the night, just use the call button for assistance."

Gavin looked at Carole in disbelief. "You *do* remember this is all a show, right?" he whispered in her ear. "We're the good guys! Healthy and good!"

Carole blushed in embarrassment. "Sorry. I got carried away."

He laughed heartily. Carole could always make him laugh.

The night proved uneventful and Gavin slept well. Awakening in the morning to the sound of an orderly pushing a cart to deliver a breakfast tray to his room, he was soon face-to-face with Caleb Blackwell.

Both men couched their words. "You worked the night shift last night?" Gavin asked innocently.

"Yes, but it was quiet. I understand you have physical therapy this afternoon. Once you get more mobile you will be able to eat your meals in the dining room."

"I can only hope."

"Just stay quiet until then. Someone will come for you."

Gavin nodded in understanding. "Can my wife join me for physical therapy?"

"It's not recommended. She should stay in your room until after your session. It won't be long."

"I understand."

An hour before the scheduled physical therapy session, Donna entered the facility and made her way to Gavin's room. Entering, she was louder than usual, for a purpose. "Hey, Cowboy! How 'ya ridin'?"

Gavin laughed. "I'm ridin' just fine, Donna. Nice of you to visit, good neighbor," Gavin replied just as loudly.

"No buckin' broncos today!" Carole brayed before sitting back in a leather recliner beside Gavin's bed with an open book in her lap. Carole then silently mouthed to Donna, "When's the action to begin?"

"Any time now," Donna silently returned.

Minutes later, Detective Leon Niles, dressed in scrubs, entered Gavin's room with a wheelchair. "Mr. Tandermann, it's time for your physical therapy session. I'll help you into the chair and then wheel you to the therapy center. I'm afraid our regular therapist called in sick today, but we have a highly capable substitute who will take good care of you and the others," Niles pronounced rather loudly as well.

Niles assisted Gavin into the chair and, once he was settled, Carole handed her husband a cane. "I won't need that," Gavin said, shunning the cane.

"Sure you will," she returned, enjoying the role she was playing. "Humor me, sweetheart," she entreated. "I'm always concerned for your welfare," she ended with a wry grin.

Gavin reluctantly took the cane, setting it across his lap while Niles wheeled him to the therapy center.

At about the same time, Lacy Sue, as hospital administrator, entered the room directly across the hall from Gavin's.

"Ms. Sylvia," she announced somewhat loudly as she entered the room of a patient recovering from a stroke, "I'm afraid we're a bit short-handed today, but I'm determined you shall have your therapy session today, dear lady."

The patient looked up in surprise to see the hospital administrator and not her usual orderly. "I put on a lot of hats, Ms. Sylvia, when the need arises. Let's get you to the therapy room."

Without a moment's hesitation, Lacy Sue swung Ms. Sylvia's chair around to face the doorway and escorted her down the hallway toward the therapy room. She could see the door to the room was open and Gavin being wheeled in by Leon Niles.

She took a quick scan of the hallway, immeasurably relieved to see the corridors patrolled by security personnel, disguised as maintenance workers, putting maintenance measures into effect that required cordoning off the area to prevent entry or use by other residents.

Reaching the doorway, Caleb Blackwell, dressed in scrubs, took charge of Ms. Sylvia. "I'll take it from here," he commented, blocking Lacy Sue's entry into the room. Lacy Sue was impressed with the attention to detail. Caleb even had a facility identification badge with his name on it hanging from his neck, indicating he was employed by the nursing home.

"Thank you, Caleb. Ms. Sylvia, your regular therapist has called in sick, but we were lucky enough to get Caleb to oversee your therapy session today. Caleb, this is Ms. Sylvia."

Caleb knelt to be at eye level with the woman who appeared to be in her mid-fifties. "Nice to meet you, Ms. Sylvia. I have reviewed your file. You're progressing very nicely, I see. We have some work to do today." With that, Lacy Sue turned away as previously instructed and went directly to join Carole and Donna, who were waiting in Gavin's room.

Ms. Sylvia looked around the therapy room and saw Gavin at the station next to hers being attended by another therapist. This therapist, however, was Ken Daniels. Gavin and Ken worked out a rough routine for the purposes of this session. They were just completing warm-ups.

"Who's that?" the woman in the wheelchair asked.

Caleb looked in the direction of Ms. Sylvia's gaze. "That is Mr. Tandermann. He entered the facility yesterday and has the room directly across from yours. The therapist's name is Ken. He and I are on loan from the hospital for the day. Shall we begin?"

Caleb, following directions he received the day before from the regular therapist, began an unexpected routine for

Ms. Sylvia. "Ms. Sylvia, I'm going to help you out of your chair to a standing position. Once we have you stable, I'm going to have you take a step. Don't be afraid, I'm going to be right beside you."

"I can't walk. Surely you must know my condition! My whole right side is bummed."

Caleb smiled brightly, pretending every step of the way. "Oh, Ms. Sylvia. 'Can't' is a nasty word. It means we are powerless. Surely you are not powerless. Let's try, shall we?"

Caleb, Ken, and even Gavin observed the conflicting expressions on Ms. Sylvia's face.

Caleb positioned himself carefully to assist Ms. Sylvia to a standing position. "Okay, Ms. Sylvia. Let's do this on the count of three. One…two…three." With that, he hoisted Ms. Sylvia to her feet and slid the wheelchair out of the way. She stood erect without wavering, but her eyes were wide-open, scanning the room for threatening signs. "Now, I'm going to let you go to see if you can stand on your own," Caleb announced.

"No! Don't do that! I will fall," the woman yelled, wobbling without support. Caleb just stepped back, not making an effort to assist. Sure enough, the woman righted herself.

Caleb smiled, stealing a glance at Ken across the room.

"Ms. Sylvia, I'm so proud of you. Look! You are standing on your own! You're speaking better as well."

"Still," the woman stammered, lost for words. "I need help!" was all she could muster, both fists tightening.

"Apparently not! You look pretty steady to me. Look at yourself!" Caleb implored.

"What is this?" the woman uttered loudly, remaining frozen in place, assessing the situation. Her face revealed alarm. All along, she had pretended helplessness. Now it was being challenged and she saw no way out. She had been set up! How could this have happened?

"What's going on here? Where's my regular therapist?" she snarled heatedly.

Her eyes displayed pure distrust, her stance was protected and guarded. It was only when she heard Caleb utter the next few words, she acted.

"Laura Miles, you are under arrest for the murders of Simon and Wanda Lundy."

With that, the woman growled loudly as if she had become a beast. Reaching into the pocket of her smock she pulled out a Smith & Wesson .38 revolver. Caleb yelled, *Gun!* Gavin, still in his wheelchair, reacted immediately, turning his chair in her direction. She instantly turned, with an expression of hate and the gun now pointed in Gavin's direction.

Ken and Caleb both had their guns drawn. "Stop or we will shoot!" Ken shouted.

Gavin held up both hands in a gesture of surrender, but in a flash picked up the cane resting across his lap and brought it down hard on the woman's hands. They heard a crack and the woman screamed. Her gun fell to the floor, her smashed hands unable to hold the loaded weapon.

Caleb and Ken pounced on the woman before she could move, taking her to the ground and bringing her arms behind her back, cuffing her securely as she lay faced down on the floor. All the while, she screamed a stream of obscenities that could be heard down the hallway.

Ken immediately transmitted to the team on site in the facility that the space was secure.

At the same time, two other arrests were being made. Within moments, Ken received texts from the other two arresting teams, confirming a successful conclusion from each.

The screaming woman was escorted out of the therapy room, down the hallway, into a secure room across the hall from Lacy Sue's office. Detectives guarded the woman while paramedics attended her hands before taking her to the hospital for X-rays. Verifying that no bones were broken, a wrap was applied and medication was administered. From the hospital she was escorted to a waiting police vehicle parked outside the emergency entrance of the hospital and taken to the county jail.

Ken returned to the nursing home to find Donna, Carole, and Gavin in the foyer, joined by Lacy Sue.

"Who is she?" Lacy Sue asked quietly, still reeling from the day's events. "We have her as Sylvia Crutcheon."

Donna answered, but didn't elaborate. "Her real name is Laura Miles."

Chapter Sixteen

The next two days were concentrated for Ken and his team. Each of the three people arrested was scheduled for interrogation. Ken was determined the arrests would be foolproof, with each one brought to justice. Donna was present at all times, watching the interrogation process through a two-way mirror, making notes where anomalies appeared among the three.

Laura Miles was interrogated first thing in the morning. Time for two sessions was allowed, with flexibility to add more, if needed. Laura was fairly uncooperative, refusing to answer questions during both sessions. Despite Laura's lack of cooperation, Donna was able to provide Ken and his team a timeline of her involvement. Each question asked of this woman, now in her mid-fifties, was answered by silence. Once or twice she even spat at her interrogators in defiance. Even so, Laura Miles betrayed her thoughts. On hearing sensitive questions, her eyes would grow big and she would tap her feet nervously in response. Following more benign questions, she would simply sit back in her chair, adopting a not-a-care-in-the-world posture. To Donna, her body language told the truth.

The two afternoons following Laura Miles morning interrogations were reserved for Blake Miles. He was obviously unhinged and nervous during both sessions, clearly the less offensive of the two, but still highly culpable.

Blake was far more cooperative and revealed the plan that evolved two years earlier.. There were times during the interrogation process when he sobbed and begged for forgiveness. Other times, he was completely silent, not answering questions…as if frozen in guilt. Donna wanted to feel sorry for him, seeing him as the weaker, more vulnerable one, but reminded herself of the role he played in the grisly deaths of two people. Regardless of the reasons for his complicity, Blake Miles was an accomplice in two murders, and brutal ones at that.

The last interrogated was Eden Parish, cousin of Blake and Laura. Donna concluded he was the toughest of the three mentally, using the emotional deficits of the other two in his favor through the whole process. He had the most to gain. By her yard-stick, he was the most dangerous, the most unforgivable of the three. He presented himself without remorse, and even, in an exalted manner, excused the other two for their crimes.

In Donna's opinion, he was a sociopath, evidencing several severe mental illnesses. Luckily, the trail implicating him was sound. It was only when they spelled out his involvement in undeniable terms that his self-induced Teflon-type façade collapsed. He crumbled to the floor, balled up in unrestrained crying.

Donna wondered whether it was an act. She was very aware that these personality types could act one way at a moment in time and then act in a completely different way moments later. It served as a tool for disarming and defusing others. It was the behavior of highly controlling and disturbed individuals. Left to their own devices, they would reassume their treacherous roles by imposing their pathological behavior on other innocents. It was the way of highly controlling and disturbed individuals. Donna could tell that Eden Parish was highly intelligent, and she fully expected him to continue in his unstable behavior. For now he was corralled. For now.

By day three, Donna and Ken were completely exhausted. They had accomplished their goal to secure an impenetrable charge against the three accomplices. Ken had ordered his team to take several days off. He had driven them hard, but now it was time for all to reconnect with their families and get some much-needed rest. Only a dire emergency would interfere with their rest period. Fortunately, such an emergency never arose.

Donna, unfettered from the details of the case, luxuriated in cooking meals and reconnecting with her home. She even looked forward to doing the laundry. Ken unwound by attending to the lawn as well as the garden, which was beginning to produce. Donna looked at him out the window now and again, noting a look of peace on Ken's face as he rode the riding lawn mower. Their lovemaking the night before was testament to full mutual surrender to each other, rather than immersion in the minutiae of the case, satisfying each other in salient manners of physical and emotional expression. They were back to normal.

Mid-afternoon, Carole called. "Hey, Gavin wants to use the new grill this evening. Are you up to joining us along with Lacy Sue, Seth, and the twins?"

"Oh, that sounds marvelous. Count us in," Donna returned. There were no finer friends and neighbors than Carole and Gavin.

After a scrumptious meal of seafood and vegetable kabobs along with hamburgers for the twins, followed by Gavin's famous lemon meringue pie, Seth took the twins home for their nightly showers before bedtime, leaving Lacy Sue to linger with the others a while longer.

Ken thought it the appropriate time to acknowledge their neighbors' contributions to the Lundy case. "Donna and I wouldn't have been able to resolve the Lundy case without your help. We so appreciate your willingness to be of support. Thank you all."

"Yes," Donna said to underscore Ken's comment. She applauded her friends. "Then to top it off, you feed us royally! It doesn't get any better than this."

Gavin, Carole, and Lacy Sue smiled. It was Gavin who put forward a question about the case. "There is always one pivotal moment when you know who the bad guy is. What was your moment, Donna?"

"Actually, I had help with that one, and it came from Herta Cohen."

"Really?" Ken said. "You never told me this."

Donna smiled. "On one of my last visits to Herta at the nursing home, I saw a woman and a man in a rather animated conversation. She even rose from her wheelchair to point a finger in his face, clearly upset about something. That same week, I saw her coming out of the physical therapy room. I completely forgot about the incident. When we interviewed Blake Miles, however, I had the feeling I had seen him somewhere before, but for the life of me I couldn't remember where. I let it go, but when Gavin did the last genealogy project for me, it all came together. The woman was Laura Miles and the guy was Blake Miles.

"During one of my last visits with Herta, I mentioned to her what I had seen, commenting how odd it was that a stroke victim rose to her feet so effortlessly. Herta told me that she had observed the same thing when she sat in her wheelchair just outside her room across the hall from Ms. Sylvia, aka, Laura Miles. At that point, I started putting the pieces together."

"Ms. Sylvia? She came to us as a stroke victim. She couldn't talk or walk very well," Lacy Sue ventured forth, still coming to terms with the patient she thought was helpless.

"The long and the short of it is that Laura Miles simply faked her stroke symptoms," Donna returned, wanting Lacy Sue to understand.

"Holy Hannah!" Carole blurted.

"She was able to pull it off for so long!" Lacy Sue exclaimed, shock registering on her face. "She truly had us all fooled."

"According to Blake Miles, she watched multiple videos on after-stroke effects and practiced them."

"I might buy that, but there are still MRIs. You can't fake them!" Gavin asserted.

Ken jumped in at this point. "You can if someone had access to archived MRIs in the Records Room of the hospital and placed several in her file. It was an ingenious way of hiding in plain sight after the crime. Laura Miles could literally use the nursing home as a cover by pretending to have a disability after a so-called stroke with no one the wiser. All she had to do was wait it out until things cooled down."

Lacy Sue shook her head in disbelief. "So her husband was her accomplice," she concluded. "He's the one who put the old MRIs in her folder, right?"

"Yes, he's the one who, without authorization, entered the hospital Records Room and stole MRIs matching her supposed stroke. You should know, however, Blake Miles is not the husband of Laura Miles. They, with the encouragement of Eden Parish, pretended to be married as a means of getting closer to Simon and Wanda Lundy. No one was the wiser. There was no cause for anyone to be suspicious of who they were. He took a position with the pharmacy at the hospital, and she did house cleaning. The fact is, Laura Miles and Blake Miles are brother and sister!"

"What? Bizarre!" Carole said. "The lengths they went to."

Donna offered additional information. "Since Blake worked for the hospital as a pharmacy tech, he had access to the Records Room. The hospital is strengthening its security in that regard as we speak."

"Why, though?" Lacy Sue asked, somewhat quietly. "Why murder two people who were just trying to help them?"

Donna and Ken looked at each other. "You have the floor, Detective," she offered.

Ken cleared his throat. "It was Donna who figured it out."

This is where Donna jumped in, "Only with Gavin's help," she interjected.

Ken nodded. "The bottom line is Laura and Blake Miles are the grandchildren of Anna, Burkhardt's first wife."

The group looked at each other bewildered. "Who?" Carole finally asked, shrugging her shoulders as if the announcement was of no import and Ken had lost his mind.

Ken turned to Donna. "You take it from here."

Donna paced the floor, gathering her thoughts. "On a hunch, I asked Gavin to do a genealogy study on Burkhardt, the second husband of the now-deceased fourth wife, Darla Straighter. Just so you know, Burkhardt is Karen Coppick's father. Her mother was Hildegarde, the second wife."

"I remember," Gavin said.

"Do you remember when you attempted a search on Anna, the first wife, and there was no trail that could be found after she left her husband and three young children in the early 40's?"

Gavin nodded, remembering. "Yes, she simply disappeared," he said upon reflection. "There was no further mention of her in the genealogy records after her marriage to Burkhardt and the birth of their three children. So you're saying these three murderers, Blake and Laura Miles, and Eden Parish are her grandchildren?"

"Precisely."

The group grew quiet. "Holy crap!" Carole said. "You can't stop there! Keep it comin', sister!"

Donna smiled at Carole's enthusiastic endorsement. "While examining the family history and genealogy, I couldn't help but note that Burkhardt moved his family from Montclair, New Jersey, to Metuchen, New Jersey, somewhere in the early 50's. At this point, he was married to Hildegarde, his second wife."

"And?" Gavin countered, eager for more information.

Donna cocked her head a bit before answering with conviction. "It simply didn't fit. Why uproot an entire family from their moorings of school, church, friends, and family in Montclair, New Jersey and drive nearly forty-five minutes to his luncheonette each morning in Elizabeth, New Jersey, and forty-five minutes back home to Metuchen, New Jersey? Before they moved, he was only ten minutes away from his place of business! He was in the cat-bird's seat with no real commute. It didn't make sense to me. There had to be a reason he decided to drive to and from his place of work, enduring one-and-one-half hours of daily inconvenience. That was when I asked Gavin to do further genealogy research. Even after Gavin provided the timeline, I was still stumped. Burkhardt and Hildegarde, the second wife, and the three children from Anna, were all presented in the timeline, but not Anna, the first wife. After 1940 she simply disappeared. Five additional children showed up in the timeline as offspring of Burkhardt and Hildegarde's marriage, though."

"So?" Carole asked, motioning for her friend to continue.

"So, what was so appealing in Metuchen, New Jersey that would cause Burkhardt to uproot his whole family? I asked myself," Donna projected.

"Your answer to yourself was…?" Carole summoned for a response.

"Anna, the first wife of Burkhardt."

"*What*!" the group erupted in unison.

The room went completely silent for a time, her listeners stunned by the revelation. Gavin, Carole, and Lacy Sue were speechless until Lacy Sue finally broke the silence after thinking through what she just heard. "That can only mean that Burkhardt reconnected with Anna."

"Oh, dear. I don't like where this is going," Carole added.

"Exactly," Ken confirmed. "Anna was living in Metuchen, New Jersey, all those years. She had two more children, a son and a daughter. The father of those children was Burkhardt as well. These two children were born in between the births of his five children with Hildegarde."

"That's why he moved his family! To be close to Anna!" Carole confirmed.

"Exactly!" Donna returned.

"How deceitful!" Lacy Sue exclaimed. "How awful for Hildegarde. Did she ever find out?"

"Oh, yes," Ken confirmed. "She became suspicious and followed him on occasion, discovering the real reason for his frequent absences from home. This much we got from Karen Coppick."

"What became of these two other children? The son and daughter born in between the other children of Burkhardt and Hildegarde?" Gavin asked.

"The son, Franklin, had a child, a boy, and the daughter, Margaret, had two children, a boy and a girl," Donna answered.

"Let me guess," Carole offered. "Blake and Laura Miles would be the two children born to Margaret, thus two of Anna's grandchildren. Who would the third grandchild be?"

"Eden Parish," Ken replied. "He was born to Anna's son, Franklin."

"The guy who wants to purchase Lundy Vintage Automotive from the Lundy's daughters?"

"One and the same. The three cousins all pretty much grew up together."

"What a cesspool!" Carole boomed. "This Burkhardt guy cheats on Hildegarde, going back to his first wife, Anna, and has two more kids with her. Years later, three grandchildren no one else knows exist...Blake, Laura, and Eden...end up killing the guy who is in charge of their grandfather's money. No wonder this case had your heads spinning!"

Gavin sat back thinking before he asked the next question. "So, did *all* three grandchildren kill the Lundys?"

Donna looked at Ken. "I'll let you answer this one."

Ken nodded. "In a manner of speaking, yes. We believe Eden Parish came up with the plan. He worked on Laura to do the actual killings by slitting the Lundys' wrists. Blake as much as said so. Blake admits to tying their wrists and ankles, after which he taped their mouths shut and placed the drip pans behind the chairs to catch the blood."

"Where was Eden Parish all this time?" Lacy Sue questioned.

"At home waiting for word from Laura and Blake that the Lundys had been executed," Donna returned. "In my opinion he was the master planner, using his cousins to do his dirty work."

"Why?" Carole asked in a subdued tone. "What drove the three of them to kill?"

"Good question. Each one presents a different mental impairment. Eden Parish used his intellect to get his two cousins to do his bidding. He is calculating, devious, and without conscience. Laura Miles is of another bent. She is highly motivated and pretty much hard-wired for anger. Her actions are probably the culmination of years of want and deprivation. She needed an outlet for her anger, and when Eden Parish gave her one, she jumped on it. Blake Miles is, in my opinion, a victim of the other two. He is highly co-dependent, relying on his sister and cousin for direction and focus. He was virtually a slave doing their bidding. They told him what to do and he did it."

"Why was Laura Miles so angry? What drove *her*?" Lacy Sue asked, still trying to wrap her head around the resident murderer who lived in her nursing home undetected.

Donna answered. "She found out that after Hildegarde discovered his secret, her grandfather, Burkhart, pretty much physically and emotionally abandoned the two children he fathered with Anna while still married to Hildegarde. It became the focus of Laura's anger. Her mother and uncle went without, while another family seemed to have had their needs met, or so she thought."

Lacy Sue shook her head. "It takes so little to create a monster," she said quietly.

"Was there anything else that tipped you off, Donna?" Lacy Sue asked, still reeling about Ms. Sylvia being a murderer, while all along faking her stroke symptoms, thus fooling everyone.

Donna thought for a bit. "Yes, there was another thing that piqued my interest. When we interviewed Blake Miles at his home, he mentioned that he went to the Lundy home earlier that evening to return a power saw. That's when he claimed to have discovered the bodies. Ken and his men made a careful inventory of the home, even taking photos during their investigation. There was no power saw on the list or in any photo. Why would he lie about that if he didn't have something to hide?"

"At the time of that interview we had no idea the moving truck he was waiting for that morning was going to take his things to the Lundy home, the very home where they committed the murders," Ken added.

"How ballsy," Carole quipped. "Stealing in plain sight!"

Gavin raised another question. "....So, if the three cousins were living in New Jersey, how did they find their way here to South Carolina? What did the Lundys ever do to them?"

"They took their money," Donna answered. "Once they understood their grandfather had willed money to all of the second-tier beneficiaries, but not their own parents, they were driven to make matters right. While their parents were now dead, they stood to inherit monies in their place per the terms of the trust. They discovered something, however, something much bigger than the trust."

"What was it?" Carole inquired.

"A path toward greater riches," Donna answered.

Chapter Seventeen

EDEN, BLAKE, AND LAURA

New Jersey – three years previously:

"Did you see this?" Laura Miles asked, handing the day's newspaper to her cousin, Eden Parish. Blake, her brother, was sitting back in a recliner completely engrossed in a TV Western, never hearing the question.

"What is it?" Parish asked offhandedly, while eating a slice of leftover pizza from the night before.

"An obituary. Our grandfather is dead. The funeral is this week," Laura replied.

"So?" Eden inquired. "Doesn't he live in South Carolina? What's his obituary doing in our local newspaper?"

"Don't you remember? He was a big shot in the church. A lot of people from up here would know him. He had children living up here as well. They were probably responsible for placing his obituary in the paper."

"So what's it to us?"

"The thing is, he had money, money we should be inheriting."

This got Eden's attention. He sat up. "How do you know?"

"I hear things. They say he married for the fourth time and set up a trust for the fourth wife. Some of that money is ours, since our parents are dead, but we won't see a dime. Our parents were not mentioned in the obituary and probably not mentioned in the will."

Eden Parish sat up straighter and thought about Laura's comment. After a time he finally said, "Don't be so sure. First we need to get a copy of the trust."

"How do we do that?" Laura inquired, eyeing Eden suspiciously.

"We can get a copy from the courthouse."

"We'll have to go to South Carolina for it."

"I think we should. We need to look into this whole thing, scope out the situation, see where the widow lives, that sort of thing, and then we need to come up with a plan."

A week later the three offspring of Burkhardt's potentially forgotten children were leaving the county courthouse with a copy of their grandfather's will and trust. Not long after that, they were eyeing Burkhardt's former residence, where the fourth wife had lived since her marriage to him. Though she was nowhere to be seen, there was a car in the driveway they presumed was hers. Another item maintained by the trust. So be it.

Next, they found out where the executor of the trust, Simon Lundy, and his wife, Wanda, lived. They noted a van in the driveway with signage that read "Lundy Vintage Automotive". Within seconds, they had an address for the business and started the short drive to its location.

"Nice house, nice place of business," was all Parish said with an evil tone after eyeing both the Lundy residence and their place of business. "I've got a feeling we can make out like bandits. Let's get something to eat first. I'm starving. We'll talk later."

Parish laid out the plot for his two cousins later that evening. Laura liked the idea, but Blake was resistant. "Why do we have to kill them? There's got to be a better way!"

Parish eyed his weak-willed cousin with a sneer. "You're either all in or all out! Make up your mind! We'll be set for life if we handle this right."

In the end, Parish won his male cousin over to his way of thinking. It didn't take much effort. Blake could be convinced of anything; he was never one to assert himself.

The very next night, they broke into Lundy's place of business. "What are we looking for?" Laura asked in a whisper as they broke the lock on a side door and entered the premises, heading toward the back of the building.

"Anything we can use as blackmail against the Lundys," came Eden's response. "Let's try to find a storage closet. I'm looking for a box of records. Could be business, personal, or estate papers. If we hit the motherlode, it will tell us all we need to know."

"What if what you're looking for is not here?" Blake asked weakly.

"Then we will find it in their home, but first I have to get myself hired by Lundy as an auto body tech. Before long we will have all the leverage we need. Mark my words."

Laura and Blake looked at each other and shrugged. They could never keep up with their cousin and his wizard-like thinking. In the end, it would cost them dearly.

Chapter Eighteen

South Carolina – Present Day

"I know you're not going to want to hear this, but I pretty much understand their situation…not that I agree with their crimes," Carole commented during another conversation with Donna and the others. "They won't qualify for sainthood, but at the same time, no one knew they existed. They were the lost ones in the family."

"That doesn't give them license to murder. Besides, it's not entirely true that no one knew they existed," Donna countered.

"The other beneficiaries knew of their existence?" Carole propelled rather loudly.

Donna, understanding her friend's need for detail, explained. "It was a question I asked Karen Coppick. According to her, several years after Burkhardt's death, her older brother received a phone call from a woman in New Jersey who claimed to be the daughter of Anna and Burkhardt. The family ignored it, thinking it was someone trying to shoulder a way into the estate. If they had pursued the claim, they may have tracked down these three grandchildren."

"Instead, they became the legacy of the lost," Carole decided quietly. "Not only were their parents lost in a web of secrets, but the grandchildren were lost, as well."

"Precisely. What they saw as exclusions fueled anger and hatred from the grandchildren," Ken added, "especially Laura Miles."

Donna then added some facts. "To make matters worse, the cousins discovered, in their review of the records stolen from the closet at the Lundy's place of business, that Simon and Wanda never claimed certain assets of the estate, omitting these assets from the official estate listing. No one knew these assets existed so no one was the wiser. Once Lundy got control of the Burkhardt's estate, they retitled these assets into their own names."

"How deceitful! No wonder the grandchildren had it out for them! Did the fourth wife know of this?" Lacy Sue asked.

"From a forensic examination of the records, it appears she did know. It's surmised she didn't want to jeopardize the benefit she would be receiving from the trust for as long as she lived, so she simply looked the other way."

"Whew! That takes balls! How much in assets did Lundy hide?" Gavin queried.

"Nearly one million dollars," Ken answered.

"Whew! That would fuel the rage for sure!" Carole quipped.

"The thing is," Donna offered, "Eden Parish found it as a way to embolden and solidify their plan. They had something on Lundy they could now use to control him. After all, the executor and his wife had committed an act of grand theft."

"Go on," Gavin encouraged.

"By this time, Parish had embedded himself with Lundy through employment, playing the repentant drug addict, obedient employee, and dedicated church goer.

"When Parish and his cousins broke into the Lundy's place of business months before the murders, they discovered a folder that held the original paperwork of hidden assets. Parish knew what he was going to do with this information. It didn't help that Lundy was often heard bragging about his yearly executor fees for managing the estate. The cousins now knew he had helped himself to more than the yearly fees… a heck of a lot more.

"At the same time, Laura and Blake played the role of interested Bible seekers, gaining valuable information about Simon and Wanda from their weekly Bible studies and their occasional attendance at Lundy's church."

"How did they manage to do that?" Carole probed.

Ken answered for Donna. "Eden convinced Laura and Blake to present themselves at the shop with an automotive body blemish they wanted fixed, which they themselves created. Eden then introduced them to Simon Lundy, who took an immediate liking to the engaging couple. Blake convincingly turned the conversation toward current affairs, which created an opening for Simon to share his church's promotion of a new order in God's due time. The Miles feigned interest in what Simon was telling them. Before long, they had agreed to study the Bible with Simon and Wanda, using it as a front to gather more information with the goal to eventually gain complete control of the assets.

"They soon discovered, through Simon Lundy's careless bragging, that Burkhardt's estate was not the only one that they had handled. There were three other elderly folks from the church who placed their affairs into Lundy's hands before their deaths."

"So, Lundy had a bit of an operation going on inside the church, using his position as a church elder to gain access to the financial affairs of the elderly," Gavin concluded. "How clever."

"How diabolical, you mean," Carole corrected her husband.

"Did Lundy declare all of the assets in these other three cases?" Lacy Sue inquired already guessing the answer.

"No, he did not, though these estates were not as large as Burkhardt's estate. Lundy's success at hiding assets from the other three estates emboldened him to acquire a bigger chunk of the pie in the larger estate once he gained control."

Carole was now leaning forward, pulled in completely by the details of the investigation.

"So they knew of these matters even before Lundy bragged of the other three estates he had managed," she forwarded for confirmation.

"Yes. They discovered them in the closet, along with Burkhardt's estate. There were three additional boxes. The cousins took all they had found, examined the contents, and copied just enough paperwork to prove their findings. They had Simon and Wanda just where they wanted them," Ken answered. "They not only had Lundy on the Burkhardt thefts, but also the thefts from the other three estates."

Donna furthered the explanation. "It wasn't long before Parish, Blake, and Laura, confronted Simon and Wanda one day at their business just after closing. The other workers had gone home for the day, and it was just the five of them. They chose the day Laura and Blake were scheduled for their

Bible study. The three cousins cornered the couple in their back office, revealing their knowledge of the Lundy thefts, even showing them proof of their discovery by handing over copies of the paperwork they had taken from the estate boxes months before.

"According to Blake, the Lundys looked as though they were going to have heart attacks. Wanda froze when she heard the accusations, and Simon began shaking and offering all sorts of excuses. Then Eden Parish offered them a way out."

"This should be good," Carole nearly shouted, still leaning forward in anticipation. Gavin placed his hand on her shoulder to calm her down.

"Oh, it is," Donna assured her friend. "The three cousins made one hell of a team. Simon and Wanda were amateurs, compared to Eden, Laura, and Blake. The first thing they made the guilty couple do was hand over the undeclared assets from Burkhardt's estate, assuming correctly that the funds had been comingled with the stolen assets of the other three estates.

"Originally, Simon Lundy deposited the assets in a bank account, but, over time, Lundy slowly withdrew the cash and stored it in a safe deposit box at another bank across town. The very next morning after their showdown with Simon and Wanda, Eden Parish accompanied Simon to the bank, and waited for Lundy to return with a satchel of cash. To ensure Simon's complete cooperation, Laura and Blake kept watch over Wanda until Parish called in with an "all clear" message. They left nothing to chance.

"The next thing they insisted on was retitling the deed to the Lundy home and the transfer of the deed to an LLC. The LLC is titled to the principals, namely, Laura and Blake Miles."

"Oh! They stole the Lundy home?" Lacy Sue gasped.

"Essentially. Not only their home, but their money. Eden Parish took possession of the cash from the safe deposit box and the business accounts, while Laura and Blake took possession of the Lundy home, along with personal and investment accounts," Ken explained.

"Payback is a bitch!" Carole blurted.

"That explains why Eden Parish was so confident he would be able to take control of Lundy Vintage Automotive from Joanna Carnes. The fact was, he had possession of the business already!" Gavin concluded.

"Indeed," Donna countered. "The Lundys had nothing left. If their deeds of crime had been discovered, they would have gone to prison, been ostracized by the church, and been rejected by family and friends. As it was, Parish offered the Lundys a way out, or so they thought."

"Yet, they were killed. Why didn't the cousins allow them to live and watch them suffer in silence?" Lacy Sue questioned.

"The short answer is that Laura Miles wanted the Lundy home for herself and Blake. It would be, in her eyes, their first real home. In her mind, it amounted to restitution for all the years she and Blake lived in squalor and want. She was determined not to look over her shoulder or answer questions as to how the home came into her possession. The Lundys knew too many people who would ask why they 'sold' the home, especially their daughter, Joanna. The only logical thing to do was to kill Simon and Wanda and then have Blake 'discover' the bodies, hoping it appeared as an attempted robbery that went bad. The thing they didn't consider was that nothing was stolen."

Carole sat reviewing the facts in her head and then her eyes lit up. "Don't tell me! Let me guess! The basins were placed beneath the Lundy's wrists to catch the blood spill because Laura didn't want their future home bloodied! Tell me I'm wrong, sister!"

"I wish I could. It seems Laura Miles thought of everything."

"Didn't Joanna Carnes, Simon and Wanda's daughter, become suspicious at any point? After all, she did the books for her father's business?" Lacy Sue asked.

"By then, Parish was funneling just enough money back into the business to make it look like everything was as usual *before* his 'purchase' of the business. The fact is, we suspect she was next on the list to be killed by the three. He as much as alluded to that plot when questioned. He did not plan on making 'payments' to Joanna Carnes for very long," Donna replied.

"The fact that the Lundy killings had become so public and were still being investigated caused the three of them to decide against murdering Joanna, rightly concluding that the death of the daughter following that of the parents would bring more suspicion and questions than they could handle," Ken shared.

"Was there anything else that made you suspicious of this group?" Lacy Sue questioned Donna.

"As a matter of fact, there was another peculiarity having to do with the personal bank statements of the fourth wife, Darla," Donna answered reflectively.

Her audience leaned forward in rapt attention. Donna paced the room, gathering the details of the financial discovery in her mind. "There was something off starting two years before Darla Straighter's death. Until then, her bank statements had been very consistent since Burkhardt's death. However, an unexplained entry appeared monthly for two years leading up to her passing. It was a $500 electronic transfer."

"Payable to whom?" Gavin inquired, his face set in a puzzled look.

"Payable to an LLC marked and coded as "maintenance". The named principal of the LLC is none other than Eden Parish."

"Holy Moly! He was fleecing the old lady! How did that happen?" Carole asked in utter disbelief.

"It happened because, from the records recovered from the back closet at the Lundy's business site closet months before, Parish discovered the fourth wife had conspired with Lundy for him to gain control of his assets through her marriage to Burkhardt upon his death. Darla, for years, transferred from her private account into a private account owned by the Lundys, a pre-arranged monthly 'thank-you' payment to supplement their yearly executor fee."

"So the old lady had been part of a low level Ponzi scheme!" Gavin exclaimed in disbelief.

"Pretty much!" Donna confirmed. "Darla, Simon, and Wanda knew Burkhardt had made money with his bank investment. Dorothy, his third wife, was now gone, and most of the children lived far away, except for Karen Coppick. Karen though, was now on the 'outs' with the church, and as he aged her father sought more support from within the church than he did from family. Enter the Lundys! They would support Burkhardt physically, emotionally, and spiritually, even encouraging a relationship with Darla Straighter! Hell, Simon Lundy even married Burkhardt and Darla in Burkhardt's home!"

"It doesn't get any more conniving than that," Gavin said sadly.

"When Parish stumbled upon the 'thank you' payments Lundy was receiving from Darla, he forced Darla to redirect the payments to his LLC, or face exposure. The old woman complied readily.

"The only innocents in this whole affair are the second-tier beneficiaries, the children of Anna, Hildegarde, and Dorothy. They had no clue of what had transpired in handling the affairs of the estate. All they were presented with was a financial statement indicating that there was nothing left of the estate upon Darla's death, except the house, which was sold for a fraction of what it could have been worth if maintained," Donna concluded.

"Mary's new home," Lacy Sue confirmed, in a subdued manner.

"Yes, I'm afraid so," Donna verified.

"What are the odds? We can't forget the other innocents in this matter are the two children of Burkhardt and Anna... Franklin and Margaret... who went undiscovered and unsupported," Lacy Sue corrected. She shook her head in disbelief.

"This all happened because, more than fifty years ago, a woman named Anna, who had three young children, left her husband and family and disappeared. Now we find out years later that she had two more children by Burkhardt and three grandchildren. What became of her?" Lacy Sue quietly asked, as was her nature.

"Good question," Carole forwarded. "It seems to me, from what I've heard so far, she helped create this legacy of the lost and bears responsibility for the three grandchildren who became murderers."

It was a question Donna had asked herself. She consulted the pages of genealogy Gavin provided. She still had questions, and needed answers. There was still work to do.

Chapter Nineteen

South Carolina – present day:

Though the case was essentially solved, Donna was not fully satisfied. Questions remained for which she needed answers. After a time, she discussed her angst with Ken. He listened thoughtfully, but knew she would pursue the answers she sought relentlessly until she had the complete picture. Then, and only then, could she walk away from this case with a sense of satisfaction and closure.

"How long will you be away?" he asked.

"Not more than a day or so. I've already been in touch with the family."

"I won't stand in your way, if this is something you feel you must do to put all of this business behind you. I'm just grateful for your help in putting this case to rest."

Newark, New Jersey – Present Day

Donna flew into Newark International Airport, one of the first municipal commercial airports in the country. She checked out a rental car, and put into the GPS the address given her by the family...a nursing home in the middle of the city.

Donna had been a Jersey girl herself and yet facing crowded Newark after years of living on the coast of South Carolina, was a reminder of the concentrated, and often chaotic city environment. Passing the waterfront, Donna remembered the port had the distinction of being one of the busiest container shipping terminals on the East Coast.

Finding the address, Donna parked the rental and glanced at her surroundings before exiting the car. The nursing home was an older building that had seen better days, although it had mature trees and, to its credit, tasteful landscaping. It was only a block or two from an established neighborhood of lower income homes.

Entering the building through the visitor's entrance door, she found an interior that was dark and dated, almost to the point of shabby. It smelled of years of bleached urine. A gentlemen in his mid-sixties rose from a worn armchair in the foyer and walked toward her.

"Dr. DeShayne?" he inquired hesitantly.

"Yes. You must be Patrick O'Connell," she replied, offering a warm handshake. "It is so kind of you to assist me, Mr. O'Connell."

"Please call me Patrick. I've informed my father of your visit. We're both intrigued by your need to ask questions about my Aunt Anna, whom I've never met. Her name came up in conversation at times, but no one in the family seemed willing to enlarge the narrative."

"I understand. It will all become clear, Patrick, when I present what I know and ask for help filling in the blanks. I hope I'm not causing any distress to your father with my visit. If so, please tell me."

"No, not at all. He is anxious to meet you. His mind is still very sharp, though he struggles physically. He is waiting for us in his room, watching his favorite morning program, reruns of *The Lucy Show*. It doesn't matter that he has seen every episode at least a dozen times, he still laughs like it's the first time. Let me show you to his room."

Donna followed Patrick O'Connell down a drab hallway toward the living quarters of Liam O'Connell, his father, shared with another resident. Patrick introduced Donna to his father, now 93 years old, who was sitting in a wheelchair with a beautifully crocheted wrap across his lap. The older man reached out with a shaky hand in greeting.

"What kind of a doctor are you, again?" Liam O'Connell asked softly.

"I'm a forensic psychiatrist, Mr. O'Connell."

"Do I need one of those?" he returned with a twinkle of a smile.

She laughed. Donna already loved this man. "No, sir. I don't think you need me at all."

The aged man smiled and nodded. "So what's this all about? Something about my sister, Anna, I understand."

"Dad, perhaps Doctor DeShayne would be more comfortable if we went down the hallway to the private alcove. It would give us more space," Patrick suggested, eyeing his father's roommate sitting just a couple of feet away.

"I suppose that would be all right," the older O'Connell replied.

Donna was relieved by the suggestion. The conversation she was about to have regarding the former Anna O'Connell was a sensitive one, and a listening roommate would limit her ability to share information and ask questions.

Patrick wheeled his father out of the room toward an unoccupied recess down the hallway. Donna followed. Once settled, Donna asked her first question of Anna's youngest brother, Liam. "Mr. O'Connell, how close were you to your sister, Anna?"

He eyed her with a pensive expression mixed with pain. "We were all real close when we were children. They're all gone now, my brothers, Patrick, Sean, and Jack. My sister Anna, is gone as well. I miss them terribly. We were quite the bunch. Hell raisers, some would say."

Donna smiled, but decided to tread lightly from this point on. "Did you all stay close as you became adults and had families of your own?"

"I did with my brothers, but my sister…" Liam eyed his son before continuing. "My sister disappeared for a time while her three children were very young."

"For a while? You mean she reappeared again?"

"You had to know our Anna. She would appear and then disappear. When she did appear, it was all the same again, as if she never left. She would stay for a while, be the life of the party, and then go off again without a warning, never sharing anything about herself. You could see the sadness and loneliness though, when she thought no one was looking," Liam shared with a strangled voice.

"Then one day, she appeared again, but this time with a little boy. His name was Franklin. When I asked her who his father was, she admitted it was Burkhardt, the father of her first three children."

"How did you feel about that?" Donna probed.

"I was shocked, of course. She had been living with another guy at the time, so I assumed the child belonged to him."

Donna had to ask her next question, hoping it wouldn't upset Anna's aged brother. "Did she ever say why she left Burkhardt and never saw her first three children again?"

"Oh, but she did see them!"

Donna looked puzzled. "Mr. O'Connell, I was under the impression she never saw her first three children again."

"Oh, that's not true. She wouldn't visit them face-to-face, mind you, but she would watch them from a distance when they went to school or played in the yard. Several times a year. She told me this herself, and she said Burkhardt knew of her visits and never tried to discourage her. I think she may have expressed her gratitude by letting him into her bed again."

"So the man she was then living with never knew the child was not his?"

"It seemed that way to me, but the guy had a violent temper and he'd beat her from time-to-time. She would come to us with the boy, broken and battered, and we would take them in, but the guy would eventually come to get her and the boy and take them back home. The beatings eventually stopped. My brothers and I had a 'come-to-Jesus-meeting' with the bastard."

"Did it help?" Donna probed.

O'Connell had a smug look on his face when he answered. "Let's just say we took matters into our own hands. He never laid a hand on Anna again, that much I can tell you."

All this time, Patrick was listening. "Dad, what did you do?"

"You don't need to know. All you have to know is he never hurt her again," Patrick's father returned defensively.

Patrick shook his head, guessing the batterer was the subject of a garbage removal project. He knew Irish gangs could be hired for such occasions. Patrick often heard his father say the Irish didn't call the police…they called family.

Donna saw the tension between father and son and changed the subject. "Mr. O'Connell, are you aware your sister Anna bore a fifth child, a girl?"

Liam looked shocked. "Are you sure you have the right person?"

"Yes sir. The birth is recorded."

Liam O'Connell looked startled, shaking his head in disbelief. "I didn't know. A girl, you say? Who was the father this time?"

Donna hesitated. "Mr. O'Connell, the father in this case was again Burkhardt."

Liam's eyes welled in tears. "He just couldn't stay away from her, our Anna. I can't blame him, really. She was addictive and he was drawn to her like so many others," he replied sadly. "What is the girl's name?"

"Margaret," Donna replied. "There were two additional children after the first three. A Margaret and a Franklin. You already knew of Franklin, but Margaret was the name of the other child. Her father was Burkhardt as well.'

"Where are they now?"

"They are both dead, I'm afraid. Franklin died in a gang-related encounter, and Margaret died of an overdose. Margaret, however, had two children, a boy and a girl. The boy's name is Blake and the girl's name is Laura. Franklin, had one son. His name is Eden."

"So our Anna had grandchildren. We didn't know," Liam said quietly, hanging his head in a gesture of shame. "Seems like we didn't know a lot of things about our red-headed wild child," he reflected. "Where are the grandchildren now?" he asked.

"I have information you will find disturbing, Mr. O'Connell." Donna proceeded to share the details of the Lundy case, Burkhardt's estate, the terms of the trust, and the charge of murder against his sister's three grandchildren, Blake, Laura, and Eden. When she finally finished, O'Connell remained quiet. For a long time he stared at the floor without saying a word.

"Dad, are you all right?" Patrick asked, eyeing his father with concern.

The old man finally looked up and nodded. "You say Burkhardt's estate went to a fourth wife?" he asked without expecting an answer. "Burkhardt wasn't a very smart man. A nice enough guy, a hard worker without a doubt, but not a smart man. He found his match in Anna, though. She couldn't get a handle on life, despite being fussed over and adored by her family. There was something gnawing at her soul, chewing at her bit by bit, eventually swallowing her life. As a distraction, she went from one man to another, seeking something she never found. Maybe Burkhardt represented a time in her life she wanted to return to, but never did.

"The fact remains, her only tried and true friend was the bottle. It was her solace and comfort in a sea of failed relationships. She died a hideous death of liver disease. The long and the short of it…my sister simply self-destructed. The unconscious desire to die is everywhere one goes, I'm afraid," Liam uttered quietly.

Donna, noting the old man's struggle, remained silent for a time, allowing Liam to gather himself before she asked her next question. "Are you aware of any other relationships Anna may have been involved with? So far, we know your sister had given birth to five children, the first three borne to Burkhardt but raised by the second wife, Hildegarde. Then two more *during* the time Burkhardt was married to Hildegarde, a boy and a girl. I'm trying to establish whether there were any more children?"

At this point, Liam O'Connell began to shudder and cry. Donna looked with alarm at Patrick, who shrugged, indicating his lack of knowledge. They both waited, observing an old man as he dealt with significant emotions related to events in the past. Dabbing his eyes he looked at his audience of two.

"There was another child. We never knew who the father was, but it wasn't Burkhardt. She was a most beautiful creature. I adored her from the moment I set eyes on her. Cherubic in every respect," Liam shared before another soulful outcry.

So shaken was Liam, that Donna decided to end the session and continue the next day. "Mr. O'Connell, perhaps my questions should be reserved for another day," Donna offered. "I'm afraid I have upset you."

"No! No!" was his adamant response through a torrent of tears.

Patrick got up from his chair and knelt before his father's chair. Placing his hands over his father's, he looked into his eyes. "Dad, what do we need to know? There is something we need to know, isn't there? Tell us. Tell us and be free!"

The old man bent over and continued to cry, his entire body drawn in as if trying to hide. Body tremors soon followed. It was some time before he quieted somewhat. The shudders had subsided, the crying was more subdued, and then not at all. Liam O'Connell sat there, a reduced version of himself, surrendering to a heretofore, secret memory.

"Tell us, Dad…" Patrick further appealed, while holding his father's hands.

Liam spoke softly at first, almost with reverence. "My niece, Anna's daughter by another relationship she never talked about, was a beauty, but no one saw her beauty but my wife and I," was his initial subdued response.

"She had a facial deformity. The result of a house fire." Liam bowed his head looking down at his hands in painful recall. His body shuddered with the memory. He labored to continue. "She was only three years old when it happened. A day I will never forget."

"What happened, Dad?" Patrick implored his father. Clearly the son was shaken by this new information. Secrets. There were too many secrets.

The old man continued, gathering strength. "My sister was drunk that night, as usual, and smoking. The house caught fire. Anna woke to the screams of her young daughter. By the time the little girl was rescued, the flames had already engulfed the home. A firefighter located her in a back bedroom and brought her to safety, but the cost was greater than anyone realized. Multiple surgical skin grafts eventually brought her to an acceptable standard of movement and appearance. The damage to her mind, however, left a very fragile person. She had suffered an unforgiving childhood of mocking and teasing, not to mention painful surgical procedures. She often railed that she never fit in."

"What was her name?" Donna asked tenderly, while placing a hand on the shoulder of Liam O'Connell.

"Keller. Keller O'Connell," Liam returned, his face laced in lines of painful memory.

Donna's head whipped up in recognition of the name. "Not the author! Keller O'Connell, the famous author?"

Liam slowly nodded with a smile. "One and the same. My wife and I took the child in after the fire and saw her through multiple surgeries. My sister went AWOL again, undone, most likely, by the shame of her neglect. We lost track of Keller and never heard from her again after high school. She simply left, with a note not to look for her. It was so much like her mother. I suppose she found an outlet for her pain by writing. She became famous, but I understand she never gives interviews. I don't think she ever got over being burned."

Liam bowed his head again. "It's the children who suffer when their parents are not well. The children absorb the illnesses of the family, whether they are physical, mental, emotional, or spiritual. It's the children who often become lost."

Donna was torn, listening to his heartbreak. She was responsible for the current state of this man. Did she have the right to upset him at this point in his life?

"Did you ever try to find her?" Donna questioned. "Keller O'Connell, I mean?"

"Her note was very clear. She wanted to be left alone. I understand she eventually married and had two children of her own and now is famous. We decided not to disturb her peace. There's not a night that goes by that I do not pray for her."

"Now I discover there were other children and grandchildren who were never connected with our family," Liam stuttered through his distress.

"Mr. O'Connell, it's not your fault," Donna said soothingly.

"You don't understand. We made a pact. We O'Connell children... my three brothers, Sean, Patrick, and Jack, and my sister, Anna... had an agreement. We made a solemn oath to always be there for each other through thick-and-thin, no matter what. Our family should have cared for Anna's grandchildren."

Donna spoke softly but convincingly to the old man bent over before her. "Mr. O'Connell, you can't keep a pact if you don't have the facts. There is no doubt in my mind you would have been there at some level for your sister's grandchildren, but you simply had no knowledge of them. The blame is not yours to bear, sir."

Liam took a deep breath and sighed. He looked out the window in the alcove, with a far-away look in his eyes. "She was a beauty, our Anna," he said quietly after a long while. "A real beauty. She could lighten hearts, sing like a song bird, and dance a jig that would bring the house down. Much like Keller. How I miss them both. It could have all been so different. Now I find that my great niece and nephews have committed murder. It could have been all so different," the old man said, his voice fading away.

Donna was suddenly stricken with guilt. She had not soothed this fragile man. If anything, she had unsettled him at a time he should be comforted by his life memories and support system.

"Mr. O'Connell," she began hesitatingly, "your sister, from what I have gleaned, was considered the family gem. The fact she lost her way at times, does not necessarily mean she was responsible for the choices of her grandchildren... Blake, Laura, and Eden."

Liam O'Connell looked hard and long at the doctor before speaking. "Doctor, every adult who has a child is responsible for that child. If that adult cannot care for the child in a responsible manner, another adult, or an agency needs to step in to do so. They would have had a home with us, if I had known."

The old man looked away. Donna was gathering her things when she heard his voice again. "I want to meet them. I want to meet Anna's grandchildren, my great-niece and nephews," he said firmly, his manner resolute.

Patrick whipped his head in his father's direction. "I don't think that's a good idea, Dad. There's no need to become involved in a matter in which you have no responsibility."

"I'll be the judge of that," Liam O'Connell firmly declared.

Chapter Twenty

By week's end, Donna had gotten permission for and arranged a teleconference between Laura and Blake Miles and Liam O'Connell. Liam's son, Patrick, was highly resistant to the idea at first, but eventually yielded, understanding his father would never rest until he was satisfied the right thing was done.

"Who is this guy to me, again?" Laura Miles asked rather caustically when Donna visited her in prison with the idea of a teleconference.

"Mr. Liam O'Connell is your grandmother's brother. He would be your great uncle."

"So?" She sat back smugly. "Why does he need to talk to me and Blake?"

Donna was about to dismiss the whole process herself. It didn't appear Laura Miles had any interest in family connections, but then remembered Liam O'Connell did. She pressed forward, wanting the old man to have the satisfaction of making a gesture, however unrecognized it may turn out to be.

"Your great-Uncle Liam recently learned of you and Blake."

"How nice," she forwarded unceremoniously. "What's in it for us?" Laura had a most disinterested air. Donna had to remind herself repeatedly this upcoming encounter was an old man's wish, a wish she had promised to support. Now she wasn't so sure she could deliver.

"Let's just say you might want to hear what the man has to say?" she offered.

Laura sat back folding her arms. "Why not? There's nothing else to do in this god-forsaken place," she spat sarcastically.

Several days later, with Donna's urging, Ken arranged for Blake and Laura Miles to be brought into a private cubicle at the prison, with one guard posted at the door and two more placed on either side of the shackled brother and sister. It was the first time in a number of months the siblings were in each other's company. They stepped toward each other to hug, but were warned by the guards to step back. Laura gnarled an unceremonious expression at the guards, not unexpected in prison environment.

Ken, not wholly in favor of this arrangement, was reminded that Donna had greatly contributed to his department, declaring a 'case-closed' ending in the here-to-fore unsolvable Lundy murder investigation. He felt he owed her this gesture of support, though he harbored reservations as to any positive results it would produce.

He ordered the siblings to take a seat. They were purposely placed on opposites sides of the room. He then took his place in a far corner of the room, keeping a watchful eye on the suspects and the anticipated proceedings. He nodded to Donna, who had been seated before the brother and sister entered the room.

Donna tended to her laptop on the table before looking up at the siblings.

"Blake and Laura Miles, I have Mr. Liam O'Connell and his son, Patrick, on audio and visual. We are now live," she announced.

"Patrick, this is Dr. DeShayne. Can you hear me?" she began, to establish a setting.

"Loud and clear, Doctor," came the reply.

"You have visual as well?" she questioned to be sure.

"Yes. It appears all is well," Patrick returned.

Donna gathered herself for a forum she was not quite sure of. It was dicey. An old man seeking contact with those connected to a beloved deceased sister.

"Then let us begin introductions," she directed bravely. "Liam O'Connell, I present the grandchildren of your late sister, Anna...Blake and Laura Miles. Blake and Laura, Mr. Liam O'Connell is your great-Uncle and is accompanied by his son, Patrick O'Connell, your second cousin."

Neither side spoke at first. For Donna, the lull was interminable. Finally, Liam made a meager offer of acknowledgement. "I didn't know," was all he said at first. "I didn't know my sister had other children, or even grandchildren. She was lost to us."

There was complete silence on the other end for an undetermined period. The dead zone of silence was finally broken by a singular voice. "What was she like, our grandmother?" Blake Miles ventured forth in a compliant manner.

"What difference does it make?" Laura spat forcefully. "She was a drunk! Don't you remember?" Laura was clearly the leader of the two.

"I just want to know. I don't remember much of her," Blake meekly returned to his irate sister.

"What possible good can it do?" Laura returned with a sneer at her brother.

Liam intervened willingly. "She was a beauty, Blake. Much like your sister. I am stunned at how much my sister looks like your sister, the flaming red hair and all. She would light up a crowd everywhere she went. She was infectious."

"That's not what we heard!" Laura interrupted. "We heard she pretty much abandoned her first three kids and drank herself to death. A lot of good she was to us!"

Liam quieted for a time. "I'm sorry you didn't have the chance to know her like I did, when she was younger. Yes, she walked away from her family. We don't know why. I wish you knew her before the darkness of her mind took over."

"Yeah, well, we didn't. Instead we were stuck with a mother who did drugs and let every jerk into her bed. Hell, if it wasn't for neighbors, we would never have eaten. Our mother would have done us a favor by walking away like her mother did!"

Donna observed Laura's seething anger. There was a lot more to Laura's story than she was telling. She suspected the now-grown woman may have been the victim of sexual abuse by her mother's lovers at a young age. She made a note to pursue this possibility in a future, but in a far more private setting, if such a setting ever presented itself.

"So what's this all about, old man?" Laura hurled. "You wanted to meet us. So you have. What's in it for you? What are you after, old man?"

Donna could see Liam was dismayed. She had warned him and his son Patrick that Laura was especially difficult, showing no remorse in her actions against Simon and Wanda Lundy and that they should not expect a warm reception.

Liam looked straight into the viewer. "I suppose I'm a foolish old man who hoped to recapture a bit of his sister and brothers again through her offspring." He bowed his head in resignation. "The wishes of an old fool, it appears," he uttered almost inaudibly.

Finally, Blake spoke up. "How many brothers?"

Liam looked up, surprised by Blake's interest. "There were five of us in all. Our sister Anna, my brothers, Patrick, Sean, and Jack. They're all gone now. You look a bit like Jack, I might add. He was very smart."

"Like our cousin, Eden?" Blake asked. "Eden is a whiz. There's nothing he can't figure out. Why, he even knew how to put the old lady out of her misery so that no one would be the wiser."

"You fool!" Laura exploded. "Shut your damn mouth!" She made an effort to lunge at her brother in unbridled fury but the shackles around her ankles prevented her from advancing toward him. The guards roughly returned her to her seat.

Donna looked in Ken's direction at his place against the far wall. Ken gave a slight nod. An unexpected confession of sorts, but Blake couldn't take back the words. It revealed another unexpected aspect of this case they hadn't figured on, but it made sense.

Blake looked scared. He knew what his sister was capable of when she got angry. The only thing protecting him from her now was the guards and the detective in the corner of the room.

Everyone remained quiet. "I think that will do for now," Ken said aloud, indicating the need to end the session.

Liam cleared his throat. "Yes, I agree. I'm so sorry that I couldn't have been more available to you both. Perhaps you will allow me to write?"

"Don't bother!" Laura firmly said, leaving no question of her position.

"Blake?" Liam queried.

Blake shrugged his shoulders. "If you want."

Immediately upon ending the conference call, the prisoners were escorted in the direction of their cells, however, Blake, was redirected. Ken had ordered he be brought to the interrogation room for further questioning. It didn't take long before they had Blake telling all he knew regarding the murder of Darla Straighter, Burkhardt's fourth wife.

Chapter Twenty-One

Six months later:

In separate trials for Eden Parish, Blake Miles, and Blake's sister, Laura, they were each found guilty of the murders of Simon and Wanda Lundy. Eden Parish was sentenced, in two separate trials, to two consecutive life terms for his role in the Lundy murders as well as the murder of Darla Straighter, the fourth wife.

Laura Miles was sentenced to life in prison for the Lundy murders, while Blake Miles, due to his cooperation, received a lesser sentence of thirty years, with the possibility for early release for good behavior.

Still, Donna held reservations. She expressed her concern to Carole over lunch a short time after the verdicts were announced.

"In retrospect, it's Laura who haunts me," she announced.

Carole, sensitive to her friend given her own years in a psychiatric practice, said quietly, "Why is that?"

Donna pushed her plate aside before answering, "I sense she is holding something in, something very painful that no one has yet heard. Any of us could have been abandoned emotionally and/or physically in our youth.

Some survive the experience and go on to lead productive lives, while others harbor bitterness."

Carole nodded in acknowledgment. "If she let it out, would it make a difference in the outcome...in her future?"

Donna shrugged. "The life sentence would, no doubt, stand. However, the prisoner just might be set free on an emotional level. Isn't that worth something?"

Carole smiled. "That's worth everything. One can be imprisoned physically, but freed emotionally and spiritually. Is that what you're thinking?"

Donna gathered herself. "Yes, if she would allow me to help her."

"Yes," Carole acknowledged. "*If* she allowed you, but how *long* will it take?"

Donna was relieved to have shared her thoughts with her friend. "Is this the right thing to do?" she asked herself.

Two months later:

Donna signed in at the prison's maximum security visitor's entrance and was escorted to a partitioned conference room. The air was dank and stale, smelling of mildew. The walls of the room were of concrete; the paint had faded long ago. The metal chairs were cold, hard, and rusted. She waited a while before she heard footsteps and the clearing of locks, along with the creak of a steel door. Looking up, she saw Laura Miles, escorted by a burly female prison guard to a table separated from her by glass.

"You have thirty minutes," the guard announced unceremoniously before going to stand against a far wall.

Donna took her seat on the other side of the glass

partition, noting immediately that Laura Miles had aged in the short time since her confinement. Her hair bore streaks of gray, her face had a haggard look, and her eyes reflected exhaustion. Her walk was bent and labored. It appeared that prison life was rough on this murderer.

Miles sat with a thump, eyeing Donna with suspicion. "So," she eventually spat, her voice derisive. "You were responsible for sending me to this hell hole, and now you visit. How nice! To what do I owe the pleasure? Any other surprises for me today, Doctor?"

Donna understood Laura had an oppositional personality, and had committed a memorable murder. Donna's first choice was to disarm the woman, but she thought better of it. She simply asked a question.

"How are you adjusting?"

Laura slumped in her chair in a signal of defiance. "What's it to you? Why do you even care?"

For the first time, Donna questioned her decision to visit Laura, but she knew she couldn't let on. She quickly found an answer. "Would this be a first? That someone cared, I mean?"

Laura adjusted herself in the chair, discomfited by the question, but she held firm. "What's it to you?" she repeated, her stare piercing.

"Your Uncle Liam O'Connell cared enough to communicate with you. He is family," Donna offered.

Laura smiled wickedly. "He's an old man who won't be here much longer. You want me to hang my heart on *his* star? Sister, you've got a lot to learn!"

Donna held firm. "Does family, regardless of who it is, not interest you?"

Laura laughed derisively. "Why should it? The whole notion of a loving and caring family is a fantasy."

"Your brother Blake; is he a fantasy?" Donna ventured cautiously.

Laura shifted uncomfortably, suddenly alarmed. "I haven't heard anything from Blake. Is he okay?"

Bingo! Donna determined immediately that Blake was Laura's Achilles' heel. Donna quickly replied. "Blake is fine. I spoke with him the other day. He sends his love. Is there a message you want me to take to him?"

Laura again drew cautious and defensive. "Why would you do that? What's in it for you? What does my brother have to do with you?" she hurled.

Donna held silent for a time, corralling her inward eagerness. "He wants you to know he is well," she said quietly.

Laura took a deep breath and exhaled. "He's not too smart. He talks too much," was all she offered. Donna could tell the information she provided Laura about Blake was a relief to her.

"You've protected him all these years," Donna pitched with an air of confidence she did not feel.

Laura looked penetratingly at her visitor. "Someone had to," she offered while folding her arms across her body.

"Oh?" Donna questioned, hoping to gain more insight.

Laura smiled knowingly. "So you want to know about our childhood, Doctor? That's it, isn't it? You want to know why a sister and brother, along with their cousin, committed murder. Didn't our trials provide enough information for you? Now you want more gritty details? Are you planning to write a book? Is that it?"

Donna was taken aback by the vitriolic tone of the prisoner. It took a moment to gather herself in a sharp response. "So, you're above the rest of us?"

Laura appeared deflated. It took some time before a response was forthcoming. She finally answered somewhat meekly. "You're out there, and I'm in here."

"Precisely," Donna returned determinedly. "I'd say your current place of residence should be your first clue that you've nurtured your own anger…pure, unadulterated anger. How's it working for you? Are there days when you take a look around and ask yourself, 'How did I end up here? How did this happen to me? Only a fool wouldn't ask those questions. I don't think you are a fool, Laura. I see you as a survivor. So tell me, what's your story?"

Laura slumped further into her chair with her arms folded defiantly across her body. Her facial features flashed a series of responses, but a prolonged silence hung in the room. Donna decided to wait it out. This gal had something to say.

"I protected him," was the quiet pronouncement.

"Blake," Donna stated, for confirmation.

Laura nodded slightly. "Our mother was absent, often because of alcohol or some drug, whichever was the favorite of the day. She definitely was not our provider or protector, I can guarantee you that much," she conveyed with condemnation.

Again, quiet followed. Donna looked at this woman who, she suspected, had survived years of degradation and want. Despite the cost, she had clawed her way to survival, taking her younger brother with her, even when she went too far.

Donna understood one's personal struggle was often independent of right or wrong. The struggle often originated from the individual's need to survive the unthinkable; a drive to preserve a sense of one's own humanity in an inhumane setting. It was the psyche's way of winning in life, however the winning translated in the mind of the doer.

During the initial years of her incarceration, Laura, with Donna's support, slowly and painfully unveiled her youth; a time during which she was used sexually on multiple occasions in exchange for her brother's protection. It was an arrangement defined by her own mother, who needed the leverage for her own drug use. Donna had expected abuse, but not on such unthinkable levels.

Donna now understood Laura's rage, a rage growing out of an inability to control events during a childhood, when she was without protection or boundaries of any kind. The adults in her young world were bottom feeders in a perpetual cycle of addiction, using anyone and anything they could to feed their cravings.

Laura, at some unexplained level, had an inkling that there was a higher order. It propelled her to escape from home at a very young age, taking her brother with her. After being on the streets for several years, Laura was eventually able to save enough money from two part-time jobs to secure housing for herself and her brother, though in a seedy neighborhood. They moved often when they ran out of money or needed to get away from threatening situations, but Laura determined they would have a place to sleep out of the weather. They slept on thrown-out mattresses they picked from the streets, dirty and worn. They clothed themselves in articles obtained from thrift stores or the Salvation Army. Their food was from whatever charity offered a meal that day. They knew their neighborhoods. They were street smart, surviving as best they could in an unforgiving environment surrounded by others just like them. At any time, just one wrong decision could end their lives. Laura wouldn't let that happen. She would rant, rage, and drag her way to survival, taking her brother with her.

All through this time, Laura and Blake kept in touch with their cousin, Eden. He had taken to selling drugs and was often unavailable, but when he did show up, he always had a wad of money. They never questioned the source when he gave them money. It was always sorely needed.

With some help from Eden and later student loans, Laura pressed Blake to get his GED and then go to college to become a pharmacist. While he did so, she herself did housekeeping and waitressing wherever she could. Blake eventually graduated and found a position with a local hospital, earning enough to allow them to live in a better neighborhood. Finally.

When Laura was in the seventh year of her life sentence, Donna asked the ultimate question of her.

"Laura, you killed two people, Simon and Wanda Lundy. Do you ever regret that?"

"You've asked me that before and the answer is still 'No'."

Donna waited, not entirely surprised by the reply.

Laura smiled. She had come to tolerate Donna almost to the point of liking her. The woman had a heart, something she had never experienced in anyone before her. She no longer suspected that the psychiatrist had an ulterior motive for her visits. Hell! What more could they do to her? After all she was in prison for life!

"Would you clarify?" Donna prompted gently.

Laura sat back, placing her hands behind her head in a self-satisfied gesture, as she looked at her counselor. Before long she said, "I get it. After all this time, you still want me to feel remorse for my deeds. Does it make me a psychopath if I don't, Doctor?"

Donna was thrown off by the question, at first, but she understood that Laura delighted in putting her interrogators off balance with her questions. "It doesn't, necessarily, but most feel people feel regret for their deeds," Donna said.

"You don't get this, do you?" Laura asked. "I still have to explain this to the Doctor!" she taunted, in a superior tone.

Donna smiled benignly. The two had developed a relationship. It wasn't professional, nor was it a friendship; perhaps a respectful recognition of each other. "Tell this Doctor a thing or two," Donna beckoned teasingly.

Laura laughed. So did Donna. The air had been cleared. "They took from me and Blake, and even Eden," she said at first in a fiery bluster.

Donna jolted. "Who took from you? You mean the trust?"

"Yes! Of course the trust! It would have included, if written correctly, recognition of Blake and myself, as well as Eden. Our damn grandfather ignored his responsibilities for fathering two of his children, as if we never happened! What a crock of shit!"

Donna sat back, following the reasoning. "So you remain angry."

Laura glared at Donna. "Damned straight I'm angry. Angry enough to punish those who not only managed the trust, but made money doing it!" Laura spat. "All those years Blake and I lived in squalor. Not our choice! Our grandfather could have made the difference, but he didn't. So why should people like Simon and Wanda Lundy benefit from our suffering? Year-after-year, after the death of our grandfather, they benefited from manipulating an old man into entrusting them with his estate, a man who conveniently ignored *all* his children. There had to be a reckoning! Am I sorry? Not one bit, Sister! I would do it again in a heartbeat!"

Donna was quiet for a moment before asking her next question. "Even though the act was against the law?"

Laura made a snarl and then laughed. Donna was taken aback by the woman's ongoing laughter. "The law!" Laura finally spat. "You are so willing to endorse the law and justice! Let me tell you about the law and justice! It can be changed in a heartbeat for political reasons, or tweaked to favor those with power and money. People with money, power, and influence have performed countless unlawful acts, and they get away with it. Your kind of law and justice, Doctor, is an illusion!"

Donna sat back after Laura's response and decided not to comment. The anger was too deep, too embedded to allow balanced thought or discussion. As she often did, on her way home from her visit, Donna, evaluated the interview. She concluded that Laura Miles would probably never release her anger. In fact, it could be that her anger was the only thing protecting her in prison. Despite Laura's often confrontational manner and caustic replies, the two had developed an understanding of sorts. That was probably as far as it would go.

Chapter Twenty-Two

Shortly after Eden's, Blake's, and Laura's trials, Karen Coppick, along with the remaining second-tier beneficiaries, at Donna's urging, filed suit against Burkhardt's estate. The family provided a list of complaints about trustees, Simon and Wanda Lundy's mismanagement, theft, misappropriation, and fraud related to estate matters.

It took nearly two years, but following a thorough court-ordered forensic financial audit, the second-tier beneficiaries were awarded a sizeable portion of estate funds collected from the hidden accounts of Eden Parish and the Miles siblings As it turned out, the amount granted to the second-tier inheritors was what they would have received upon Burkhardt's death had there been no fourth wife or trustee obligations.

Another portion of the funds was granted to Joanna Carnes and her sister. The house owned by their parents and the Lundy's investment accounts were returned to the daughters along with the business assets of Lundy Vintage Automotive, now managed by Sam Carpetta.

The remaining funds, though small by comparison, were distributed across the three families whose assets

Simon and Wanda Lundy stole while they had oversight of those estates, allocated in proportions aligned with each estate's loss.

The one remaining loss scenario where Donna hoped to see closure was going to be a challenge. She began by writing a letter and waited. After some weeks she had given up on receiving a response, but most unexpectedly there was a reply awaiting her one morning when she opened her email. As invited, she made a phone call. The conversation turned out to be a lengthy one, followed by a second and third call during the following ten days. In the end, the conversations were cathartic and healing. An accord was reached and Donna went about setting the wheels in motion.

Liam's son, Patrick wheeled him into the courtyard. Patrick's visit was a surprise. It was not the usual day for his weekly visits. Within minutes, a woman approached the wheelchair. "Uncle Liam," she spoke softly, so as not to startle him. The old man looked up, protecting his eyes from the glaring sun with his hand. The woman looked familiar. He looked away, though. His mind was playing tricks on him again.

"Uncle Liam, it's me. Keller," the woman prompted quietly.

He turned toward her and stared. His mouth dropped open, finally recognizing the visitor.

"My Keller! Is it really you?" He began to cry.

She knelt and took him into her arms. "It is me, Uncle. I am so sorry I stayed away so long. Please forgive me."

"You are here now, my dear one. You are here now."

One afternoon Donna received a phone call from Patrick O'Connell informing her of his father's death. Liam O'Connell had passed away two days before. "I'm so sorry for your loss, Patrick. I so enjoyed getting to know your father."

"Your intervention made all the difference in the world, Dr. DeShayne. We are forever grateful. He died a happy man."

Donna and Ken attended the funeral, along with a small showing of family. Patrick insisted they sit next to him and his wife. After the funeral Patrick introduced them to his cousin, Keller O'Connell.

"Your reaching out was a god-send, Dr. DeShayne. I now have my family back and was able to spend time with Uncle Liam and eventually say goodbye. What a wonderful man! I just wish I hadn't wasted so much time running from my past."

"I'm glad I could be of help," Donna returned warmly.

"Oh," Keller commented before turning away, "you may be pleased to know I've made a connection with Blake Miles. We write. It was a request from Uncle Liam that I reach out to him and his sister, Laura. While Laura has not responded, Blake has. We've established a rapport of sorts. I plan to visit him in the fall. He tells me his cousin Eden died recently."

Donna looked at Ken questioningly. "I didn't know. Ken, did you?"

"This is the first I've heard. I'll look into it," he replied, taking out his cell phone.

On the way home, Ken updated Donna with the information that Eden Parish had died in prison of a stabbing. "Apparently he got on someone's bad side," Ken concluded.

"Do they know who did it?" Donna inquired.

"Not yet, and they probably never will." Ken looked at Donna again before he spoke. "It's prison life, Donna. There's a code. Parish violated the code, no doubt, and suffered the consequences."

Two weeks before Christmas

Donna opened a Christmas card from Keller O'Connell. The women kept in touch, having become long-distance friends. Keller's card contained her usual yearly update on happenings. She mentioned the launch of another book, which was being well received. She shared that once again, during Thanksgiving weekend, she had visited Blake Miles. It was her fourth visit to the cousin she grown to like.

"He's not a bad guy, Donna," she wrote. "I believe he was under the control of his sister, feeling he owed her his allegiance. I'm not excusing him, mind you. He's paying dearly for his crime. The good news is that, with his pharmacy background, he is being used in the prison clinic as an assistant to the nurses. He's gained some respect among the inmates. They trust him with their health issues. Blake recently saved a prisoner who had choked on his food and stopped breathing. He has a bit of status, perhaps for the first time in his life."

During their regular card game later that week with Gavin, and Carole, Donna shared the letter she received from Keller. They listened without interruption, an unusual occurrence for Carole, especially.

"It's sad," Carole commented when Donna finished, "that he had to go to prison to build a bit of status. What's wrong with this picture? Does Keller mention their sister, Laura?"

"Just that Laura and Blake speak to each other twice a month by phone, but nothing more."

"Have you seen her recently?" Gavin asked.

"No, I'm overdue for a visit. I mailed her a Christmas card just this morning."

Ken was shuffling the deck of cards and was just about ready to deal another hand when he paused and looked at Donna, "So is this it, then? After all this time, is this case closed for you?"

Donna smiled. "Yes. It is finally closed."

"Whew!" was all Ken said.

"Was the investment of time and energy worth it?" Gavin probed before popping a handful of M-&-M's into his mouth.

"Yes it was. When I understood the depth of the secrets and those who were lost over the years, it was worth further effort. Liam O'Connell, before he died reconnected with his beloved niece Keller after many years of separation.

"After that, Keller connected with other family members and has established a relationship with many of them. That has to count for something."

"It's major!" Carole confirmed. "Did she ever tell you why she chose to distance herself from her Uncle Liam and his wife?"

"Yes, she did, in fact. The facial surgeries, as she told it, were ongoing through most of her youth. She missed a great deal of school, but when she did attend she would be teased and taunted for her looks. It got to the point where she almost welcomed the surgeries as a way of escaping the insults. As time went by she isolated herself more and more, not trusting anyone. Even after her face was restored to something acceptable, her guard was always up, and she distrusted everyone around her."

"The teasing and taunting left the bigger scar on her heart," Carole commented sadly.

"Precisely. Although her Uncle Liam and his wife were good to her and supported her throughout the entire ordeal, she was so scarred by her experience that she just wanted to be left to herself. They honored her wish to make no effort to find her. For them, it was an agonizing decision."

"How sad," Gavin said. "Yet, she became a famous author and chose to be identified with the O'Connell name by taking it as a pen name. That's an interesting twist."

"I asked her about that very thing. Apparently, during her college years, she went into therapy with the encouragement of her then boyfriend, whom she eventually married. With her husband's loving support and through therapy, over time, she eventually found balance. However, reuniting with her aunt and uncle would also have meant a connection with extended family with reputations for aberrant behavior. She wanted no part of her mother, her grandmother, or her cousins, and so she stayed away. Her means of reconnection, it turns out, was through her pen name, in acknowledgment of her Uncle Liam and his wife."

"Wow," Carole said quietly, awed by the explanation. "Did she ever mention that fact to her uncle before he died?"

"She did. Keller said it was a watershed moment for both of them."

Carole and Gavin's eyes teared. "I can only imagine. At least her uncle died in peace," Gavin said.

"What other benefits can you see for dogging-the-trail on this case?" Ken asked. Though he knew already, he wanted Donna to tell their friends and be proud of her accomplishments. He was certainly proud of her.

"In the end, the second-tier beneficiaries were fairly dealt with by the courts. Karen Coppick has thanked me numerous times for my involvement. Apparently, a couple of the aging second-tier individuals were in dire financial straits. The funds from the settlement were sorely needed."

"Any disappointments?" Gavin prodded while sorting his cards.

"Laura Miles is my biggest disappointment. She still has no remorse for murdering the Lundys or for her role in the death of Burkhardt's fourth wife, Darla. On the several occasions when I reminded her of her life sentence in prison, her argument remains that prison is far better than the streets. She commented she would rather die in prison, with shelter and food, than be on the streets fighting for her needs every day."

"It is what it is, Donna. I'd say you did all you could do and then some," Gavin commented while refilling the bowl of M-&-Ms.

Years Later

Donna had just returned from another on-site consultation on a crime in Las Vegas. It felt good to be home again. Ken had ordered Chinese take-out while she showered. Just as she donned a robe, her cell phone rang. She was surprised to see the caller's name.

"Keller! Wow! What a surprise!" Donna said in greeting. "To what do I owe the pleasure?"

"Donna, it's so lovely to hear your voice. This is a quick phone call. I'll fill you in at a later time, but I thought you would like to know that Blake Miles has been granted an early parole because of his exceptional behavior. Apparently, last year he saved a guard's life when a prison riot broke out and the guard was held hostage by the inmates. Blake convinced them to release the guard, acting as a mediator between prison officials and the rioters. He's being released tomorrow. I'll be serving as his advocate."

"What wonderful news, Keller."

"I know. Got to go. I'll call when the smoke clears."

Donna reviewed her conversation with Keller O'Connell as she exchanged her robe for an old pair of sweatpants and a t-shirt. "Not all were lost," she said to herself with a smile of satisfaction.

IN GRATEFUL APPRECIATION

I wish to thank the following for their support through the writing process of *Legacy of the Lost*:

- The Carolina Authors' Club of Myrtle Beach, South Carolina for their manuscript review along with suggestions, observations, and encouragement. They are a dedicated group whose goal is to support the writing process. I value each one of them.

- Caroline Rohr, Star Editors, for her diligent proof reading.

- Kathy Dunker, for her review in timing, sequence, and consistency. What an eye!

- Jessica Tilles, TWA Solutions, for the book cover design and interior layout.

ABOUT THE AUTHOR

Bella Fayre, a former New Jersey resident, enjoys traveling, reading, and spending time with grandchildren. She currently resides in South Carolina.

Other Works by Bella Fayre

Maelstroms of the Silent
Guardian of the Damned
Sisters of the Scorned

CPSIA information can be obtained
at www.ICGtesting.com
Printed in the USA
FSHW010503100220
66988FS

מסורה

ArtScroll Mesorah Series®

Rabbi Nosson Scherman / Rabbi Meir Zlotowitz

General Editors

SHIRAS YEHUDAH ❖ שירת יהודה

הָא לַחְמָא עַנְיָא דִי אֲכָלוּ אַבְהָתָנָא
בְּאַרְעָא דְמִצְרָיִם. כָּל דִכְפִין
יֵיתֵי וְיֵיכוֹל, כָּל דִצְרִיךְ יֵיתֵי וְיִפְסַח.
הָשַּׁתָּא הָכָא, לְשָׁנָה הַבָּאָה

Published by

Mesorah Publications, ltd

הגדה של פסח

SHIRAS YEHUDAH ◆ שירת יהודה
PESACH HAGGADAH

by

Rabbi Eliezer Ginsburg

FIRST EDITION
First Impression . . . February 1994

Published and Distributed by
MESORAH PUBLICATIONS, Ltd.
4401 Second Avenue
Brooklyn, New York 11232

Distributed in Europe by
J. LEHMANN HEBREW BOOKSELLERS
20 Cambridge Terrace
Gateshead, Tyne and Wear
England NE8 1RP

Distributed in Israel by
SIFRIATI / A. GITLER — BOOKS
4 Bilu Street
P.O.B. 14075
Tel Aviv 61140

Distributed in Australia & New Zealand by
GOLD'S BOOK & GIFT CO.
36 William Street
Balaclava 3183, Vic., Australia

Distributed in South Africa by
KOLLEL BOOKSHOP
22 Muller Street
Yeoville 2198, Johannesburg, South Africa

ARTSCROLL MESORAH SERIES®
HAGGADAH SHIRAS YEHUDAH
© *Copyright 1994, by* MESORAH PUBLICATIONS, Ltd.
4401 Second Avenue / Brooklyn, N.Y. 11232 / (718) 921-9000

ISBN
0-89906-424-8 (hard cover)
0-89906-443-4 (paperback)

Typography by Compuscribe at ArtScroll Studios, Ltd.

Printed in the United States of America by Noble Book Press
Bound by Sefercraft, Quality Bookbinders, Ltd. Brooklyn, N.Y.

In memory of
Grandparents and Relatives

יוסף בן נפתלי הי״ד
אשתו דאברא בת יצחק הי״ד

בניהם
אברהם ואפרים הי״ד
נשותיהם ומשפחתם

בנותיהם
טויבע הי״ד
ופייגא הי״ד

Frommer

יעקב בן שמואל הי״ד
אשתו מלכה בת שלמה זלמן ע״ה

בנם
חיים בן ציון ארי׳ הי״ד

Benedikt

יצחק בן אלימלך הי״ד
אשתו רייזיל בת דוד הי״ד

Tag

אהרן בן יוסף פנחס הי״ד
אשתו אסתר בת יוסף ע״ה

Greenberg

Dedicated by
Mr. and Mrs. Yosef Frommer

✒️ Preface

> *It is more precious in my eyes to teach a fundamental principle of our religion and belief than any other subject I may teach.*
>
> Commentary of the Rambam, Mishnayos Berachos

From whose pen did these words originate? From none other than the great codifier whose all-encompassing *Mishneh Torah* serves as a primary basis for the *Shulchan Aruch*; the towering genius whose Mishnah commentary has enlightened the generations; the unending source of guidance and comfort whose letters and responsa were sought and sent to all the outposts of Jewish settlement. Yet he found no pursuit more fulfilling than teaching *emunah* (faith).

All of Torah and mitzvos are rooted in *emunah*; all character traits are shaped and formed by a deep-rooted faith in Hashem. The prophet *Habbakuk* established *emunah* as the bedrock of everything: וְצַדִּיק בֶּאֱמוּנָתוֹ יִחְיֶה, *The righteous one lives by his faith* (*Habbakuk* 2:4, see *Makkos* 23b). In the words of the *Alter of Kelm* "One who possesses *emunah* possesses all."

The first wellspring of *emunah* is the Exodus experience. It is for this reason that the mitzvah of *emunah*, which is the opening statement of the Ten Commandments spells out the Exodus experience: אָנֹכִי ה׳ אֱלֹקֶיךָ אֲשֶׁר הוֹצֵאתִיךָ מֵאֶרֶץ מִצְרַיִם מִבֵּית עֲבָדִים , *"I am Hashem, your G-d, Who has taken you out of the land of Egypt, from the house of slavery."*

"All the miracles performed by Hashem in Egypt and in the desert were performed not only for the people of that generation but were given to Jews of all generations to strengthen their faith" (*Ohr Yechezkel*). It is for this reason that "every man must see himself as if he left Egypt."

In order to strengthen and deepen my own sense of *emunah* I chose to focus my efforts on the issues and ideas of the Exodus, with the hope that through studying this fundamental area my faith in the *Ribbono Shel Olam* would grow and become more deeply internalized. In publicizing the fruits of this effort I only pray to Hashem that my wish be granted. It is only in the merit of my forefathers and the merit of *Klal Yisrael,* who are thirsty for *emunah*, that I dare to attempt such a difficult undertaking.

I have entitled this work [and the Hebrew work from which it is adapted] *Shiras Yehudah* since the Haggadah is the score provided us by our Sages so that we may raise our voices in praise and song to

Hashem, adding our heartfelt melody to that of the angels who say a special *shirah* on this night (see *Targum Yonason, Bereishis* 27:1).

Furthermore, with the name *Shiras Yehudah* I hope to memorialize the memory of my older brother, Yehudah Tzvi Hirsh a"h, who passed away when only nine-years-old. His life was short yet his days were long, filled with Torah and spiritual pursuits. Before his passing, he consoled my mother תחי׳ when, with wisdom beyond his years, he told her, "Hitler *yms"h* destroyed bodies; the decadence of America destroys souls; what does this life *really* have to offer?"

The staff at the hospital were amazed at the tenacity he displayed never to be without head covering and constantly reciting *Tehillim* by heart. On the Shabbos before his *petirah*, lying in his hospital bed, he told my father *zt"l*, "I just reviewed *Parashas Bo* by heart; I hope to review all of Torah [though not in this world]."

This young giant of spirit whose crown was his fear of Heaven, returned his unblemished soul to his Maker during the week of the *Parashah* of the Exodus, 8 Shevat 5712.

❧ ❧ ❧

I write these few words with deep gratitude to the *Ribbono Shel Olam* who has granted me the privilege to present this Haggadah to the English speaking public. I am indeed fortunate to have such a close friend as Rabbi Meir Zlotowitz who undertook to publish this *sefer*. With leadership and loyalty he provided two gifted and talented *talmidei chachamim*, Rabbi Yaakov Blinder and Rabbi Moshe Lieber, to translate, adapt and edit the *sefer*. Without their priceless work and skills this *sefer* could not have been completed. To all the Mesorah/ArtScroll staff whose professionalism is incomparable, I owe my thanks.

I would like to express my great appreciation to Rabbi Berl Mittelmann and Rabbi Yitzchak Kasnett who selflessly gave of their time to review the manuscript.

I would like in just a few words to express my debt of gratitude to Mr. Yossi Frommer and his wife for their support of all my literary Torah efforts.

Finally, I would like to express my deep appreciation for the constant support and assistance I have always received from my נוה בית שתחי׳, who has had more than a major share in all aspects of all my publications. May we be זוכה to achieve great heights in serving Hashem and his people, כלל ישראל.

May we merit to speedily see the day when all who have left this world will arise to join in singing a new song, the song of Yehudah revived, as we see the comforting of *Tzion* and Yerushalayim with the advent of the true liberator, *Mashiach Tzidkeinu*.

SHIRAS YEHUDAH ❖ שירת יהודה

בדיקת חמץ

On the night of 14 Nissan, the night before the Pesach *Seder,* the search for *chametz,* leaven, is made. It should be done with a candle as soon as possible after nightfall. Due to the fact that our houses are highly flammable (carpets, drapes, etc.), after starting with a candle, a flashlight *should* be used. [When the first *Seder* is on Saturday night, the search is conducted on Thursday night (13 Nissan).]

Before the search is begun, ten pieces of *chametz,* wrapped well, should be placed around the house. One should make a written note as to the location of each piece in order to avoid misplacing it. The following blessing is recited.

If several people assist in the search, only one recites the blessing for all.

בָּרוּךְ אַתָּה יהוה, אֱלֹהֵינוּ מֶלֶךְ הָעוֹלָם, אֲשֶׁר קִדְּשָׁנוּ בְּמִצְוֹתָיו, וְצִוָּנוּ עַל בִּעוּר חָמֵץ.

After the search, the *chametz* is wrapped and put aside in a safe place
to be burned in the morning. Then the following declaration is made:

כָּל חֲמִירָא וַחֲמִיעָא דְּאִכָּא בִרְשׁוּתִי, דְּלָא חֲמִתֵּהּ וּדְלָא בַעַרְתֵּהּ וּדְלָא יְדַעְנָא לֵהּ, לִבָּטֵל וְלֶהֱוֵי הֶפְקֵר כְּעַפְרָא דְאַרְעָא.

ביעור חמץ

In the morning, after the *chametz* has been burned, the following declaration is made:

כָּל חֲמִירָא וַחֲמִיעָא דְּאִכָּא בִרְשׁוּתִי, דַּחֲזִתֵּהּ וּדְלָא חֲזִתֵּהּ, דַּחֲמִתֵּהּ וּדְלָא חֲמִתֵּהּ, דְּבַעַרְתֵּהּ וּדְלָא בַעַרְתֵּהּ, לִבָּטֵל וְלֶהֱוֵי הֶפְקֵר כְּעַפְרָא דְאַרְעָא.

עירוב תבשילין

When Pesach falls on Thursday and Friday, an *eruv tavshilin* is made on Wednesday.
The *eruv*-foods are held while the following blessing and declaration are recited:

בָּרוּךְ אַתָּה יהוה אֱלֹהֵינוּ מֶלֶךְ הָעוֹלָם, אֲשֶׁר קִדְּשָׁנוּ בְּמִצְוֹתָיו, וְצִוָּנוּ עַל מִצְוַת עֵרוּב.

בַּהֲדֵין עֵרוּבָא יְהֵא שָׁרֵא לָנָא לַאֲפוּיֵי וּלְבַשּׁוּלֵי וּלְאַטְמוּנֵי וּלְאַדְלוּקֵי שְׁרָגָא וּלְתַקָּנָא וּלְמֶעְבַּד כָּל צָרְכָּנָא, מִיּוֹמָא טָבָא לְשַׁבַּתָּא [לָנָא וּלְכָל יִשְׂרָאֵל הַדָּרִים בָּעִיר הַזֹּאת].

THE SEARCH FOR CHAMETZ

On the night of 14 Nissan, the night before the Pesach *Seder,* the search for *chametz,* leaven, is made. It should be done with a candle as soon as possible after nightfall. Due to the fact that our houses are highly flammable (carpets, drapes, etc.), after starting with a candle, a flashlight *should* be used. [When the first *Seder* is on Saturday night, the search is conducted on Thursday night (13 Nissan).]
Before the search is begun, ten pieces of *chametz,* wrapped well, should be placed around the house. One should make a written note as to the location of each piece in order to avoid misplacing it. The following blessing is recited.
If several people assist in the search, only one recites the blessing for all.

Blessed are You, HASHEM, our God, King of the universe, Who has sanctified us with His commandments and has commanded us concerning the removal of chametz.

> After the search, the *chametz* is wrapped and put aside in a safe place
> to be burned in the morning. Then the following declaration is made:

Any chametz or leaven that is in my possession which I have not seen, have not removed and do not know about, should be annulled and become ownerless, like dust of the earth.

BURNING THE CHAMETZ

In the morning, after the *chametz* has been burned, the following declaration is made:

Any chametz or leaven that is in my possession, whether I have recognized it or not, whether I have seen it or not, whether I have removed it or not, should be annulled and become ownerless, like dust of the earth.

ERUV TAVSHILIN

When Pesach falls on Thursday and Friday, an *eruv tavshilin* is made on Wednesday. The *eruv*-foods are held while the following blessing and declaration are recited:

Blessed are You, HASHEM, our God, King of the universe, Who has sanctified us with His commandments and has commanded us concerning the mitzvah of eruv.

Through this eruv may we be permitted to bake, cook, insulate, kindle flame, prepare, and do anything necessary on the Festival for the sake of the Sabbath [for ourselves and for all Jews who live in this city].

הַדְלָקַת הַנֵּרוֹת

On each Yom Tov night of Pesach two blessings are recited. When Pesach coincides with
the Sabbath, light the candles, then cover the eyes and recite the blessings. Uncover the
eyes and gaze briefly at the candles. When Pesach falls on a weekday, some follow the
above procedure, while others recite the blessings before lighting the candles. When
Pesach coincides with the Sabbath, the words in brackets are added.
[It is forbidden to create a new flame — for example, by striking a match —
on Yom Tov. Therefore, on the second night the candles must be lit
from a flame that has been burning from before Yom Tov.]

בָּרוּךְ אַתָּה יהוה אֱלֹהֵינוּ מֶלֶךְ הָעוֹלָם, אֲשֶׁר קִדְּשָׁנוּ
בְּמִצְוֹתָיו, וְצִוָּנוּ לְהַדְלִיק נֵר שֶׁל [שַׁבָּת וְשֶׁל]
יוֹם טוֹב.

בָּרוּךְ אַתָּה יהוה אֱלֹהֵינוּ מֶלֶךְ הָעוֹלָם, שֶׁהֶחֱיָנוּ וְקִיְּמָנוּ
וְהִגִּיעָנוּ לַזְּמַן הַזֶּה.

It is customary to recite the following prayer after the kindling.
The words in brackets are included as they apply.

יְהִי רָצוֹן לְפָנֶיךָ, יהוה אֱלֹהַי וֵאלֹהֵי אֲבוֹתַי, שֶׁתְּחוֹנֵן
אוֹתִי [וְאֶת אִישִׁי, וְאֶת בָּנַי, וְאֶת בְּנוֹתַי,
וְאֶת אָבִי, וְאֶת אִמִּי] וְאֶת כָּל קְרוֹבַי; וְתִתֶּן לָנוּ וּלְכָל
יִשְׂרָאֵל חַיִּים טוֹבִים וַאֲרוּכִים; וְתִזְכְּרֵנוּ בְּזִכְרוֹן טוֹבָה
וּבְרָכָה; וְתִפְקְדֵנוּ בִּפְקֻדַּת יְשׁוּעָה וְרַחֲמִים; וּתְבָרְכֵנוּ
בְּרָכוֹת גְּדוֹלוֹת; וְתַשְׁלִים בָּתֵּינוּ; וְתַשְׁכֵּן שְׁכִינָתְךָ בֵּינֵינוּ.
וְזַכֵּנִי לְגַדֵּל בָּנִים וּבְנֵי בָנִים חֲכָמִים וּנְבוֹנִים, אוֹהֲבֵי
יהוה, יִרְאֵי אֱלֹהִים, אַנְשֵׁי אֱמֶת, זֶרַע קֹדֶשׁ, בַּיהוה
דְּבֵקִים, וּמְאִירִים אֶת הָעוֹלָם בַּתּוֹרָה וּבְמַעֲשִׂים טוֹבִים,
וּבְכָל מְלֶאכֶת עֲבוֹדַת הַבּוֹרֵא. אָנָּא שְׁמַע אֶת תְּחִנָּתִי
בָּעֵת הַזֹּאת, בִּזְכוּת שָׂרָה וְרִבְקָה וְרָחֵל וְלֵאָה אִמּוֹתֵינוּ,
וְהָאֵר נֵרֵנוּ שֶׁלֹּא יִכְבֶּה לְעוֹלָם וָעֶד, וְהָאֵר פָּנֶיךָ
וְנִוָּשֵׁעָה. אָמֵן.

KINDLING LIGHTS

On each Yom Tov night of Pesach two blessings are recited. When Pesach coincides with the Sabbath, light the candles, then cover the eyes and recite the blessings. Uncover the eyes and gaze briefly at the candles. When Pesach falls on a weekday, some follow the above procedure, while others recite the blessings before lighting the candles. When Pesach coincides with the Sabbath, the words in brackets are added.
[It is forbidden to create a new flame — for example, by striking a match — on Yom Tov. Therefore, on the second night the candles must be lit from a flame that has been burning from before Yom Tov.]

Blessed are You, HASHEM, our God, King of the universe, Who has sanctified us with His commandments, and has commanded us to kindle the light of [the Sabbath and of] the Festival.

Blessed are You, HASHEM, our God, King of the universe, Who has kept us alive, sustained us, and brought us to this season.

It is customary to recite the following prayer after the kindling.
The words in brackets are included as they apply.

May it be Your will, HASHEM, my God and God of my forefathers, that You show favor to me [my husband, my sons, my daughters, my father, my mother] and all my relatives; and that You grant us and all Israel a good and long life; that You remember us with a beneficent memory and blessing; that You consider us with a consideration of salvation and compassion; that You bless us with great blessings; that You make our households complete; that You cause Your Presence to dwell among us. Privilege me to raise children and grandchildren who are wise and understanding, who love HASHEM and fear God, people of truth, holy offspring, attached to HASHEM, who illuminate the world with Torah and good deeds and with every labor in the service of the Creator. Please, hear my supplication at this time, in the merit of Sarah, Rebecca, Rachel, and Leah, our mothers, and cause our light to illuminate that it be not extinguished forever, and let Your countenance shine so that we are saved. Amen.

⋳§Preparing for the Seder

The *Seder* preparations should be made in time for the *Seder* to begin as soon as the synagogue services are finished. It should not begin before nightfall. However, when Pesach falls on motzaei *Shabbos*, preparations, may not begin until *Shabbos* is over. Matzah, bitter herbs and several other items of symbolic significance are placed on the *Seder* plate in one of the arrangements shown below.

According to *Arizal*

According to *Rama*

According to *Vilna Gaon*

Matzah — Three whole matzos are placed one atop the other; Matzah must be eaten three times during the *Seder*: by itself, with *maror,* and as the *afikoman.* Each time, the minimum portion of matzah for each person should have a volume equivalent to half an egg. Where many people are present, enough matzos should be available to enable each participant to receive a proper portion.

Maror and **Chazeres** — Bitter herbs are eaten twice during the *Seder,* once by themselves and a second time with matzah. Each time a minimum portion, equal to the volume of half an egg, should be eaten. The Talmud lists several vegetables that qualify as *maror,* two of which are put on the *Seder* plate in the places marked *chazeres* and *maror.* Many people use romaine lettuce for *chazeres,* and horseradish (whole or grated) for *maror*, although either may be used for the mitzvah of eating *maror* later in the

---

◆§ הקערה – The Seder Plate

The *Seder* plate contains ten items — three matzos, two roasted foods (traditionally a bone and an egg), *maror* and *charoses*, the fresh vegetable (כרפס) and the saltwater, and *chazeres.* This is certainly not a coincidence; the number ten is significant and recurring in the context of Pesach. The *Gemara* tells us (*Rosh HaShanah* 16a) that on Pesach, Hashem passes judgment on the grain crops which will grow that year — if they will be plentiful, what their quality will be, etc. The *Midrash* says that before the sin of Adam, bread would grow from the ground, ready to eat; it was only after he was punished with the curse of בְּזֵעַת אַפֶּיךָ תֹּאכַל לֶחֶם, "By the sweat of your brow shall you eat bread" (*Bereishis* 3:19), that the current situation arose — namely, that wheat must be sown and harvested and threshed, etc., entailing a total of ten *melachos* (activities) mentioned in the list of forbidden labor on the Sabbath (see *Shabbos* 73a). This is why, according to kabbalistic teachings, there are ten mitzvos in the Torah which are done with bread, there are ten words in the blessing said over bread, and one should hold the bread so that all ten fingers touch it while he is reciting the blessing. All this is intended to "correct" the primeval sin of Adam (a kabbalistic concept) which expressed itself in the curse of the toil required in preparing bread. On Pesach, when we are judged concerning the grain growing in the fields, we make an additional symbolic gesture in this connection, by setting the centerpiece of the *Seder* table with ten components.[1]

---

1. In this context, it may be noted also that the word פסח (Pesach) has the same numerical value (גימטריא 148) as the word קמח (flour).

Seder. Due to the problem of insects, those using romaine lettuce should use only the stalks and only after checking each one under a light, prior to Yom Tov.

Charoses — The bitter herbs are dipped into *charoses* (a mixture of grated apples, nuts, other fruit, cinnamon and other spices, mixed with red wine). The *charoses* has the appearance of mortar to symbolize the lot of the Hebrew slaves, whose lives were embittered by hard labor with brick and mortar.

Z'roa [Roasted bone or a chicken wing and **Beitzah** [Roasted egg] — On the eve of Passover in the Holy Temple in Jerusalem, two sacrifices were offered and their meat roasted and eaten at the *Seder* feast. To commemorate these two sacrifices, we place a roasted bone (with some meat on it) and a roasted hard-boiled egg on the *Seder* plate.

The egg, a symbol of mourning, is used in place of a second piece of meat as a reminder of our mourning for the destruction of the Temple — may it be rebuilt speedily in our day.

Karpas — A vegetable (celery, parsley, boiled potato) other than bitter herbs completes the *Seder* plate. It will be dipped in salt water and eaten. (The salt water is not put on the *Seder* plate, but it, too, should be prepared beforehand, and placed near the *Seder* plate.)

Kittel — A *kittel* should be worn at the *Seder* by the head of the household.

קַדֵּשׁ וּרְחַץ וכו׳ — The first few steps of the *Seder* are given in the imperative, rather than the descriptive form: Recite *Kiddush*! Wash! etc. Rabbi Yerucham Levovitz (*Mashgiach* of the Mirrer Yeshiva in Europe) used to say that the goal of the *Seder* service is to increase one's awareness of his servitude to Hashem. We should be cognizant that this is the night when we "ceased being the servants of Pharaoh and became the servants of Hashem, and for this reason we must sing the praises of Hallel, which begin, 'Praise Hashem! Praise, servants of Hashem' " (*Yalkut Shimoni Parashas Bo* 208). It is, therefore, fitting that the order of the *Seder* start off in the imperative mode, a tone suggestive of the master speaking to his servant.

❧ The Order of the Seder

KADDESH	Sanctify the day with the recitation of *Kiddush*.	קדש
URECHATZ	Wash the hands before eating *karpas* without reciting a blessing	ורחץ
KARPAS	Eat a **vegetable** dipped in salt water.	כרפס
YACHATZ	**Break** the middle matzah. Put away the larger half for *afikoman*.	יחץ
MAGGID	**Narrate** the story of the Exodus from Egypt.	מגיד
RACHTZAH	**Wash** the hands prior to the meal, and recite the blessing, *al netilas yadaim*.	רחצה
MOTZI	Recite the blessing, **Who brings forth,** over matzah as a food.	מוציא
MATZAH	Recite the blessing over **matzah.**	מצה
MAROR	Recite the blessing for the eating of the **bitter herbs.**	מרור
KORECH	Eat the **sandwich** of matzah and bitter herbs.	כורך
SHULCHAN ORECH	The **table is prepared** with a festive meal.	שלחן עורך
TZAFUN	Eat the *afikoman* which has been **hidden** all during the *Seder*.	צפון
BARECH	Recite *Bircas HaMazon*, the **blessings** after the meal.	ברך
HALLEL	Recite the *Hallel*, Psalms of praise.	הלל
NIRTZAH	Pray that God **accept** our observance and speedily send *Mashiach*.	נרצה

⋒ *Halachic Pointers for the Seder*

⋒ קדש

1) In order to avoid a doubt regarding the *berachah* of "הטוב והמטיב," only the types of wine which were on the table at the time of *Kiddush* should be used for all the remaining cups [או"ה סימן קע"ה שער הציון ג].

2) At the time of *Kiddush,* one should bear in mind that he is fulfilling the mitzvah of the first of the four cups, besides the mitzvah of *Kiddush.* [או"ח תע"ג מ"ב ס"ק א בשם החיי אדם].

3) One should bear in mind that the *berachah* of *shehechianu* includes all the mitzvos of the night (recitation of the Haggadah, eating the matzah eating the *maror,* drinking the four cups) as well as the general Yom Tov [סידור יעב"ץ וברכי יוסף].

⋒ ורחץ

1) One should specifically have in mind, [פרי מגדים מ"ז סק"א], *not* to fulfill the obligation of washing for the meal with this washing. An announcement should be made to wash *without a berachah.*

2) Even though we are permitted to talk after this washing, we should limit our conversation to matters concerning the

---

לֵיל הַסֵּדֶר — *Divrei Negidim* attributes to the *Maharal* the explanation of the *kittel,* which is traditionally worn at the *Seder,* as symbolic of the white robe worn by the *Kohen Gadol* on Yom Kippur. In a similar vein, the *Shlah* writes that one should not engage in idle conversation on *Seder* night, but should continuously and fervently involve himself in the *mitzvah* of retelling the story of the Exodus from Egypt. The inner-connection between these two nights reveals that just as the Kohen Gadol was focused on the all-pervasive sense of לְפְנֵי ה' (being in the presence of Hashem) and was forbidden to think of anything else on Yom Kippur, so too, we should dedicate ourselves by focusing on the immediacy of the revelation of the *Shechinah* on this night. (See *Targum Yonasan Bereishis* 27:1.) In this respect, the sanctity of Yom Kippur pervades this evening as well.

dipping in order not to be distracted from the washing, thus
necessitating a new נטילה [או"ח קס"ד סעיף א].

כרפס §ּ

1) Bear in mind that the *berachah* of בורא פרי האדמה should
also include the מרור [או"ח תע"ג במ"ב ס"ק נ"ה].

2) The *karpas* vegetable should be taken in hand without use
of any utensil since the purpose of washing is to permit this
contact.

מגיד §ּ

1) Prior to the Haggadah reading, all participants should be
reminded that everyone is required to read the Haggadah
— *even women!* If they need to leave the table, they should,
upon returning, resume the Haggadah reading from the
point where they left off [או"ח תע"ב סעיף יד].

2) The Haggadah should be read in question-answer form. We
must be attentive to the children asking the *mah nishtanah,*
and read the Haggadah as if we were answering them [בשם
הגר"ח מבריסק זצ"ל].

3) One must be careful not to interrupt between reciting the
berachah of *Ga'al Yisrael* and drinking the second cup.
Therefore one should fill the cup *before* the *berachah,* in
order to recite the *berachah* over a full cup, like all cups of
berachah [או"ח קס"ג סעיף ו].

רחצה §ּ

1) One should touch some part of the body generally covered
(e.g. above the elbow) in order to be required to wash again
with a *berachah* [ביאור הלכה סימן תע"ה].

2) All participants should be reminded that *this* washing *does*
require a *berachah.* One should attempt to limit the delay
between the washing and the *bircas hamotzi.*

מוציא מצה §ּ

1) The one who actually makes the *bircas hamotzi* (generally
the head of the household) needs to eat two *kezaysim*

(olive-size volume) of matzah — one from the complete matzah, and one from the partial matzah over which he made the berachah of *al achilas matzah*. The participants need not eat more than one *kezayis* [ע״פ או״ח תע״ה סעיף א בהסכמת הגאון הרב ש״ך שליט״א].

2) All participants, including women, should be reminded that they must eat the *kezayis,* and that it should be eaten without undue delay [או״ח תע״ה סעיף א].

3) All should keep in mind that the *berachah* covers the matzah of *achilas matzah,* and the matzah of *korech*. Hence, one should refrain from speaking until after *korech*. [שם].

מרור ⚬§

1) *All* particpants receive a *kezayis*. If one is nauseous after eating the *maror,* he may only drink water, However, while eating the *kezayis* of *maror* — he may *not* swallow it with water [ע״פ או״ח תעב סעיף ג].

2) When reciting the berachah on *maror* one should have in mind to include the *maror* of *korech.*

כורך ⚬§

1) The *korech* sandwich should be comprised of a *kezayis* of matzah and a *kezayis* of *maror* [או״ח תע״ה סעיף א].

2) R' Yechezkel Levenstein zt"l used to recite ״זכר למקדש כהלל״ *after* eating the *Korech* in order not to interrupt between the *berachah* of *al achilas matzah* and eating *korech.*

שלחן ערוך ⚬§

1) In order to eat the *afikoman* before midnight (*chatzos*) one should not prolong the meal.

2) Preferably one should eat the *entire* meal reclining toward the left side [או״ח תע״ב סעיף ז].

3) Neither roast, nor pot roast (poultry or meat) should be eaten on the Seder night. [או״ח תע״ו מ״ב ס״ק א].

צפון ⚬§

1) All participants must eat a *kezayis* of *matzah* for afikoman [או״ח תע״ז סעיף א].

&§ ברך

1) All cups should be rinsed out prior to *Bircas HaMazon* [או"ח קפ"ג סעיף א].
2) One should not interrupt with speaking between the end of *Bircas HaMazon* and the *berachah* on the third cup [שם סעיף ו].

&§ הלל

1) Preferably one should hold the cup throughout the entire recitation of the Hallel, since Hallel should be recited over wine [סברת המחבר].

&§ נרצה

1) This section should be recited joyously and with song.
2) The author finishes the *Seder* with a jubilant dance, in order to show that we conduct it with a sense of enjoyment, not merely to discharge an obligation.

קדש

Kiddush should be recited and the *Seder* begun as soon after synagogue services as possible — however, not before nightfall. Each participant's cup should be poured by someone else to symbolize the majesty of the evening, as though each participant had a servant.

On Shabbos begin here:

(וַיְהִי עֶרֶב וַיְהִי בֹקֶר)

יוֹם הַשִּׁשִּׁי: וַיְכֻלּוּ הַשָּׁמַיִם וְהָאָרֶץ וְכָל צְבָאָם. וַיְכַל אֱלֹהִים בַּיּוֹם הַשְּׁבִיעִי מְלַאכְתּוֹ אֲשֶׁר עָשָׂה, וַיִּשְׁבֹּת בַּיּוֹם הַשְּׁבִיעִי מִכָּל מְלַאכְתּוֹ אֲשֶׁר עָשָׂה. וַיְבָרֶךְ אֱלֹהִים אֶת יוֹם הַשְּׁבִיעִי וַיְקַדֵּשׁ אֹתוֹ, כִּי בוֹ שָׁבַת מִכָּל מְלַאכְתּוֹ אֲשֶׁר בָּרָא אֱלֹהִים לַעֲשׂוֹת.[1]

On all nights other than Friday, begin here; on Friday night include all passages in parentheses.

סַבְרִי מָרָנָן וְרַבָּנָן וְרַבּוֹתַי:

בָּרוּךְ אַתָּה יהוה אֱלֹהֵינוּ מֶלֶךְ הָעוֹלָם, בּוֹרֵא פְּרִי הַגָּפֶן:

בָּרוּךְ אַתָּה יהוה אֱלֹהֵינוּ מֶלֶךְ הָעוֹלָם, אֲשֶׁר בָּחַר בָּנוּ מִכָּל עָם, וְרוֹמְמָנוּ מִכָּל לָשׁוֹן, וְקִדְּשָׁנוּ בְּמִצְוֹתָיו. וַתִּתֶּן לָנוּ יהוה אֱלֹהֵינוּ בְּאַהֲבָה (שַׁבָּתוֹת לִמְנוּחָה וּ)מוֹעֲדִים לְשִׂמְחָה, חַגִּים וּזְמַנִּים לְשָׂשׂוֹן, אֶת יוֹם (הַשַּׁבָּת הַזֶּה וְאֶת יוֹם) חַג הַמַּצּוֹת הַזֶּה, זְמַן חֵרוּתֵנוּ (בְּאַהֲבָה) מִקְרָא קֹדֶשׁ, זֵכֶר לִיצִיאַת מִצְרָיִם, כִּי בָנוּ בָחַרְתָּ וְאוֹתָנוּ קִדַּשְׁתָּ מִכָּל הָעַמִּים, (וְשַׁבָּת) וּמוֹעֲדֵי קָדְשֶׁךָ (בְּאַהֲבָה וּבְרָצוֹן) בְּשִׂמְחָה וּבְשָׂשׂוֹן הִנְחַלְתָּנוּ. בָּרוּךְ אַתָּה יהוה, מְקַדֵּשׁ (הַשַּׁבָּת וְ)יִשְׂרָאֵל וְהַזְּמַנִּים.

KIDDUSH CONTINUES ON THE NEXT PAGE.

מְקַדֵּשׁ יִשְׂרָאֵל וְהַזְּמַנִּים — **Who sanctifies Israel and the Festivals.** On Yom Tov, unlike Shabbos, the concluding blessing of *Kiddush* mentions the sanctity of Israel in addition to that of the Yom Tov. The reason for this, as explained by *Rashi (Beitzah* 17a), is that the exact time of the

KADDESH

Kiddush should be recited and the *Seder* begun as soon after synagogue services as possible — however, not before nightfall. Each participant's cup should be poured by someone else to symbolize the majesty of the evening, as though each participant had a servant.
On Shabbos begin here:

(And there was evening and there was morning)

T he sixth day. And the heavens and the earth and all their array were completed. And God completed on the seventh day His work which He had done. And He rested on the seventh day from all His work which He had done. And God blessed the seventh day and sanctified it, for on it He rested from all His work which God created to make.[1]

On all nights other than Friday, begin here; on Friday night include all passages in parentheses.

By your leave, my masters and teachers:

B lessed are You, HASHEM, our God, King of the Universe, Who creates the fruit of the vine.

B lessed are You, HASHEM, our God, King of the Universe, Who has chosen us from among all peoples, raised us above all languages, and sanctified us with His commandments. And You have given us, HASHEM, our God, lovingly, (Sabbaths for rest, and) appointed times for gladness, festivals and holidays for rejoicing, this day of (the Sabbath and this day of) the Festival of Matzos, the time of our freedom, (lovingly,) a holy assembly in commemoration of the Exodus from Egypt. For You have chosen us and sanctified us from among all peoples and (the Sabbath and) Your sacred holidays (with love and goodwill) with gladness and joy You have granted us a heritage. Blessed are You, HASHEM, Who sanctifies (the Sabbath and) Israel and the Festivals.

KIDDUSH CONTINUES ON THE NEXT PAGE.

---

(1) *Genesis* 1:31-2:3.

---

holidays is determined by the *Sanhedrin*, through their sanctification of *Rosh Chodesh*. Thus the sanctity of Israel, as represented by the *Sanhedrin*,[1] is a prerequisite to the holiness of the Yom Tov itself.

1. This idea, that the *Sanhedrin* represents the sanctity of Israel, helps to clarify a difficult *midrash*. In *Bereishis Rabbah Parashas Vayeira* (quoted by *Rashi* 18:1), the *Midrash* teaches that Hashem informed Abraham that his descendants would be the future members of the

בָּרוּךְ אַתָּה יהוה אֱלֹהֵינוּ מֶלֶךְ הָעוֹלָם, בּוֹרֵא מְאוֹרֵי הָאֵשׁ.

בָּרוּךְ אַתָּה יהוה אֱלֹהֵינוּ מֶלֶךְ הָעוֹלָם, הַמַּבְדִּיל בֵּין קֹדֶשׁ לְחוֹל, בֵּין אוֹר לְחֹשֶׁךְ, בֵּין יִשְׂרָאֵל לָעַמִּים, בֵּין יוֹם הַשְּׁבִיעִי לְשֵׁשֶׁת יְמֵי הַמַּעֲשֶׂה. בֵּין קְדֻשַּׁת שַׁבָּת לִקְדֻשַּׁת יוֹם טוֹב הִבְדַּלְתָּ, וְאֶת יוֹם הַשְּׁבִיעִי מִשֵּׁשֶׁת יְמֵי הַמַּעֲשֶׂה קִדַּשְׁתָּ, הִבְדַּלְתָּ וְקִדַּשְׁתָּ אֶת עַמְּךָ יִשְׂרָאֵל בִּקְדֻשָּׁתֶךָ. בָּרוּךְ אַתָּה יהוה, הַמַּבְדִּיל בֵּין קֹדֶשׁ לְקֹדֶשׁ.

On all nights conclude here:

בָּרוּךְ אַתָּה יהוה אֱלֹהֵינוּ מֶלֶךְ הָעוֹלָם, שֶׁהֶחֱיָנוּ וְקִיְּמָנוּ וְהִגִּיעָנוּ לַזְּמַן הַזֶּה.

The wine should be drunk without delay, while reclining on the left side.
It is preferable to drink the entire cup but at the very least,
most of the cup should be drained.

וּרְחַץ

The head of the household washes his hands as if to eat bread [pouring water from a cup, twice on the right hand and twice on the left], but without reciting a blessing. It is preferable to bring water and a basin to the head of the household at the head of the table. The custom of my father's and grandfather's house was for all participants to wash their hands.

It would seem that only a material object — such as a place, a vessel or an animal — could be invested with a status of holiness, but not something as completely abstract as "time." HaRav Yonasan David, *shlita,* explained that there are instances where "concepts" can actually be given a degree of tangible reality. For instance, concerning *olam haba* (the World to Come), it is said, לְהַנְחִיל אֹהֲבַי יֵשׁ, *to impart substance unto those who love Me* (*Mishlei* 8:21). That is, *olam haba*, which is now only conceptualized in thought, will one day become a tangible reality for the righteous. The Shabbos day is said to contain an element of *olam haba* (מֵעֵין עוֹלָם הַבָּא). By extension, this element of the Shabbos also possesses the potential to assume a material reality in spite of being

---

Sanhedrin. The *Beis HaLevi* questions the significance of this particular revelation occurring while Abraham was recovering from his circumcision. In light of what we have shown, that the *Sanhedrin* is a manifestation of Israel's sanctity, the connection becomes clear. Since the circumcision rite is also a purveyor of sanctity and Jewish holiness, this was the proper time to inform Abraham that his descendants would sit on the *Sanhedrin.*

On Saturday night, add the following two paragraphs:

Blessed are You, HASHEM, our God, King of the Universe, Who creates the lights of the fire.

Blessed are You, HASHEM, our God, King of the Universe, Who distinguishes between the sacred and the profane, between light and darkness, between Israel and the other peoples, between the seventh day and the six days of labor. You have made a distinction between the sanctity of the Sabbath and the sanctity of a holiday, and sanctified the seventh day over the six days of labor. You have separated and sanctified Your people Israel with Your holiness. Blessed are You, HASHEM, Who distinguishes between one sanctity and another.

On all nights conclude here:

Blessed are You, HASHEM, our God, King of the Universe, Who has kept us alive, and maintained us and enabled us to reach this time.

The wine should be drunk without delay, while reclining on the left side. It is preferable to drink the entire cup but at the very least, most of the cup should be drained.

URECHATZ

The head of the household washes his hands as if to eat bread [pouring water from a cup, twice on the right hand and twice on the left], but without reciting a blessing. It is preferable to bring water and a basin to the head of the household at the head of the table. The custom of my father's and grandfather's house was for all participants to wash their hands.

---

intrinsically an intangible time period. In view of this, the idea of our investing time with sanctity to time (such as Yom Tov, whose holiness emanates from that of Shabbos) is no longer difficult to comprehend.

Another interesting note may be added in this connection. We find that Pesach is called "Shabbos" — וּסְפַרְתֶּם לָכֶם מִמָּחֳרַת הַשַּׁבָּת, *You shall count for yourselves — from the morrow of the Sabbath (Vayikra 23:15).* Although Pesach may be considered a "Sabbath" because of the required cessation from labor, we may wonder why it is the only one of the Yomim Tovim so designated. The connection between Shabbos and Pesach may be explained by recalling the exhortation in the Haggadah: "In every generation one is obligated to view himself as if he himself has gone out of Egypt." Of all the holidays of the year it is only on Pesach that we are obligated to take an event from the past and relive

כרפס

All participants take a vegetable other than *maror* in hand (see Halachic Pointers p. 11) and dip it into salt water. A piece smaller in volume than half an egg should be used. The following blessing is recited [with the intention that it also applies to the *maror* which will be eaten during the meal] before the vegetable is eaten.

בָּרוּךְ אַתָּה יהוה אֱלֹהֵינוּ מֶלֶךְ הָעוֹלָם, בּוֹרֵא פְּרִי הָאֲדָמָה.

יחץ

The head of the household breaks the middle matzah in two. He puts the smaller part back between the two whole matzos, and wraps up the larger part for later use as the *afikoman*. Some briefly place the *afikoman* portion on their shoulders, in accordance with the Biblical verse (*Exodus* 12:34) recounting that Yisrael left Egypt carrying their matzos on their shoulders, and say בִּבְהִלוּ יָצָאנוּ מִמִּצְרָיִם, *In haste we went out of Egypt*.

---

it as if it were actually taking place in the present. The past is gone, yet by reliving it in the present we are concretizing the abstract. Here, then, is the common theme between Pesach and Shabbos, which is not shared by other Yomim Tovim.

יַחַץ — **Breaking the middle matzah.** The reason the matzah is broken at this point in the *Seder* is so that the narrative and discussion of the Exodus from Egypt may revolve around poor man's bread, for the Gemara (*Pesachim* 115b) interprets the words לֶחֶם עֹנִי, *poor man's bread* (*Devarim* 16:3), to mean that the Pesach matzah should be broken, just as a poor man eats from a broken loaf. To this idea, the *Vilna Gaon* (*Biur HaGra* 473:30) adds that the *afikoman* is also taken from the broken piece so that each time the matzah is eaten (once following *hamotzi* and once at the end of the meal) it should come from a "poor" (broken) piece.

This comment of the *Vilna Gaon's* seems to be somewhat puzzling. It is quite understandable that the matzah over which the Haggadah is recited be "poor" bread. However, the *afikoman*, as the *Sefas Emes* explains, represents the future Redemption[2] and is thus hidden away until the very end of the meal, symbolic of the finale of history. Certainly at that time the differences of poverty and wealth are immaterial and meaningless.

There is a difference of opinion among the commentators as to whether matzah symbolizes bondage and exile, or deliverance and

---

1. See מוֹצִיא מַצָּה for elaboration of this theme.

KARPAS

All participants take a vegetable other than *maror* in hand (see Halachic Pointers p. 11) hand dip it into salt water. A piece smaller in volume than half an egg should be used. The following blessing is recited [with the intention that it also applies to the *maror* which will be eaten during the meal] before the vegetable is eaten.

Blessed are You, HASHEM, our God, King of the Universe, Who creates the fruit of the soil.

YACHATZ

The head of the household breaks the middle matzah in two. He puts the smaller part back between the two whole matzos, and wraps up the larger part for later use as the *afikoman*. Some briefly place the *afikoman* portion on their shoulders, in accordance with the Biblical verse (*Exodus* 12:34) recounting that Yisrael left Egypt carrying their matzos on their shoulders, and say בְּהִלּוּ יָצָאנוּ מִמִּצְרַיִם, *In haste we went out of Egypt.*

redemption. The *Sefas Emes* is of the opinion that matzah has within it *both* aspects. This is borne out by the fact that the Haggadah refers to matzah as "the bread which our forefathers ate in the land of Egypt," yet it explains that the reason we eat matzah today is to recall that when our salvation came about, it was so swift that there was not even enough time to prepare regular bread — making it the ultimate symbol of Redemption. Thus the matzah eaten at the beginning of the meal represents the bondage aspect, whereas the *afikoman* stands for the aspect of freedom and deliverance.

However, upon closer scrutiny, there is a very important moral lesson to be derived from this comment of the *Vilna Gaon*. Even in the times of our greatest euphoria we must comport ourselves with humility and modesty, recalling our humble past. For if we act with haughtiness and conceit we are liable to lose the benefits of the great spiritual uplifting which will come with the final Redemption. Therefore, even when eating the *afikoman*, which represents deliverance, we eat it as would a poor man.

This may also explain the idea behind *Rashi's* comment on the verse, וְהִתְהַלַּכְתִּי בְּתוֹכְכֶם, *I will walk among you* (*Vayikra* 26:12): "I will walk together with you (the righteous), as one of you, in Paradise, and you will not be overawed by My presence. One might infer from this that you (the righteous in Paradise) would not be fearful of Me; for this reason the verse continues וְהָיִיתִי לָכֶם לֵאלֹקִים , *and I will be unto you as God* (i.e. My fear will still be upon you)." Here, too, we see that even upon achieving this lofty experience of intimacy with Hashem, humility and meekness are necessary.

יַחַץ — The three matzos on the *Seder* plate are said to represent the three types of Jews — Kohen, Levi and Yisrael. Why is it specifically the middle matzah — the "Levi" — which is to be broken in half at יַחַץ?

Along with the covenant of *bris bein habesarim* (*Bereishis* 15), three decrees were related to Abraham regarding his descendants: They would be strangers in a land not their own they would be slaves in that land; and they would be persecuted there. *Rashi* tells us (*Shemos* 5:4) that the tribe of Levi was not enslaved to the Egyptians nor persecuted by them at all. Thus, of the three decrees, only the one that spoke about being strangers in a foreign land was applicable to the Levites. It is perhaps for this reason that this particular matzah is the one chosen to be broken: The smaller piece, representing the one decree (of three) which the Levites also suffered, is left on the table as the focal point of the discussion of our hardships in Egypt, while the larger piece, representing the other two decrees which did *not* affect that tribe, is removed from the table.

It remains to be explained, however, why this larger broken piece of "Levi" is chosen specifically as the *afikoman*. It is said that the reason that the *afikoman* is referred to as צָפוּן ("hidden thing") is to allude to the verse (*Tehillim* 31:20), מָה רַב טוּבְךָ אֲשֶׁר צָפַנְתָּ לִירֵאֶיךָ, *How great* (רַב) *is Your goodness that You have hidden away* (צָפַנְתָּ) *for those who fear You.* The *larger* piece is put away as an allusion to the greatness (i.e. largeness) of the hidden goodness expressed by the word רַב. The *Rambam* (*Avodah Zarah* 1:3) writes that the Levites were unique in that they were the only Jews who did not succumb to copying the idolatrous practices of their Egyptian neighbors. Hence, the tribe of Levi truly represents the trait of fear of Hashem and devotion to His Torah.[1] It is thus most appropriate that the *afikoman*, which represents the hidden future reward (צָפוּן) of God-fearing people, be taken from the middle, "Levi" matzah.

Others ascribe a different symbolism to the three matzos — namely, that they represent the three Patriarchs, Abraham, Isaac and Jacob. According to this approach we must ask once again why it is specifically the middle matzah — that of Isaac — which is broken.

There is a Sephardic custom, based on the Arizal, to break the matzah of יַחַץ in such a way that the small and large pieces should resemble the letters יו"ד (*yud*) and דל"ת (*daled*) respectively, as if the letter ה"א (*hei*) — which is shaped like a דל"ת with a יו"ד inserted in its corner — was being broken up into its constituent parts. The Vilna Gaon explains that if we compare the letters which make up "matzah" — ה, מ, צ — with those that spell *chametz* — ח, מ, ץ — we find that the

---

1. In fact, the *Rambam* writes (*Shemittah V'Yovel* 13:13) that *all* people who dedicate their lives to sacred pursuits and to the teaching of Torah are considered to be the spiritual descendants of Levi.

only difference between these two complete opposites is the minuscule difference between the letters חי״ת (ches) and ה״א (hei). Thus the letter ה״א represents matzah. If this יו״ד inside the ה״א would expand just a bit upward, the ה״א would become a חי״ת, and the "matzah" would become "chametz," just as a tiny amount of leaven causes dough to ferment and become chametz. It should also be noted that יו״ד, being the smallest and simplest letter, represents the trait of modesty; if the יו״ד swells in size, it is symbolic of the swelling of one's ego from the state of unassuming humility to arrogance and conceit. It is arrogance, symbolized by chametz, the swelling of the humble יו״ד, that brings out in man the urge to satisfy his greed and lust, which spoils the purity of the soul. For this reason, leaven, which causes dough to sour, is used by the Sages (Berachos 17a) as a metaphor for the yetzer hara. Hence, the difference in spelling distinguishing the word "matzah" from "chametz" mirrors the actual physical characteristics of these two items and their symbolic meanings.

The Gemara (Shabbos 89b) relates that in the future Hashem will confront the three Patriarchs and protest to them that their descendants, the children of Israel, have sinned, in hope that they, the Patriarchs, will stand in defense of their offspring. Abraham and Jacob will respond that if the Jews have sinned to such a degree, they should be obliterated in order to preserve the sanctity of Hashem's holy Name. Only Isaac will plead for Hashem to show mercy and forgive their sins. Included in his plea will be a proposal that the burden of their transgression should be "half Yours and half mine." [This aggadah, as many others, is replete with allegory and symbolism.] The idea that Isaac and Hashem should share the burden of Israel's guilt is especially perplexing.

Rabbi Yitzchak ("Peterburger") Blaser advances the following explanation: The Gemara (Berachos 17a) quotes the prayer of R' Alexandrei, one of the Sages: "It is our will to do Your will, Hashem, but two impediments prevent us from always doing so: the 'leaven in the dough' (i.e. the yetzer hara) and 'our subservience to the nations.' " The yetzer hara, the Sages tell us (Berachos 31b), was implanted in man by Hashem Himself, and thus He is, as it were, "to blame" for this phenomenon. Subjugation to the nations, on the other hand, comes about as the result of their hatred for Israel, as exemplified by Esau, who was favored by his father Isaac. Thus, Isaac's argument was that of the two causes of sin, "half (the yetzer hara) is Yours, and half (subservience to the nations) is mine (i.e. my fault)."

As mentioned earlier, the Arizal wrote that the breaking of the matzah symbolizes the breaking away of the leg (the "יו״ד") of the ה״א from its main body (the דל״ת). Thus, יחץ may be understood as an act of prayer, that the small leg not be given the opportunity to become

מַגִּיד

The broken matzah is lifted for all to see as the head of the household begins with the following brief explanation of the proceedings.

הָא לַחְמָא עַנְיָא דִי אֲכָלוּ אַבְהָתָנָא בְּאַרְעָא דְמִצְרָיִם.

enlarged until it would transform the ה"א into a חי"ת; that is, not to allow the "matzah" (the pure soul) to be soured by the "leaven" (the *yetzer hara*). Since, of all the Patriarchs, Isaac was the one who defended us from being punished for our *yetzer hara*, it is appropriate that "his" matzah — the middle one — be chosen to convey this prayer.

There is perhaps another symbolic reference involved in the breaking of the "ה"א"; that is, an allusion to the final Redemption, the "end of days." (As pointed out earlier, the *Sefas Emes* explains that the *afikoman* matzah, which is taken from one of these broken pieces, represents the Messianic period.) The Gemara (*Menachos* 29b) says that "this world," i.e. the natural, present-day world that we live in, was created with the letter ה"א, to signify that just as a ה"א is completely open on the bottom, so too the world has an "opening" so that anyone who wishes to leave (i.e. to lead an immoral and sinful life) can "drop out." And just as a ה"א has a small space near the top, so too the world was created in such a manner that if someone who has dropped out wishes to return to the fold, there is a "breach" left for him through which he may enter — i.e. *teshuvah* (repentence).

The *Ramban* explains the verse (*Devarim* 30:6), *And Hashem, your God, will then [in the days of the Mashiach] circumcise your hearts and the hearts of your children to love Hashem, your God*, as an expression of the idea that in the future world there will be no more desire to do evil (*yetzer hara*). Based on this interpretation, it may be said that breaking off the leg of the ה"א is a symbolic reference to this world, when the leaven in the dough (the *yetzer hara*) will finally be vanquished and the repentant masses shall return through the wide open gate.

הָא לַחְמָא עַנְיָא — **This is the poor bread. . .** *The Belzer Rebbe, zatzal,* explained that the reason the opening statement of the Haggadah (הָא לַחְמָא עַנְיָא) is in Aramaic (whereas the rest of the Haggadah is in Hebrew) is based on the Gemara (*Shabbos* 12a). It teaches that although prayers should not normally be said in Aramaic, as this language is not recognized by the angels, and leaves them unable to, so to speak, to "convey" the prayers to Hashem, nonetheless a prayer said in the presence of a sick person may be recited in Aramaic, since Hashem Himself is present at the bedside of the ill, and no interceding angels are needed. So too on this night of Pesach, Hashem's Presence is with

MAGGID

The broken matzah is lifted for all to see as the head of the household
begins with the following brief explanation of the proceedings.

This is the poor bread which our fathers ate in the land of Egypt.

us at the *Seder* table, and we are לְפָנָי ה׳. As such, our prayer this evening
may be recited in Aramaic. It is to emphasize this idea that the opening
statement of the Haggadah is formulated in Aramaic.

◂§ This introductory statement to the Haggadah presents several difficulties. Firstly, what is the connection between the public invitation —
Let anyone who is needy come in and make Pesach — and the prayer
which follows it — that we be speedily redeemed and brought to *Eretz
Yisrael*? Secondly, since this paragraph was apparently composed in
Babylonia (judging from the Aramaic employed), why is an invitation
issued to "make Pesach," i.e. to partake of the paschal sacrifice, when
no sacrifices may ever be brought outside of the Temple in Jerusalem?
  An answer to these questions may be found by examining the verses
in *Malachi* (3:22-23), which are in fact from the very last verses in the
Prophets: "Remember the Torah of Moses my servant, which I
commanded him . . .for all of Israel . . . .Behold, I send unto you Elijah
the prophet before the coming of the great and awesome Day of
Hashem." These verses need clarification on several accounts. First,
what is the relationship of the remembering of Moses' Torah to the
coming of the end of days? Second, why is the expression "*all* of Israel"
used, instead of the more usual "people" or "children of Israel"?
Finally, what is the significance of these particular verses being the
closing statement of all the Prophets?
  The Torah in its entirety is the spiritual possession of all of Israel.
While not every Jew can fulfill every mitzvah (women cannot fulfill
men's mitzvos nor may Israelites do the mitzvos of Kohanim), the
nation as a whole has the ability to do all of Hashem's commandments.
Through the national corpus every individual has a share in the entire
Torah. This is but one aspect of עֲרֵבוּת (communal responsibility and
interconnectedness).
  Today, however, with the destruction of the Temple, there are
mitzvos — sacrificial and purification rituals, for instance — which are
not being fulfilled by *any* Jew, thus leaving some parts of Torah
fulfillment inaccessible.
  This may be the message of *Malachi*: As the prophetic era draws to
a close we must realize that an even more devastating blow to our
closeness to Hashem will occur. The Torah that Moses gave to *all* of

כָּל דִּכְפִין יֵיתֵי וְיֵכוֹל, כָּל דִּצְרִיךְ יֵיתֵי וְיִפְסַח. הָשַׁתָּא

Israel, which all the individuals of Israel could in the past fulfill through the national corpus, will now, with the destruction of the Temple, become partially inaccessible. If we take this realization seriously and feel the appropriate sorrow and pain over it, we will merit the ultimate Redemption to be ushered in by Elijah. Thus the closing message of the Prophets relates: If you are genuinely distressed at your lack of ability to fully carry out Hashem's commandments, you will be deserving of His deliverance.

This may be the key to understanding the transition of ideas in the paragraph הָא לַחְמָא עַנְיָא. As we perform the mitzvos of the *Seder*, we are saddened by the fact that we cannot fulfill the mitzvah of the *pesach* sacrifice; we allude to this by wishfully inviting everyone to join us in this mitzvah, and pray that as a result of our remorse we may merit to celebrate Pesach — replete with all of its mitzvos — *next year in the Land of Israel*.

Another insight into this paragraph is revealed if we examine the meaning of the seemingly redundant expressions employed by the *Baal Haggadah*. *Let anyone who is needy come in and make Pesach* seems superfluous after we have just said, *Let anyone who is hungry come in and eat*. Also, *Now we are slaves. . .* sounds repetitious after *This year we are here. . . .*

A person's needs fall within one of two categories: those that are physical in nature and those that are spiritual. It is these two categories that are alluded to in this paragraph. If one is hungry — a physical need — he is invited to eat. If he is "needy" — in a spiritual sense — let him join us in the Pesach service.

In what sense do we offer these two invitations? Perhaps we have here an instance of the idea expressed in the words of King David: ה׳ צִלְּךָ , *Hashem is your shadow* (*Tehillim* 121:5). The *Midrash* (see *Nefesh HaChaim* 1:7) explains that Hashem, so to speak, serves as the shadow and mirror-image of man. Hashem "imitates" man's actions toward his fellow man. For example, only after "Moses grew up and saw the affliction of his people" (*Shemos* 2:11), *then* "Hashem saw the children of Israel, and Hashem knew (of their suffering)" (*Shemos* 2:25) (see *Ohr RaShaz* Chapter 194).

The invitations proffered here might be understood in this vein: Since we have shown concern for our fellow Jews' physical needs, may we next year be released from our physical bondage to hostile nations; and as we have expressed our care for their spiritual necessities, so may You lead us to *Eretz Yisrael* to partake of its spiritual bounty.

Yet another approach is found in the *Migdal Eder Haggadah*, which quotes a *midrash* in *Eichah* which comments on the verse גָּלְתָה יְהוּדָה

Let anyone who is hungry come in and eat. Let anyone who is needy come in and make Pesach. This year we are here;

מֵעֹנִי, *Judah went into exile due to poverty* (*Eichah* 1:3). The *Midrash* says that it was because the Jews did not fulfill the mitzvah of eating matzah (לֶחֶם עֹנִי) that the Jews were driven into exile.[1] The connection of ideas is now clear: Since we are now carefully observing the laws of Pesach, as evidenced by our declaration, *here is the poor bread* (הָא לַחְמָא עַנְיָא), may we merit that next year the exile will be over and we will be in *Eretz Yisrael*. (It should be noted that the first day of Pesach always occurs on the same day of the week as Tishah B'Av.)

Another pertinent question about this section of the Haggadah concerns its placement at this particular point in the *Seder*, before the lengthy *maggid* section. Would it not be more appropriate to issue this invitation to eat immediately prior to the meal? The answer to this may be that Pesach, the first of the three festivals of the year, corresponds to Abraham, the first of the three Patriarchs, as explained in the *Tur* (*Orach Chaim* 417). The *Yalkut Shimoni* points out that it was on the fifteenth of Nisan (i.e. Pesach) that the covenant of *bris bein habesarim* between Hashem and Abraham took place, and that it was on this date that Sarah was informed that she would have a child in her old age, and on this date that child — Isaac — was born.

One of the major messages which we derive from Abraham's way of life is that of the supreme importance of *hachnasas orchim*, welcoming guests. We learn from his actions (*Bereishis* 18:3) that welcoming guests takes precedence even over communion with Hashem. To recall this connection between Abraham and Pesach, we issue the invitation to our Pesach *Seder* even before we turn to the words of song and praise of Hashem, thus illustrating that kindness to guests must even come before service of God.

This motif is mirrored in the opening Mishnah of the tenth chapter of *Pesachim* which deals with the laws of the *Seder*. As opposed to the *Rambam* who first states the general laws of the *Seder* and afterwards details the special considerations to be shown to the poor, the Mishnah, at the outset, delineates the care of the poor. "Even the poor man should not eat on this night unless he reclines"; "The poor must be given at least four cups of wine, even those who are sustained by the public kitchen" (*Pesachim* 99b).

---

1. The story is told of a man who had eaten *chametz* on Pesach and went to R' Shalom of Belz to ask him to suggest an appropriate penance for his sin. The course prescribed was two years in self-exile. The reason given for this particular punishment was that throughout the Torah the word וְנִכְרְתָה (*and he shall be cut off*) never appears with the *trop* (cantillation sign) of גֵּרְשַׁיִם — except for the two times the word is used in connection with eating *chametz* on Pesach (in *Shemos* 12). The word גֵּרְשַׁיִם is from the root גרש, meaning "to drive out"; hence its appearance twice indicates two years of exile.

הָכָא, לְשָׁנָה הַבָּאָה בְּאַרְעָא דְיִשְׂרָאֵל. הָשַׁתָּא עַבְדֵי, לְשָׁנָה הַבָּאָה בְּנֵי חוֹרִין.

Having discovered the connection between Abraham, the personification of *chessed* (kindness) and Pesach, we can understand why the motif of care for the needy is so prominent, being mentioned first in the Mishnah's discussion and likewise in the Haggadah.[1]

הָשַׁתָּא הָכָא לְשָׁנָה הַבָּאָה בְּאַרְעָא דְיִשְׂרָאֵל — **This year we are here; next year we will be in the Land of Israel.** In the Gemara (*Rosh Hashanah* 11a) we find the statement, "In Nisan they (the Jewish people) were redeemed (from Egypt); in Nisan they will be redeemed again (in Messianic times)." In *Targum Yonasan* (*Shemos* 12:42) the predicted time for the future Redemption is further narrowed down to the night of Pesach, the fifteenth of Nisan.[2]

Being that this night is singled out as being a particularly appropriate one for the ultimate Redemption, it seems strange that we express the hope that we will be in the Land of Israel *next* year. It would be much more fitting to express our desire that *Mashiach* should come immediately, even on this very night! The explanation for this is that while indeed we eagerly await *Mashiach*'s coming even on this night, even if he would come at this very moment, we would not be privileged to celebrate *this* Pesach in the Land of Israel, since just as the deliverance from Egypt was followed by many years of traveling before the Promised Land was reached, so too *Mashiach* will not take us instantly to *Eretz Yisrael*, but will first lead us through the "wilderness of the

---

1. The preeminence of *hachnasas orchim* is highlighted by a most beautiful incident. R' Chaim Ozer Grodzenski, *zt'l*, once received a guest at his home on a cold Succos day. Since R' Chaim Ozer was ill, he begged the guest's forgiveness and invited him to go alone into the *succah* to partake of some refreshments. The guest complied and went out into the cold *succah*. But a few minutes later, who but R' Chaim Ozer appeared in the *succah* wrapped snugly in a warm overcoat. His guest objected, "But Rebbe, you are exempt from coming into the *succah*, you are מִצְטַעֵר (pained and distressed) due to the cold." R' Chaim Ozer replied: "Yes, being מִצְטַעֵר absolves me from the mitzvah of *succah*, but not from the mitzvah of *hachnasas orchim*."

2. The idea of having a set time for the future Redemption would seem to contradict the well-known article of our faith that we must at all times believe that the day of our salvation is imminent. As the Gemara puts it, "If someone takes a vow that he will become a *nazir* on the day that the son of David (i.e., *Mashiach*) comes, he may never drink wine (because of the real possibility that *that* day will be the day of the *Mashiach*'s coming)." The *Turei Even* (*Rosh Hashanah* 11a) answers this question based on the Gemara in *Sanhedrin* (98a) which interprets the verse, "I am Hashem; at its time I will hasten it (the Redemption) (*Yeshayahu* 60:22)," to mean that if Israel is especially meritorious, "I will hasten it"; if not, it will take place at a particular set time. Thus the *Targum Yonasan* refers to the time set for the final salvation to come if all else fails. We, however, are obligated to hope and believe that we will be deserving of an earlier deliverance.

next year we will be in the Land of Israel. Now we are slaves; next year we will be free men.

---

nations" as prophesied by Yechezkel (20:35).[1] Thus, even under the most favorable of circumstances — that *Mashiach* would come immediately — we can only pray to be in the Land of Israel *next year*.

מַגִּיד — **The narrative of the Exodus from Egypt.** The *Rambam (Chametz U'Matzah* 10:1) defines the mitzvah of relating the story of the Exodus with the following statement: "It is a positive Biblical commandment to tell of the miracles and wonders that were wrought to our forefathers in Egypt, on the night of the fifteenth of Nisan, as it says (*Shemos* 13:3), 'Remember this day on which you have left Egypt,' just as it says (ibid. 20:8), 'Remember the Sabbath day, to sanctify it.' " The analogy to Shabbos is seemingly not contextual and based merely on a similarity of terminology (*remember*). What insight into the mitzvah of recounting the Exodus does the Rambam expect us to gain by comparing it to the mitzvah of Shabbos?

Rabbi Meir Simchah HaCohen (the *"Meshech Chochmah"*) derives a novel idea from this analogy of the *Rambam* (which is actually paraphrased from the *Mechilta*). He explains that on Shabbos there is a Biblical commandment, known to us as *Kiddush,* to sanctify Shabbos by making a verbal declaration of its holiness, based on the aforementioned verse "Remember the Sabbath day...." This mitzvah, as Rabbinically defined, is performed over a cup of wine. The mitzvah of recounting the Exodus revolves around the matzah, which is referred to (in *Devarim* 16:3) as לֶחֶם עֹנִי, interpreted by the Sages as "the bread about which many words are uttered." Yet, suggests the *Meshech Chochmah,* the Rabbis here, too, ordained that the mitzvah be performed over a cup of wine just like the *Kiddush* of Shabbos.[2] Accordingly, the second cup of wine is poured before מַה נִּשְׁתַּנָּה, though we do not drink it until

---

1. This idea that Israel's salvation (past and future) is always followed by a certain interlude of time before they actually enter the Land of Israel is found in the *Raavad's* commentary on *Eduyos* 2:9.

2. *Rabbi Chaim Soloveitchik,* however, offers a different explanation of the *Rambam's* comparison of the remembrances of Shabbos and the Exodus, explaining that one must not only tell the story of the Exodus on Pesach night, but must emphasize that the events being discussed transpired on *this* night, the fifteenth of Nisan, just as the purpose of *Kiddush* on Shabbos is to declare that it is *now* Shabbos. The only place in the Haggadah where this idea is actually mentioned is the phrase זְמַן חֵרוּתֵנוּ (*this [is] the season of our freedom*) in *Kiddush*. Thus, the *Kiddush* of Pesach night, aside from being a regular Yom Tov *Kiddush,* is also an integral part of the *Seder* service emphasizing that *now* is the season of our freedom. Perhaps, for this reason the *Shulchan Aruch* (*Orach Chaim* 472:1) rules that unlike on Shabbos or other Yomim Tovim, *Kiddush* on Pesach should not be recited until nightfall since, as the Haggadah itself teaches (quoting from the *Mechilta*), the mitzvah of recounting the Exodus may not be fulfilled until nighttime.

The *Seder* plate may either be moved to the far end of the table or completely removed from the table, and the second of the four cups of wine is poured.
The youngest present asks the reasons for the unusual proceedings of the evening.

מַה נִּשְׁתַּנָּה הַלַּיְלָה הַזֶּה מִכָּל הַלֵּילוֹת?

the conclusion of the מַגִּיד section, since the entire section must be recited over this cup of wine. Another difficulty solved by the approach of the *Meshech Chochmah* concerns the glaring omission of the drinking of the four cups of wine from the קַדֵּשׁ וּרְחַץ which describes the steps of the *Seder*. Now that we have shown that the מַגִּיד section is recited over the second cup of wine, it may be said that the four cups of wine are indeed included as elemental parts of the steps of קַדֵּשׁ, מַגִּיד, בָּרֵךְ, הַלֵּל, since each of these steps is recited over a cup of wine. (Similarly, the two "dippings" are not specifically mentioned because they are part and parcel of the proper fulfillment of כַּרְפַּס and מָרוֹר.)

מַה נִּשְׁתַּנָּה וכו׳ — **Why is this night different ...** The *Mishnah* says of this stage in the *Seder*, "At this point the son asks (these four questions)." The *Rambam*, paraphrasing the Gemara, tells us what should be done if there is no son present: "If he has no son, his wife should ask the questions; if he has no wife, the participants should ask one another — even if they are all scholars."

This preference of sons over others is also found in connection with the mitzvah of teaching Torah. In the Laws of *Talmud Torah* (1:2) the *Rambam* writes: "A father is obligated to teach the Torah to his son, as it says, 'and you shall teach them (i.e. the words of the Torah) to your sons'....Similarly, every scholar is obligated to teach disciples, as it says, 'You shall teach them diligently unto your sons,' and we have a tradition that *sons* in this verse means *students*, for disciples are often referred to as sons [in the *Tanach*]."

Comparing these two selections from the *Rambam*, a question arises. Since, as the *Rambam* points out concerning *talmud Torah*, disciples are almost the equivalent of one's own children, preference should seemingly be given to one's student over all of the others mentioned except, of course, for the person's son. Why, then, does the *Rambam*, regarding the four questions, skip directly from son to wife, not mentioning students at all?

The same question may be asked concerning the following quote from the *Tosefta* (*Pesachim* 10,8): "One must occupy himself with discussing the laws of Pesach the whole night — with his son, or even by

The *Seder* plate may either be moved to the far end of the table or completely removed from the table, and the second of the four cups of wine is poured.
The youngest present asks the reasons for the unusual proceedings of the evening.

Why is this night different from all other nights?

himself, or with his student." Here also we find that the student enjoys no special status, being mentioned after the case of studying by oneself!

Apparently the mitzvah of וְהִגַּדְתָּ לְבִנְךָ ("and you shall tell [the story of the Exodus from Egypt] to your son"), unlike the mitzvah of studying the Torah, applies only to one's actual children, with students having no more status in this area than any other participant in the *Seder*. The discrepancy in these two areas of *halachah* requires explanation.

One possible reason for this difference may be based on the fact that the principle that "one's disciples are like his own sons" did not take effect until after the Revelation at Mount Sinai. This is alluded to in the following verses (*Bamidbar* 3:1-2) which are the sources for this concept: *These are the descendants of Moses and Aaron on the day that Hashem spoke to Moses on Mount Sinai. These are the names of the sons of Aaron: the firstborn was Nadab, and Abihu* .... Moses' children are not mentioned at all, yet the statement begins with "These are the descendants of *Moses* and Aaron." *Rashi,* quoting the Gemara, explains that from this verse it may be inferred that "if someone teaches Torah to another man's children it is as if he were their father." Since the verse refers to "the day that Hashem spoke to Moses on Mount Sinai," it conveys the implication that the disciple-son relationship did not begin until that day.[1]

The *Rambam* remarks that on Pesach night we are obliged to see ourselves as if we now had personally experienced the Exodus from Egypt. Correspondingly, since the Exodus preceded the Revelation at Mount Sinai, this mitzvah intentionally disregards the disciple-son relationship which took effect only with the Revelation.

Another explanation of this difference in status accorded a student regarding the mitzvos of *talmud Torah* and וְהִגַּדְתָּ לְבִנְךָ (recounting the

---

1. This assertion, that disciples are tantamount to sons only after the giving of the Torah, may be explained as follows. The concept of a teacher being like a father is based on the idea that just as a father has given the gift of physical life to his children, so too one who teaches Torah gives life — *spiritual* life — to his students. This analogy can only be valid after the Torah became the source of our spiritual existence, namely at Sinai.

שֶׁבְּכָל הַלֵּילוֹת אָנוּ אוֹכְלִין חָמֵץ וּמַצָּה,
הַלַּיְלָה הַזֶּה – כֻּלּוֹ מַצָּה.

שֶׁבְּכָל הַלֵּילוֹת אָנוּ אוֹכְלִין שְׁאָר יְרָקוֹת,
הַלַּיְלָה הַזֶּה – מָרוֹר.

שֶׁבְּכָל הַלֵּילוֹת אֵין אָנוּ מַטְבִּילִין אֲפִילוּ פַּעַם אֶחָת,
הַלַּיְלָה הַזֶּה – שְׁתֵּי פְעָמִים.

שֶׁבְּכָל הַלֵּילוֹת אָנוּ אוֹכְלִין בֵּין יוֹשְׁבִין וּבֵין מְסֻבִּין,
הַלַּיְלָה הַזֶּה – כֻּלָּנוּ מְסֻבִּין.

---

story of the Exodus) may be suggested as follows. One might have thought to explain the mitzvah of recounting the Exodus as a particular subcategory of the general mitzvah of studying the Torah (i.e. on the night of the fifteenth of Nisan we are required to study the specific topic of the Exodus) with its attendant rules and laws. This, however, is not the case, for as I once heard from *Rav Yitzchak Hutner, z"tl*, the mitzvah of וְהִגַּדְתָּ לְבִנְךָ is actually completely independent from that of learning Torah. The purpose of this mitzvah, *Rav Hutner* explained, is not to teach, but rather to perpetuate the testimonies and traditions about our miraculous deliverance from Egypt which are then handed down from generation to generation. This idea is borne out by a statement in the Mishnah (*Pesachim*, chap. 10) which says: "The father should gear his discussion (of the Exodus) according to the intellect of the son." Were the mitzvah of וְהִגַּדְתָּ לְבִנְךָ to be merely an instance of *talmud Torah* with a didactic purpose alone, this statement would be completely superfluous. Certainly when one teaches Torah — or any other subject matter — he should employ whatever methods and ideas are most suitable for the individual student! And in fact no such rule is found in the *halachos* of *talmud Torah*. However, since the mitzvah of recounting the Exodus is not simply the teaching of Torah but rather the perpetuation and transmission of our traditions and testimonies, one could assume that these need be transmitted in a particular form and system in order to maintain their authenticity. Hence, the completeness of the transmission rather than its full comprehension may have been seen as the goal of וְהִגַּדְתָּ לְבִנְךָ. It is in contradistinction to this perception of וְהִגַּדְתָּ לְבִנְךָ that the Mishnah had to tell us that the discussion must "be geared according to the intellect of the son." Nonetheless, since this mitzvah is not the intellectual exercise of *talmud Torah* but rather a transmittal of fundamentals, the student-teacher relationship plays no special role

1. *On all other nights we eat chametz and matzah. On this night — only matzah.*

2. *On all other nights we eat all kinds of vegetables. On this night — maror.*

3. *On all other nights we do not dip even once. On this night — twice.*

4. *On all other nights we eat either sitting straight or reclining. On this night we all recline.*

(the student is just one more participant at the *Seder*) while the natural father-son connection is the perfect vehicle for this mitzvah.

◄§ The *Sefas Emes* writes that the four questions correspond to the four kinds of sons (discussed later in the Haggadah) mentioned in the Torah, with each question paralleling one of the sons.

Following the approach of the *Sefas Emes,* we may explain that the question about matzah, which is symbolic of a leaven-free existence, may be related to the wise, righteous son, who seeks to rid himself of the souring effect of the symbolic *chametz.*

The evil son, for whom the mitzvos and the Torah have a bitter taste, is reflected in the question about *maror* (the bitter herbs).

The question about immersing vegetables in a flavored dip may be associated with the simple son, whose lack of enthusiasm in service of Hashem might be rectified if the Torah is presented to him in an "appetizing" way.

The son who "is unable to ask" has an attitude of total indifference to the Torah, having no "taste" for spirituality at all, bitter or sweet. The only remedy for his situation is to induce in him a complete change of "position" and posture regarding spiritual matters. This corresponds to the question about the unusual posture (reclining) adopted at the *Seder*.

◄§ Many commentators have asked why the four cups, possibly the most noticeable *Seder* departure from an ordinary meal, find no place in the מַה נִּשְׁתַּנָה.

The answer may be that these four questions are in reality one series with four parts. The child's attention is drawn to the fact that in the myriad of symbols and rituals of the *Seder* table there appears to be a contradiction of themes. On the one hand we have the bitter herbs and the "bread of affliction" which are vivid reminders of our enslavement, yet we also adopt the eating posture and dining habits (dipping the food) of freemen and nobles. In reality the four symbols we focus on are a study in contrasts.

The *Seder* plate is returned. The matzos are kept uncovered as the Haggadah is recited in unison. The Haggadah should be translated if necessary, and the story of the Exodus should be amplified upon.

עֲבָדִים הָיִינוּ לְפַרְעֹה בְּמִצְרָיִם, וַיּוֹצִיאֵנוּ יהוה אֱלֹהֵינוּ מִשָּׁם בְּיָד חֲזָקָה וּבִזְרֹעַ נְטוּיָה. וְאִלּוּ לֹא הוֹצִיא הַקָּדוֹשׁ בָּרוּךְ הוּא אֶת אֲבוֹתֵינוּ

The drinking of wine, however, is associated with either of two functions: It "gladdens the heart of man" (*Tehillim* 104:15), yet it is, as well, the beverage used to console mourners (*Kesubos* 8b) and other ill-fated people from their anguish (*Sanhedrin* 43a). In the words of King Solomon, "give strong drink to him that is doomed, and wine to men of bitter souls" (*Mishlei* 31:6). Therefore, due to its duality in function, wine is not mentioned in the four questions! The drinking of wine does not arouse in the child any questions of contradiction.

עֲבָדִים הָיִינוּ — **We were slaves.** *Shulchan Aruch* (*Mishneh Berurah* 472 §50) rules that after reciting the עֲבָדִים הָיִינוּ in response to the מַה נִּשְׁתַּנָּה, one may allow children to go to sleep, indicating that this short answer encapsulates a full response to the child's questions.

As previously noted, the theme of the מַה נִּשְׁתַּנָּה is the amazement of the child at the mixed signals sent by the different *Seder* rituals and symbols. This seeming contradiction is explained by this pithy phrase, *We were slaves to Pharaoh in Egypt* which we express with matzah, the bread of affliction, and *maror*, the bitter herbs. *And Hashem, our God, took us out of there....* hence, the symbols of freedom.

◆§ Were *we* slaves in Egypt? It was our distant ancestors who were enslaved, not we! This is an example of our fulfilling the Haggadah's dictum: "In every generation it is one's duty to regard himself as though he personally had gone out of Egypt." This is not merely an exercise in imagination, since the souls of the 600,000 Jews who were slaves in Egypt contained within themselves the souls of all the future generations of *Klal Yisrael.* All of the Jewish souls throughout the generations are intertwined and interconnected. Thus, in a spiritual sense, we were indeed enslaved in Egypt.

◆§ In Tractate *Pesachim* (116a) the *Mishnah* instructs that when telling the story of the Exodus at the *Seder*, one should "begin with גְּנוּת (the diminished status of Israel) and end with שֶׁבַח (their subsequent elevated situation)." There is a difference of opinion in the Gemara as to what exactly these two terms are referring. Rav says גְּנוּת is a reference to מִתְּחִלָּה עוֹבְדֵי עֲבוֹדָה זָרָה הָיוּ אֲבוֹתֵינוּ, *At first our forefathers were idolaters,* and שֶׁבַח means וְעַכְשָׁו קֵרְבָנוּ הַמָּקוֹם לַעֲבוֹדָתוֹ, *but now the Omnipresent has*

W e were slaves unto Pharaoh in Egypt, and HASHEM, our God, took us out of there with a strong hand and an outstretched arm. If the Holy One, Blessed is He, had not taken our forefathers

brought us close to His worship. Shmuel, on the other hand, holds that גְּנוּת denotes the present section, עֲבָדִים הָיִינוּ, We were slaves unto Pharaoh in Egypt, and שֶׁבַח refers to מִשָּׁם...וַיּוֹצִיאֵנוּ, but Hashem, our God, took us out of there.

The positions of Rav and Shmuel are not exclusive. The argument is only one of emphasis and in fact both opinions have been incorporated into our Haggadah, thus addressing two distinct perspectives of the Exodus from Egypt.

The Jewish people are distinguished by a duality of character. On the one hand, in a biological sense they are the *children of Israel* — the descendants of the Patriarchs — and are referred to by this name even before the Exodus. On the other hand they are possessed of a spiritual sanctity, having been chosen by Hashem to be מַמְלֶכֶת כֹּהֲנִים וְגוֹי קָדוֹשׁ, *a kingdom of priests and a holy nation* (Shemos 19:6). This second aspect was bestowed upon them upon leaving Egypt. (See *Yevamos* 46a, Rashi ad loc.) It is in respect to these elements that Rav and Shmuel express their opinions. Regarding their biological status we note (according to Rav) that from our ignominious family origins we achieved the distinction of being the children of hallowed Patriarchs — "Your forefathers... Terach, the father of Abraham and the father of Nachor, and they worshiped other gods. And I took your father Abraham... and I led him throughout all the Land of Canaan... and I gave Isaac unto him, and I gave Jacob... unto Isaac." With respect to the second characteristic — the "sanctity of Israel" — we mention (according to Shmuel) the indignity of "we were slaves unto Pharaoh..." and the subsequent elevation of "Hashem, our G-d, took us out of there," to be His holy sanctified nation.

Based on this idea we can now understand why the Haggadah continues, "Had not the Holy One, Blessed is He, taken our fathers out of Egypt, then we and our children... would have remained subservient to Pharaoh in Egypt." (It does not use the word עֲבָדִים ("enslaved"), despite the fact that the paragraph began using this word, but rather "subservient.") This choice of terminology is to indicate that while actually we would not have remained enslaved in permanent physical servitude, since a state of permanent slavery could not be reconciled with our exalted status as the "children of Israel" (which already existed at the time of the enslavement in Egypt), we would have nevertheless re-

מִמִּצְרַיִם, הֲרֵי אָנוּ וּבָנֵינוּ וּבְנֵי בָנֵינוּ מְשֻׁעְבָּדִים
הָיִינוּ לְפַרְעֹה בְּמִצְרָיִם. וַאֲפִילוּ כֻּלָּנוּ חֲכָמִים,

mained *subservient* to the Egyptians, never having been able to attain the state of "sanctity of Israel."

עֲבָדִים הָיִינוּ . . . וַיּוֹצִיאֵנוּ ה' אֱלֹקֵינוּ . . . בְּיָד חֲזָקָה וּבִזְרֹעַ נְטוּיָה — We were slaves . . . and Hashem, our G-d, took us out . . . with a strong hand, and with an outstretched arm. This is a verbatim quote from *Devarim* 6:21, except for the addition of the last two words — *and with an outstretched arm*. Why did the *Baal HaHaggadah* add these words from *Devarim* 4:34 to the Biblical verse quoted here?

Based on a verse in *Shir HaShirim* (2:8), we are taught that the Jews in Egypt had sunk to such a low level of impurity through imitation of their Egyptian neighbors' idolatrous ways that Hashem had to liberate them far in advance of the four hundred years they were to have been enslaved, lest they sink to an even lower state from which they would not have been able to emerge (cf. *Bereishis* 15:13). אִלּוּ לֹא הוֹצִיא וכו', "If the Holy One had not taken our fathers out of Egypt" — at that exact time — "then we and our children ... would have remained subservient to Pharaoh in Egypt."

While early redemption was beneficial, in a sense it unleashed some later difficulties. The *Beis HaLevi* explains that had Hashem not been "compelled" (as it were) to redeem the Israelites before the set time, no evil would have befallen them in the desert, or at any time thereafter.

Concerning the verse (*Devarim* 4:34) that Hashem took us out of Egypt "with trials, with signs and with wonders...and with an outstretched arm," the *Sforno* explains that the *outstretched arm* — implying a continuous, relentless vengeance — was necessary to protect the Jews from any further misfortune that might come their way *after* the Exodus. Since these misfortunes were a result of the early release from Egypt, the protection afforded us from the resultant calamities by the "outstreched hand" is also part of the salvation Hashem provided with the Exodus. For this reason did the Haggadah embellish our text with the phrase "and with an outstreched hand."

Another explanation for the additional phrase may be offered. Commenting on the verse "You have begun to show Your servant (Moses) ... Your mighty hand" (*Devarim* 3:24), Rashi interprets this as a reference to Hashem's right "hand," which is always open to all human beings to mercifully accept those who seek Him with true contrition (cf. *Sifsei Chachamim* ibid.). The "outstretched arm," as noted, signifies Hashem's continuous vigilance in retribution of His people's enemies.

The *Zohar* points out that each of the ten plagues visited upon the

out of Egypt, we and our children and our children's children
would still be subservient to Pharaoh in Egypt. Even if all of us

Egyptians actually served two purposes: punishment for Egypt, and salvation for the Children of Israel. It may be in order to reflect this parallelism that the Haggadah adds here that the Exodus from Egypt took place not only with *a mighty hand* of mercy, vis-a-vis the Israelites, but also with an *outstretched arm* of retribution, vis-a-vis the Egyptians.

וְאִלּוּ לֹא הוֹצִיא לֹא הַקב״ה אֶת אֲבוֹתֵינוּ מִמִּצְרַיִם הֲרֵי אָנוּ . . . מְשֻׁעְבָּדִים הָיִינוּ לְפַרְעֹה בְּמִצְרָיִם — **If the Holy One, Blessed is He, had not taken our forefathers out of Egypt, we . . . would still be subservient to Pharaoh in Egypt.** The *question* is often asked: Surely over the centuries and millennia that have passed since the time of the Exodus the Jewish people would have been granted their emancipation through some natural or political means even without the miraculous intervention of Hashem?! Why then does the Haggadah state with such certainty that "we would still be subservient to Pharoh in Egypt"?

Rav Shlomo Harkavy of Grodno answered this question by pointing out that the Haggadah does not say that we would still be *slaves* (עֲבָדִים) unto Pharaoh, but rather that we would be מְשֻׁעְבָּדִים (translated here as *subservient*, but it could also mean "beholden," or "indebted") to him. Even if some agreement had been worked out with the Egyptians over the ages, we would nevertheless be מְשֻׁעְבָּדִים, *indebted*, to the Pharaohs, or to their successors, for their graciously granting us emancipation.

Another question arises regarding this passage. Our Sages tell us (*Nedarim* 32a), based on a verse in *Yirmiyahu* 33:25, that if the Torah had not been given to mankind, the Universe would cease to exist, having been deprived of the purpose of its creation. Rashi quotes a similar *midrash* in his commentary on the verse, "and it was evening and it was morning, *the* sixth day"(*Bereishis* 1:31): At the close of the six days of creation, Hashem made it clear that creation's very existence was dependent on Israel's eventual acceptance of the Torah on the sixth of Sivan (the festival of Shavuos, when the Revelation on Mount Sinai took place). If this is the case, how can it be said that if there had been no Exodus — and hence no giving of the Torah at Sinai — we would still be enslaved to the Egyptians? In fact, if we had not left Egypt there would be no world left at all!

Actually, as previously noted, this sentence is puzzling for another reason: Even if Hashem had not taken us out of Egypt Himself, would we not have found some other manner of being released from bondage by now? The *Zichron Niflaos* explains that the Haggadah does not intend to say that the Jewish people as such would still be enslaved to the Egyptians physically. Rather, the Haggadah means that if Hashem had

כֻּלָּנוּ נְבוֹנִים, כֻּלָּנוּ זְקֵנִים, כֻּלָּנוּ יוֹדְעִים אֶת הַתּוֹרָה,
מִצְוָה עָלֵינוּ לְסַפֵּר בִּיצִיאַת מִצְרָיִם. וְכָל הַמַּרְבֶּה לְסַפֵּר

not redeemed us *before the appointed time* but had waited the full four hundred years, many Israelites would have become completely assimilated, and their descendants would today be ordinary Egyptians. Only a select, tenacious few would have survived the terrible ordeal, to fulfill Hashem's promise to Abraham that his seed would return to the Promised Land after four generations.

According to this approach, our other question is also answered. There would indeed have been a Revelation on Mount Sinai, even if Hashem had not taken us out of Egypt *earlier than the appointed time* — but only for a small group of extraordinary individuals.

וַאֲפִילוּ כֻּלָּנוּ חֲכָמִים ... מִצְוָה עָלֵינוּ לְסַפֵּר בִּיצִיאַת מִצְרָיִם — **Even if all of us were wise . . . we would still be commanded to tell the story of the Exodus from Egypt.** We have the daily obligation to recall the Exodus from Egypt, as stated in the verse (*Devarim* 16:3), "that you should remember the day of your going out of Egypt all the days of your life." We also have the mitzvah to tell the story of the Exodus on the first night of Pesach. The Biblical source for *this* commandment is found in *Shemos* 13:8: "And you shall tell your son on that day [Pesach], saying, 'because of this Hashem did so for me when I went out of Egypt.'"

Bearing this in mind, several questions concerning the order of the Haggadah become apparent. First, why does the Haggadah mention the statements of R' Elazar ben Azariah and the Sages, which presumably illustrates the Biblical source for the mitzvah of זְכִירָה, to remember *daily* the events of *Yetzias Mitzrayim*, when the entire discussion pertains to the *other* mitzvah, וְהִגַּדְתָּ, retelling the story of the Exodus on Pesach night? Second, having asserted that there is a mitzvah to discuss the Exodus at Pesach time (מִצְוָה עָלֵינוּ לְסַפֵּר בִּיצִיאַת מִצְרָיִם), the Haggadah should have immediately addressed the question of when exactly this mitzvah is to be performed (יָכוֹל מֵראֹשׁ חֹדֶשׁ), instead of leaving this issue hanging for several paragraphs, until after the discussion of the four sons.

Finally, there is even greater confusion regarding the distinction between these two mitzvos. We find a third verse (*Shemos* 13:3) that says, "Remember this day, on which you have gone out of Egypt." Which of the two mitzvos under discussion is this verse referring to — the daily remembrance or the once-yearly recounting of the Exodus? The *Mechilta* clearly interprets it as a reference to the former, while Rambam (*Chametz U'Matzah*) brings it as a source for the latter. The question how the Rambam can contradict the authoritative *Mechilta* is raised by *were wise, all of us understanding, all of us aged, all of us learned in Torah, we would still be commanded to tell the story of the Exodus from Egypt, and whoever enlarges upon the tale*

the *Maharal of Prague* (*Gevaros HaShem* 2). In fact, this question is further reinforced since the *Mechilta itself* quotes this verse elsewhere in connection with the Pesach mitzvah (*Mechilta Bo* 13)!

Let us resolve the last difficulty first. Actually the verse in question, by stressing the phrase "Remember *this day*," lends itself to two possible interpretations. First, "this *day*" could be taken to intimate that the remembrance referred to applies only during the day, but not at nights. In this case, it would be referring to the daily mitzvah, and would be in accordance with the view of the Sages (who argue with Ben Zoma), as quoted in the coming paragraphs of the Haggadah. Alternatively, "*this* day" may be understood as a reference to one particular day in the year — Pesach — to the exclusion of all other days; in this sense it would obviously be relating to the Pesach mitzvah. The *Rambam,* who rules (*Krias Shema* 1:3) in accordance with the opinion of Ben Zoma that the daily remembrance of the Exodus must be done at night as well as during the day, is forced to reject the first of these two explanations and hence he adopts the second, relating the verse to the Pesach mitzvah. The *Mechilta*, however, does not take a definitive stand in the dispute between the Sages and Ben Zoma, and thus interprets the verse according to both opinions — once in accordance with the view of Ben Zoma, and once with that of the Sages.

If the verse, "Remember this day, etc.," refers to the Pesach mitzvah, as the Rambam and the *Mechilta* contend, what does it add to the "main" verse, quoted above which tells of the commandment to recount the story of *Yetzias Mitzrayim* on Pesach, "and you shall tell your son on that day, etc."? The *Mechilta* addresses this question as follows: "If we only had the verse, 'and you shall tell your son, etc.' we might think that the mitzvah is only applicable to someone who has a son; would we know that there is an obligation for one who has no children? For this reason the Torah states a second verse, "Remember this day, etc." where no mention is made of a son."

Now we can answer the questions posed earlier, concerning the order of topics in the Haggadah to this point. First the Haggadah asserts that there is a mitzvah of telling the Exodus story which is unique to Pesach, besides the daily mitzvah of remembering the Exodus. It then goes on to say that this mitzvah applies *even if we* — the participants in the *Seder* — *are all wise men* — i.e. even when it is not a father-and-son situation. The Biblical source for this idea (that the telling of the story of the Exodus is not limited to fathers and sons) is, as seen in the *Mechilta*, the

בִּיצִיאַת מִצְרַיִם, הֲרֵי זֶה מְשֻׁבָּח.

מַעֲשֶׂה בְּרַבִּי אֱלִיעֶזֶר וְרַבִּי יְהוֹשֻׁעַ וְרַבִּי אֶלְעָזָר בֶּן
עֲזַרְיָה וְרַבִּי עֲקִיבָא וְרַבִּי טַרְפוֹן שֶׁהָיוּ מְסֻבִּין
בִּבְנֵי בְרַק, וְהָיוּ מְסַפְּרִים בִּיצִיאַת מִצְרַיִם כָּל אוֹתוֹ

verse of "Remember this day, etc." But how can we be sure that this verse is really referring to the Pesach mitzvah, and not to the daily mitzvah (in which case it can not be used to prove that there is a mitzvah even in the absence of children)? For this reason the Haggadah's next step is to quote the exegesis of Ben Zoma, who shows that the daily mitzvah of remembering the Exodus is binding at nighttime as well as daytime, thus proving (as shown in the previous paragraph) that the verse in question — "Remember this day, etc." — is referring to the Pesach mitzvah. Next, the Haggadah alludes to the other verse which deals with the Pesach mitzvah — "and you shall tell your son, etc." — by explaining the four kinds of sons spoken of in the Torah. But why is this second verse necessary altogether, since we have already been told, "Remember this day, etc."? To answer this question the Haggadah goes on to show (שֶׁיָכוֹל מֵראשׁ חֹדֶשׁ) that this verse, in its continuation, tells us a crucial fact — the precise time during the Pesach season the mitzvah is to be performed — namely, on the night of the fifteenth of Nisan.

וַאֲפִילוּ כֻּלָּנוּ חֲכָמִים . . . כֻּלָּנוּ יוֹדְעִים אֶת הַתּוֹרָה מִצְוָה עָלֵינוּ לְסַפֵּר בִּיצִיאַת מִצְרַיִם — Even if all of us were wise . . . all of us learned in Torah, we would still be commanded to tell the story of the Exodus from Egypt. Why might I have thought otherwise? Is a Torah scholar exempt from any other mitzvah in the Torah?

Based on the previous comment, we may suggest an answer to this problem. The mitzvah of telling the story of the Exodus to one's son is derived from the verse, "and you shall tell your son, etc." A second verse, "Remember (זָכוֹר) this day, etc.," extends this mitzvah to cases where there is no son. The Gemara (*Megillah* 18a) says, in connection with the mitzvah of remembering Amalek, that the word זָכוֹר ("Remember") may imply mere mental contemplation unless the Torah specifically requires a verbal utterance (which it does in the case of remembering Amalek). Since the mitzvah to discuss the story of *Yetzias Mitzrayim*, even when there are no children, is derived from the word זָכוֹר ("Remember"), we might have supposed that if we — the participants at the *Seder* — are not children but rather all are "wise . . . learned in Torah" — we may fulfill our obligation by merely meditating on the Exodus. Therefore, the Haggadah informs us that *even if all of us were of the Exodus merits praise.*

An incident took place in which Rabbi Eliezer, Rabbi Yehoshua, Rabbi Elazar ben Azariah, Rabbi Akiva, and Rabbi Tarfon were reclining in Bnei Brak and recounting the tale of the Exodus from Egypt all that night,

wise . . . we would still be commanded to **tell** — verbally — the Exodus from Egypt.

מִצְוָה עָלֵינוּ לְסַפֵּר — *Kedushas Levi* asks why is it on the night of Pesach more than any other time that the mitzvah of recalling the miracles of the Exodus should be done in a father-to-son dialogue. On Succos we are told to reside in *succos* (huts) "so that your future generations may know that I had the children of Israel dwell in huts when I took them out of the land of Egypt" (*Vayikra* 23:43), yet there is no specific mitzvah to discuss the symbolism of the *succah* with one's children.

In assuring Jacob of His constant guiding presence in the descent to Egypt and in the eventual emergence to freedom, Hashem says, "I shall descend with you to Egypt and I shall also surely bring you up" (*Bereishis* 46:4). Not only is this a Divine assurance, it is also descriptive of the process of redemption. Moses' descent to the people engendered the response of Hashem to "go down," so to speak, among His people in order to redeem them. When "Moses grew up and saw the affliction of his people" (*Shemos* 2:11), his descent from the royal palace of Egypt elicited a mirroring by Hashem and "Hashem saw the children of Israel and Hashem knew (of their suffering)" (*Shemos* 2:25). The "descent" of Hashem's presence signaled the beginning of redemption.

The Sages tell us that the month of Nisan is especially suited for redemption — past as well as future. The night of the fifteenth is thus a particularly auspicious time to beseech Hashem to hasten the day of our deliverance. The idea of a mature man — even a scholarly sage — descending from his peak level of wisdom to relate stories and simple traditons to his son is reminiscent of the sort of spiritual descent mentioned above. Thus, the act of coming down to the level of the child arouses and catalyzes a Heavenly reaction that Hashem also allow His Shechinah to descend to us as a harbinger of the final Redemption. Accordingly, this theme is exceptionally appropriate to this evening's mitzvah.

מַעֲשֶׂה בְּרַבִּי אֱלִיעֶזֶר וְכוּ׳. . . וְהָיוּ מְסַפְּרִים בִּיצִיאַת מִצְרַיִם כָּל אוֹתוֹ הַלַּיְלָה —
An incident took place in which Rabbi Eliezer . . . and recounting the tale of the Exodus from Egypt all that night.

The Haggadah (p. 52) informs us that the mitzvah of discussing *Yetzias Mitzrayim* must take place at the time when matzah and *maror*

הַלַּיְלָה. עַד שֶׁבָּאוּ תַלְמִידֵיהֶם וְאָמְרוּ לָהֶם, רַבּוֹתֵינוּ הִגִּיעַ זְמַן קְרִיאַת שְׁמַע שֶׁל שַׁחֲרִית.

אָמַר רַבִּי אֶלְעָזָר בֶּן עֲזַרְיָה, הֲרֵי אֲנִי כְּבֶן שִׁבְעִים שָׁנָה, וְלֹא זָכִיתִי שֶׁתֵּאָמֵר יְצִיאַת מִצְרַיִם בַּלֵּילוֹת, עַד שֶׁדְּרָשָׁהּ בֶּן זוֹמָא, שֶׁנֶּאֱמַר, לְמַעַן תִּזְכֹּר אֶת יוֹם צֵאתְךָ מֵאֶרֶץ מִצְרַיִם כֹּל יְמֵי חַיֶּיךָ.[1] יְמֵי חַיֶּיךָ הַיָּמִים, כֹּל יְמֵי חַיֶּיךָ הַלֵּילוֹת. וַחֲכָמִים אוֹמְרִים, יְמֵי

are to be eaten. Since the proper time for these mitzvos is only up until midnight, it is logical to conclude that this should be the true time frame for discussing the Exodus as well. What, then, was the point of these sages staying awake all night to perform a mitzvah whose time had already elapsed? Furthermore, the expression "that night" is noteworthy. One would expect the more common "the entire night of the fifteenth of Nisan."

Rav Hutner zt"l (*Pachad Yitzchak*, *Pesach* 72), answered this question by positing that the mitzvah of recalling the Exodus on Pesach night is twofold: Besides the mitzvah of "and you shall tell your son on that day, etc." (*Shemos* 13:8), there is a further commandment that "this night shall be unto Hashem, a [night of] watching for all the Children of Israel, for [all] their generations" (ibid. 12:42). Rambam explains this verse to mean that this night, the fifteenth of Nisan (i.e. the first night of Pesach), should be dedicated to worship of Hashem and to telling of the wonders and miracles He did for us when we left Egypt. The time restriction imposed on the mitzvah of discussing *Yetzias Mitzrayim* is derived from the wording of the *first* verse (13:8), but there is not necessarily any such limitation regarding the mitzvah described in the *second* verse (12:42). Thus, it is indeed justified, and even meritorious, to continue on with this mitzvah even after midnight. Perhaps this is the implication of the term "that night", a reference to the לֵיל שְׁמוּרִים, *the night of watching.*

אָמַר רַבִּי אֶלְעָזָר בֶּן עֲזַרְיָה הֲרֵי אֲנִי כְּבֶן שִׁבְעִים שָׁנָה וְלֹא זָכִיתִי. . . — Rabbi Elazar ben Azariah said: "Behold, I am like a seventy-year-old man, yet I have never been privileged. . . .

The Gemara (*Berachos* 28a) explains the phrase "I am *like* a seventy year old man" as a cryptic reference to a historical incident: Rabbi Elazar was a very young man (eighteen years old) when he was appointed *Nasi* (Head Sage). He was concerned that due to his youth he would not command the respect so vital for such an exalted position.

until their students came and told them: "Our Rabbis! The time for the recitation of the morning Shema has arrived."

Rabbi Elazar ben Azariah said: "Behold, I am like a seventy-year-old man, yet I have never been privileged to show that the Exodus from Egypt must be said at night until Ben Zoma explained it. It says: 'So that you will remember the day of your departure from Egypt all the days of your life.'[1] 'The days of your life' indicates the days. 'All the days of your life' indicates the nights. The other Sages say, 'the days of*

---

1. *Devarim* 16:3.

Miraculously his beard turned white on that very day of his appointment. This is the meaning of his statement: Although I am quite young, I have been vested with the authority and appearance of a venerable sage, and I am *like* a seventy-year-old man.

Although this story explains Rabbi Elazar's choice of words, his statement nonetheless remains puzzling. Of what relevance is this incident in connection with this particular discussion, that it should be mentioned here as opposed to the scores of other places that this sage's opinion is cited throughout the Talmud?

The answer is that Rabbi Elazar is pointing out a certain basic Torah truth. Despite the fact that he was the head of the yeshivah that now stood in place of the great *Sanhedrin*, and thus the leader of all the Sages of Israel, and despite the fact that he had been granted a miraculous sign as an indication of Heavenly approbation, he was unable to persuade his colleagues to adopt his opinion by virtue of his authority, and succeeded only on the merit of Ben Zoma's exegetical derivation. The Gemara (*Bava Metzia* 59b) states the cardinal principle that the Torah is "not in Heaven" (*Devarim* 30:12), and all the supernatural signs in the world are insufficient to counterbalance even one vote in the *Beis Din* here on earth.[1]

In addition to explaining why it is in this specific context that Rabbi Elazar's unique personal situation is mentioned, this idea may also explain the connection between this paragraph and the next one in the Haggadah, extolling Hashem for having given the Torah to His people, Israel — to be the exclusive province of man and his intellect.

כָּל יְמֵי חַיֶּיךָ – הַלֵּילוֹת. וַחֲכָמִים אוֹמְרִים . . . כָּל יְמֵי חַיֶּיךָ – לְהָבִיא לִימוֹת

---

1. Someone once asked the *Chazon Ish* why the Gemara (*Chullin* 67b) bothers proving that the *livyasan* is a kosher species of seafood. After all, the tradition is that in the future Hashem will personally (as it were) give the righteous to eat of this creature's flesh. The *Chazon Ish* replied that, apparently, unless the Torah clearly permits something, one may not even partake of a meal prepared by the Creator Himself!

חַיֶּיךָ הָעוֹלָם הַזֶּה, כֹּל יְמֵי חַיֶּיךָ לְהָבִיא לִימוֹת הַמָּשִׁיחַ.

בָּרוּךְ הַמָּקוֹם, בָּרוּךְ הוּא. בָּרוּךְ שֶׁנָּתַן תּוֹרָה לְעַמּוֹ

הַמָּשִׁיחַ — [Ben Zoma explained it]: "all the days of your life" includes the nights as well. But the Sages declare that [the addition of] "all" includes the era of Mashiach.

It was mentioned earlier (p. 36) that there are actually two distinct mitzvos in the Torah concerning the remembrance of the Exodus — a daily recitation, and the special retelling of the story of the Exodus which is required once a year, on Pesach night. It is the *daily* mitzvah that Rabbi Elazar and Ben Zoma were discussing, and according to Ben Zoma there will be no mitzvah of remembering *Yetzias Mitzrayim* in the times of *Mashiach* (see *Berachos* 12b).

Many commentators have noted that the *Rambam* does not count this daily mitzvah of recalling the Exodus in his list of 613 mitzvos, and many possible explanations have been proposed. The following answer is related in the name of *Rav Chaim Soloveitchik*. Since the *Rambam* rules (*Krias Shema* 1:3) that the *halachah* is in accordance with the view of Ben Zoma that mentioning *Yetzias Mitzrayim* is obligatory at nights as well, it follows that this mitzvah will no longer be in practice in Messianic days, as mentioned above. One of the Rambam's fourteen guidelines for a commandment's inclusion in the list of 613 mitzvos is that one which is not binding for all generations should not be counted. Thus, due to its "temporary" status, the daily mitzvah of recalling the Exodus is not listed.

However, this explanation presents a difficulty. The reason Ben Zoma gives for this mitzvah becoming nullified in the Messianic era is based on the verse in *Yirmiyahu* 23:7: "Behold, the days will come when it will no longer be said, 'Praise be to Hashem Who brought up the Children of Israel from the land of Egypt,' but rather, 'Praise be to Hashem Who has brought up . . . the descendants of the House of Israel . . . from all the lands to which I have banished them, that they should [again] dwell in their Land.' " That is, the miraculous, contemporary events of this future epoch will overshadow the events of the Exodus, which are only remote historical memories. Given this reasoning, we would expect Ben Zoma to hold that the *other* mitzvah — the once-yearly obligation to retell the story of *Yetzias Mitzrayim*, on Pesach — should also be rescinded in the Messianic age. Yet we find that the *Rambam* does indeed include this mitzvah on his list of 613! Why is there a difference between these two mitzvos?

your life' indicates the world in its present state. *'All the days of your life'* includes the days of the Messiah."

B lessed is the Omnipresent. Blessed is He. Blessed is He Who gave the Torah to His people, Israel. Blessed is He.

This question is raised by the *Pachad Yitzchak*, who suggests the following answer. We are enjoined on Pesach to feel *ourselves* as if we have personally experienced the bondage and liberation of our ancestors in Egypt. Thus, regarding the mitzvah to retell the Exodus story on the *Seder* night, it cannot be said that "contemporary" experiences will dwarf "remote" ones in this case, since the events of the Exodus are always viewed as the most contemporary of all — "taking place" anew every year.

בָּרוּךְ הַמָּקוֹם בָּרוּךְ הוּא ... — **Blessed is the Omnipresent; Blessed is He ...**

Some commentators suggest that this fourfold benediction corresponds to the four kinds of sons which the Haggadah is about to discuss. In order to establish how each expression relates to a particular one of the sons, it is necessary to first clarify the term מָקוֹם (translated here as "Omnipresent," but literally "place") as a reference to Hashem!

The name מָקוֹם is used to refer to the attribute of self-constraint — i.e. just as a "place" is an area with clearly delineated boundaries, so Hashem causes His Presence to be concentrated within delineated parameters. When Moses wished to "see" (i.e. perceive) Hashem, He told him, "Behold, there is a place (מָקוֹם) with Me" (*Shemos* 33:21). The words "there is a מָקוֹם with Me" are interpreted to mean that since Hashem's Presence, in Its true dimensions, is too overwhelming to be beheld by any human being (ibid.), He told Moses that He would cause a "contraction," as it were, of His Presence so that He could be "seen" by him.

According to *Ramban* (*Shemos* 25:1), the *Mishkan* (Tabernacle) in the desert (and, for that matter, the Temple in Jerusalem) was to serve in this role, as a perpetuation of the Revelation of Hashem on Mount Sinai. In the *Mishkan* He would cause His Presence to "dwell" (be concentrated) over the Tablets of the Covenant in the Holy Ark, from where He would communicate with Moses. As such it would serve as a focal point through which Torah wisdom may be attained. In this sense a Torah scholar may also be considered as a sort of resting place for the *Shechinah* (Divine Presence). Thus it is quite appropriate that the term מָקוֹם be used to parallel the wise and righteous son.

יִשְׂרָאֵל, בָּרוּךְ הוּא. כְּנֶגֶד אַרְבָּעָה בָנִים דִּבְּרָה תוֹרָה: אֶחָד חָכָם, וְאֶחָד רָשָׁע, וְאֶחָד תָּם, וְאֶחָד שֶׁאֵינוֹ יוֹדֵעַ לִשְׁאוֹל.

The plain, unembellished praise of "Blessed is He," which is repeated twice, corresponds to the wicked son and the son unable to question, for one is obligated to praise Hashem for any misfortune which befalls him just as he does when good fortune comes to him (*Berachos* 54a). Even the unfortunate occurrence of a *wicked* or apathetic son demands thanks and praise of Hashem. (See *Shemos* 12:27 and Rashi ad loc.)

The simple son, whose question is a crude "What is this," is searching for direction from his parents and teachers. He has no idea how to find his bearings in a complicated and confusing world. Of such a child we say, "Blessed is the One Who has given the Torah (the source of eternal guidance) to His people." For the Gemara, (*Sotah* 21), expounding upon the verses "a mitzvah is a candle and the Torah is light" (*Mishlei* 6:23) and "when you are walking, it will guide you" (ibid. 6:22), explains that the Torah protects man from pitfalls and erroneous decisions, as a light does for a man who is traveling in the dead of night. Thus, this simple son, who is stranded at the crossroads of life, will have the light of Torah to guide him on the correct path.

בָּרוּךְ הַמָּקוֹם . . . בָּרוּךְ שֶׁנָּתַן תּוֹרָה לְעַמּוֹ יִשְׂרָאֵל . . . כְּנֶגֶד אַרְבָּעָה בָנִים דִּבְּרָה תוֹרָה וכו' — **Blessed is the Omnipresent . . . Blessed is He Who gave the Torah to His people, Israel . . . The Torah addresses itself to four sons, etc.**

What is the connection of ideas from one sentence to the next in this section of the Haggadah and why is this benediction a preface to the discussion of the four sons?

In reference to the wicked son, the verse in *Shemos* (12:26) states, "And it shall be, when your children will say to you, 'What is this service of yours?' that you should say, 'It is a *pesach* sacrifice, . . .' And the people bowed down and prostrated themselves." On this verse the *Yalkut Shimoni* (*Bo* 18) comments that the children of Israel were thus told a distressing prophecy — that the Torah would one day be forgotten by their descendants [for otherwise, why would they not know of the paschal sacrifice on their own?]. Despite the distressing news, the people "bowed down and prostrated themselves." Perhaps the explanation for this ties into the fact that it was a relief for them to hear that the wicked among their descendants would not be wicked

The Torah addresses itself to four sons — one is wise, one is wicked, one is naive, and one is unable to ask.

---

because of some inherent baseness or corruption of the spirit, but, rather, because of sheer ignorance of the Torah. In its own way this was reassuring, for the study of Torah can rectify this shortcoming. The people, therefore, gave thanks to Hashem for having given Torah to His people Israel, and through the Torah we know that we will, with Hashem's help, always be able to redirect even those of our children who may stray. It is in this vein that this blessing serves as the lead into the discussion of the full gamut of children.

בָּרוּךְ שֶׁנָּתַן תּוֹרָה לְעַמּוֹ יִשְׂרָאֵל — **Blessed is He Who gave the Torah to His people, Israel.**

In his explanation of the Blessing over the Torah that is recited daily, the *Vilna Gaon* writes that the phrase אֲשֶׁר בָּחַר בָּנוּ... וְנָתַן לָנוּ אֶת תּוֹרָתוֹ (Who has chosen us . . . and has given us the Torah) expresses two distinct stages in the sanctification process of Israel. First the Jews were "chosen" on the second of Sivan when told by Hashem that they were to be a "kingdom of priests and a holy nation" (*Shemos* 19:6), and then they were given the Torah during the Revelation at Mount Sinai, four days later.

The expression employed by the Hagaddah suggests both elements of this double theme, i.e. שֶׁנָּתַן תּוֹרָה, *Who gave the Torah,* suggests the actual giving of Torah, and לְעַמּוֹ יִשְׂרָאֵל, *to His people, Israel,* suggests the choice of Israel as Hashem's nation.

Further, relative to its placement at this point, before the exegetical section of the Hagaddah begins, it may be that this paragraph constitutes an abbreviated form of the daily Torah blessing itself.

אֶחָד חָכָם וְאֶחָד רָשָׁע וכו' — **one is wise, one is wicked, etc.**

The *Baal Haggadah* introduces each of the four types of sons with the term אֶחָד, *one.* Would a straightforward listing of the four sons without the introductory אֶחָד (one) not be sufficient?

The *Maharal of Prague* notes that all of the verses cited regarding the different types of sons are couched in the singular, בִּנְךָ, (your son), while the text for the wicked son refers to בְּנֵיכֶם (your sons) in the plural.

On this basis, perhaps the significance of this specific use of language comes to teach us two important insights about child rearing. Firstly, each child must be regarded as an individual (בִּנְךָ), with his own strengths, weaknesses, unique needs and concerns in his relationship with his parents. Secondly, our failure to approach our children in such an individualistic and sensitive manner is likely to

חָכָם מַה הוּא אוֹמֵר? מָה הָעֵדֹת וְהַחֻקִים וְהַמִּשְׁפָּטִים אֲשֶׁר צִוָּה יהוה אֱלֹהֵינוּ אֶתְכֶם?[1] וְאַף אַתָּה אֱמָר לוֹ כְּהִלְכוֹת הַפֶּסַח, אֵין מַפְטִירִין אַחַר הַפֶּסַח אֲפִיקוֹמָן.

רָשָׁע מַה הוּא אוֹמֵר? מָה הָעֲבֹדָה הַזֹּאת לָכֶם?[2] לָכֶם וְלֹא לוֹ, וּלְפִי שֶׁהוֹצִיא אֶת עַצְמוֹ מִן הַכְּלָל, כָּפַר בְּעִקָּר — וְאַף אַתָּה הַקְהֵה אֶת שִׁנָּיו וֶאֱמָר לוֹ,

---

result in the disastrous בְּנֵיכֶם situation, akin to what we find so prevalent in society today.

Another approach may be taken to explain why the apparently extraneous word אֶחָד is used. The Gemara (*Shabbos* 138b) quotes a verse from *Amos* 8:12: "Behold, days are coming . . . and they will travel from sea to sea . . . to seek out the word of Hashem, but they will not find it." Rabbi Shimon bar Yochai commented on this verse, "Heaven forbid that the Torah should ever be forgotten from Israel! Is it not stated, 'It shall not be forgotten from the mouths of their descendants'? Rather, the prophet means to say that people will not be able to find a clear halachic opinion or a lucid explanation of the *mishnayos* in one place (i.e. Torah knowledge will not be forgotten, but it will not be concentrated in any particular place)."

The *Maharal of Prague,* in his commentary on this Gemara, explains that since Israel and the Torah are "one and the same" (i.e. their essences are inextricably bound together), they share historical fate. Just as Israel, the ultimate "*one* nation in the world" (*Shmuel II* 7:23), has been forced into exile, being scattered in small groups throughout the earth, so too the Torah has been forced into a situation where it is fragmented into many small "pieces," and dispersed throughout the land.

Rav Hutner, zt"l, carries this comparison one step further. Just as the dispersion of the Jewish people weakens it physically, causing it to be vulnerable to harsh treatment by its host nations, so, too, the Torah, through its dispersal, becomes more susceptible to attacks from foreign cultures and ideas, making it impossible for seekers of the truth to find clear explanations and rulings.

As previously explained (p. 44), the wickedness of the "wicked son" is not due to any inherent spiritual depravity or corruption, but, rather, to the Torah's having been forgotten during the last two millennia of exile. In light of Maharal's teaching that a major cause of the forgetting of the Torah is the breakup and dispersal of the Jewish people, the Haggadah uses the expression אֶחָד חָכָם וְאֶחָד רָשָׁע וכו׳, *one is wise, one*

W hat does the wise son say? "What are the testimonies, the statutes, and the laws which HASHEM, our God, has commanded you?"[1] And you, too, should tell him the laws of Pesach: "It is forbidden to eat anything after the korban pesach."

W hat does the wicked son say? "What is this service to you?"[2] "To you," but not to himself. Since he excludes himself from the group, he denies everything. You, too, should set his teeth on edge, and say to him: "It

---

(1) *Devarim* 6:20. (2) *Shemos* 12:26.

---

is wicked, etc.), breaking up the sons into four distinct divisions, to emphasize that it is because of the isolation of people into small distinct and unconnected groups that the phenomenon of the "wicked son" occurs.

חָכָם מַה הוּא אוֹמֵר ''מָה הָעֵדֹת וכו' . . . וְאַף אַתָּה אֱמָר לוֹ כְּהִלְכוֹת הַפֶּסַח וכו' — **What does the wise son say? "What are the testimonies, the statutes, etc." . . . And you, too, should tell him the laws of pesach etc.** What is it about this question that indicates that it is asked by a wise son? Also, in what way is our answer relevant to the concerns of this son?

As explained later (p. 48), the wicked son's use of the word "you" is understood in a negative sense, the implication being that he is withdrawing himself from the rest of the congregation of Israel. This is because he asks, "What is this service to you?" — "to you," but not to me. When the wise, righteous son uses the word, however, it is in an entirely different sense: "What are the testimonies . . . which Hashem. . . has commanded you?" — the *commandment* was issued to you, but not to me. Due to his intense humility he does not see himself as being worthy of being a part of the sacred community to whom Hashem communicates His commandments, although he certainly has every intention to scrupulously carry out those commandments.

The response to the wise son's exaggerated humility is that everything — even virtuous actions and attitudes — has a limit. Eating the meat of the *pesach* sacrifice is a mitzvah, but the Torah forbids it after eating the *afikoman*. So too humility is a desirable trait, yet there comes a time when it is counter-productive and even destructive. The wise son must also learn the boundaries of modesty and understand that he, like all Jews, is a vital member of the Covenant of Hashem, and not a tangential participant.

רָשָׁע מַה הוּא אוֹמֵר . . . וְאַף אַתָּה . . . וְאֱמָר לוֹ בַּעֲבוּר זֶה וכו' — **What does**

בַּעֲבוּר זֶה עָשָׂה יהוה לִי בְּצֵאתִי מִמִּצְרָיִם.' לִי וְלֹא לוֹ,
אִלּוּ הָיָה שָׁם לֹא הָיָה נִגְאָל.

תָּם מָה הוּא אוֹמֵר? מַה זֹּאת? וְאָמַרְתָּ אֵלָיו, בְּחֹזֶק יָד

---

the wicked son say? ... You, too, ... and say to him: "It is because
of this, etc."

The wicked son's question is described in the Torah as follows: "And
it shall be, when your children say to you, 'What is this service to you?'
(Shemos 12:26-27) And you shall say, It is a pesach sacrifice unto God,
Who passed over the houses of the Children of Israel in Egypt when He
smote the Egyptians and saved our houses.' " Surprisingly, when the
Haggadah discusses the answer to be given to the wicked son, it does
not mention the response given in this passage of the Torah but rather
quotes from a verse in the next chapter (Shemos 13:8), concerning the
answer to the "son who is unable to ask." Why does the Haggadah
choose to ignore the answer specifically prescribed by the Torah for the
wicked son?

The Netziv, in his commentary on the Chumash, explains that of the
four responses to the various sons mentioned in the Torah, all of them
begin with the phrase, "You shall tell him," or "You shall say unto your
son" — all, that is, except for the wicked son, whose response is
prefaced only by "And you shall say." The Haggadah perceives in this
change of wording an implication that the statement "It is a pesach
sacrifice ..." is not meant to be addressed to the wicked son as a
response, but is meant to be proclaimed by the father, to reinforce his
own faith in the Pesach rituals, after having been challenged by the
heretical scoffing of the wicked son.[1]

There is another interesting linguistic difference, noted by Chasam
Sofer in the responses of the three other sons as opposed to that of the
wicked one. The wicked son's answer is the only one which mentions
the "houses" of the Children of Israel. Perhaps this could be explained
by the fact that the phrasing of his question is, as the Haggadah
explains, an indication of his desire to separate himself from the
community of Israel. Thus, it is especially appropriate that the question
is dealt with by stressing that the sole reason the Jews merited salvation
was that they were undivided and considered themselves a united

---

1. This sort of self-strengthening response to blasphemous statements made by the
irreverent actually has a precedent in the Tanach. In Malachi 3:14 it says: "You have said,
'It is worthless to worship God. What have we gained by keeping his watch and by walking
with obsequious humility before Him?' ... Then the God-fearing people spoke to one
another, etc." The God-fearing people did not bother to respond to the sacrilege of these
scoffers, but rather turned and "spoke to one other," in order to uphold their own beliefs.

is because of this that HASHEM did so for me when I went out of Egypt."[1] "For me," but not for him. Had he been there, he would not have been redeemed.

What does the naive son say? "What is this?" Say to him:

---

(1) *Shemos* 13:8.

---

community. This concept of national unity is implied by the use of the word "house," for a house is what combines a group of individuals into one integrated unit.[1]

מָה הָעֲבוֹדָה הַזֹּאת לָכֶם — **What is this service to you?**

The *Yalkut Shimoni* (Bo 18) derives from this verse that the bad tidings the nation of Israel received that day will come when the Torah would be forgotten by their descendants (see p. 44). What exactly in this verse indicates that the wickedness of the "wicked" sons would be based upon ignorance of the Torah rather than upon spiritual degeneracy and corruption of character?

The *Beis HaLevi* (in his commentary on the *Chumash*, *Parashas Bo*) derives from the word הַזֹּאת, *this*, that the wicked son does not wish to say that we should not believe in God or worship Him. Rather, he does not believe that *this* particular service, of the Pesach sacrifice, is the appropriate manner of showing our devotion to Hashem; he thinks a more meaningful, perhaps more contemporary, form of worship should be employed.

It is largely because of forgetfulness of the Torah that such an attitude develops. If the real reasons and true significance of the mitzvos — both revealed and hidden — were retained, people would never feel the necessity to supplant the Torah's prescribed methods of worship with new innovations. The study of Torah has the ability to invigorate one's mitzvah performance with a sense of freshness and meaning which negates the need to seek the "new and thrilling." Perhaps it is this implication of the word זאת that prompted the *Yalkut* to comment that the "wickedness" dicussed here is based on ignorance rather than on evil intent.

תָּם מַה הוּא אוֹמֵר? מַה זֹּאת? — **The simple son — what does he say? "What is this?"**

This son does not choose the rebellious ways of the wicked son. He does follow the Torah's word; but he asks, "Why do it *this* way?" implying that he has alternate ideas in mind, unlike the wise and righteous son who is unwavering in his devotion to the ways of the Torah.

---

1. See *Rashi* (*Shemos* 12:46) where he defines "house" as the group who congregate to eat of the *pesach* offering.

הוֹצִיאָנוּ יהוה מִמִּצְרַיִם מִבֵּית עֲבָדִים.[1]

וְשֶׁאֵינוֹ יוֹדֵעַ לִשְׁאוֹל, אַתְּ פְּתַח לוֹ. שֶׁנֶּאֱמַר, וְהִגַּדְתָּ לְבִנְךָ בַּיּוֹם הַהוּא לֵאמֹר, בַּעֲבוּר זֶה עָשָׂה יהוה לִי בְּצֵאתִי מִמִּצְרָיִם.[2]

יָכוֹל מֵרֹאשׁ חֹדֶשׁ, תַּלְמוּד לוֹמַר בַּיּוֹם הַהוּא. אִי בַּיּוֹם הַהוּא, יָכוֹל מִבְּעוֹד יוֹם, תַּלְמוּד לוֹמַר בַּעֲבוּר

To such an attitude, the response must be *With a strong hand did Hashem take us out of Egypt.* Just as Hashem's salvation was powerful and unequivocal, so you, simple son, must free yourself of your hesitation and doubts to find personal redemption in powerful and unflinching faith.

וְשֶׁאֵינוֹ יוֹדֵעַ לִשְׁאוֹל אַתְּ פְּתַח לוֹ — **And regarding the one who is unable to ask, you open conversation with him.**

The word אַתְּ ("you") employed here is the word generally used for the feminine gender. This is to insinuate that the proper method for dealing with this type of child is to speak softly and lovingly to him; as *Rashi* comments (*Shemos* 19:3), Hashem told Moses to speak forcefully to the men, but to speak to the women in a softer tone. Unlike the "simple" son, this one is completely innocent and comes with no preconceived notions. If dealt with in a warm and compassionate manner, he will respond to the Torah's message.

Another explanation for the unusual use of the word אַתְּ in this context may be that since this son seems to be lacking even the slightest knowledge of his heritage, he must be taught everything from the beginning — from אלף till תיו (from "A to Z")!

יָכוֹל מֵרֹאשׁ חֹדֶשׁ — **We might have held . . . from the first of the month.**

Why would anyone have thought that this mitzvah should take place on *Rosh Chodesh?* Is there any particular significance of this day which would suggest that this day is an appropriate time for a discussion of *Yetzias Mitzrayim?*

The chapter (*Shemos* 12) from which the quoted verse (בַּעֲבוּר זֶה וכו', *Because of this . . .*) is taken begins with the commandment to "sanctify" the New Moon (i.e. to have the *Sanhedrin* officially declare it as *Rosh Chodesh*): "And Hashem spoke to Moses and Aaron, saying, 'This [part of the] month shall be [sanctified] unto you as *Rosh*

"HASHEM took us out of Egypt, from the house of slaves, by strength of hand."[1]

A nd regarding the one who is unable to ask, you open conversation with him, as it is said: *"And you will tell your son on that day, saying, 'It is because of this that HASHEM did so for me when I went out of Egypt.' "*[2]

W e might have held [that we should begin telling the son who is unable to ask of the redemption from Egypt] from the first of the month, but the Torah tells us: *"On that day."* Since it says *"on that day,"* we might have held that we should begin while it is still day. But the Torah says: *"Because*

---

(1) *Shemos* 13:14. (2) Ibid. v. 8.

Chodesh.' " (This is the traditional Rabbinical interpretation of the verse — see Rashi ad loc. although it is not the simple translation.) It was previously mentioned (p. 15) that the sanctification of specific times of the year by the Jewish court takes place only by virtue of the Jewish people's own intrinsic sanctity. (It is for this reason that the blessings for *Rosh Chodesh* and the festivals — whose dates are also determined by the fixing of *Rosh Chodesh* — end off with, "Blessed is Hashem, Who has sanctified *Israel and Rosh Chodesh*," or ". . . has sanctified *Israel and* the festivals.)

It was also mentioned (p. 33) that although the appellation of "Children of Israel" in a biological sense was used for the Jews long before the Exodus (see *Shemos* 1:7, 1:9, 1:12, 2:23, et al.), the spiritual concept of the "sanctity of Israel" was not applicable until the Exodus (see *Rashi* on *Yevamos* 46a) or possibly until the giving of the Torah (see *Rambam, Issurei Biah* 13:1). Given this duality of Israel's identity, we are presented with a difficulty. If the Jews lacked the crucial ingredient of "sanctity of Israel" at the time, how could they be given the law of sanctifying the New Moon two weeks prior to the Exodus? What was the point in giving a mitzvah to people who were incapable of carrying it out? Apparently we must conclude that the status of "sanctity of Israel" did not come into effect all at one time; there was a preliminary stage when they were partially imbued with this dimension to be culminated at a later date. The initial "installment" of our sanctified status was the giving of the very first mitzvah — that of sanctifying the New Moon. Since this important milestone in our assumption of sanctity took place on *Rosh Chodesh* Nisan, we might entertain the idea that the mitzvah to discuss *Yetzias*

זֶה. בַּעֲבוּר זֶה לֹא אָמַרְתִּי אֶלָּא בְּשָׁעָה שֶׁיֵּשׁ מַצָּה
וּמָרוֹר מֻנָּחִים לְפָנֶיךָ.

מִתְּחִלָּה, עוֹבְדֵי עֲבוֹדָה זָרָה הָיוּ אֲבוֹתֵינוּ, וְעַכְשָׁו
קֵרְבָנוּ הַמָּקוֹם לַעֲבוֹדָתוֹ. שֶׁנֶּאֱמַר, וַיֹּאמֶר

Mitzrayim — the events that effected our total transformation into
the *"Am Kadosh"* (sanctified nation) — should take place on that very
day.

תַּלְמוּד לוֹמַר בַּעֲבוּר זֶה — But the Torah says: "Because of this."

The words בַּעֲבוּר זֶה, *because of this*, are excerpted from the answer
of the "son who is unable to ask." One wonders of what import it is
that the source for the mitzvah of retelling the story of the Exodus is
rooted in the answer provided this particular son. The question is
made even sharper when we consider that one of the main characteristics of this mitzvah — as opposed to the daily mitzvah of remembering
the Exodus — is that it should be carried out through question-and-an-
swer dialogue. Yet the source for the mitzvah of questions and
answers is from the response to the one son whose discussion of the
Exodus involves no question at all!

One of the basic patterns that can be discerned in the Torah's
mitzvos is that Hashem commands us to dedicate to Him the first
products of any of our endeavors. By doing so we indicate that all our
creativity and abilities are harnessed to His service. The firstborn child
and animal are consecrated to Him; the first of the fruits are brought
to the Temple; the first portion separated from produce or from dough
is given to the Kohen, etc. The son who is unable to ask is also at the
beginning of a process — he has never thought out matters before and
is just starting to formulate his outlook on life. The Torah teaches us
that we should ensure that this initial formulation of life's path finds its
root in the basic faith regarding the sanctity and special mission of our
nation, as exemplified by the story of the Exodus. The fact that
Hashem took us out of Egypt to be His people forms the "preamble"
to the Ten Commandments, and is mentioned scores of times in the
admonishments of the Prophets, because it is the cornerstone of
Jewish history and faith. Thus, the son who cannot even ask a proper
question and has no preconceptions is especially suited to integrate
the message of Torah faith. It is he who is therefore the prototype
vehicle through which the mitzvah to remember *Yetzias Mitzrayim* is
conveyed to us.

of this." I only say "because of this" at a time when matzah and maror are placed before you.

At first our forefathers were idolaters, but now the Omnipresent has brought us close to His worship, as it says:

מִתְּחִלָּה עוֹבְדֵי עֲבוֹדָה זָרָה הָיוּ אֲבוֹתֵינוּ — **At first our forefathers were idolaters.**

Is it really appropriate for us to disparage our ancestors by bringing up this embarrassing chapter of their past? Granted that this information helps to amplify our debt of gratitude to Hashem, by portraying the contrast, but does our obligation to praise Hashem have to come at the expense of our forefathers' prestige?

The *Baal Haggadah,* commenting on the verse in *Shemos* (12:12), points out (p. 82), that the salvation of the Children of Israel was done "personally" by Hashem, and not through some heavenly messenger or earthly agent. This may be explained in the following manner: Through the "judgments that were done against the gods of the Egyptians" (ibid.), everyone understood that Hashem alone is in control of the Universe, and that the forces of nature and other agents of His will are totally subservient to Him (see *Ramban, Shemos* 13:16), and that the deification of any material object is an absolute falsehood. This is one of the main themes of the *Seder* service — to emphasize our realization of the utter Unity of Hashem in the Universe.

The *midrash* offers an interesting interpretation for a verse in *Iyov* (14:4), which states, מִי יִתֵּן טָהוֹר מִטָּמֵא לֹא אֶחָד, *Who can bring forth the pure from the impure — no one* (לֹא אֶחָד)!: Who could possibly cause Abraham to emerge from Terach, Hezekiah out of Ahaz, etc? Was it not the "One" of the Universe (Hashem)? The *Ohr Gedalyahu* explains this *midrash* as follows: Under natural circumstances it is impossible for something as holy and pure as the Patriarch Abraham to emerge from a Terach. Normally, impure breeds only impure. The fact that Abraham came from an idolatrous background and ancestry is a proof that there was supernatural, Divine intervention in his life, and is thus testimony to the "One" of the Universe. It is thus indeed appropriate to mention this seemingly ignoble item of history at the *Seder*.

וְעַכְשָׁיו קֵרְבָנוּ הַמָּקוֹם לַעֲבוֹדָתוֹ — **But now the Omnipresent has brought us close to His worship.**

This phrase implies that Hashem took the initiative and brought Abraham close to Him. This seems to contradict the well-known *midrash* (*Bereishis Rabbah* 39:1) that Abraham came to know his Creator through logical deduction and honest soul-searching.

יְהוֹשֻׁעַ אֶל כָּל הָעָם, כֹּה אָמַר יהוה אֱלֹהֵי יִשְׂרָאֵל,
בְּעֵבֶר הַנָּהָר יָשְׁבוּ אֲבוֹתֵיכֶם מֵעוֹלָם, תֶּרַח אֲבִי אַבְרָהָם
וַאֲבִי נָחוֹר, וַיַּעַבְדוּ אֱלֹהִים אֲחֵרִים. וָאֶקַּח אֶת אֲבִיכֶם
אֶת אַבְרָהָם מֵעֵבֶר הַנָּהָר, וָאוֹלֵךְ אוֹתוֹ בְּכָל אֶרֶץ כְּנָעַן,
וָאַרְבֶּה אֶת זַרְעוֹ, וָאֶתֶּן לוֹ אֶת יִצְחָק. וָאֶתֵּן לְיִצְחָק אֶת
יַעֲקֹב וְאֶת עֵשָׂו, וָאֶתֵּן לְעֵשָׂו אֶת הַר שֵׂעִיר לָרֶשֶׁת
אוֹתוֹ, וְיַעֲקֹב וּבָנָיו יָרְדוּ מִצְרָיִם.[1]

In reality there is no inconsistency here. My grandfather (the *Ohr
Yechezkel*) writes that even though a basic tenet of Judaism is that
every man has free will to choose for himself between good and evil,
we should not think that a person would be capable of arriving at the
proper decision were he not equipped with the logical mind and pure
spirit granted to him by Hashem. "If the Holy One, Blessed is He,
would not help [man] he would be unable to [vanquish] him, i.e. [the
yetzer hara]" (*Succah* 52b).

וָאֶקַּח אֶת . . . אַבְרָהָם . . . וָאֶתֵּן לוֹ אֶת יִצְחָק. וָאֶתֵּן לְיִצְחָק אֶת יַעֲקֹב וְאֶת עֵשָׂו
— **And I took . . . Abraham . . . and I gave Isaac unto him, and I gave
Jacob and Esau unto Isaac.**

The *Radak,* in his commentary (on *Yehoshua* 24:3), explains why
Ishmael is not mentioned in this historical outline [although Esau is].
The reason, he suggests, is the result of Sarah's request to Abraham,
גָּרֵשׁ הָאָמָה הַזֹּאת וְאֶת בְּנָהּ כִּי לֹא יִירַשׁ בֶּן הָאָמָה הַזֹּאת עִם בְּנִי עִם יִצְחָק, *Drive away
this maidservant and her son (Ishmael), for the son of that maidservant
he shall not inherit with my son, with Isaac* (*Bereishis* 21:10), and Abraham's compliance (ibid.). Thus, we see that with these words Ishmael
was effectively and permanently disowned from the house of Abraham. Esau, on the other hand, is considered to be a rightful heir of
Abraham's, as it says in this verse, quoted in the Haggadah: "to Esau
I gave Mount Seir to inherit" (*Yehoshua* 24:4).[1]

---

1. The *Pachad Yitzchak* (*Sefer HaZikaron* p. 56) expands on this theme, explaining with this
idea why the Torah refers to the tribes of Esau, אֵלֶּה אַלּוּפֵי אֱדוֹם לְמשְׁבֹתָם בְּאֶרֶץ אֲחֻזָּתָם, *according
to their settlements, in the land of their inheritance* (*Bereishis* 36:43), whereas concerning the
family of Ishmael it says, וְאֵלֶּה שְׁמֹתָם בְּחַצְרֵיהֶם וּבְטִירֹתָם, *And these are their names by their
encampments and their strongholds* (*Bereishis* 25:16). Esau has a legitimate right of possession in his land, but Ishmael has no permanent foothold, only temporary "encampments and
strongholds." He adds further that it is thus understandable why the modern descendants
of Ishmael (the Arab nations), as opposed to those of Edom (the European nations), are
constantly striving violently to assert some sort of sovereignty over the Land of Israel — the
hallmark of a son who has been disinherited and stops at nothing to acquire what he believes
to be his rightful share of that from which, in his eyes, he has been unjustly excluded.

"And Joshua said to all of the people, So says HASHEM the God of Israel, Of old, your forefathers dwelt beyond the river — Terach, the father of Abraham and the father of Nachor, and they worshiped other gods. And I took your father Abraham from beyond the river, and I led him throughout all the Land of Canaan, and I multiplied his seed, and I gave Isaac unto him, and I gave Jacob and Esau unto Isaac, and I gave unto Eisau Mount Seir to inherit, and Jacob and his sons went down to Egypt."[1]

(1) *Yehoshua* 24:2-4.

Another possible answer to this question is based on an explanation I once heard from my grandfather (the *Ohr Yechezkel*) as to why the verse quoted here refers to the wicked Esau with the verb וָאֶתֵּן ("and I gave"), which generally has the connotation of a benevolent gift. Since Esau and Jacob were in the womb together, he explained, it was possible for all the negative traits which might have genetically found their way into Jacob's character to be screened out and cast onto Esau. (This idea is also mentioned by the *Metzudas David*, ad loc.) Thus, in effect, Esau was indeed a great boon to the Patriarchs in that he served as a filter in purifying the soul of his brother. Hence, his birth was a benevolent gift. Accordingly, it is clear why Esau finds a place in this verse while Ishmael does not.

וָאַרְבֶּה אֶת זַרְעוֹ וָאֶתֶּן לוֹ אֶת יִצְחָק — **And I multiplied his seed, and I gave him Isaac.**

In order for this phrase not to be redundant we must interpret "offspring" to be a reference to Abraham's other children — those from Hagar and Keturah. The verse seems to present these descendants in a positive light, to serve as an illustration of the bounty Hashem showered upon the revered Patriarch. Yet, in *Bereishis* 25:6 we are told that Abraham effectively cut all these children off from contact with him and his primary family so that, as Rashi explains, they would not have an adverse effect on their spiritual development. How could this multitude of children, estranged by Abraham himself, be considered a blessing to him? We may add to this the question raised earlier, i.e. why Esau is considered to have been a "gift" to Isaac.

The *Zichron Niflaos* explains that Abraham was promised two things by Hashem: His descendants would be physically numerous; and that they would be spiritually superior, dedicating themselves to Hashem's service. One could argue that Isaac and Jacob should not be considered so righteous and deserving of the special privileged status and

בָּרוּךְ שׁוֹמֵר הַבְטָחָתוֹ לְיִשְׂרָאֵל, בָּרוּךְ הוּא. שֶׁהַקָּדוֹשׁ בָּרוּךְ הוּא חִשַּׁב אֶת הַקֵּץ, לַעֲשׂוֹת כְּמָה שֶׁאָמַר

---

reverence accorded them scores of times throughout Scripture and thereafter. After all, their righteousness was foretold, and hence guaranteed, by Hashem to Abraham; they achieved nothing on their own merit.

The answer to this claim is similar to that given by the Rambam (*Teshuvah* 6:5) regarding a similar question: Why were the Egyptians so severely penalized for persecuting the Israelites? Was their oppression not foretold, and thus pre-ordained by Hashem at the בְּרִית בֵּין הַבְּתָרִים, *Covenant Between the Parts* (*Bereishis* 15:13)? The *Rambam* refutes this argument by pointing out that the exact identities of the oppressors, and the extent of the oppression, were not established, and thus the Egyptians, by "volunteering" to play the role — and play it exceedingly cruelly — were indeed liable for the harsh punishments meted out to them.

Here too, the promise made to Abraham that his descendants would become a holy nation could have been fulfilled through any of his numerous offspring. The fact that it was Isaac and Jacob, rather than their siblings, who chose the role of piety and devotion to Hashem for themselves makes them praiseworthy and deserving of our veneration. Thus the "other" children played a positive role in the development of the Patriarchs' spiritual achievements, since Isaac and Jacob, by ignoring the example of their siblings and freely choosing to follow their father's path, merited all the promises given Abraham.

בָּרוּךְ שׁוֹמֵר הַבְטָחָתוֹ — Blessed is He Who keeps His promise.

Usually the verb used for keeping one's word is מְקַיֵּם, whereas שׁוֹמֵר is used in the sense of "keeping something in mind," without necessarily acting upon it. Seemingly, מְקַיֵּם would be a more apt usage. Moreover, it is certainly not much of a praise to say of someone who has promised something that he "keeps his pledge," and if this is so for mortal man, how much more so for Hashem, Who "is not a man, that He should be deceitful" (*Bamidbar* 23:19). Why, then, is this praise deemed appropriate at this point?

An explanation of the usage of the term שׁוֹמֵר, which I heard from Rabbi Groinem Lazewnik, *shlita,* may be given. As mentioned earlier, the Jews at the time of the Exodus did not, strictly speaking, merit redemption; they were on an exceedingly low spiritual level. Hashem "had to" (as it were) liberate them immediately, lest they sink

Blessed is He Who keeps His promise to Israel. Blessed is He. For the Holy One, Blessed is He, calcu-lated the end [of the exile], to do as He said to

---

to an even lower level, to a point where it would have been, so to speak, absolutely impossible to redeem them. Such an "early" salvation could not be done randomly, however; a period of tribulations of four hundred years had been decreed upon the Jews at the Covenant between the Parts, and this could not simply be abrogated. What Hashem did was to allow the period, between the birth of Isaac and the beginning of the enslavement to the Egyptians, to be included in this period of suffering, since this time could technically serve as a fulfilment of the decree, כִּי גֵר יִהְיֶה זַרְעֲךָ בְּאֶרֶץ לֹא לָהֶם, *your seed will be a wanderer in a land not their own. (Bereishis* 15:13). Thus, Hashem did more than just "keep" (מְקַיֵּם) his pledge; He *"ensured"* (שׁוֹמֵר) that it would be able to be kept by having it take place "ahead of schedule."[1]

שֶׁהַקָּדוֹשׁ בָּרוּךְ הוּא חִשַׁב אֶת הַקֵּץ וכו' — **For the Holy One, Blessed is He, calculated the end, etc.**

I have seen it written that the Heavenly advocate of the Egyptians complained to Hashem that it was unfair to release the Jews from their service to his people before the full "contract" was expired. The answer given to him was that a precedent had been set for such an interpretation by Pharaoh himself, many years earlier. When Jacob was first introduced to Pharaoh, the monarch, awed by his extraordinarily aged appearance, asked him how old he was. Jacob replied that he was really not so old, but that the many hardships and worries he had gone through made him look older than his 130 years (see *Bereishis* 47:8-9.) This explanation was apparently accepted by Pharaoh, and the precedent was set for reckoning a lesser amount, but painful time, as though it were more.

---

1. Rabbi Lazewnik offered a beautiful parable for this concept: A wealthy man, before his death, deposited a large sum of money with a trustee stipulating that it be used only for the purpose of marrying off his lone orphan daughter. The daughter came of marriageable age but suddenly took ill. Her mother approached the trustee and requested funds to pay for medical procedures needed to cure the daugher. The trustee refused, citing the deathbed instruction of the father. "Yes," the mother replied, "but if we don't cure her, there will be no daughter to marry."

Initially, Jews were supposed to be in Egypt for four hundred years but if they had stayed any longer, there would ח"ו not be a Jewish people left to redeem. This is reminiscent of the words of the *Rambam (Avodah Zarah* 1:3): "Yet a bit more and the the root that Abraham planted would have been uprooted and the children of Jacob would have reverted to the mistakes of the world and its [spiritual] wanderings."

לְאַבְרָהָם אָבִינוּ בִּבְרִית בֵּין הַבְּתָרִים, שֶׁנֶּאֱמַר, וַיֹּאמֶר
לְאַבְרָם, יָדֹעַ תֵּדַע כִּי גֵר יִהְיֶה זַרְעֲךָ בְּאֶרֶץ לֹא לָהֶם,
וַעֲבָדוּם וְעִנּוּ אֹתָם, אַרְבַּע מֵאוֹת שָׁנָה. וְגַם אֶת הַגּוֹי
אֲשֶׁר יַעֲבֹדוּ דָן אָנֹכִי, וְאַחֲרֵי כֵן יֵצְאוּ בִּרְכֻשׁ גָּדוֹל.

וַיְהִי מִקֵּץ שְׁלֹשִׁים שָׁנָה וְאַרְבַּע מֵאוֹת שָׁנָה וַיְהִי בְּעֶצֶם הַיּוֹם הַזֶּה יָצְאוּ כָּל צִבְאוֹת ה' מֵאֶרֶץ מִצְרָיִם, *And it was at the end of 430 years [after the Covenant between the Parts], and it was on that very day that all the legions of Hashem left the land of Egypt* (Shemos 12:41). *Rashi,* quoting the *Mechilta* , comments, "When the End came, Hashem did not delay even one moment. It was on the fifteenth of Nisan that the angels informed Abraham that he would have a son the following year (*Bereishis* 18:14). It was on that day (a year later) that Isaac was born, and it was on that day (several years earlier) that the edict of the Covenant Between the Parts (ibid. chap. 15) was decreed (that Abraham's descendants would be enslaved and per-secuted)."

The implication of the *Mechilta* is that the predictions of the Covenant Between the Parts became fulfilled *in their entirety* on this day, the 430th anniversary of its announcement — including the prophecy, וְאַחֲרֵי כֵן יֵצְאוּ בִּרְכֻשׁ גָּדוֹל, *and after this they shall leave (the land of their persecution) with great wealth* (ibid. 15:14). This seems to contradict the assertion of the *Vilna Gaon* (*Kol Eliyahu-Bo*) and the *Perashas Derachim* that the true redemption of the Israelites was not complete until the Splitting of the Red Sea seven days after the Exodus. At that time, when the Egyptians were punished by drowning "measure for measure" for having drowned the Jewish infants at the beginning of the period of persecution, and then the promise of "and after this they will leave with great wealth" was fulfilled when the riches of the drowned Egyptian soldiers were washed ashore at the feet of the Israelites. According to this, the final fulfillment of the Covenant did not take place on the exact anniversary of its enactment.

There may be no contradiction, however, if we consider the *Vilna Gaon's* comment in his *siddur* on the words מִמִּצְרַיִם גְּאַלְתָּנוּ וכו' וּמִבֵּית עֲבָדִים פְּדִיתָנוּ, *You redeemed us from Egypt and liberated us from the house of bondage.* He explains the seemingly repetitive expressions as an indica-tion that there were actually two distinct redemptions from the hands of the Egyptians: One, which took place on the fifteenth of Nisan, was from enslavement to them, and is referred to as "liberation from the house of bondage"; the other, which took place on the twenty-first of the month, at the Splitting of the Red Sea, was from general sub-servience and submission to the Egyptian authority, and is called

Avraham our father at the Covenant Between the Parts, as it is said, "And He said to Avram, Know that your offspring will be a stranger in a land not theirs, and they will serve them and they will torment them for four hundred years. But also the nation whom they will serve I will judge. Afterward, they will go out with great possessions."[1]

_____

(1) *Bereishis* 15:13-14.

_____

"redemption from Egypt." Thus, both positions can coexist: Freedom from bondage and persecution was indeed secured on the anniversary of the Covenant, as stated in the verse, and "it was on that very day that all the legions of Hashem left the land of Egypt"; however, a second stage, completely severing the Israelites' connection with Egyptians, took place a week later.

בָּרוּךְ שׁוֹמֵר הַבְטָחָתוֹ לְיִשְׂרָאֵל . . . שֶׁהַקּבָּ״ה חִשַּׁב אֶת הַקֵּץ . . . וְהִיא שֶׁעָמְדָה לַאֲבוֹתֵינוּ — Blessed is He Who keeps His promise to Israel . . . For the Holy One, Blessed is He, calculated the end . . . It [the Covenenat Between the Parts] has stood firm for our fathers. . . .

The Gemara in *Megillah* 10b states, "We have a tradition from the Men of the Great Assembly (a group of sages who lived in the fifth and fourth centuries B.C.E.) that whenever the word וַיְהִי ("and it was" or "and it happened") is employed, it is an implication of some misfortune that is involved in the narrative being presented." Quite a few counterexamples are produced by the Gemara, and in (almost) each case some negative angle is found in the story in question to explain the use of this sorrowful term. One verse in particular, which is *not* cited in the Gemara's discussion, seems to clearly contradict the rule: וַיְהִי מִקֵּץ (וַיְהִי), *And it was* שְׁלֹשִׁים שָׁנָה וְאַרְבַּע מֵאוֹת שָׁנָה וכו׳ יָצְאוּ כָּל צִבְאוֹת ה׳ מֵאֶרֶץ מִצְרָיִם at the end 430 years . . . that all the legions of Hashem left Egypt (*Shemos* 12:41). What possible note of pessimism could be found in this instance to justify the negative connotation of וַיְהִי?

As previously discussed, Hashem's redemption of the Children of Israel after only 210 years was justified on the grounds that the 400 years stipulated in the Covenant between the Parts (*Bereishis* 15) were reckoned from the time of Isaac's birth, when the phrase "your offspring will be a stranger in a land not theirs" (ibid. 15:13) was first realized. This in itself would be insufficient, since the 400-year time frame related to *all* facets of the decree — including "they will enslave and persecute them" — not only to the decree that they would be strangers.[1] In addition, the intensity of the enslavement and the

_____

1. See *Ramban* ad loc. for a textual answer to this question.

large numbers of Jews subject to it were so great that Hashem considered it a mitigating factor that allowed Him to count the 210 "concentrated" years of hardship as being equivalent to 400 years of "plain" persecution.

Nevertheless, since the four hundred-year decree was not fulfilled in its literal sense, the Jews became liable to many future persecutions, all "outgrowths," as it were, of the Covenant. Had the Israelites been able to withstand the literal implementation of the entire prophecy, they would not have experienced any further travail in the desert nor after their entry to the Promised Land *(Beis HaLevi — Shemos)*. Since these future oppressions, which the people were destined to experience, were a result of the premature Exodus from Egypt, the use of the word וַיְהִי, which conveys misfortune, is justified in this context.

With this in mind we may better understand the connection of ideas from this paragraph to the next. Because "the Holy One, Blessed is He, calculated the end of the bondage" the way He did, we were destined to experience the cruelty of the nations who "rise against us to annihilate us, but it is this (the Covenant) that has stood by our fathers and us, and the Holy One, Blessed is He, rescues us from their hand."

כְּמוֹ שֶׁאָמַר לְאַבְרָהָם אָבִינוּ בִּבְרִית בֵּין הַבְּתָרִים — **as He said to our father Abraham at the Covenant Between the Parts . . ..**

The choice of name — the Covenant between the Parts — seems rather unusual, yet this name, coined by the *Baal HaHaggadah,* has remained its name throughout Rabbinic literature. Would the events of that chapter not be more aptly described by the momentous prophecies which it entailed rather than by the physical method used to symbolically seal the covenant?

The *Aruch HaShulchan*, in a novel fashion, explains that in this covenant of the one-half of one animal was placed across from the half of *another* animal (rather than across from its corresponding piece). Based on his interpretation, we may suggest that this was to show Abraham a prophecy of comfort regarding the future of his children in exile. As Rashi points out there, the animals represented the various nations that would subdue Israel; perhaps the cutting and separation of the pieces was to show Abraham that their very dispersal to the far corners of the earth would serve to protect them from annihilation. Whenever they would be persecuted by one nation, there would always remain some other country where they would be safe. By separating them and not having them remain concentrated in one area, under one ruler, their safety would be assured. Thus, the appellation "Covenant Between the Parts" is quite an appropriate one, since it symbolizes one of the basic means by which Hashem would protect His people throughout all their bitter tribulations and in their many exiles.

וְגַם אֶת הַגּוֹי אֲשֶׁר יַעֲבֹדוּ דָּן אָנֹכִי — but also upon the nation which they shall serve will I execute judgment.

Rashi, in his commentary on this verse (Bereishis 15:14), explains "Will I execute judgment" as referring to the ten plagues inflicted upon the Egyptians. The Haggadah proves that the punishments the Egyptian army suffered at the Red Sea were ten times worse than anything they endured in Egypt. If so, asks the *Pachad Yitzchak*, why does the prophecy at the Covenant between the Parts mention the plagues in Egypt, which were the lesser of the two forms of punishments?

Another question is raised by the *Avnei Neizer*. We are told (*Shem MiShmuel* p.113) that the Israelites, being in an exceptionally low spiritual state, could not be redeemed from Egypt until they elevated their status by performing two mitzvos — circumcision and the paschal sacrifice. At the Red Sea, however, in spite of the angelic protest that the Jews were undeserving of salvation, Moshe was told, מַה תִּצְעַק אֵלָי דַּבֵּר אֶל בְּנֵי יִשְׂרָאֵל וְיִסָּעוּ, "Why do you cry out to Me? Speak unto the Children of Israel and let them journey forth (into the sea)" (*Shemos* 14:15). Why was no process of purification or expiation necessary there?

In the *Chasam Sofer's* commentary *Toras Moshe*, the author discusses the different roles played by Abraham and Isaac in the *Akeidah*, when Abraham was commanded to sacrifice his only son to Hashem (*Bereishis* 22). He proposes that Abraham's actions represented the aspect of תּוֹרָה שֶׁבִּכְתָב, the Written Torah, whereas Isaac's part exemplified the idea of תּוֹרָה שֶׁבְּעַל פֶּה, the Oral, interpretational, Torah. Abraham was obeying a specific decree communicated to him directly by Hashem, much like the Written Torah — a clearly elucidated statement from Hashem Himself. Isaac's consent to be sacrificed, however, was not based on a direct command heard from Hashem, but rather on his complete faith in his father to comprehend, interpret and carry out the word of Hashem, reminiscent of the concept of the Oral Law.

The *Avnei Neizer* suggests that whereas the course of action exhibited at the crossing of the Red Sea was an example of following not the apparent Divine directive (Written Torah) but rather the interpretation of the legitimate bearers of Hashem's will (Oral Torah). We read that the pillar of smoke, which symbolized the Presence of Hashem, moved from in front of the camp of the Israelites to their rear, to cause a separation between the Egyptian ranks and theirs (*Shemos* 14:19). Since the Jews were supposed to follow after this cloud of smoke wherever it went (ibid. 13:21 and *Bamidbar* 9:15-23), a literal understanding of the word of Hashem would have caused them to turn around and begin marching towards the Egyptians, yet Moses led them in the opposite direction, towards the sea. Here then, was an example of the interpretational power of the Oral Law, where we put our trust in those who are authorized to override the seemingly literal intent of God's directive and help us penetrate the reality of His will.

As previously discussed the deliverance from the Egyptians was a two-step process: one, the Exodus from Egypt; and two, the Splitting of the Sea. The former was by the merit of Abraham, and this is the reason it alone is mentioned in the Covenant Between the Parts. The latter, however, where the Jews showed their faith in the concept of the Oral Law, was through the merit of Isaac, who was the initiator of this kind of belief.

The verse in *Vayikra* (26:42) starts, וְזָכַרְתִּי אֶת בְּרִיתִי יַעֲקוֹב וְאַף אֶת בְּרִיתִי יִצְחָק וְאַף אֶת בְּרִיתִי אַבְרָהָם אֶזְכֹּר, *And I will remember My covenant with Jacob, and also My covenant with Isaac, and I will also remember My covenant with Abraham.* Noting that the verb "remember" is used in connection with both Jacob and Abraham, but not in connection with Isaac, Rashi comments that a special remembrance is not necessary because "his ashes are heaped upon the altar (of the *Akeidah*)." (Obviously this is not meant literally; Isaac was in fact never sacrificed on the altar. Rather, the meaning is that the merit of Isaac's consent to be sacrificed gave him an extra degree of presence and concreteness that the other Patriarchs did not have.) This is why the Israelites, who through their actions at the Red Sea recalled this special merit of Isaac, needed no particular mitzvos to invoke Hashem's remembrance of them. In the Egyptian Exodus, however, it was the merit of Abraham that came to fore. To elicit his merit, active forms of mitzvos are needed.

וְאַחֲרֵי כֵן יֵצְאוּ בִּרְכֻשׁ גָּדוֹל — **and afterwards they shall leave with great wealth.**

"And Hashem said to Moses. . ., '*Please* speak in the ears of the people that each person borrow from his [Egyptian] neighbor . . . silver vessels and gold vessels' " (*Shemos* 11:2). Why was the "Please" necessary? Rashi explains that Hashem told Moses that He wanted to ensure that the promise of "and afterwards they shall leave with great wealth," made in the Covenant Between the Parts, was fulfilled. Nevertheless, it would seem that encouragement and prodding are unnecessary when it comes to an action from which a person stands to benefit substantially.

The *Midrash* (*Shemos Rabbah*) teaches that in the verse, "And Hashem gave the people favor in the eyes of the Egyptians, so that they lent to them [silver vessels, golden vessels and garments]" (*Shemos* 12:36), this favorable perception of the Jews was a result of their scrupulously *honorable behavior* during the plague of darkness, when the Egyptians were rendered sightless but the Jews were not; they could easily have used the opportunity to loot and completely despoil their Egyptian oppressors, yet they did not take a single item.

Accordingly, we see how much this despoiling of the Egyptians went against the nature of the Jews who were scrupulously careful regarding money and thus we understand why this encouragement was necessary.

◦§ It is difficult to understand why such a great emphasis is placed on the despoiling of the Egyptians, both upon the Jews' leaving Egypt and at the Red Sea. After all, the Exodus is one of the pinnacles in our spiritual development, to ultimately prepare us for receiving the Torah; greed and avarice are the very antitheses of Torah.

The Torah says, כִּי הַשֹּׁחַד יְעַוֵּר עֵינֵי חֲכָמִים, *for the bribe will blind the eyes of the wise* (*Devarim* 16:19) — i.e. as the "Alter" of Kelm used to paraphrase it, love of money and love of wisdom cannot coexist. Certainly this promise of wealth should not be understood as a concession to a material weakness on the part of the Jews, for a lust for wealth was not an ingrained trait in the Israelite personality. On the contrary, as noted above, the people actually needed to be prodded to take the possessions of their Egyptian taskmasters. Furthermore, this overabundance of wealth in the Israelite camp proved to be a major cause in the catastrophic episode of the Golden Calf, as explained in the Gemara (*Berachos* 32).

The Gemara (*Berachos* 9b) introduces a parable to explain why the Jews were hesitant about plundering the Egyptians: A man was held a prisoner [for many years]. One day someone came to him and told him that the following day he would be freed and receive a great fortune as well. The man's response was, "I would rather forego the money and be released today!" So too the Jews' attitude was, "Would that we could just escape with our lives!"

The *Noda B'Yehudah,* in his *Tzlach* commentary to *Berachos,* points out that the parable does not exactly parallel the situation to which it is compared. Taking the spoils of Egypt did not delay the exodus of the Jews in any way, nor did the Jews suggest "would that we escape with our lives, as long as we escape immediately."

The answer to this question may become clear if we make some observations about the subject. Firstly, we should realize that the prisoner in the parable is obviously in a situation of mortal danger every moment of his imprisonment; otherwise, why would he be so anxious to turn down the monetary gift for just one more day of freedom? We must also realize that the Jews were well aware of the moral danger involved if they would acquire the riches of the Egyptians, for just as

The matzos are covered and the cups lifted as the following paragraph is proclaimed joyously. Upon its conclusion, the cups are put down and the matzos are uncovered.

וְהִיא שֶׁעָמְדָה לַאֲבוֹתֵינוּ וְלָנוּ, שֶׁלֹּא אֶחָד בִּלְבָד עָמַד עָלֵינוּ לְכַלּוֹתֵנוּ. אֶלָּא שֶׁבְּכָל דּוֹר וָדוֹר עוֹמְדִים עָלֵינוּ לְכַלּוֹתֵנוּ, וְהַקָּדוֹשׁ בָּרוּךְ הוּא מַצִּילֵנוּ מִיָּדָם.

---

a slave is subservient to his master, so, too, a rich man is in danger of becoming enslaved to his wealth. Now we can better understand the parable and its message. In both cases the arguments of the prisoners are that they would rather leave their incarceration in a matter that is not life-threatening — in the parable this means leaving a day earlier, and in the case of the Exodus this means leaving without taking the money of the Egyptians — than be freed under perilous circumstances. This explanation of the Gemara's parable, illustrating as it does the aversion of the Israelites to taking the Egyptians' possessions, only serves to make the original question even more poignant: Why was Hashem so adamant that the Jews should despoil the Egyptians?

I once heard from the Ponevezher Rav an explanation of the Sages' interpretation of the verse, "One who loves money will never be satiated with money" (Koheles 5:9), which the Sages interpret to mean that one who loves Torah will never be satiated with Torah. Why did the Sages insist on taking this maxim out of its very appropriate literal meaning and interpret money as a reference to Torah? Furthermore, what similarity does money share with Torah that it may serve as a metaphor for something so exalted?

Hashem created within man the capability to develop intense passions and desires and imbedded these cravings deep in his psyche. The reason He did this, explained the Rav, was that these emotions should serve man in a positive fashion — causing him to yearn and thirst for spiritual fulfillment. They provide man with the sense of ambition and initiative through which he may better himself through spiritual pursuits. Man, however tends to misuse these gifts and applies them to less noble purposes, addressing his physical needs instead.[1] This is what the Sages meant to tell us in their interpretation of the verse from Koheles. The craving for money and the craving for Torah are really two sides of the same coin, for they both emerge from the same source: man's yearnings. The two ideas can readily be compared: Just as the

---

1. This is similar to the idea the Sages put forth in the Midrash (Bereishis Rabbah 9:7) that "were it not that Hashem had implanted in mankind the yetzer hara (the inclination to sin), no one would ever marry or have children or pursue a livelihood." These noble undertakings and the yetzer hara are two manifestations of the same impulse in man's soul.

The matzos are covered and the cups lifted as the following paragraph is proclaimed joyously. Upon its conclusion, the cups are put down and the matzos are uncovered.

It *[the Covenant Between the Parts] has stood firm for our fathers and for us. For it was not one alone who rose against us to annihilate us, but in every generation there are those who rise against us to annihilate us. But the Holy One, Blessed is He, saves us from their hand.*

---

thirst for material comfort is insatiable, so is the more noble drive to draw close to Hashem through His Torah.

Now we can resolve the original difficulty presented above. The Jews, after centuries of slavery, humiliation and torment, were drained of any sense of ambition and aspiration toward any goal at all, be it physical or spiritual — a common consequence of prolonged, severe repression. This is why Hashem sought to stir up these latent emotions in them, in order that the people be capable of craving and hence of receiving and internalizing the new, profound spiritual heights they were about to experience. The exposure to wealth would serve as a catalyst to awaken a dormant sense of ambition which could then be channeled to a higher purpose.

וְהִיא שֶׁעָמְדָה — It . . . has stood firm.

At this point the matzos are covered and the cup of wine is taken in the hand. This may be interpreted symbolically. Matzah (the "bread of affliction") represents the tribulations experienced by the Jews throughout the ages. The way they traditionally react to such episodes of suffering is to "cover them up" in their hearts, not allowing them to disorient them or to distract them from their constant service of Hashem; rather, they continue to worship and sing praises to Him. *It is this* sort of response — covering up the "matzah" of hard times and lifting up the "cup" of praise — "that has stood by our fathers and us" to ensure our survival as a people.

וְהִיא שֶׁעָמְדָה לַאֲבוֹתֵינוּ וְלָנוּ — It . . . has stood firm for our fathers and for us.

It is interesting to note that although the usual formula used in the liturgy (and in the Torah — see *Shemos* 15:2) refers to Hashem as "our God and God of our fathers," here the order is reversed: First "our fathers" are mentioned, and then "us". Why the departure from the regular wording? It would seem more logical to express one's feelings about his own experiences before mentioning those of his fathers.

It would appear that the Haggadah is trying to teach us a lesson. Our privilege of Divine protection, as promised in the Covenant Between

צֵא וּלְמַד מַה בִּקֵּשׁ לָבָן הָאֲרַמִּי לַעֲשׂוֹת לְיַעֲקֹב אָבִינוּ, שֶׁפַּרְעֹה לֹא גָזַר אֶלָּא עַל הַזְּכָרִים, וְלָבָן בִּקֵּשׁ לַעֲקוֹר אֶת הַכֹּל. שֶׁנֶּאֱמַר:

אֲרַמִּי אֹבֵד אָבִי, וַיֵּרֶד מִצְרַיְמָה וַיָּגָר שָׁם בִּמְתֵי מְעָט,

---

the Parts, is not an automatic right, but is rather due to the merits of our forefathers, and is dependent on the extent to which we emulate their righteous ways. Since it is only through our ancestors that we are entitled to this special status, they are mentioned first.

צֵא וּלְמַד — Go and ascertain.

What is the momentous lesson the Haggadah seeks to have us "go and ascertain"? What follows is seemingly nothing more than a straightforward restatement of the events of *Bereishis* 31:23.

The *Baal HaHaggadah* is perhaps showing us a very important principle of our daily lives as Jews. Many people believe that the key to a Jew's success in developing a favorable relationship with the non-Jews surrounding him is through becoming involved with non-Jews in a personal manner, sharing experiences and demonstrating to them how much we actually resemble them. The story of Jacob's relationship with Laban highlights the fallacy in this approach. Jacob took up residence with Laban only reluctantly; he was Laban's son-in-law and father of his grandchildren; he worked for him with uncompromising dedication despite the fact that he was not dealt with fairly. And yet, when it came to a parting of ways, when the interests of the two parties were no longer reconcilable, Laban came with his army and *intended to uproot everything*, to kill his own son-in-law who had shared his home and life with him for over twenty years. This is the lesson we are instructed to "go and learn" from Laban. The true way to develop a healthy relationship with the gentile world is through mutual respect — from a distance — of the *differences* between the two ways of life.[1]

מַה בִּקֵּשׁ לָבָן הָאֲרַמִּי לַעֲשׂוֹת לְיַעֲקֹב אָבִינוּ — What Laban the Aramean intended to do to Jacob our father.

---

1. A beautiful analogy to this situation is given by the *Ridvaz* in his commentary on the Torah. The Jewish nation is compared to fire אֵשׁ וְהָיָה בֵית יַעֲקֹב, *and the house of Jacob shall be fire* (Obadiah 1:18), while the gentile nations are likened to water: מַיִם רַבִּים לֹא יוּכְלוּ, *Many waters are unable to extinguish the love* (see *Shir HaShirim* 8:7 and the commentaries ad loc.). When fire and water are brought into direct contact, it is the water which extinguishes the flame; yet if there is a solid object, such as a pan, separating the two, the fire is unaffected by the water, and even effects it, boiling it away. So too, a clear division between Jews and non-Jews allows for the two to co-exist properly.

Go and ascertain what Laban the Aramean intended to do to Jacob our father, for Pharaoh decreed destruction only for the males, but Lavan intended to eradicate all. As it is said, **"An Aramean would destroy my father, and he went down to Egypt, and he sojourned there with few people, and he**

Why, of the many tribulations faced by Jacob throughout his lifetime, is the example of Laban chosen as the archetypical enemy who wished to "uproot everything"? Certainly Esau's enmity for Jacob is more well known, and his desire to kill him more clearly stated (*Bereishis* 27:41).

Ramban, in his commentary on the Torah (*Bereishis* 12:6), teaches that מַעֲשֵׂה אָבוֹת סִימָן לַבָּנִים — the events which the Torah relates to us concerning the lives of the Patriarchs foreshadow parallel occurrences in the history of their descendants, the Jewish people. Regarding the Patriarchal precedent for the events of the Exodus from Egypt, there seem to be two opinions. It is related in the name of the *Vilna Gaon* that Jacob's distressing experience in Laban's distant household, and his eventual escape with enormous wealth, was the forerunner of the Exodus from Egypt. *Ramban,* however (ibid. on *Bereishis* 12:10), interprets the episode of Abraham's molestation at the hands of Pharaoh, and his subsequent expulsion from Egypt laden with great riches, as the harbinger of the events of the Exodus. I believe that these two opinions may be complementary, rather than exclusive, and refer to two different aspects of the Exodus.

As previously mentioned (p. 20) there were two distinct elements to the Jews' subjugation to the Egyptians — for once, they were persecuted foreigners exiled to a foreign land, and in addition, they were physically enslaved. The tribe of Levi, for instance, experienced only the first of these two facets. It is thus possible that the events that transpired between Abraham and Pharaoh foreshadowed the first of these two elements, for Abraham was merely ill treated but not enslaved; whereas the Jacob-Laban episode was the forerunner of the *slavery* aspect, since Jacob's position in the house of Laban was, for all intents and purposes, tantamount to slavery.

Since Laban's treatment of Jacob was a forerunner of the events of the Exodus, it, rather than Esau's enmity for Jacob, is chosen by the Torah to be mentioned in conjunction with the suffering and deliverance of the Jews in Egypt.

וַיֵּרֶד מִצְרַיְמָה וַיָּגָר שָׁם בִּמְתֵי מְעָט — **And he went down to Egypt and he sojourned there, with few people.**

וַיְהִי שָׁם לְגוֹי, גָּדוֹל עָצוּם וָרָב.[1]

וַיֵּרֶד מִצְרַיְמָה – אָנוּס עַל פִּי הַדִּבּוּר.

וַיָּגָר שָׁם – מְלַמֵּד שֶׁלֹּא יָרַד יַעֲקֹב אָבִינוּ לְהִשְׁתַּקֵּעַ
בְּמִצְרַיִם, אֶלָּא לָגוּר שָׁם. שֶׁנֶּאֱמַר, וַיֹּאמְרוּ אֶל פַּרְעֹה,
לָגוּר בָּאָרֶץ בָּאנוּ, כִּי אֵין מִרְעֶה לַצֹּאן אֲשֶׁר לַעֲבָדֶיךָ,

"With few people," as explained later (p.70), is a reference to the seventy souls who originally traveled to Egypt with Jacob. Accordingly, we would expect the verse to be phrased, "He descended to Egypt with few people, and sojourned there." Why is the phrase "with few people" positioned so that it appears to modify the phrase "and sojourned there"?

It seems that as long as Jacob or one of his sons was still alive, the people remained in the original "ghetto" that was set aside for them in Goshen, despite the fact that the *Midrash* says that Jacob himself lived to see thousands of descendants. Nonetheless, only after "Joseph died, and all his brothers and that entire generation" are we taught that "the land became full of them" (*Shemos* 1:6); until that point their abundance was apparently not so conspicuous.

This may explain why, as the *Midrash* (quoted by *Rashi*) notes, the enslavement did not begin until after the deaths of Joseph and his brothers. The people, although extremely numerous, were not perceived as a threat until they spread out throughout the land. It is for this reason that the phrase "with few people" is used to modify "and sojourned there," since it also indicates that the manner in which the Jews survived was by maintaining a "low profile."

שֶׁנֶּאֱמַר אֲרַמִּי אֹבֵד אָבִי וכו' — as it is said, "An Aramean would destroy my father, etc."

In this section of the Haggadah, a passage of the Torah called מִקְרָא בִּכּוּרִים (*Devarim* 26:5-8), which is a brief synopsis of the story of the Jews' sojourn in and Exodus from Egypt, is thoroughly analyzed, verse by verse. In most cases a verse is cited from the actual story of the Exodus in *Shemos* to "corroborate" the version in *Devarim*. Many commentators have questioned what the point of these supporting verses are. It is absurd to think that we are trying to authenticate the accuracy of the Torah in the latter account; and even if this were so, how could one verse be verified through citing another one in the same Torah?!

The Haggadah later on (p. 84) asserts that the Exodus from Egypt was carried out directly by Hashem, and not through the medium of

became there a nation, great, mighty, and formidable." [1]

"And he went down to Egypt" — *forced by HASHEM's word.*

"And he sojourned there" — *This teaches us that Jacob our father did not go down to settle permanently in Egypt, but merely to sojourn there, as it is said, "And they said to Pharaoh, We have come to sojourn in the land, for there is no pasture for the sheep of your servants,*

---

1. *Devarim* 26:5.

---

any earthly agent.[1] It is interesting to note that in fact, as if to emphasize this point, the name of Aaron is not mentioned at all, and that of Moses only once — and even then incidentally — throughout the Haggadah, despite the fact that they ostensibly played a crucial role in the events of the Exodus.

The salient difference between the Book of *Devarim* and the other four Books of the Torah is that the former is written in first person, with Moses as narrator (this, of course, in no way diminishes the Divine nature or authenticity of this part of the Torah), whereas the rest of the Torah is presented as the direct word of Hashem — "and Hashem spoke to Moses, saying. . .," etc. As mentioned above, although the apparent role of Moses in the redemption process from Egypt was central, in reality this was only the superficial appearance of the events; in fact it was Hashem Who "personally" delivered them. By quoting verses from the other Books of the Torah to confirm, as it were, the verses spoken by Moses in *Devarim*, the Haggadah is accentuating this theme that while Moses gives the appearance of acting on his own, much like he seems to be speaking *Devarim* on his own, in reality he was only serving as the instrument of Hashem's direct action, just as the words of *Shemos* are clearly those of Hashem.

מְלַמֵּד שֶׁלֹּא יָרַד יַעֲקֹב אָבִינוּ לְהִשְׁתַּקֵּעַ — **This teaches that Jacob our father did not go down to settle permanently.**

The word מְלַמֵּד, *this teaches*, has the implication that the Haggadah teaches us a lesson which is applicable to our own lives, in all future generations.

---

1. The Brisker Rav explains that this was what Moses intended, when he originally declined Hashem's charge sending him as His messenger to Pharaoh to release the people. His objection was, מִי אָנֹכִי כִּי אֵלֵךְ אֶל פַּרְעֹה וְכִי אוֹצִיא אֶת בְּנֵי יִשְׂרָאֵל, *Who am I that I should go to Pharaoh and that I should take the Children of Israel out of Egypt* (*Shemos* 3:11), to which Hashem replied, "For I will be with you, and this is your sign that I sent you, etc." Moses was actually saying, "Did you not promise my forefathers that You would 'personally' redeem us, without an intermediary, so who am I etc.?" Hashem's response was that actually it was indeed *He* Who was redeeming them, and Moses was only to be His spokesman.

כִּי כָבֵד הָרָעָב בְּאֶרֶץ כְּנָעַן, וְעַתָּה יֵשְׁבוּ נָא עֲבָדֶיךָ בְּאֶרֶץ גֹּשֶׁן.[1]

בִּמְתֵי מְעָט — כְּמָה שֶׁנֶּאֱמַר, בְּשִׁבְעִים נֶפֶשׁ יָרְדוּ אֲבֹתֶיךָ מִצְרָיְמָה, וְעַתָּה שָׂמְךָ יהוה אֱלֹהֶיךָ כְּכוֹכְבֵי הַשָּׁמַיִם לָרֹב.[2]

וַיְהִי שָׁם לְגוֹי — מְלַמֵּד שֶׁהָיוּ יִשְׂרָאֵל מְצֻיָּנִים שָׁם.

גָּדוֹל עָצוּם — כְּמָה שֶׁנֶּאֱמַר, וּבְנֵי יִשְׂרָאֵל פָּרוּ וַיִּשְׁרְצוּ וַיִּרְבּוּ וַיַּעַצְמוּ בִּמְאֹד מְאֹד, וַתִּמָּלֵא הָאָרֶץ אֹתָם.[3]

וָרָב — כְּמָה שֶׁנֶּאֱמַר, רְבָבָה כְּצֶמַח הַשָּׂדֶה נְתַתִּיךְ, וַתִּרְבִּי וַתִּגְדְּלִי וַתָּבֹאִי בַּעֲדִי עֲדָיִים, שָׁדַיִם נָכֹנוּ וּשְׂעָרֵךְ צִמֵּחַ, וְאַתְּ עֵרֹם וְעֶרְיָה; וָאֶעֱבֹר עָלַיִךְ וָאֶרְאֵךְ מִתְבּוֹסֶסֶת בְּדָמָיִךְ, וָאֹמַר לָךְ, בְּדָמַיִךְ חֲיִי, וָאֹמַר לָךְ, בְּדָמַיִךְ חֲיִי.[4]

Rav Meir Simchah of Dvinsk took note of this expression, explaining it as follows: "This verse (וַיְהִי שָׁם) teaches *us* that throughout our history, in all our various exiles, we should realize that we are not living in our host countries as permanent residents, but rather as sojourners until the time comes for Hashem to redeem us. This is the meaning of the Gemara (*Sotah* 11a) that interprets the word וַיָּקֻצוּ (*Shemos* 1:12 — lit., 'they [the Egyptians] were repulsed') as 'they regarded them as thorns' — just as thorns and weeds do not intermingle with the other vegetation in the garden or orchard, and do not strike permanent roots there, so too was the Jews' presence there regarded as temporary and completely detached from the other people who lived there" (*Meshech Chochmah* on *Vayikra* 26:44). A similar expression is found in the next passage of the Haggadah: "This teaches that Israel were distinctive there." Here again the term מְלַמֵּד is employed since the *Baal Haggadah* come to teach a timeless life lesson. The secret of Jewish survival and continuity in exile is the art of remaining distinctively Jewish in all areas of life.

וְאַתְּ עֵרֹם וְעֶרְיָה . . . וָאֹמַר לָךְ בְּדָמַיִךְ חֲיִי — But you were naked and bare . . . and I said to you: "Through your blood shall you live!"

This verse is interpreted allegorically by the Sages (in the *Mechilta*, quoted by *Rashi* in *Shemos* 12:6) to mean that when the time had come to redeem the Israelites from bondage, Hashem saw that they were "naked" of any mitzvos which might have provided them with the merit for the famine is severe in the Land of Canaan. And now, may your servants please live in the Land of Goshen.'"[1]

"With few people" — as it is said, "With seventy souls your fathers went down to Egypt, but now HASHEM, your God, has made you numerous as the stars of the heavens."[2]

"And he became there a nation" — This teaches us that the Jews were distinguishable there.

"Great, mighty" — as it is said, "And the Children of Israel were fruitful and fertile, and they multiplied and became very, very mighty, and the land became full of them."[3]

"And formidable" — as it is said, "Like the plants of the field I made tens of thousands of you, and you increased and grew, and became mature. Your breasts were full, and your hair had grown, but you were naked and bare. I passed over you and saw you downtrodden in your blood and I said to you: 'Through your blood you shall live!' And I said to you: 'Through your blood you shall live!' "[4]

---

(1) Bereishis 47:4. (2) Devarim 10:22. (3) Shemos 1:7. (4) Yechezkel 16:7,6.

---

necessary to justify Divine intervention. He therefore gave them two mitzvos to perform on that night — circumcision and the *pesach* sacrifice, and it was "through the blood" of these two actions they might gain the required merit to be delivered from Egypt. This is why the phrase, בְּדָמַיִךְ חֲיִי, *Through your blood shall you live,* is repeated twice: to allude to the two types of blood shed that night. [It should be noted that we are graced by the presence of Elijah the Prophet on two occasions, a *Bris Milah* and at any *Seder* table. The presence of Elijah the Prophet at these occasions clearly points to these mitzvos as harbingers of redemption.]

Several questions arise when we examine this interpretation. Why were two mitzvos necessary to remove this "nakedness" rather than one? And why these particular mitzvos rather than any of the other 611 in the Torah?

In *Toras Refael*, R' Refael Hamburger, zt"l, points out a contradiction between two statements in the *Talmud Yerushalmi*. In one place it states, responding to the question of why the Jews waited until the parting of the Red Sea to praise Hashem with the famous Song of *Az Yashir* and did not do so upon leaving Egypt a week earlier, that the Exodus from Egyptian bondage was not actually complete until the Egyptian army was decimated at the sea.[1] In another place, however, it says that the Jews did indeed say Hallel (praise) to Hashem on the night of the Exodus: When Pharaoh declared to the people, "Heretofore you have been *my* servants; as of now you are free men and you are servants of Hashem, and it behooves you to sing praises to Him, saying, 'Praise Hashem, you servants of Hashem' (the opening verse of the Hallel)." (See *Yalkut Shimoni Bo* 12:06.)

To resolve this apparent contradiction, Rav Refael notes our previously mentioned point, that the Jews in Egypt were actually subject to a twofold persecution: They were exiled in a country not their own, subjects of an openly hostile government and, in addition to this, they were actually *enslaved* by the Egyptians. The *enslavement* came to an end on the first night of Passover, and the people celebrated this occasion by singing the Hallel. But the end of their political subjugation to the Egyptians as an alien, despised people was not until the vanquishing of Pharaoh's soldiers at the sea: This final and total break with Egyptian dominion is expressed clearly in the words: כִּי אֲשֶׁר רְאִיתֶם אֶת מִצְרַיִם הַיּוֹם לֹא תֹסִפוּ לִרְאֹתָם עוֹד עַד עוֹלָם, *for as you have seen Egypt today, you shall not see them ever again!* (*Shemos* 14:13). It was for this reason tha the singing of Hashem's praises for *this* milestone (the Song of *Az Yashir*) was postponed until seven days after the Exodus.

It was mentioned earlier (67) that this dual nature of the Jews' exile in Egypt explains why there are apparently two separate events in the Torah to portend the eventual enslavement and deliverance in Egypt: one, experienced by Abraham, corresponding to exile and subservience to a foreign, hated power; and the other, undergone by Jacob, paralleling the enslavement aspect. The significance of these two particular mitzvos in establishing a basis by which the Jews could be deserving of redemption may also be rooted in this duality. Circumcision is an unalterable seal in the very flesh of the Jew, and is reminiscent of the fact that slaves were usually "branded" in some way to prevent them from fleeing their masters. Thus this mitzvah represents the end of the enslavement to the Egyptians and then affirmation of their being subservient to Hashem. The *pesach* (passover) sacrifice is interpreted by many commentators as a symbol of the fact that Hashem "passed over" the option of waiting the full 400 years to redeem His people, choosing rather to intervene earlier on their behalf. The mitzvah of the *pesach* sacrifice thus represented to the people that the time had come when Hashem was about to fulfill His promise to Abraham

---

1. *Rav Chaim (Brisker) Soloveitchik* explained the following verse in *Tehillim* (13:6) along the lines of this *Yerushalmi:* וַאֲנִי בְּחַסְדְּךָ בָטַחְתִּי יָגֵל לִבִּי בִּישׁוּעָתֶךָ אָשִׁירָה לַה׳ כִּי גָמַל עָלָי, *But as for me, I trust in Your kindness; my heart will exult in Your salvation. I will sing to Hashem, for He has dealt kindly with me.* Although "my heart will exult" even when I am only hoping and praying for Your mercy, the time for song is only when Hashem is *actually* "has dealt kindly with me."

and lead His people back to the Promised Land. Both of these mitzvos played an important symbolic role in the Exodus, each one representing one of the two aspects of the domination of the Egyptians over the Jews: circumcision reflecting the conclusion of the enslavement aspect, and the *pesach* sacrifice connoting the end of the general exile and subjugation.

My grandfather, the *Ohr Yechezkel*, questioned how one may say that the Jews had no merits of their own without these new mitzvos. When Moses protested to Hashem that the Jews would not believe him that He was about to redeem them, Hashem reprimanded him for underestimating their resolute and steadfast faith in Him (*Shabbos* 97a). Furthermore, the *midrash* (*Vayikra Rabbah* 34:5) states that the Jews merited redemption because of their tenacity in maintaining their ancestral language, names and mode of dress, and thus averting any assimilation with Egyptian culture. The Jews then *did* possess certain crucial spiritual virtues. What was the necessity of introducing new opportunities for merit?

He answered this question by developing an idea introduced by the Alter of Kelm. The world was created, says the Torah, "to do," to act — אֲשֶׁר בָּרָא אֱלֹקִים לַעֲשׂוֹת (*Bereishis* 2:3). Ours is the world of accomplishing and achieving real, concrete goals. This is true for the mitzvos of the Torah as well, spiritual though they may be. Even the mitzvah of donning *tefillin*, whose purpose is for man to subordinate his heart and brain to the service of Hashem, must be concretized. If someone does not actually put them on his body, all the noble and lofty thoughts in the world cannot serve as a substitute for the actual performance of the mitzvah. So too with the Jews in Egypt — although their attitudes and outlooks were perfectly wholesome, this was no replacement for actual, tangible actions. There two concrete mitzvos were necessary.

Yet another difficulty arises from this *midrash*. The law is that a circumcision which is performed at night is invalid. If so, how can it be that the Jews performed this mitzvah on the *night* of the first Pesach?

It is possible that this *midrash* (and *Rashi*, who quotes it) follows of the opinion that this law — that circumcision may be done only during the daytime — was not in effect before the giving of the Torah. The source for this rule, in fact, is derived from the brief statement of the mitzvah (given at Mount Sinai) in *Vayikra* 12:3, וּבַיּוֹם הַשְּׁמִינִי יִמּוֹל בְּשַׂר עָרְלָתוֹ, *And on the eighth day the flesh of his foreskin shall be circumcised*, rather than from the lengthy discussion of its details as given to Abraham in *Bereishis* 17.[1]

---

1. That *Rashi* indeed is of this opinion can be shown from his comment to *Bereishis* 17:23. On the verse, וַיָּמָל אֶת בְּשַׂר עָרְלָתָם בְּעֶצֶם הַיּוֹם הַזֶּה, *and he [Abraham] circumcised the flesh of their surplusage [all the males of his household] on that very day.* *Rashi* explains this last phrase

Another possible explanation of this halachic anomaly may be offered, based on an idea found in the commentary *Chanukas HaTorah*. The *midrash* comments on the verse, וַיִּקְרָא אֱלֹקִים לָאוֹר יוֹם וְלַחֹשֶׁךְ קָרָא לָיְלָה, *And God called the light "day," and the darkness He called "night"* (*Bereishis* 1:5), that the name of God is mentioned in the first part of the sentence but not repeated in the second part, since Hashem does not wish to associate His Name with the idea of "night" (which represents imperfection and evil). Nevertheless, says the aforementioned commentary, we find that the night of Pesach is called "a night of watching *unto Hashem*"; the name of God is indeed mentioned in connection with the night. He explains, based on the *Zohar*, that that night of the Exodus was "as bright as a summer day," i.e. in a metaphysical sense it had the attributes of daytime. This being the case, we may understand that even if nighttime circumcisions were forbidden even *before* the Revelation at Sinai, this particular night was an exception to this rule.

The two kinds of blood referred to in this verse (בְּדָמַיִךְ חֲיִי וכו׳ בְּדָמַיִךְ חֲיִי, *Through your blood you shall live! . . . Through your blood you shall live!*), as noted earlier, are the blood of the *pesach* sacrifice and the blood of circumcision, which were to be smeared on the doorposts of all the Jewish homes so that the "Destroyer" would "pass over" them (*Shemos* 12:23). The question may be asked: Why were these *two* signals necessary to prevent evil from befalling the Jewish homes? Would not smearing *one* kind of blood over the door have provided sufficient protection?

The Torah says in *Shemos* 12:23, וְעָבַר ה׳ לִנְגֹּף אֶת מִצְרַיִם וְרָאָה אֶת הַדָּם עַל הַמַּשְׁקוֹף וכו׳ וּפָסַח ה׳ עַל הַפֶּתַח וְלֹא יִתֵּן הַמַּשְׁחִית לָבֹא אֶל בָּתֵּיכֶם לִנְגֹּף, *'And Hashem will pass through to smite Egypt, and He will see the blood that is on the lintel . . . and Hashem will pass over the entrance and He will not permit the Destroyer to enter your houses to smite*. The *Vilna Gaon*, in his commentary *Divrei Eliyahu*, asks a penetrating question: The Haggadah (p. 84) tells us unequivocally that the events of the night of the Exodus took place through Hashem Himself, rather than through the agency of any angel or mortal intermediary. In fact, the verse in question itself begins by saying that "*Hashem* will pass through to smite. . ." What, then, could the role of the "Destroyer" mentioned in this verse possibly be? The *Vilna Gaon* answers: The smiting of the firstborn was indeed administered by Hashem. However, among the

---

to mean that Abraham did not delay until evening in order to hide his actions from his pagan neighbors, who might ridicule or scorn him; rather, he performed the mitzvah in broad daylight to show his pride and zeal in carrying out Hashem's bidding. This clearly implies that the option of performing the circumcision at night was indeed available to Abraham, had he chosen to do so.

multitude of Jews who were living there at the time, there were surely some whose natural time of death was due to occur on that evening. It was to take the souls of *these* people that the Destroyer — the Angel of Death — had come, and it was such encounters with natural death that Hashem wished to avoid, in order to prevent the Egyptians from falsely surmising that the plague was affecting the Israelites as well. Thus, the sign of the blood served a dual purpose: It was indicative that through the performance of His mitzvos, the Jews had achieved the merit necessary to earn redemption, and should thus be spared from the Divinely invoked plague of the smiting of the firstborn; and it also was a reminder to the "Destroyer" to refrain from inflicting "natural" death.

It would appear that the two types of blood corresponded to this twofold purpose. The sign of the sacrificial blood was to protect them from the plague, as is clear from *Shemos* 12:27, while the blood of circumcision was that which warded off the Angel of Death. [1]

One may ponder, since these two mitzvos — namely, circumcision and the *pesach* sacrifice — were both performed on that night of the Exodus, and are seemingly of equal significance, why is it that the story of the *pesach* sacrifice is told in such great detail in the Torah, whereas circumcison is not mentioned at all, except for a very veiled, oblique reference in the Book of *Yechezkel*. Several approaches seem pertinent in addressing this question.

The *midrash* (*Shemos Rabbah* 19) relates that when the Jews were told to circumcise themselves, they were hesitant to do so. Hashem made the idea more appealing to them by causing Moses' paschal lamb, which he had already slaughtered and begun to roast, to emit a pleasant aroma. When the Jews in Egypt requested that they be allowed to partake of this feast, he replied that, וְכָל עָרֵל לֹא יֹאכַל בּוֹ, *no uncircumcised person may eat from it* (*Shemos* 12:48). They thereupon consented to undergo the ritual. On the other hand, we find no such apprehension on the part of the Jews when it came to obeying the command to prepare the *pesach* sacrifice (see ibid. 12:28 and Rashi ad loc.), despite the fact that it involved great personal risk, as the lamb was an Egyptian deity (see *Shemos* 8:22). Because the people eagerly accepted the mitzvah of the sacrifice, but were reluctant to assent to circumcision, the former was mentioned explicitly, while the latter was left to oral tradition.

---

1. This power of circumcision to ward off physical death may be explained as follows. The *midrash* (*Tanchuma*, *Tzav*) says that when a person is lacking circumcision, it is as if Hashem's Name of Sha—d—ai (שׁ־ד־י) is missing the letter יוד, leaving שד, which refers to the diabolical forces of evil in the world. Thus, through the blood of this mitzvah, the Israelites negated the influence of these harmful forces, of which Death is the archetypical example.

וַיָּרֵעוּ אֹתָנוּ הַמִּצְרִים, וַיְעַנּוּנוּ, וַיִּתְּנוּ עָלֵינוּ עֲבֹדָה קָשָׁה.[1]

וַיָּרֵעוּ אֹתָנוּ הַמִּצְרִים – כְּמָה שֶׁנֶּאֱמַר, הָבָה נִתְחַכְּמָה לוֹ, פֶּן יִרְבֶּה, וְהָיָה כִּי תִקְרֶאנָה מִלְחָמָה, וְנוֹסַף גַּם הוּא עַל שֹׂנְאֵינוּ, וְנִלְחַם בָּנוּ, וְעָלָה מִן הָאָרֶץ.[2]

Another possible answer, suggested by my brother, R' Chaim Yerucham Ginsberg shlita, is based on the midrash (Shemos Rabbah 1:10) which teaches that the subjugation to the Egyptians began only when the descendants of the twelve sons of Jacob began to disregard the mitzvah of circumcision. Thus, the mass circumcision which took place on the night of the Exodus was in reality only a "correction" of a previous deviation from the norm. The pesach sacrifice, however, was a new mitzvah, and was an important factor in the Israelites' attainment of the spiritual purification necessary to undergo redemption. By offering the deity of Egypt as a sacrifice to Hashem, they sought to uproot the last vestiges of idolatry and Egyptian culture to which they had been exposed. It is for this reason that it is dealt with explicitly and extensively in the Exodus narrative, while the circumcision of the people is not.

וַיָּרֵעוּ אֹתָנוּ הַמִּצְרִים — And the Egyptians made us evil.

Why did the Torah use the phrase וַיָּרֵעוּ אֹתָנוּ, meaning "they made us evil," as opposed to the more grammatical expression of וַיָּרֵעוּ לָנוּ, meaning "they did evil to us"?

The Torah means to tell us that the Egyptians portrayed us in an evil light. They suspected the Israelites of infidelity, believing that they would join forces with any enemy army who might come to fight against Egypt (Shemos 1:10).

My grandfather, Rav Yechezkel Levenstein, pointed out that the Egyptians, who possessed a highly advanced level of civilization, were certainly aware of the simple rule of decency that one does not repay goodness with evil. How is it possible, then, that after Joseph's death it was "forgotten" how he had saved the country from disaster and ruin (Shemos 1:8), and his brethren became subject to such severe persecution? The answer is provided by the following verse: First, Pharaoh convinced the people that it was the Israelites who were repaying kindness with malice, for after all the generous, favorable terms that were granted to them when they first came to settle in Egypt (Bereishis 47), their loyalty to their benevolent host government was suspect. Since they demonstrated such a contemptible lack of grati-

"And the Egyptians made us evil, and they tormented us, and laid hard labor upon us."[1]

"And the Egyptians made evil of us" — *as it is said, "Come, let us devise plans against him lest he increase. Then, if war will befall us, he will join our enemies and wage war against us and go up out of the land."*[2]

(1) *Devarim* 26:6. (2) *Shemos* 1:10.

---

tude to their patrons, the Egyptians felt that they were released of any moral obligation to show appreciation to the Jews for what their ancestors had done; on the contrary, they felt that perfidy deserves to be repaid in kind.[1]

Another explanation of why the Torah used the phrase "they made us evil" may be offered. The Gemara (*Sotah* 11a) says, based on the verse in *Shemos* 1:10, that Pharaoh's plan for dealing with the Jews was to "outsmart" their Savior, by oppressing them in such a way that Hashem would not exact punishment from their tormentors. While there the reference is to the form of punishment, the same outsmarting process, so to speak, could be accomplished by causing the Jews to be undeserving of salvation. In fact, we find in the *midrash* (*Yalkut* 234) that when Hashem was about to save the Israelites at the Red Sea, the Accuser protested in Heaven that they were not deserving of His salvation, since they were as much idolaters as the Egyptians. It might be said that the Egyptian plan was to cause the Jews to degenerate from their lofty spiritual level by persuading them to adopt the idolatrous ways of their hosts and abandon their forefathers' customs, such as circumcision. By doing so they would weaken their entitlement to Divine protection, and "negate" the influence of Hashem to intervene. Thus the Egyptians indeed "made us evil."

I heard from my father, *HaRav HaGaon Rav Ephraim Mordechai Ginsberg zt"l,* that it was due to the deep insidious influence of the Egyptians on our character that Hashem *personally* redeemed us from Egypt. Had He not done so, we would have remained internally and morally enslaved to Egypt and the evil character they induced in us. It is for this freedom from "Egyptianism" that we thank and praise Hashem.

---

1. Perhaps it is because Pharaoh used the idea of "retribution in kind" (מִדָּה כְּנֶגֶד מִדָּה) so effectively that we find that Hashem used this method of punishment against him in a revealed fashion. In *Shemos Rabbah* (e.g. 9:10), it is shown how the plagues were each a form of "punishment in kind" for Pharaoh's actions. See also *Shemos* 18:11 and Rashi ad loc., concerning the drowning of the Egyptians in the sea as an example of this type of retribution. Perhaps this is the intent of the Torah in using the expression "they made us [appear] evil."

וַיְעַנּוּנוּ — כְּמָה שֶׁנֶּאֱמַר, וַיָּשִׂימוּ עָלָיו שָׂרֵי מִסִּים, לְמַעַן עַנֹּתוֹ בְּסִבְלֹתָם, וַיִּבֶן עָרֵי מִסְכְּנוֹת לְפַרְעֹה, אֶת פִּתֹם וְאֶת רַעַמְסֵס.

וַיִּתְּנוּ עָלֵינוּ עֲבֹדָה קָשָׁה — כְּמָה שֶׁנֶּאֱמַר, וַיַּעֲבִדוּ מִצְרַיִם אֶת בְּנֵי יִשְׂרָאֵל בְּפָרֶךְ.

וַנִּצְעַק אֶל יהוה אֱלֹהֵי אֲבֹתֵינוּ, וַיִּשְׁמַע יהוה אֶת קֹלֵנוּ, וַיַּרְא אֶת עָנְיֵנוּ, וְאֶת עֲמָלֵנוּ, וְאֶת לַחֲצֵנוּ.

וַיְעַנּוּנוּ – כְּמָה שֶׁנֶּאֱמַר, וַיָּשִׂימוּ עָלָיו וכו׳ — **And they tormented us — as it is said, They set taskmasters over them etc.**

In the quoted verse (*Shemos* 1:11) the Torah describes the development of the process of Egypt's subjugation of the Israelites. It is interesting to note that there seems to be one verse out of place in this description. In verse 8-11 the beginning of the persecution of the people is depicted. In verses 13-16 this discussion is continued. In between these two halves of the story, verse 12, seemingly unattached, is inserted: וְכַאֲשֶׁר יְעַנּוּ אֹתוֹ כֵּן יִרְבֶּה וְכֵן יִפְרֹץ וַיָּקֻצוּ, *But as much as they would afflict it, so it would increase and so it would spread out; and they became disgusted* (*Shemos* 1:12). Why is this description of the Jews' *reaction* to their affliction placed in the middle of the depiction of the oppression itself?

I believe that the Torah outlines the prototype of the attitude of gentile governments towards their Jewish subjects throughout the ages, as exemplified by the Egyptians. First (several generations after the Jews have settled somewhere under cordial and amicable terms) comes jealousy: הִנֵּה עַם בְּנֵי יִשְׂרָאֵל רַב וְעָצוּם מִמֶּנּוּ, *Behold, the people, the Children of Israel, are more numerous and stronger than we* (v. 9). Then a plan is devised to check their growth and strength — all for the legitimate purpose of improving the well-being of the state, of course הָבָה נִתְחַכְּמָה לוֹ, פֶּן וכו׳ וְנוֹסַף גַּם הוּא עַל שֹׂנְאֵינוּ וְנִלְחַם בָּנוּ, *Come, let us outsmart it lest . . . it too, may join our enemies, and wage war against us* (v. 10). But whatever measures are enacted, the Jews seem to overcome the hardships and remain as steadfast as ever, all the more strengthened by the ordeal (v. 12): "But as much as they would afflict it, so it would increase and so it would spread out." At this point the host nation abandons their pretext of protecting their legitimate self-interests, and their true motivation — pure, intractable, irrational hatred of Hashem's people — surfaces: "And they became disgusted because of the Children of Israel"

"And they tormented us" — *as it is said, "And they put over him taskmasters to torment him with their burdens. And he built store-cities for Pharaoh — Pisom and Raamses."[1]*

"And laid hard labor upon us" — *as it is said, "And the Egyptians made the Children of Israel work at racking labor."[2]*

"And we cried out unto HASHEM the God of our fathers, and HASHEM heard our voice, and He saw our distress, and our travail, and our oppression."[3]

---

(1) *Shemos* 1:11. (2) 1:13. (3) *Devarim* 26:7.

(ibid.). This hate lead to unbridled harassment and oppression (vs. 13-16), until their wickedness reaches a point where Hashem intervenes to avenge His servant's suffering, punishing the guilty regime which began the whole process.

Thus, the description of the oppression of the Israelites is split into two halves: one which tells of the "legitimate" concerns of the regime for the welfare of the state, and the other which describes the hysterical hatred which comes after the "civilized" solutions fail and the facade falls. The two halves are aptly separated by the crucial "and they became disgusted etc."

וַנִּצְעַק אֶל ה' — **And we cried out unto Hashem.**

At the Red Sea, the Torah tells us, the Israelites found themselves trapped, with the Egyptian army at their rear, and the vast expanse of the sea in front of them. They cried out to Hashem and He heard their plea. He told Moses to lead the people into the sea, which would split apart for them. Why was it necessary for Hashem to put the people in such a desperate situation, and to perform the miracle only after hearing their cries of anguish? Could not Hashem have parted the waters for them as soon as they arrived at the sea? The answer to this question, the *midrash* tells us, is that Hashem longs to hear the prayers of Israel.[1]

This teaches us an interesting lesson about prayer. We would have thought that an unsolicited prayer, offered voluntarily without pressure from external factors, is more desirable and pleasing to Hashem. The *midrash* informs us otherwise. A person in distress automatically abandons any courses of action which are not absolutely productive and beneficial; he will turn instead to means of proven efficacy. If that person resorts to prayer, it is an indication of the importance he attaches to this course and of the extent to which he believes in its effectiveness. It is to such a sincere prayer that Hashem is most likely to react with favor.

---

1. See *Shemos Rabbah* 21:5.

וַנִּצְעַק אֶל יהוה אֱלֹהֵי אֲבֹתֵינוּ — כְּמָה שֶׁנֶּאֱמַר, וַיְהִי בַיָּמִים הָרַבִּים הָהֵם, וַיָּמָת מֶלֶךְ מִצְרַיִם, וַיֵּאָנְחוּ בְנֵי יִשְׂרָאֵל מִן הָעֲבֹדָה, וַיִּזְעָקוּ, וַתַּעַל שַׁוְעָתָם אֶל הָאֱלֹהִים מִן הָעֲבֹדָה.[1]

וַיִּשְׁמַע יהוה אֶת קֹלֵנוּ — כְּמָה שֶׁנֶּאֱמַר, וַיִּשְׁמַע אֱלֹהִים אֶת נַאֲקָתָם, וַיִּזְכֹּר אֱלֹהִים אֶת בְּרִיתוֹ אֶת אַבְרָהָם, אֶת יִצְחָק, וְאֶת יַעֲקֹב.[2]

וַיַּרְא אֶת עָנְיֵנוּ — זוֹ פְּרִישׁוּת דֶּרֶךְ אֶרֶץ, כְּמָה שֶׁנֶּאֱמַר, וַיַּרְא אֱלֹהִים אֶת בְּנֵי יִשְׂרָאֵל, וַיֵּדַע אֱלֹהִים.[3]

וְאֶת עֲמָלֵנוּ — אֵלּוּ הַבָּנִים, כְּמָה שֶׁנֶּאֱמַר, כָּל הַבֵּן הַיִּלּוֹד הַיְאֹרָה תַּשְׁלִיכֻהוּ, וְכָל הַבַּת תְּחַיּוּן.[4]

וַיִּשְׁמַע ה' אֶת קֹלֵנוּ – כְּמָה שֶׁנֶּאֱמַר, וַיִּשְׁמַע אֱלֹקִים אֶת נַאֲקָתָם, וַיִּזְכֹּר אֱלֹקִים אֶת בְּרִיתוֹ אֶת אַבְרָהָם, אֶת יִצְחָק, וְאֶת יַעֲקֹב — "And Hashem heard our voice — as it is said: And God heard their groaning, and God remembered His covenant with Abraham, with Isaac, and with Jacob.

As a support text from *Shemos,* the Haggadah cites the verse, "God heard their groaning."(*Shemos* 2:24) This would seem to buttress the point. Why then does it continue to cite the end of the verse, that He remembered His covenant with the Patriarchs? Of what relevance is the covenantal rememberance to show that *"Hashem heard our voice"?*

Perhaps the *Baal HaHaggadah* means to intimate to us that had it not been for the merit of the sainted Patriarchs, the prayers of the Israelites might not have been accepted by Hashem. As the *Rambam* says (*Teshuvah* 7:7), "a man's sins can create a barrier between himself and Hashem, preventing his prayers from being received favorably by Him, as it says (*Yeshayahu* 1:15), גַּם כִּי תַרְבּוּ תְפִלָּה אֵינֶנִּי שׁוֹמֵעַ, *even if you pray profusely, I will not listen."* As has been explained earlier in this commentary (p 70) the Jews at that time were in many ways deficient in their spiritual condition, and had even allowed the mitzvah of circumcision to fall into disuse. Hence it was entirely possible that their prayers might go unheeded. Nevertheless, the Gemara (*Rosh Hashanah* 11a) tells us that Hashem מְדַלֵּג עַל הֶהָרִים, *skipped over the mountains"* (*Shir HaShirim* 2:8) in Egypt, which the Sages interpret homiletically to mean that only because of the merit of the Patriarchs (who are referred to here — and elsewhere — as mountains due to their immense spiritual stature), Hashem "skipped over" almost two

"And we cried out unto HASHEM the God of our fathers"
— *as it is said, "During those many days, the king of Egypt died, and the Children of Israel sighed because of the labor and cried out, and their moaning rose up to God from the labor."[1]*

"And HASHEM heard our voice" — *as it is said, "And God heard their groaning. And God remembered His covenant with Abraham, with Isaac and with Jacob."[2]*

"And He saw our distress" — *that means forced abstinence from normal family life, as it is said, "And God saw the Children of Israel, and God knew."[3]*

"And our travail" — *that means the sons, as it is said, "Every son that is born you will cast into the river, and every daughter you will let live."[4]*

---

(1) *Shemos* 2:23. (2) 2:24. (3) 2:25. (4) 1:22.

---

centuries of the foreordained four hundred years to redeem the Israelites before their time. (See *Pachad Yitzchak*, *Pesach* Chapter 70.) Thus, it was only through the merit of the Patriarchs that the Jews' prayers became acceptable to Hashem: The second part of the verse is quite appropriately quoted to illustrate how "Hashem heard our voice" since it was in fact the key to open the doors of Heaven for our prayers.

וְאֶת עֲמָלֵנוּ – אֵלּוּ הַבָּנִים, כְּמָה שֶׁנֶּאֱמַר וכו' — **And our travail — that means the sons, as it is said, etc.**

The association of the word "travail" with children requires explanation.

The Gemara (*Sotah* 12a) asserts that Pharaoh's decree to drown all male Jewish babies (*Shemos* 1:22) was in effect for only a short time. It was issued on advice of Pharaoh's astrologers, who foresaw that the savior of Israel was to meet his downfall through water (a reference to the events of *Bamidbar* 20:7-14), but after Moses was born and was successfully spared from Pharaoh's evil decree, the sorcerers saw that the opportunity to avert the arrival of this savior had been missed, and the decree was rescinded.

Accordingly, the Haggadah's interpretation of this verse as referring to Pharaoh's decree regarding the Jewish children seems implausible. Since the "crying out" referred to occurred long after the birth of Moses (see *Shemos* 2:23) and the subsequent abolition of the decree, how could the Haggadah *say* that Hashem "saw our burden" refers to the decree to kill all male Jewish newborns, a practice which had long since been discontinued?

וְאֶת לַחֲצֵנוּ – זוֹ הַדַּחַק, כְּמָה שֶׁנֶּאֱמַר, וְגַם רָאִיתִי
אֶת הַלַּחַץ אֲשֶׁר מִצְרַיִם לֹחֲצִים אֹתָם.[1]

וַיּוֹצִאֵנוּ יהוה מִמִּצְרַיִם בְּיָד חֲזָקָה, וּבִזְרֹעַ נְטוּיָה,
וּבְמֹרָא גָּדֹל, וּבְאֹתוֹת וּבְמֹפְתִים.[2]

וַיּוֹצִאֵנוּ יהוה מִמִּצְרַיִם – לֹא עַל יְדֵי מַלְאָךְ, וְלֹא
עַל יְדֵי שָׂרָף, וְלֹא עַל יְדֵי שָׁלִיחַ, אֶלָּא הַקָּדוֹשׁ

The answer to this question is perhaps that although the decree itself had been annulled long before, its effect was still felt. A Jewish man laboring in the field or on the construction site would think to himself that if only the lives of his infant boys had been spared, they would now be able to assist him in fulfilling his overwhelming quota of work, for, as the Gemara (*Kiddushin* 31b) sets forth, one of the ways in which a child is obligated to honor his father is by taking his place in doing any arduous tasks assigned him by governmental authorities. Thus, the intent is not that the children are the burden, but rather that through their "burden," meaning *literally* their physically laborious tasks, they would recall the children they had been deprived of as a result of Pharaoh's decree.

Another explanation of the connection between "our burden" and children may be as follows. In *Shemos* 1:22 we are told, וַיְצַו פַּרְעֹה לְכָל עַמּוֹ לֵאמֹר כָּל הַבֵּן הַיִּלּוֹד הַיְאֹרָה תַּשְׁלִיכֻהוּ, *Pharaoh commanded his entire people, saying, "Every son that will be born — into the river shall you throw him!"* Rashi comments on this verse that it would appear that Pharaoh's decree was directed against *all* boys, not just those born to the Israelites. Rashi explains this by quoting a *midrash* that says that on the day of Moses' birth Pharaoh's astrologers advised him that this was the day that the liberator of the Jews would be born, although they could not tell whether this deliverer would be an Israelite or an Egyptian. Accordingly, for that one day the decree was issued that *all* newborn boys be drowned. This being the case, however, we would expect the wording of the verse to be a bit different from the way it is. Firstly, instead of וַיְצַו פַּרְעֹה, *Pharaoh commanded*, the Torah should have written "the *king of Egypt* commanded," as it does in other places where it discusses his particularly heartless, cruel decrees (*Shemos* 1:8; 1:15,17,18; 2:23). Also, rather than לְכָל עַמּוֹ, *his entire people*, we would expect לְכָל הָעָם, *the entire people*, since in this particular decree of infanticide he was certainly not relating to them as one of their own countrymen, but rather as a distant, heartless autocrat.

"And our oppression" — *that means stress, as it is said, "I have also seen the oppression by which the Egyptians are oppressing them."*[1]

"And HASHEM took us out of Egypt with a strong hand, and with an outstretched arm, and with great terror, and with signs, and with wonders."[2]

"And HASHEM took us out of Egypt" — *not through an angel, nor through a seraph, nor through a messenger. Rather the Holy*

---

(1) *Shemos* 3:9. (2) *Devarim* 26:8.

Apparently Pharaoh deliberately issued his decree in the manner described by the Torah in order to accomplish his goal. He did not wish to give the impression that this edict was being issued by the mighty "king of Egypt," the cruel and ruthless dictator, for then his people would surely not have cooperated and would have gone to any extreme to save the lives of their children. Rather, he explained to the people, speaking as a concerned member of the Egyptian nation, this unfortunate step had to be taken for their own good, in order to prevent the loss of their most valuable asset — Jewish slavepower. Through carrying out this seemingly brutal command they would ensure their future prosperity and comfortable life-style, for these slaves, so scrupulously honest and hard working, could never be replaced if they ever left their service.

Thus, when the Torah mentions our "burden" (עֲמָלֵנוּ, better translated as "our unfaltering, dedicated work"), it is reminiscent of Pharaoh's evil decree, since this loyal dedication to hard work was what enabled him to convince his people to carry it out.

וַיּוֹצִיאֵנוּ יי מִמִּצְרַיִם – לֹא עַל יְדֵי מַלְאָךְ — And Hashem took us out of Egypt — not through an angel.

The *Baal Haggadah* emphasizes here that the Exodus from Egypt in general, and the plague of the firstborn in particular, were carried out directly by Hashem, and not through any heavenly or mortal proxies. This would seem to contradict Rashi's comment in *Shemos* 12:29, that the seemingly superfluous "and" in the verse, וַיְהִי בַּחֲצִי הַלַּיְלָה וַה' הִכָּה כָל בְּכוֹר בְּאֶרֶץ מִצְרַיִם, *It was at midnight and Hashem smote every firstborn in the land of Egypt,* is written to signal that it was not Hashem acting alone, but rather in conjunction with (*and*) His Heavenly court. How can these two interpretations be reconciled?

The killing of the firstborn includes two aspects. On the one hand this was one of the many punishments meted out to the Egyptians; in addition it was this event that imparted an elevated status of holiness

בָּרוּךְ הוּא בִּכְבוֹדוֹ וּבְעַצְמוֹ. שֶׁנֶּאֱמַר, וְעָבַרְתִּי בְאֶרֶץ מִצְרַיִם בַּלַּיְלָה הַזֶּה, וְהִכֵּיתִי כָל בְּכוֹר בְּאֶרֶץ מִצְרַיִם מֵאָדָם וְעַד בְּהֵמָה, וּבְכָל אֱלֹהֵי מִצְרַיִם אֶעֱשֶׂה שְׁפָטִים, אֲנִי יהוה.[1]

וְעָבַרְתִּי בְאֶרֶץ מִצְרַיִם בַּלַּיְלָה הַזֶּה — אֲנִי וְלֹא מַלְאָךְ. וְהִכֵּיתִי כָל בְּכוֹר בְּאֶרֶץ מִצְרַיִם — אֲנִי וְלֹא שָׂרָף. וּבְכָל אֱלֹהֵי מִצְרַיִם אֶעֱשֶׂה שְׁפָטִים — אֲנִי וְלֹא הַשָּׁלִיחַ. אֲנִי יהוה — אֲנִי הוּא, וְלֹא אַחֵר.

בְּיָד חֲזָקָה — זוֹ הַדֶּבֶר, כְּמָה שֶׁנֶּאֱמַר, הִנֵּה יַד יהוה הוֹיָה בְּמִקְנְךָ אֲשֶׁר בַּשָּׂדֶה, בַּסּוּסִים בַּחֲמֹרִים בַּגְּמַלִּים בַּבָּקָר וּבַצֹּאן, דֶּבֶר כָּבֵד מְאֹד.[2]

---

to the Jewish nation as a whole. The birth of "My firstborn son Israel" was a result of the plague of the firstborn. As we say in the prayer עֶזְרַת אֲבוֹתֵינוּ, "All their firstborn You slew, but Your firstborn, Israel, You redeemed."

The *Maharal of Prague* asserts that just as childbirth is one of the three things which Hashem oversees "personally," not assigning it to any angel or other agent (*Taanis* 2a), so too the birth of a nation, especially His own holy people, is carried out directly by Hashem Himself. It is for this reason that Hashem was not accompanied by any angel or seraph when He delivered the Jewish people from the Egyptians.

However, when Hashem passes judgment He does so through consulting (as it were) with His Heavenly court, as *Rashi* points out in his commentary to *Bereishis* 11:7. Therefore, in inflicting judgment on the Egyptians, Hashem involved his Heavenly Court.

Thus, we may reconcile the two statements of the Haggadah and of *Rashi* in *Shemos*. Hashem acted alone in the sanctification of the emerging Jewish people; when He passed judgment and executed the sentence upon the firstborn, Hashem did so in conjunction (as it were) with His celestial court.

אֲנִי וְלֹא מַלְאָךְ — I, and not an angel.

On this night of the Exodus, Hashem revealed His true Unity, and demonstrated equivocally that אֵין עוֹד מִלְּבַדּוֹ, *There is* none other than *beside Him (Devarim* 4:35) Why, of all events, was this night chosen to

One, Blessed is He, Himself, in His glory, as it is said, "And I will pass through the land of Egypt this night, and I will kill every firstborn in the land of Egypt from man to beast, and upon all the gods of Egypt I will inflict judgments. I am HASHEM."[1]

"And I will pass through the land of Egypt this night" — I, and not an angel. "And I will kill every firstborn in the land of Egypt" — I, and not a seraph. "And upon all the gods of Egypt I will inflict judgments" — I and not any messenger. "I am HASHEM" — I am He, and none other.

"With a strong hand" — that means the pestilence, as it is said, "Behold, the hand of HASHEM is against your livestock in the fields, against the horses, the donkeys, the camels, the cattle, and the flocks, a very heavy pestilence."[2]

---

(1) *Shemos* 12:12. (2) Ibid. 9:3.

---

showcase Hashem's Unity, whereas at other times He acts through intermediaries or agents?

When Moses presented himself and his case to Pharaoh for the first time (כֹּה אָמַר ה' וכו' שַׁלַּח אֶת עַמִּי, *So said Hashem* . . . "Send out My people. . ." — *Shemos* 5:1), Pharaoh denied the existence of Hashem by saying, מִי ה' אֲשֶׁר אֶשְׁמַע בְּקֹלוֹ, *Who is Hashem that I should heed His voice. . .?* לֹא יָדַעְתִּי אֶת ה' וְגַם אֶת יִשְׂרָאֵל לֹא אֲשַׁלֵּחַ, *I do not know Hashem, nor will I send out Israel!* (ibid. v.2). In reaction to Pharaoh's blasphemous denial of His very being, on the night of the Exodus Hashem answered Pharaoh's "question" by showing that "Hashem" — acting entirely by Himself — is the One Who was sending out the Children of Israel.

Another thought may be offered to explain the appropriateness of this demonstration of unity at this juncture. We find that there is a profound correspondence between the mitzvos Israel performs and Hashem's course of actions. Just as the nation of Israel fulfills the Torah, Hashem, so to speak, "fulfills" the Torah. Thus, the Sages[1] tell us that just as the Jews don *tefillin* which contain selections from the Torah extolling the greatness and unity of Hashem (שְׁמַע יִשְׂרָאֵל ה' אֱלֹקֵינוּ ה' אֶחָד), so does Hashem — in an allegorical sense — "don" His own *tefillin* containing verses that speak the praise of unity of Israel (וּמִי כְעַמְּךָ יִשְׂרָאֵל גּוֹי אֶחָד בָּאָרֶץ).

The *Meshech Chochmah* questions why we are told that the angels protested Hashem's rescue of the Israelites at the Red Sea (arguing that the people had insufficient merit to warrant His intervention), yet we do not find any such protest when Hashem delivered the people out of

---

1. Berachos 6.

וּבִזְרֹעַ נְטוּיָה – זוֹ הַחֶרֶב, כְּמָה שֶׁנֶּאֱמַר, וְחַרְבּוֹ
שְׁלוּפָה בְּיָדוֹ, נְטוּיָה עַל יְרוּשָׁלָיִם.[2]

וּבְמֹרָא גָּדֹל – זוֹ גִּלּוּי שְׁכִינָה, כְּמָה שֶׁנֶּאֱמַר, אוֹ
הֲנִסָּה אֱלֹהִים לָבוֹא לָקַחַת לוֹ גוֹי מִקֶּרֶב גּוֹי, בְּמַסֹּת,
בְּאֹתֹת, וּבְמוֹפְתִים, וּבְמִלְחָמָה, וּבְיָד חֲזָקָה, וּבִזְרוֹעַ

Egypt. The key difference, he explains, is that on the night of the Exodus the nation stood united, with mutual regard and respect for each other (see *Mechilta* 5:28). This unity was a tremendous source of merit for them, not allowing for any prosecution on the part of the angels. At the Red Sea, however, we are taught (*Mechilta* 14:13) that the people were divided into four contentious factions, wrangling with each other over which course of action should be taken. This cantankerous behavior opened the door to the prosecution of the angels.

The command that each household was to join together in celebrating the *pesach* sacrifice communally was a vehicle to ingrain this spirit of unity among the people.

As a reflection of this human unity, so central to the Passover ritual, Hashem also "fulfilled" (as it were) this precept by demonstrating His complete Unity on this night, acting without any angelic assistance.

וּבְמֹרָא גָּדֹל – זוֹ גִּלּוּי שְׁכִינָה, כְּמָה שֶׁנֶּאֱמַר, אוֹ הֲנִסָּה וכו׳ — And with great terror — that means the revelation of the Shechinah
The verse following that quoted by the proof text states, אַתָּה הָרְאֵתָ לָדַעַת כִּי ה׳ הוּא הָאֱלֹקִים אֵין עוֹד מִלְּבַדּוֹ, *You have been shown in order to know that Hashem, He is the God! There is none beside Him!* (*Devarim* 4:35). The reference, explains *Rashi,* is to the Revelation at Mount Sinai. *Baal HaTurim* adds that since this verse is juxtaposed to the words כְּכֹל אֲשֶׁר עָשָׂה לָכֶם ה׳ אֱלֹקֵיכֶם בְּמִצְרַיִם לְעֵינֶיךָ, *such as everything that Hashem, your God, did for you in Egypt,* at the end of the preceding passage, an allusion to the revelation of Hashem's might at the Exodus is also intended. Accordingly, the revelation of Hashem on the night of the first Pesach is put on par with the great Revelation at the time of the Giving of the Torah, where we are told (see *Rashi* ibid.) that Hashem "tore open the seven heavens" and showed His glory to the Children of Israel, so manifest was the splendor of Hashem at the time.[1]

One wonders why the Torah states explicitly that "we were shown"

1. According to this explanation, we may better understand the use of the plural in the quoted verse (*Devarim* 4:34) — וּבְמוֹרָאִים גְּדֹלִים, *and with great terrors* — while in the verse being expounded (*Devarim* 26:8) the singular וּבְמֹרָא גָּדֹל, *and with great terror* is used. In the first case, there is a dual reference — one to the Exodus and the other to the Revelation at Sinai — while in the second, only the Exodus is mentioned.

"And with an outstretched arm" — *that means the sword, as it is said, "And his sword is drawn in his hand, outstretched over Jerusalem."[1]*

"And with great terror" — *that means the revelation of the Shechinah, as it is said, "Or has God ever tried to come to take unto Himself a nation [other than you] from the midst of another nation, with trials, with signs and with wonders, and with battle, and with a strong hand, and with an outstretched*

(1) *Divrei HaYamim I* 21:16.

Hashem's Unity, at the Sinaitic Revelation, whereas the equally compelling experience at the Exodus is left to an oblique inference.

The *Mechilta* comments on verse 34 — לָקַחַת לוֹ גוֹי מִקֶּרֶב גוֹי, *to take unto Himself a nation from the midst of another nation . . .* — that the process of the Exodus was like childbirth, where one person is "taken out" of another person. The *Maharal of Prague* develops this idea further, suggesting that the period of the Israelites' enslavement to the Egyptians is likened to the embryonic stage in a person's life.

The Sages tell us (*Niddah* 30b) that while yet unborn, every Jewish child undergoes an intensely thorough spiritual experience — he "is taught the entire Torah by an angel." Just before birth, the angel smites the child on his lips, causing him to forget — on the conscious level — all that he has learned.

Concerning the Revelation at Sinai, we find that the experience was completely internalized into the national psyche. In fact, we are enjoined (*Devarim* 4:9-10) never to forget this event for an instant and to pass on the impression it made on us to future generations. There is no evidence of any such lasting impression caused by the revelation of Hashem's glory in Egypt; this spiritually elevating experience, like that of the unborn child, was erased from the national consciousness. Thus, it is not mentioned — except by indirect implication — along with the experience of Mount Sinai.[1]

בְּמַסֹּת בְּאֹתֹת וּבְמוֹפְתִים וכו׳ וּבְמוֹרָאִים גְּדֹלִים — **With trials, with signs and with wonders . . . and with great terrors.**

1. It was actually to the Israelites' benefit that the extent of Hashem's revelation was not internalized. The reason Hashem does not reveal Himself at all times is that such an obvious Divine Presence would deprive people of the choice between doing good or evil, and thereby remove any possibility of earning merit and reward. We find that the Jewish people are praised by the prophet Jeremiah (2:2) for their unbounded faith in following Hashem's command to leave the relative security of Egypt and venture forth into the barren and perilous desert. Had the people been fully aware of the extent of Hashem's proposed revelation, they would not be deserving of such lavish praise for following His word, for this would have been the only logically sound course to take.

נְטוּיָה, וּבְמוֹרָאִים גְּדֹלִים, כְּכֹל אֲשֶׁר עָשָׂה לָכֶם יהוה אֱלֹהֵיכֶם בְּמִצְרַיִם לְעֵינֶיךָ.[1]

וּבְאֹתוֹת — זֶה הַמַּטֶּה, כְּמָה שֶׁנֶּאֱמַר, וְאֶת הַמַּטֶּה הַזֶּה תִּקַּח בְּיָדֶךָ, אֲשֶׁר תַּעֲשֶׂה בּוֹ אֶת הָאֹתֹת.[2]

וּבְמֹפְתִים — זֶה הַדָּם, כְּמָה שֶׁנֶּאֱמַר, וְנָתַתִּי מוֹפְתִים בַּשָּׁמַיִם וּבָאָרֶץ —

As each of the words דָּם, *blood,* אֵשׁ, *fire,* and עָשָׁן, *smoke,* is said, a bit of wine is removed from the cup, with the finger or by pouring.

דָּם וָאֵשׁ וְתִמְרוֹת עָשָׁן.[3]

דָּבָר אַחֵר — בְּיָד חֲזָקָה, שְׁתַּיִם. וּבִזְרֹעַ נְטוּיָה, שְׁתַּיִם. וּבְמֹרָא גָּדֹל, שְׁתַּיִם. וּבְאֹתוֹת, שְׁתַּיִם. וּבְמֹפְתִים, שְׁתַּיִם.

אֵלּוּ עֶשֶׂר מַכּוֹת שֶׁהֵבִיא הַקָּדוֹשׁ בָּרוּךְ הוּא עַל הַמִּצְרִים בְּמִצְרַיִם, וְאֵלּוּ הֵן:

There are seven expressions for the miracles wrought in Egypt in this verse. What is the significance of this number in this context? *Baal HaTurim* suggests that it corresponds to the seven days of Pesach. If each expression is matched with the respective day of the holiday, וּבְמוֹרָאִים גְּדֹלִים, *and with greatly awesome deeds,* which the Haggadah tells us refers to the revelation of the *Shechinah*, corresponds to the seventh day. Thus, it is possible that the "revelation of the *Shechinah*," of which the *Baal HaHaggadah* speaks, is actually the miracle of the Splitting of the Sea, where רָאֲתָה שִׁפְחָה עַל הַיָּם, מַה שֶּׁלֹּא רָאָה יְחֶזְקֵאל בֶּן בּוּזִי בַּמַּחֲזֶה, *a simple maidservant at the sea perceived more than the prophet Ezekiel ben Buzi in his Heavenly vision* (Ramban, *Bereishis* 18:2).

These seven levels of Divine intervention in Egypt might also parallel the seven days of creation. The *midrash* (*Bereishis Rabbah* 1:1) tells us that the whole purpose of creation was for the nation of Israel. Thus, the seven-step "formation" of the Jewish nation in Egypt parallels the seven days of formation of the universe.[1] (It is interesting to note that there are also seven expressions for Israel's being chosen by Hashem in the Yom Tov prayer אַתָּה בְחַרְתָּנוּ.)

---

1. *Rav Hutner, zt"l,* was fond of referring to the birth of the nation of Israel at the Exodus as the מַהֲדוּרָא תִּנְיָנָא (the second edition) of Man.

arm, and with great terrors, like all that HASHEM, your God, has done for you in Egypt before your eyes?"[1]

"And with signs" — that means the staff, as it says, "Take in your hand this staff with which you will perform the signs."[2]

"And with wonders" — that means the blood, as it says, "And I will display wonders in the heavens and on the earth:

As each of the words דָּם, blood, אֵשׁ, fire, and עָשָׁן, smoke, is said, a bit of wine is removed from the cup, with the finger or by pouring.

Blood, and fire, and pillars of smoke."[3]

An alternative explanation is: "With a strong hand" means two plagues. "And with an outstretched arm" — two more plagues. "And with great terror" — two more. "And with signs" — two more. "And with wonders" — two more.

These are the ten plagues which the Holy One, Blessed is He, brought upon the Egyptians in Egypt:

---

(1) *Devarim* 4:34 (2) *Shemos* 4:17. (3) *Yoel* 3:3.

לָבוֹא לָקַחַת לוֹ גוֹי מִקֶּרֶב גּוֹי בְּמַסֹּת בְּאֹתֹת וכו' כְּכֹל אֲשֶׁר עָשָׂה ה' אֱלֹקֵיכֶם בְּמִצְרַיִם לְעֵינֶיךָ — To come to take unto Himself a nation . . . from the midst of another nation, with trials, with signs. . . all that Hashem, your God, has done for you in Egypt before your eyes.

The seven expressions for "wonders" in this verse are intended to illustrate the assertion of *Devarim* 4:31: כִּי קֵל רַחוּם ה' אֱלֹקֶיךָ לֹא יַרְפְּךָ וְלֹא יַשְׁחִיתֶךָ, *For Hashem, your God, is a merciful God, He will not abandon you nor destroy you,* which is a sevenfold description of the miraculous Divine intervention in Egypt offered as proof to the Israelites that Hashem would always protect them. The last phrase in the verse — *Hashem. . . did for you. . . before your eyes* — may also be understood as part of this assurance as follows:

It has been asserted (see, for example, *B'nei Yisaschar*, p. 37) that if a person is miraculously saved from some calamity due to personal merit, he will live to see the downfall of the enemy from whose hands he was delivered. If, on the other hand, he was unworthy of salvation, but by Hashem's grace he was saved nonetheless, he will not merit seeing his foe's destruction.[1]

---

1. It is for this reason that Lot was prohibited from turning around and witnessing the destruction of Sodom. Lot's salvation was due to the merit of Abraham the Patriarch (*Rashi, Bereishis* 19:17). This concept may explain verses in *Tehillim* (58:11,12): יִשְׂמַח צַדִּיק כִּי חָזָה נָקָם וכו' וְיֹאמַר אָדָם אַךְ פְּרִי לַצַּדִּיק, *The righteous one shall rejoice when he sees vengeance etc. And*

As each of the plagues is mentioned, a bit of wine is removed from the cup.
The same is done at each word of Rabbi Yehudah's mnemonic.

דָּם. צְפַרְדֵּעַ. כִּנִּים. עָרוֹב. דֶּבֶר. שְׁחִין. בָּרָד. אַרְבֶּה. חֹשֶׁךְ. מַכַּת בְּכוֹרוֹת.

The Israelites at the time of the Exodus were sorely lacking in spiritual virtue, and did not, strictly speaking, deserve to be saved by Hashem. Thus, according to the above-stated principle, they should not have merited to see the terrible punishments meted out to the Egyptians. Hence, the fact that the "wonders and awesome deeds" were performed "before their eyes" was an added proof of the special consideration Hashem in His mercy showed for His people on that night.

◆§ The Ten Plagues

דָּם — Blood.

A few points of interest arise regarding the plague of blood. We are told (*Shemos* 7:21) that after the waters of the River turned to blood, וְהַדָּגָה אֲשֶׁר בַּיְאֹר מֵתָה וַיִּבְאַשׁ הַיְאֹר וְלֹא יָכְלוּ מִצְרַיִם לִשְׁתּוֹת מַיִם מִן הַיְאֹר, *the fish-life that was in the river died, and the river became foul, and the Egyptians could not drink water from the river.* From the phrasing of this verse, it is clear that the fact that the water became blood was insufficient to deter the people from drinking from the river; it was only once it "became foul" that they could not drink its water. Were the Egyptians perhaps, used to drinking blood?

Furthermore, during the Great Flood at the time of Noah, the Torah states: כֹּל אֲשֶׁר נִשְׁמַת רוּחַ חַיִּים בְּאַפָּיו מִכֹּל אֲשֶׁר בֶּחָרָבָה מֵתוּ, *All in whose nostrils was the breath of the spirit of life, of everything that was on dry land, died* (*Bereishis* 7:22), implying that the sea life did not perish (see *Rashi* ad loc.). *Sifsei Chachamim* explains (*Bereishis* 6:22 §12) that whereas the other animals "acted immorally," and thus deserved to be punished along with mankind, the fish did nothing wrong and were therefore spared. Being that Divine justice extends even to the animal kingdom, we must question why, in this plague, the fish were also condemned to die, making it, in a sense, an even more severe punishment than the Flood.

In his classic work *Mesillas Yesharim* (Chapter 1), *Rabbi Moshe Chaim Luzzatto* writes that the entirety of the Universe was created to serve the needs of mankind: When man stains his soul by sinning, he also, indirectly, causes damage to the world around him. This may be

---

mankind shall say, "There is, indeed, a reward for the righteous." When men see that the righteous have personally witnessed vengeance being exacted upon their enemies, they realize that their salvation was indeed earned by their virtuous deeds.

1. Blood 2. Frogs 3. Lice 4. Wild Beasts 5. Pestilence 6. Boils 7. Hail 8. Locusts 9. Darkness 10. Killing of the Firstborn.

compared to a person who has a highly contagious and deadly disease. All articles that come into contact with him must be discarded or purged, and sometimes even a whole building must be razed in order to be rid of any trace of the disease, so intense is man's influence upon his surroundings.[1]

We find that the prophet Ezekiel reprimands Pharaoh for his hubris, quoting him as saying, לִי יְאֹרִי וַאֲנִי עֲשִׂיתִנִי, *Mine is the river and I have created it* (*Yechezkel* 29:3). This self-deification and Pharoah's claim to being the "god" of the river had to be repudiated by Hashem: Therefore, Hashem had no choice but to strike at the river, rendering it useless and even noxious, and destroying all its life forms.

צְפַרְדֵּעַ — Frogs.

It is written (*Shemos* 8:2), וַתַּעַל הַצְפַרְדֵּעַ וַתְּכַס אֶת אֶרֶץ מִצְרָיִם, *The frog rose up and covered the land of Egypt.* Commenting on the seemingly incongruous use of the singular word "frog," Rabbi Akiva suggested that there was at first only one frog, but that when struck it split miraculously into two more frogs, continuously multiplying until they covered the entire land. Rabbi Elazar ben Azariah rejected this interpretation, explaining instead that the plague indeed began with one frog, but that this frog, through his croaking, signaled to hordes of others to come from all over to join him, until Egypt was swarming with them. (See *Sanhedrin* 67b.)

On what basis did Rabbi Elazar object to Rabbi Akiva's interpretation? The *Chasam Sofer* explains: The Sages tell us (*Pesachim* 53b) that when Chananiah, Mishael and Azariah were ordered by Nebuchadnezzar to worship his giant golden idol or face being burned alive in a fiery furnace (*Daniel* 3:13-18), they took inspiration from the frogs of the plague in Egypt. "If these mere animals, who are not bound by any commandments, risked their lives (by entering the ovens of the Egyptians — see *Shemos* 7:28) to do the will of their Creator," they reasoned, "then how much more so should we, who, as Jews, are enjoined to sanctify the Name of Hashem!" According to Rabbi Akiva, the entire episode of the frogs was supernatural: It must have been that Hashem created special creatures just for the purpose of carrying out this plague, since normal frogs obviously could not have multiplied in this

---

1. The power of man, to impact positively on his enviroment, is certainly not to be underestimated.

hydra-like fashion. If so, explains the *Chasam Sofer,* the logic of Chananiah and his colleagues was faulty. The frogs in Egypt may have sacrificed their lives to participate in sanctifying Hashem's Name because they had been created solely for this purpose. For human beings, however, who are created to sanctify Hashem through their *lives*, by performing mitzvos and the like, this may not necessarily be the correct course of action. It is for this reason that Rabbi Elazar ben Azariah rejected Rabbi Akiva's interpretation and explained the verse to be dealing with ordinary, natural frogs.

We may, however, understand Rabbi Akiva's interpretation as an extension of his own opinion and outlook as seen in a different context. We are told (*Berachos* 61b) that Rabbi Akiva died a martyr's death at the hands of the Romans, because he refused to obey their edict outlawing the practice and promulgation of Judaism. His persecutors tortured him by scraping off his flesh with iron combs. Despite the intense pain, he continuously declared his loyalty to Hashem and his unremitting acceptance of His will. When his students questioned how he managed to direct his mind to such sublime thoughts under such dire circumstances, he replied, "All my life I was troubled by the commandment, וְאָהַבְתָּ אֵת ה' אֱלֹקֶיךָ בְּכָל לְבָבְךָ וּבְכָל נַפְשְׁךָ, *You shall love Hashem, your God, with all your soul (Devarim* 6:5) (which demands "even if it means giving up one's life"), fearing that I would be unable to fulfill this mitzvah. Now that I have been granted the opportunity to carry it out, shall I not do so?!"

Based on this life perspective, there is no logical objection to the comparison which Chananiah, Mishael and Azariah drew between themselves and the frogs of Egypt, even if the latter were supernatural creatures created for this express purpose, for *all* men are also created for just this purpose. Both natural and supernatural were brought into being to sanctify the name of the Creator.

The *sefer Shiras HaChayos*, which develops the idea that all creatures in some way "sing praises" of Hashem in thier lives, states that the song of the frog expresses the praise, בָּרוּךְ שֵׁם כְּבוֹד מַלְכוּתוֹ לְעוֹלָם וָעֶד, *Blessed is the Name of His glorious kingdom for ever and ever*. This is the very verse we recite immediately after the declaration of faith of שְׁמַע יִשְׂרָאֵל (*Hear, O Israel: Hashem is our God, Hashem is the One and Only — Devarim* 6:4).

R' Chaim of Volozhin in *Nefesh HaChaim* (3:7) asserts that the verse שְׁמַע יִשְׂרָאֵל, *Hear O Israel, etc.*, constitutes our acceptance of Hashem's reign above, in the Heavens, while the following passage of בָּרוּךְ שֵׁם, *Blessed is the Name, etc.*, is a declaration of our acceptance of His dominion on earth — i.e. that He "condenses" or "mitigates" His Divine Presence in such a way that it may relate to and be perceived in our physical, mundane world. Why, of all the endless praises of Hashem, does this praise of Hashem's immanence find its way into the mouths of the frogs?

The *Ramban* comments that the "fire" described at the "burning bush" (*Shemos* 3:2) is not the ordinary earthly fire with which we are familiar from everyday life, but rather a Heavenly fire representing the Presence of Hashem, which does not burn objects with which it comes into contact.

Regarding the plague of frogs, the Torah states (*Shemos* 7:28) that they were found בְּבֵיתֶךָ וּבְתַנּוּרֶיךָ וּבְמִשְׁאֲרוֹתֶיךָ, *into your* [the Egyptians'] *houses. . . and into your ovens and into your kneading bowls;* yet at their death, it states only that they perished, מִן הַבָּתִּים מִן הַחֲצֵרֹת וּמִן הַשָּׂדֹת, *from the houses, from the courtyards, and from the fields* (ibid. 8:9), omitting any reference to the frogs of the ovens. *Baal HaTurim* explains that because of their willingness to sacrifice their lives for Hashem's sake by jump-ing into burning ovens, Hashem spared their lives. This occurred when Hashem miraculously changed the fire of these ovens from or-dinary fire to the kind of Heavenly fire which is not destructive and does not burn things. Since the frogs witnessed the fire of the ovens being "mitigated" and transformed into the Heavenly fire, it was fitting for them to sing this praise of "Blessed is the Name, etc.," which is (as ex-plained by *Nefesh HaChaim*) representative of this mitigation process.

שְׁחִין — Boils.

The Torah tells us of the reaction of Pharaoh's servants upon hearing about the impending plague of locusts: וַיֹּאמְרוּ עַבְדֵי פַרְעֹה אֵלָיו עַד מָתַי יִהְיֶה זֶה לָנוּ לְמוֹקֵשׁ שַׁלַּח אֶת הָאֲנָשִׁים וכו׳, *Pharaoh's servants said to him, "How long will this be a snare for us? Send out the men. . ."* (*Shemos* 10:7). Seemingly, these "servants" are not his sorcerers and magicians who had initially advised him (see ibid. 7:11,22; 8:3,14,15; 9:11). What happened to these experts now? Why is Pharaoh now being advised by his ordinary "servants" at large?

We are told: וְלֹא יָכְלוּ הַחַרְטֻמִּים לַעֲמֹד לִפְנֵי מֹשֶׁה מִפְּנֵי הַשְּׁחִין, *The sorcerers were not able to stand before Moses because of the boils* (*Shemos* 9:11). The *Ramban* explains that during the plague of boils, the sorcerers remained in their homes and out of shame of their helplessness did not appear at Pharaoh's court. It may be that these sorcerers were never healed of their boils and therefore never again were found offering advice to Pharaoh.

Ramban asks (*Shemos* 7:3): How it could be that the Torah states repeatedly וַיְחַזֵּק ה׳ אֶת לֵב פַּרְעֹה, *Hashem hardened the heart of Pharaoh?* Does this not contradict the basic axiom that a person can never be punished for actions that he was compelled to take? He solves this dilemma by noting that during the first five plagues it is written that it was *Pharaoh* who hardened his *own* heart, defiantly refusing to recognize Hashem's dominion over the world, himself included. After giving a sinner several chances at mending his ways, and seeing these opportunities disregarded, Hashem regards the sinner as being in an unrepentant state and ceases to provide these opportunities to him. Thus, it is only with regard to the last five of the ten plagues that we find that Hashem hardened Pharaoh's heart — after it was already abundantly clear that he was not the least bit remorseful.

One of the major causes of Pharaoh's lack of contrition was the advice of the sorcerers, who assured him that all of Moses' signs could be explained as ordinary phenomena of nature — or magic — although they must have known full well that Moses was indeed drawing upon supernatural, Divine powers. The first of the final five plagues, boils, occurred when Hashem began to punish Pharaoh for his long-standing defiant attitude. As such, it was the most appropriate occasion to penalize the sorcerers for their deception and impiety which was a major cause of Pharaoh's downfall. Perhaps for this reason the sorcerers left the stage at this juncture to indicate that Pharaoh's punishment of losing his free choice was a result of the sorcerers' bad advice.

בָּרָד — Hail.

הִנְנִי מַמְטִיר כָּעֵת מָחָר בָּרָד כָּבֵד מְאֹד — [Hashem said,] Behold, at this time tomorrow I shall cause a very heavy hail to rain down (*Shemos* 9:18). The word used for "to rain down" is מַמְטִיר, which has the connotation of an ordinary rainfall. Considering the ferocity of the hailstorm — וַה׳ נָתַן קֹלֹת וּבָרָד וַתִּהֲלַךְ אֵשׁ אָרְצָה, *Hashem sent out thunder and hail, and fire went earthward* (ibid. v. 23) — we would expect a more forceful verb, such as מַשְׁלִיךְ or מוֹרִיד, to be used.

The answer to this may be found by comparing this episode to a somewhat similar situation at the time of the Great Flood. There (*Bereishis* 7:12) the moderate word גֶּשֶׁם ("rain") is used at first, but afterwards (ibid. 7:17) the more severe מַבּוּל ("deluge") appears. *Rashi* (ibid. 7:14) explains that at first the downpour was like a rain (not so deadly), so as to give one last chance to the generation to repent and avoid the impending catastrophe altogether. When Hashem saw that no one took the initiative to repent, the water began to fall more vehemently, as a deluge. Perhaps the same course of events took place in Egypt: At first, it rained —מַמְטִיר — a hail of regular proportion — in order to signal to the Egyptians that there was still time to change and follow the word of Hashem. Only afterwards, when the opportunity was not seized, did it turn into a deadly, destructive storm.

Concerning the advent of this plague, the Torah tells us: הַיָּרֵא אֶת דְּבַר ה׳, מֵעַבְדֵי פַרְעֹה הֵנִיס אֶת עֲבָדָיו וְאֶת מִקְנֵהוּ אֶל הַבָּתִּים, *Whoever of Pharaoh's servants feared the word of Hashem hurried his servants and livestock* indoors (*Shemos* 9:20). Why does the verse refer exclusively to "Pharaoh's servants"? Were there no people in Egypt who had learned by now to fear Hashem's word other than among Pharaoh's servants? Furthermore, the appellation "fearer of the word of Hashem" seems a misnomer. Is someone who acts out of pragmatic self-interest, solely in order to avoid incurring a great monetary loss, deserving of the distinctive and honorable title? Surely they feared nothing but financial ruin!

Commenting on the description of Pharaoh's initial reaction to the plague of hail: [Pharaoh] said to [Moses and Aaron]. . . "הֹ הַצַּדִּיק וַאֲנִי וְעַמִּי הָרְשָׁעִים, *Hashem is the Righteous One, and I and my people are the wicked ones* (ibid. 9:27)," the *midrash* teaches that Pharaoh alone, of all his household, brought his livestock indoors, but not his servants and attendants. Based on this, *Chasam Sofer* suggests that it is possible to translate the words מֵעַבְדֵי פַרְעֹה (usually translated as "of Pharaoh's servants") in another way: "*more than* Pharaoh's servants." (The prefix מֵ can mean either "of" or "more than.") The sense of the verse would then be: "Those who feared Hashem more than Pharaoh's servants (who ignored Hashem's warning) hurried their servants and livestock indoors." These Egyptians truly deserved the title "fearers of Hashem" on account of their resolve to heed the admonishments of Moses and Aaron. However, the members of Pharaoh's household, who were eyewitnesses to, yet ignored, all the miracles were far from being "fearers of Hashem."

אַרְבֶּה — Locusts.

Regarding the verse, וְאָכַל אֶת כָּל עֵשֶׂב הָאָרֶץ אֵת כָּל אֲשֶׁר הִשְׁאִיר הַבָּרָד, *and it [the plague of locusts] shall devour all the grass of the land, everything that the hail had left* (*Shemos* 10:12), *Baal HaTurim* points out that the word וְיֹאכַל ("it/he shall devour/eat") appears in connection with a person who, although not entirely righteous, received recognition and reward for some act of generosity.[1] Thus the word וְיֹאכַל is found in connection with Jethro, קִרְאֶן לוֹ וְיֹאכַל לָחֶם (*Shemos* 2:20), who was present when Pharaoh devised his plans to persecute the Jews (as related in *Sotah* 11a). Jethro was spared because he ran away and later had Moses brought to his house, and Jethro fed him. One wonders, then, why Pharaoh was not granted some sort of reprieve in recognition of the gracious acceptance and sponsorship of the hungry and homeless Israelites by his predecessors several generations earlier. Was not the sustaining of the entire extended household of Jacob (*Bereishis* 47:12) worth at least as much as the meal Jethro gave Moses?

This query is compounded by a comment of the *Meshech Chochmah*. In connection with the first plague, the Torah states: וַיִּפֶן פַּרְעֹה וַיָּבֹא אֶל בֵּיתוֹ וְלֹא שָׁת לִבּוֹ גַּם לָזֹאת, *Pharaoh turned away and came to his house,*

---

1. See *Bereishis* 27:31.

and he did not take this to heart either (Shemos 7:23). Based on the Midrash, Meshech Chochmah explains that the water in Pharaoh's own house was not affected by the plague of blood. This was so, he explains, because unlike the rest of the Egyptians who had to purchase unaffected water from the Israelites, Pharaoh, having raised Moses and supported him in his own house, was considered to have already "paid" the price to the Jews for his water. Here then we find that Pharaoh's generosity did indeed serve him in good stead. Why was this not so regarding his hospitality?

It would appear that Pharaoh — or his ancestors, to be precise — had built up a good deal of merit from their previous generous treatment of the Jews. Nonetheless, this credit was more than expended when he changed his policy to harsh repression and enslavement of his former beneficiaries, thus indicating that this generosity was in fact self-serving — in order to further enslave the Jews.

חֹשֶׁךְ — Darkness.

Rashi (Shemos 10:22) offers two reasons (from Midrash Rabbah) for the timing of this particular plague to punish the Egyptians. Firstly, there were many Israelites who were exceedingly wicked and not worthy of being redeemed from Egypt with their compatriots. In order that a large-scale carnage in the Israelite camp not be witnessed by the Egyptians (thereby obscuring one of the central messages of the ten plagues: namely, that Hashem was punishing the Egyptians specifically, while miraculously protecting His own people from each form of destruction), the Egyptians were plunged into total darkness. The other explanation is that the Israelites, whose Exodus was already imminent, used this opportunity to enter their Egyptian neighbors' homes while they could not be seen, and search for valuables which they would later confiscate. This set the scene so that if the Egyptians, when asked to produce these items, would deny having them, the Israelites would be able to correct this "lapse of memory," pointing out the exact locations of everything requested.

These midrashic explanations pose several difficulties. For one thing, keeping in mind the extent of the casualties among the Israelites (Rashi [Shemos 13:18] puts the figure in the millions), it would seem that there was widespread bereavement throughout the camp; there was probably not a single family that did not lose a loved one. Was this not a rather inopportune moment for the people to be thinking about spoils and financial gain? Could they not wait just a few more days to deal with such mundane matters?

Perhaps the timing of these events was intentional and entirely appropriate. We have noted elsewhere in this commentary (p. 62) that the Jews were not eager to loot their Egyptian neighbors — although they rightfully earned every penny of this booty through generations of slave labor — and in fact Hashem had to plead with them (as it were) to do so. Furthermore, this act (the despoiling of Egypt) was fraught with spiritual danger, for the people, used to the abject poverty of slavery, were liable to misuse their newfound wealth — as was proven in time.[1] Therefore, in order to forestall any possibility that the Israelites would be led by their newly acquired wealth to euphoria and hence to haughtiness and inappropriate behavior, Hashem intentionally introduced the idea of despoiling the Egyptians when the people were not in a frame of mind to enjoy this act. It is well known that when a person encounters any kind of experience while he is severely distressed, this experience, whenever it recurs in the future, will always be associated with the troubled disposition the person originally felt while undergoing the experience. By having the gathering of wealth take place at this inopportune time, they would always regard this wealth with a bittersweet recollection, associating it with the great personal tragedy through which it had been acquired.

A comment of *Rashi* (based on another *Midrash*) seems to stand in direct contradiction to the *Midrash* cited above. In *Shemos* 12:36 we read, וַה' נָתַן אֶת חֵן הָעָם בְּעֵינֵי מִצְרַיִם וַיַּשְׁאִלוּם , *And Hashem gave the people [the Israelites] favor in the eyes of the Egyptians, and they gave them [their valuables]. Rashi* comments that the Egyptians were so eager to be rid of the Israelites at that point that they would say, "You ask for *one* golden vessel? Take *two* and just be gone!" Thus we find that there really was no necessity for the Jews to search out the hiding places of the Egyptians' valuables during the plague of darkness — the latter gave up their belongings more than willingly, without any need to "be reminded" of their locations.

Perhaps this seeming contradiction can be resolved if illuminated by a theme concerning the performance of mitzvos. The *Ramban,* commenting on *Bereishis* 6:20, says that when Noah was gathering all the animals of the world into the ark, he found that both a male and a female of each species that was to survive found their way by themselves, through Divine guidance, to the ark. However, when it came to those *"clean" species,* of which Noah took *seven* pairs in order to use them as offerings after the Flood, he had to actively search them out and bring them to the ark himself, since he was commanded to prepare these animals for this purpose. When a person has a Divine commandment to fulfill, he must invest his own effort in performing it; the mitzvah cannot be left to happen automatically, without any personal exertion or strain.

Another example of this principle can be found in *Bereishis* 24:17.

---

1. See *Berachos* 32a.

Rashi (quoting Midrash Rabbah) teaches that Eliezer, Abraham's servant who was searching for an appropriate mate for Isaac, was so impressed with the young Rebecca because when she came to the well, the level of water miraculously rose so that she would not have to exert herself to draw water from it. The Ramban (ad loc.) surmises that the source in the text for this midrashic interpretation is the fact that the verse (Bereishis 24:16) says only, וַתֵּרֶד ... וַתְּמַלֵּא כַדָּהּ וַתָּעַל, she went down. . ., filled her pitcher, and came up, and not ". . .she drew water, filled her pitcher, and came up." If so, continues the Ramban, this miracle only happened one time, for in v. 20 where Eliezer requests more water, the verse does indeed say, וַתִּשְׁאַב לְכָל גְּמַלָּיו, and she drew [water] for all his camels.

The explanation for this change may be that the second time, when the drawing was in response to a request of a wayfarer, and thus constituted the performance of a mitzvah (גְּמִילוּת חֲסָדִים), automatic, miraculous feats were no longer appropriate; the good deed had to be carried out through personal effort and toil.

The Torah tells us (Shemos 11:2) that it was the express wish of Hashem that the Israelites loot the precious belongings of the Egyptians. (The reasons for this are discussed elsewhere in this commentary — see page 62.) Nonetheless, since this act constituted the fulfillment of a commandment, and had to be done with an element of self-exertion and toil, the Israelites had to search out the valuables of the Egyptians. Of course, in actuality, this effort was not necessary for the procurement of these objects, since they were eventually surrendered quite willingly.

The Midrash (Shemos Rabbah 14:1) tells us that unlike the other nine plagues, Hashem consulted with the angels whether or not He should bring this plague upon the Egyptians. What was so unique about this punishment that necessitated such consultation?

We find that after the Great Flood, Hashem took an oath never to overturn the natural cycle of day and night (Bereishis 8:22). Thus, Hashem had to be "released from His vow" (as it were) in order to carry out this particular punishment, as it involved an interruption of the natural order of the day. It was to obtain such a release that He turned to the angels. Since the Children of Israel were the purpose of Creation, בְּרֵאשִׁית בִּשְׁבִיל יִשְׂרָאֵל שֶׁנִּקְרָא רֵאשִׁית, and the Israelites would now benefit from this unnatural darkness (see above), this aberration from the natural order of light and darkness was necessary; therefore the oath should not be binding.

King David in Tehillim (105:28) describes the Children of Israel's sojourn in Egypt, שָׁלַח חֹשֶׁךְ וַיַּחְשִׁךְ וְלֹא מָרוּ אֶת דְּבָרוֹ, He sent darkness and made it dark, and they did not defy His word. The Chasam Sofer explains this to mean that although the sightless Egyptians were completely powerless to restrain them, the Israelites did not exploit the situation and leave before the appointed time, since this would have displayed a rebellious disregard of Hashem's wishes.

This teaches us a fundamental lesson about the importance of temperance. The fervent longing of the Jews to leave the "house of bondage," remove themselves from their idolatrous and immoral surroundings and acquire their freedom was certainly a commendable emotion, yet they realized that they could not allow this yearning and desire — as purely motivated as they were — to overpower them and lead them to overstep the limits of propriety. Even the most praiseworthy attitudes and sentiments can become harmful if they are not expressed with moderation. In fact, the very word מִדָּה, which means "trait," also means "a measure," for even positive qualities are commendable only as long as they are properly "measured."

מַכַּת בְּכוֹרוֹת — Smiting of the Firstborn.

Prior to the plague of the smiting of the firstborn, the Jews were commanded to smear the blood of the *pesach* sacrifice on their doorposts as a sign in order to ensure that death would not enter into their houses. The commentators ask why it was necessary for the people to mark their homes in this fashion. After all, even without external markings, the previous plagues had not affected the Israelite population (see *Shemos* 8:19; 9:4,6,7,26; 10:23; 11:7).

As was explained elsewhere in this commentary (p. 83), the smiting of the firstborn actually played a dual role in the Exodus process. It was the last of the ten plagues through which Hashem fulfilled the prophecy to Abraham: וְגַם אֶת הַגּוֹי אֲשֶׁר יַעֲבֹדוּ דָּן אָנֹכִי, *But also the nation that they shall serve, I shall judge* (*Bereishis* 15:14). *Rashi* (ad loc.) comments that this is a specific reference to the ten plagues. In addition, it was the definitive act of redemption and consecration of the Jewish people, through which the concept of "the sanctity of Israel" came about. (See *Bamidbar* 3:13; 8:17.) It is interesting to note that when Moses first appeared before Pharaoh he was told to warn Pharaoh that if he did not agree to an exodus, his firstborn son would be killed (*Shemos* 4:23). The fact that this plague alone was specifically mentioned of all the punishments suffered by the Egyptians testifies to the unique role it played in the process of the redemption.

The other plagues which befell Egypt had no such dual function, but were intended solely as punishment to the Egyptians for their brutal enslavement and persecution of the Jews. Hence, there was no need for the Israelites to "ward off" the penetration of these plagues; they had no relevance to them at all. The smiting of the firstborn, however, since it also acted as the birthstone of the nascent Jewish people, left the

רַבִּי יְהוּדָה הָיָה נוֹתֵן בָּהֶם סִמָּנִים:
דְּצַ״ךְ • עֲדַ״שׁ • בְּאַחַ״ב.

people vulnerable to the reservations and protestations of Hashm's Heavenly court, who argued that the Jews did not merit this distinction. For this reason the mitzvah of the *pesach* sacrifice was given to them, and its blood used as a symbol, to show that the people were willing and capable of scrupulously following Hashem's commandments.

רַבִּי יְהוּדָה הָיָה נוֹתֵן בָּהֶם סִמָּנִים: דְּצַ״ךְ עֲדַ״שׁ בְּאַחַ״ב — Rabbi Yehudah abbreviated them thus: D'tzach, Adash, B'achav.

The commentators offer various possibilities as to what the significance of this system of abbreviation is. The *Baal HaHaggadah* would certainly not have bothered to record Rabbi Yehudah's arrangement if it were merely a convenient mnemonic.

Perhaps the division of the plagues into three groupings symbolizes the three types of decrees often used in the persecution of Jews, as evidenced throughout the ages almost until our very day. [The beastly persecution by the Nazis ימ״ש serves as a vivid example of these three elements.] Undoubtedly the oppression by the Egyptians followed the same pattern which may be described as follows: First an attempt is made to undermine and delegitimize Judaism as a valid religion — institutions of Jewish learning are closed and various facets of religious observance are outlawed. This is what the Sages referred to when they said, נִסְתַּמּוּ עֵינֵיהֶם וְלִבָּם מִצָּרַת הַשִּׁעְבּוּד, *Their eyes and hearts were blinded* [i.e. from seeing the light of the Torah] by the hardships of the enslavement (*Rashi, Bereishis 47:28*). Second, laws are enacted to impose physical hardships on the Jewish population, such as forced labor or random incarceration. Lastly, actual annihilation, especially of "non-productive" children, is put into action: כָּל הַבֵּן הַיִּלּוֹד הַיְאֹרָה תַּשְׁלִיכֻהוּ, *Every son that will be born — into the river shall you throw him* (*Shemos 1:22*).

Hashem punished the Egyptians מִדָּה כְּנֶגֶד מִדָּה, *measure for measure* for each of these phases, beginning with the last and most severe step. The first group of plagues — blood, frogs and vermin — were in retribution for murdering the Jewish babies. The connection of the plague of blood to this context of bloodshed is obvious. The plague of frogs, whose major annoyance is their constant croaking noise, was a punishment for the Egyptians callously ignoring the cries of their victims and the passionate pleas of their parents to spare them. It is interesting to note that concerning these two plagues the Torah says that they created a great stench (ibid. 7:21; 8:11). This is because the method of execution used by the Egyptians — drowning in the River — was probably chosen because it alleviated the difficulty faced very often by the

Rabbi Yehudah abbreviated them thus:
D'tzach, Adash, B'achav.

Nazis יִמַ"ש — how to dispose of such a huge number of corpses without creating a sanitary problem.

When the Patriarch Jacob requested not to be buried in Egypt, one of the reasons given for this appeal (*Rashi, Bereishis* 47:29) was that since Jacob knew that the dust of Egypt would later be transformed into vermin, he did not want his body to be subjected to the indignity that these insects would surely cause to all buried in there. Thus, the plague of vermin, when the very ground of Egypt crawled with these pests, can be seen as a sort of retribution for the fact that the helpless victims of Egyptian brutality were not even given the opportunity to have a decent burial.

The second grouping — wild beasts, pestilence and boils — corresponded to the second phase of the Egyptian persecution — physical enslavement. The plague of wild animals was a fitting punishment for the inhuman cruelty and harshness with which the Egyptians drove their hapless slaves — an appropriate precedent of the animalistic sadism of the Nazi beasts of our own time. Since the heartless enslavement of the Israelites must certainly have had a deleterious effect on their health, affecting both their external bodies which were directly involved in the backbreaking labor as well as their general fitness and resistance to disease, they were punished with both skin disease (boils) and illness (pestilence).

The last division — hail, locusts, darkness and plague of the firstborn — corresponded to the first type of repression — namely, religious persecution. When anti-Jewish legislation is first promulgated, religious institutions are usually not immediately shut down, but are allowed to operate for a time on a limited basis, catering only to those who are already enrolled in these institutions, without allowing new people to enter. For this reason the Egyptians were punished with the plague of hail which forced them [those among them who had learned to take Hashem's threats seriously] to gather all their livestock and servants and squeeze them into indoor quarters. The plague of locusts, which "covered the landscape, so that the land could not be seen" (*Shemos* 10:5), as well as the plague of darkness, symbolized the fact that the Egyptians attempted to extinguish the "light of the Torah" (cf. *Mishlei* 6:23). It is also noteworthy that concerning these two plagues the Torah stresses the damage done to the major food crops (ibid. 9:31; 10:15). This corresponds to the famous saying (*Pirkei Avos* 3:21), אִם אֵין קֶמַח אֵין תּוֹרָה, *if there is no flour [i.e. food], there is no [study of] Torah.*

It is a basic tenet of Judaism that the distinction of being elevated

The cups are refilled. The wine that was removed is not used.

רַבִּי יוֹסֵי הַגְּלִילִי אוֹמֵר: מִנַּיִן אַתָּה אוֹמֵר שֶׁלָּקוּ הַמִּצְרִים בְּמִצְרַיִם עֶשֶׂר מַכּוֹת, וְעַל הַיָּם לָקוּ חֲמִשִּׁים מַכּוֹת? בְּמִצְרַיִם מָה הוּא אוֹמֵר, וַיֹּאמְרוּ הַחַרְטֻמִּם אֶל פַּרְעֹה, אֶצְבַּע אֱלֹהִים הוּא.¹

---

above the other nations, as the "chosen people," being on a higher level than the other nations, is based solely on the Jews' acceptance of and adherence to the laws of the Torah. וּשְׁמַרְתֶּם וַעֲשִׂיתֶם כִּי הִוא חָכְמַתְכֶם וּבִינַתְכֶם לְעֵינֵי הָעַמִּים אֲשֶׁר יִשְׁמְעוּן אֵת כָּל הַחֻקִּים הָאֵלֶּה וְאָמְרוּ רַק עַם חָכָם וְנָבוֹן הַגּוֹי הַגָּדוֹל הַזֶּה, *You shall safeguard and perform them, for it is your wisdom and understanding in the eyes of the nations, who shall hear all these decrees and who shall say, "Surely a wise and discerning people is this great nation!"* (*Devarim* 4:6).[1] The nation of Israel is considered Hashem's firstborn in the same sense as the firstborn son who has an exalted position over all his siblings by virtue of the fact that he is generally the one who acts as assistant to his father in all family matters and in fulfillment of his responsibilities.[2]

Corresponding to the Egyptians' attempt to eliminate the source of Israel's unique status by depriving them of their Torah tradition which teaches them how to "assist their Father" in the realization of His goals, the Egyptians were punished with the slaying of their firstborn.

רַבִּי יוֹסֵי הַגְּלִילִי אוֹמֵר וכו׳ — Rabbi Yosi the Galilean says etc.

In this section the *Baal Haggadah* discusses the extent of extra severity of punishment the Egyptians experienced at the Red Sea beyond that of the ten plagues visited upon them in Egypt. One wonders, then, why the "lighter" plagues are described in such lengthy detail in the Torah (*Shemos*, Chaps. 7-12), while the extent of the Egyptians' "heavier" ordeal at the sea is intimated only by a subtle textual allusion.

In *Shemos* 11:1 we read, עוֹד נֶגַע אֶחָד אָבִיא עַל פַּרְעֹה וְעַל מִצְרַיִם אַחֲרֵי כֵן יְשַׁלַּח אֶתְכֶם מִזֶּה, *One more plague [i.e., that of the firstborn] shall I bring upon Pharaoh and upon Egypt; after that he shall send you forth from*

---

1. *Rabbi Moshe Feinstein* commented that it is apparent from the passage in the Sabbath liturgy, אַתָּה אֶחָד וְשִׁמְךָ אֶחָד וּמִי כְּעַמְּךָ יִשְׂרָאֵל גּוֹי אֶחָד בָּאָרֶץ, *You [Hashem] are One and Your Name is One; and who is like Your people Israel, one [i.e. a unique] nation on earth,* that the "uniqueness" of Israel is not because of some innate facet of their character or some physical trait, but only because they are the ones who testify to *Hashem's* uniqueness.
2. The *Maharal of Prague* notes that the word בְּכֹר ("firstborn") consists of the letters whose numerical values are 2, 20 and 200, respectively, all numbers which are second, i.e. "2" is the second number in the single digits, "20" is the second in the tens, and "200" is the second in the hundreds, because the firstborn is in the "number-two" position of the family right behind the father.

The cups are refilled. The wine that was removed is not used.

R abbi Yosi the Galilean says: "What is the source for the idea that the Egyptians suffered ten plagues in Egypt and suffered fifty plagues on the sea? What does it say concerning Egypt? 'And the sorcerers said to Pharaoh: It is the finger of God.'[1]

---

(1) *Shemos* 8:15.

---

here. The *Lashon Chachamim* explains that it was this prophecy that emboldened Pharaoh to chase after the Children of Israel after their escape. After all, he was not a careless or capricious ruler, and had a staff of astrologers and sorcerers, whom the Sages credit with having provided him with some rather accurate information. What could have led him to pursue such a foolhardy course of action, which eventually led to utter disaster for him and his people? He relied on the word of Moses that Hashem had only "one more plague" to visit upon the Egyptians. When he heard that the Israelites were apparently lost in the desert (ibid. 14:3), he was certain that the God of Israel had "run out of strength."

In truth, a more basic issue must be pursued. Why, indeed, did Hashem speak of only "one more plague," if yet another disaster of even greater proportions was actually in store for the Egyptians?

The key to answering this question lies in a comment made by the *Ramban* on *Bereishis* 46:15. The Torah had just finished enumerating the descendants of Leah, and sums up, כָּל נֶפֶשׁ ... שְׁלֹשִׁים וְשָׁלֹשׁ, *All the souls . . . numbered thirty-three.* A perusal of the list of names, however, shows that only thirty-two persons were mentioned. The Sages explain the discrepancy as follows: Levi's wife was pregnant with Yocheved when she departed the Land of Canaan, and gave birth to her upon arriving in Egypt. Thus, she was not listed by name among those who left Canaan with Jacob's camp, but she was counted among the total population of those who reached Egypt. The commentator Ibn Ezra points out that this would make Yocheved an astounding 130 years old at the time she gave birth to Moses! Why, he asks, would such a miraculous occurrence not even be given mention in the Torah, considering the significant amount of attention the Torah devotes to Sarah's miraculous childbirth at merely ninety years of age? The answer to this, asserts the Ramban, is that it is not the purpose of the Torah to record every unusual or miraculous event that ever took place in the lives of the righteous. Rather, the Torah shows that Hashem "decrees and carries out." Only when a particular miracle is foretold by Hashem or His prophet to demonstrate a specific lesson or moral is the outcome pre-

וְעַל הַיָּם מָה הוּא אוֹמֵר, וַיַּרְא יִשְׂרָאֵל אֶת הַיָּד הַגְּדֹלָה
אֲשֶׁר עָשָׂה יהוה בְּמִצְרַיִם, וַיִּירְאוּ הָעָם אֶת יהוה,
וַיַּאֲמִינוּ בַּיהוה וּבְמֹשֶׁה עַבְדּוֹ.¹ כַּמָּה לָקוּ בָּאֶצְבַּע? עֶשֶׂר
מַכּוֹת. אֱמוֹר מֵעַתָּה, בְּמִצְרַיִם לָקוּ עֶשֶׂר מַכּוֹת, וְעַל הַיָּם
לָקוּ חֲמִשִּׁים מַכּוֹת.

---

served in the Torah, as in the case of the Splitting of the Red Sea here. Since the events were not foretold to Pharaoh by Moses, it is not the Torah's function to describe all miracles which occur for the salvation of Hashem's chosen saints. As far as the declaration, "One more plague [i.e., that of the firstborn] shall I bring upon Pharaoh and Egypt," it meant that Hashem had only one more *declared* punishment to mete out to the Egyptians.

Rav Yitzchak Hutner, zt"l, questioned why the Splitting of the Sea is not mentioned in the "Covenant Between the Parts" (*Bereishis* 15), which was the prophecy which encapsulated the future of Abraham's descendants for the following few centuries, until their reentry into the Promised Land. After all, the ten plagues as well as the despoiling of Egypt are mentioned there (ibid. v. 14; cf. *Rashi*), though the judgment of the Egyptians at the Sea was of a much greater scope than these plagues. The *Mechilta* (quoted by *Rashi* to *Shemos* 15:22) asserts further that the booty gathered by the Israelites at the sea dwarfed that taken from the Egyptians in Egypt.

A further question (quoted in *Zichron Niflaos*) is posed in the *Zohar Chadash*: Why is it that we are told to go to such great lengths to show our gratitude to Hashem for the Exodus from Egypt? Was it not preordained generations earlier, and sealed in a covenant between Abraham and Hashem, just as the persecution and enslavement by the Egyptians were?

The answer to these questions is that while the tribulations and the Exodus were preordained events, the experiences at the sea were not part of this predestined, promised plan. This was an "extra dosage" of salvation granted by Hashem, solely out of His love for Israel. Through this miraculous event the Jews saw that they were indeed beloved to Hashem, and realized that *all* the experiences they had undergone in the process of the Exodus were a result of this love. These events were not merely the actions of the God of Truth redeeming the promise He made to their worthy forebears. For this reason, no prophecy concerning the Splitting of the Sea was included in the Covenant with Abraham. This event was intended to serve exclusively as an expression of

And what does it say concerning the sea? 'And Israel saw the great hand which HASHEM manifested against Egypt, and the people feared HASHEM, and they believed in HASHEM and in Moses, His servant.'[1] How much were they scourged by one finger? Ten plagues. Thus you can conclude that in Egypt they suffered ten plagues, and on the sea they suffered fifty plagues."

---

(1) *Shemos* 14:31.

---

love to the Jews. Hashem was acting out of true concern for them, and not merely to fulfill ancient promises. Consequently, we are especially indebted to Hashem and we are obligated to express our gratitude to Him for the Exodus from Egypt.

וַיַּרְא יִשְׂרָאֵל אֶת הַיָּד הַגְּדֹלָה אֲשֶׁר עָשָׂה ה' בְּמִצְרַיִם וַיִּירְאוּ הָעָם אֶת ה' וַיַּאֲמִינוּ בַּה' וּבְמֹשֶׁה עַבְדּוֹ — **And Israel saw the great hand which Hashem manifested against Egypt, and the people feared Hashem, and they believed in Hashem and in Moses, His servant.**

Under examination, this passage presents several questions. Firstly, why does the verse begin by referring to "Israel," but change to "the people" afterwards? The *Chasam Sofer* repeatedly stresses that the appellation יִשְׂרָאֵל, *Israel*, refers to the Jews when they are on an elevated spiritual plane, while עַם, *people*, which can also mean "waning" or "losing vitality," alludes to a diminished spiritual status. Why the change in mid verse? Furthermore, after seeing Hashem's unbounded love and dedication to them, it would seem that the Israelites' response should have been to *love* Hashem, rather than to *fear* Him.

In *Shemos* 3:14, Hashem reveals Himself to Moses by the Name אֶהְיֶה אֲשֶׁר אֶהְיֶה (I Shall Be As I Shall Be), but then immediately modifies this Name to אֶהְיֶה (I Shall Be). *Rashi,* quoting the Gemara (*Berachos* 9a), explains that originally Hashem wanted Moses to tell the people that *He would be* with them at this time of distress, *as He would be* with them in future times of suffering; He later omitted the reference to future troubles, in order to avoid disheartening the people by arousing thoughts of more travails to come their way. Why did Hashem originally think it necessary to mention the future troubles that would beleaguer the Jewish people?

The exile and suffering in Egypt were the prototype for all similar episodes in times to come. Just as the seed of a fruit tree carries within it the germ and the "blueprint" of the thousands of fruits that this tree will produce in its lifetime, so did the events in Egypt bear within them the "buds" of all similar travails of the future. This is also the reason

רַבִּי אֱלִיעֶזֶר אוֹמֵר: מִנַּיִן שֶׁכָּל מַכָּה וּמַכָּה שֶׁהֵבִיא הַקָּדוֹשׁ בָּרוּךְ הוּא עַל הַמִּצְרִים בְּמִצְרַיִם הָיְתָה שֶׁל אַרְבַּע מַכּוֹת? שֶׁנֶּאֱמַר, יְשַׁלַּח בָּם חֲרוֹן אַפּוֹ — עֶבְרָה, וָזַעַם, וְצָרָה, מִשְׁלַחַת מַלְאֲכֵי רָעִים.[1] עֶבְרָה, אַחַת. וָזַעַם, שְׁתַּיִם. וְצָרָה, שָׁלֹשׁ. מִשְׁלַחַת מַלְאֲכֵי רָעִים, אַרְבַּע. אֱמוֹר מֵעַתָּה, בְּמִצְרַיִם לָקוּ אַרְבָּעִים מַכּוֹת, וְעַל הַיָּם לָקוּ מָאתַיִם מַכּוֹת.

רַבִּי עֲקִיבָא אוֹמֵר: מִנַּיִן שֶׁכָּל מַכָּה וּמַכָּה שֶׁהֵבִיא הַקָּדוֹשׁ בָּרוּךְ הוּא עַל הַמִּצְרִים בְּמִצְרַיִם הָיְתָה שֶׁל חָמֵשׁ מַכּוֹת? שֶׁנֶּאֱמַר, יְשַׁלַּח בָּם חֲרוֹן אַפּוֹ, עֶבְרָה, וָזַעַם, וְצָרָה, מִשְׁלַחַת מַלְאֲכֵי רָעִים. חֲרוֹן אַפּוֹ, אַחַת. עֶבְרָה, שְׁתַּיִם. וָזַעַם, שָׁלֹשׁ. וְצָרָה, אַרְבַּע. מִשְׁלַחַת מַלְאֲכֵי רָעִים, חָמֵשׁ. אֱמוֹר מֵעַתָּה, בְּמִצְרַיִם לָקוּ חֲמִשִּׁים מַכּוֹת, וְעַל הַיָּם לָקוּ חֲמִשִּׁים וּמָאתַיִם מַכּוֹת.

כַּמָּה מַעֲלוֹת טוֹבוֹת לַמָּקוֹם עָלֵינוּ.

אִלּוּ הוֹצִיאָנוּ מִמִּצְרַיִם, וְלֹא עָשָׂה בָהֶם שְׁפָטִים, דַּיֵּנוּ.

אִלּוּ עָשָׂה בָהֶם שְׁפָטִים, וְלֹא עָשָׂה בֵאלֹהֵיהֶם, דַּיֵּנוּ.

---

that Hashem's retribution against the Egyptians was stretched out over such a long period of time, even though it was obviously within His power to decimate them with one mighty, deadly blow (as He did to the armies of Sennacherib centuries later); Hashem wanted these punishments to also act as precursors of similar acts of retribution in the future.

Despite the fact that the people were not informed of Hashem's full Name — i.e., the travails of future times were not mentioned to them — those Jews who were attuned to a higher spiritual level (יִשְׂרָאֵל) realized from the lengthy procedure of redemption that the events taking place were not merely for the "here and now," but were an allusion to more persecutions and salvations in the future. The simpler

Rabbi Eliezer says: "What is the source for the idea that each plague which the Holy One, Blessed is He, brought upon the Egyptians in Egypt consisted of four plagues? As it is said, 'He did send upon them the kindling of His wrath, rage, and misery, and trouble, a legation of angels of calamity.'[1] 'Rage' — one; 'and misery' — two; 'and trouble' — three; 'a legation of angels of calamity' — four. Thus you can conclude that they suffered forty plagues in Egypt and two-hundred plagues on the sea."

Rabbi Akiva says: "What is the source for the idea that each plague that the Holy One, Blessed is He, brought upon the Egyptians in Egypt consisted of five plagues? As it is said, 'He did send upon them the kindling of His wrath, rage, and misery, and trouble, a legation of angels of calamity.' 'The kindling of His wrath' — one; 'rage' — two; 'and misery' — three; 'and trouble' — four; 'a legation of angels of calamity' — five. Thus you can conclude that they suffered fifty plagues in Egypt and two hundred and fifty plagues on the sea."

How indebted we are to the Omnipresent for all the levels of good He has done for us!
Had He taken us out of Egypt
  and not inflicted judgments upon them
                    — it would have been enough for us.
Had He inflicted judgments upon them
  and not upon their gods —
                    it would have been enough for us.

---

(1) *Tehillim* 78:49.

---

people (עַם), however, did not understand this subtle indication. However, upon the Splitting of the Sea, even these common folk recognized from the awesome power unleashed by Hashem that this was not the last time Hashem would have to come to their rescue. Thus the verse tells us that "Israel" — the more spiritual people — "saw the great hand which Hashem inflicted upon Egypt," while the more common people did not realize this until the Splitting of the Sea, at which point even "the people (עַם) feared Hashem," understanding for

אִלּוּ עָשָׂה בֵאלֹהֵיהֶם, וְלֹא הָרַג אֶת בְּכוֹרֵיהֶם, דַּיֵּנוּ.
אִלּוּ הָרַג אֶת בְּכוֹרֵיהֶם, וְלֹא נָתַן לָנוּ אֶת מָמוֹנָם, דַּיֵּנוּ.

the first time that there would be more difficulties and salvations in the future. The verse cited finished with the ultimate tool of survival and strength in the long exile. וַיַּאֲמִינוּ בַּה׳ וּבְמשֶׁה עַבְדּוֹ, *and they believed in Hashem and in Moses, His servant.* It is our firm belief and reliance on Hashem, and the Torah leaders He provides us in all generations that has given us the ability to persevere.

אִלּוּ עָשָׂה בֵאלֹהֵיהֶם וְלֹא הָרַג אֶת בְּכוֹרֵיהֶם — **Had He inflicted judgments upon their gods, and not killed their firstborn.**

This stich is based on the verse, וּבְכָל אֱלֹהֵי מִצְרַיִם אֶעֱשֶׂה שְׁפָטִים אֲנִי ה׳, *and upon all the gods of Egypt shall I inflict judgments; I am Hashem"* (Shemos 12:12). *Sefas Emes* questions the all-encompassing scope of this verse: How can the Torah state that Hashem destroyed *all* the gods of Egypt, when in fact there was one deity which was left intact — that of *Baal Tzefon* (see ibid. 14:2 and *Rashi* ad loc.)? Surely the Torah does not speak in approximations or exaggerations!

The matter may become clear in light of an interpretation of this verse, offered by *Rabbi Yitzchak of Volozhin.* He explained that Moses was surprised to hear that Hashem intended to "personally" descend to Egypt to attend to the smiting of the firstborn. After all, Moses was forbidden to so much as *pray* to Hashem in Pharaoh's city due to the inundation of idolatrous images found there (*Rashi, Shemos* 9:29). Did Hashem intend to descend to a place of such abomination, where even mentioning His Name was considered improper? Hashem responded to Moses' bewilderment by explaining that He of course planned to rid Egypt of its idolatry — "upon all the gods of Egypt shall I inflict judgments" — *before* descending to Egypt. In this fashion He would then be able to "enter" Egypt to smite their firstborn. Accordingly, it was only the lowly gods in Egypt proper that needed to be eliminated; *Baal Tzefon*, located in the wilderness (adjacent to the Red Sea), far from urban population centers, was not included in this decree. Thus, Hashem's statement that He would "inflict judgments against all the gods of Egypt" — in Egypt proper — was indeed accurate.

אִלּוּ הָרַג אֶת בְּכוֹרֵיהֶם — **Had He killed their firstborn.**

Jews are commanded to observe certain mitzvos indicative that the firstborn (boys as well as animals) of Israel possess a heightened level of sanctification. All these mitzvos, given in commemoration of the slaying of the Egyptian firstborn, are limited to those males who are firstborn to their mothers — פֶּטֶר רֶחֶם, *first issue of the womb (Shemos*

Had He inflicted judgments upon their gods
and not killed their firstborn
— it would have been enough for us.
Had He killed their firstborn and not given us their riches
— it would have been enough for us.

13:12). A father's first offspring is specifically excluded (see *Shemos* 13:2,12,15; 34:19; *Bamidbar* 3:12; 8:16; 18:15). The *Ramban* (*Shemos* 12:30) questions this distinction since the Sages tell us that Hashem killed all Egyptian firstborn, whether paternal or maternal. Since the sanctity of the Jewish firstborn is rooted in the Egyptian firstborn plague (see *Bamidbar* 3:13; 8:17), one would expect the full spectrum of Jewish firstborn to be accorded this sanctity, yet this is not the case.

As mentioned earlier, *Rav Hutner zt"l,* categorized the plague of the killing of the firstborn as serving a dual role in the events of the Exodus. On the one hand, it was the tenth in a series of punishments against the Egyptians, in retribution for their sinful treatment of the Jews. On the other hand, it also serves as a seminal event in the formation of Jewish nationhood, infusing the nation as a whole with the "sanctity of Israel" and conferring an elevated status of holiness upon the Jewish firstborn. This latter sanctified status was put into effect through the medium of the slaying of the Egyptian firstborn. Hashem declared before Moses' first meeting with Pharaoh: בְּנִי בְכֹרִי יִשְׂרָאֵל, . . . וַתְּמָאֵן לְשַׁלְּחוֹ הִנֵּה אָנֹכִי הֹרֵג אֶת בִּנְךָ בְּכֹרֶךָ, *My firstborn son is Israel!* . . . *but you have refused to send him out; behold, I shall slay your firstborn son* (*Shemos* 4:22-23). Pharaoh and his people were punished measure for measure: They abused Hashem's firstborn, and thus had to forfeit their own.

It would seem that regarding the punitive aspect of the tenth plague, the definition of "firstborn" was taken in a very broad sense, and the fathers' firstborn were also included. (In fact, the Sages tell us that even the senior member of the family — one who managed family affairs together with or in the absence of the father — was killed in the plague, even when he was not biologically the firstborn of either parent.) Regarding the second facet of this plague, in which the slaying of the firstborn is seen as a unique measure-for-measure action to avenge the maltreatment of Hashem's "firstborn," only those who were firstborn according to the narrower definition — those who were "the first issue of the womb" — were included in this symbolic act. *Ramban* (ibid.) states clearly that the custom among royalty was to have the firstborn of the mother as the heir apparent to the throne. In a similar vein the *royal status* of Jewish firstborn is unique to those who have "opened the womb."

אִלּוּ נָתַן לָנוּ אֶת מָמוֹנָם, וְלֹא קָרַע לָנוּ אֶת הַיָּם, דַּיֵּנוּ.

This definition of the two aspects of the slaying of the firstborn may help us solve a seeming chronological inconsistency in our daily liturgy. In the morning, R' Hutner zt"l, points out that in the prayer עֶזְרַת אֲבוֹתֵינוּ, in which the Exodus from Egypt is recalled, we say, מִמִּצְרַיִם גְּאַלְתָּנוּ וּמִבֵּית עֲבָדִים פְּדִיתָנוּ כָּל בְּכוֹרֵיהֶם הָרָגְתָּ וּבְכוֹרְךָ גָּאָלְתָּ, *You redeemed us from Egypt . . . and from the house of slavery You liberated us. You slew all their firstborn, but Your firstborn [i.e. Israel] You redeemed.* In the parallel prayer in the evening service, the order of events is reversed, הַמַּכֶּה בְעֶבְרָתוֹ כָּל בְּכוֹרֵי מִצְרָיִם וַיּוֹצֵא אֶת עַמּוֹ יִשְׂרָאֵל מִתּוֹכָם לְחֵרוּת עוֹלָם, *Who smote in His wrath all the firstborn of Egypt, and took His people Israel out from their midst to eternal freedom.* Since the descriptions of the other events of the Exodus in both paragraphs follow strict chronological order, the chronological reversal of these particular phrases is quite puzzling.

This problem, however, can be solved if we recall the dual nature of the plague of the killing of the firstborn. In the evening prayer, where we speak of Hashem "smiting in His wrath the Egyptian firstborn," we refer to the plague as one of the "Ten Plagues," a punitive act of retribution. This took place prior to the physical Exodus, following the schedule described at the Covenant Between the Parts (*Bereishis* 15): וְגַם אֶת הַגּוֹי אֲשֶׁר יַעֲבֹדוּ דָּן אָנֹכִי וְאַחֲרֵי כֵן יֵצְאוּ בִּרְכֻשׁ גָּדוֹל, *But also the nation that they shall serve, I shall judge* ["a reference to the ten plagues" — Rashi] *and afterwards they shall leave with great wealth* (ibid. v. 14). In the morning prayer, on the other hand, we focus on the other aspect of the killing of Egypt's firstborn — i.e. the relationship of the Egyptians' firstborn's fate to that of the Israelites' firstborn: "You slew all their firstborn, but Your firstborn You redeemed." This unique relationship between Hashem and His people — "My firstborn son is Israel!" — did not fully emerge until *after* the Jews succeeded in casting off the yoke of slavery to Egypt; only then did it become clear to the Egyptian people — and to the world — that this was truly Hashem's chosen nation. Hence, in this prayer the Exodus is mentioned before the killing of the firstborn, for while the physical death of the Egyptian firstborn occurred before the Israelites left Egypt, their resultant elevated status occurred only afterward, on the morrow of the redemption.

אִלּוּ נָתַן לָנוּ אֶת מָמוֹנָם — **Had He given us their riches . . ..**

In *Shemos* 11:2, Hashem tells Moses, דַּבֶּר נָא בְּאָזְנֵי הָעָם וְיִשְׁאֲלוּ אִישׁ מֵאֵת רֵעֵהוּ. . . כְּלֵי כֶסֶף וּכְלֵי זָהָב, *Please speak in the ears of the people that they request each man from his [Egyptian] neighbor . . . silver vessels*

Had He given us their riches and not split the sea for us
— it would have been enough for us.

and golden vessels. Commenting on the puzzling use of the word "please" in this context, *Rashi* explains that Hashem was especially eager (as it were) that the Israelites despoil the Egyptians, so that "that righteous man" (Abraham) not protest to Hashem saying, "You have implemented the decree of וַעֲבָדוּם וְעִנּוּ אֹתָם אַרְבַּע מֵאוֹת שָׁנָה, *and they shall enslave them and oppress them four hundred years* (*Bereishis* 15:13), but the promise of וְאַחֲרֵי כֵן יֵצְאוּ בִּרְכֻשׁ גָּדוֹל, *and afterwards they shall leave with great wealth* (ibid. v. 14), You did not fulfill."

The commentators raise an obvious question. Is not the mere desire that Hashem's promise be kept, sufficient cause for Him to encourage the Jews to take the spoils of the Egyptians? Was it only to avoid being confronted by an indignant Abraham that He wished His promise to be realized? We may also question the appellation for Abraham here, of all the many places he is mentioned in Rabbinic literature, as "that righteous man."

Tosefes Berachah asserts that the promise of "afterwards they shall leave with great wealth" is [as implied by the word "afterwards,"] dependent on the total fulfillment of the previous verse — "and they shall enslave them . . . four hundred years." Since the full four-hundred-year decree was not carried out in its literal sense, he continues, the pledge of "great wealth" was not really binding. Why, then, did Hashem grant the Israelites these riches if they were not entitled to them? It was because of the great merits and righteousness of their sainted ancestors — particularly Abraham, who was so careful to avoid taking the spoils of war, no matter how deserving he was of them (see *Bereishis* 14:22-23). Abraham, having forgone wealth that he did deserve in order to honor Hashem as the only true source of wealth, was deserving of reward (see *Bereishis* ibid.). It is for this reason that Abraham is referred to, regarding this matter, as "that righteous man."

וְלֹא קָרַע לָנוּ אֶת הַיָּם. . . — . . .and not split the sea for us.

In the "Song at the Sea" the Torah says, ה׳ אִישׁ מִלְחָמָה ה׳ שְׁמוֹ, *"Hashem is a Man of war, Hashem is His Name"* (*Shemos* 15:3). The Name "Hashem" always signifies God's attribute of *mercy,* whereas "Elokim" connotes the attribute of strict judgment. It seems incongruous that the name "Hashem" should be emphasized in this context of war and death.

Just before the miraculous events at the sea, Hashem said He was acting וְיָדְעוּ מִצְרַיִם כִּי אֲנִי ה׳, *"so that Egypt may know that I am Hashem"*

אִלּוּ קָרַע לָנוּ אֶת הַיָּם,
וְלֹא הֶעֱבִירָנוּ בְתוֹכוֹ בֶּחָרָבָה,
דַּיֵּנוּ.

אִלּוּ הֶעֱבִירָנוּ בְתוֹכוֹ בֶּחָרָבָה,
וְלֹא שִׁקַּע צָרֵינוּ בְּתוֹכוֹ,
דַּיֵּנוּ.

(Shemos 14:18). *Ibn Ezra* explains: Hashem wanted the Egyptians to recognize His dominion even though it would be just as they were dying. One wonders what exactly would be gained by having the Egyptian army find out the truth moments before their death. My grandfather (the *Ohr Yechezkel*) explained this as an act of mercy — by recognizing the existence and omnipotence of Hashem, even if only for a few seconds, the Egyptians merited that their souls would have some measure of reprieve in the afterlife. It is for this reason that the verse concludes "that I am *Hashem*" — again using the Name associated with Hashem's attribute of mercy. Similarly in the "Song at the Sea" what on the surface appeared only as war and retribution was in fact also an expression of Divine mercy. It is the merciful Hashem who is the Man of war.

Why, however, should the wicked and vicious blasphemers of Hashem's Name and tormentors of His people be deserving of such Divine mercy? The matter may be clarified by applying a principle developed by the *Alter of Kelm* in *Chochmah U'Mussar* (Vol. II p. 344). He questions of why the firstborn merited their special exalted status accorded them by Torah. Prior to being replaced by the Levites and Kohanim at the time of the sin of the Golden Calf, it was the firstborn who were the practitioners of the sacrificial services. The *Alter of Kelm* answers that the Torah tells us (*Bamidbar* 3:13; 8:17) that this status was given them because when Hashem smote the Egyptian firstborn, those of the Israelites were spared. They performed no meritorious deeds, they exhibited no special sublime spiritual characteristics; the only reason they were consecrated is because they were a *vehicle* through which Hashem sanctified His name by miraculously preserving them while all Egyptian firstborn perished. This teaches that even an inactive catalyst for increased honor of Heaven deserves recognition and reward. The Egyptians as well, although completely wicked and thoroughly deserving of the highest levels of punishment, nevertheless served as a medium through which Hashem was able to show the entire world His mastery over mighty kingdoms and the seemingly immutable forces of nature. For this reason alone they were entitled to a small measure of benevolence from Hashem, at least posthumously.

Had He split the sea for us
and not let us pass through it on dry land
>> *— it would have been enough for us.*
Had He let us pass through it on dry land
and not sunk our foes in it
>> *— it would have been enough for us.*

אִלּוּ קָרַע לָנוּ אֶת הַיָּם וְלֹא הֶעֱבִירָנוּ בְּתוֹכוֹ בֶּחָרָבָה דַּיֵּנוּ — **Had He split the Sea for us, and not let us pass through it on dry land — it would have been enough for us.**

The question is obvious: Of what good would have been the parting of the Red Sea waters if we had not been permitted to cross through them? In what way would this situation have been sufficient to require our gratitude to Hashem?

I found in the work *Toras Tzion* a reference to a liturgical poem apparently based on midrashic sources recited on the last day of Pesach, which describes the Splitting of the Sea as follows: The top third of the water split open, וְהַמַּיִם לָהֶם חוֹמָה מִימִינָם וּמִשְּׂמֹאלָם, *and the water was a wall for them, on their right and on their left* (Shemos 14:22). The middle third of the water hardened into a solid, over which the Jews passed, as a sort of bridge — נִצְבוּ כְמוֹ נֵד נוֹזְלִים קָפְאוּ תְהֹמֹת בְּלֶב יָם, *straight as a wall stood the running water, the deep waters congealed in the heart of the sea* (ibid. 15:8). The bottom third of the sea remained fluid, like ordinary water. When the Egyptians tried to pass over the "bridge," they sank instead into the bottom third of the sea and drowned there, while the Israelites looked on from above, personally witnessing the downfall of their erstwhile tormentors and executioners.

According to this detailed portrayal of the events at the sea, this stich may now be clearly understood. Had Hashem only split the sea in its entirety, enabling us to pass through, but had not, additionally, divided the waters into three levels, creating the solid "bridge" that enabled us to witness the destruction of the wicked Egyptians, that too would have been sufficient for us to thank Him.

אִלּוּ הֶעֱבִירָנוּ בְתוֹכוֹ בֶּחָרָבָה — **Had He let us pass through it on dry land.**

Two similar verses in the Torah describe the splitting of the waters of the Red Sea: וַיָּבֹאוּ בְנֵי יִשְׂרָאֵל בְּתוֹךְ הַיָּם בַּיַּבָּשָׁה וְהַמַּיִם לָהֶם חוֹמָה מִימִינָם וּמִשְּׂמֹאלָם, *And the Children of Israel came within the sea on dry land; and the water was as a wall* (חוֹמָה) *for them, on their right and on their left* (Shemos 14:22); וּבְנֵי יִשְׂרָאֵל הָלְכוּ בַיַּבָּשָׁה בְּתוֹךְ הַיָּם וְהַמַּיִם לָהֶם חֹמָה מִימִינָם וּמִשְּׂמֹאלָם, *And the Children of Israel went on dry land in the midst of the*

אִלּוּ שִׁקַּע צָרֵינוּ בְּתוֹכוֹ,

וְלֹא סִפֵּק צָרְכֵּנוּ בַּמִּדְבָּר אַרְבָּעִים שָׁנָה,   דַּיֵּנוּ.

אִלּוּ סִפֵּק צָרְכֵּנוּ בַּמִּדְבָּר אַרְבָּעִים שָׁנָה,

וְלֹא הֶאֱכִילָנוּ אֶת הַמָּן,   דַּיֵּנוּ.

---

sea; and the water was a wall (חֹמָה) *for them, on their right and on their left* (ibid. 14:29). Commenting on the shortened spelling of the word חֹמָה (missing a ו"י) in the second verse, the *Baal HaTurim* explains that, spelled this way, the word can also be read as חֵמָה, meaning "wrath." He points out that the Sages tell us that the idolatrous image known as the "idol of Michah," which became an object of worship in later generations (see *Shoftim* 17), actually was brought from Egypt and was transported by the Israelites to the Promised Land upon their Exodus from Egypt. The wrath of the sea was, as it were, a reaction to the treacherous behavior of those responsible for this act of disloyalty. One wonders, nonetheless, why this incident, and the resultant wrath, are alluded to in the second verse, while in the first verse the word is spelled in the usual manner.

Perhaps a solution might emerge if we take note of another subtle difference in phrasing between the verses. In the first verse we are told that the people came "within the midst of the sea on dry land," whereas the latter verse reverses the phrase: They went "on dry land in the midst of the sea." This difference in order brings to mind the well known *midrash* (*Midrash Tehillim* 114) that describes the course of events at the Splitting of the Sea. At first, Hashem commanded the Jews to march straight into the sea, not revealing to them His intention to divide the waters. The Israelites were, not surprisingly, apprehensive about carrying out Hashem's command, until a group of them, led by Nachshon ben Aminadav, the intrepid leader of the tribe of Judah, jumped into the raging sea, whereupon Hashem parted its waters for the remainder of the people to pass through. Thus, when the first verse mentions "the midst of the sea" *before* "on dry land," the reference is, most likely, to the heroic behavior of Nachshon's "leader" group, who entered the *midst of the sea* even before there was any *dry land* there. In the second verse, however, where "the midst of the sea" is mentioned *after* the phenomenon of the "dry land," the reference is more likely to the Israelite "followers" *passing through* the midst of the sea — between its "walls." Thus the first verse, which focuses on the noble and heroic among the Israelites, does not allude to the less virtuous among them. The second verse, however, which clearly refers to those Jews

Had He sunk our foes in it
and not satisfied our needs in the desert for forty years
— it would have been enough for us.
Had He satisfied our needs in the desert for forty years
and not fed us the manna
— it would have been enough for us.

---

who initially lacked full faith, alludes with the shortened spelling
(חמה) to the "wrath" of the sea caused by those who "exported" the
"idol of Michah."

This concept may help answer another question, posed by the
Meshech Chochmah, which has been addressed elsewhere in this
commentary. Why do we find that at the Red Sea the angels tried to
dissuade Hashem from granting the Israelites salvation, owing to their
sin of idol worship, whereas we find no such opposition at the time of
the Exodus from Egypt the previous week? According to the idea
mentioned in the preceding paragraph, this can be explained by the
fact that at the time of the Exodus, all Jews displayed a heroic and
praiseworthy attitude of trust in Hashem to lead them through the
perilous desert: כֹּה אָמַר ה' זָכַרְתִּי לָךְ חֶסֶד נְעוּרַיִךְ אַהֲבַת כְּלוּלֹתָיִךְ לֶכְתֵּךְ אַחֲרַי
בַּמִּדְבָּר בְּאֶרֶץ לֹא זְרוּעָה, *Thus says Hashem: I have remembered for*
you the righteousness of your youth, the love of your bridal days
— your going after Me into the desert, into an arid land (Yirmiyahu
2:2). This trusting and loving attitude was enough to neutralize any
attempts by accusing angels to point out the negative aspects of Israel's spiritual state. When the Jews were encamped at the Red Sea
(before Nachshon's "leap of faith"), however, there was no virtuous
behavior on their part to offset the criticisms of their heavenly detrac-
tors.

Had — אִלוּ סִפֵּק צָרְכֵּנוּ בַּמִּדְבָּר אַרְבָּעִים שָׁנָה, וְלֹא הֶאֱכִילָנוּ אֶת הַמָּן, דַּיֵּנוּ
He satisfied our needs in the desert for forty years and not fed us
the manna, it would have been enough for us.

By virtue of the separate reckoning of manna, we must assume that
the "satisfying of our needs in the desert" apparently alludes to the
other extraordinary forms of protection and care afforded the Israelites by the "Clouds of Glory." During their forty years of wander-
ing: שִׂמְלָתְךָ לֹא בָלְתָה מֵעָלֶיךָ וְרַגְלְךָ לֹא בָצֵקָה זֶה אַרְבָּעִים שָׁנָה, *Your garment*
did not wear out upon you and your feet did not swell, these forty years
(Devarim 8:4). These forms of Divine sustenance come in the form of
"hidden (or unobvious) miracles" (that is, they did not involve any
overt, abrupt change in the laws of nature), unlike the phenomenon of

אִלּוּ הֶאֱכִילָנוּ אֶת הַמָּן,

וְלֹא נָתַן לָנוּ אֶת הַשַּׁבָּת, דַּיֵּנוּ.

אִלּוּ נָתַן לָנוּ אֶת הַשַּׁבָּת,

וְלֹא קֵרְבָנוּ לִפְנֵי הַר סִינַי, דַּיֵּנוּ.

אִלּוּ קֵרְבָנוּ לִפְנֵי הַר סִינַי,

וְלֹא נָתַן לָנוּ אֶת הַתּוֹרָה, דַּיֵּנוּ.

אִלּוּ נָתַן לָנוּ אֶת הַתּוֹרָה,

וְלֹא הִכְנִיסָנוּ לְאֶרֶץ יִשְׂרָאֵל, דַּיֵּנוּ.

אִלּוּ הִכְנִיסָנוּ לְאֶרֶץ יִשְׂרָאֵל,

וְלֹא בָנָה לָנוּ אֶת בֵּית הַבְּחִירָה, דַּיֵּנוּ.

עַל אַחַת כַּמָּה, וְכַמָּה טוֹבָה כְפוּלָה וּמְכֻפֶּלֶת לַמָּקוֹם עָלֵינוּ. שֶׁהוֹצִיאָנוּ מִמִּצְרַיִם, וְעָשָׂה בָהֶם שְׁפָטִים, וְעָשָׂה בֵאלֹהֵיהֶם, וְהָרַג אֶת בְּכוֹרֵיהֶם, וְנָתַן לָנוּ אֶת

the manna, which was clearly a "revealed (or perceptible) miracle."[1]

In comparing these two classes of miracles, "revealed" ones are of greater potency than "hidden" ones, since they involve a more unambiguous testimony to Hashem's mastery over the world. Hence, the thrust of this stitch is as follows: *Had He satisfied our needs in the desert for forty years* with the hidden miracles that generally sustain life, but not exposed us to the "revealed miracle of the manna," it would still be sufficient reason for us to thank Hashem.[2]

אִלּוּ קֵרְבָנוּ לִפְנֵי הַר סִינַי וְלֹא נָתַן לָנוּ אֶת הַתּוֹרָה דַּיֵּנוּ — Had He brought us before Mount Sinai and not given us the Torah, it would have been enough for us.

Of what benefit would being brought to Mount Sinai have been, if not for the giving of the Torah?

In *Shemos* 19:4, speaking of a time prior to the giving of the Torah, Hashem tells us, וָאֶשָּׂא אֶתְכֶם עַל כַּנְפֵי נְשָׁרִים וָאָבִא אֶתְכֶם אֵלָי, *I [Hashem]*

---

1. See *Ramban, Shemos* 12:17 for a breathtaking exposure to this fundamental idea.

2. Indeed, the *Ramban* points out (in his commentary to *Parashas Lech Lecha*) that the Patriarchs never experienced the kind of overt "revealed miracles" that their less worthy descendants did. It is for this reason that the manna is described as *"that you did not know, nor did your forefathers know"* (*Devarim* 8:3). Since the manna was a "revealed miracle," it was not "known" (experienced) by our saintly ancestors, the Patriarchs.

Had He fed us the manna and not given us the Sabbath
　　　　　　　— it would have been enough for us.
Had He given us the Sabbath
　and not brought us before Mount Sinai
　　　　　　　— it would have been enough for us.
Had He brought us before Mount Sinai
　and not given us the Torah
　　　　　　　— it would have been enough for us.
Had He given us the Torah
　and not brought us into the Land of Israel
　　　　　　　— it would have been enough for us.
Had he brought us into the Land of Israel
　and not built for us the Beis HaMikdash
　　　　　　　— it would have been enough for us.

H*ow multiple, then, is our debt to the Omnipresent. For He took us out of Egypt, and inflicted judgments upon them and upon their gods, and killed their firstborn, and gave us*

---

have borne you on the wings of eagles and brought you to Me. The Targum renders "I have brought you to Me" as "I have brought you to My service." The *Mechilta*, however, offers a different interpretation: "I have brought you to Mount Sinai." Apparently their mere presence at the mountain was of great spiritual significance and left a lasting influence on their national character. The Sages point out, for instance, that when the Torah states, וַיִּחַן שָׁם יִשְׂרָאֵל נֶגֶד הָהָר, *Israel encamped there, opposite the mountain [Sinai]* (*Shemos* 19:2), the verb וַיִּחַן, *encamped*, is in the singular form, implying that the diverse people of the entire nation were at peace with each other, united in brotherhood, in their eagerness to accept the Torah. This is but one element of the significance of the Sinai experience. The Israelites were able to internalize this sense of unity and its concomitant trait of selflessness. We may say that Mount Sinai itself, which the Sages say (*Megillah* 29a) was a symbol of humility and modesty, was the teacher of this lesson through its unpretentious and unassuming nature. Hence, coming to Mount Sinai was in itself an experience of great spiritual growth for which we thank Hashem.

עַל אַחַת כַּמָּה וְכַמָּה טוֹבָה וכו' לַמָּקוֹם עָלֵינוּ וכו' וְנָתַן לָנוּ אֶת הַתּוֹרָה — How multiple, then, is our debt to the Omnipresent. . . . and

מָמוֹנָם, וְקָרַע לָנוּ אֶת הַיָּם, וְהֶעֱבִירָנוּ בְתוֹכוֹ בֶּחָרָבָה,
וְשִׁקַּע צָרֵינוּ בְּתוֹכוֹ, וְסִפֵּק צָרְכֵּנוּ בַּמִּדְבָּר אַרְבָּעִים
שָׁנָה, וְהֶאֱכִילָנוּ אֶת הַמָּן, וְנָתַן לָנוּ אֶת הַשַּׁבָּת, וְקֵרְבָנוּ
לִפְנֵי הַר סִינַי, וְנָתַן לָנוּ אֶת הַתּוֹרָה, וְהִכְנִיסָנוּ לְאֶרֶץ
יִשְׂרָאֵל, וּבָנָה לָנוּ אֶת בֵּית הַבְּחִירָה, לְכַפֵּר עַל כָּל
עֲוֹנוֹתֵינוּ.

gave us the Torah.

In *Shemos* 15:22, we are taught, וַיֵּלְכוּ שְׁלֹשֶׁת יָמִים בַּמִּדְבָּר וְלֹא מָצְאוּ מָיִם, *and they [the Children of Israel] went for a three-day period in the desert, but they did not find water.* The Sages (*Bava Kamma* 22b), interpreting water allegorically as Torah (see *Isaiah* 55:1), explain that when the Jews traveled for three days without Torah they became "thirsty," that is, weakened in a spiritual sense. To slake this spiritual thirst it was ordained that the Torah should be read publicly at intervals not exceeding three days. This is the source of our custom to read from the Torah every Shabbos, Monday, and Thursday in the synagogue.

Considering that שְׁלוּחֵי מִצְוָה אֵינָן נִיזּוֹקִין הֵיכָא דִּשְׁכִיחַ הֶיזֵּיקָא שָׁאנֵי, *One never suffers any misfortune while engaged in a mitzvah, unless he goes to a particularly dangerous place* (*Pesachim* 8b), one wonders how it could happen that the people met upon ill fortune, since during this entire time they were "encamping and journeying according to the word of Hashem" (*Bamidbar* 9:20). There is no greater mitzvah than following the express commands of Hashem, and there is no greater misfortune than experiencing a spiritual decline! The two are conceptually incompatible. We must conclude, therefore, that for the Jewish people a situation without Torah is considered a "particularly dangerous situation," leaving them, as noted above, vulnerable to misfortune. The Evil Inclination (יֵצֶר הָרַע) seeks relentlessly to destroy man by weakening his moral fiber, but Hashem Who created it has given us the antidote to this scourge — the Torah (see *Kiddushin* 30b). Without Torah, we are truly in mortal danger, prey to the wiles of the Evil Persuader.[1]

וּבָנָה לָנוּ אֶת בֵּית הַבְּחִירָה — and built for us the Beis HaMikdash.

This entry appears to be inappropriate. While all the other items mentioned in this paragraph refer to some miracle or kindness that Hashem, in His infinite benevolence, granted us, the Temple was built

---

1. This is the thrust of the famous parable of Rabbi Akiva (*Berachos* 61b) where he compares Jews forsaking Torah to fish forsaking water.

their riches, and split the sea for us, and let us pass through it on dry land, and sank our foes in it, and satisfied our needs in the desert for forty years, and fed us the manna, and gave us the Sabbath, and brought us near Him at Mount Sinai, and gave us the Torah, and brought us into the Land of Israel, and built for us the Beis HaMikdash to atone for all of our sins.

entirely through natural means, by the hands of mortal men. Why is this included on the list of blessings for which we are grateful to the Omnipresent?

The *Meshech Chochmah* (*Shemos* 19:13) explains the significance of the fact that after the departure of the *Shechinah* (Divine Presence) from Mount Sinai, the people were immediately permitted to ascend the mountain and even to graze their animals there. A central objective of the Torah and its laws is to uproot idolatrous ideas from the minds of the Israelites. Hashem wished to impress upon them the notion that the sanctity associated with any material object, no matter how great, is not innate. When the source of sanctity leaves, that object reverts completely to its previous, unconsecrated and mundane state. The awesome sanctity of Mount Sinai during the giving of the Torah, לֹא תִגַּע בּוֹ יָד כִּי סָקוֹל יִסָּקֵל אוֹ יָרֹה יִיָּרֶה אִם בְּהֵמָה אִם אִישׁ לֹא יִחְיֶה, *A hand shall not touch it [the mountain], for he shall surely be stoned or thrown down; whether animal or person, he shall not live* (*Shemos* 19:13), was due solely to the presence of Hashem's Glory; the mountain *per se* had no holiness attached to it, and returned to its prior state when that Glory departed. This is the antithesis of idolatry, a doctrine based upon the idea that there is innate godliness in material objects, be they icons, heavenly objects, or imposing natural formations. Similarly, the *halachah* states that a person who is ritually impure, even with the most severe level of contamination, may touch the stones of the actual Temple building — from the *outside*; only *entering* the sacred premises is forbidden to such people. It is only Hashem's Presence which dwells there that gives the Temple its sanctity; the bricks and walls of the edifice have no innate sanctity whatsoever.

Accordingly, the *Beis HaMikdash* is indeed built by Hashem, not the construction of stones and bricks itself, but its most vital sustaining ingredient — the Presence of the *Shechinah*.

וּבָנָה לָנוּ אֶת בֵּית הַבְּחִירָה, לְכַפֵּר עַל כָּל עֲוֹנוֹתֵינוּ — **and built for us the Beis HaMikdash, to atone for all of our sins.**

The *Rambam* (*Beis HaBechirah* 1:1) describes the commandment to build a Temple to Hashem with the following words: "It is a positive mitzvah to make a House for Hashem, equipped for the offering of

רַבָּן גַּמְלִיאֵל הָיָה אוֹמֵר: כָּל שֶׁלֹּא אָמַר שְׁלֹשָׁה
דְּבָרִים אֵלּוּ בַּפֶּסַח, לֹא יָצָא יְדֵי
חוֹבָתוֹ, וְאֵלּוּ הֵן,

---

sacrifices, and [furthermore] this is where we must come to celebrate [the festivals] three times a year." The *Beis HaMikdash* thus serves two main purposes: the offering of sacrifices and the celebration of the three pilgrim festivals. The words *to atone for all our sins* would seem to refer to the first function of the *Beis HaMikdash* — to be the location where sacrifices took place. One wonders, however, why no reference is made here to the second reason for building the Temple — to be the locus for the national pilgrimages on the festivals.

We have noted earlier that the *Seder* evening is imbued with an element of solemnity reminiscent of Yom Kippur eve. A further correlation of this Yom Kippur theme may be seen in the commandment to avoid all leaven on Pesach, which parallels the powerlessness of the *Yetzer Hara* over Israel on Yom Kippur (see *Yoma* 20b). (Leaven is employed by the Sages as a metaphor for the *Yetzer Hara*.) In light of this Yom Kippur-*Seder* nexus, it is now apparent why the Haggadah emphasizes this particular aspect of the function of the *Beis HaMikdash* — namely, that it is the place *to atone for all of our sins*.

Another explanation for the emphasis on the atonement for sins may be offered, as follows: It is well known that Hashem applies a stricter standard of justice to righteous people than to ordinary men; in the words of the Sages, הַקָּבָּ"ה מְדַקְדֵּק עִם סְבִיבָיו כְּחוּט הַשַּׂעֲרָה *He is exacting with those who surround him [the righteous] even down to a hair's breadth* (*Yevamos* 121b). The *Shem MiShmuel* extends this concept and asserts that even the same person, when on a higher spiritual plane, is subject to a higher standard than when his spirituality is less exemplary. The many privileges we have been granted by Hashem are certainly evidence of our exalted status in His eyes. However, this exalted status, in addition to earning us a unique level of protection from Hashem, subjects us to a unique level of scrutiny for our deeds. We therefore mention the expiatory aspect of the *Beis HaMikdash*.

עַד כָּאן אוֹמְרִים בְּשַׁבָּת הַגָּדוֹל — On Shabbos HaGadol, the recitation of the Haggadah stops at this point.

Several theories have been offered by the commentators as to why the Sabbath before Pesach is known as *Shabbos HaGadol*, "the great (or, long) Sabbath." One reason, given by *Rashi* in his *Sefer HaPardes*, is that it is customary that the rabbi of the community deliver a sermon

On Shabbos HaGadol, the recitation of the Haggadah stops at this point.

Rabban Gamliel used to say: Whoever has not discussed these three things on Pesach has not fulfilled his obligation, namely:

on this Sabbath, thereby adding significantly to the length of the service; hence the name "the long Sabbath"! Why is this custom particular to Pesach?

The midrash (Yalkut Shimoni, Malachi 3:50) says, "If Israel neglects to repent, they will not be redeemed. And one is not generally led to feel repentant unless he experiences some degree of pain, displacement or lack of financial security. And they are not destined to repent until Elijah comes (to herald the Messianic era), as it says (Malachi 3:23-24), הִנֵּה אָנֹכִי שֹׁלֵחַ לָכֶם אֵת אֵלִיָּה הַנָּבִיא לִפְנֵי בּוֹא יוֹם ה׳ הַגָּדוֹל וְהַנּוֹרָא וְהֵשִׁיב לֵב אָבוֹת עַל בָּנִים וכו׳, Behold, I am sending to you Elijah the prophet before the coming of the great and terrible Day of Hashem; and he will turn the heart of the father to the children. . ."

Rav Dessler zt"l, in his classic Michtav MeEliyahu (3:23) explains: The underlying theme of the midrash is that when one experiences suffering, it helps him shift focus from his material desires to become more spiritually oriented. It takes a great religious leader to ensure that this spiritual potential is not lost, and that this message is properly assimilated and acted upon. It is therefore unlikely that this great spiritual revival will occur until Elijah himself comes to initiate it.

In a similar vein, the Gemara (Megillah 11a) homiletically interprets the verse, וְאַף גַּם זֹאת בִּהְיוֹתָם בְּאֶרֶץ אֹיְבֵיהֶם לֹא מְאַסְתִּים וְלֹא גְעַלְתִּים, But despite all this, while they will be in the land of their enemies, I will not have been revolted by them nor will I have rejected them (Vayikra 26:44), as reference to the great religious leaders (e.g. Daniel, Chananiah, and Shimon HaTzaddik) who inspired and gave direction to the Jewish people in periods of exile and dispersion. Hashem, in His unbounded love for His people, always ensures that there is a religious figure with the ability to stimulate the people to return to Him and regain His good graces.

The Pesach season is one of redemption and freedom: בְּנִיסָן נִגְאֲלוּ וּבְנִיסָן עֲתִידִים לִיגָּאֵל, In Nisan they were redeemed from Egypt, and in Nisan they will again be redeemed (in Messianic times) (Rosh Hashanah 11a). Thus, it is the appropriate time to hear words of inspiration from our religious leaders, since their words have the ability to engender the spiritual uplifting which will enable us to merit the ultimate redemption.[1]

---

1. It should be noted that the passage which serves as the source for this idea — the penultimate verse of Malachi — is found in the Haftarah reading of this Sabbath.

פֶּסַח. מַצָּה. וּמָרוֹר.

פֶּסַח מַצָּה וּמָרוֹר — pesach offering, matzah, and maror.

If we examine the symbolic meanings of the above-mentioned three items, we note that the matzah and the *pesach* offering are to remind us of the Exodus, for they recall miraculous events that happened on the way out of Egypt, whereas the *maror* represents circumstances that were in effect during the period of enslavement itself. In that sense, *maror* should seemingly precede the *pesach* offering and matzah.

Yet, it is also possible to see *maror*, too, as reminiscent of the miracles of the Exodus. The *midrash* (*Shir HaShirim Rabbah* 4:17), on the verse אִתִּי מִלְּבָנוֹן כַּלָּה אִתִּי מִלְּבָנוֹן תָּבוֹאִי, *With Me from Lebanon, O bride — come with Me from Lebanon* (*Shir HaShirim* 4:8), comments that although the usual custom is to allow a girl a full year to prepare for her marriage following her betrothal (see *Kesubos* 57a), Hashem did not delay even one day when He took Israel from Egypt to be His "bride." [1] "I did not wait," says Hashem. "While you were yet toiling with mortar and bricks [and far from being a glamorous bride], I hastened to redeem you." The meaning of the *midrash* is that although a slave mentality is certainly far from being the optimum frame of mind for the climb to yet unattained lofty spiritual heights, Hashem nevertheless redeemed the Israelites and brought them to Sinai without first requiring them to undergo an appropriately lengthy purification process. Based on this *midrash*, it may be said that the *maror*, which represents the bitter toil forced upon our ancestors in Egypt, is also symbolic of the miracle of their hasty Exodus from there. Even before they had a chance to spiritually overcome their longstanding state of slavery, their "Groom," out of His great love for them, redeemed them.

פֶּסַח מַצָּה — the pesach offering, matzah.

In the *sefer Beis Moed* the author asserts that each of these two mitzvos — the *pesach* offering and matzah — represents the Torah in its entirety. He shows that by using the *gematria malei* system, whereby each letter's name is completely spelled out and then the values of *all* these component letters are added up, both מַצָּה, *matzah,* and פֶּסַח, *pesach,* equal 613, the number of mitzvos in the Torah.[2] Exactly how these two mitzvos are an embodiment of the whole Torah, however, needs some clarification.

---

1. It is well known that the "groom and bride" of *Shir HaShirim* are allegories for Hashem and His Chosen People.

2. The word מַצוֹת, *matzos*, consists of the four letters מם,צדי,ואו,תיו. The numerical value of these eleven letters equals 613. פֶּסַח, *pesach*, consists of the three letters פה,סמך,חת, which also adds up to 613.

the pesach offering, matzah, and maror.

A Jew may not own a slave unless the slave has undergone circumcision (if male) and ritual immersion to enter, at least partially, into the
covenant of the Jewish religion. The slave can, however, if he is clever,
undergo this immersion with the intent to become a regular convert to
Judaism, thereby preventing his would-be master from enslaving him
further, since a full-fledged Jew cannot be a slave to another Jew. For
this reason, the master should be careful to demonstrate his domination over the slave in some manner as he is immersing, thus preventing
such a ruse (see *Rambam*, *Issurei Biah* 13:11). The *Bnei Yisaschar* writes
that Hashem did the same with the Children of Israel as they were
leaving Egypt: He demonstrated His mastery over them by commanding them to observe the many laws of the *pesach* offering [among them,
וְאַתֶּם לֹא תֵצְאוּ אִישׁ מִפֶּתַח בֵּיתוֹ עַד בֹּקֶר, and as for you, you shall not leave the
entrance of the house until morning (Shemos 12:22)], so that the people
could not claim afterwards that now that they had escaped from Egypt
they were free men; even free, God forbid, from Heavenly rule. At the
very moment the redemption from the Egyptians was taking place,
Hashem allowed no gap and assured that the Jews were made subservient to Him instead of to their former taskmasters.

In the Gemara (*Berachos* 9a) there is a difference of opinion as to
when the redemption took place. According to Rabbi Elazar ben
Azariah, it was at midnight, when Pharaoh officially *declared* the Jews
free to leave; Rabbi Akiva holds it it was at daybreak, when they *actually*
left the country. Seemingly, the concept of the *Bnei Yisaschar*, that
Hashem wanted to enforce His own dominion over the Israelites at the
moment of their emancipation from the Egyptians, is viable only according to Rabbi Elazar's opinion; if the redemption actually occurred
the next morning, as Rabbi Akiva asserts, the mitzvah of the *pesach*
offering which served as the binder to Hashem was already finished by
that time. In what way did Hashem show His mastery over the people
according to Rabbi Akiva's view? Perhaps the answer is that it was
through the mitzvah of matzah, which the Jews were commanded to
keep as *they were driven from Egypt* (Shemos 12:39).

Thus, according to R' Akiva the mitzvah of matzah was the act that
turned us from slaves of Pharaoh into servants of Hashem while according to R' Elazar it was the *pesach* offering that effected this transformation. Hence, matzah and *pesach* are indeed unique among the mitzvos,
and may be taken to represent the entire Torah, since they were the
original expressions of servitude to Hashem, instituted at our initiation
into Jewish nationhood. Perhaps it is for this reason that the punishment for eating *chametz* or not offering the *pesach* is *kareis* (excision

One should not point to the roasted meat on the *Seder* plate when the following is recited

פֶּסַח שֶׁהָיוּ אֲבוֹתֵינוּ אוֹכְלִים בִּזְמַן שֶׁבֵּית הַמִּקְדָּשׁ
הָיָה קַיָם, עַל שׁוּם מָה? עַל שׁוּם שֶׁפָּסַח הַקָּדוֹשׁ
בָּרוּךְ הוּא עַל בָּתֵּי אֲבוֹתֵינוּ בְּמִצְרַיִם. שֶׁנֶּאֱמַר,
וַאֲמַרְתֶּם, זֶבַח פֶּסַח הוּא לַיהוה, אֲשֶׁר פָּסַח עַל בָּתֵּי בְּנֵי
יִשְׂרָאֵל בְּמִצְרַיִם בְּנָגְפוֹ אֶת מִצְרַיִם, וְאֶת בָּתֵּינוּ הִצִּיל,
וַיִּקֹּד הָעָם וַיִּשְׁתַּחֲווּ.¹

---

of the soul), usually found in connection with violations of commandments which involve blasphemy or severe immorality. Since these were
the catalysts to initiate Jewish nationhood, negating their fulfillment
rends asunder the ties to the nation.

פֶּסַח — the pesach offering.

Regarding the *pesach* offering the Torah teaches: וְהָיָה כִּי תָבֹאוּ אֶל הָאָרֶץ
אֲשֶׁר יִתֵּן ה׳ לָכֶם וכו׳ וּשְׁמַרְתֶּם אֶת הָעֲבֹדָה הַזֹּאת, *It shall be that when you come
to the Land that Hashem will give you. . ., you shall observe this service*
(*Shemos* 12:25). *Rashi* points out that this verse clearly implies that the
pesach offering was one of the several mitzvos which were not
applicable until the conquest of *Eretz Yisrael*; it was not practiced
during the years of wandering in the desert, except on one occasion —
the year after the Exodus — when it was mandated by a special
command from Hashem, as described in *Bamidbar* 9:1. Rashi (ad loc.),
however, seems to explain matters in a totally different light. He
comments that the story of the *pesach* offering of the second year was
deliberately written by the Torah in an inconspicuous place because
this episode casts the Israelites of that generation in a negative light,
showing that throughout the entire forty-year period of wandering in
the desert they only sacrificed the *pesach* sacrifice that year. This seems
to be a glaring contradiction to the comment of *Rashi* in *Shemos* which
asserts — on the basis of straightforward Scriptural implication — that
the observation of the *pesach* offering was never *supposed* to apply to
the Jews of the desert!

The passage in *Bamidbar* contains the laws of the "remedial" *pesach*
offering, to be offered by those who were ritually unfit to participate in
the offering at the prescribed time. But, in a rare departure from the
usual form of transmission of laws, these rules were not given to Moses
until he was approached by a group of men who were distressed by the
fact that they were not able to participate in the sacrifice, owing to their
ritual impurity. Moses brought their plight before Hashem, and *only
then* was informed of the laws of the "remedial" *pesach* offering. The

W hat is the reason for the pesach offering that our ancestors used to eat at the time that the Beis HaMikdash was standing? Because the Holy One, Blessed is He, passed over the houses of our ancestors in Egypt, as it says, "You will say: It is a sacrifice of Pesach unto Hashem, for He passed over the houses of the Children of Israel in Egypt when He smote Egypt, and He saved our houses. And [upon hearing this] the people bowed down and prostrated themselves."[1]

_____
(1) *Shemos* 12:27.

Sages explain this unusual course of events by saying that because of this group's enthusiasm and zeal in their desire to find some way to perform Hashem's mitzvah, they earned the merit of acting as catalysts through which this entire portion of the Torah was given. Perhaps it is this aspect of the incident which Rashi refers to when he says that there is a disparagement of the Jews of the time. Throughout all the years of wandering in the desert, when the Jews were in fact exempt from observing the *pesach* offering, there was no one who ever felt the sincere longing for carrying out Hashem's word to the extent that he sought to *create* an obligation for himself where it was not required, except for this one instance, where this group of earnest men regarded being *exempt* as being "*deprived*" (ibid. 9:7). The disparaging view of the generation was not for not *bringing* the offering but rather for not *wanting* to bring it.

פֶּסַח שֶׁהָיוּ אֲבוֹתֵינוּ אוֹכְלִים וכו׳ עַל שׁוּם מָה? עַל שׁוּם שֶׁפָּסַח הַקָּדוֹשׁ בָּרוּךְ הוּא עַל בָּתֵּי אֲבוֹתֵינוּ וכו׳ — **What is the reason for the pesach offering that our ancestors used to eat . . .? Because the Holy One, Blessed is He, passed over the houses of our ancestors etc.**

On the eve of the first Pesach, the Jews were occupied with the observance of the *pesach* offering while the Egyptians were weeping over their loved ones. These two acts were more than just two contemporaneous events, however, as the verse quoted here implies: וַאֲמַרְתֶּם זֶבַח פֶּסַח הוּא לה׳ אֲשֶׁר פָּסַח עַל בָּתֵּי בְנֵי יִשְׂרָאֵל בְּמִצְרַיִם בְּנָגְפּוֹ אֶת מִצְרַיִם וְאֶת בָּתֵּינוּ הִצִּיל, *It is a pesach feast-offering to Hashem, Who passed over the houses of the Children of Israel in Egypt when He smote Egypt* (Shemos 12:27). The very name of the "Passover" offering testifies to its connection with the plague of the killing of the firstborn. This relationship needs to be explored.

Let us examine the special nature of the *pesach* offering. There are several unique *halachos* which distinguish this offering from all other sacrifices. For one thing, it may be eaten only after it is roasted; other offerings may be prepared by any form of cooking. Also, the animal must be roasted as one, without cutting it into pieces; even its entrails must be tied to it and roasted together with the flesh. Another anomaly of the *pesach* offering is that it must be eaten together with a predetermined group of company, and the meat may not be transported away from the group. This extensive list of halachic distinguishing details undoubtedly indicates some sort of symbolic significance.

When Moses and Aaron first came to Pharaoh, telling him, כֹּה אָמַר ה׳ אֱלֹקֵי יִשְׂרָאֵל שַׁלַּח אֶת עַמִּי, "So said Hashem, the God of Israel, 'Send out my people. . .,'" Pharaoh replied, וַיֹּאמֶר פַּרְעֹה מִי ה׳ אֲשֶׁר אֶשְׁמַע בְּקֹלוֹ וכו׳ לֹא יָדַעְתִּי אֶת ה׳, "Who is Hashem that I should heed His voice. . .? I do not know Hashem. . ." (Shemos 5:1-2). The *midrash* (*Yalkut Shimoni, Shemos* 4:175) tells of a huge ledger listing all the gods of the various nations, in which Pharaoh searched for, but could not find, the name of Hashem. Moses and Aaron explained this: "Of course Hashem is not on your list! The gods in your 'catalogue' are dead and powerless; our God is the living God, King of the Universe!" What the *midrash* implies is that heathen nations cannot grasp the notion that there is one Supreme Power over all the Universe — the world is too complex and full of apparent, surface contradictions for this concept to be easily understood. Because of this failure to comprehend the idea of Hashem's Unity — that He *alone* is the source of all forces of nature and of all events — the name of Hashem was not even entered into their directory of gods.

The *Maharal of Prague* explains that all of the unusual laws of the *pesach* offering are reflective of this Unity theme. The requirement that the animal be left whole may easily be seen to reflect the idea of oneness. And unlike boiled meat, which disintegrates into small pieces in the process of cooking, broiling preserves the meat in one solid piece. The fact that it must be eaten only in a specific group and only inside the house, where several individuals join together to form one unit, again illustrates this theme. These symbolic acts are meant to help us inculcate this idea of the Unity of Hashem into our minds and spirits, for Pesach eve is the night during which Hashem revealed this Unity most distinctly. This is the meaning of Moses' statement (*Shemos* 12:21), מִשְׁכוּ וּקְחוּ לָכֶם צֹאן, *Draw forth or buy for yourselves sheep [for the pesach],* which the Sages interpret, "Draw yourselves away from the idolatrous practices that have found their way into your midst, and only then may you prepare the *pesach* offering." The *pesach* offering, whose entire message was the Unity of Hashem and the non-relevance of any other force, cannot co-exist with its very antithesis — any vestige of idolatrous leanings.[1]

1.There is another offering brought specifically on the Passover festival — the *Omer* meal offering. It is interesting to note that this offering also had to be toasted on a fire, which

We read in *Bereishis* 2:24, עַל כֵּן יַעֲזָב אִישׁ אֶת אָבִיו וְאֶת אִמּוֹ דָּבַק בְּאִשְׁתּוֹ וְהָיוּ לְבָשָׂר אֶחָד, *Therefore a man shall leave his father and his mother and cling to his wife, and shall become one flesh.* These two distinct human beings merge and become one person in the form of offspring. The first child born to a couple is the realization of this Biblical statement, uniting the qualities of his parents into a new, single entity. Thus the firstborn child also personifies the concept of unity. Bearing this in mind we can perhaps better appreciate the appropriateness of the punishment of the slaying of the firstborn. Pharaoh and his people, who so arrogantly denied the idea of Hashem's Unity, suffered by losing their own firstborn, who embodied this very concept.

The connection between the *pesach* offering and the plague of the killing of the firstborn now becomes quite clear. Both events are illustrative of the same theological concept — recognition of the absolute Unity of Hashem.

Perhaps this idea can be used to shed light on a somewhat difficult verse in the Torah. In *Parashas Shemos* (12:28) we are told, וַיֵּלְכוּ וַיַּעֲשׂוּ בְּנֵי יִשְׂרָאֵל כַּאֲשֶׁר צִוָּה ה' אֶת משֶׁה וְאַהֲרֹן כֵּן עָשׂוּ, *The Children of Israel went and did* [the *pesach* offering] *as Hashem commanded Moses and Aaron, so did they do.* The seemingly superfluous phrase *so did they do* at the end of this verse is explained by *Rashi* as a reference to Moses and Aaron. Not only did the Children of Israel carry out the commandments exactly as they were commanded, but so did Moses and Aaron themselves. *The Belzer Rebbe zt"l* is reported to have asked: Why would the Torah make a point of telling us that these two sainted leaders of the Jewish people *also* did what they were told? Were they not already included in the general statement just written: *The Children of Israel went and did as Hashem commanded?* Why would I have thought that they were exempt from, or remiss in, the obligation to offer the *pesach* offering?

Perhaps the verse by saying, *so did they do*, of Moses and Aaron expresses not only their fulfillment of the *pesach* rite, but that they did it exactly as the Children of Israel did. Although they were the leaders of Israel, and of a spiritual stature that towered over the rest of the nation, they never acted in a manner that would keep them apart from the concerns and needs of the people. Rather, they retained an intimate relationship with their fellow Jews, participating with them in the performance of this mitzvah as well as in all other aspects of their lives.

---

solidified and hardened the moist grains. Also the kernels for this offering were sifted through thirteen progressively finer sieves to ensure that the grain *by itself* — with absolutely no impurities mixed in with it — would go into the flour. (Incidentally, the Hebrew word for "one" — אֶחָד — has the numerical value of thirteen.) This is one more instance of the "Unity — One" theme of Passover.

The middle matzah is lifted and displayed while the following paragraph is recited.

מַצָּה זוּ שֶׁאָנוּ אוֹכְלִים, עַל שׁוּם מָה? עַל שׁוּם שֶׁלֹּא
הִסְפִּיק בְּצֵקָם שֶׁל אֲבוֹתֵינוּ לְהַחֲמִיץ,

⸙§ In *Shemos* 12:11 we read, וְכָכָה תֹּאכְלוּ אֹתוֹ מָתְנֵיכֶם חֲגֻרִים נַעֲלֵיכֶם בְּרַגְלֵיכֶם
וּמַקֶּלְכֶם בְּיֶדְכֶם וַאֲכַלְתֶּם אֹתוֹ בְּחִפָּזוֹן פֶּסַח הוּא לַה', *So shall you eat it [the original pesach offering]: your loins girded, your shoes on your feet, and your staff in your hand; you shall eat it in haste — it is a pesach offering to Hashem.* How does the fact that "it is a *pesach* offering to Hashem" explain why it must be eaten with such hastiness? *Rashi* (ad loc.) explains: "The offering is called *pesach*, which connotes leaping and skipping over, for Hashem went from one Egyptian household to the other, so to speak, skipping over any Israelite homes in between. Hence, you, too, perform all of its service in a manner of leaping and skipping (i.e., hastily)." While Rashi defines the obligation, he does not explain why the Israelites had to simulate the manner of actions performed by Hashem. Why are we here enjoined to "imitate" Hashem's actions?

I learned the following important principle from my grandfather (the *Ohr Yechezkel*). Our life in this world is a life of deeds; nothing is accomplished in our mundane world without some kind of physical action. This is the meaning of the verses (*Bereishis* 2:2-3), וַיִּשְׁבֹּת בַּיּוֹם
הַשְּׁבִיעִי מִכָּל מְלַאכְתּוֹ אֲשֶׁר עָשָׂה וכו' אֲשֶׁר בָּרָא אֱלֹקִים לַעֲשׂוֹת, *and He abstained on the seventh day from all His work which He had done. . . which God created to make* — the creation was intended to function only through "doing" and "acting." In concert with this, we find that Hashem Himself, even when He acts in a completely supernatural and miraculous way, does so through some physical action on earth. This is why we often find prophets acting out their prophecies with some physical activity. Similarly, before each of the ten plagues began, there was a commandment to Moses or Aaron to "stretch out your hand over the water," to "throw some dirt into the air," or some other physical equivalent of the upcoming plague. Although Hashem certainly did not need any "help" from these physical acts to perform His supernatural deeds, He nevertheless carries out His miraculous feats in this way, as if to create a connection or conduit between the Heavenly, metaphysical world and our earthly, physical world. [1] This was the purpose of the demonstrative manner in which the Israelites were commanded to

---

1. This concept is discussed by the *Ramban* on the verse, וַיַּעֲבֹר אַבְרָם בָּאָרֶץ, *And Abram passed into the Land* (*Bereishis* 12:6), where he comments that Abraham's traversing the width and breadth of the Land was meant to be a sort of "preparatory step" for the miraculous conquest of *Eretz Yisrael* by his future descendants.

The middle matzah is lifted and displayed while the following paragraph is recited.

What is the reason behind this matzah which we eat? Because the dough of our ancestors did not have enough time to be

partake of the *pesach* offering — to "pave the way," as it were, for the miraculous events of that fateful night, when Hashem slew the Egyptians, while "skipping over" the Israelite households.

◄§ Regarding the precautions to be taken by the Israelites on the night of the slaying of the firstborn, the Torah cautions (*Shemos* 12:22): וְאַתֶּם לֹא תֵצְאוּ אִישׁ מִפֶּתַח בֵּיתוֹ עַד בֹּקֶר, *and as for you, you shall not leave the entrance of the house until morning.* Rashi explains that since nighttime is given over to destructive forces, the "Agent of Destruction" would not bother to distinguish between righteous and evil people that night. From this comment it would seem that this prohibition on leaving the house was related to the fact that the "Destroyer" was on the loose, administering the plague of the firstborn; it is not an intrinsic requirement of the observance of the *pesach* sacrifice. *Rav Yitzchak Zev Soloveitchik, the Brisker Rav,* noted that the Tosefta (*Pesachim* 8:7) lists the many laws which were unique to the first *pesach* offering in Egypt, but were not required for subsequent observances of the ritual, among them that only at the first *pesach* offering was it forbidden to leave the house. From the inclusion of this prohibition on this list it would appear that, unlike *Rashi's* interpretation, it was a feature of the laws of the *pesach* offering rather than a safety precaution from the "Destroyer." [If it was protective, as Rashi understands, its exclusion from subsequent Pesach observance is obvious and need not be spelled out.]

According to the explanation of the *Brisker Rav,* however, we must understand why the prohibition lasted the whole night long, since the fulfillment of the mitzvah of the *pesach* offering was only until midnight (according to the accepted opinion). How could one of the laws of the offering be of a longer duration than the sacrificial ritual itself?

This difficulty may be resolved in view of another halachic ruling of the *Brisker Rav* (this time, in the name of his father, Rav Chaim). He asserts that although the meat of the *korban pesach* may not be eaten after midnight as a fulfillment of the *pesach* sacrifice, it may nevertheless be eaten as an ordinary *kodashim kalim* sacrifice, whose consumption time extends until daybreak. Hence, while this prohibition of leaving the house is a function of the offering and not (as *Rashi* explains) a protective measure, it still extends until morning since this sacrifice in its general (non-*pesach*) role is not deemed *nosar* until morning.

עַד שֶׁנִּגְלָה עֲלֵיהֶם מֶלֶךְ מַלְכֵי הַמְּלָכִים הַקָּדוֹשׁ בָּרוּךְ הוּא וּגְאָלָם. שֶׁנֶּאֱמַר, וַיֹּאפוּ אֶת הַבָּצֵק אֲשֶׁר הוֹצִיאוּ מִמִּצְרַיִם עֻגֹת מַצּוֹת כִּי לֹא חָמֵץ, כִּי גֹרְשׁוּ מִמִּצְרַיִם, וְלֹא יָכְלוּ לְהִתְמַהְמֵהַּ, וְגַם צֵדָה לֹא עָשׂוּ לָהֶם.¹

The *maror* is lifted and displayed while the following paragraph is recited.

מָרוֹר זֶה שֶׁאָנוּ אוֹכְלִים, עַל שׁוּם מָה? עַל שׁוּם שֶׁמֵּרְרוּ הַמִּצְרִים אֶת חַיֵּי אֲבוֹתֵינוּ בְּמִצְרַיִם.

עַד שֶׁנִּגְלָה עֲלֵיהֶם מֶלֶךְ מַלְכֵי הַמְּלָכִים הַקָּדוֹשׁ בָּרוּךְ הוּא — before the Ulti-mate King, the Holy One, Blessed is He, revealed Himself to them.

We see from this phrase that there was a revelation of Hashem's Glory at the time of the Exodus from Egypt. This fact can be used to help ex-plain the difficulties presented in the following passage from the Torah.

In *Bamidbar* 33:3-4 we read: מִמָּחֳרַת הַפֶּסַח יָצְאוּ בְנֵי יִשְׂרָאֵל בְּיָד רָמָה לְעֵינֵי כָּל מִצְרָיִם: וּמִצְרַיִם מְקַבְּרִים אֶת אֲשֶׁר הִכָּה ה׳, בָּהֶם כָּל בְּכוֹר, *on the day after the pesach offering, the Children of Israel went forth with an upraised hand (i.e. proudly, and from a position of strength), before the eyes of all Egypt. And the Egyptians were burying those whom Hashem had struck among them, every firstborn.* Of what relevance is the fact that the Egyptians were burying their firstborn? This phrase is particularly puzzling because it appears in *Sefer Bamidbar*, in a very abbreviated review of the travels of Israel; hardly the place to mention a seemingly insignificant historical fact. Rashi explains that the verse teaches that since the Egyptians were so preoccupied with their own personal tragedies they did not have the opportunity to restrain the Israelites from leaving the country. This explanation is a bit puzzling, since it implies that had the Egyptians cared to, they could have prevented the Exodus from taking place, a prospect that seems highly unlikely.

Bearing in mind the Haggadah's assertion that there was a revelation of the Glory of Hashem when the Jews left Egypt, perhaps a different explanation might be offered. Whenever the Presence of Hashem manifests itself — as, for instance, when a great miracle takes place — even the wicked are inspired to recognize and praise Him. The Gemara points this out (*Sanhedrin* 92b) in connection with Nebuchadnezzar and the miracle of Chananiah and his companions who were miraculously saved from the fiery furnace. We would have expected the same of the Egyptians who experienced a lofty spiritual awakening, having witnessed the manifestation of Hashem's Glory. It is to explain the absence of this spiritual arousal that the verse teaches us of the *leavened before the Ultimate King, the Holy One, Blessed is He, revealed Himself to them and redeemed them, as it says, "They baked the dough which they took out of Egypt into cakes of matzah as it did not rise, for they were driven from Egypt and could not linger; nor had they prepared any provisions for themselves."[1]*

The *maror* is lifted and displayed while the following paragraph is recited.

What is the reason behind this maror which we eat? Because the Egyptians embittered the lives of our ancestors in Egypt,

_____
(1) *Shemos* 12:39.

Egyptian preoccupation. Had the Egyptians undergone such a spiritual wake-up, they would have been deserving of just reward. Hashem, however, did not wish to grant them this opportunity to redeem themselves from their wickedness, and, thus, saw to it that the Egyptians were "too busy" to notice the revelation that was going on right in their midst.

עַל שׁוּם שֶׁמֵּרְרוּ הַמִּצְרִים אֶת חַיֵּי אֲבוֹתֵינוּ בְּמִצְרָיִם — Because the Egyptians embittered the lives of our ancestors in Egypt.

The words "in Egypt" seem to be superfluous; the embitterment by the Egyptians certainly took place in Egypt!

It has been previously mentioned that originally the Jews intended to dwell only in the area of Goshen. In this way they would be able to retain their distinct identities and way of life without fear of excessive assimilation toward Egyptian culture. In time, however, they spread out throughout the cities of Egypt, and as a result began to emulate the ways of the local inhabitants, a turn which led to a great spiritual decline. This is reflected in the juxtaposition of the following two verses: וּבְנֵי יִשְׂרָאֵל פָּרוּ וַיִּשְׁרְצוּ וכו' וַתִּמָּלֵא הָאָרֶץ אֹתָם, *And the Children of Israel were fruitful and spread out. . .and the land became filled with them* (*Shemos* 1:7), and וַיָּקָם מֶלֶךְ חָדָשׁ עַל מִצְרָיִם, *A new king arose over Egypt* [who began to persecute the Jews] (ibid. v. 8). If the people had abided by their original intention and remained isolated in Goshen, rather than "spread out," they might not have been subjected to the harsh suffering forced upon them by the Egyptians. Although there was an outstanding decree upon the people to be oppressed for four hundred years, this oppression could have taken many other (and more gentle) forms, such as some spiritual or even mild physical discomfiture.[1] Indeed the first

_____
1. *Rabbi Moshe Feinstein* commented that this is one of the messages of *maror*. The Mishnah mentions five types of vegetables which may be used for this mitzvah. The first on the list (and hence the most preferred — *Pesachim* 39a) is romaine lettuce; only later is horseradish

שֶׁנֶּאֱמַר, וַיְמָרְרוּ אֶת חַיֵּיהֶם, בַּעֲבֹדָה קָשָׁה, בְּחֹמֶר וּבִלְבֵנִים, וּבְכָל עֲבֹדָה בַּשָּׂדֶה, אֵת כָּל עֲבֹדָתָם אֲשֶׁר עָבְדוּ בָהֶם בְּפָרֶךְ.[1]

בְּכָל דּוֹר וָדוֹר חַיָּב אָדָם לִרְאוֹת אֶת עַצְמוֹ כְּאִלּוּ הוּא יָצָא מִמִּצְרָיִם. שֶׁנֶּאֱמַר, וְהִגַּדְתָּ לְבִנְךָ בַּיּוֹם הַהוּא לֵאמֹר, בַּעֲבוּר זֶה עָשָׂה יהוה לִי, בְּצֵאתִי מִמִּצְרָיִם.[2] לֹא אֶת אֲבוֹתֵינוּ בִּלְבָד גָּאַל הַקָּדוֹשׁ בָּרוּךְ הוּא, אֶלָּא אַף אוֹתָנוּ גָּאַל עִמָּהֶם. שֶׁנֶּאֱמַר, וְאוֹתָנוּ הוֹצִיא מִשָּׁם, לְמַעַן הָבִיא אֹתָנוּ לָתֶת לָנוּ אֶת הָאָרֶץ אֲשֶׁר נִשְׁבַּע לַאֲבוֹתֵינוּ.[3]

---

190 years of the decree consisted only of the wandering and occasional perilous and painful incidents of the Patriarchs. Thus it was only because of the fact that the Israelites dwelt *in Egypt* (as opposed to remaining in Goshen) that their lives became so embittered by the persecution of the Egyptians.

וַיְמָרְרוּ אֶת חַיֵּיהֶם בַּעֲבֹדָה קָשָׁה בְּחֹמֶר וּבִלְבֵנִים — **They embittered their lives with hard labor, etc.**

The *Zohar* interprets this verse homiletically as referring to the difficulties involved in Torah study: בַּעֲבֹדָה קָשָׁה, *with hard labor*, refers to Talmudic questions and objections (קוּשְׁיָא); בְּחֹמֶר, *with mortar*, refers to the hermeneutic principle known as קַל וָחֹמֶר; וּבִלְבֵנִים, *and bricks,* refers to clarification of the final halachic ruling (לִיבּוּן הֲלָכָה); עֲבֹדָה בַּשָּׂדֶה, *and all sorts of work in the field*, refers to non-mishnaic Tannaic statements (known as *beraisa*, which can also mean "outdoors"), and, finally, אֵת כָּל עֲבֹדָתָם אֲשֶׁר עָבְדוּ בָהֶם בְּפָרֶךְ, *all of the work which they made them do was rigorous,* refers to unresolved Talmudic queries (תֵּיקוּ) over which the scholars toil, ceaselessly seeking solutions. What is the connection of Torah study to the context of

---

listed. Since horseradish is obviously much more bitter than romaine lettuce why should the order of preference be lettuce before horseradish? Rav Moshe answers that this represents Hashem's method of reproaching sinners. First He sends a "hint" through some minor discomfort or frustration, hoping that the person will realize through this that he should improve his ways. If this fails, He goes on to progressively harsher "messages," until a severe punishment is administered. This is why the least irritating herb is mentioned first, and only afterwards are the harsher ones listed.

as it says, "They embittered their lives with hard labor at mortar and bricks, and all sorts of work in the field. All of the work which they made them do was rigorous."[1]

In each and every generation one is obligated to view himself as though he has gone out of Egypt, as it is said, "And you shall tell your son on that day, saying, 'It is because of this that HASHEM did so for me when I went out of Egypt.' "[2] Not only did the Holy One, Blessed is He, redeem our ancestors, but He redeemed us, too, with them, as it is said, "He took us out of there to bring us to and give us the land which He had sworn to our fathers."[3]

---

(1) *Shemos* 1:14. (2) 13:8. (3) *Devarim* 6:23.

---

this verse, which describes the hardships of the Israelites in Egypt, that prompted the *Zohar* to read this interpretation into the passage?

In the *sefer Shem MiShmuel*, the author suggests that the word וַיְמָרֲרוּ ("they embittered") be understood as related to the word בְּמַר, meaning "instead of" (see *Chullin* 94a). The meaning of the phrase would thus be "and they exchanged their lives for hard labor, etc." Accordingly, the verse is referring to the Jews themselves who, through their callous abandonment of the moral exhortations and religious traditions bequeathed to them by their sainted ancestor Jacob, exchanged their fate to one much harsher than was necessary. Although a four-hundred-year period of hardship was already decreed upon them at the Covenant Between the Parts, had they remained faithful to Jacob's legacy they could have endured this decree of "suffering" in a spiritual and academic sense. The Sages tell us that when Jacob died the people's spiritual level began to ebb, and "their eyes became blinded" to the truths of the Torah. What caused Hashem to decide that the decree had to be carried out through *physical* suffering and affliction was the fact that the people had spurned Jacob's teachings and allowed themselves to sink to a perilously low level of spirituality. Thus the Israelites "exchanged" the milder form of affliction that could have been their lot for the more severe physical distress that actually befell them. The *Zohar's* homiletic rendering of the passage as a reference to the hardships of Talmudic study is an expression of an alternate form the decree might have assumed had the Jews merited it.

The matzos are covered and the cup is lifted and held until it is to be drunk. According to some customs, however, the cup is put down after the following paragraph, in which case the matzos should once more be uncovered.

לְפִיכָךְ אֲנַחְנוּ חַיָּבִים לְהוֹדוֹת, לְהַלֵּל, לְשַׁבֵּחַ, לְפָאֵר, לְרוֹמֵם, לְהַדֵּר, לְבָרֵךְ, לְעַלֵּה, וּלְקַלֵּס, לְמִי שֶׁעָשָׂה לַאֲבוֹתֵינוּ וְלָנוּ אֶת כָּל הַנִּסִּים הָאֵלּוּ, הוֹצִיאָנוּ מֵעַבְדוּת לְחֵרוּת, מִיָּגוֹן לְשִׂמְחָה, וּמֵאֵבֶל לְיוֹם טוֹב, וּמֵאֲפֵלָה לְאוֹר גָּדוֹל, וּמִשִּׁעְבּוּד לִגְאֻלָּה, וְנֹאמַר לְפָנָיו שִׁירָה חֲדָשָׁה, הַלְלוּיָהּ.

לְפִיכָךְ אֲנַחְנוּ חַיָּבִים לְהוֹדוֹת לְהַלֵּל לְשַׁבֵּחַ וכו' — **Therefore it is our duty to thank, praise, laud, etc.**

There are ten synonyms for the verb "to praise" in this passage — nine at the beginning of the paragraph and one at the end: וְנֹאמַר לְפָנָיו שִׁירָה חֲדָשָׁה הַלְלוּיָהּ, *Let us say before Him a new song, Praise Hashem!* The *Vilna Gaon*, in his Haggadah commentary, asserts that each expression corresponds to one of the ten plagues inflicted upon Egypt. The last one thus parallels the plague of the slaying of the firstborn. This may be understood if we recall the words of the *midrash* (*Yalkut Shimoni* 103): When the plague started [at midnight] Pharaoh went to Moses and exclaimed, "Arise and go out." Moses protested, "Are we thieves that we should leave stealthily in the middle of the night? We will leave in the morning [in broad daylight]!" Pharaoh thereupon cried out, "You are hereby freed! Until now you have been my slaves, but now you are the servants of the Holy One, Blessed is He, and you must therefore praise Him, as it says, 'Praise Hashem! Praise, servants of Hashem.'" Thus, it was specifically at the time of the plague of the Slaying of the Firstborn that the Jews first attained the status of "servants of Hashem," and became "eligible" to sing הַלְלוּיָהּ, הַלְלוּ עַבְדֵי ה', *Praise Hashem! Praise, servants of Hashem.*

Another explanation of the significance of these ten synonyms of praise may be offered in light of the Biblical ten expressions used for "praying" (see *Bamidbar Rabbah* 2:1). Paralleling the ten forms of prayer uttered by our forefathers when וַיֵּאָנְחוּ בְנֵי יִשְׂרָאֵל מִן הָעֲבֹדָה וַיִּזְעָקוּ וכו' אֶל הָאֱלֹהִים, *And the children of Israel sighed . . . because of the labor and cried out . . . to Hashem* (Shemos 2:23), we now have the privilege of expressing our *praise* for Hashem in ten different ways.

הוֹצִיאָנוּ . . . וּמֵאֲפֵלָה לְאוֹר גָּדוֹל — **He has brought us forth . . . from darkness to great light.**

The matzos are covered and the cup is lifted and held until it is to be drunk. According to some customs, however, the cup is put down after the following paragraph, in which case the matzos should once more be uncovered.

Therefore it is our duty to thank, praise, laud, glorify, aggrandize, extol, bless, exalt and acclaim the One who performed all of these miracles for our ancestors and for us. He has brought us out from slavery to freedom, from anguish to joy, from mourning to festivity, from darkness to great light, and from servitude to redemption. Let us say before Him a new song, Praise HASHEM!

The Torah, in describing the Exodus of the Jews from Egypt, uses the following analogy: אוֹ הֲנִסָּה אֱלֹהִים לָבוֹא לָקַחַת לוֹ גוֹי מִקֶּרֶב גּוֹי וכו׳ אֲשֶׁר עָשָׂה לָכֶם ה׳ וכו׳ בְּמִצְרַיִם וכו׳?, Or has any god ever miraculously come to take for himself a nation from amidst a nation . . . as Hashem did for you in Egypt? (Devarim 4:34). The expression "from amidst," says the midrash, suggests that it was like a fetus emerging from the womb. It is this "birth" process, explains the Maharal of Prague, that the Sages of the Haggadah had in mind when they said that Hashem "brought us forth . . . from darkness to great light."

The meaning of this imagery of the fetus being born requires some explanation. The midrash explains the verse, מִי יִתֵּן טָהוֹר מִטָּמֵא לֹא אֶחָד, Who can bring out the pure from the impure? Is it not the One [Hashem]? (Iyov 14:4), to be an expression of amazement at the fact that Hashem manages to produce righteous saints despite their ignominious origins: Abraham's father Terach was an idolater, Hezekiah was the son of the wicked Ahaz, Josiah came from the evil Amon, Mordechai was descended from the infamous Shimi, and Israel comes from the nations of the world. The illustrations of this principle given by the midrash are all quite clear examples of how a son can break away from the erroneous ways of his family's traditions to follow a path of righteousness and piety — except for the last case. Who was the "evil family" which Israel veered away from?

In Shir HaShirim (1:6) the "maiden" of the poem (Israel) laments, אַל תִּרְאֻנִי שֶׁאֲנִי שְׁחַרְחֹרֶת שֶׁשְּׁזָפַתְנִי הַשָּׁמֶשׁ בְּנֵי אִמִּי נִחֲרוּ בִי שָׂמֻנִי נֹטֵרָה אֶת הַכְּרָמִים, Do not view me with contempt despite my swarthiness, for it is but the sun which has glared upon me. The alien children of my mother were incensed with me and made me a keeper of the vineyards of idols. Rashi explains the "children of my mother" to be an allegorical reference to the עֵרֶב רַב (the Egyptian "riffraff" who tagged along with the Israelites when they left Egypt — Shemos 12:38), who antagonized the Israelites throughout the years in the desert by constantly interjecting their idolatrous ideologies and irreverent attitudes. If the Egyptians were the "children of my mother," then the "mother" is Egypt itself. The Israelites were so steeped in Egyptian culture before the Exodus that it was as if they were truly native sons of "mother Egypt," figuratively tied by the Egyptian umbilical cord, unexposed to the spiritual light of Torah.

But once Israel was "born," i.e. redeemed from the immorality that was Egypt, וָאֶשְׁטֹף דָּמַיִךְ מֵעָלָיִךְ וָאֲסֻכֵךְ בַּשָּׁמֶן: וָאַלְבִּישֵׁךְ רִקְמָה וָאֶנְעֲלֵךְ תָּחַשׁ, *Then I [Hashem] washed your blood from you, and I anointed you with oil. I clothed you also with embroidered cloth, and shod you with tachash hide* (Yechezkel 16:9-10), as one does with a newborn baby. The *midrash* (*Yalkut* 527) tells us that the angels protested when Hashem wanted to save the seemingly unworthy Jews from the hands of the Egyptian army at the Red Sea. Hashem replied, "They are only infants, and one cannot hold an infant responsible for his deeds. Just as an infant emerges from the womb covered in blood and must be cleaned and cared for, so is Israel sullied, but I shall cleanse them, as it says, 'Then I washed your blood from you, etc.' (ibid.)." Despite their unworthiness, Hashem chose to extend His miraculous salvation to them and, like a baby just emerged from the womb, to nurse them with manna, the well of Miriam and the clouds of glory.

◦§ The *Vilna Gaon* explains these five parallel expressions of salvation as corresponding to five crucial stages in Jewish history: "From slavery to freedom" applies to the actual Exodus from Egypt; "from anguish to joy" is a reference to the miraculous Splitting of the Red Sea, when the Jews were relieved from their great distress and anguish; "from mourning" gives expression to the episode of the Golden Calf (where וַיִּשְׁמַע הָעָם אֶת הַדָּבָר הָרָע הַזֶּה וַיִּתְאַבָּלוּ, *The people heard this bad tiding [of Hashem's anger at them] and they mourned — Shemos* 33:4); with "festivity" focusing on Yom Kippur, the joyous day several months afterwards when the Jews were forgiven for that calamity (see *Taanis* 26b); "from darkness to light" is an allusion to the Israelites' triumphant entry into *Eretz Yisrael* after decades of wandering in the desert, "and from servitude to redemption" corresponds to the emergence of the Israelites from an ungovernable mass, in the period of the Judges, to a stable, united nation under a glorious monarchy in the days of David and his dynasty.

Perhaps another explanation of these five terms is that they are meant to signify the same symbolism as the cups of wine drunk at the *Seder* — reminiscent of the verse in *Tehillim* (116:13), כּוֹס יְשׁוּעוֹת אֶשָּׂא וּבְשֵׁם ה' אֶקְרָא, *I will raise the cup of salvations and the Name of Hashem*

I will invoke [in praise]." Although we are accustomed to speak of the *four* cups of wine, there is a reading in the Gemara (*Pesachim* 118a) that a fifth cup is to be poured for the recitation of the *Hallel HaGadol* (*Tehillim* 136). Although the opinion that five cups *should* be drunk is not the accepted *halachah*, the fifth cup *is* mentioned on an *optional* basis (see *Rama, Orach Chaim* 481:1).

The *Netziv* explains the significance of this fifth optional cup as follows. The four main cups, as explained in the *midrash*, represent the four expressions of redemption which Hashem invoked when He sent Moses to tell the Israelites of their impending liberation: וְהוֹצֵאתִי אֶתְכֶם, *and I shall take you out;* וְהִצַּלְתִּי אֶתְכֶם מֵעֲבֹדָתָם, *I shall rescue you from their service;* וְגָאַלְתִּי אֶתְכֶם, *I shall redeem you,* and וְלָקַחְתִּי אֶתְכֶם לִי לְעָם, *I shall take you to Me for a people* (*Shemos* 6:6,7). There is a fifth expression in this verse, however — וִידַעְתֶּם כִּי אֲנִי ה' אֱלֹקֵיכֶם *and you shall know that I am Hashem, your God.* This last statement, unlike the first four which were addressed to the Jewish population at large, was applicable to only the most spiritually inclined members of the community. The spiritually less-sophisticated would be incapable of attaining such an elevated level of recognition of Hashem. It is for this reason, according to the *Netziv,* that the fifth cup, which parallels this expression, is optional and not an absolute requirement for all Jews. In fact, he continues, this is the basis for the tradition of setting aside an extra "cup of Elijah" nowadays. Since we live in a time when Divine Inspiration (רוּחַ הַקֹּדֶשׁ) has ceased to manifest itself among us, we pray for the advent of the Messianic era, to be ushered in by Elijah, when we may once again be blessed with this extraordinary spiritual gift, and drink of the cup of "knowing Hashem" once more.

According to this interpretation, the five expressions of salvation used by the Haggadah correspond exactly to the five expressions of redemption found in *Shemos,* chapter 6. The fifth expression (the "extra" one) which, as shown above, alludes to the future redemption is "from servitude to redemption."

The choice of terminology is most appropriate for this theme. The Sages teach us (*Berachos* 34b) that there will be no changes in the natural order of things when the *Mashiach* comes. The only difference in world order will be the removal of Israel's subservience to the nations. The *Rambam*, expanding on this idea, describes the nature of this change in Messianic times: "and the main interest of all peoples in the world at this time will be only to know Hashem..." (*Hilchos Melachim* 12:5), clearly a restatement of the "extra expression" in *Shemos*: "and you shall know that I am Hashem, your God."

הַלְלוּיָה הַלְלוּ עַבְדֵי יהוה, הַלְלוּ אֶת שֵׁם יהוה. יְהִי שֵׁם יהוה מְבֹרָךְ, מֵעַתָּה וְעַד עוֹלָם. מִמִּזְרַח שֶׁמֶשׁ עַד מְבוֹאוֹ, מְהֻלָּל שֵׁם יהוה. רָם עַל כָּל גּוֹיִם יהוה, עַל הַשָּׁמַיִם כְּבוֹדוֹ. מִי כַּיהוה אֱלֹהֵינוּ, הַמַּגְבִּיהִי לָשָׁבֶת. הַמַּשְׁפִּילִי לִרְאוֹת, בַּשָּׁמַיִם וּבָאָרֶץ. מְקִימִי מֵעָפָר דָּל, מֵאַשְׁפֹּת יָרִים אֶבְיוֹן. לְהוֹשִׁיבִי עִם נְדִיבִים, עִם נְדִיבֵי עַמּוֹ. מוֹשִׁיבִי עֲקֶרֶת הַבַּיִת, אֵם הַבָּנִים שְׂמֵחָה, הַלְלוּיָה.¹

בְּצֵאת יִשְׂרָאֵל מִמִּצְרָיִם, בֵּית יַעֲקֹב מֵעַם לֹעֵז. הָיְתָה יְהוּדָה לְקָדְשׁוֹ, יִשְׂרָאֵל מַמְשְׁלוֹתָיו. הַיָּם רָאָה

מְקִימִי מֵעָפָר דָּל מֵאַשְׁפֹּת יָרִים אֶבְיוֹן — He raises the impoverished from the dust. From the trash heaps He lifts the indigent.

When the Patriarch Jacob was about to descend with his family to Egypt, he was greatly distressed at having to leave *Eretz Yisrael*. This disappointment is reflected in the reassurance that Hashem gave him saying: אַל תִּירָא מֵרְדָה מִצְרַיְמָה כִּי לְגוֹי גָּדוֹל אֲשִׂימְךָ שָׁם אָנֹכִי אֵרֵד עִמְּךָ מִצְרַיְמָה וְאָנֹכִי אַעַלְךָ גַם עָלֹה וְיוֹסֵף יָשִׁית יָדוֹ עַל עֵינֶיךָ, *Do not fear going down to Egypt. . . . I shall go down with you to Egypt and also bring you back, and Joseph shall place his hand upon your eyes* (Bereishis 46:3-4). What exactly was the cause of Jacob's fear, and how was Hashem's response that "Joseph shall place his hand upon your eyes" meant to alleviate this apprehension?

It appears that Jacob, being aware of the prophecy of the Covenant Between the Parts, in which centuries of exile and subjugation by a foreign power were decreed, was apprehensive about having this formative stage of the fledgling Israelite nation take place in Egypt. After all, Egypt was known for its immorality and corruption; how could this spiritually contaminated country possibly serve as the proper environment for the embryonic stage of Hashem's holy people? The proof that Egypt could indeed spawn a righteous personality, responded Hashem, was Jacob's own son, Joseph. When he left *Eretz Yisrael* he was described as an immature lad (ibid. 37:2, see *Sforno* ad loc.), but in Egypt he became renowned for his righteousness and piety (see ibid. 49:24 and *Devarim* 33:16). Eventually he achieved a level of spirituality unrivaled by any of his brothers,

Praise HASHEM! Praise, servants of HASHEM. Praise the Name of HASHEM! May the Name of HASHEM be blessed from now unto eternity. From the dawning place of the sun to its setting place, praised is the Name of HASHEM. Exalted above all nations is HASHEM. Above the heavens is His glory. Who is like HASHEM our God, Who dwells on high, Who lowers Himself to scrutinize the heavens and the earth? He raises the impoverished from the dust. From the trash heaps He lifts the indigent. To seat them with nobles, with the nobles of His people. He transforms a barren woman into a happy mother of children. Praise HASHEM![1]

When Israel went out of Egypt, the house of Jacob from a people of alien tongue, then Judah became His holy one, Israel His dominion. The sea saw and

_____

(1) *Tehillim* 113.

---

when he himself became the progenitor of two tribes of Israel, thus attaining near Patriarchal status. It was precisely the hostile spiritual environment in which he found himself in Egypt that forced him to strengthen his religious resolve. Thus, the Divine reassurance that Joseph "*shall place* his hand on your eyes" may be understood as, "with your own eyes you will see from Joseph's accomplishments that your fears for the spiritual wellbeing of your descendants are unfounded." The fostering of holiness and purity in the midst of this environment of moral depravity and degradation is illustrative of the Divine personal salvation and guidance that Hashem grants the downtrodden, for which King David praised Him in this psalm: "He raises the impoverished from the dust. From the trash heaps He lifts the indigent."

בְּצֵאת יִשְׂרָאֵל מִמִּצְרַיִם וכו' הָיְתָה יְהוּדָה לְקָדְשׁוֹ וכו' — **When Israel went out of Egypt . . . then Judah became His holy one, etc.**

There is a *midrash* cited in *Damesek Eliezer* that associates the verse וַיַּסֵּב אֱלֹקִים אֶת הָעָם דֶּרֶךְ הַמִּדְבָּר יַם סוּף, *So God turned the people toward the way of the wilderness to the Red Sea (Shemos* 13:18), with the *mishnah* that states that "even the poorest person in Israel (who does not customarily eat in such luxurious fashion) must recline (יָסֵב)" while eating the matzah (and drinking the wine) at the *Seder*. Is this merely a play on words or is there some deeper connection between the route of the Exodus and the mitzvah of reclining?

וַיָּנֻס, הַיַּרְדֵּן יִסֹב לְאָחוֹר. הֶהָרִים רָקְדוּ כְאֵילִים, גְּבָעוֹת
כִּבְנֵי צֹאן. מַה לְּךָ הַיָּם כִּי תָנוּס, הַיַּרְדֵּן תִּסֹב לְאָחוֹר.
הֶהָרִים תִּרְקְדוּ כְאֵילִים, גְּבָעוֹת כִּבְנֵי צֹאן. מִלְּפְנֵי אָדוֹן
חוּלִי אָרֶץ, מִלִּפְנֵי אֱלוֹהַּ יַעֲקֹב. הַהֹפְכִי הַצּוּר אֲגַם מָיִם,
חַלָּמִישׁ לְמַעְיְנוֹ מָיִם.¹

According to all customs the cup is lifted and the matzos are covered during the recitation
of this blessing. On Saturday substitute the bracketed phrase for the preceding phrase.
All cups should be fully refilled before reciting the blessing on the second cup

בָּרוּךְ אַתָּה יהוה אֱלֹהֵינוּ מֶלֶךְ הָעוֹלָם, אֲשֶׁר גְּאָלָנוּ
וְגָאַל אֶת אֲבוֹתֵינוּ מִמִּצְרַיִם, וְהִגִּיעָנוּ הַלַּיְלָה
הַזֶּה לֶאֱכָל בּוֹ מַצָּה וּמָרוֹר. כֵּן יהוה אֱלֹהֵינוּ וֵאלֹהֵי

As previously mentioned, the Israelites' Exodus from Egypt actually
was a two-stage event. The first stage was the actual leaving the land
of Egypt after the slaying of the firstborn on the fifteenth of Nisan, while
the second stage occured a week later when the entire Egyptian army
was drowned in the Red Sea. Although the two "Exoduses" share certain aspects (they both produced great amounts of monetary spoils),
there are several striking differences between the two episodes which
require explanation. Firstly, the Sages tell us that at the Splitting of the
Sea the angels protested to Hashem that the Israelites were not deserving of such salvation. Considering that they presented no such protestations during the actual Exodus, one wonders: What objection did
these angels only now perceive that they were unaware of before? (This
question was discussed on page 9). Furthermore, we find that the Jews
at the sea had the privilege of witnessing the Glory of Hashem manifested "in a more explicit manner than that witnessed by the prophet
Ezekiel" (see *Mechilta* 15:2). Why were the people granted this sublime
revelation only at the sea, rather than at the first stage in their deliverance on the night of the Exodus? Furthermore, would it not have suf-
ficed to have the Egyptian army routed, thus saving the Jews from their
destruction and enslavement, without this unprecedented revelation?

The answer to these questions is that each of the two "Exoduses"
functions in a different role in the liberation of the Jews from Egypt. On
the night of the fifteenth of Nisan the Jews were officially released from
the bondage of their Egyptian masters when Pharaoh declared that they
were free to go. The liberation at the Red Sea, however, was their
spiritual "Exodus," when their souls were freed from the grip of Egyptian culture and religious ideology. It was then that they began their

fled. The Jordan turned back. The mountains skipped like rams; the hills — like lambs. What is it, sea, that makes you flee? Jordan, what makes you turn back? Mountains, why do you prance like rams? Hills, why do you skip like lambs? Tremble before the Master, earth. Before the God of Jacob; Who turns the rock into a pond of water, the flintrock into a fountain of water. [1]

According to all customs the cup is lifted and the matzos are covered during the recitation of this blessing. On Saturday substitute the bracketed phrase for the preceding phrase.
All cups should be fully refilled before reciting the blessing on the second cup

Blessed are You, HASHEM, our God, King of the universe, Who has redeemed us and redeemed our ancestors from Egypt, and enabled us to live to this night, to eat on it matzah and maror. So, HASHEM, our God and the God of

---

(1) *Tehillim* 114.

---

development as a *kingdom of priests and a holy nation*, מַמְלֶכֶת כֹּהֲנִים וְגוֹי קָדוֹשׁ (*Shemos* 19:6), which would receive the Torah a few weeks hence. The development of the Jewish nation at this critical stage could only be accomplished through an extraordinary revelation of Hashem's Presence, providing the necessary spiritual input with which to purify themselves from any taint of Egyptian culture. It was this exceptional manifestation of Hashem's splendor that the "accusing angels" felt was undeserved by the Israelites at that point.

The physical release from bondage commemorated on Pesach is something that not all people can appreciate at all times. At times of anti-Semitic persecution, or in a situation when an individual is faced with severe physical or financial stress, it is often difficult to celebrate the escape from peril experienced by our distant ancestors. But the *spiritual* deliverance which they underwent is something that any Jew, in any situation, can fully relate to and feel grateful for "even the poorest person (spiritually) in Israel must recline." The single event which marked the beginning of this spiritual liberation is the Splitting of the Red Sea; hence the connection between reclining (יָסֵב) and the roundabout route (וַיַּסֵּב) to the Red Sea taken by the Israelites.

Bearing in mind the "dual phase" nature of the Exodus, we may better appreciate the meaning of the following two verses quoted from the *Hallel*: "When Israel went out of Egypt, Jacob's household from a people of alien tongue" refers to the physical redemption, the actual leaving of the physical boundaries of Egypt. "Judah became His holy one, Israel His dominion" is a reference to the spiritual deliverance,

אֲבוֹתֵינוּ, יַגִּיעֵנוּ לְמוֹעֲדִים וְלִרְגָלִים אֲחֵרִים הַבָּאִים לִקְרָאתֵנוּ לְשָׁלוֹם, שְׂמֵחִים בְּבִנְיַן עִירֶךָ וְשָׂשִׂים בַּעֲבוֹדָתֶךָ, וְנֹאכַל שָׁם מִן הַזְּבָחִים וּמִן הַפְּסָחִים [מִן הַפְּסָחִים וּמִן הַזְּבָחִים] אֲשֶׁר יַגִּיעַ דָּמָם עַל קִיר מִזְבַּחֲךָ לְרָצוֹן. וְנוֹדֶה לְךָ שִׁיר חָדָשׁ עַל גְּאֻלָּתֵנוּ וְעַל פְּדוּת נַפְשֵׁנוּ. בָּרוּךְ אַתָּה יהוה, גָּאַל יִשְׂרָאֵל.

בָּרוּךְ אַתָּה יהוה אֱלֹהֵינוּ מֶלֶךְ הָעוֹלָם, בּוֹרֵא פְּרִי הַגָּפֶן.

The second cup is drunk while leaning on the left side —
preferably the entire cup, but at least most of it.

---

when, as mentioned above, the Jews began to assume their role as "a holy nation." Since the purpose of Creation was realized with Israel's acceptance of this role as the bearers of Torah, this acceptance indeed elevated them to a position of "His dominion," ensuring Creation's continued existence, and the extension of Hashem's dominion on earth.

So — כֵּן ה׳ אֱלֹהֵינוּ . . . יַגִּיעֵנוּ לְמוֹעֲדִים וְלִרְגָלִים וכו׳ וְנֹאכַל שָׁם מִן הַזְּבָחִים Hashem, our God . . . may You enable us to live to other festivals and holidays. . .. May we eat there of the offerings.

Our prayer here is that we be enabled to celebrate all the רְגָלִים (translated here as "holidays," but actually referring specifically to the three *pilgrim* festivals) by fulfilling the mitzvah of going to the *Beis HaMikdash* and offering sacrifices there. Since this prayer includes all of the festivals, why is it recited on Pesach alone?

Further, we read in *Parashas Shemos* (23:15): אֶת חַג הַמַּצּוֹת תִּשְׁמֹר וכו׳, *You shall observe the Festival of Matzos,* etc., וְלֹא יֵרָאוּ פָנַי רֵיקָם, *and you shall not be seen before me emptyhanded.* The next verse continues, וְחַג הַקָּצִיר, *And the Festival of the Harvest,* etc., וְחַג הָאָסִף, *and the Festival of the Ingathering.* Why is the prohibition of not coming to the Temple emptyhanded, which certainly applies to all three pilgrim festivals, mentioned specifically in association with Pesach, before the other holidays are even mentioned? Apparently some relationship between the concept of festival sacrifice and Pesach gives this obligation a heightened applicability regarding Pesach.

The Tur (*Orach Chaim* 417) cites an opinion that the three festivals of the year correspond to the three Patriarchs — Pesach to Abraham, Shavuos to Isaac, and Succos to Jacob. Abraham, who took his son to Mount Moriah, where the Temple would later be built, to offer him up *our fathers, may You enable us to live to other festivals and holidays which will come to meet us in peace, happy in the reconstruction of Your city and joyful in Your service. May we eat there of the sacrifices and pesach offerings [the pesach offerings and the sacrifices] whose blood will reach the wall of Your altar for acceptance. And may we thank You with a new song for our redemption and the liberation of our soul. Blessed are You, HASHEM, Who redeemed Yisrael.*

B*lessed are You, HASHEM, our God, King of the Universe, Who creates the fruit of the vine.*

The second cup is drunk while leaning on the left side — preferably the entire cup, but at least most of it.

---

as an actual sacrifice, was, in a sense, the forerunner of the masses of Jewish pilgrims that would some day throng to that very place. Moreover, the name Abraham gave this site after being told not to carry out the actual sacrifice of Isaac was ה׳ יִרְאֶה, *Hashem Yireh*, meaning, as the verse itself (*Bereishis* 22:14) explains, אֲשֶׁר יֵאָמֵר הַיּוֹם בְּהַר ה׳ יֵרָאֶה, *as it is said this day, on the mountain Hashem will be seen.* Abraham prayed that this place, where he demonstrated such unprecedented and total dedication to Hashem, should serve as the spiritual focal point for his descendants in the distant future, when the Temple would be built. The Gemara (*Chagigah* 3a) further reinforces this connection between Abraham and the pilgrim festivals, in its homiletical interpretation of a verse from *Shir HaShirim* (7:2): מַה יָּפוּ פְעָמַיִךְ בַּנְּעָלִים בַּת נָדִיב, *How beautiful are your feet in shoes, O daughter of the noble one.* The Gemara renders, "How beautiful are the footsteps of Israel when they perform the mitzvah of going up (עוֹלִים) to Jerusalem for the pilgrim festivals (שָׁלֹשׁ פְּעָמִים — see *Shemos* 23:17); they are the daughters of Abraham, who is called 'the noble one.'" [1] In this light we can understand why the Torah seems to consider Pesach, more than any other holiday, as the premier pilgrim festival, stating the prohibition of coming empty-handed to the Temple more emphatically for this holiday than for the others. By extension, it is for this reason that our prayer that Hashem grant us the privilege to once again celebrate the pilgrim festivals is more fitting for the Pesach liturgy than for any other occasion.

---

1. It is interesting to note the expression used for Israel in this connection — "O *daughter* of the noble one." The *Mesbech Chochmah* (in *VaEschanan*) quotes a *midrash* that points out that in *Shir HaShirim*, Israel is first referred to as "daughter," then "sister," then "mother." He explains that each of these three expressions corresponds to one of the festivals, with "daughter" paralleling Pesach. Thus, there is a further connection between this verse and the holiday of Pesach.

רחצה

The hands are washed for matzah and the following blessing is recited.
It is preferable to bring water and a basin to the head of the household at the *Seder* table.

בָּרוּךְ אַתָּה יהוה אֱלֹהֵינוּ מֶלֶךְ הָעוֹלָם, אֲשֶׁר קִדְּשָׁנוּ בְּמִצְוֹתָיו, וְצִוָּנוּ עַל נְטִילַת יָדָיִם.

מוֹצִיא / מַצָּה

The following two blessings are recited over matzah; the first is recited over matzah as food, and the second for the special mitzvah of eating matzah on the night of Pesach. [The latter blessing is to be made with the intention that it also apply to the *korech* "sandwich" and the *afikoman*.] The head of the household raises all the matzos on the *Seder* plate and recites the following blessing:

בָּרוּךְ אַתָּה יהוה אֱלֹהֵינוּ מֶלֶךְ הָעוֹלָם, הַמּוֹצִיא לֶחֶם מִן הָאָרֶץ.

The bottom *matzah* is put down and the following blessing is recited while the top (whole) *matzah* and the middle (broken) piece are still raised.

בָּרוּךְ אַתָּה יהוה אֱלֹהֵינוּ מֶלֶךְ הָעוֹלָם, אֲשֶׁר קִדְּשָׁנוּ בְּמִצְוֹתָיו, וְצִוָּנוּ עַל אֲכִילַת מַצָּה.

Each participant is required to eat an amount of matzah equal in volume to an egg. Since it is usually impossible to provide a sufficient amount of matzah from the two matzos for all members of the household, other matzos should be available at the head of the table from which to complete the required amounts. However, each participant should receive a piece from each of the top two matzos. The matzos are to be eaten while reclining on the left side and without delay; they need not be dipped in salt.

מוֹצִיא מַצָּה — **Motzi / Matzah.**

The general custom (among Ashkenazim) is to use three matzos at the *Seder.* The *Daas Zekeinim* (*Shemos* 12:8) suggests that this is done in order to recall the three *se'ah* of flour that Abraham had Sarah prepare for the three "wayfarers" who came to him *(Bereishis* 18), which, as Rashi points out (quoting the *midrash*), took place on Pesach. What is the connection between these two matters — the eating of matzah and Abraham's hospitality — other than the historical coincidence that they both occur on the same day?

When the Jews left Egypt we are told that (*Shemos* 12:39): וַיֹּאפוּ אֶת הַבָּצֵק אֲשֶׁר הוֹצִיאוּ מִמִּצְרַיִם עֻגֹת מַצּוֹת כִּי לֹא חָמֵץ כִּי גֹרְשׁוּ מִמִּצְרַיִם וְלֹא יָכְלוּ לְהִתְמַהְמֵהַּ, *They baked the dough that they took out of Egypt into unleavened cakes, for they could not be leavened, for they were driven from*

RACHTZAH

The hands are washed for matzah and the following blessing is recited.
It is preferable to bring water and a basin to the head of the household at the *Seder* table.

B*lessed are You, HASHEM, our God, King of the Universe, Who has sanctified us with His commandments and com-manded us with regard to washing the hands.*

MOTZI / MATZAH

The following two blessings are recited over matzah; the first is recited over matzah as food, and the second for the special mitzvah of eating matzah on the night of Pesach. [The latter blessing is to be made with the intention that it also apply to the *korech* "sandwich" and the *afikoman*.] The head of the household raises all the matzos on the *Seder* plate and recites the following blessing:

B*lessed are You, HASHEM, our God, King of the Universe, Who brings forth bread from the earth.*

The bottom *matzah* is put down and the following blessing is recited
while the top (whole) *matzah* and the middle (broken) piece are still raised.

B*lessed are You, HASHEM, our God, King of the Universe, Who has sanctified us with His commandments and com-manded us with regard to eating matzah.*

Each participant is required to eat an amount of matzah equal in volume to an egg. Since it is usually impossible to provide a sufficient amount of matzah from the two matzos for all members of the household, other matzos should be available at the head of the table from which to complete the required amounts. However, each participant should receive a piece from each of the top two matzos. The matzos are to be eaten while reclining on the left side and without delay; they need not be dipped in salt.

Egypt for they could not delay. The word "cakes" seems superfluous. The point of the verse is that due to the great urgency they could not ferment their dough, but of what import is it that they made this dough into cakes?

It is an established principle of the Torah that the events in the times of the Patriarchs portend, in some manner, the events that will befall the Jewish nation at some time in the future (מַעֲשֵׂה אָבוֹת סִימָן לַבָּנִים). Thus, for example, when Abraham and Sarah were maltreated by Pharaoh and afterwards were sent away with a large monetary gift, this foreshadowed the events experienced by their descendants at the hands of the Egyptians many years later.

When the three "men" came to Abraham, he told Sarah, "Quickly prepare three *se'ah* of fine flour; knead it and make cakes." Perhaps it

מרור

The head of the household takes a half-egg volume of the *maror*, dips it into *charoses*, and gives each participant a like amount. The following blessing is recited with the intention that it also apply to the *maror* of the "sandwich." The *maror* is eaten without reclining, and without delay.

בָּרוּךְ אַתָּה יהוה אֱלֹהֵינוּ מֶלֶךְ הָעוֹלָם, אֲשֶׁר קִדְּשָׁנוּ בְּמִצְוֹתָיו, וְצִוָּנוּ עַל אֲכִילַת מָרוֹר.

כורך

The bottom (thus far unbroken) matzah is now taken. From it, with the addition of other *matzos*, each participant receives a half-egg volume of matzah with an equal volume of *maror* (dipped into *charoses* which is shaken off). The following paragraph is recited and the "sandwich" is eaten while reclining.

זֵכֶר לְמִקְדָּשׁ כְּהִלֵּל. כֵּן עָשָׂה הִלֵּל בִּזְמַן שֶׁבֵּית הַמִּקְדָּשׁ הָיָה קַיָּם. הָיָה כּוֹרֵךְ (פֶּסַח) מַצָּה וּמָרוֹר וְאוֹכֵל בְּיַחַד. לְקַיֵּם מַה שֶּׁנֶּאֱמַר, עַל מַצּוֹת וּמְרֹרִים יֹאכְלֻהוּ.[1]

was the alacrity with which Abraham hurried to perform the mitzvah of taking care of wayfarers (an act of kindness, חֶסֶד) which presaged, and provided merit for, the hasty manner in which the Israelites went out of Egypt. That they left without preparing adequate provisions for a lengthy trek in the desert, trusting in Hashem to provide for them, is considered as a source of great merit for them, for in *Yirmiyahu* 2:2 it states: כֹּה אָמַר ה' זָכַרְתִּי לָךְ חֶסֶד נְעוּרַיִךְ אַהֲבַת כְּלוּלֹתָיִךְ לֶכְתֵּךְ אַחֲרַי בַּמִּדְבָּר בְּאֶרֶץ לֹא זְרוּעָה, *Thus says Hashem, "I have remembered for you the righteousness* (חֶסֶד) *of your youth, the love of your bridal days: your following after Me in the desert, in a barren land."* The spiritual impetus to perform this righteous deed was provided by the actions of their ancestor, Abraham.

Perhaps to hint that Abraham's "haste" foreshadowed and resulted in the haste with which the Israelites left Egypt, the Torah tells us that the Jews baked "cakes," the same preparation made by Sarah for her "guests." These cakes, made in haste, are hence directly linked to the three matzos of the *Seder*.

מַצָּה — Matzah.

The *Rambam* writes in the laws of Pesach (*Chametz U'Matzah* 6:12): "The early sages used to starve themselves on the day before Pesach

MAROR

The head of the household takes a half-egg volume of the *maror,* dips it into *charoses,* and gives each participant a like amount. The following blessing is recited with the intention that it also apply to the *maror* of the "sandwich." The *maror* is eaten without reclining, and without delay.

B*lessed are You, HASHEM, our God, King of the Universe, Who has sanctified us with His commandments and commanded us with regard to eating maror.*

KORECH

The bottom (thus far unbroken) matzah is now taken. From it, with the addition of other *matzos,* each participant receives a half-egg volume of matzah with an equal volume of *maror* (dipped into *charoses* which is shaken off). The following paragraph is recited and the "sandwich" is eaten while reclining.

I*n commemoration of the Beis HaMikdash according to Hillel: This is what Hillel would do when the Beis HaMikdash was in existence — He would join the korban pesach, matzah, and maror, and eat them together to fulfill that which is written, "With matzos and maror they should eat it."*[1]

_____

(1) *Bamidbar* 9:11.

so that they could fulfill the mitzvah of eating the matzah that night with greater appetite and enthusiasm." Would not this fasting be counterproductive with the Sages eating matzah out of ravenous hunger rather than with zest and enthusiasm for the mitzvah?

At the core of this question lies an important principle of Judaism — and of life in general — as formulated in the classic *mussar* text, *Mesillas Yesharim*. The author asserts that the way a person comports himself externally in his manner of dress, behavior and general demeanor, even if this is performed with total insincerity, will eventually have a significant influence on his innermost thoughts and beliefs. If a person is forced to play the role of a criminal or idiot long enough, even if it is orginally a facade, in the long run it will affect his morality or sanity. Thus, advises the *Mesillas Yesharim*, a person should strive to adopt certain pious actions and habits even if these seem to smack of hypocrisy at first, for ultimately this will transform him. As he begins to internalize these practices, they will become a natural aspect of his behavior and thoughts.

Thus, if a person can arrange that his performance of a mitzvah, such

שֻׁלְחָן עוֹרֵךְ

The meal should be eaten in a combination of joy and solemnity, for the meal, too, is a part of the *Seder* service. While it is desirable that *zemiros* and discussion of the laws and events of Pesach be part of the meal, extraneous conversation should be avoided. It should be remembered that the *afikoman* must be eaten while there is still some appetite for it. In fact, if one is so sated that he must literally force himself to eat it, he is not credited with the performance of the mitzvah of *afikoman*. Therefore, it is unwise to eat more than a moderate amount during the meal. At the start of the meal a piece of egg should be eaten to commemorate the loss of the Beis HaMikdash. A hard egg is taken for this purpose since it is used for the *seudas havraah* of mourners.

צָפוּן

From the *afikoman* matzah (and from additional matzos to make up the required amount) a half-egg volume portion — according to some, a full egg's volume portion — is given to each participant. It should be eaten before midnight, while reclining, without delay, and uninterruptedly. Nothing may be eaten or drunk after the *afikoman* (with the exception of water and the like) except for the last two *Seder* cups of wine.

בָּרֵךְ

The third cup is poured and *Bircas HaMazon* (Grace After Meals) is recited.
According to some customs, the Cup of Elijah is poured at this point.

שִׁיר הַמַּעֲלוֹת, בְּשׁוּב יהוה אֶת שִׁיבַת צִיּוֹן, הָיִינוּ כְּחֹלְמִים. אָז יִמָּלֵא שְׂחוֹק פִּינוּ וּלְשׁוֹנֵנוּ רִנָּה, אָז יֹאמְרוּ בַגּוֹיִם, הִגְדִּיל יהוה לַעֲשׂוֹת עִם אֵלֶּה. הִגְדִּיל יהוה לַעֲשׂוֹת עִמָּנוּ, הָיִינוּ שְׂמֵחִים. שׁוּבָה יהוה אֶת שְׁבִיתֵנוּ, כַּאֲפִיקִים בַּנֶּגֶב. הַזֹּרְעִים בְּדִמְעָה בְּרִנָּה יִקְצֹרוּ. הָלוֹךְ יֵלֵךְ וּבָכֹה נֹשֵׂא מֶשֶׁךְ הַזָּרַע, בֹּא יָבֹא בְרִנָּה, נֹשֵׂא אֲלֻמֹּתָיו.

תְּהִלַּת יהוה יְדַבֶּר פִּי, וִיבָרֵךְ כָּל בָּשָׂר שֵׁם קָדְשׁוֹ לְעוֹלָם וָעֶד.¹ וַאֲנַחְנוּ נְבָרֵךְ יָהּ, מֵעַתָּה וְעַד עוֹלָם, הַלְלוּיָהּ.² הוֹדוּ לַיהוה כִּי טוֹב, כִּי לְעוֹלָם חַסְדּוֹ.³ מִי יְמַלֵּל גְּבוּרוֹת יהוה, יַשְׁמִיעַ כָּל תְּהִלָּתוֹ.⁴

as eating matzah, is carried out with great enthusiasm and zeal, even though this ardor is due to motives which are not entirely noble — e.g.

SHULCHAN ORECH

The meal should be eaten in a combination of joy and solemnity, for the meal, too, is a part of the *Seder* service. While it is desirable that *zemiros* and discussion of the laws and events of Pesach be part of the meal, extraneous conversation should be avoided. It should be remembered that the *afikoman* must be eaten while there is still some appetite for it. In fact, if one is so sated that he must literally force himself to eat it, he is not credited with the performance of the mitzvah of *afikoman*. Therefore, it is unwise to eat more than a moderate amount during the meal. At the start of the meal a piece of egg should be eaten to commemorate the loss of the Beis HaMikdash. A hard egg is taken for this purpose since it is used for the *seudas havraah* of mourners.

TZAFUN

From the *afikoman* matzah (and from additional matzos to make up the required amount) a half-egg volume portion — according to some, a full egg's volume portion — is given to each participant. It should be eaten before midnight, while reclining, without delay, and uninterruptedly. Nothing may be eaten or drunk after the *afikoman* (with the exception of water and the like) except for the last two *Seder* cups of wine.

BARECH

The third cup is poured and *Bircas HaMazon* (Grace After Meals) is recited. According to some customs, the Cup of Elijah is poured at this point.

A song of the steps. When HASHEM will bring the exiles back to Zion, it will be as if we were dreaming. Then our mouth will be filled with laughter and our tongue with joy. Then they will say among the nations, "HASHEM is the One Who has done great things with these." HASHEM has indeed done great things with us. We have been made happy. HASHEM, return our captives like dry streams that run again in the south. Those who sow in tears will reap in song. He who goes crying, carrying his load of seed, will return singing, carrying his sheaves of grain.

May my mouth declare the praise of HASHEM and may all flesh bless His Holy Name forever.[1] We will bless HASHEM from this time and forever. Praise HASHEM![2] Give thanks to God for He is good, His kindness endures forever.[3] Who can express the mighty acts of HASHEM? Who can declare all His praise?[4]

---

(1) *Tehillim* 145:21. (2) 115:18. (3) 118:1. (4) 106:2.

---

hunger — nonetheless, these "feigned" emotions will eventually be internalized, resulting in a deeper emotional performance of mitzvos.

If three or more males, aged thirteen or older, participate in the meal, the leader is required to formally invite the others to join him in the recitation of *Bircas HaMazon*.

Following is the *zimun*, or formal invitation.

The leader begins:

רַבּוֹתַי נְבָרֵךְ.

The group responds:

יְהִי שֵׁם יהוה מְבֹרָךְ מֵעַתָּה וְעַד עוֹלָם.[1]

The leader continues:

[If ten men join the *zimun*, the words in parentheses are included.]

יְהִי שֵׁם יהוה מְבֹרָךְ מֵעַתָּה וְעַד עוֹלָם.[1]

בִּרְשׁוּת מָרָנָן וְרַבָּנָן וְרַבּוֹתַי,

נְבָרֵךְ (אֱלֹהֵינוּ) שֶׁאָכַלְנוּ מִשֶּׁלּוֹ.

The group responds:

בָּרוּךְ (אֱלֹהֵינוּ) שֶׁאָכַלְנוּ מִשֶּׁלּוֹ וּבְטוּבוֹ חָיִינוּ.

The leader continues:

בָּרוּךְ (אֱלֹהֵינוּ) שֶׁאָכַלְנוּ מִשֶּׁלּוֹ וּבְטוּבוֹ חָיִינוּ.

The following line is recited if ten men join the *zimun*.

בָּרוּךְ הוּא וּבָרוּךְ שְׁמוֹ.

בָּרוּךְ אַתָּה יהוה אֱלֹהֵינוּ מֶלֶךְ הָעוֹלָם, הַזָּן אֶת הָעוֹלָם כֻּלּוֹ, בְּטוּבוֹ, בְּחֵן בְּחֶסֶד וּבְרַחֲמִים, הוּא נֹתֵן לֶחֶם לְכָל בָּשָׂר, כִּי לְעוֹלָם חַסְדּוֹ.[1] וּבְטוּבוֹ הַגָּדוֹל, תָּמִיד לֹא חָסַר לָנוּ, וְאַל יֶחְסַר לָנוּ מָזוֹן לְעוֹלָם וָעֶד. בַּעֲבוּר שְׁמוֹ הַגָּדוֹל, כִּי הוּא אֵל זָן וּמְפַרְנֵס לַכֹּל, וּמֵטִיב לַכֹּל, וּמֵכִין מָזוֹן לְכָל בְּרִיּוֹתָיו אֲשֶׁר בָּרָא. (כָּאָמוּר: פּוֹתֵחַ אֶת יָדֶךָ, וּמַשְׂבִּיעַ לְכָל חַי רָצוֹן.[2]) . בָּרוּךְ אַתָּה יהוה, הַזָּן אֶת הַכֹּל.

נוֹדֶה לְךָ יהוה אֱלֹהֵינוּ, עַל שֶׁהִנְחַלְתָּ לַאֲבוֹתֵינוּ אֶרֶץ חֶמְדָּה טוֹבָה וּרְחָבָה. וְעַל שֶׁהוֹצֵאתָנוּ יהוה אֱלֹהֵינוּ מֵאֶרֶץ מִצְרַיִם, וּפְדִיתָנוּ מִבֵּית עֲבָדִים, וְעַל

If three or more males, aged thirteen or older, participate in the meal, the leader is required to formally invite the others to join him in the recitation of Grace After Meals.

Following is the *zimun,* or formal invitation.

The leader begins:

Gentlemen, let us make the blessing.

The group responds:

May the name of Hashem be blessed from this moment and forever![1]

The leader continues:

[If ten men join the *zimun,* the words in parentheses are included.]

May the name of Hashem be blessed from this moment and forever![1]

With the permission of the distinguished people present, let us bless [our God], for we have eaten from what is His.

The group responds:

Blessed is [our God] He of Whose we have eaten and through Whose goodness we live.

The leader continues:

Blessed is [our God] He of Whose we have eaten and through Whose goodness we live.

The following line is recited if ten men join the *zimun.*

Blessed is He and Blessed is His Name.

B*lessed are You, HASHEM, our God, King of the Universe, Who feeds the entire world with His goodness, with grace, kindness, and mercy. He gives bread to all flesh, for His kindness is eternal.*[1] *And in His great goodness, food has never been lacking for us, nor may it ever be, for the sake of His great name. For He feeds and supports all and does good to all and readies food for all His creatures that He created. (As it is said: "You open Your hand and satisfy the wants of every living thing."*[2]*) Blessed are You, HASHEM, Who feeds all.*

W*e thank You, HASHEM, our God, because You bequeathed to our forefathers, a desirable, good, and spacious land, and for taking us out, HASHEM, our God, from the land of Egypt, and redeeming us from the house of bondage, and for Your*

---

(1) *Tehillim* 136:25. (2) 145:16.

בְּרִיתְךָ שֶׁחָתַמְתָּ בִּבְשָׂרֵנוּ, וְעַל תּוֹרָתְךָ שֶׁלִּמַּדְתָּנוּ, וְעַל חֻקֶּיךָ שֶׁהוֹדַעְתָּנוּ, וְעַל חַיִּים חֵן וָחֶסֶד שֶׁחוֹנַנְתָּנוּ, וְעַל אֲכִילַת מָזוֹן שָׁאַתָּה זָן וּמְפַרְנֵס אוֹתָנוּ תָּמִיד, בְּכָל יוֹם וּבְכָל עֵת וּבְכָל שָׁעָה.

וְעַל הַכֹּל יהוה אֱלֹהֵינוּ אֲנַחְנוּ מוֹדִים לָךְ, וּמְבָרְכִים אוֹתָךְ, יִתְבָּרַךְ שִׁמְךָ בְּפִי כָּל חַי תָּמִיד לְעוֹלָם וָעֶד. כַּכָּתוּב. וְאָכַלְתָּ וְשָׂבָעְתָּ, וּבֵרַכְתָּ אֶת יהוה אֱלֹהֶיךָ, עַל הָאָרֶץ הַטֹּבָה אֲשֶׁר נָתַן לָךְ.[1] בָּרוּךְ אַתָּה יהוה, עַל הָאָרֶץ וְעַל הַמָּזוֹן.

רַחֵם נָא יהוה אֱלֹהֵינוּ עַל יִשְׂרָאֵל עַמֶּךָ, וְעַל יְרוּשָׁלַיִם עִירֶךָ, וְעַל צִיּוֹן מִשְׁכַּן כְּבוֹדֶךָ, וְעַל מַלְכוּת בֵּית דָּוִד מְשִׁיחֶךָ, וְעַל הַבַּיִת הַגָּדוֹל וְהַקָּדוֹשׁ שֶׁנִּקְרָא שִׁמְךָ עָלָיו. אֱלֹהֵינוּ אָבִינוּ רְעֵנוּ זוּנֵנוּ פַּרְנְסֵנוּ וְכַלְכְּלֵנוּ וְהַרְוִיחֵנוּ, וְהַרְוַח לָנוּ יהוה אֱלֹהֵינוּ מְהֵרָה מִכָּל צָרוֹתֵינוּ. וְנָא אַל תַּצְרִיכֵנוּ יהוה אֱלֹהֵינוּ, לֹא לִידֵי מַתְּנַת בָּשָׂר וָדָם, וְלֹא לִידֵי הַלְוָאָתָם, כִּי אִם לְיָדְךָ הַמְּלֵאָה הַפְּתוּחָה הַקְּדוֹשָׁה וְהָרְחָבָה, שֶׁלֹּא נֵבוֹשׁ וְלֹא נִכָּלֵם לְעוֹלָם וָעֶד.

On Shabbos add the following paragraph.

רְצֵה וְהַחֲלִיצֵנוּ יהוה אֱלֹהֵינוּ בְּמִצְוֹתֶיךָ, וּבְמִצְוַת יוֹם הַשְּׁבִיעִי הַשַּׁבָּת הַגָּדוֹל וְהַקָּדוֹשׁ הַזֶּה, כִּי יוֹם זֶה גָּדוֹל וְקָדוֹשׁ הוּא לְפָנֶיךָ, לִשְׁבָּת בּוֹ וְלָנוּחַ בּוֹ בְּאַהֲבָה כְּמִצְוַת רְצוֹנֶךָ, וּבִרְצוֹנְךָ הָנִיחַ לָנוּ יהוה אֱלֹהֵינוּ, שֶׁלֹּא תְהֵא צָרָה וְיָגוֹן וַאֲנָחָה בְּיוֹם מְנוּחָתֵנוּ, וְהַרְאֵנוּ יהוה אֱלֹהֵינוּ בְּנֶחָמַת צִיּוֹן עִירֶךָ, וּבְבִנְיַן יְרוּשָׁלַיִם עִיר קָדְשֶׁךָ, כִּי אַתָּה הוּא בַּעַל הַיְשׁוּעוֹת וּבַעַל הַנֶּחָמוֹת.

covenant which You sealed into our flesh, and for Your Torah which You taught us, and for Your laws which You made known to us, and for life, grace, and kindness which You have bestowed upon us, and for the food with which You feed and sustain us constantly every day, at every time, at every moment.

For it all, HASHEM, our God, we thank You and bless You. May Your name be blessed by the mouths of all who live constantly, forever, as it is written, "You will eat and you will be satisfied and you will bless HASHEM, your God, for the good land which He has given you."[1] Blessed are You, HASHEM, for the land and the food.

Have mercy, please HASHEM, our God, on Yisrael, Your people, and on Jerusalem, Your city, and on Zion, the abode of Your glory, and on the kingdom of David, Your Mashiach, and on the great and holy house upon which Your name has been called. Our God, our Father, pasture us, feed us, support us, sustain us, and rescue us. And rescue us, HASHEM, our God, speedily from all of our troubles. Please, HASHEM, our God, do not put us in need of gifts or loans from men. May we need only Your full, open, holy, and ample hand, so that we may never be ashamed or embarrassed.

On Shabbos add the following paragraph.

May it be Your will, HASHEM, our God, that You fortify us through Your mitzvos and through the mitzvah of the seventh day, this great and sacred Sabbath. For this day is great and sacred before You, to desist from work on it, and to rest on it lovingly, in accordance with the command of Your will. May it be Your will, HASHEM, our God, that You spare us any trouble, anguish, or sorrow on the day of our rest, and that You show us, HASHEM, our God, the consolation of Zion, Your city, and the reconstruction of Jerusalem, Your sacred city, for You are the Master of salvations and the Master of consolations.

___

(1) Devarim 8:10.

אֱלֹהֵינוּ וֵאלֹהֵי אֲבוֹתֵינוּ, יַעֲלֶה, וְיָבֹא, וְיַגִּיעַ, וְיֵרָאֶה, וְיֵרָצֶה, וְיִשָּׁמַע, וְיִפָּקֵד, וְיִזָּכֵר זִכְרוֹנֵנוּ וּפִקְדוֹנֵנוּ, וְזִכְרוֹן אֲבוֹתֵינוּ, וְזִכְרוֹן מָשִׁיחַ בֶּן דָּוִד עַבְדֶּךָ, וְזִכְרוֹן יְרוּשָׁלַיִם עִיר קָדְשֶׁךָ, וְזִכְרוֹן כָּל עַמְּךָ בֵּית יִשְׂרָאֵל לְפָנֶיךָ, לִפְלֵיטָה לְטוֹבָה לְחֵן וּלְחֶסֶד וּלְרַחֲמִים, לְחַיִּים וּלְשָׁלוֹם בְּיוֹם חַג הַמַּצּוֹת הַזֶּה. זָכְרֵנוּ יהוה אֱלֹהֵינוּ בּוֹ לְטוֹבָה, וּפָקְדֵנוּ בוֹ לִבְרָכָה, וְהוֹשִׁיעֵנוּ בוֹ לְחַיִּים. וּבִדְבַר יְשׁוּעָה וְרַחֲמִים, חוּס וְחָנֵּנוּ וְרַחֵם עָלֵינוּ וְהוֹשִׁיעֵנוּ, כִּי אֵלֶיךָ עֵינֵינוּ, כִּי אֵל (מֶלֶךְ) חַנּוּן וְרַחוּם אָתָּה.[1]

וּבְנֵה יְרוּשָׁלַיִם עִיר הַקֹּדֶשׁ בִּמְהֵרָה בְּיָמֵינוּ. בָּרוּךְ אַתָּה יהוה, בּוֹנֵה בְרַחֲמָיו יְרוּשָׁלָיִם. אָמֵן.

בָּרוּךְ אַתָּה יהוה אֱלֹהֵינוּ מֶלֶךְ הָעוֹלָם, הָאֵל אָבִינוּ מַלְכֵּנוּ אַדִּירֵנוּ בּוֹרְאֵנוּ גּוֹאֲלֵנוּ יוֹצְרֵנוּ קְדוֹשֵׁנוּ קְדוֹשׁ יַעֲקֹב, רוֹעֵנוּ רוֹעֵה יִשְׂרָאֵל, הַמֶּלֶךְ הַטּוֹב וְהַמֵּטִיב לַכֹּל, שֶׁבְּכָל יוֹם וָיוֹם הוּא הֵטִיב, הוּא מֵטִיב, הוּא יֵיטִיב לָנוּ. הוּא גְמָלָנוּ הוּא גוֹמְלֵנוּ הוּא יִגְמְלֵנוּ לָעַד, לְחֵן וּלְחֶסֶד וּלְרַחֲמִים וּלְרֶוַח הַצָּלָה וְהַצְלָחָה, בְּרָכָה וִישׁוּעָה נֶחָמָה פַּרְנָסָה וְכַלְכָּלָה וְרַחֲמִים וְחַיִּים וְשָׁלוֹם וְכָל טוֹב, וּמִכָּל טוּב לְעוֹלָם אַל יְחַסְּרֵנוּ.

הָרַחֲמָן הוּא יִמְלוֹךְ עָלֵינוּ לְעוֹלָם וָעֶד. הָרַחֲמָן הוּא יִתְבָּרַךְ בַּשָּׁמַיִם וּבָאָרֶץ. הָרַחֲמָן הוּא יִשְׁתַּבַּח לְדוֹר דּוֹרִים, וְיִתְפָּאַר בָּנוּ לָעַד וּלְנֵצַח נְצָחִים, וְיִתְהַדַּר בָּנוּ לָעַד וּלְעוֹלְמֵי עוֹלָמִים. הָרַחֲמָן הוּא יְפַרְנְסֵנוּ

Our God and the God of our fathers, may there arise, come, arrive, be seen, be accepted, be heard, be taken note of, and be remembered a remembrance and recollection of us, and a remembrance of our ancestors, and a remembrance of Mashiach the son of David Your servant, and a remembrance of Jerusalem, Your sacred city, and a remembrance of all of Your people, the House of Israel, before You, for deliverance, for goodness, for grace, for kindness and for mercy, for life, and for peace, on this day of the Festival of Matzos. Remember us on it, HASHEM, our God, for good, take us into account for blessing, and save us so that we may live. And with a word of salvation and mercy, have pity and be gracious to us, and have mercy upon us and save us, for our eyes look to You, for You are a merciful and gracious God (King).[1]

And build Jerusalem, the city of sanctity, quickly in our days. Blessed are You, HASHEM, Who builds Jerusalem in His mercy. Amen.

Blessed are You, HASHEM, our God, King of the Universe, the Powerful One, our Father, our King, our Mighty One, our Creator, our Redeemer, our Shaper, our Holy One, the Holy One of Yaakov, our Shepherd, the Shepherd of Israel, the Sovereign Who is good and does good to all, Who in each and every day has done good, is doing good, and will do good to us. He has bestowed upon us, is bestowing upon us, and will forever bestow upon us grace, kindness, mercy, rescue, deliverance, success, blessing, salvation, consolation, livelihood, sustenance, mercy, life, peace, and all that is good. May He never let us lack for any good thing.

May the Merciful One rule over us forever. May the Merciful One be blessed in the heavens and the earth. May the Merciful One be praised for all generations, and may He take pride in us for eternity, and may we be a source of glory to Him forever and ever. May the Merciful One provide us an honor-

(1) Cf. *Nechemiah* 9:31.

בִּכְבוֹד. הָרַחֲמָן הוּא יִשְׁבּוֹר עֻלֵּנוּ מֵעַל צַוָּארֵנוּ, וְהוּא
יוֹלִיכֵנוּ קוֹמְמִיּוּת לְאַרְצֵנוּ. הָרַחֲמָן הוּא יִשְׁלַח לָנוּ
בְּרָכָה מְרֻבָּה בַּבַּיִת הַזֶּה, וְעַל שֻׁלְחָן זֶה שֶׁאָכַלְנוּ עָלָיו.
הָרַחֲמָן הוּא יִשְׁלַח לָנוּ אֶת אֵלִיָּהוּ הַנָּבִיא זָכוּר לַטּוֹב,
וִיבַשֶּׂר לָנוּ בְּשׂוֹרוֹת טוֹבוֹת יְשׁוּעוֹת וְנֶחָמוֹת.

The following text — for a guest to recite at his host's table —
appears in *Shulchan Aruch, Orach Chaim* 201.

יְהִי רָצוֹן שֶׁלֹּא יֵבוֹשׁ וְלֹא יִכָּלֵם בַּעַל הַבַּיִת הַזֶּה, לֹא בָעוֹלָם
הַזֶּה וְלֹא בָעוֹלָם הַבָּא, וְיַצְלִיחַ בְּכָל נְכָסָיו, וְיִהְיוּ נְכָסָיו
וּנְכָסֵינוּ מוּצְלָחִים וּקְרוֹבִים לָעִיר, וְאַל יִשְׁלוֹט שָׂטָן בְּמַעֲשֵׂה יָדָיו,
וְאַל יִזְדַּקֵּק לְפָנָיו שׁוּם דְּבַר חֵטְא וְהִרְהוּר עָוֹן, מֵעַתָּה וְעַד עוֹלָם.

Those eating at their own table recite the following,
adding the appropriate parenthesized phrases:

הָרַחֲמָן הוּא יְבָרֵךְ אוֹתִי
(וְאֶת אִשְׁתִּי /בַּעְלִי וְאֶת זַרְעִי) וְאֶת כָּל אֲשֶׁר לִי.

Guests recite the following.
Children at their parents' table add the words in parentheses.

הָרַחֲמָן הוּא יְבָרֵךְ
אֶת (אָבִי מוֹרִי) בַּעַל הַבַּיִת הַזֶּה,
וְאֶת (אִמִּי מוֹרָתִי) בַּעֲלַת הַבַּיִת הַזֶּה,

All guests recite the following:

אוֹתָם וְאֶת בֵּיתָם וְאֶת זַרְעָם וְאֶת כָּל אֲשֶׁר לָהֶם.

All continue here:

אוֹתָנוּ וְאֶת כָּל אֲשֶׁר לָנוּ, כְּמוֹ שֶׁנִּתְבָּרְכוּ אֲבוֹתֵינוּ
אַבְרָהָם יִצְחָק וְיַעֲקֹב בַּכֹּל מִכֹּל כֹּל,[1] כֵּן יְבָרֵךְ אוֹתָנוּ
כֻּלָּנוּ יַחַד בִּבְרָכָה שְׁלֵמָה, וְנֹאמַר, אָמֵן.

בַּמָּרוֹם יְלַמְּדוּ עֲלֵיהֶם וְעָלֵינוּ זְכוּת, שֶׁתְּהֵא לְמִשְׁמֶרֶת
שָׁלוֹם. וְנִשָּׂא בְרָכָה מֵאֵת יהוה, וּצְדָקָה
מֵאֱלֹהֵי יִשְׁעֵנוּ, וְנִמְצָא חֵן וְשֵׂכֶל טוֹב בְּעֵינֵי אֱלֹהִים
וְאָדָם.[2]

able livelihood. May the Merciful One break the yoke upon our shoulders and lead us upright to our land. May the Merciful One send us great blessing in this house, and upon this table at which we have eaten. May the Merciful One send us Eliyahu the prophet, who is remembered for the good, and may he bring us good tidings, salvations, and consolations.

The following text — for a guest to recite at his host's table — appears in *Shulchan Aruch, Orach Chaim* 201.

M *ay it be God's will that this host not be shamed nor humiliated in This World or in the World to Come. May he be successful in all his dealings. May his dealings and our dealings be successful and conveniently close at hand. May no evil impediment reign over his handiwork, and may no semblance of sin or iniquitous thought attach itself to him from this time and forever.*

Those eating at their own table recite the following, adding the appropriate parenthesized phrases:

May the Merciful One bless me, (my wife/husband and children) and all that is mine.

Guests recite the following. Children at their parents' table add the words in parentheses.

May the Merciful One bless (my father, my teacher) the master of this house, and (my mother, my teacher) the mistress of this house,

All guests recite the following:

them, their house, their family, and all that is theirs,

All continue here:

ours and all that is ours — just as our forefathers Avraham, Yitzchak, and Yaakov were blessed with every sort of blessing.[1] *So may He bless us all together with perfect blessing, and let us say: Amen.*

M *ay there be a favorable report (of them and) of us in heaven that should preserve peace. May we receive blessing from* HASHEM, *and charity from the God of our salvation, and may we find favor and good regard in the eyes of God and man.*[2]

---

(1) Cf. *Bereishis* 24:1; 27:33; 33:11. (2) Cf. *Mishlei* 3:4.

On *Shabbos* add the following sentence:

הָרַחֲמָן הוּא יַנְחִילֵנוּ יוֹם שֶׁכֻּלּוֹ שַׁבָּת וּמְנוּחָה לְחַיֵּי הָעוֹלָמִים.

The words in parentheses are added on the two *Seder* nights in some communities.

הָרַחֲמָן הוּא יַנְחִילֵנוּ יוֹם שֶׁכֻּלּוֹ טוֹב (יוֹם שֶׁכֻּלּוֹ אָרוּךְ, יוֹם שֶׁצַּדִּיקִים יוֹשְׁבִים וְעַטְרוֹתֵיהֶם בְּרָאשֵׁיהֶם וְנֶהֱנִים מִזִּיו הַשְּׁכִינָה, וִיהִי חֶלְקֵנוּ עִמָּהֶם).

הָרַחֲמָן הוּא יְזַכֵּנוּ לִימוֹת הַמָּשִׁיחַ וּלְחַיֵּי הָעוֹלָם הַבָּא. מִגְדּוֹל יְשׁוּעוֹת מַלְכּוֹ וְעֹשֶׂה חֶסֶד לִמְשִׁיחוֹ לְדָוִד וּלְזַרְעוֹ עַד עוֹלָם.[1] עֹשֶׂה שָׁלוֹם בִּמְרוֹמָיו, הוּא יַעֲשֶׂה שָׁלוֹם עָלֵינוּ וְעַל כָּל יִשְׂרָאֵל. וְאִמְרוּ, אָמֵן.

יְראוּ אֶת יהוה קְדֹשָׁיו, כִּי אֵין מַחְסוֹר לִירֵאָיו. כְּפִירִים רָשׁוּ וְרָעֵבוּ, וְדֹרְשֵׁי יהוה לֹא יַחְסְרוּ כָל טוֹב.[2] הוֹדוּ לַיהוה כִּי טוֹב, כִּי לְעוֹלָם חַסְדּוֹ.[3] פּוֹתֵחַ אֶת יָדֶךָ, וּמַשְׂבִּיעַ לְכָל חַי רָצוֹן.[4] בָּרוּךְ הַגֶּבֶר אֲשֶׁר יִבְטַח בַּיהוה, וְהָיָה יהוה מִבְטַחוֹ.[5] נַעַר הָיִיתִי גַּם זָקַנְתִּי, וְלֹא רָאִיתִי צַדִּיק נֶעֱזָב, וְזַרְעוֹ מְבַקֶּשׁ לָחֶם.[6] יהוה עֹז לְעַמּוֹ יִתֵּן, יהוה יְבָרֵךְ אֶת עַמּוֹ בַשָּׁלוֹם.[7]

Upon completion of *Bircas HaMazon*, the blessing over wine is recited and the third cup is drunk while reclining on the left side. It is preferable to drink the entire cup, but at the very least, most of the cup should be drained.

בָּרוּךְ אַתָּה יהוה אֱלֹהֵינוּ מֶלֶךְ הָעוֹלָם, בּוֹרֵא פְּרִי הַגָּפֶן.

The fourth cup is poured. According to most customs, the Cup of Elijah is poured at this point, (some have the custom to pour wine from the cup of Elijah into all the cups of the participants so that all participants should use some wine from that cup) after which the door is opened in accordance with the verse, "It is a guarded night." Then the following paragraph is recited.

שְׁפֹךְ חֲמָתְךָ אֶל הַגּוֹיִם אֲשֶׁר לֹא יְדָעוּךָ וְעַל מַמְלָכוֹת אֲשֶׁר בְּשִׁמְךָ לֹא קָרָאוּ. כִּי אָכַל אֶת יַעֲקֹב וְאֶת

שְׁפֹךְ חֲמָתְךָ אֶל הַגּוֹיִם וכו' — **Pour out Your wrath upon the nations, etc.**

It was explained earlier (p. 131), in the name of the *Netziv*, that the custom to pour the "cup of Elijah" is meant to correspond to the fifth ex-

On *Shabbos* add the following sentence:
*May the Merciful One grant us a day which
is all Sabbath and rest for eternal life.*

The words in parentheses are added on the two *Seder* nights in some communities.

M ay the Merciful One grant us a day which is entirely good
(that everlasting day, the day when the righteous sit with
crowns on their heads, enjoying the reflection of God's majesty —
and may our portion be with them)!

M ay the Merciful One let us live to the days of the Mashiach
and the life of the world to come. He is a tower of salvation
to His king, and does kindness to His Mashiach, to David and his
offspring forever.[1] May He Who makes peace in His heights make
peace over us and over all of Yisrael. Now respond: Amen.

F ear HASHEM, holy ones of His! For those who fear Him lack
nothing.[2] Young lions may be poor and hungry, but those
who seek HASHEM will not be in need of any good thing. Praise
HASHEM for He is good, for His kindness is eternal.[3] You open
Your hand and satisfy the wants of every living thing.[4] Blessed
is the man who trusts HASHEM; then HASHEM will be his
security.[5] I was once a young man and I have since aged, but
I have never seen someone righteous abandoned, nor his
children in want of bread.[6] HASHEM will grant strength to His
people. HASHEM will bless His people with peace.[7]

Upon completion of *Bircas HaMazon* the blessing over wine is recited and the third cup is
drunk while reclining on the left side. It is preferable to drink the entire cup, but at the very
least, most of the cup should be drained.

B lessed are You, HASHEM, our God, King of the Universe, Who
creates the fruit of the vine.

The fourth cup is poured. According to most customs, the Cup of Elijah is poured at this point,
(some have the custom to pour wine from the cup of Elijah into all the cups of the participants
so that all participants should use some wine from that cup) after which the door is opened
in accordance with the verse, "It is a guarded night." Then the following paragraph is recited.

P our out Your wrath upon the nations who do not know
You and upon the kingdoms who call not upon Your
name, for they have consumed Yaakov and laid waste his

---

(1) *Tehillim* 18:51. (2) 34:10-11. (3) 136:1 et al. (4) 145:16.
(5) *Yirmiyahu* 17:7. (6) *Tehillim* 37:25. (7) 29:11.

---

pression of deliverance used by Hashem (*Shemos* 6), just as the four regular cups drunk at the *Seder* parallel the first four terms used there. The

נָוֵהוּ הֵשַׁמּוּ.¹ שָׁפַךְ עֲלֵיהֶם זַעְמֶךָ וַחֲרוֹן אַפְּךָ יַשִּׂיגֵם.² תִּרְדֹּף בְּאַף וְתַשְׁמִידֵם מִתַּחַת שְׁמֵי יהוה.³

הלל

The door is closed and the recitation of the Haggadah is continued.

לֹא לָנוּ יהוה לֹא לָנוּ, כִּי לְשִׁמְךָ תֵּן כָּבוֹד, עַל חַסְדְּךָ עַל אֲמִתֶּךָ. לָמָּה יֹאמְרוּ הַגּוֹיִם, אַיֵּה נָא אֱלֹהֵיהֶם. וֵאלֹהֵינוּ בַשָּׁמָיִם, כֹּל אֲשֶׁר חָפֵץ עָשָׂה. עֲצַבֵּיהֶם כֶּסֶף וְזָהָב, מַעֲשֵׂה יְדֵי אָדָם. פֶּה לָהֶם וְלֹא יְדַבֵּרוּ, עֵינַיִם לָהֶם וְלֹא יִרְאוּ. אָזְנַיִם לָהֶם וְלֹא יִשְׁמָעוּ, אַף לָהֶם וְלֹא יְרִיחוּן. יְדֵיהֶם וְלֹא יְמִישׁוּן, רַגְלֵיהֶם וְלֹא יְהַלֵּכוּ, לֹא יֶהְגּוּ בִּגְרוֹנָם. כְּמוֹהֶם יִהְיוּ עֹשֵׂיהֶם, כֹּל אֲשֶׁר בֹּטֵחַ בָּהֶם. יִשְׂרָאֵל בְּטַח בַּיהוה, עֶזְרָם וּמָגִנָּם הוּא. בֵּית אַהֲרֹן בִּטְחוּ בַיהוה, עֶזְרָם וּמָגִנָּם הוּא. יִרְאֵי יהוה בִּטְחוּ בַיהוה, עֶזְרָם וּמָגִנָּם הוּא.

reason this fifth cup is not drunk like the others is because the fifth expression, וִידַעְתֶּם כִּי אֲנִי ה׳, *And you shall know that I am Hashem* (*Shemos* 6:7), speaks of Hashem's Essence that is possible only for the spiritual elite, and is altogether unattainable nowadays, when Divine Inspiration (רוּחַ הַקֹּדֶשׁ) is lacking among us. Only when Elijah will usher in the Messianic era will this level of spirituality again become achievable — hence the appellation "cup of Elijah." *The Netziv* continues to explain that this is why it is also customary to recite these three verses at this point. These verses highlight the difference between us and the nations of the world. They are ,,הַגּוֹיִם אֲשֶׁר לֹא יְדָעוּךָ, *the nations that do not recognize You*, seeking to ignore Your presence in human affairs and the concurrent obligation to serve You. They are מַמְלָכוֹת אֲשֶׁר בְּשִׁמְךָ לֹא קָרָאוּ, *kingdoms that do not invoke Your Name*. We, however, constantly seek You and call out to Your name.

While the Temple stood it was a beacon of light, not only to us but even to the nations of the world. וְגַם אֶל הַנָּכְרִי אֲשֶׁר לֹא מֵעַמְּךָ יִשְׂרָאֵל הוּא וּבָא מֵאֶרֶץ רְחוֹקָה לְמַעַן שְׁמֶךָ, *And also the foreigner, that is not of Your peo-*

dwelling.[1] *Pour Your fury on them and may Your rage overtake them.*[2] *Pursue them with anger and obliterate them from under* HASHEM'S *skies.*[3]

HALLEL

The door is closed and the recitation of the Haggadah is continued.

Not for us, HASHEM, not for us, but for Your name give glory, for Your kindness and Your truth. Why should the nations say: Where is their God? Our God in the heavens does whatever He desires. Their idols are silver and gold, the work of man's hands. They have a mouth, but do not speak. They have eyes, but do not see. They have ears, but do not hear. They have a nose, but do not smell. Their hands do not feel. Their feet do not walk. They do not utter sound with their throat. Their makers will be like them, all those who trust them. Israel, trust HASHEM — He is their help and shield. House of Aharon, trust HASHEM — He is their help and shield. Those who fear HASHEM, trust HASHEM — He is their help and shield.

---

(1) *Tehillim* 79:6-7. (2) 69:25. (3) *Eichah* 3:66.

---

ple, will come from a distant land for the sake of Your name (Melachim I 8:41).

Since the nations of the world sought total disassociation from Hashem, they felt a need to sever and destroy the Temple that connects them to Hashem. כִּי אָכַל אֶת יַעֲקֹב וְאֶת נָוֵהוּ הֵשַׁמּוּ, *For they have devoured Jacob* [the nation of Israel] and *destroyed His habitation* [the Temple].

We therefore ask Hashem to revenge our honor as well as His: "Pour out Your wrath upon the nations."

יִשְׂרָאֵל בְּטַח בַּה' עֶזְרָם וּמָגִנָּם הוּא — **Israel, trust Hashem; He is their help and shield.**

The word בְּטַח is in the singular form (as opposed to the following two verses, where it appears in the plural, בִּטְחוּ), to convey that it is precisely because Israel is capable of joining together as one collective essence that they are deserving of Hashem's protection as *"their help and shield."*

יהוה זְכָרָנוּ יְבָרֵךְ, יְבָרֵךְ אֶת בֵּית יִשְׂרָאֵל, יְבָרֵךְ אֶת בֵּית אַהֲרֹן. יְבָרֵךְ יִרְאֵי יהוה, הַקְּטַנִּים עִם הַגְּדֹלִים. יֹסֵף יהוה עֲלֵיכֶם, עֲלֵיכֶם וְעַל בְּנֵיכֶם. בְּרוּכִים אַתֶּם לַיהוה, עֹשֵׂה שָׁמַיִם וָאָרֶץ. הַשָּׁמַיִם שָׁמַיִם לַיהוה, וְהָאָרֶץ נָתַן לִבְנֵי אָדָם. לֹא הַמֵּתִים יְהַלְלוּ יָהּ, וְלֹא כָּל יֹרְדֵי דוּמָה. וַאֲנַחְנוּ נְבָרֵךְ יָהּ, מֵעַתָּה וְעַד עוֹלָם, הַלְלוּיָהּ.[1]

אָהַבְתִּי כִּי יִשְׁמַע יהוה, אֶת קוֹלִי תַּחֲנוּנָי. כִּי הִטָּה אָזְנוֹ לִי, וּבְיָמַי אֶקְרָא. אֲפָפוּנִי חֶבְלֵי מָוֶת, וּמְצָרֵי שְׁאוֹל מְצָאוּנִי, צָרָה וְיָגוֹן אֶמְצָא. וּבְשֵׁם יהוה אֶקְרָא, אָנָּה יהוה מַלְּטָה נַפְשִׁי. חַנּוּן יהוה וְצַדִּיק, וֵאלֹהֵינוּ מְרַחֵם. שֹׁמֵר פְּתָאיִם יהוה, דַּלּוֹתִי וְלִי יְהוֹשִׁיעַ. שׁוּבִי נַפְשִׁי לִמְנוּחָיְכִי, כִּי יהוה גָּמַל עָלָיְכִי. כִּי חִלַּצְתָּ נַפְשִׁי מִמָּוֶת, אֶת עֵינִי מִן דִּמְעָה, אֶת רַגְלִי מִדֶּחִי. אֶתְהַלֵּךְ לִפְנֵי יהוה, בְּאַרְצוֹת הַחַיִּים. הֶאֱמַנְתִּי כִּי אֲדַבֵּר, אֲנִי עָנִיתִי מְאֹד. אֲנִי אָמַרְתִּי בְחָפְזִי, כָּל הָאָדָם כֹּזֵב.

מָה אָשִׁיב לַיהוה, כָּל תַּגְמוּלוֹהִי עָלָי. כּוֹס יְשׁוּעוֹת אֶשָּׂא, וּבְשֵׁם יהוה אֶקְרָא. נְדָרַי לַיהוה אֲשַׁלֵּם, נֶגְדָה נָּא לְכָל עַמּוֹ. יָקָר בְּעֵינֵי יהוה, הַמָּוְתָה לַחֲסִידָיו. אָנָּה יהוה כִּי אֲנִי עַבְדֶּךָ, אֲנִי עַבְדְּךָ, בֶּן אֲמָתֶךָ, פִּתַּחְתָּ לְמוֹסֵרָי. לְךָ אֶזְבַּח זֶבַח תּוֹדָה,

---

לְךָ אֶזְבַּח זֶבַח תּוֹדָה — I will sacrifice to you an offering of thanksgiving.
The Sages (Berachos 54b), tell us that offerings of thanksgiving must be brought by anyone who experienced the following experiences: a journey by sea, crossing a desert, being released from captivity, or recovering from serious physical infirmity. The Israelites, upon leaving Egypt, were thus duty bound by their salvation to offer sacrfices of thanksgiving for all four reasons! It was with such thanksgiving offerings in mind that Moses told Pharaoh, גַּם אַתָּה תִּתֵּן בְּיָדֵנוּ זְבָחִים וְעֹלֹת, *Even you will place in our hands feast offerings and burnt*

Hashem, Who has been mindful of us, He will bless. He will bless the house of Israel. He will bless the house of Aharon. He will bless those who fear HASHEM, the small with the great. HASHEM will add unto you, unto you and your children. You are blessed unto HASHEM, the Maker of the heavens and the earth. The heavens are the heavens of HASHEM, but the earth He has given to man. The dead will not praise HASHEM, nor all those who descend into silence. But we will praise HASHEM forever. Praise HASHEM![1]

I love Him, because HASHEM hears my voice, my supplications. For He has inclined His ear to me. In all my days I will call upon Him. Pangs of death have encompassed me, and the distress of the pit has found me. I meet with trouble and sorrow. I call on the name of HASHEM: Please, HASHEM, rescue my soul! Gracious is HASHEM, and righteous. Our God has mercy. HASHEM guards the simple. I was poor, and He saved me. Return, my soul, to your rest, for HASHEM has been bountiful to you. You have delivered my soul from death, my eye from tears, my foot from stumbling. I will walk before HASHEM in the lands of life. I believe that I will say: I was greatly afflicted. I said in my despondency: All men lie.

How can I repay HASHEM for all His bounties to me? I will lift up a cup of salvations, and I will call out the name of HASHEM. I will pay my vows to HASHEM in the presence of all His people. Precious in the eyes of HASHEM is death for His pious ones. I beseech You, HASHEM, for I am Your slave. I am Your slave, the son of Your slavewoman. You have loosened my fetters. I will sacrifice to You an offering of thanksgiving,

---

(1) *Tehillim* 115.

---

offerings, and we shall offer them to Hashem (*Shemos* 10:25). There is a difference of opinion among the commentators concerning the exact meaning of this verse. *Ibn Ezra* (ad loc.) takes this statement at face value: Pharaoh would give the Israelites sacrificial animals to offer to Hashem on his behalf. The *Ohr HaChaim*, however, rejects this interpretation on the grounds that זֶבַח רְשָׁעִים תּוֹעֵבָה, *An*

וּבְשֵׁם יהוה אֶקְרָא. נְדָרַי לַיהוה אֲשַׁלֵּם, נֶגְדָה נָּא לְכָל
עַמּוֹ. בְּחַצְרוֹת בֵּית יהוה, בְּתוֹכֵכִי יְרוּשָׁלָיִם הַלְלוּיָהּ.[1]

הַלְלוּ אֶת יהוה, כָּל גּוֹיִם, שַׁבְּחוּהוּ כָּל הָאֻמִּים. כִּי גָבַר
עָלֵינוּ חַסְדּוֹ, וֶאֱמֶת יהוה לְעוֹלָם, הַלְלוּיָהּ.[1]

כִּי לְעוֹלָם חַסְדּוֹ.	**הוֹדוּ** לַיהוה כִּי טוֹב,
כִּי לְעוֹלָם חַסְדּוֹ.	יֹאמַר נָא יִשְׂרָאֵל,
כִּי לְעוֹלָם חַסְדּוֹ.	יֹאמְרוּ נָא בֵית אַהֲרֹן,
כִּי לְעוֹלָם חַסְדּוֹ.	יֹאמְרוּ נָא יִרְאֵי יהוה,

מִן הַמֵּצַר קָרָאתִי יָּהּ, עָנָנִי בַמֶּרְחָב יָהּ. יהוה לִי לֹא
אִירָא, מַה יַּעֲשֶׂה לִי אָדָם. יהוה לִי בְּעֹזְרָי,
וַאֲנִי אֶרְאֶה בְשֹׂנְאָי. טוֹב לַחֲסוֹת בַּיהוה, מִבְּטֹחַ בָּאָדָם.
טוֹב לַחֲסוֹת בַּיהוה, מִבְּטֹחַ בִּנְדִיבִים. כָּל גּוֹיִם סְבָבוּנִי,
בְּשֵׁם יהוה כִּי אֲמִילַם. סַבּוּנִי גַם סְבָבוּנִי, בְּשֵׁם יהוה כִּי
אֲמִילַם. סַבּוּנִי כִדְבֹרִים דֹּעֲכוּ כְּאֵשׁ קוֹצִים, בְּשֵׁם יהוה
כִּי אֲמִילַם. דָּחֹה דְחִיתַנִי לִנְפֹּל, וַיהוה עֲזָרָנִי. עָזִּי וְזִמְרָת
יָהּ, וַיְהִי לִי לִישׁוּעָה. קוֹל רִנָּה וִישׁוּעָה, בְּאָהֳלֵי צַדִּיקִים,
יְמִין יהוה עֹשָׂה חָיִל. יְמִין יהוה רוֹמֵמָה, יְמִין יהוה עֹשָׂה
חָיִל. לֹא אָמוּת כִּי אֶחְיֶה, וַאֲסַפֵּר מַעֲשֵׂי יָהּ. יַסֹּר יִסְּרַנִי
יָּהּ, וְלַמָּוֶת לֹא נְתָנָנִי. פִּתְחוּ לִי שַׁעֲרֵי צֶדֶק, אָבֹא בָם

---

offering of a wicked person is an abomination (*Mishlei* 21:27), and is
halachically unacceptable as a sacrifice. He explains that Moses only
meant to tell Pharaoh to give over large amounts of livestock to his
erstwhile slaves, from which many would be brought as sacrifices.
Even so, why did such an evildoer and blasphemer of God's name
deserve to participate in the service of Hashem, even indirectly?

Perhaps this occurred in the merit of Pharaoh's ancestor who
presented Abraham with many valuable gifts, including herds of
livestock, when Abraham and Sarah left Egypt so many centuries
before (*Bereishis* 13:2). Presumably these animals were used by
Abraham as sacrifices on the altar near Bethel, which took place

and I will call out the name of HASHEM. I will pay my vows to HASHEM in the presence of all His people. In the courtyards of the house of HASHEM, in you, Jerusalem. Praise HASHEM.[1]

Praise HASHEM! *Praise HASHEM, all nations! Laud Him, all states. For His love for us is strong, and the truth of HASHEM is eternal. Praise HASHEM!*[1]

Give thanks to HASHEM for He is good,
                                    for His kindness is eternal.
Let Yisrael say   for His kindness is eternal.
Let the house of Aharon say   for His kindness is eternal.
Let those who fear HASHEM say   for His kindness is eternal.

Out of distress I called HASHEM. *He responded to me expansively. HASHEM is for me. I shall not fear. What can man do to me? HASHEM is for me through my helpers, and I shall see the downfall of my enemies. It is better to take shelter in HASHEM than to trust in man. It is better to take shelter in HASHEM than to trust in princes. All nations have beset me. In the name of HASHEM I cut them down. They have surrounded me and beset me. In the name of HASHEM I cut them down. They have surrounded me like bees. They were extinguished like a fire of thorns — in the name of HASHEM I cut them down. You have pushed at me to topple me, but HASHEM has assisted me. The strength and vengeance of HASHEM has been my salvation. There is a voice of song and salvation in the tents of the righteous. The right hand of HASHEM does valiantly. The right hand of HASHEM is raised high. The right hand of HASHEM does valiantly. I shall not die, for I shall live and tell of the deeds of HASHEM. HASHEM has chastised me, but He has not let me die. Open for me the gates of righteousness; I will enter them; I*

---

(1) *Tehillim* 116. (1) *Tehillim* 117.

---

immediately after he left Egypt. Thus, the earlier Pharaoh — through his sincere, wholehearted magnanimity to Abraham, which resulted (albeit indirectly) in enhancing the Patriarch's worship of Hashem — paved the way for his less-deserving descendant to merit participation in the service of Hashem as well.

אוֹדֶה יָּהּ. זֶה הַשַּׁעַר לַיהוה, צַדִּיקִים יָבֹאוּ בוֹ. אוֹדְךָ
כִּי עֲנִיתָנִי, וַתְּהִי לִי לִישׁוּעָה. אוֹדְךָ כִּי עֲנִיתָנִי, וַתְּהִי
לִי לִישׁוּעָה. אֶבֶן מָאֲסוּ הַבּוֹנִים, הָיְתָה לְרֹאשׁ פִּנָּה.
אֶבֶן מָאֲסוּ הַבּוֹנִים, הָיְתָה לְרֹאשׁ פִּנָּה. מֵאֵת יהוה
הָיְתָה זֹּאת, הִיא נִפְלָאת בְּעֵינֵינוּ. מֵאֵת יהוה הָיְתָה
זֹּאת, הִיא נִפְלָאת בְּעֵינֵינוּ. זֶה הַיּוֹם עָשָׂה יהוה,
נָגִילָה וְנִשְׂמְחָה בוֹ. זֶה הַיּוֹם עָשָׂה יהוה, נָגִילָה וְנִשְׂמְחָה
בוֹ.

אָנָּא יהוה הוֹשִׁיעָה נָּא. אָנָּא יהוה הוֹשִׁיעָה נָּא.
אָנָּא יהוה הַצְלִיחָה נָּא. אָנָּא יהוה הַצְלִיחָה נָּא.

בָּרוּךְ הַבָּא בְּשֵׁם יהוה, בֵּרַכְנוּכֶם מִבֵּית יהוה. בָּרוּךְ
הַבָּא בְּשֵׁם יהוה, בֵּרַכְנוּכֶם מִבֵּית יהוה.
אֵל יהוה וַיָּאֶר לָנוּ, אִסְרוּ חַג בַּעֲבֹתִים, עַד קַרְנוֹת
הַמִּזְבֵּחַ. אֵל יהוה וַיָּאֶר לָנוּ, אִסְרוּ חַג בַּעֲבֹתִים,
עַד קַרְנוֹת הַמִּזְבֵּחַ. אֵלִי אַתָּה וְאוֹדֶךָּ, אֱלֹהַי אֲרוֹמְמֶךָּ.
אֵלִי אַתָּה וְאוֹדֶךָּ, אֱלֹהַי אֲרוֹמְמֶךָּ. הוֹדוּ לַיהוה כִּי
טוֹב, כִּי לְעוֹלָם חַסְדּוֹ. הוֹדוּ לַיהוה כִּי טוֹב, כִּי לְעוֹלָם
חַסְדּוֹ.[1]

יְהַלְלוּךָ יהוה אֱלֹהֵינוּ כָּל מַעֲשֶׂיךָ, וַחֲסִידֶיךָ צַדִּיקִים
עוֹשֵׂי רְצוֹנֶךָ, וְכָל עַמְּךָ בֵּית יִשְׂרָאֵל בְּרִנָּה
יוֹדוּ וִיבָרְכוּ וִישַׁבְּחוּ וִיפָאֲרוּ וִירוֹמְמוּ וְיַעֲרִיצוּ וְיַקְדִּישׁוּ
וְיַמְלִיכוּ אֶת שִׁמְךָ מַלְכֵּנוּ, כִּי לְךָ טוֹב לְהוֹדוֹת וּלְשִׁמְךָ
נָאֶה לְזַמֵּר, כִּי מֵעוֹלָם וְעַד עוֹלָם אַתָּה אֵל.

הוֹדוּ לַיהוה כִּי טוֹב	כִּי לְעוֹלָם חַסְדּוֹ.
הוֹדוּ לֵאלֹהֵי הָאֱלֹהִים	כִּי לְעוֹלָם חַסְדּוֹ.

will thank HASHEM. This is the gate of HASHEM, the righteous will enter it. I thank You, for You have answered me and become my salvation. I thank You, for You have answered me and become my salvation. The stone the builders despised has become the cornerstone. The stone the builders despised has become the cornerstone. This emanated from HASHEM; it is wondrous in our eyes. This emanated from HASHEM; it is wondrous in our eyes. This is the day HASHEM made; let us rejoice and be glad on it. This is the day HASHEM made; let us rejoice and be glad on it.

We beseech You, HASHEM, save us!
    We beseech You, HASHEM, save us!
We beseech You, HASHEM, grant us success!
    We beseech You, HASHEM, grant us success!

Blessed is he who comes in the name of HASHEM; we bless you from the house of HASHEM. Blessed is he who comes in the name of HASHEM; we bless you from the house of HASHEM. HASHEM is God and He will give us light. Bind the festival sacrifice with cords, leading it up to the corners of the altar. HASHEM is God and He will give us light. Bind the festival sacrifice with cords, leading it up to the corners of the altar. You are my God and I will thank You. My God — I will exalt You. You are my God and I will thank You. My God — I will exalt You. Give thanks to HASHEM for He is good, for His kindness is eternal. Give thanks to HASHEM for He is good, for His kindness is eternal. [1]

All Your works, HASHEM, our God, will praise You, and Your pious ones, the righteous who perform Your will. And all Your people, the house of Israel, with song, will thank, bless, laud, glorify, exalt, adulate, sanctify, and acknowledge the majesty of Your name, our King, for to You it is good to give thanks, and to Your name it is proper to sing, because You are God for eternity.

Give thanks to HASHEM for He is good
                                     — for His kindness is eternal.
Give thanks to the God of gods   — for His kindness is eternal.

---

(1) *Tehillim* 118.

כִּי לְעוֹלָם חַסְדּוֹ.	הוֹדוּ לַאֲדֹנֵי הָאֲדֹנִים
כִּי לְעוֹלָם חַסְדּוֹ.	לְעֹשֵׂה נִפְלָאוֹת גְּדֹלוֹת לְבַדּוֹ
כִּי לְעוֹלָם חַסְדּוֹ.	לְעֹשֵׂה הַשָּׁמַיִם בִּתְבוּנָה
כִּי לְעוֹלָם חַסְדּוֹ.	לְרֹקַע הָאָרֶץ עַל הַמָּיִם
כִּי לְעוֹלָם חַסְדּוֹ.	לְעֹשֵׂה אוֹרִים גְּדֹלִים
כִּי לְעוֹלָם חַסְדּוֹ.	אֶת הַשֶּׁמֶשׁ לְמֶמְשֶׁלֶת בַּיּוֹם
	אֶת הַיָּרֵחַ וְכוֹכָבִים לְמֶמְשָׁלוֹת בַּלָּיְלָה
כִּי לְעוֹלָם חַסְדּוֹ.	
כִּי לְעוֹלָם חַסְדּוֹ.	לְמַכֵּה מִצְרַיִם בִּבְכוֹרֵיהֶם
כִּי לְעוֹלָם חַסְדּוֹ.	וַיּוֹצֵא יִשְׂרָאֵל מִתּוֹכָם
כִּי לְעוֹלָם חַסְדּוֹ.	בְּיָד חֲזָקָה וּבִזְרוֹעַ נְטוּיָה
כִּי לְעוֹלָם חַסְדּוֹ.	לְגֹזֵר יַם סוּף לִגְזָרִים
כִּי לְעוֹלָם חַסְדּוֹ.	וְהֶעֱבִיר יִשְׂרָאֵל בְּתוֹכוֹ
כִּי לְעוֹלָם חַסְדּוֹ.	וְנִעֵר פַּרְעֹה וְחֵילוֹ בְיַם סוּף
כִּי לְעוֹלָם חַסְדּוֹ.	לְמוֹלִיךְ עַמּוֹ בַּמִּדְבָּר
כִּי לְעוֹלָם חַסְדּוֹ.	לְמַכֵּה מְלָכִים גְּדֹלִים
כִּי לְעוֹלָם חַסְדּוֹ.	וַיַּהֲרֹג מְלָכִים אַדִּירִים
כִּי לְעוֹלָם חַסְדּוֹ.	לְסִיחוֹן מֶלֶךְ הָאֱמֹרִי
כִּי לְעוֹלָם חַסְדּוֹ.	וּלְעוֹג מֶלֶךְ הַבָּשָׁן
כִּי לְעוֹלָם חַסְדּוֹ.	וְנָתַן אַרְצָם לְנַחֲלָה
כִּי לְעוֹלָם חַסְדּוֹ.	נַחֲלָה לְיִשְׂרָאֵל עַבְדּוֹ
כִּי לְעוֹלָם חַסְדּוֹ.	שֶׁבְּשִׁפְלֵנוּ זָכַר לָנוּ
כִּי לְעוֹלָם חַסְדּוֹ.	וַיִּפְרְקֵנוּ מִצָּרֵינוּ
כִּי לְעוֹלָם חַסְדּוֹ.	נֹתֵן לֶחֶם לְכָל בָּשָׂר
כִּי לְעוֹלָם חַסְדּוֹ.[1]	הוֹדוּ לְאֵל הַשָּׁמַיִם

Give thanks to the Master of masters — for His kindness is eternal.
To Him Who does great wonders alone — for His kindness is eternal.
To Him Who makes the heavens with understanding
                            — for His kindness is eternal.
To Him Who stretches the earth over the water
                            — for His kindness is eternal.
To Him Who makes the great lights   — for His kindness is eternal.
The sun to govern the day   — for His kindness is eternal.
The moon and the stars to govern the night
                            — for His kindness is eternal.
To Him Who smote the firstborn of the Egyptians
                            — for His kindness is eternal.
And brought Israel out from among them
                            — for His kindness is eternal.
With a strong hand and an outstretched arm
                            — for His kindness is eternal.
To Him Who divided the Red Sea into parts
                            — for His kindness is eternal.
And had Israel pass through it   — for His kindness is eternal.
And tossed Pharaoh and his army into the Red Sea
                            — for His kindness is eternal.
To Him Who led His people through the desert
                            — for His kindness is eternal.
To Him Who smote great kings   — for His kindness is eternal.
And killed mighty kings   — for His kindness is eternal.
Sichon, the king of the Emorites   — for His kindness is eternal.
And Og, the king of the Bashan   — for His kindness is eternal.
And gave their lands as an inheritance — for His kindness is eternal.
An inheritance to Israel, His slave   — for His kindness is eternal.
Who remembered us in our lowliness — for His kindness is eternal.
And redeemed us from our enemies   — for His kindness is eternal.
He gives food to all flesh   — for His kindness is eternal.
Give thanks to the God of the heavens
                            — for His kindness is eternal. [1]

---

(1) *Tehillim* 136.

נִשְׁמַת כָּל חַי תְּבָרֵךְ אֶת שִׁמְךָ יהוה אֱלֹהֵינוּ, וְרוּחַ כָּל בָּשָׂר תְּפָאֵר וּתְרוֹמֵם זִכְרְךָ מַלְכֵּנוּ תָּמִיד. מִן הָעוֹלָם וְעַד הָעוֹלָם אַתָּה אֵל, וּמִבַּלְעָדֶיךָ אֵין לָנוּ מֶלֶךְ גּוֹאֵל וּמוֹשִׁיעַ. פּוֹדֶה וּמַצִּיל וּמְפַרְנֵס וּמְרַחֵם בְּכָל עֵת צָרָה וְצוּקָה. אֵין לָנוּ מֶלֶךְ אֶלָּא אָתָּה. אֱלֹהֵי הָרִאשׁוֹנִים וְהָאַחֲרוֹנִים אֱלוֹהַּ כָּל בְּרִיּוֹת אֲדוֹן כָּל תּוֹלָדוֹת הַמְהֻלָּל בְּרֹב הַתִּשְׁבָּחוֹת הַמְנַהֵג עוֹלָמוֹ בְּחֶסֶד וּבְרִיּוֹתָיו בְּרַחֲמִים וַיהוה לֹא יָנוּם וְלֹא יִישָׁן. הַמְעוֹרֵר יְשֵׁנִים וְהַמֵּקִיץ נִרְדָּמִים וְהַמֵּשִׂיחַ אִלְּמִים וְהַמַּתִּיר אֲסוּרִים וְהַסּוֹמֵךְ נוֹפְלִים וְהַזּוֹקֵף כְּפוּפִים לְךָ לְבַדְּךָ אֲנַחְנוּ מוֹדִים. אִלּוּ פִינוּ מָלֵא שִׁירָה כַיָּם וּלְשׁוֹנֵנוּ רִנָּה כַּהֲמוֹן גַּלָּיו וְשִׂפְתוֹתֵינוּ שֶׁבַח כְּמֶרְחֲבֵי רָקִיעַ וְעֵינֵינוּ מְאִירוֹת כַּשֶּׁמֶשׁ וְכַיָּרֵחַ וְיָדֵינוּ פְרוּשׂוֹת כְּנִשְׁרֵי שָׁמָיִם וְרַגְלֵינוּ קַלּוֹת כָּאַיָּלוֹת, אֵין אֲנַחְנוּ מַסְפִּיקִים לְהוֹדוֹת לְךָ יהוה אֱלֹהֵינוּ וֵאלֹהֵי אֲבוֹתֵינוּ וּלְבָרֵךְ אֶת שְׁמֶךָ עַל אַחַת מֵאֶלֶף אֶלֶף אַלְפֵי אֲלָפִים וְרִבֵּי רְבָבוֹת פְּעָמִים הַטּוֹבוֹת שֶׁעָשִׂיתָ עִם אֲבוֹתֵינוּ וְעִמָּנוּ. מִמִּצְרַיִם גְּאַלְתָּנוּ יהוה אֱלֹהֵינוּ וּמִבֵּית עֲבָדִים פְּדִיתָנוּ בְּרָעָב זַנְתָּנוּ וּבְשָׂבָע כִּלְכַּלְתָּנוּ מֵחֶרֶב הִצַּלְתָּנוּ וּמִדֶּבֶר מִלַּטְתָּנוּ וּמֵחֳלָיִם רָעִים וְנֶאֱמָנִים דִּלִּיתָנוּ. עַד הֵנָּה עֲזָרוּנוּ רַחֲמֶיךָ וְלֹא עֲזָבוּנוּ חֲסָדֶיךָ וְאַל תִּטְּשֵׁנוּ יהוה אֱלֹהֵינוּ לָנֶצַח. עַל כֵּן אֵבָרִים שֶׁפִּלַּגְתָּ בָּנוּ וְרוּחַ וּנְשָׁמָה שֶׁנָּפַחְתָּ בְּאַפֵּינוּ וְלָשׁוֹן אֲשֶׁר שַׂמְתָּ בְּפִינוּ הֵן הֵם יוֹדוּ וִיבָרְכוּ וִישַׁבְּחוּ וִיפָאֲרוּ וִירוֹמְמוּ וְיַעֲרִיצוּ וְיַקְדִּישׁוּ וְיַמְלִיכוּ אֶת שִׁמְךָ מַלְכֵּנוּ. כִּי כָל פֶּה לְךָ יוֹדֶה וְכָל לָשׁוֹן לְךָ תִשָּׁבַע וְכָל בֶּרֶךְ לְךָ תִכְרַע וְכָל קוֹמָה לְפָנֶיךָ תִשְׁתַּחֲוֶה וְכָל לְבָבוֹת יִירָאוּךָ וְכָל קֶרֶב וּכְלָיוֹת יְזַמְּרוּ לִשְׁמֶךָ. כַּדָּבָר שֶׁכָּתוּב כָּל עַצְמֹתַי תֹּאמַרְנָה יהוה מִי כָמוֹךָ מַצִּיל עָנִי מֵחָזָק מִמֶּנּוּ וְעָנִי וְאֶבְיוֹן

The soul of every living being will praise Your name, HASHEM, our God, and the spirit of all flesh will constantly glorify and exalt Your remembrance, our King. You are God forever, and besides You we have no king, redeemer, savior, liberator, deliverer, supporter, or source of mercy at any time of trouble or distress. We have no God but You, God of the first and the last, God of all creatures, Master of all generations, extolled with many praises, Who conducts His world with kindness and His creatures with mercy. HASHEM does not doze or slumber. He wakes those who sleep and arouses those who slumber. He makes the mute speak. He releases the imprisoned, supports those who fall, and straightens those who are bent over. You alone we thank. Even if our mouths were as full of song as the sea, and our tongue full of joyous melody as its many waves, and our lips full of praise as the expanses of the firmament, and our eyes illuminating as the sun and the moon, and our arms spread wide as the eagles of the skies, and our feet as fleet as antelopes, we still could not sufficiently thank You or bless Your name, HASHEM, our God and the God of our fathers, for even a thousandth or a ten-thousandth of the good that You have done for our ancestors and for us. You redeemed us from Egypt, HASHEM, our God, and delivered us from the house of bondage. You have fed us in famine and sustained us in plenty. You have saved us from the sword, rescued us from epidemic, and spared us from evil, deadly, diseases. Your mercy has helped us until this time and Your kindness has not abandoned us. HASHEM, our God, do not ever desert us. Therefore the limbs which You have carved in us, the spirit and soul that You have blown into our nostrils, the tongue that You have put into our mouths — they will thank, bless, laud, glorify, exalt, adulate, sanctify, and acknowledge the majesty of Your name, our King. For every mouth gives thanks to You, every tongue vows allegiance to You, every knee bends to You, every stature bows before You, every heart fears You, and all internal organs sing out to Your name. As it is written: "All my bones say, 'HASHEM: Who is like You?' You save the indigent from one stronger than he, and the poor and impoverished from the one

מִגְּזֹלּוֹ.[1] מִי יִדְמֶה לָּךְ וּמִי יִשְׁוֶה לָּךְ וּמִי יַעֲרָךְ לָּךְ הָאֵל הַגָּדוֹל הַגִּבּוֹר וְהַנּוֹרָא אֵל עֶלְיוֹן קֹנֵה שָׁמַיִם וָאָרֶץ. נְהַלֶּלְךָ וּנְשַׁבֵּחֲךָ וּנְפָאֶרְךָ וּנְבָרֵךְ אֶת שֵׁם קָדְשֶׁךָ כָּאָמוּר לְדָוִד בָּרְכִי נַפְשִׁי אֶת יהוה וְכָל קְרָבַי אֶת שֵׁם קָדְשׁוֹ.[2]

הָאֵל בְּתַעֲצֻמוֹת עֻזֶּךָ הַגָּדוֹל בִּכְבוֹד שְׁמֶךָ הַגִּבּוֹר לָנֶצַח וְהַנּוֹרָא בְּנוֹרְאוֹתֶיךָ הַמֶּלֶךְ הַיּוֹשֵׁב עַל כִּסֵּא רָם וְנִשָּׂא.

שׁוֹכֵן עַד מָרוֹם וְקָדוֹשׁ שְׁמוֹ. וְכָתוּב רַנְּנוּ צַדִּיקִים בַּיהוה לַיְשָׁרִים נָאוָה תְהִלָּה.[3] בְּפִי יְשָׁרִים תִּתְהַלָּל וּבְדִבְרֵי צַדִּיקִים תִּתְבָּרַךְ וּבִלְשׁוֹן חֲסִידִים תִּתְרוֹמָם וּבְקֶרֶב קְדוֹשִׁים תִּתְקַדָּשׁ:

וּבְמַקְהֲלוֹת רִבְבוֹת עַמְּךָ בֵּית יִשְׂרָאֵל בְּרִנָּה יִתְפָּאַר שִׁמְךָ מַלְכֵּנוּ בְּכָל דּוֹר וָדוֹר שֶׁכֵּן חוֹבַת כָּל הַיְצוּרִים לְפָנֶיךָ יהוה אֱלֹהֵינוּ וֵאלֹהֵי אֲבוֹתֵינוּ לְהוֹדוֹת לְהַלֵּל לְשַׁבֵּחַ לְפָאֵר לְרוֹמֵם לְהַדֵּר לְבָרֵךְ לְעַלֵּה וּלְקַלֵּס עַל כָּל דִּבְרֵי שִׁירוֹת וְתִשְׁבָּחוֹת דָּוִד בֶּן יִשַׁי עַבְדְּךָ מְשִׁיחֶךָ.

יִשְׁתַּבַּח שִׁמְךָ לָעַד מַלְכֵּנוּ הָאֵל הַמֶּלֶךְ הַגָּדוֹל וְהַקָּדוֹשׁ בַּשָּׁמַיִם וּבָאָרֶץ כִּי לְךָ נָאֶה יהוה אֱלֹהֵינוּ וֵאלֹהֵי אֲבוֹתֵינוּ שִׁיר וּשְׁבָחָה הַלֵּל וְזִמְרָה עֹז וּמֶמְשָׁלָה נֶצַח גְּדֻלָּה וּגְבוּרָה תְּהִלָּה וְתִפְאֶרֶת קְדֻשָּׁה וּמַלְכוּת בְּרָכוֹת וְהוֹדָאוֹת מֵעַתָּה וְעַד עוֹלָם: בָּרוּךְ אַתָּה יהוה אֵל מֶלֶךְ גָּדוֹל בַּתִּשְׁבָּחוֹת אֵל הַהוֹדָאוֹת אֲדוֹן הַנִּפְלָאוֹת הַבּוֹחֵר בְּשִׁירֵי זִמְרָה מֶלֶךְ אֵל חֵי הָעוֹלָמִים.

who seeks to rob him."[1] Who can resemble You? Who can compare to You? Who can estimate You? The great, mighty, and awesome God, the supreme God, Creator of heavens and earth. We will praise You, laud You, glorify You, and bless Your holy name, as it says: "Of David: my soul blesses HASHEM, and all my insides bless His holy name."[2]

O God, in the supremacies of Your might! You Who are great in the glory of Your name, Who are mighty forever and fearful through Your awe-inspiring deeds! The King Who sits upon a high and exalted throne!

He Who dwells in eternity, high and holy is His name. As it is written, "Let the righteous rejoice in HASHEM. It is fitting for the upright to extol."[3] By the mouth of the upright You are praised. And by the words of the righteous You are blessed. And by the tongue of the pious You are exalted. And among the holy You are sanctified.

And in the assemblies of the myriads of Your people, the house of Israel, Your name will be extolled in song, our King, in each and every generation. For it is the duty of all that is created — in Your presence, HASHEM, our God and the God of our fathers, to thank, praise, laud, glorify, exalt, adorn, bless, elevate, and celebrate beyond all the songs and praises of David the son of Jesse, Your servant, Your Mashiach.

May Your name be praised forever, our King, the God and King, great and holy, in the heavens and the earth. For hymn and praise befit You, HASHEM, our God and the God of our fathers — accolade and song, strength and sovereignty, eternity, greatness and might, fame and glory, sanctity and majesty, blessing and thanksgiving, for all eternity. Blessed are You, HASHEM, God, King, great in praises, the God to whom we owe thanks, the Master of wonders, Who is pleased with melodious song, the King, the God, Life of the worlds.

---

(1) *Tehillim* 35:10. (2) 103:1. (3) 33:1.

The blessing over wine is recited and the fourth cup is drunk while reclining to the left side.
It is preferable that the entire cup be drunk; if not, one should drink at least most of it.

בָּרוּךְ אַתָּה יהוה אֱלֹהֵינוּ מֶלֶךְ הָעוֹלָם, בּוֹרֵא פְּרִי הַגָּפֶן.

After drinking the fourth cup, the concluding blessing is recited.
On Shabbos include the passage in parentheses.

בָּרוּךְ אַתָּה יהוה אֱלֹהֵינוּ מֶלֶךְ הָעוֹלָם, עַל הַגֶּפֶן וְעַל פְּרִי הַגֶּפֶן וְעַל תְּנוּבַת הַשָּׂדֶה וְעַל אֶרֶץ חֶמְדָּה טוֹבָה וּרְחָבָה שֶׁרָצִיתָ וְהִנְחַלְתָּ לַאֲבוֹתֵינוּ לֶאֱכוֹל מִפִּרְיָהּ וְלִשְׂבּוֹעַ מִטּוּבָהּ. רַחֶם נָא יהוה אֱלֹהֵינוּ עַל יִשְׂרָאֵל עַמֶּךְ וְעַל יְרוּשָׁלַיִם עִירֶךְ וְעַל צִיּוֹן מִשְׁכַּן כְּבוֹדֶךְ וְעַל מִזְבְּחֶךְ וְעַל הֵיכָלֶךְ. וּבְנֵה יְרוּשָׁלַיִם עִיר הַקֹּדֶשׁ בִּמְהֵרָה בְיָמֵינוּ וְהַעֲלֵנוּ לְתוֹכָהּ וְשַׂמְּחֵנוּ בְּבִנְיָנָהּ וְנֹאכַל מִפִּרְיָהּ וְנִשְׂבַּע מִטּוּבָהּ וּנְבָרֶכְךָ עָלֶיהָ בִּקְדֻשָּׁה וּבְטָהֳרָה. [וּרְצֵה וְהַחֲלִיצֵנוּ בְּיוֹם הַשַּׁבָּת הַזֶּה] וְשַׂמְּחֵנוּ בְּיוֹם חַג הַמַּצּוֹת הַזֶּה. כִּי אַתָּה יהוה טוֹב וּמֵטִיב לַכֹּל וְנוֹדֶה לְּךָ עַל הָאָרֶץ וְעַל פְּרִי הַגָּפֶן. בָּרוּךְ אַתָּה יהוה עַל הָאָרֶץ וְעַל פְּרִי הַגָּפֶן.

נרצה

חֲסַל סִדּוּר פֶּסַח כְּהִלְכָתוֹ. כְּכָל מִשְׁפָּטוֹ וְחֻקָּתוֹ. כַּאֲשֶׁר זָכִינוּ לְסַדֵּר אוֹתוֹ. כֵּן נִזְכֶּה לַעֲשׂוֹתוֹ. זָךְ שׁוֹכֵן מְעוֹנָה. קוֹמֵם קְהַל עֲדַת מִי מָנָה. בְּקָרוֹב נַהֵל נִטְעֵי כַנָּה. פְּדוּיִם לְצִיּוֹן בְּרִנָּה.

לְשָׁנָה הַבָּאָה בִּירוּשָׁלָיִם.

The blessing over wine is recited and the fourth cup is drunk while reclining to the left side. It is preferable that the entire cup be drunk; if not, one should drink at least most of it.

Blessed are You, Hashem, our God, King of the Universe, Who creates the fruit of the vine.

After drinking the fourth cup, the concluding blessing is recited.
On Shabbos include the passage in parentheses.

Blessed are You, Hashem, our God, King of the universe, for the vine and the fruit of the vine, and the produce of the field, and for the precious, good, and spacious land that You willed to give as an inheritance to our ancestors, to eat of its fruit and to be sated by its goodness. Have mercy, we beg You, HASHEM, our God, on Israel, Your people, and on Jerusalem, Your city, and on Zion, the abode of Your glory, and on Your altar and on Your Temple. Rebuild Jerusalem, the city of sanctity, speedily in our lifetimes. Bring us up into it and let us rejoice in its reconstruction. Let us eat of its fruits and be sated by its goodness. May we bless You over it in holiness and purity (and may it be Your will to fortify us on this day of the Sabbath), and may You bring us joy on this day of the Festival of Matzos. For You, HASHEM, are good and do good to all, and we thank You for the land and the fruit of the vine. Blessed are You, HASHEM, for the land and the fruit of the vine.

NIRTZAH

The order of Pesach has come to its end in accordance with its Halachah, in accordance with all of its laws and statutes. Just as we have been worthy of making the Seder this year, so may we merit performing it in the future. Pure One, Who dwells in His heavenly abode, raise up the uncountable congregation of Israel. In the near future, lead the shoots You have planted to Zion, redeemed, joyously.

Next year in Jerusalem!

On the first night recite the following. On the second night continue on page 178.

וּבְכֵן וַיְהִי בַּחֲצִי הַלַּיְלָה.

אָז רוֹב נִסִּים הִפְלֵאתָ בַּלַּיְלָה.

בְּרֹאשׁ אַשְׁמוּרֶת זֶה הַלַּיְלָה.

גֵּר צֶדֶק נִצַּחְתּוֹ כְּנֶחֱלַק לוֹ לַיְלָה.

וַיְהִי בַּחֲצִי הַלַּיְלָה.

דַּנְתָּ מֶלֶךְ גְּרָר בַּחֲלוֹם הַלַּיְלָה.

הִפְחַדְתָּ אֲרַמִּי בְּאֶמֶשׁ לַיְלָה.

וַיָּשַׂר יִשְׂרָאֵל לְמַלְאָךְ וַיּוּכַל לוֹ לַיְלָה.

וַיְהִי בַּחֲצִי הַלַּיְלָה.

זֶרַע בְּכוֹרֵי פַתְרוֹס מָחַצְתָּ בַּחֲצִי הַלַּיְלָה.

חֵילָם לֹא מָצְאוּ בְּקוּמָם בַּלַּיְלָה.

טִיסַת נְגִיד חֲרוֹשֶׁת סִלִּיתָ בְכוֹכְבֵי לַיְלָה.

וַיְהִי בַּחֲצִי הַלַּיְלָה.

וַיְהִי בַּחֲצִי הַלַּיְלָה — **It happened at midnight.**

The Torah emphasizes that the Exodus took place exactly at midnight (*Shemos* 11:4,12:29). What is the significance of this particular time that it should have been chosen — and stressed — as the time for this momentous event? This is the first time in the Torah that midnight, as a point in time, assumes significance.

I once heard in the name of *Rav Hutner, zt"l,* that the times "midday" and "midnight" (both of which are called חֲצוֹת in Hebrew) are unique in that they are considered to be the turning points of the day or night, respectively. Thus we find that immediately after midday begins the period of בֵּין הָעַרְבַּיִם, the Biblical equivalent of "afternoon" [literally, it means "towards evening"]. Similarly, King David says in *Tehillim* (119:62), חֲצוֹת לַיְלָה אָקוּם לְהוֹדוֹת לָךְ, *At midnight I arise to thank you.* It is well known, however, that nighttime is not considered an auspicious time for prayer and supplication, since it is the time when Hashem sits in strict judgment over the world. Apparently, then, after midnight has passed, it is considered as if morning is already imminent and as if the

On the first night recite the following. On the second night continue on page 178.

It happened at midnight.

Then You performed wondrous miracles at	*night.*
At the first watch of this	*night.*
You brought victory to the righteous convert	
[Avraham] when divided for him was the	*night.*
It happened at midnight.	
You judged the king of Gerar [Abimelech]	
in a dream of the	*night.*
You terrified the Aramean [Laban] in the dark of	*night.*
And Israel fought with an angel and overcame him at	*night.*
It happened at midnight.	
You bruised the firstborn seed of Pasros [Egypt] at	*midnight.*
They did not find their legions when they arose at	*night.*
The swift armies of the prince of Charoshes	
[Sisera] You crushed with the stars of	*night.*
It happened at midnight.	

period of Hashem's grace has already begun. (This is why *Selichos*, when recited at night, are always delayed until after midnight.) Thus midnight is the time which symbolizes the idea that another period, although it has not actually come yet, is already exhibiting its latent potential.

The *Midrash,* quoted by Rashi, explains that when Moses asked Hashem, וְכִי אוֹצִיא אֶת בְּנֵי יִשְׂרָאֵל מִמִּצְרַיִם , *". . . and that I should take the Children of Israel out of Egypt?"* (*Shemos* 3:11), his intent was to question, "By what right are the Children of Israel deserving of deliverance from Egypt?" Hashem answered him (ibid. v. 12), בְּהוֹצִיאֲךָ אֶת הָעָם מִמִּצְרַיִם תַּעַבְדוּן אֶת הָאֱלֹקִים עַל הָהָר הַזֶּה, *"When you take the people out of Egypt, you will serve God on this mountain [i.e. Sinai]."* The *Midrash* paraphrases: "Although they have no merits *as of yet*, after they leave they will come to this place and receive the Torah. I will count this in their favor even now, before the event actually happens." Thus Hashem redeemed the people "on credit," as it were. The timing of the Exodus, precisely at midnight, was intended to symbolize this willingness of Hashem to reckon with the latent potential of the Jews and consider a time in the future — the Revelation at Sinai — as if it had already arrived.

	יָעֵץ מְחָרֵף לְנוֹפֵף אִוּי הוֹבַשְׁתָּ פְגָרָיו
בַּלַּיְלָה.	
לַיְלָה.	כָּרַע בֵּל וּמַצָּבוֹ בְּאִישׁוֹן
לַיְלָה.	לְאִישׁ חֲמוּדוֹת נִגְלָה רָז חֲזוֹת
	וַיְהִי בַּחֲצִי הַלַּיְלָה.

	מִשְׁתַּכֵּר בִּכְלֵי קֹדֶשׁ נֶהֱרַג בּוֹ
בַּלַּיְלָה.	
לַיְלָה.	נוֹשַׁע מִבּוֹר אֲרָיוֹת פּוֹתֵר בִּעֲתוּתֵי
בַּלַּיְלָה.	שִׂנְאָה נָטַר אֲגָגִי וְכָתַב סְפָרִים
	וַיְהִי בַּחֲצִי הַלַּיְלָה.

	עוֹרַרְתָּ נִצְחֲךָ עָלָיו בְּנֶדֶד שְׁנַת
לַיְלָה.	
מִלַּיְלָה.	פּוּרָה תִדְרוֹךְ לְשׁוֹמֵר מַה
לַיְלָה.	צָרַח כַּשּׁוֹמֵר וְשָׂח אָתָא בֹקֶר וְגַם
	וַיְהִי בַּחֲצִי הַלַּיְלָה.

	קָרֵב יוֹם אֲשֶׁר הוּא לֹא יוֹם וְלֹא
לַיְלָה.	
הַלַּיְלָה.	רָם הוֹדַע כִּי לְךָ הַיּוֹם אַף לְךָ
הַלַּיְלָה.	שׁוֹמְרִים הַפְקֵד לְעִירְךָ כָּל הַיּוֹם וְכָל
לַיְלָה.	תָּאִיר כְּאוֹר יוֹם חֶשְׁכַּת
	וַיְהִי בַּחֲצִי הַלַּיְלָה.

On the first night continue on page 182.
On the second night recite the following.

וּבְכֵן וַאֲמַרְתֶּם זֶבַח פֶּסַח:

	אֹמֶץ גְּבוּרוֹתֶיךָ הִפְלֵאתָ
בַּפֶּסַח.	
פֶּסַח.	בְּרֹאשׁ כָּל מוֹעֲדוֹת נִשֵּׂאתָ
פֶּסַח.	גִּלִּיתָ לְאֶזְרָחִי חֲצוֹת לֵיל
	וַאֲמַרְתֶּם זֶבַח פֶּסַח.

The blasphemer [Sennacherib] schemed to raise
  his hand menacingly [over the precious city].
    You made his corpses rot at   *night.*
Bel [the Babylonian pagan deity] and his
  pedestal fell in the black of   *night.*
To the beloved man [Daniel] was revealed
  the secret of the visions of   *night.*
            It happened at midnight.

He who guzzled out of the sacred vessels
  [Belshazzar, king of Babylonia] was killed on that   *night.*
The one who was saved from the lions' den
  interpreted the terrors of the   *night.*
The Agagite [Haman] nurtured hatred
  and wrote decrees at   *night.*
            It happened at midnight.

You initiated Your triumph against him
  by disturbing the sleep [of Ahasverus] at   *night.*
You will tread a winepress [in peace after victory]
  for him who cries out [Israel]: Our Guardian!
    What will be of this   *night?*
Like a guardian You will call out in response:
    The morning has come, as well as the   *night.*
            It happened at midnight.

The day is approaching which is neither day nor   *night.*
High one! Make it known that Yours are
  both the day and the   *night.*
Appoint watchmen over Your city all day and all   *night.*
Illuminate like the light of day the darkness of   *night.*
            It will happen at midnight.

On the first night continue on page 182.
On the second night recite the following.

And you will say: A feast of Pesach.

The power of Your mighty deeds
  You showed wondrously on   *Pesach.*
Foremost of all festivals You exalted   *Pesach.*
You revealed to the oriental [Abraham]
  the events of the night of   *Pesach.*
        And you will say: A feast of Pesach.

דְּלָתָיו דָּפַקְתָּ כְּחֹם הַיּוֹם   בַּפֶּסַח.

הִסְעִיד נוֹצְצִים עֻגוֹת מַצּוֹת   בַּפֶּסַח.

וְאֶל הַבָּקָר רָץ זֵכֶר לְשׁוֹר עֵרֶךְ   פֶּסַח.

וַאֲמַרְתֶּם זֶבַח פֶּסַח.

זוֹעֲמוּ סְדוֹמִים וְלוֹהֲטוּ בָּאֵשׁ   בַּפֶּסַח.

חֻלַּץ לוֹט מֵהֶם וּמַצּוֹת אָפָה בְּקֵץ   פֶּסַח.

טִאטֵאתָ אַדְמַת מוֹף וְנוֹף בְּעָבְרְךָ   בַּפֶּסַח.

וַאֲמַרְתֶּם זֶבַח פֶּסַח.

יָהּ רֹאשׁ כָּל אוֹן מָחַצְתָּ בְּלֵיל שִׁמּוּר   פֶּסַח.

כַּבִּיר עַל בֵּן בְּכוֹר פָּסַחְתָּ בְּדַם   פֶּסַח.

לְבִלְתִּי תֵּת מַשְׁחִית לָבֹא בִּפְתָחַי   בַּפֶּסַח.

וַאֲמַרְתֶּם זֶבַח פֶּסַח.

מְסֻגֶּרֶת סֻגְּרָה בְּעִתּוֹתֵי   פֶּסַח.

נִשְׁמְדָה מִדְיָן בִּצְלִיל שְׂעוֹרֵי עֹמֶר   פֶּסַח.

שׂוֹרְפוּ מִשְׁמַנֵּי פּוּל וְלוּד בִּיקַד יְקוֹד   פֶּסַח.

וַאֲמַרְתֶּם זֶבַח פֶּסַח.

עוֹד הַיּוֹם בְּנֹב לַעֲמוֹד עַד גָּעָה עוֹנַת   פֶּסַח.

פַּס יַד כָּתְבָה לְקַעֲקֵעַ צוּל   בַּפֶּסַח.

צָפֹה הַצָּפִית עָרוֹךְ הַשֻּׁלְחָן   בַּפֶּסַח.

וַאֲמַרְתֶּם זֶבַח פֶּסַח.

You knocked on his doors during the heat of the day on
Pesach.

He gave bright angels a meal of cakes
   of matzah on   *Pesach.*
He ran to fetch an ox in commemoration of
   the ox sacrificed [as the festival offering] on   *Pesach.*
        And you will say: A feast of Pesach.
The people of Sodom felt the wrath of Hashem
   and were set ablaze on   *Pesach.*
Lot escaped from them and baked matzos at the end of
Pesach.

You swept clean the land of Mof and Nof
   [Egyptian cities] on   *Pesach.*
        And you will say: A feast of Pesach.
Hashem, the first issue of strength You bruised
   on the watch night of   *Pesach.*
Mighty One, You skipped over the firstborn son
   because of the blood of   *Pesach,*
So as not to let the destroyer enter my doors on   *Pesach.*
        And you will say: A feast of Pesach.

The closed city [Jericho] was handed over
   [to the Jews] at the time of   *Pesach.*
Midian was destroyed [by the Jews under the leadership of
   Gideon] through the merit of a cake of the omer on   *Pesach.*
The fat people of Pul and Lud [the Assyrians in the days
   of King Hezekiah] were burnt in a conflagration on   *Pesach.*
        And you will say: A feast of Pesach.

He [Sennacherib] would have stood at Nob,
   but the time of Pesach arrived.
A hand wrote the decree of annihilation against Tzul
   [Babylonia] on   *Pesach.*
Their scout went to look for the enemy while their table
   was festively set on   *Pesach.*
        And you will say: A feast of Pesach.

קָהָל כִּנִּסָּה הֲדַסָּה צוֹם לְשַׁלֵּשׁ   בַּפֶּסַח.

רֹאשׁ מִבֵּית רָשָׁע מָחַצְתָּ בְּעֵץ חֲמִשִּׁים   בַּפֶּסַח.

שְׁתֵּי אֵלֶּה רֶגַע תָּבִיא לְעוּצִית   בַּפֶּסַח.

תָּעֹז יָדְךָ וְתָרוּם יְמִינְךָ כְּלֵיל הִתְקַדֵּשׁ חַג   פֶּסַח.

וַאֲמַרְתֶּם זֶבַח פֶּסַח.

On both nights continue here:

כִּי לוֹ נָאֶה, כִּי לוֹ יָאֶה:

אַדִּיר בִּמְלוּכָה, **בָּחוּר** כַּהֲלָכָה, **גְּדוּדָיו** יֹאמְרוּ לוֹ, לְךָ וּלְךָ, לְךָ כִּי לְךָ, לְךָ אַף לְךָ, לְךָ יהוה הַמַּמְלָכָה, כִּי לוֹ נָאֶה, כִּי לוֹ יָאֶה.

דָּגוּל בִּמְלוּכָה, **הָדוּר** כַּהֲלָכָה, **וָתִיקָיו** יֹאמְרוּ לוֹ, לְךָ וּלְךָ, לְךָ כִּי לְךָ, לְךָ אַף לְךָ, לְךָ יהוה הַמַּמְלָכָה, כִּי לוֹ נָאֶה, כִּי לוֹ יָאֶה.

זַכַּאי בִּמְלוּכָה, **חָסִין** כַּהֲלָכָה, **טַפְסְרָיו** יֹאמְרוּ לוֹ, לְךָ וּלְךָ, לְךָ כִּי לְךָ, לְךָ אַף לְךָ, לְךָ יהוה הַמַּמְלָכָה, כִּי לוֹ נָאֶה, כִּי לוֹ יָאֶה.

יָחִיד בִּמְלוּכָה, **כַּבִּיר** כַּהֲלָכָה, **לִמּוּדָיו** יֹאמְרוּ לוֹ, לְךָ וּלְךָ, לְךָ כִּי לְךָ, לְךָ אַף לְךָ, לְךָ יהוה הַמַּמְלָכָה, כִּי לוֹ נָאֶה, כִּי לוֹ יָאֶה.

מוֹשֵׁל בִּמְלוּכָה, **נוֹרָא** כַּהֲלָכָה, **סְבִיבָיו** יֹאמְרוּ לוֹ, לְךָ וּלְךָ, לְךָ כִּי לְךָ, לְךָ אַף לְךָ, לְךָ יהוה הַמַּמְלָכָה, כִּי לוֹ נָאֶה, כִּי לוֹ יָאֶה.

Hadassah [Esther] gathered an assembly for
   a three-day fast on   Pesach.
The head of the evil house [Haman] You killed
   on a fifty-cubit pole on   Pesach.
Bring bereavement and widowhood to Utzis
   [Edom] in an instant on   Pesach.
Strengthen Your hand, raise Your right hand
   as on the night that the festival of Pesach was sanctified.
        And you will say: A feast of Pesach.

On both nights continue here:

To Him it is fitting. To Him it is due.

Mighty in royalty, chosen by right, His legions say to Him: Yours and only Yours; Yours, yes Yours, Yours, surely Yours; Yours, HASHEM, is the sovereignty of the world. To Him it is fitting. To Him it is due.

Distinguished in royalty, glorious of right. His faithful say to Him: Yours and only Yours; Yours, yes Yours; Yours, surely Yours; Yours, HASHEM, is the sovereignty of the world. To Him it is fitting. To Him it is due.

Pure in royalty, firm of right. His courtiers say to Him: Yours and only Yours; Yours, yes Yours; Yours, surely Yours; Yours, HASHEM, is the sovereignty of the world. To Him it is fitting. To Him it is due.

Unique in royalty, mighty of right. His disciples say to Him: Yours and only Yours; Yours, yes Yours; Yours, surely Yours; Yours, HASHEM, is the sovereignty of the world. To Him it is fitting. To Him it is due.

Ruling in royalty, feared of right. Those who surround Him say to Him: Yours and only Yours; Yours, yes Yours; Yours, surely Yours; Yours, HASHEM, is the sovereignty of the world. To Him it is fitting. To Him it is due.

עֲנָיו בִּמְלוּכָה, **פּ**וֹדֶה כַּהֲלָכָה, **צ**דִּיקָיו יֹאמְרוּ לוֹ, לְךָ
וּלְךָ, לְךָ כִּי לְךָ, לְךָ אַף לְךָ, לְךָ יהוה הַמַּמְלָכָה, כִּי לוֹ
נָאֶה, כִּי לוֹ יָאֶה.

קדוֹשׁ בִּמְלוּכָה, **ר**חוּם כַּהֲלָכָה, **שׁ**נְאַנָּיו יֹאמְרוּ לוֹ, לְךָ
וּלְךָ, לְךָ כִּי לְךָ, לְךָ אַף לְךָ, לְךָ יהוה הַמַּמְלָכָה, כִּי לוֹ
נָאֶה, כִּי לוֹ יָאֶה.

תּקִּיף בִּמְלוּכָה, **תּ**וֹמֵךְ כַּהֲלָכָה, **תּ**מִימָיו יֹאמְרוּ לוֹ, לְךָ
וּלְךָ, לְךָ כִּי לְךָ, לְךָ אַף לְךָ, לְךָ יהוה הַמַּמְלָכָה, כִּי לוֹ
נָאֶה, כִּי לוֹ יָאֶה.

אַדִּיר הוּא יִבְנֶה בֵיתוֹ בְּקָרוֹב, בִּמְהֵרָה, בִּמְהֵרָה,
בְּיָמֵינוּ בְּקָרוֹב. אֵל בְּנֵה, אֵל בְּנֵה, בְּנֵה
בֵיתְךָ בְּקָרוֹב.

בָּחוּר הוּא. **גָּ**דוֹל הוּא. **דָּ**גוּל הוּא. יִבְנֶה בֵיתוֹ בְּקָרוֹב,
בִּמְהֵרָה, בִּמְהֵרָה, בְּיָמֵינוּ בְּקָרוֹב. אֵל בְּנֵה, אֵל בְּנֵה, בְּנֵה
בֵיתְךָ בְּקָרוֹב.

הָדוּר הוּא. **וָ**תִיק הוּא. **זַ**כַּאי הוּא. **חָ**סִיד הוּא. יִבְנֶה
בֵיתוֹ בְּקָרוֹב, בִּמְהֵרָה, בִּמְהֵרָה, בְּיָמֵינוּ בְּקָרוֹב. אֵל בְּנֵה,
אֵל בְּנֵה, בְּנֵה בֵיתְךָ בְּקָרוֹב.

טָהוֹר הוּא. **יָ**חִיד הוּא. **כַּ**בִּיר הוּא. **לָ**מוּד הוּא. **מֶ**לֶךְ
הוּא. **נ**וֹרָא הוּא. **ס**גִּיב הוּא. **ע**זּוּז הוּא. **פּ**וֹדֶה הוּא. **צ**דִּיק
הוּא. יִבְנֶה בֵיתוֹ בְּקָרוֹב, בִּמְהֵרָה, בִּמְהֵרָה, בְּיָמֵינוּ
בְּקָרוֹב. אֵל בְּנֵה, אֵל בְּנֵה, בְּנֵה בֵיתְךָ בְּקָרוֹב.

קדוֹשׁ הוּא. **ר**חוּם הוּא. **שַׁ**דַּי הוּא. **תּ**קִּיף הוּא. יִבְנֶה
בֵיתוֹ בְּקָרוֹב, בִּמְהֵרָה, בִּמְהֵרָה, בְּיָמֵינוּ בְּקָרוֹב. אֵל בְּנֵה,
אֵל בְּנֵה, בְּנֵה בֵיתְךָ בְּקָרוֹב.

Humble in royalty, redeeming by right. His righteous ones say to Him: Yours and only Yours; Yours, yes Yours; Yours, surely Yours; Yours, HASHEM, is the sovereignty of the world. To Him it is fitting. To Him it is due.

Holy in royalty, merciful of right. His angels say to Him: Yours and only Yours; Yours, yes Yours; Yours, surely Yours; Yours, HASHEM, is the sovereignty of the world. To Him it is fitting. To Him it is due.

Powerful in royalty, sustaining of right. His perfect ones say to Him: Yours and only Yours; Yours, yes Yours; Yours, surely Yours; Yours, HASHEM, is the sovereignty of the world. To Him it is fitting. To Him it is due.

M*ighty is He. May He build His house soon; quickly, quickly, in our lifetimes, soon. God, build; God, build; build Your house soon.*

Exalted is He, great is He, distinguished is He. May He build His house soon; quickly, quickly, in our lifetimes, soon. God, build; God, build; build Your house soon.

Glorious is He, faithful is He, guiltless is He, righteous is He. May He build His house soon; quickly, quickly, in our lifetimes, soon. God, build; God, build; build Your house soon.

Pure is He, unique is He, powerful is He, all-wise is He, the King is He, awesome is He, sublime is He, all-powerful is He, the Redeemer is He, all-righteous is He. May He build His house soon; quickly, quickly, in our lifetimes, soon. God, build; God, build; build Your house soon.

Holy is He, compassionate is He, Almighty is He, Omnipotent is He. May He build His house soon; quickly, quickly, in our lifetimes, soon. God, rebuild; God, build; build Your house soon.

ספירת העומר

The *Omer* is counted from the second night of Pesach until the night before Shavuos.

בָּרוּךְ אַתָּה יהוה אֱלֹהֵינוּ מֶלֶךְ הָעוֹלָם, אֲשֶׁר קִדְּשָׁנוּ בְּמִצְוֹתָיו וְצִוָּנוּ עַל סְפִירַת הָעוֹמֶר.

הַיּוֹם יוֹם אֶחָד בָּעוֹמֶר.

יְהִי רָצוֹן מִלְּפָנֶיךָ, יהוה אֱלֹהֵינוּ וֵאלֹהֵי אֲבוֹתֵינוּ, שֶׁיִּבָּנֶה בֵּית הַמִּקְדָּשׁ בִּמְהֵרָה בְיָמֵינוּ, וְתֵן חֶלְקֵנוּ בְּתוֹרָתֶךָ. וְשָׁם נַעֲבָדְךָ בְּיִרְאָה כִּימֵי עוֹלָם וּכְשָׁנִים קַדְמוֹנִיּוֹת.

סְפִירַת הָעוֹמֶר — **The counting of the Omer.**
The name of the meal offering performed on the second day of Pesach was the *Omer*, so called because of the amount of grain contained in the offering: וְהָעוֹמֶר עֲשִׂרִית הָאֵיפָה הוּא, *The omer is a tenth of an ephah* (Shemos 16:36). Usually a sacrifice or meal offering is named after its function (חַטָּאת, *sin offering*; אָשָׁם, *guilt offering*, etc.) or its method of preparation ("burnt offering," "fine-flour offering," "meal offering of the pan," etc.). Why should this one sacrifice derive its name from a seemingly casual characteristic such as the measure of its ingredients?

The lesson that the mitzvah of the counting of the *Omer* teaches us is to appreciate the importance of time and its passage. The Torah tells us, וּסְפַרְתֶּם לָכֶם וכו׳ חֲמִשִּׁים יוֹם, *You shall count for yourselves . . . fifty days* (Vayikra 23:15-16). There is a difference between the way a man's money is counted out by an accountant and the way it is counted by the owner himself; every dollar has precious significance to the one who has earned it. So, too, the Torah wants us to count these days realizing that they are our own days, and that each individual day is precious, providing us with infinite oppportunities to better ourselves spiritually and to strive for perfection. Perhaps the name of the *Omer* offering also imparts a similar message, namely that everything in life — a person's life span, the amount of free time he has, the amount of financial security he is granted, etc. — is in specific, measured quantities,[1] and we must learn to appreciate the opportunities that life affords us and use them to the utmost.

The *Omer* offering is unique among all other meal offerings in that

---

1. Even one's words and steps are given in specific measure. In his later years my grandfather, the *Ohr Yechezkel*, stopped delivering *mussar* talks in the yeshivah. He is reported to have said that he sensed that the Heavenly mandate to be an influence on the public had been rescinded. Even this was given with an exact measure.

COUNTING THE OMER

The *Omer* is counted from the second night of Pesach until the night before Shavuos.

B lessed are You, HASHEM, our God, King of the universe, Who has sanctified us with His commandments and has commanded us regarding the counting of the Omer.

Today is one day of the Omer.

M ay it be Your will, HASHEM, our God and the God of our forefathers, that the Holy Temple be rebuilt,* speedily in our days, and grant us our share in Your Torah, and may we serve You there with reverence as in days of old and in former years.

---

it consists of barley flour rather than the more commonly used wheat flour. The Gemara (*Sotah* 12a) comments on the meal offering of the *sotah* (a licentious woman who is suspected of adultery), which consists of barley flour, that this ingredient is intended to teach a lesson: She acted in an animal-like fashion (following only her passions and physical desires, without paying attention to the spirituality of her conscience) and therefore brings an offering of the food usually fed to animals, that is, barley. The *Aruch HaShulchan* extends this symbolism to the *Omer* offering as well. At the end of the fifty-day period of the "counting of the *Omer*," on the Shavuos festival, another meal offering — the "two breads" — is offered, this one being of the usual wheat flour. The *Aruch HaShulchan* says that this arrangement is intended to show that without the Torah we are no better than barley-eating animals; only after the Giving of the Torah (which took place on Shavuos) can we consider ourselves as wheat-eating human beings.

Yet another explanation of the use of barley in the *Omer* sacrifice may be suggested as follows. The Gemara (*Sanhedrin* 96) praises the loyalty of the Patriarchs, stating that they "ran before Hashem like horses run through marshland (so great was their stamina and steadfastness in their service of Hashem)." The comparison of these great saints to the actions of animals seems incongruous.

Rav Hutner, zt"l, explained that many animals have admirable "character traits" — ants are industrious, cats are modest and sanitary (see *Eruvin* 110a). It is obvious, however, that these are not acquired characteristics but are part of the inborn nature of the animal, passed on genetically from one generation to the next. What the Sages taught us with their comparison of the Patriarchs' actions to the galloping of horses is that they so inculcated their dedication to righteousness and fear of Hashem into their characters that these traits became ingrained in their natures to the point that they no longer required conscious effort. Furthermore, these attributes, having become intrinsic to the

אֶחָד מִי יוֹדֵעַ? אֶחָד אֲנִי יוֹדֵעַ. אֶחָד אֱלֹהֵינוּ שֶׁבַּשָּׁמַיִם וּבָאָרֶץ.

שְׁנַיִם מִי יוֹדֵעַ? שְׁנַיִם אֲנִי יוֹדֵעַ. שְׁנֵי לֻחוֹת הַבְּרִית, אֶחָד אֱלֹהֵינוּ שֶׁבַּשָּׁמַיִם וּבָאָרֶץ.

שְׁלֹשָׁה מִי יוֹדֵעַ? שְׁלֹשָׁה אֲנִי יוֹדֵעַ. שְׁלֹשָׁה אָבוֹת, שְׁנֵי לֻחוֹת הַבְּרִית, אֶחָד אֱלֹהֵינוּ שֶׁבַּשָּׁמַיִם וּבָאָרֶץ.

אַרְבַּע מִי יוֹדֵעַ? אַרְבַּע אֲנִי יוֹדֵעַ. אַרְבַּע אִמָּהוֹת, שְׁלֹשָׁה אָבוֹת, שְׁנֵי לֻחוֹת הַבְּרִית, אֶחָד אֱלֹהֵינוּ שֶׁבַּשָּׁמַיִם וּבָאָרֶץ.

חֲמִשָּׁה מִי יוֹדֵעַ? חֲמִשָּׁה אֲנִי יוֹדֵעַ. חֲמִשָּׁה חֻמְשֵׁי תוֹרָה, אַרְבַּע אִמָּהוֹת, שְׁלֹשָׁה אָבוֹת, שְׁנֵי לֻחוֹת הַבְּרִית, אֶחָד אֱלֹהֵינוּ שֶׁבַּשָּׁמַיִם וּבָאָרֶץ.

שִׁשָּׁה מִי יוֹדֵעַ? שִׁשָּׁה אֲנִי יוֹדֵעַ. שִׁשָּׁה סִדְרֵי מִשְׁנָה, חֲמִשָּׁה חֻמְשֵׁי תוֹרָה, אַרְבַּע אִמָּהוֹת, שְׁלֹשָׁה אָבוֹת, שְׁנֵי לֻחוֹת הַבְּרִית, אֶחָד אֱלֹהֵינוּ שֶׁבַּשָּׁמַיִם וּבָאָרֶץ.

שִׁבְעָה מִי יוֹדֵעַ? שִׁבְעָה אֲנִי יוֹדֵעַ. שִׁבְעָה יְמֵי שַׁבַּתָּא, שִׁשָּׁה סִדְרֵי מִשְׁנָה, חֲמִשָּׁה חֻמְשֵׁי תוֹרָה, אַרְבַּע אִמָּהוֹת, שְׁלֹשָׁה אָבוֹת, שְׁנֵי לֻחוֹת הַבְּרִית, אֶחָד אֱלֹהֵינוּ שֶׁבַּשָּׁמַיִם וּבָאָרֶץ.

שְׁמוֹנָה מִי יוֹדֵעַ? שְׁמוֹנָה אֲנִי יוֹדֵעַ. שְׁמוֹנָה יְמֵי מִילָה, שִׁבְעָה יְמֵי שַׁבַּתָּא, שִׁשָּׁה סִדְרֵי מִשְׁנָה, חֲמִשָּׁה חֻמְשֵׁי

Patriarchs' very essence, were passed on from generation to generation, as an animal's instinctive traits are passed on to its offspring.

In *Yirmiyahu* 2:2, the prophet praises the Israelites of the generation of the Exodus for putting their complete trust in Hashem, taking the seemingly irrational step of embarking on a lengthy trip in the desert without adequate provisions: כֹּה אָמַר ה' זָכַרְתִּי לָךְ חֶסֶד נְעוּרַיִךְ אַהֲבַת כְּלוּלֹתָיִךְ לֶכְתֵּךְ אַחֲרַי בַּמִּדְבָּר בְּאֶרֶץ לֹא זְרוּעָה, *Thus says Hashem, "I have remembered for you the righteousness of your youth, the love of your bridal days: your following after Me in the desert, in a barren land."* That is, the Jews of that time did not act rationally, but rather in an impulsive,

Who knows one? *I know one.*
One is our God in the heavens and the earth.

Who knows two? *I know two. Two are the Tablets of the Covenant. One is our God in the heavens and the earth.*

Who knows three? *I know three. Three are the fathers. Two are the Tablets of the Covenant. One is our God in the heavens and the earth.*

Who knows four? *I know four. Four are the mothers. Three are the fathers. Two are the Tablets of the Covenant. One is our God in the heavens and the earth.*

Who knows five? *I know five. Five are the books of the Torah. Four are the mothers. Three are the fathers. Two are the Tablets of the Covenant. One is our God in the heavens and the earth.*

Who knows six? *I know six. Six are the orders of the Mishnah. Five are the books of the Torah. Four are the mothers. Three are the fathers. Two are the Tablets of the Covenant. One is our God in the heavens and the earth.*

Who knows seven? *I know seven. Seven are the days of the week. Six are the orders of the Mishnah. Five are the books of the Torah. Four are the mothers. Three are the fathers. Two are the Tablets of the Covenant. One is our God in the heavens and the earth.*

Who knows eight? *I know eight. Eight are the days of circumcision. Seven are the days of the week. Six are the orders of the Mishnah. Five are the books of the*

---

instinctive way, as an animal follows its shepherd. Because of this unquestioning loyalty they earned the merit of having the spiritual gains which they experienced at the Exodus, the Splitting of the Sea, the Giving of the Torah, etc., become part of the legacy genetically transmitted to their children and future descendants.

Perhaps *this* is the symbolism of the barley, the food of animals, used in the *Omer* sacrifice. It is to recall that the Exodus from Egypt was undertaken by the Jews with complete, absolute submissiveness, reminiscent of an animal who relies totally and blindly on its master.

תּוֹרָה, אַרְבַּע אִמָּהוֹת, שְׁלֹשָׁה אָבוֹת, שְׁנֵי לֻחוֹת הַבְּרִית, אֶחָד אֱלֹהֵינוּ שֶׁבַּשָּׁמַיִם וּבָאָרֶץ.

תִּשְׁעָה מִי יוֹדֵעַ? תִּשְׁעָה אֲנִי יוֹדֵעַ. תִּשְׁעָה יַרְחֵי לֵדָה, שְׁמוֹנָה יְמֵי מִילָה, שִׁבְעָה יְמֵי שַׁבַּתָּא, שִׁשָּׁה סִדְרֵי מִשְׁנָה, חֲמִשָּׁה חֻמְשֵׁי תוֹרָה, אַרְבַּע אִמָּהוֹת, שְׁלֹשָׁה אָבוֹת, שְׁנֵי לֻחוֹת הַבְּרִית, אֶחָד אֱלֹהֵינוּ שֶׁבַּשָּׁמַיִם וּבָאָרֶץ.

עֲשָׂרָה מִי יוֹדֵעַ? עֲשָׂרָה אֲנִי יוֹדֵעַ. עֲשָׂרָה דִבְּרַיָּא, תִּשְׁעָה יַרְחֵי לֵדָה, שְׁמוֹנָה יְמֵי מִילָה, שִׁבְעָה יְמֵי שַׁבַּתָּא, שִׁשָּׁה סִדְרֵי מִשְׁנָה, חֲמִשָּׁה חֻמְשֵׁי תוֹרָה, אַרְבַּע אִמָּהוֹת, שְׁלֹשָׁה אָבוֹת, שְׁנֵי לֻחוֹת הַבְּרִית, אֶחָד אֱלֹהֵינוּ שֶׁבַּשָּׁמַיִם וּבָאָרֶץ.

אַחַד עָשָׂר מִי יוֹדֵעַ? אַחַד עָשָׂר אֲנִי יוֹדֵעַ. אַחַד עָשָׂר כּוֹכְבַיָּא, עֲשָׂרָה דִבְּרַיָּא, תִּשְׁעָה יַרְחֵי לֵדָה, שְׁמוֹנָה יְמֵי מִילָה, שִׁבְעָה יְמֵי שַׁבַּתָּא, שִׁשָּׁה סִדְרֵי מִשְׁנָה, חֲמִשָּׁה חֻמְשֵׁי תוֹרָה, אַרְבַּע אִמָּהוֹת, שְׁלֹשָׁה אָבוֹת, שְׁנֵי לֻחוֹת הַבְּרִית, אֶחָד אֱלֹהֵינוּ שֶׁבַּשָּׁמַיִם וּבָאָרֶץ.

שְׁנֵים עָשָׂר מִי יוֹדֵעַ? שְׁנֵים עָשָׂר אֲנִי יוֹדֵעַ. שְׁנֵים עָשָׂר שִׁבְטַיָּא, אַחַד עָשָׂר כּוֹכְבַיָּא, עֲשָׂרָה דִבְּרַיָּא, תִּשְׁעָה יַרְחֵי לֵדָה, שְׁמוֹנָה יְמֵי מִילָה, שִׁבְעָה יְמֵי שַׁבַּתָּא, שִׁשָּׁה סִדְרֵי מִשְׁנָה, חֲמִשָּׁה חֻמְשֵׁי תוֹרָה, אַרְבַּע אִמָּהוֹת, שְׁלֹשָׁה אָבוֹת, שְׁנֵי לֻחוֹת הַבְּרִית, אֶחָד אֱלֹהֵינוּ שֶׁבַּשָּׁמַיִם וּבָאָרֶץ.

שְׁלֹשָׁה עָשָׂר מִי יוֹדֵעַ? שְׁלֹשָׁה עָשָׂר אֲנִי יוֹדֵעַ. שְׁלֹשָׁה עָשָׂר מִדַּיָּא, שְׁנֵים עָשָׂר שִׁבְטַיָּא, אַחַד עָשָׂר כּוֹכְבַיָּא, עֲשָׂרָה דִבְּרַיָּא, תִּשְׁעָה יַרְחֵי לֵדָה, שְׁמוֹנָה יְמֵי מִילָה, שִׁבְעָה יְמֵי שַׁבַּתָּא, שִׁשָּׁה סִדְרֵי מִשְׁנָה, חֲמִשָּׁה חֻמְשֵׁי תוֹרָה, אַרְבַּע אִמָּהוֹת, שְׁלֹשָׁה אָבוֹת, שְׁנֵי לֻחוֹת הַבְּרִית, אֶחָד אֱלֹהֵינוּ שֶׁבַּשָּׁמַיִם וּבָאָרֶץ.

Torah. Four are the mothers. Three are the fathers. Two are the Tablets of the Covenant. One is our God in the heavens and the earth.

Who knows nine? *I know nine. Nine are the months of pregnancy. Eight are the days of circumcision. Seven are the days of the week. Six are the orders of the Mishnah. Five are the books of the Torah. Four are the mothers. Three are the fathers. Two are the Tablets of the Covenant. One is our God in the heavens and the earth.*

Who knows ten? *I know ten. Ten are the commandments. Nine are the months of pregnancy. Eight are the days of circumcision. Seven are the days of the week. Six are the orders of the Mishnah. Five are the books of the Torah. Four are the mothers. Three are the fathers. Two are the Tablets of the Covenant. One is our God in the heavens and the earth.*

Who knows eleven? *I know eleven. Eleven are the stars [of Joseph's dream]. Ten are the commandments. Nine are the months of pregnancy. Eight are the days of circumcision. Seven are the days of the week. Six are the orders of the Mishnah. Five are the books of the Torah. Four are the mothers. Three are the fathers. Two are the Tablets of the Covenant. One is our God in the heavens and the earth.*

Who knows twelve? *I know twelve. Twelve are the tribes. Eleven are the stars. Ten are the commandments. Nine are the months of pregnancy. Eight are the days of circumcision. Seven are the days of the week. Six are the orders of the Mishnah. Five are the books of the Torah. Four are the mothers. Three are the fathers. Two are the Tablets of the Covenant. One is our God in the heavens and the earth.*

Who knows thirteen? *I know thirteen. Thirteen are the attributes of Hashem. Twelve are the tribes. Eleven are the stars. Ten are the commandments. Nine are the months of pregnancy. Eight are the days of circumcision. Seven are the days of the week. Six are the orders of the Mishnah. Five are the books of the Torah. Four are the mothers. Three are the fathers. Two are the Tablets of the Covenant. One is our God in the heavens and the earth.*

חַד גַּדְיָא, חַד גַּדְיָא, דְּזַבִּין אַבָּא בִּתְרֵי זוּזֵי, חַד גַּדְיָא חַד גַּדְיָא.

וְאָתָא **שׁוּנְרָא** וְאָכְלָה לְגַדְיָא, דְּזַבִּין אַבָּא בִּתְרֵי זוּזֵי, חַד גַּדְיָא חַד גַּדְיָא.

וְאָתָא **כַלְבָּא** וְנָשַׁךְ לְשׁוּנְרָא, דְּאָכְלָא לְגַדְיָא, דְּזַבִּין אַבָּא בִּתְרֵי זוּזֵי, חַד גַּדְיָא חַד גַּדְיָא.

וְאָתָא **חוּטְרָא** וְהִכָּה לְכַלְבָּא, דְּנָשַׁךְ לְשׁוּנְרָא, דְּאָכְלָה לְגַדְיָא, דְּזַבִּין אַבָּא בִּתְרֵי זוּזֵי, חַד גַּדְיָא חַד גַּדְיָא.

וְאָתָא **נוּרָא** וְשָׂרַף לְחוּטְרָא, דְּהִכָּה לְכַלְבָּא, דְּנָשַׁךְ לְשׁוּנְרָא, דְּאָכְלָה לְגַדְיָא, דְּזַבִּין אַבָּא בִּתְרֵי זוּזֵי, חַד גַּדְיָא חַד גַּדְיָא.

וְאָתָא **מַיָּא** וְכָבָה לְנוּרָא, דְּשָׂרַף לְחוּטְרָא, דְּהִכָּה לְכַלְבָּא, דְּנָשַׁךְ לְשׁוּנְרָא, דְּאָכְלָה לְגַדְיָא, דְּזַבִּין אַבָּא בִּתְרֵי זוּזֵי, חַד גַּדְיָא חַד גַּדְיָא.

וְאָתָא **תּוֹרָא** וְשָׁתָה לְמַיָּא, דְּכָבָה לְנוּרָא, דְּשָׂרַף לְחוּטְרָא, דְּהִכָּה לְכַלְבָּא, דְּנָשַׁךְ לְשׁוּנְרָא, דְּאָכְלָה לְגַדְיָא, דְּזַבִּין אַבָּא בִּתְרֵי זוּזֵי, חַד גַּדְיָא חַד גַּדְיָא.

וְאָתָא **הַשּׁוֹחֵט** וְשָׁחַט לְתוֹרָא, דְּשָׁתָא לְמַיָּא, דְּכָבָה לְנוּרָא, דְּשָׂרַף לְחוּטְרָא, דְּהִכָּה לְכַלְבָּא, דְּנָשַׁךְ לְשׁוּנְרָא, דְּאָכְלָה לְגַדְיָא, דְּזַבִּין אַבָּא בִּתְרֵי זוּזֵי, חַד גַּדְיָא חַד גַּדְיָא.

וְאָתָא **מַלְאַךְ הַמָּוֶת** וְשָׁחַט לְשׁוֹחֵט, דְּשָׁחַט לְתוֹרָא, דְּשָׁתָה לְמַיָּא, דְּכָבָה לְנוּרָא, דְּשָׂרַף לְחוּטְרָא, דְּהִכָּה לְכַלְבָּא, דְּנָשַׁךְ לְשׁוּנְרָא, דְּאָכְלָה לְגַדְיָא, דְּזַבִּין אַבָּא בִּתְרֵי זוּזֵי, חַד גַּדְיָא חַד גַּדְיָא.

וְאָתָא **הַקָּדוֹשׁ בָּרוּךְ הוּא** וְשָׁחַט לְמַלְאַךְ הַמָּוֶת, דְּשָׁחַט לְשׁוֹחֵט, דְּשָׁחַט לְתוֹרָא, דְּשָׁתָה לְמַיָּא, דְּכָבָה לְנוּרָא, דְּשָׂרַף לְחוּטְרָא, דְּהִכָּה לְכַלְבָּא, דְּנָשַׁךְ לְשׁוּנְרָא, דְּאָכְלָה לְגַדְיָא, דְּזַבִּין אַבָּא בִּתְרֵי זוּזֵי, חַד גַּדְיָא חַד גַּדְיָא.

One kid, *one kid that father bought for two zuzim. One kid, one kid.*

And the cat *came and ate the kid that father bought for two zuzim. One kid, one kid.*

And the dog *came and bit the cat that ate the kid that father bought for two zuzim. One kid, one kid.*

And the stick *came and beat the dog that bit the cat that ate the kid that father bought for two zuzim. One kid, one kid.*

And the fire *came and burned the stick that beat the dog that bit the cat that ate the kid that father bought for two zuzim. One kid, one kid.*

And the water *came and doused the fire that burned the stick that beat the dog that bit the cat that ate the kid that father bought for two zuzim. One kid, one kid.*

And the ox *came and drank the water that doused the fire that burned the stick that beat the dog that bit the cat that ate the kid that father bought for two zuzim. One kid, one kid.*

And the slaughterer *came and slaughtered the ox that drank the water that doused the fire that burned the stick that beat the dog that bit the cat that ate the kid that father bought for two zuzim. One kid, one kid.*

And the Angel of Death *came and slaughtered the slaughterer who slaughtered the ox that drank the water that doused the fire that burned the stick that beat the dog that bit the cat that ate the kid that father bought for two zuzim. One kid, one kid.*

And the Holy One, Blessed is He, *came and slaughtered the Angel of Death who slaughtered the slaughterer who slaughtered the ox that drank the water that doused the fire that burned the stick that beat the dog that bit the cat that ate the kid that father bought for two zuzim. One kid, one kid.*

שיר השירים ‏‫‎
Shir Hashirim

שִׁיר הַשִּׁירִים

א שִׁיר הַשִּׁירִים אֲשֶׁר לִשְׁלֹמְה: ב יִשָּׁקֵנִי מִנְּשִׁיקוֹת פִּיהוּ כִּי־טוֹבִים דֹּדֶיךָ מִיָּיִן: ג לְרֵיחַ שְׁמָנֶיךָ טוֹבִים שֶׁמֶן תּוּרַק שְׁמֶךָ עַל־כֵּן עֲלָמוֹת אֲהֵבְוּךָ: ד מָשְׁכֵנִי אַחֲרֶיךָ נָּרוּצָה הֱבִיאַנִי הַמֶּלֶךְ חֲדָרָיו נָגִילָה וְנִשְׂמְחָה בָּךְ נַזְכִּירָה דֹדֶיךָ

עַל כֵּן עֲלָמוֹת אֲהֵבְוּךָ — Therefore do the maidens love you (1:3).

Rashi sees the "maidens" in this verse as an allegory for the nations of the world, from whose ranks come proselytes who show their "love" for Hashem by joining the Jewish people. As examples, he cites two people who were moved by the miraculous events surrounding the Exodus from Egypt to enter into Hashem's covenant — Jethro, and Rahab the harlot. In the case of Jethro, *Rashi* (*Shemos* 2:16) points out that long before the Jews left Egypt he abandoned the idolatrous practices of his countrymen, and began to worship Hashem. Yet, in *Shemos* 18 we are taught that what prompted Jethro to join the ranks of the Jewish people was his having heard of the miraculous deliverance of the Israelites from the hands of the Egyptians. These accounts seem irreconcilable. When did Jethro really embrace the true faith in God?

Apparently there are two different levels of conviction which bring a person to convert to Judaism. The lower of these two levels is when someone realizes that he owes his existence and sustenance to Hashem. This was the level of faith of the "mixed multitude" (עֶרֶב רַב) who accompanied the Jews when they left Egypt (*Shemos* 12:38): The Sages tell us that they were not protected by the עֲנָנֵי הַכָּבוֹד, *Clouds of Glory,* along with the Jews, nor did the manna fall for them. The mixed multitude realized that Hashem controlled the forces of nature and that the survival of man is dependent upon Him, and thus decided to cast their lot with His people. Although this is considered sufficient motivation to accept a convert, it is not the optimum situation. For this reason this type of convert is not afforded the full measure of Divine protection experienced by the Jewish nation as a whole, nor are his actions deemed as praiseworthy and deserving of special mention as those of a true, "righteous convert."

The second, more elevated level is when a man yearns to worship Hashem and to know Him not merely out of recognition that Hashem provides for his physical existence, but due to the clarity of perspective that there is no other important goal in life other than to fulfill the will of God. This deep emotional commitment entitles the proselyte to the

מִיַּיִן מֵישָׁרִים אֲהֵבוּךָ: ה שְׁחוֹרָה אֲנִי וְנָאוָה בְּנוֹת
יְרוּשָׁלַיִם כְּאָהֳלֵי קֵדָר כִּירִיעוֹת שְׁלֹמֹה: ו אַל־תִּרְאֻנִי
שֶׁאֲנִי שְׁחַרְחֹרֶת שֶׁשְּׁזָפַתְנִי הַשָּׁמֶשׁ בְּנֵי אִמִּי נִחֲרוּ־בִי
שָׂמֻנִי נֹטֵרָה אֶת־הַכְּרָמִים כַּרְמִי שֶׁלִּי לֹא נָטָרְתִּי: ז הַגִּידָה
לִּי שֶׁאָהֲבָה נַפְשִׁי אֵיכָה תִרְעֶה אֵיכָה תַּרְבִּיץ בַּצָּהֳרָיִם
שַׁלָּמָה אֶהְיֶה כְּעֹטְיָה עַל עֶדְרֵי חֲבֵרֶיךָ: ח אִם־לֹא תֵדְעִי

full status of a member of the community of Israel, and his actions are considered to be most laudable, worthy of being publicized.

Jethro's initial step in embracing the faith in the true God was based on the first type of motive; this is why the Torah does not mention it specifically, but only hints at it (by saying that his daughters were shunned by the other shepherds — *Shemos* 2:16-17, see *Rashi* ibid.). After contemplating the awesome magnitude of Hashem's actions during the Exodus and the Splitting of the Sea, however, he was moved to recognize Hashem on a much higher level. It was then that וַיִּחַדְּ יִתְרוֹ עַל כָּל הַטּוֹבָה אֲשֶׁר עָשָׂה ה' לְיִשְׂרָאֵל, *Jethro rejoiced over all the good that Hashem had done for Israel* (*Shemos* 18:9), and yearned to know and worship Hashem on a higher plane. At that point the Torah devotes considerable attention to the arrival of Jethro to the Israelite camp and to his actions and accomplishments there.

נַזְכִּירָה דֹדֶיךָ מִיַּיִן — We recall your love more than wine (1:4).

Rashi explains this as follows: Even during our times of disaster, we fondly remember earlier, more fortunate periods, such as the period described by the prophet Jeremiah, כֹּה אָמַר ה' זָכַרְתִּי לָךְ חֶסֶד נְעוּרַיִךְ אַהֲבַת כְּלוּלֹתָיִךְ לֶכְתֵּךְ אַחֲרַי בַּמִּדְבָּר בְּאֶרֶץ לֹא זְרוּעָה, *Thus says Hashem, "I have remembered for you the righteousness of your youth, the love of your bridal days: your following after Me in the desert, in a barren land"* (*Yirmiyahu* 2:2).

Midrash Tehillim (*Tehillim* 36) illustrates this description of Jeremiah with a parable: "Rabbi Yannai said: If someone lights a candle during the day, what good is it? [Obviously none at all.] When does this candle begin to benefit him? When darkness sets in. Similarly, the righteousness of the Israelites at the time of the Exodus, when they blindly and obediently followed the command of Hashem to march into the vast desert without preparing adequate supplies, produced a great deal of merit for them. Although it was not necessary to derive benefit from it at that time, it stood them in good stead during a later, 'dark' chapter

לָךְ הַיָּפָה בַּנָּשִׁים צְאִי־לָךְ בְּעִקְבֵי הַצֹּאן וּרְעִי אֶת־
גְּדִיֹּתַיִךְ עַל מִשְׁכְּנוֹת הָרֹעִים: ט לְסֻסָתִי בְּרִכְבֵי פַרְעֹה
דִּמִּיתִיךְ רַעְיָתִי: י נָאווּ לְחָיַיִךְ בַּתֹּרִים צַוָּארֵךְ בַּחֲרוּזִים:
יא תּוֹרֵי זָהָב נַעֲשֶׂה־לָּךְ עִם נְקֻדּוֹת הַכָּסֶף: יב עַד־שֶׁהַמֶּלֶךְ

---

of their history, in the days of Jeremiah." The reward for their devotion
and unbounded faith during the Exodus was granted to the Jews at the
time of their exile from Jerusalem, when Hashem granted His protection to them and safeguarded them from harm. In the scheme of מִדָּה
כְּנֶגֶד מִדָּה, where Divine reward is symmetrically reflective of the good
deed that engenders it, we must understand the connection between
these two events.

When the Jews left Egypt they exhibited an extraordinary measure
of trust in Hashem's protection. This sort of blind faith is characteristic
of the father-son relationship. When a child goes on a trip with his father
or mother he need not be concerned about food or lodging arrangements; these concerns are the domain of the parents. The Sages taught:
חֲבִיבִין יִשְׂרָאֵל שֶׁנִּקְרְאוּ בָּנִים לַמָּקוֹם, *Israel is beloved, for they are referred to
as children of Hashem (Pirkei Avos* 3:18). Although all of mankind is also
beloved, only Israel has this unique, intense and emotional relationship
with their "Father in Heaven." The Exodus from Egypt was the genesis
of this relationship.

Another distinctive aspect of the parent-child relationship is that
even while punishing a child, the father will do all he can to care for his
son and to protect him from harm. Parental punishment is not meant
to be detrimental to the child's welfare, but rather to ultimately benefit
his character and behavior in some positive way. It, unlike governmental or judicial punishment, is uniquely able to chastise and love at the
same time. This aspect of the relationship found expression in the days
of Jeremiah.

As a son follows his father, with full faith that his father is always there
for him, so did the Israelites follow Hashem into the desert. They reaped
their reward in the days of Jeremiah, when Hashem repaid them in kind
by showing His compassion for them even while punishing them.[1]

**תּוֹרֵי זָהָב נַעֲשֶׂה לָּךְ עִם נְקֻדּוֹת הַכָּסֶף — Circlets of gold we will make for
you, together with spangles of silver (1:11).**

---

1. The Rebbe of Kotsk explained why the month in which the Temple was destroyed is
called Av (lit. father): "If you see a lad come into the *beis midrash* and a Jew caresses his
face, he may or may not be the boy's father. But if you see the man slap him, you can be
sure it is his father." The loving reproof of the Temple destruction is the greatest indicator
of our Father's love.

בְּמִסְבּוֹ נִרְדִּי נָתַן רֵיחוֹ: יִּ צְרוֹר הַמֹּר l דּוֹדִי לִי בֵּין שָׁדַי
יָלִין: יִ אֶשְׁכֹּל הַכֹּפֶר l דּוֹדִי לִי בְּכַרְמֵי עֵין גֶּדִי: טו הִנָּךְ יָפָה
רַעְיָתִי הִנָּךְ יָפָה עֵינַיִךְ יוֹנִים: טז הִנְּךָ יָפֶה דוֹדִי אַף נָעִים
אַף־עַרְשֵׂנוּ רַעֲנָנָה: יי קֹרוֹת בָּתֵּינוּ אֲרָזִים רַהִיטֵנוּ
בְּרוֹתִים:

Rashi explains this as a reference to the vast riches that the Israelites looted from the Egyptian soldiers who were drowned in the Red Sea, interpreting the verse as follows: "I and My Heavenly court decided to persuade Pharaoh and their men to adorn their horses and soldiers with all the treasures of Egypt, so that I would thus provide you with circlets of gold and spangles of silver." *Rashi's* interpretation that this action was taken by Hashem together with His Heavenly court is based on the use of the plural form of the verb נַעֲשֶׂה, *we will make* (see *Sifsei Chachamim* ibid.). A similar inference is made in *Bereishis* 1:26: וַיֹּאמֶר אֱלֹקִים נַעֲשֶׂה אָדָם בְּצַלְמֵנוּ, *And God said, "Let us make Man in Our image"* where *Rashi* comments that the plural usage indicates that Hashem consulted (as it were) with the angels regarding the Creation of Man.

It is no mere coincidence that we find Hashem conferring with the Hosts of Heaven specifically in these two contexts: the Creation of Man, and the final stage of Israel's liberation from Egypt. The Sages teach that the entire purpose of Creation was to create an environment for the acceptance of the Torah and fulfillment of its precepts by Israel (see *Rashi, Bereishis* 1:1). Thus the Exodus, the milestone which marked the genesis of Israel as the sanctified nation (who would shortly receive the Torah at Sinai), was an event as momentous and significant as Creation itself, inasmuch as the entire existence of the universe was dependent on the emergence of this holy nation.[1]

I once heard a beautiful explanation of a *midrash* based on this idea. In *Tanna DeVei Eliahu* it is written: Amalek once asked his father Elifaz (who was the son of Esau), "Who is destined to inherit both this world and the World to Come?" Elifaz replied, "The Children of Israel.

---

1. In a similar vein we can understand a statement made by *Rashi* in his commentary on the Torah. In *Bamidbar* 10:35, Moses prays, וְיָנֻסוּ מְשַׂנְאֶיךָ מִפָּנֶיךָ, *Let those who hate You flee from before You.* Who are the enemies of Hashem? *Rashi* explains: "These are the enemies of Israel, for anyone who hates Israel also, by definition, hates He Who Created the World through His word." *Rashi* speaks of Hashem as Creator rather than the far more common "Master of the Universe" or "Holy One, Blessed is He," for one who opposes the Jewish nation and its sacred mission stands in opposition to the realization of the Creator's goals in Creation.

א אֲנִי חֲבַצֶּלֶת הַשָּׁרוֹן שׁוֹשַׁנַּת הָעֲמָקִים: ב כְּשׁוֹשַׁנָּה בֵּין הַחוֹחִים כֵּן רַעְיָתִי בֵּין הַבָּנוֹת: ג כְּתַפּוּחַ בַּעֲצֵי הַיַּעַר כֵּן דּוֹדִי בֵּין הַבָּנִים בְּצִלּוֹ חִמַּדְתִּי וְיָשַׁבְתִּי וּפִרְיוֹ מָתוֹק לְחִכִּי: ד הֱבִיאַנִי אֶל־בֵּית הַיָּיִן וְדִגְלוֹ עָלַי אַהֲבָה: ה סַמְּכוּנִי בָּאֲשִׁישׁוֹת רַפְּדוּנִי בַּתַּפּוּחִים כִּי־חוֹלַת אַהֲבָה אָנִי: ו שְׂמֹאלוֹ תַּחַת לְרֹאשִׁי וִימִינוֹ תְּחַבְּקֵנִי: ז הִשְׁבַּעְתִּי אֶתְכֶם בְּנוֹת יְרוּשָׁלַם בִּצְבָאוֹת אוֹ בְּאַיְלוֹת הַשָּׂדֶה אִם־תָּעִירוּ | וְאִם־תְּעוֹרְרוּ אֶת־הָאַהֲבָה עַד שֶׁתֶּחְפָּץ: ח קוֹל דּוֹדִי הִנֵּה־זֶה בָּא מְדַלֵּג עַל־הֶהָרִים מְקַפֵּץ עַל־הַגְּבָעוֹת: ט דּוֹמֶה דוֹדִי לִצְבִי אוֹ לְעֹפֶר הָאַיָּלִים הִנֵּה־זֶה עוֹמֵד אַחַר כָּתְלֵנוּ מַשְׁגִּיחַ מִן־הַחַלֹּנוֹת מֵצִיץ מִן־הַחֲרַכִּים: י עָנָה דוֹדִי וְאָמַר לִי קוּמִי לָךְ רַעְיָתִי יָפָתִי וּלְכִי־לָךְ: יא כִּי־הִנֵּה הַסְּתָו עָבָר הַגֶּשֶׁם חָלַף הָלַךְ לוֹ: יב הַנִּצָּנִים נִרְאוּ בָאָרֶץ עֵת הַזָּמִיר הִגִּיעַ וְקוֹל הַתּוֹר נִשְׁמַע בְּאַרְצֵנוּ: יג הַתְּאֵנָה חָנְטָה פַגֶּיהָ וְהַגְּפָנִים | סְמָדַר נָתְנוּ רֵיחַ קוּמִי לָךְ רַעְיָתִי יָפָתִי וּלְכִי־לָךְ: יד יוֹנָתִי בְּחַגְוֵי הַסֶּלַע בְּסֵתֶר הַמַּדְרֵגָה הַרְאִינִי אֶת־מַרְאַיִךְ הַשְׁמִיעִנִי אֶת־קוֹלֵךְ כִּי־קוֹלֵךְ עָרֵב וּמַרְאֵיךְ נָאוֶה: טו אֶחֱזוּ־לָנוּ שׁוּעָלִים שׁוּעָלִים קְטַנִּים

Therefore go now and dig wells and repair the roads [to facilitate their journey from Egypt to the Land of Israel], and you too will merit a share of their reward [for assisting them]." But Amalek did not heed this advice; instead he set out to destroy the world, as it says, וַיָּבֹא עֲמָלֵק וַיִּלָּחֶם עִם יִשְׂרָאֵל בִּרְפִידִם, And Amalek came and battled Israel in Rephidim (Shemos 17:8).

Rav Shmuel Brudny, zt"l, pointed out a seeming exaggeration in the wording of this midrash. If Amalek decided to "battle Israel," as the quoted verse states, why does the midrash call this "setting out to destroy the world"? He explained that since Amalek had just been told that Israel represents the entire purpose of Creation (evidenced by the fact that it is they who are destined to inherit the World to Come), his decision to attack them was in essence an intent to destroy the world entirely.

מְחַבְּלִים כְּרָמִים וּכְרָמֵינוּ סְמָדַר: טוּדוֹדִי לִי וַאֲנִי לוֹ
הָרֹעֶה בַּשּׁוֹשַׁנִּים: יוּעַד שֶׁיָּפוּחַ הַיּוֹם וְנָסוּ הַצְּלָלִים סֹב
דְּמֵה־לְךָ דוֹדִי לִצְבִי אוֹ לְעֹפֶר הָאַיָּלִים עַל־הָרֵי בָתֶר:

פרק ג

א עַל־מִשְׁכָּבִי בַּלֵּילוֹת בִּקַּשְׁתִּי אֵת שֶׁאָהֲבָה נַפְשִׁי
בִּקַּשְׁתִּיו וְלֹא מְצָאתִיו: בּאָקוּמָה נָּא וַאֲסוֹבְבָה בָעִיר
בַּשְּׁוָקִים וּבָרְחֹבוֹת אֲבַקְשָׁה אֵת שֶׁאָהֲבָה נַפְשִׁי בִּקַּשְׁתִּיו
וְלֹא מְצָאתִיו: גמְצָאוּנִי הַשֹּׁמְרִים הַסֹּבְבִים בָּעִיר אֵת
שֶׁאָהֲבָה נַפְשִׁי רְאִיתֶם: דכִּמְעַט שֶׁעָבַרְתִּי מֵהֶם עַד
שֶׁמָּצָאתִי אֵת שֶׁאָהֲבָה נַפְשִׁי אֲחַזְתִּיו וְלֹא אַרְפֶּנּוּ
עַד־שֶׁהֲבֵיאתִיו אֶל־בֵּית אִמִּי וְאֶל־חֶדֶר הוֹרָתִי:
ההִשְׁבַּעְתִּי אֶתְכֶם בְּנוֹת יְרוּשָׁלַ͏ִם בִּצְבָאוֹת אוֹ בְּאַיְלוֹת
הַשָּׂדֶה אִם־תָּעִירוּ | וְאִם־תְּעוֹרְרוּ אֶת־הָאַהֲבָה עַד
שֶׁתֶּחְפָּץ: ומִי זֹאת עֹלָה מִן־הַמִּדְבָּר כְּתִימְרוֹת עָשָׁן
מְקֻטֶּרֶת מוֹר וּלְבוֹנָה מִכֹּל אַבְקַת רוֹכֵל: זהִנֵּה מִטָּתוֹ
שֶׁלִּשְׁלֹמֹה שִׁשִּׁים גִּבֹּרִים סָבִיב לָהּ מִגִּבֹּרֵי יִשְׂרָאֵל: חכֻּלָּם
אֲחֻזֵי חֶרֶב מְלֻמְּדֵי מִלְחָמָה אִישׁ חַרְבּוֹ עַל־יְרֵכוֹ מִפַּחַד
בַּלֵּילוֹת: טאַפִּרְיוֹן עָשָׂה לוֹ הַמֶּלֶךְ שְׁלֹמֹה מֵעֲצֵי הַלְּבָנוֹן:
יעַמּוּדָיו עָשָׂה כֶסֶף רְפִידָתוֹ זָהָב מֶרְכָּבוֹ אַרְגָּמָן תּוֹכוֹ
רָצוּף אַהֲבָה מִבְּנוֹת יְרוּשָׁלָ͏ִם: יאצְאֶינָה | וּרְאֶינָה בְּנוֹת
צִיּוֹן בַּמֶּלֶךְ שְׁלֹמֹה בָּעֲטָרָה שֶׁעִטְּרָה־לּוֹ אִמּוֹ בְּיוֹם
חֲתֻנָּתוֹ וּבְיוֹם שִׂמְחַת לִבּוֹ:

צְאֶינָה וּרְאֶינָה בְּנוֹת צִיּוֹן בַּמֶּלֶךְ שְׁלֹמֹה בָּעֲטָרָה שֶׁעִטְּרָה לּוֹ אִמּוֹ בְּיוֹם חֲתֻנָּתוֹ
וּבְיוֹם שִׂמְחַת לִבּוֹ — Go forth and gaze, O daughters of Zion, upon King
Solomon in the crown with which his mother crowned him on his
wedding day and on the day of his heart's rejoicing (3:11).

It is axiomatic that *Shir HaShirim* is an allegory describing the love
between Hashem and His beloved, the people of Israel. Reflected here
are the three stages in a human marriage. בָּעֲטָרָה שֶׁעִטְּרָה לּוֹ אִמּוֹ, *The*

א הִנָּךְ יָפָה רַעְיָתִי הִנָּךְ יָפָה עֵינַיִךְ יוֹנִים מִבַּעַד לְצַמָּתֵךְ
שַׂעְרֵךְ כְּעֵדֶר הָעִזִּים שֶׁגָּלְשׁוּ מֵהַר גִּלְעָד: ב שִׁנַּיִךְ כְּעֵדֶר
הַקְּצוּבוֹת שֶׁעָלוּ מִן־הָרַחְצָה שֶׁכֻּלָּם מַתְאִימוֹת וְשַׁכֻּלָה
אֵין בָּהֶם: ג כְּחוּט הַשָּׁנִי שִׂפְתוֹתַיִךְ וּמִדְבָּרֵךְ נָאוֶה כְּפֶלַח
הָרִמּוֹן רַקָּתֵךְ מִבַּעַד לְצַמָּתֵךְ: ד כְּמִגְדַּל דָּוִיד צַוָּארֵךְ בָּנוּי

---

crown with which his mother crowned him, is a reference to the festival of Pesach and the miracles of the Exodus which took place during the week of the first Passover. This parallels the engagement stage when the bride-groom relationship is established. The *Midrash* (*Shir HaShirim Rabbah* 4:17), commenting on the verse, אִתִּי מִלְּבָנוֹן כַּלָּה אִתִּי מִלְּבָנוֹן תָּבוֹאִי, *With Me from Lebanon, O bride — Come with me from Lebanon* (ibid. v. 8), says: "Normally a girl is given twelve months to prepare her trousseau, but I [Hashem] did not do so; while you were yet smeared with plaster and bricks [from your toiling in Egypt] I immediately took you and redeemed you." Thus we see that it was at the time of the Exodus that Israel is first described as Hashem's "bride." The revelation of Hashem's Glory to Israel at the time of the Exodus was by way of introduction, much like a bride and groom meeting each other even before they are betrothed. The Exodus, then, represents the שִׁדּוּכִין, *engagement*, as it were, between Israel and its Divine "Groom."

בְּיוֹם חֲתֻנָּתוֹ, *On his wedding day*, explains Rashi, refers to the day of the Giving of the Torah. This may be compared to the stage of קִדּוּשִׁין, *betrothal*, when the bride and groom become legally and irrevocably bound to each other. At the time of the Giving of the Torah, on the Shavuos festival, the Gemara (*Kreisos* 9a) tells us that the Jews underwent a type of ritual conversion, consisting of immersion, circumcision for males, and a sacrificial rite. It was through this "conversion" that the Jews "entered the covenant" with Hashem at Sinai. At this juncture the relationship between Hashem and Israel became irrevocable, sealed with a covenant.

וּבְיוֹם שִׂמְחַת לִבּוֹ, And on *the day of his heart's rejoicing*, according to *Rashi,* alludes to the day the Tabernacle was dedicated in the desert, namely the first of Nisan of the second year of the Israelites' leaving Egypt. This is analogous to the final stage in the joining of a man and his wife, נִשּׂוּאִין וְחוּפָּה, *the bridal canopy*, when the bride symbolically enters the home of the groom. With the dedication of the Tabernacle, Hashem brought Israel into His "house," so that they would be forever protected and sheltered by Him.

לְתַלְפִּיּוֹת אֶלֶף הַמָּגֵן תָּלוּי עָלָיו כֹּל שִׁלְטֵי הַגִּבֹּרִים: ה שְׁנֵי
שָׁדַיִךְ כִּשְׁנֵי עֳפָרִים תְּאוֹמֵי צְבִיָּה הָרֹעִים בַּשּׁוֹשַׁנִּים: ו עַד
שֶׁיָּפוּחַ הַיּוֹם וְנָסוּ הַצְּלָלִים אֵלֶךְ לִי אֶל־הַר הַמּוֹר
וְאֶל־גִּבְעַת הַלְּבוֹנָה: ז כֻּלָּךְ יָפָה רַעְיָתִי וּמוּם אֵין בָּךְ:
ח אִתִּי מִלְּבָנוֹן כַּלָּה אִתִּי מִלְּבָנוֹן תָּבוֹאִי תָּשׁוּרִי ׀ מֵרֹאשׁ
אֲמָנָה מֵרֹאשׁ שְׂנִיר וְחֶרְמוֹן מִמְּעֹנוֹת אֲרָיוֹת מֵהַרְרֵי
נְמֵרִים: ט לִבַּבְתִּנִי אֲחֹתִי כַלָּה לִבַּבְתִּנִי בְּאַחַת מֵעֵינַיִךְ
בְּאַחַד עֲנָק מִצַּוְּרֹנָיִךְ: י מַה־יָּפוּ דֹדַיִךְ אֲחֹתִי כַלָּה מַה־טֹּבוּ

לִבַּבְתִּנִי אֲחֹתִי כַלָּה וכו׳ בְּאַחַד עֲנָק מִצַּוְּרֹנָיִךְ — You captured my heart,
my sister, O bride. . . with but one ornament of your neck (4:9).

This verse describes the love expressed by Hashem towards His
beloved, the Congregation of Israel. *Rashi* explains the metaphor as
referring to Abraham (with the word עֲנָק [*ornament*] meaning "giant").
The sense of the verse in thus: ". . .with but one of the sainted Patriarchs, referring to the unique one (אֶחָד), Abraham, who is called עֲנָק
(giant) because of his towering [spiritual] greatness."

This appellation of singularity would seemingly be more suited for
Jacob. It is Jacob who is referred to as the בְּחִיר הָאָבוֹת, "choicest one of
the Patriarchs"; it is only Jacob whom, the Sages tell us, was given a
Divine Name (קֵל) by Hashem (*Megillah* 18a). *Daas Zekeinim* (*Bereishis*
28:13) cites a *midrash* that compares Abraham to the farmer who plows
the land (קוּם הִתְהַלֵּךְ בָּאָרֶץ לְאָרְכָּהּ וּלְרָחְבָּהּ, *Arise, walk about in the Land*,
through its width and breadth — Bereishis 13:17); Isaac to the farmer who
sows the land (וַיִּזְרַע יִצְחָק בָּאָרֶץ הַהִיא, *And Isaac sowed in that land . . .* —
ibid. 26:12), and Jacob to the finished, processed grain (קֹדֶשׁ יִשְׂרָאֵל לַה׳
רֵאשִׁית תְּבוּאָתֹה, *Israel* [= *Jacob*] *is holy unto Hashem, the first of His
produce — Yirmiyahu* 2:3). Why, then, is Abraham taken to represent
the "giant" among the Patriarchs in this particular context?

The *Rambam* (*Avodah Zarah* 1:2) calls Abraham the "pillar of the
world,"[1] indicative of his towering stature and pivotal role in the development of the *raison d'etre* of Creation. The explanation of this central-
ity of Abraham in the world may be seen from a statement made by the
Rambam in his *Sefer HaMitzvos*: "This commandment [to love Hashem
(*Devarim* 6:5)] includes within it the idea that we should encourage

---

1. Similarly the *Baal HaTurim* points out that when the Torah says, "These are the events
of the heavens and the earth *when they were* created (בְּהִבָּרְאָם)," it is actually an allusion to
Abraham (אַבְרָהָם), in whose merit the universe was created.

דֹּדַ֫יִךְ מִיַּ֫יִן וְרֵ֫יחַ שְׁמָנַ֫יִךְ מִכָּל־בְּשָׂמִֽים: יֹא נֹ֫פֶת תִּטֹּ֫פְנָה שִׂפְתוֹתַ֫יִךְ כַּלָּ֑ה דְּבַ֤שׁ וְחָלָב֙ תַּ֣חַת לְשׁוֹנֵ֔ךְ וְרֵ֥יחַ שַׂלְמֹתַ֖יִךְ כְּרֵ֥יחַ לְבָנֽוֹן: יֹב גַּ֣ן ׀ נָע֤וּל אֲחֹתִי֙ כַלָּ֔ה גַּ֥ל נָע֖וּל מַעְיָ֥ן חָתֽוּם: יֹג שְׁלָחַ֙יִךְ֙ פַּרְדֵּ֣ס רִמּוֹנִ֔ים עִ֖ם פְּרִ֣י מְגָדִ֑ים כְּפָרִ֖ים עִם־נְרָדִֽים: יֹד נֵ֣רְדְּ ׀ וְכַרְכֹּ֗ם קָנֶה֙ וְקִנָּמ֔וֹן עִ֖ם כָּל־עֲצֵ֣י לְבוֹנָ֑ה מֹ֚ר וַאֲהָל֔וֹת עִ֖ם כָּל־רָאשֵׁ֥י בְשָׂמִֽים: יֹה מַעְיַ֣ן גַּנִּ֔ים

other [non-Jewish] people to recognize Hashem and worship Him. . .
just as we find that Abraham used to draw people to belief in Hashem
[1] out of his deep love for Him, as it says, "Abraham, who loved me"
(*Yeshayahu* 41:8). Just as his intense love for Hashem moved him to
persuade others to join him in worshiping Hashem, so should our love
for Him be so strong that we feel compelled to persuade other people."
It is axiomatic (see *Ramban* to *Shemos* 13:16) that the entire purpose
of Hashem's creating the world was to bring into being man, who is
capable of recognizing and worshiping his Creator. Hence, the role of
Abraham, who encouraged the fulfillment of this objective, was pivotal
in the scheme of Creation. It is thus quite fitting that the *Rambam* refer
to Abraham as the "pillar of the [entire] world."

In the context of *Shir HaShirim*, the expression of enthusiastic unbounded love between Hashem and His beloved, Israel, it is only proper
that Abraham, who so excelled in making Hashem beloved, be distinguished from among the other Patriarchs.

---

1. The words of the *Rambam* shed light on a *midrash* quoted by *Rashi* on the verse, וְאֶעֶשְׂךָ
לְגוֹי גָּדוֹל וַאֲבָרֶכְךָ וַאֲגַדְּלָה שְׁמֶךָ וֶהְיֵה בְּרָכָה, *And I will make of you a great nation; and I will bless
you, and make your name great, and you shall be a blessing* (*Bereishis* 12:2). The *midrash*
interprets these four promises as follows:
  "*And I will make of you a great nation*" — this is exhibited by the fact that your
  descendants will pray to Hashem [in the *Shemoneh Esrei* prayer] referring to Him as
  "the God of Abraham." "*And I will bless you*" — this refers to the phrase [ibid.] "the
  God of Isaac." "*And make your name great*" — this refers to the phrase [ibid.] "the
  God of Jacob." One would have thought that the conclusion of this section of the
  prayer should also mention all three Patriarchs; therefore the verse continues "*and
  you shall be [you by yourself] a blessing*" — the concluding words of the prayer
  mention only you (מָגֵן אַבְרָהָם, *Shield of Abraham*).
Abraham's mission was to bring men of all nationalities to recognize Hashem, as shown
above. This task cannot possibly be accomplished completely in this world. As *Rashi* points
out in his commentary to the verse שְׁמַע יִשְׂרָאֵל ה' אֱלֹקֵינוּ ה' אֶחָד, *Hear O Israel Hashem is our
God, Hashem is One* (*Devarim* 6:4), in the present world He is only "*our God*" (that is, His
Divinity is recognized only by Israel), and only in the future, in Messianic times, will it be
realized by all that "Hashem is One," as it says, בַּיּוֹם הַהוּא יִהְיֶה ה' אֶחָד וּשְׁמוֹ אֶחָד, *On that day
Hashem will be One and His Name will be One* (*Zechariah* 14:9). Thus the "conclusion" of the
prayer, symbolizing the concluding chapter of history, is devoted to Abraham alone, who
strove to bring about this universal knowledge of Hashem in his own time. The fulfillment
of Abraham's mission will be realized with the advent of the Messianic era.

בְּאֵר מַיִם חַיִּים וְנֹזְלִים מִן־לְבָנוֹן: טז עוּרִי צָפוֹן וּבוֹאִי תֵימָן הָפִיחִי גַנִּי יִזְּלוּ בְשָׂמָיו יָבֹא דוֹדִי לְגַנּוֹ וְיֹאכַל פְּרִי מְגָדָיו:

פרק ה

א בָּאתִי לְגַנִּי אֲחֹתִי כַלָּה אָרִיתִי מוֹרִי עִם־בְּשָׂמִי אָכַלְתִּי יַעְרִי עִם־דִּבְשִׁי שָׁתִיתִי יֵינִי עִם־חֲלָבִי אִכְלוּ רֵעִים שְׁתוּ וְשִׁכְרוּ דּוֹדִים: ב אֲנִי יְשֵׁנָה וְלִבִּי עֵר קוֹל | דּוֹדִי דוֹפֵק פִּתְחִי־לִי אֲחֹתִי רַעְיָתִי יוֹנָתִי תַמָּתִי שֶׁרֹאשִׁי נִמְלָא־טָל קְוֻצּוֹתַי רְסִיסֵי לָיְלָה: ג פָּשַׁטְתִּי אֶת־כֻּתָּנְתִּי אֵיכָכָה אֶלְבָּשֶׁנָּה רָחַצְתִּי אֶת־רַגְלַי אֵיכָכָה אֲטַנְּפֵם: ד דּוֹדִי שָׁלַח יָדוֹ מִן־הַחוֹר וּמֵעַי הָמוּ עָלָיו: ה קַמְתִּי אֲנִי לִפְתֹּחַ לְדוֹדִי וְיָדַי נָטְפוּ־מוֹר וְאֶצְבְּעֹתַי מוֹר עֹבֵר עַל כַּפּוֹת הַמַּנְעוּל:

קוֹל דּוֹדִי דוֹפֵק וכו' פָּשַׁטְתִּי אֶת כֻּתָּנְתִּי אֵיכָכָה אֶלְבָּשֶׁנָּה וכו' קַמְתִּי אֲנִי לִפְתֹּחַ לְדוֹדִי — The sound of my Beloved knocking... "I have doffed my robe; how can I don it?"... I arose to open [the door] for my Beloved (5:2-5).

First the "maiden" (an allegory for Israel) explains that she cannot open the door for her Beloved (Hashem) for she has already gone to bed. Then she arises to open the door for Him anyway. What happened in between these two verses? Why does the maiden suddenly realize that she really can answer the door?

The intervening verse supplies the answer to this question. דּוֹדִי שָׁלַח יָדוֹ מִן הַחוֹר וּמֵעַי הָמוּ עָלָיו, My Beloved sent forth His hand from the portal, and my innards churned with longing for Him (verse 4). Even though our actions at first betrayed an attitude of indifference towards Hashem, the presence of Hashem and the realization that He is always there, willing to accept us if we are truly penitent, inspires us to seek Him out and draw nearer to Him. One mitzvah leads to another (מִצְוָה גּוֹרֶרֶת מִצְוָה), and a minor spiritual experience, a slight exposure to the goodness of his "Beloved," spurs the Jew on to pursue an even more meaningful relationship with Him. Every Jew, no matter how far removed from spirituality, has this potential to reconnect to Torah and its mitzvos.

Rav Yerucham Levovitz, zt"l (the Mirrer Mashgiach), points out that of the four sons discussed in the Haggadah, the one who "is unable to ask" is listed last, even after the wicked son, seeming to imply that this son

ה פָּתַחְתִּי אֲנִי לְדוֹדִי וְדוֹדִי חָמַק עָבָר נַפְשִׁי יָצְאָה בְדַבְּרוֹ בִּקַּשְׁתִּיהוּ וְלֹא מְצָאתִיהוּ קְרָאתִיו וְלֹא עָנָנִי: ז מְצָאֻנִי הַשֹּׁמְרִים הַסֹּבְבִים בָּעִיר הִכּוּנִי פְצָעוּנִי נָשְׂאוּ אֶת־רְדִידִי מֵעָלַי שֹׁמְרֵי הַחֹמוֹת: ח הִשְׁבַּעְתִּי אֶתְכֶם בְּנוֹת יְרוּשָׁלָם אִם־תִּמְצְאוּ אֶת־דּוֹדִי מַה־תַּגִּידוּ לוֹ שֶׁחוֹלַת אַהֲבָה אָנִי:

---

is worse off than all the others. The wicked son possesses drive and vitality which, although presently channeled into destructive criticism and cynicism towards his religion, are the very traits which may one day bring him to repent from his evil ways and seek the truth. The son who is unable to ask, however, shows, by his apathy and indifference, that even if he were exposed to some positive spiritual experience he would not build on this to draw closer to Godliness.

קַמְתִּי אֲנִי לִפְתֹּחַ לְדוֹדִי וכו' וְדוֹדִי חָמַק עָבָר וכו' — I arose to open [the door] for my Beloved. . . but my Beloved had turned and slipped away. . . (5:5-6).

The "maiden" (Israel) in the end mustered up enough spiritual energy to seek out Hashem and draw near to Him (see above), but He was no longer there; her overtures to Him were rebuffed. What happened? Why did Hashem reject the actions of the maiden He had Himself come to meet? It appears that although the maiden was moved and achieved a more elevated spiritual level than she had had previously, her actions were insufficient to merit Divine attention. Once a person arrives at a higher plane of spirituality, his actions must keep pace with his new gains; if not, he is deemed to have fallen short of his obligation. The maiden should have *jumped* out of bed and *run* to the door, full of exuberance and enthusiasm. When Hashem did not detect any such alacrity in her actions, He left.

A similar idea is advanced by the *Sefas Emes* in explanation of an enigmatic *midrash* on the verse וַיַּאֲמִינוּ בַּה' וּבְמֹשֶׁה עַבְדּוֹ, *and they [Israel] believed in Hashem and in Moses, His servant* (*Shemos* 14:31). The *midrash* says as follows: וַיַּאֲמֵן הָעָם, "Even though it says 'the people believed [when Moses first approached them in Egypt]' (ibid. 4:31), they soon lapsed and lost faith, as it says (*Tehillim* 106:12-13), וַיַּאֲמִינוּ בִדְבָרָיו יָשִׁירוּ תְּהִלָּתוֹ: מִהֲרוּ שָׁכְחוּ מַעֲשָׂיו, *Then they believed in His words, they sang His praise [at the Red Sea]. Swiftly they forgot His deeds, etc.* The *midrash* implies that after the Splitting of the Sea, when "the humble maidser-vant saw [Hashem's Glory] more clearly than the prophet Ezekiel," the people's faith declined to a level even lower than the level to which they had sunk in Egypt. Even allowing for the frailty of human nature and

ט מַה־דּוֹדֵךְ מִדּוֹד הַיָּפָה בַּנָּשִׁים מַה־דּוֹדֵךְ מִדּוֹד שֶׁכָּכָה הִשְׁבַּעְתָּנוּ: י דּוֹדִי צַח וְאָדוֹם דָּגוּל מֵרְבָבָה: יא רֹאשׁוֹ כֶּתֶם פָּז קְוֻצּוֹתָיו תַּלְתַּלִּים שְׁחֹרוֹת כָּעוֹרֵב: יב עֵינָיו כְּיוֹנִים עַל־אֲפִיקֵי מָיִם רֹחֲצוֹת בֶּחָלָב יֹשְׁבוֹת עַל־מִלֵּאת: יג לְחָיָו כַּעֲרוּגַת הַבֹּשֶׂם מִגְדְּלוֹת מֶרְקָחִים שִׂפְתוֹתָיו שׁוֹשַׁנִּים נֹטְפוֹת מוֹר עֹבֵר: יד יָדָיו גְּלִילֵי זָהָב מְמֻלָּאִים בַּתַּרְשִׁישׁ מֵעָיו עֶשֶׁת שֵׁן מְעֻלֶּפֶת סַפִּירִים: טו שׁוֹקָיו

---

its tendency to allow the impact of major emotional events to recede, it seems incredible that the Israelites deteriorated to yet an even *lower* level than they originally had. The *Sefas Emes* explains that since each person is expected to perceive Hashem and believe in Him according to his own level of spirituality, the *midrash* speaks in a relative sense: *relative to their level* the people fell far short of the faith they should have shown — even more than was the case in Egypt.

This concept may be used to explain yet another difficult passage in the words of the Sages (*Sotah* 48b): Rabbi Eliezer the Great used to say: Anyone who has enough bread to eat that day and is concerned about what he will eat the next day is considered to be deficient in his faith in Hashem. This is in accordance with Rabbi Elazar's homiletic interpretation of the verse, כִּי מִי בַז לְיוֹם קְטַנּוֹת, *What wastes the day? Small things do* (*Zechariah* 4:10), as Rabbi Elazar explained this to mean, "What causes the righteous to lose their full reward in the Days to Come [i.e. the Hereafter]? The meagerness of their trust in Hashem's Providence."

Since Rabbi Elazar is discussing people whose faith in Hashem is lacking, it is surprising that he uses the expression "What causes the *righteous* to lose, etc." If a man is righteous, does this not imply that his faith in Hashem is at least satisfactory, if not exemplary? Furthermore, he says only that these people will not receive their "full reward" in the World to Come, implying that they will be entitled to some reward, albeit diminished (see *Rashi* ad loc.). Being that faith in Hashem is the quintessence of Judaism (see *Makkos* 24a), how can someone who lacks this basic element be entitled to any share at all in the Hereafter? The answer is that here again the element of relativity is involved. For a simple person, thinking about where the *next* meal will come from certainly shows no inadequacy of faith. For the truly righteous, however, an entirely different level of belief and trust in Hashem is demanded, far above that of what is expected of the average person. Thus they will merit ample reward in the Next World, since they have im-

עַמּוּדֵי שֵׁשׁ מְיֻסָּדִים עַל־אַדְנֵי־פָז מַרְאֵהוּ כַּלְּבָנוֹן בָּחוּר
כָּאֲרָזִים: טז חִכּוֹ מַמְתַקִּים וְכֻלּוֹ מַחֲמַדִּים זֶה דוֹדִי וְזֶה רֵעִי
בְּנוֹת יְרוּשָׁלָ͏ִם:

פרק ו

א אָנָה הָלַךְ דּוֹדֵךְ הַיָּפָה בַּנָּשִׁים אָנָה פָּנָה דוֹדֵךְ וּנְבַקְשֶׁנּוּ
עִמָּךְ: ב דּוֹדִי יָרַד לְגַנּוֹ לַעֲרוּגוֹת הַבֹּשֶׂם לִרְעוֹת בַּגַּנִּים
וְלִלְקֹט שׁוֹשַׁנִּים: ג אֲנִי לְדוֹדִי וְדוֹדִי לִי הָרֹעֶה בַּשּׁוֹשַׁנִּים:
ד יָפָה אַתְּ רַעְיָתִי כְּתִרְצָה נָאוָה כִּירוּשָׁלָ͏ִם אֲיֻמָּה
כַּנִּדְגָּלוֹת: ה הָסֵבִּי עֵינַיִךְ מִנֶּגְדִּי שֶׁהֵם הִרְהִיבֻנִי שַׂעְרֵךְ

---

mense faith in Hashem (according to the normal definition of the term), but this reward is somewhat modified by the fact that they did not live up to the degree of faith called for by their particular spiritual plateau.

הָסֵבִּי עֵינַיִךְ מִנֶּגְדִּי שֶׁהֵם הִרְהִיבֻנִי — Turn your eyes away from Me, for they have endeared Me to you (6:5).

Rashi explains the metaphor: Hashem tells Israel: I cannot grant you that the Holy Ark and the Cherubim upon it will be present in the Second Temple as they were in Solomon's Temple, for the presence of these sacred items in the First Temple caused Me to show you too great a measure of love, which ultimately led to your rebelling against Me.

In *Mesillas Yesharim*, the classic work of Jewish devotional philosophy, the author points out that virtually every situation in the world turns out to be a challenge to man's spiritual fortitude. If he is financially secure, there is danger that his comfortable position will lead to complacency and moral decadence. If, on the other hand, he is under financial strain, the temptation of resorting to dishonest means of gaining money is a constant potential pitfall. All the various situations and vicissitudes of life are but a series of challenges and tests to man's moral stamina.

I heard from *Rav Hutner zt"l* that we see from *Rashi's* interpretation of this verse that not only monetary poverty or affluence can have adverse effects on man's spiritual well-being, but even an overabundance of spiritual bounty can be harmful. Through the presence of the symbols of Hashem's Divine Glory dwelling in Israel's midst — namely, the Holy Ark and the Cherubim — the Jews developed a sense of self-assurance and spiritual smugness, which led to moral decline. Hashem informs them that, for their own good, He would not allow

כְּעֵדֶר הָעִזִּים שֶׁגָּלְשׁוּ מִן־הַגִּלְעָד: ۱ שִׁנַּיִךְ כְּעֵדֶר הָרְחֵלִים
שֶׁעָלוּ מִן־הָרַחְצָה שֶׁכֻּלָּם מַתְאִימוֹת וְשַׁכֻּלָה אֵין בָּהֶם:
۷ כְּפֶלַח הָרִמּוֹן רַקָּתֵךְ מִבַּעַד לְצַמָּתֵךְ: ח שִׁשִּׁים הֵמָּה
מְלָכוֹת וּשְׁמֹנִים פִּילַגְשִׁים וַעֲלָמוֹת אֵין מִסְפָּר: ט אַחַת
הִיא יוֹנָתִי תַמָּתִי אַחַת הִיא לְאִמָּהּ בָּרָה הִיא לְיוֹלַדְתָּהּ
רָאוּהָ בָנוֹת וַיְאַשְּׁרוּהָ מְלָכוֹת וּפִילַגְשִׁים וַיְהַלְלוּהָ:

---

these tokens of His affection to be restored in the Second Temple.

A similar thought is expressed by *Rashi* in his commentary on the verse (*Bamidbar* 11:20), יַעַן כִּי מְאַסְתֶּם אֶת ה' אֲשֶׁר בְּקִרְבְּכֶם, *because you have rejected Hashem Who is in your midst.* *Rashi* comments: It is precisely because He planted His Divine Presence "in your midst" that you could become so arrogant as to enter into this type of rebellious activity.

Perhaps this concept can help explain why it was that immediately after the Splitting of the Sea, Hashem presented Israel with a trial: וַיָּבֹאוּ מָרָתָה וְלֹא יָכְלוּ לִשְׁתֹּת מַיִם מִמָּרָה כִּי מָרִים הֵם וכו' שָׁם שָׂם לוֹ חֹק וּמִשְׁפָּט וְשָׁם נִסָּהוּ, *And they came to Marah, but they could not drink the waters of Marah because they were bitter. There He establisehd for [the nation] a decree and an ordinance, and there He tested it* (*Shemos* 15:23-25). In order to prevent a sense of spiritual self-assurance after having witnessed the unparalleled revelation of Hashem's Glory at the Red Sea, Hashem deemed it necessary to humble their spirits with the trial at Marah.

With this understanding of the events at Marah, perhaps we can provide an answer to a question raised by the *Ramban* in his commentary on the Torah (ad loc.). Why, asks the *Ramban,* does the Torah refer to the mitzvos given at Marah (the Sages say that these were Sabbath observance, the rite of Red Heifer, and monetary laws) in such a vague manner? It should have said, "And Hashem spoke unto Moses at Marah saying: Speak unto the Children of Israel and command them to observe the Sabbath," explicitly, as it does for all the other commandments in the Torah.

The Sages tell us (*Beitzah* 25a): "Why were the people of Israel chosen to be the recipients of the Torah? Because they are strong-minded (עַזִּין). . . The Torah is like fire; if it had been given to any other nation they would not have been able to bear it." The Torah was given to Israel to help temper their strong-mindedness and to channel it into spiritually constructive energy. Perhaps this is why several mitzvos had to be given to them immediately after their experiences at the sea — in order to break their natural tendency toward self-assuredness, bolstered by

יֹ מִי־זֹאת הַנִּשְׁקָפָה כְּמוֹ־שָׁחַר יָפָה כַלְּבָנָה בָּרָה כַּחַמָּה אֲיֻמָּה כַּנִּדְגָּלוֹת: יֹא אֶל־גִּנַּת אֱגוֹז יָרַדְתִּי לִרְאוֹת בְּאִבֵּי הַנָּחַל לִרְאוֹת הֲפָרְחָה הַגֶּפֶן הֵנֵצוּ הָרִמֹּנִים: יֹב לֹא יָדַעְתִּי נַפְשִׁי שָׂמַתְנִי מַרְכְּבוֹת עַמִּי נָדִיב:

פרק ז

א שׁוּבִי שׁוּבִי הַשּׁוּלַמִּית שׁוּבִי שׁוּבִי וְנֶחֱזֶה־בָּךְ מַה־תֶּחֱזוּ בַּשּׁוּלַמִּית כִּמְחֹלַת הַמַּחֲנָיִם: בֹ מַה־יָּפוּ פְעָמַיִךְ בַּנְּעָלִים בַּת־נָדִיב חַמּוּקֵי יְרֵכַיִךְ כְּמוֹ חֲלָאִים מַעֲשֵׂה יְדֵי אָמָּן:

---

the extraordinary measure of revelation which Hashem had just granted them. Since these commandments were given not only for their usual purpose of upholding them and studying them (the *Ramban* [*Shemos* 15:25] seems to imply that they assumed the status of obligatory mitzvos only upon repetition at Sinai), but also as a means of character tempering, they are not recorded in the usual manner. Portraying mitzvos in this fashion would be degrading (however slightly) to the sanctity of those mitzvos.

מַה יָּפוּ פְעָמַיִךְ בַּנְּעָלִים בַּת נָדִיב — How beautiful are your feet in shoes, O daughter of the noble one (7:2).

The *Gemara* (*Succah* 49b) interprets this praise of Israel allegorically: "How lovely are the feet of Israel which walk together to fulfill the mitzvah of the pilgrimage to Jerusalem during the three festivals. *Daughter of Israel* — daughter of Abraham, who is called נָדִיב (nobleman), as it says, נְדִיבֵי עַמִּים נֶאֱסָפוּ עַם אֱלֹקֵי אַבְרָהָם, *The nobles of the nations gathered, [with] the nation of the G-d of Abraham* (*Tehillim* 47:10). Why are the Jews referred to here as 'the nation of the God of Abraham,' and not that 'of the God of Isaac or Jacob'? Because Abraham was the first proselyte (and the 'nobles of the nations' referred to in the verse, who 'gathered' with the Jews, are obviously proselytes)."

The *Maharsha* points out a rather obvious difficulty with the proof from the verse in *Tehillim*. The Gemara sets out to prove that Abraham is referred to as נָדִיב (noble), but the verse adduced shows only that the proselytes of the "nations" are called "nobles," not Abraham. He answers that the Gemara interprets the word נָדִיב not as "nobleman" but as "one who offers oneself, or dedicates himself, to a particular purpose" (from the word נדב, *to volunteer, to donate*). All proselytes are not Jewish by dint of birth but rather "volunteer" to join the nation of Israel.

שָׁרְרֵךְ אַגַּן הַסַּהַר אַל־יֶחְסַר הַמָּזֶג בִּטְנֵךְ עֲרֵמַת חִטִּים
סוּגָה בַּשּׁוֹשַׁנִּים: ד שְׁנֵי שָׁדַיִךְ כִּשְׁנֵי עֳפָרִים תָּאֳמֵי צְבִיָּה:
ה צַוָּארֵךְ כְּמִגְדַּל הַשֵּׁן עֵינַיִךְ בְּרֵכוֹת בְּחֶשְׁבּוֹן עַל־שַׁעַר
בַּת־רַבִּים אַפֵּךְ כְּמִגְדַּל הַלְּבָנוֹן צוֹפֶה פְּנֵי דַמָּשֶׂק:
ו רֹאשֵׁךְ עָלַיִךְ כַּכַּרְמֶל וְדַלַּת רֹאשֵׁךְ כָּאַרְגָּמָן מֶלֶךְ אָסוּר
בָּרְהָטִים: ז מַה־יָּפִית וּמַה־נָּעַמְתְּ אַהֲבָה בַּתַּעֲנוּגִים:
ח זֹאת קוֹמָתֵךְ דָּמְתָה לְתָמָר וְשָׁדַיִךְ לְאַשְׁכֹּלוֹת: ט אָמַרְתִּי

Thus they clearly fall under this description, as does Abraham, the original proselyte and "spiritual father" of all later converts. This designation of Abraham in this context of *Shir HaShirim* remains unexplained. What is the relationship between the pilgrimage festivals and Abraham in particular? Perhaps the connection is because he was the first to make a pilgrimage to Mount Moriah in Jerusalem, traveling to the *Akeidah*.

The *Meshech Chochmah* suggests another approach. Abraham was tested with ten trials (*Pirkei Avos* 5:4). The mitzvah of going on the pilgrimage is one of the most trying of all the commandments in the Torah. We are tested on the extent of our trust in Hashem to protect our property while we make the festival pilgrimage. The entire (male) population is required to abandon their homes, farms, businesses, etc. and travel — sometimes a trip of up to fifteen days — to Jerusalem. In terms of national security, economic factors, etc. (leaving one's land and possessions unattended for such a long period of time, at such frequent intervals), the risk is tremendous. Thus the people who withstand the tempting trial of personal security and nevertheless undertake this pilgrimage are referred to as the "daughter of the נָדִיב (Abraham)."

Hashem guarantees us, however, that in the merit of our ignoring the risks involved and participating in this mitzvah and thus putting our trust in Him, He will grant His protection over our possessions, as it says, וְלֹא־יַחְמֹד אִישׁ אֶת־אַרְצְךָ בַּעֲלֹתְךָ לֵרָאוֹת אֶת־פְּנֵי ה' אֱלֹהֶיךָ שָׁלֹשׁ פְּעָמִים בַּשָּׁנָה, *And no man will covet your land when you go up to appear before Hashem, your God, three times a year* (*Shemos* 34:24). As an illustration, the *Midrash* relates a tale about two non-Jewish tenants of a Jewish man, who planned to rob their landlord while he was away on the pilgrimage. Angels miraculously appeared in the house to protect the man's property, and the flabbergasted gentiles exclaimed, "Blessed be the God of the Jews!" (*Yalkut Shimoni Shemos* 404).

אֶעֱלֶה בְתָמָר אֹחֲזָה בְּסַנְסִנָּיו וְיִהְיוּ־נָא שָׁדַיִךְ כְּאֶשְׁכְּלוֹת הַגֶּפֶן וְרֵיחַ אַפֵּךְ כַּתַּפּוּחִים: יּוְחִכֵּךְ כְּיֵין הַטּוֹב הוֹלֵךְ לְדוֹדִי לְמֵישָׁרִים דּוֹבֵב שִׂפְתֵי יְשֵׁנִים: יאאֲנִי לְדוֹדִי וְעָלַי תְּשׁוּקָתוֹ: יבלְכָה דוֹדִי נֵצֵא הַשָּׂדֶה נָלִינָה בַּכְּפָרִים: יגנַשְׁכִּימָה לַכְּרָמִים נִרְאֶה אִם פָּרְחָה הַגֶּפֶן פִּתַּח הַסְּמָדַר הֵנֵצוּ הָרִמּוֹנִים שָׁם אֶתֵּן אֶת־דֹּדַי לָךְ: ידהַדּוּדָאִים נָתְנוּ־רֵיחַ וְעַל־פְּתָחֵינוּ כָּל־מְגָדִים חֲדָשִׁים גַּם־יְשָׁנִים דּוֹדִי צָפַנְתִּי לָךְ:

פרק ח

אמִי יִתֶּנְךָ כְּאָח לִי יוֹנֵק שְׁדֵי אִמִּי אֶמְצָאֲךָ בַחוּץ אֶשָּׁקְךָ גַּם לֹא־יָבֻזוּ לִי: באֶנְהָגֲךָ אֲבִיאֲךָ אֶל־בֵּית אִמִּי תְּלַמְּדֵנִי אַשְׁקְךָ מִיַּיִן הָרֶקַח מֵעֲסִיס רִמֹּנִי: גשְׂמֹאלוֹ תַּחַת רֹאשִׁי וִימִינוֹ תְּחַבְּקֵנִי: דהִשְׁבַּעְתִּי אֶתְכֶם בְּנוֹת יְרוּשָׁלִָם מַה־תָּעִירוּ ׀ וּמַה־תְּעֹרְרוּ אֶת־הָאַהֲבָה עַד שֶׁתֶּחְפָּץ: המִי זֹאת עֹלָה מִן־הַמִּדְבָּר מִתְרַפֶּקֶת עַל־דּוֹדָהּ תַּחַת הַתַּפּוּחַ עוֹרַרְתִּיךָ שָׁמָּה חִבְּלַתְךָ אִמֶּךָ שָׁמָּה חִבְּלָה יְלָדַתְךָ: ושִׂימֵנִי כַחוֹתָם עַל־לִבֶּךָ כַּחוֹתָם עַל־זְרוֹעֶךָ כִּי־עַזָּה כַמָּוֶת אַהֲבָה קָשָׁה כִשְׁאוֹל קִנְאָה, רְשָׁפֶיהָ רִשְׁפֵּי אֵשׁ, שַׁלְהֶבֶתְיָה. זמַיִם רַבִּים לֹא יוּכְלוּ לְכַבּוֹת אֶת־הָאַהֲבָה, וּנְהָרוֹת לֹא יִשְׁטְפוּהָ, אִם יִתֵּן אִישׁ אֶת כָּל־הוֹן בֵּיתוֹ בָּאַהֲבָה, בּוֹז יָבוּזוּ לוֹ. חאָחוֹת לָנוּ קְטַנָּה, וְשָׁדַיִם אֵין לָהּ, מַה־נַּעֲשֶׂה לַאֲחוֹתֵנוּ בַּיּוֹם שֶׁיְּדֻבַּר־בָּהּ. טאִם־חוֹמָה הִיא, נִבְנֶה עָלֶיהָ טִירַת כָּסֶף, וְאִם־דֶּלֶת הִיא, נָצוּר עָלֶיהָ לוּחַ אָרֶז. יאֲנִי חוֹמָה, וְשָׁדַי כַּמִּגְדָּלוֹת, אָז הָיִיתִי בְעֵינָיו כְּמוֹצְאֵת שָׁלוֹם. יאכֶּרֶם הָיָה לִשְׁלֹמֹה בְּבַעַל הָמוֹן, נָתַן אֶת הַכֶּרֶם לַנֹּטְרִים, אִישׁ יָבִא בְּפִרְיוֹ אֶלֶף כָּסֶף. יבכַּרְמִי

שֶׁלִּי לְפָנָי, הָאֶלֶף לְךָ שְׁלֹמֹה, וּמָאתַיִם לְנֹטְרִים אֶת־פִּרְיוֹ. ‏יּהַיּוֹשֶׁבֶת בַּגַּנִּים, חֲבֵרִים מַקְשִׁיבִים לְקוֹלֵךְ, הַשְׁמִיעִנִי. ‏יּבְּרַח דּוֹדִי, וּדְמֵה לְךָ לִצְבִי, אוֹ לְעֹפֶר הָאַיָּלִים, עַל הָרֵי בְשָׂמִים.

One should continue to occupy himself with the story of the Exodus and the laws of Pesach, until sleep overtakes him.

This volume is part of
THE ARTSCROLL SERIES®
an ongoing project of
translations, commentaries and expositions
on Scripture, Mishnah, Talmud, Halachah,
liturgy, history and the classic Rabbinic writings;
and biographies, and thought.

For a brochure of current publications
visit your local Hebrew bookseller
or contact the publisher:

Mesorah Publications, ltd

4401 Second Avenue
Brooklyn, New York 11232
(718) 921-9000